The Village Notary

Front cover: *Anthony Oberman*,
Still-life with books and writing instruments. 1814.

József Eötvös

The Village Notary

Translated by Bernard Adams

CEEOL Press 2022

Originally published in Hungarian as A *'falu' jegyzője* in 1845
Translation is based on the fourth edition, 1891,
published by Mór Ráth, Budapest.

Translated by Bernard Adams

Published in 2022 by CEEOLPRESS, Frankfurt am Main, Germany

Typesetting: CEEOL GmbH, CEEOLPress
Layout: Alexander Neroslavsky

ISBN: 978-3-949607-14-1
E-ISBN: 978-3-949607-15-8

Table of Contents

Retranslator's note

If the literary translator's fundamental motive is the desire to share with others his delight in the strangeness of alien things, the retranslator's purpose is more complex. He shares the first translator's enthusiasm, but more is clearly needed. He may be aware of technical errors in a previous translation – mistranslations, omissions, or factual mistakes – that he is able to correct; he may even be unaware of a previous translation; or, as in this case, feel that the literary language of 170 years ago may strike the modern reader as quaint but not always easy to understand, and that something should be done to remedy this situation. There are then two possibilities: either a revision of the previous translation, retaining as much of it as possible while correcting errors and revising archaisms, or a complete fresh start ab initio. The latter is what I chose.

The retranslator also has to be convinced that the original work has a quality that makes his efforts worthwhile. That a book is translated in the first place indicates that it has a certain intrinsic worth, a durable value that will resound beyond its domestic readership; the retranslator seeks to reassert that quality but at international level. The Village Notary is the second of Eötvös's four novels; the third, Hungary in 1514, is generally felt to be his best, but it was The Village Notary which made his name as a writer, that for which he is best remembered in Hungary, and that which, in the words of the literary historian Géza Hegedűs, was the first work of Hungarian literature to attract international acclaim; it was translated into German and English. Hungarian art prose may be dated from Kelemen Mikes's Letters from Turkey, first published in 1791, scarcely fifty years before The Village Notary in 1845. Just as the modern English reader will struggle with Shakespeare, the modern Hungarian may find Eötvös hard going, and may even find an English translation easier to read than the original.

A slight mystery surrounds the previous English translation, that made by Otto von Wenckstern in 1850. A member of an ancient Prussian family, his mother-tongue was German. He was working as a journalist in London at the time, and his English is the literary language of the period. From his biography (see Wikipedia) it appears that he had learned English and Italian, and in fact was at one time a teacher of both – but we are not told that he ever studied Hungarian. To do so would have been unusual, and so the biographical omission is serious if in fact he did; nor is it recorded that he ever visited Hungary. It is clear that he had friends among the exile Hungarian community in London, one of whom was Kossuth's emissary Ferenc Pulszky, who contributed notes to the translation. A reference to von Wenckstern in Dickens Notes Online says that he translated from German and Hungarian, and contemporary English reviewers of The Village Notary say that he translated "from the Hungarian". I cannot deny that this is possible, but it appears rather unlikely, and it would certainly have been easy for him to use the German version by Johann Mailath which appeared in 1846 and, like von Wenckstern's, is distinctly abridged.

Any two translations of the same text must inevitably have a certain amount in common, and I have refrained from consulting von Wenckstern for fear of making my translation differ to no other purpose. I have, however, seen him quoted, and on one point I have resolutely taken a different approach – that concerning personal and place names. In Eötvös, many of these are meaningful and allude to the nature of person or place – e.g. Nyúzó (from nyúz 'to flay') for the grasping magistrate, Porvár ('dust castle') for the county town. Von Wenckstern is not entirely consistent, however, and the imaginary county where the action takes place is allegorically named Taksony, after the legendary Magyar chieftain, and distant places in Hungary and beyond, e.g. Tokaj and Heidelberg, are not disguised with pseudonyms. I have preferred not to follow this style, fashionable enough in mid-nineteenth century English, but rather to call characters and places by the names given in the text, and if a name is meaningful to add a note explaining it. Official titles such as *táblabíró*, *alispán*, and *főispán* too are left untranslated but are explained in notes, as they have no precise English equivalents, as are a number of other points likely to be unclear to the English reader unversed in Hungarian affairs.

Acknowledgement

I would like to acknowledge the unfailing encouragement and assistance of Veronica Jamset in the production of this translation.

Introduction

The Village Notary
a Hungarian classic resurrected in retranslation

Born in 1813 into a Catholic Hungarian aristocratic family, Baron József Eötvös was educated typically for his class at the Királyi Egyetemi Gimnázium and Pest University, where he studied Law and Philosophy. His paternal ancestors had been high-ranking civil servants, while his mother was of Austrian descent; it was from her, an educated woman, that he inherited a sensitive nature and love of literature.

In 1833 Eötvös entered the civil service, but then interrupted his career to travel in Western Europe in 1836–37. On returning to Hungary he lived on his father's estate at Sály in north-eastern Hungary, devoting himself to literature, before moving back to Buda and parliament in 1840.

He had already published some poetry (including his well-known Frozen Child of 1833) and some drama; in 1835 he became a corresponding member of the Hungarian Academy, a full member in 1839, and eventually in 1870 its president.

Eötvös served as Minister for Religion and Education in the Kossuth government, but left Hungary in 1848 and spent the next two years in Munich. Returning to Hungary after the War of Independence was over, he divided his time between public service and writing, serving once again as Minister for Religion and Education under Ferenc Deák. Notable among his political interests were the reform of the prisons, the emancipation of the Jews, the 'nationality question', and the foundation of Kolozsvár University. He wrote no more after 1860, and died in 1871.

Baron Jozsef's four novels arouse the interest of the reader from several perspectives. The casual reader will find in them entertaining narratives, life's struggles and passions; he that reads more deeply will see judgement passed on society; the reader given to reflection will detect a moral and the facts of life, the teachings of a great heart and a wise brain.

These novels differ widely in terms of subject, and yet clearly belong to a single world of ideas. The first – *The Carthusian* (1841) – is derived from pure imagination, and shows the influence of its author's time spent abroad; the second – *The Village Notary* (1845) – turns on the great questions of the age, indeed, the author's core political ideals, validated by their trueness to life – yet the book is not outdated, as it depicts the response of the human spirit to the perpetual struggles of life. The third – *Hungary in 1514* (1847) – is a historical novel set in the peasant revolution led by György Dózsa, casting light on the parallel phenomena of two eras: the excesses of passion that lurk in it, however, are to be found in all times. The fourth – *The Sisters* (1857) – brings up questions of education; are those not as relevant today as they were at the time of writing and always will be? Eötvös considered that literature sank to the level of a pleasant pastime if it became detached from the great concerns of the age; the human spirit and life are fundamentally always the same; the same problems, passions, desires and ambitions torment them, though in different guises, just as the human species changes its clothing from age to age.

The Carthusian is the work of a youthful writer and has been compared to a first glass of champagne, fizzing under its own power from the bottle as soon as it is opened! It contains, however, the same elements of political disappointment and the conflict between noble and non-noble that feature in *The Village Notary*. By 1845 Eötvös was prominent in the opposition in the upper house of parliament, the centralist faction intent on reform. What he argued about in his political writings is encapsulated in this novel: the woes of the common people, the antiquated legal system, the tyranny of inferior officials, the corruption of electioneering, the verbose ineffectualness of ignorant reformers, the whole futile network of selfishness. That was what Ferenc Deák meant by his famous comment that the fictional Taksony county in which the book is set resembled the horse on the title-page of a veterinary textbook, with every possible disease indicated; the diseases all existed, but there was no horse on earth that had them all at once! There are two large groups in the book, the suffering and the powerful: their conflict produces the action; everyone is a type, representing a category the portrayal of which is all the sharper for being described through its individual member. Eötvös's intention is not merely to entertain but also to instruct, and he values lessons above artistic pleasure. He turns the miracle of St Erzsébet of Hungary around: in his hands, roses become bread.

Eötvös's primary purpose was to expose the unsatisfactory nature of the traditional county administration. Hungary could hardly be considered a nation when so few of the people derived benefit or protection from the way that affairs were handled. In *The Village Notary* he presented a cross-section of society in which the ruling elite were all too often lazy and self-seeking while the lesser lights, whatever their sterling qualities, were at their mercy and open to abuse. There was a commendable solidarity among the lower orders – "We poor people don't desert one another," says an inhabitant of Tiszarét – but if the basic function of law is the regulation of relationships between citizens, Hungarian law was heavily weighted in favour of the nobility – in fact, only they were effectively citizens – a point to which the English reader of the 1850 translation by Otto von Wenckstern was very sensitive.

Small wonder, then, that the influential Hungarian ears on which Eötvös's socially advanced call for greater equality fell were all too often deaf and unenlightened, and the propaganda element of the book was not well received. His secondary purpose, however, that of entertaining the reader, was much more successful, and in 1865 led to a second, revised edition, in which the amount of discursive material was reduced and the work was more in line with what became the great Hungarian tradition of racy tales. To this day the book is not forgotten in Hungary, and though relatively few will have read it (a classic book is one that people know that they should read but somehow fail to), many will have met with excerpts or at least the option to study it, or will have seen the filmed version. In the West, Otto von Wenckstern's translation is now a rarity, not unknown in the better sort of library, and is even offered for sale by the internet bookseller *Forgotten Books* – though when I asked them for a copy they were unable to supply one.

The Village Notary is thus a *Tendenzroman or roman à thèse*, and was seen by many of the Hungarian nobility as an attack on not only the status quo in general but their privileged position in particular. Even the great reformer Kossuth regarded the counties as bastions of the constitution. Power in Hungary lay in the counties, in which the local common nobility – a minority with rights but almost no obligations – wielded power over the non-nobility and peasantry – a majority with obligations but no rights at all. This is illustrated in the book by the theft of notary Tengelyi's certificate of nobility, which brings with it the loss of his rights and his helpless exposure to the malice of those that wish him ill. In 1845, however, the Romantic period is in full swing and right must triumph; Tengelyi is rescued, but not before we have been shown the state of the prisons and the faults in the legal system. The young lovers too – there had to be a romantic interest! – overcome unjust prejudice and marry, but the reader must decide for himself to what extent he should sympathise with the outlaw Viola.

The Village Notary was first published by the newspaper *Pesti Hírlap* in monthly instalments in 1845 (which earned it the description of 'an eight-volume leading article'), and the complex plot turns mainly on the lives of the eponymous notary, Jónás Tengelyi, and the outlaw Viola, and on the meshing of the two. Both men are to some extent the authors of their own misfortunes through their uncompromising natures; Tengelyi starts life as the son of a Calvinist pastor, studies law at Heidelberg and begins to practise, but his career is blighted by an adherence to strict principles which leaves him short of the right kind of friends, and he sinks from post to post until he reaches the bottom of the legal profession – a man respected but, outside his immediate family, unloved, and with powerful enemies. Viola is introduced as a fearsome bandit, the terror of the district; previously a capable peasant farmer, he has been outlawed as the result of a hasty act in which, under the severest provocation, he accidentally killed a man; love for his wife and children, however, keeps him near the village even though he can do nothing for them. When Mrs Viola is sick and reduced to utter penury the family is taken in by the Tengelyis. Soon afterwards comes the county election, at which Tengelyi's enemies cast doubt on his noble status and eligibility to vote; they have caused his 'dog-skin' certificate of nobility to be stolen. Viola discovers where it is, but, in retrieving it, once again kills a man and is forced to flee. Tengelyi is falsely accused of this murder and is imprisoned. Viola, now safely far away, learns of this and comes back to return the document but is killed in hot pursuit by a gendarme – in fact, one of those who had robbed Tengelyi – almost before he can do so. On this framework hangs more – the weak *alispán* and his wicked wife and lawyer, the love of his son for Tengelyi's beautiful daughter, the long purple passage of Viola's trial, the mystery surrounding the Reverend Vándory, numerous discourses on Eötvös's views on the medical profession, prison conditions, public education, the office of *szolgabíró*, etc. etc.

In addition to his outspokenness on political subjects, Eötvös's prose style too raised some hackles. Narrative passages move along very smoothly, and in places there is even a sharp snap that verges on the journalistic. From time to time, however, there are quite lengthy and carefully composed sections of a descriptive or discursive nature, and then Eötvös will break into long, polished, periods, the authorship of which might have pleased Tacitus. Such is the Hungarian or, as some will have it, Prussian oratorical style. The Hungarian reader is likely to require a deep breath, two attempts, or both to find his way through such a sentence, while the translator is faced with a jig-saw puzzle – but all the pieces will be there! Whether it is advisable – or even possible – to transplant such oratory whole into English depends entirely on the context, but my feeling is that the attempt is always worth making. Such a marked stylistic feature is an important element of the text. Professor Cushing (*Hungarian Prose and Verse*, Athlone Press, 1956) finds this "ponderous and didactic", while D. Mervyn Jones in *Five Hungarian Writers* (Clarendon Press, 1966, p.185) prefers "often brilliantly written", but the (frequently ironic) humour that distinguishes much of the work is not missing from these passages.

East European literature has a long tradition of seeking to inform the reader as well as to entertain him. Writing in particular of the Russian novel, the vicomte E.-M. de Vogüé likens the Western reader to one strolling in a shopping street, glancing at the shop windows on the off chance of spotting something of interest, while the East European reader has a more serious purpose in mind. Eötvös is quite explicit about what he is doing: the writer of history compiles facts, from which he deduces principles, while the novelist begins with a principle and devises a narrative to illustrate it. He refrains expressly from descriptions that his reader will not require, and at the same time states repeatedly that he is not writing history.

Antal Szerb describes Eötvös's political conviction as 'compensatory': as the scion of an aristocratic, German-speaking family, he benefited from having as tutor József Pruzsinszky, who had been imprisoned for involvement in the 'Jacobite' anti-Habsburg Martinovics plot of 1794–5. Pruzsinszky, however, was clearly unreformed, and along with Hungarian and Latin planted liberal ideas in his pupil, resulting in the weakening in him of the family's traditional pro-Austrian stance. Eötvös therefore came to the view that although, as a country conquered by the Turks and then annexed by the Austrians, Hungary had been well served by the independence of the county administrations – almost mini-kingdoms, so independent that in 1848 Ung county felt able to refuse to acknowledge the coronation of Franz Josef I – nevertheless the country would be better off with a strong central government. The county system allowed too much room for inbred incompetence and self-seeking to the 5% of the population that exercised day-to-day political power. Those with vested interests and less liberal attitudes could hardly be expected to support this view.

Despite the acclaim with which its translation met in the English press – one reviewer wrote "I envy anyone that has not read this book, as they have that pleasure in store" – *The Village Notary* was not well received in Hungary. After the War of Independence of 1848–9 many in England had a certain sympathy with the Hungarians' attempt to cast off the Austrian yoke, and all the more so as Russian intervention had a lot to do with their eventual failure. Much can be found in the book that derives both from Eötvös's position as a leading figure in the centralist party in parliament, and more precisely from A karthausi and his only play to achieve success on stage *Éljen az egyenlőség! – Up with equality!* – of 1844, some of the characters of which reappear in *The Village Notary*. His essay *Reform* (1846) also echoes the sentiments on which the novel is based.

Political enlightenment is, however, to be found in *The Village Notary* in the person of the *főispán*, the aristocratic representative of the crown in the county, as he comes to Taksony to preside over the three-yearly election. His status makes it hard for him to mingle with *hoi polloi* but his secretary goes out and about and reports back, while he himself insists on talking to the eponymous notary. Their conversation presents a summing-up of Eötvös's own views – "The nobility have used the county system to build defences around themselves, behind which they've been able to shelter for centuries even against the law" – and gives a realistic assessment of why it is so hard to take effective action.

The book holds a balance, therefore, between racy tale and the author's frequently trenchant commentary on the Hungary of his time. In the English translation of 1850 it is significantly abridged in favour of the racy tale, thus diluting Eötvös's purpose not a little, and, although contemporary English reviews make no mention of the point, appears to have been made from the 1846 German version by Johann Mailath. The present translation is made from the unabridged Hungarian, and one must hope that while being better informed of Eötvös's aims the reader of this version will suffer no loss of entertainment.

The Village Notary

I

Anyone who has been to the part of our Alföld[1] beside the Tisza, or spent even a couple of days anywhere in it, can safely say that he knows the whole. As in the faces of certain families it's possible to detect individual differences only on closer inspection, so it is here with individual regions, and when the traveller whom sleep overcomes in his carriage on our sandy plains wakes a couple of hours later he'll only realise that he's progressed because the horses are sweating and the sun is lower in the sky. The general nature of the countryside, and indeed individual details of it, will remind him of as little as the middle of the sea does him that moves with swelling sails. The meadows extending into the distance, the unchanging nature of which is only relieved here and there by a sweep-well without a bucket, or a stork strolling round a half-dried-up marsh, the ill-kept plough-lands, the maize and wheat on which are protected, after God, only by the fact that to steal them would require an effort, here and there an isolated farmstead where shaggy kuvaszes proclaim by their barks the sanctity of the property, and where the hay- and straw-ricks left from the previous year allude to the owner's very great thriftiness or very few cattle – these the traveller could see when he closed his eyes and can see when he opens them again. The very church towers which, when he last looked round, stood like pointed columns on the distant edge of the plain have, it seems, travelled with him, or at least there's as little difference between them and those that he can see now as between the village that he was then approaching and the place (it might be a town) towards which his horses are now trotting. And when he learns from his driver that he has slept from noon till six in the evening and has advanced several miles he's amazed at the miracle. It's a well known fact that nothing has more effect on our mood than the character of those whose company we keep, and therefore it's natural that, just as the law student, on appointment as *táblabíró*,[2] forgets or repents of his youthful excesses in Máramaros, so the Tisza too finally acquires the character of the region – through which it travels by sinuous

---

1   'Lowland' – the 'Great Plain' of central Hungary.
2   In pre-1848 county administration, an official appointed and accredited by the *főispán*'s office (therefore in effect by the crown) to preside over committees and especially act as judge in county courts of law. Rather like the English Recorder, but the term won't be translated.

3

ways – and, with the exception of those instances when it loses patience because of immoderate goading, or is forced unjustly from its bed by some planning authority, even in its floods it retains that measured and dignified sloth which nothing that takes its course in this wide world can display apart from the ruminations of the committee appointed to deal with it and cases in progress at Hungarian law: so that even those floods, the seasons of which we know and the extent of which is marked on our maps, we may term excesses as little as we may the tendency of men of standing in official positions to become thoroughly intoxicated at installations, elections or weddings. When the time of the flood is over the waters, having come soundlessly, depart without a murmur, and the light brown Tisza flows calmly on between its low banks like the best citizen of our country (for how many are there among our great men that dispense their treasures only on their fatherland!),[3] and so it's the most fortunate of the great rivers of Europe, as it's the only one with the liberty of which no one interferes, and it alone can say with noble self-awareness that it has remained entirely as God created it.

Somewhere on the Alföld beside the Tisza, then – that I may at last turn to my tale – in a county which we shall call Taksony County, on the nearer or farther side of the river, close to the bank, where it bends in a great S, not far from where three birch-trees stand on a sandy hillock some two fathoms high (note that particularly, reader, since there isn't a hillock for miles around, least of all one on which trees stand, and by this symbol the scene of our tale may most easily be found) lies the hamlet of Tiszarét, property of the Réty family since it was first occupied by the Magyars, as the lawyer of this clan, the worthy Jónás Macskaházy, is at all times ready to confirm with documents reliable and at the same time fabricated, if, that is to say, he should encounter anyone in Taksony County so bold as to cast doubts on the Asiatic origins[4] of the Réty family.

The Rétys are among the wealthiest of families. Their sons are born *táblabírós*. As the late father of the present head of the family once said, with noble pride: not a single one of them has died in whom the County

---

3   The river rises in northern Transylvania and joins the Danube to the east of Újvidék/ Novi Sad, both of which areas – now in Romania and Serbia respectively – were in Hungary at the time of writing. Also true at the time of writing is that no attempt had yet been made to regulate the Tisza and prevent the considerable flooding for which it was noted.

4   The Hungarians are in origin a nomadic people from Central Asia who arrived in the region in the 9th century.

didn't mourn its alispán[5] (after their deaths, one hopes); and so it's natural if individual rays of the brilliance that has surrounded that family have also flooded the hamlet of Tiszarét and charmed its region – according to the statement of the County engineer, who surveyed it and found nothing out of true other than the aforementioned hillock – into a veritable paradise.

The very extensive English park, the trees of which, planted in the sandy soil almost thirty years ago now, have grown to an incredible height; the big lake, the waters of which have in fact subsided somewhat, but the little of which that remains is a finer green than the lawn itself, while the latter, especially on rainy days, is sandier than the paths which, although supplied with ever more fresh soil, have at times been, to the gardener's surprise, considered by strangers to be muddy; the magnificent mansion, its domed roof adorned by golden balls, on the porch of which the *alispán* is accustomed to smoke his pipe of an afternoon while a whole host of petitioners kick their heels outside the Gothic portal; the great courtyard, with the stables to the right, the great greenhouse to the left, and next to it the several storeys of the chicken coops, not to mention the magnificent midden here, extending to almost half the height of the stables – everything bears the marks of luxury and magnificence; and when, especially as one goes out of the gate, one suddenly finds oneself on a causeway which leads from the house straight to the seat of the County and has been built for the sake of this one house alone – one has the feeling that one is in the vicinity of *alispáns*.

Everything that the Rétys have built is of a monumental character, and if, in the public memory, one of its principal distinguishing features is that it has been built at public expense, that again is one of those facts of which, like the family's ancient nobility in Taksony County, no one is in any doubt, and of which, even if a number find fault, the wise majority approve in accordance with the just opinion that, as the proverb has it, one hand washes the other, and in this case no one could state that by that operation – which has continued for so long a time between the Rétys and the tax-payers of the County – the hands of the alispáns have become clean.

But as, in the course of this tale, I shall have the opportunity to acquaint my readers with the Réty residence and all the beauties and conveniences of the hamlet of Tiszarét, permit me for now to walk down the street all the way to the open country, to the hillock that I have men-

---

5   Until 1950 the highest-ranking elected official in a Hungarian county.

tioned, which stands some quarter of a *mérföld* from the village and is called *Törökdomb*, Turk's Hill; and even if there weren't three trees on it, it would be worth visiting all the same, because on completely clear days – such as that on which our tale begins – from its summit the top of the hill of Tokaj can be seen like a blue hayrick.

The warm rays of the October sun were pouring their light upon the broad acres of Tiszarét. There was not a cloud in the sky to mar its deep blue; as far as the eye could see there wasn't a cart to envelop the green of the land in a cloud of dust, and only the sound of a thousand lark-songs that filled the heaven, the distant lowing of the village cattle as they grazed, and here and there an occasional worker, as he strolled homeward singing, scythe on shoulder, broke the solemn silence in which the sun sank toward the horizon. On the hillock, from where the view extends to the forest of St-Vilmos, and if we look beyond the acacias surrounding the houses of Tiszarét we can follow the course of the Tisza for miles, two men were sitting side by side, immersed in the view of the countryside, or perhaps in such thoughts as involuntarily seize the heart of man at the sight of landscapes frequently seen, and call to mind memories of days long past. There is a feeling somewhat akin to nostalgia that rises in the human breast when one has passed one's prime, and which beckons one approaching the end of his career to the finer days of childhood; the narrower the circle to which our age confines us, the less we seem to have done or experienced that is really worthy of memory: we look all the more kindly on the age when at least our expectations were glorious, and in so doing see that if not among the chosen, then at least among the called is where we too have belonged. And there is really nothing at which we should wonder if the men that we find here on the hillock, having spent their lives in an Alföld village, sometimes sigh as they look around in their old age at the place of their lengthy toil because they remember how at one time life extended around them too like a spreading plain on which the eye encountered no obstacle, and they had been able to go only to such a little part of that broad expanse! because here too there had stood previously unsuspected frontier hills beyond which they were unable to extend their working lives. But be that as it may, thoughts that are often the master rather than the property of him that they fill don't belong in the province of the historian, and so without disturbing our new friends in their comfortable reverie I shall merely undertake to acquaint my reader with their persons.

A man's appearance is part of his destiny. The face with which we step into society gives rise now to sympathy, now to alienation, and as in

6

England the day on which it is to be eaten is written on the turtle's back, so on the faces of many, unaware of it though they themselves may be, their end is plainly inscribed; perhaps my readers, after my sketchy description, will look at my characters with greater interest as I introduce them on the Turk's Hill, and I shall merely say succinctly that they have met Jónás Tengelyi, notary of Tiszarét, and Boldizsár Vándory, Calvinist pastor of that village.

What I said previously about the effect of our appearance on the course of our lives no longer actually applies to these men; their faces are no more going to open or close the doors of fortune before them. We can see from their grizzled locks that they have reached that time of life when, however comfortless the bed made by fate may be, there is nothing to be done but to lie down and wait for sleep; but if the judge of human nature finds no opportunity for prophecy in the faces of these men, what he can read of the past in their features is all the more, and all the more interesting, while time – which always leaves its stamp on the human face as on the coinage of kings – has perhaps never left behind more recognisable traces than on the honest faces of these two, simply because it may never have exercised its influence on nobler material.

Every aristocracy has marks which distinguish its members from the crowd. Here long finger-nails, there a tattooed face; in one country, as in Turkey, green clothing, in another, as in Venice, black; in some places a button on the hat, in another a ribbon in the buttonhole, a weapon at the side, or, as was the case with the Persians of old, a stick carried with an apple on it, tassels on their horses or a peacock feather on themselves. Who could enumerate the long list of those signs and privileges each of which arouses desires, jealousies and hatreds, and which, if they elevate men beyond the natural state – that is, as a savant friend of mine is accustomed to say: if they develop from wild animals to domesticated – from the moment of birth until their last hour sets them apart one from another, and which in some places, where civilisation has advanced further still, reminds the passer-by at the gibbet: he that hangs there hadn't only been a thief but also ignoble. Nature too has its nobility, and it too gives its nobles marks by which its chosen can be recognised among the crowd, however much our godless age may rant about equality. I don't mean that nature can attain its goals as perfectly as can our nation-states. Nature has never extended its powers of ennoblement in the way that among the Chinese one's deceased ancestors, or elsewhere one's posterity yet unborn, may be elevated to the nobility at a stroke; as regards distinguishing signs, only our higher civilisation has attained

7

such perfection in these details that we can perceive the rank of every individual more clearly before they descend from their carriage than after talking with them. There are, however, cases in which natural nobility reveals itself by clear indications in a number of individuals, and anyone, for example, that has once seen Jónás Tengelyi, the village notary, will no doubt acknowledge that in respect of him my statement is correct, in explanation of which I see it as further necessary to mention that, as he is a nobleman[6] of ancient stock, in the present case nature is assisted by custom.

If you came to Tiszarét to change horses, drove past the notary's neat house, and happened to meet Tengelyi, dressed in his old-fashioned but trim caftan, the ringing tones in which we usually address those of a lower order – as if we considered that nature had bestowed on them fewer ears than on ourselves – softened involuntarily. In his presence the military commissioner didn't invoke his saints and the *szolgabíró*[7] himself – to which, incredible though it seems, I could call eye-witnesses – would doff his hat, which he was never seen to do before other notaries (perhaps in order to seem taller or so as not to expose the weakest part of his body to the evil influence of the air), although on such occasions, lest his status be impaired, he was always at pains to explain this extraordinary deference by the unusual warmth or the need to straighten his hair. Tengelyi must have been about fifty years of age, and the thinning locks, which had long turned to grey, and the deep furrows which time had ploughed on his forehead made him appear even older. But as the rugged bark and gnarled branches of the oak speak of centuries, while if you look upwards the bright green of its foliage hints only at spring and proclaims the abundant life-force in the ancient tree, so, if you looked at the gleaming eye beneath that wrinkled brow, and after the grey locks considered the tall, manly bearing, you were convinced that you stood before one of those whom time had hardened rather than broken, and who, in the long battle of life, had, like colours in the midst of the fray, merely been stripped of their decoration.

---

6   In the Hungary of the time it is important to distinguish between *aristocrat* and *noble*. The aristocrat, like his English counterpart, had a heritable title – baron, count or duke – whereas the 'common nobility' had no such title but was the equivalent of the ancient freeman class – distinguished from the servile class by the possession of a *dog-skin* or letters patent of nobility, and exercising certain privileges. The status was heritable, but the common nobility were in appearance not always clearly distinguishable from the peasantry, and might follow menial occupations.

7   See note 13 below.

The man sitting at Tengelyi's side as he fixed his eyes on the ever bluer hill of Tokaj was studying the seed heads of a couple of flowers – he appeared somewhat older, and the mild expression on his regular features seemed to contrast with the serious sternness that you have observed on Tengelyi's. If on the latter's interesting face you noticed the imprint of long struggles, which time hadn't yet concealed, and while the darkling fire of his eyes hinted that though the passions in his bosom were dormant it wouldn't be impossible for them to be rekindled, Vándory's cheeks smiled before you in undisturbed calm, like the sky on which passing danger has left no trace. In the former you saw the fighter, the man who, sensing the injustice of fate, didn't allow himself to be overcome and struggled without hope but courageously, like the champion who fights on only in order that he may not have to surrender. With Vándory the priestly robe was unnecessary for you to realise that you were faced with one of those whom God has sent to this earth as his vicars, to be the consolation of their suffering fellow men, and if the sight of the former aroused in you the doleful thought that you had once more met with an honest man that had not achieved happiness in the world, from the face of the latter there smiled upon you the consoling conviction that not only did the particular sufferings of virtue walk the earth, but so too did its peculiar delights that pass all understanding.

At last Vándory put down his flowers and broke the silence in which the friends had been sitting side by side for almost half an hour.

"A penny for your thoughts, my friend."

"I was thinking of all sorts of things," replied Tengelyi; "of my schooldays, of Heidelberg, of the time when I was a law student. Do you still remember Heidelberg, my friend? It's been a good while since we saw it, close on thirty years since I left the university, but now and then I come up onto this hillock and see the top of Tokaj hill, and the beloved town appears in my memory; the green hills, the vineyards, the magnificent ruins that rise above, and if I compare it with the monotony of our region I could weep for the huge injustice of a fate that has given human beings a plain like this to live on."

"You're disparaging our beloved region once again," said Vándory with a smile, seizing his friend's hand, "isn't this meadow here as green as any in the world? The river which winds its way there between waving grasses, the darkness of yonder forest, the distant church towers, the hill of Tokaj – isn't it all lovely? If you won't look up to the sky, and are forgetting that its pure blue and the rays of the declining sun are equally

9

beautiful everywhere, it's you that are unjust, my friend, you refuse to recognise and enjoy the gifts that your fortune brings."

"You're the greatest of optimists!" Tengelyi interrupted him with a laugh. "Isn't it sufficient that there is no man whose good qualities you can't enumerate, if you extend your protection even to the region of Tiszarét? Really, I'm beginning to think that God Himself, with all His omnipotence, wouldn't be able to create anything in which you wouldn't find something very good."

"And am I any the worse or less fortunate for being content with the wise dispensations of God?" said Vándory, and smiled. "And because I look for as much good as possible on this plain and in those people among whom I live? The region, which inspires admiration by its splendour, is for the most part poor, if you consider it in detail; and you'll find the same in close acquaintance with so-called great men. The plain, the boring flatness of which wearies the eye, on closer examination displays such fertility, so many points of beauty, that you almost forget how poor the whole is seen to be. From the stars on high to the bowels of the earth, where gold branches out along hidden veins, there's nothing in which one mightn't take delight; why then shouldn't we seek those treasures that are hidden from us? Why shouldn't we choose a position from which the most beautiful view lies before our eyes?"

"That is, if we're able to do that."

"We are so able," replied Vándory, gently pressing his friend's hand. "Believe me, we are, we're all born optimists, you and I and everyone else. God has made his creatures for happiness, and as, according to Holy Scripture, hell and heaven were peopled from paradise, so all suffering and pleasure are the work not of our nature but of our free will."

"What of our experience?" interposed Tengelyi.

"That only proves what we wish it to prove," said Vándory. "Anyone that can discover the good side of the present will come upon plenty in the past too that will confirm him in his cheerful view of life. Anyone that looks on the river of life with a cheerful face will see a cheerful face smiling back from its smooth mirror, and everywhere on earth pleasure will re-echo from the groves if you have sent pleasurable sounds towards them."

"I see that I can't get the better of you," Tengelyi laughed. "I hope that Macskaházy's canonised in the near future and that you'll appear for the angels and testify that never was a man a greater cause of virtue, since everyone that didn't give him a hiding won a very great victory over themselves; and that very hare which those young gentlemen have put

10

up," said he, pointing with a finger to the west, where in the distance a number of riders were approaching at the gallop with their greyhounds, "if it asks you, will receive the answer that a hare can have no finer death than to be hunted down. Because when you remind your faithful on Sundays of their salvation, and of everything for which they owe gratitude to Providence," he added with a wry smile, "your task isn't much easier."

"That's a vulgar entertainment, unworthy of man," said Vándory, turning his full attention to the hunters, who were making for the Turk's Hill. "I can't conceive of how civilised men take pleasure in it."

"Can't you? and yet you can't prevent its attracting your attention," said Tengelyi, "and you watch the unequal contest with interest."

There will be few among my readers who, if only in their youth, haven't enjoyed the delights of coursing. The first hare that he catches leaves as indelible an impression on a man as his first love-affair, and indeed, there are those who can hardly tell which of the two memories is the more pleasant. The weak women, however, who dignify this rustic tale with their attention have surely heard detailed accounts of the delights of coursing from much dearer lips – so that on this occasion I can safely omit the heroic feats of Szellő and Czigány,[8] how many twists and turns the hare made, how it finally doubled back and was then caught by the last and slowest greyhound.

The hare had at last been caught, the company of coursers dismounted and petted the hounds as they lay around panting, and Tengelyi cast a wistful eye at the hunters as he sighed: "Ah, my friend, ah, these are happy men!"

"For my own part," Vándory repeated, "I can't conceive what pleasure civilised men can find in so uncouth a pastime."

"I believe you, my friend," said Tengelyi with a smile, "we can seldom understand the woes of others, and more rarely still their pleasures; but all in all, how much more mindless is this than the other pleasures that we find in testing our imagined strength. Anyone that feels the goal that he has set himself approaching moment by moment as he watches it, and is finally able to attain it, is a happy man; whether it be the catching of a hare or the conquest of a world that he has set himself, the feeling's the same. The only difference lies in the ways that spectator and performer see things."

---

8   'Breeze' and 'Gypsy', names of greyhounds.

"And the cruelty," said Vándory. "Doesn't it occur to you how the poor animal suffers, how unequal the contest is, all those horses and hounds in pursuit of a single terrified hare! It's little short of disgusting."

"The inequality of the contest," Tengelyi sighed. "It's true, but where in the great struggling world can you actually find equal forces opposed? The English factory-owner versus his employee, the American plantation-owner versus his slave, is there in any part of this world a more equal contest between rich and poor than what you have just seen? And as you consider the things that happen around you every day don't you realise that the Roman emperor who killed unarmed slaves in the circus for his amusement, however great the disgust with which we speak his name today, had more followers than any other of his kind that has come down to us in the history books? Oh, believe me, my friend, the cruellest of gentlemanly amusements isn't coursing: there are some in which the prey hasn't, like this hare, lived on its pursuer's crops, and couldn't run from the cruelty."

Vándory could only respond to these harsh words with a deep sigh, and if, perhaps, as an optimist he thought inwardly that Tengelyi was mistaken, he said nothing.

The hunt was over, and so Ákos Réty, who had seen our friends in the distance, came up to them on the Turk's Hill with his fellow huntsmen, bade them a good evening, and so brought their conversation to an end.

If my gentle readers could see for themselves the company which gathered round the old pastor and the notary, I'm in no doubt that Ákos Réty and Kálmán Kislaky would attract their attention. Handsomer young men, it was said in Taksony County, weren't to be seen in six counties around, and especially after the hunt, when their youthful faces were flushed and their dark locks, once they had doffed their little round caps, framed their foreheads even more handsomely in their disorder, and their upright figures showed to good effect in the blue coursing jackets – what female eye wouldn't linger in delight on these young friends? Quite as many good things were to be read in their smooth, youthful faces as in the wrinkled cheeks of Tengelyi and Vándory, but etched in finer lines; the honest gaze of the eyes was warmer too.

As a Hungarian writer, I know my trade and am aware that in Hungary no one can compare with the *szolgabíró* in his own *járás*,[9] and shall turn my attention first of all to this official and his clerk,[10] who had followed Réty in the hunt and now to the Turk's Hill.

---

9   A ward, the area for which a *szolgabíró* has responsibility.
10   In Hungarian *esküdt* 'sworn man', the lay assistant of the *szolgabíró*.

According to our men of learning Scythian blood lives in Hungary.[11] There are times when we may be forgetful of this, and indeed, among those whose names offer the clearest evidence of their Asiatic origins we non-philologists sometimes think of quite different things.[12] Pál Nyúzó, however, *szolgabíró* of the *járás,* who had taken part in the hunt on his bay and was now lighting his pipe, stands before us as reassurance that the Scythian blood from which our race springs hasn't yet dried up in Hungary.

If I were writing for foreigners I would at this point insert a footnote with a neat article on the duties of the *szolgabíró;*[13] perhaps the fair sex, who spend so much of their lives in the company of *szolgabírós,* don't even suspect all the weighty burdens that lie on the shoulders of their favourite dancing partners, and which it has taken a diligent writer two thick volumes to describe; as, however, all political aims are far from my tale let it suffice for me to inform those that are in ignorance that the office of *szolgabíró* is beyond all question the most onerous undertaken by anyone in this wide world, and the one beset with the most woes and the greatest fatigue. The *szolgabíró* is the maintainer of public order, defender of rich and poor, judge and father of his *járás,* without whose intervention no one can obtain justice, through whose hands pass every complaint from below and every order from above. He is the regulator of waterways, causes roads and bridges to be maintained, takes the part of the poor, is chief inspector of schools, head huntsman if wolves make an appearance, chief medical officer if plague looms, justice of the peace, ultimate authority concerning bills of exchange, inspector of criminal law, police-court magistrate, military commissioner for billeting soldiers, rural policeman, superintendent of hospitals – in brief, everything *in quo vivimus, movemur et sumus.*[14]

If one of the five or six hundred men in Hungary that bear this office fails, through negligence, to fulfil his obligations, thousands suffer. If one

---

11   An erroneous belief, once held by some to account for the Asiatic origins of the Magyars.

12   The names of characters are frequently allegorical, derived so far from *(Tisza)rét* '(Tisza) meadow', *macskaház* 'cat-house', *vándor* 'wanderer' and *tengely* 'pivot'. *Nyúzó* means 'skinner'.

13   I *am* writing for foreigners, though, and must point out that the Hungarian term *bíró* doesn't always translate smoothly into its usual modern equivalent 'judge'. As here explained by Eötvös, the *szolgabíró* had responsibilities at least as much administrative as judicial in his *járás.*

14   . . . in which we live, move, and have our being. Acts 17:28.

of them shows prejudice, the administration of justice ceases for several square miles around. If one is ignorant, the Hungarian parliament lays down its laws in vain, at least as far as the tax-paying population is concerned. And if my gracious readers assess the *szolgabíró*'s rewards for these burdens, and consider that, apart from an annual salary of a hundred or a hundred and fifty forints, he has the certain prospect that, if he has discharged his office impartially, in three years' time he will be deprived of it by a powerful enemy and appointed *táblabíró*,[15] they will admit that in Hungary there are five or six hundred living saints, or at the very least just as many hundred thousand suffering citizens.

The office of *szolgabíró* has, therefore, as all can see, two great shortcomings: too much work and insufficient payment; and unless individuals that bear this office ease this constitutional woe and neglect a good part of the one – I mean the work – while taking more of the other – I mean the payment – than they would be obliged by law to accept, indeed, unless the cleverest, once initiated into the secrets of their office, don't very wisely combine two improvements by which to amend our faulty civil framework, so that what their office offers so abundantly – work – they only undertake if at the same time they can reckon on some of the other – payment – I can't make out how His Worship Pál Nyúzó can bring up his four sons as pillars of the fatherland, and how he can conduct himself with the dignity that his office demands and which keeps in wholesome dread every time that he enters it the whole *járás* of Tiszarét – or rather, its humblest part, that which seeks free of charge that most valuable treasure of civic liberty, justice.

But it wasn't even necessary to know these things for everyone to be filled, in the presence of Pál Nyúzó, with the holy fear necessary for the maintenance of public order. By then his very appearance filled with foreboding not only the guilty but also the innocent. His figure was gaunt and bony, the grim expression of his wrinkled face was enhanced by a dark beard and long, pendulous moustache, and his green, gleaming eyes seemed created by God not merely for seeing but also for wounding; added to that the short-stemmed pipe without which no one had ever seen him except at angariation assemblies, and which therefore seemed to be reckoned among the parts of his body, and the harsh voice, which reduced entire villages to trembling at every interrogation or other legal proceedings, constituted a whole at which everyone in the

---

15 The *táblabíró*'s salary would depend on his appointment, but might be as much as 3,000 Ft.

járás trembled – with the exception of evil-doers; and above all, anyone that saw him in his carriage was forced to admit that nowhere did justice assume a more formidable guise. Let certain clever people say what they will, but the four coach-horses with their garrulous coachman might furnish the clearest evidence of how quickly the Hungarian judiciary moved: behind the mounted coachman was a gaudily plumed liveryman and behind him – *post equitem sedet atra cura*[16] – a bundle of rods which could not fail to remind anyone that had delved into Classical antiquity of the lictors of Rome: after the rods came the *szolgabíró*, smoking his pipe and swearing from time to time; and finally the empty and oh! so ample leather bag which – *quia natura abhorret vacuum*[17] – travelled with its owner in order to be filled; the whole represented a gradation from great to greater before which even the bravest couldn't stand firm.

A *szolgabíró* without a clerk is inconceivable. As nature has created in pairs, so the Hungarian constitution, which, as we know, is entirely based on natural principles, brings justice into being only by the joint operation of two: the *szolgabíró* and the clerk; and as I have spoken of Nyúzó, it's what Kant calls the *postulatum* of the practical mind that I should present to my readers Kenyházy,[18] who, not quite at his side but a little to the rear, was engaging in the most interesting conversation with one of his master's greyhounds, in the kindness of his heart making use of certain colloquial expressions by means of which a shepherd had been threatened during the last court session.

András Kenyházy, or old Bandi, as he was generally called by his most intimate friends, was his master's right hand, but not the sort sometimes found among clerks, who, in the words of scripture, don't know what the left hand – the *szolgabíró* – has done, and do the precise opposite; he was the sort that knew his superior's every wish and strove only to perform what constituted half of the whole. As a good Christian, Kenyházy the clerk framed his life entirely in accordance with those words of scripture in which it's ordained that if we're struck on the one cheek we should proffer the other . . . and every time that his master was insulted – by insult, meaning the greatest that a magistrate can suffer, to wit, a bribe – he too would hold out his hand, and indeed was prepared

---

16 Black care sits behind the man on horseback. Horace, Carmina 3, 1, 40.

17 . . . because Nature abhors a vacuum . . . Coined by Rabelais in *Gargaantua* (book I ch 5).

18 *Keny-* is perhaps out of *kény* = *kéj*, 'pleasure, gratification' and *ken* 'to bribe' and *ház* 'house'.

to fly into the greatest rage if that insult wasn't perpetrated on him too. Anyone, however, that thought Kenyházy easily bribed was mistaken; indeed, nothing in this world was more difficult, little short of more dangerous, and anyone that had witnessed the abuse with which the clerk, in his righteous indignation, turned on any briber, would offer his gift to the mild-natured *szolgabíró* with a certain trepidation: even after such affronts, however, Kenyházy never forgot his oath, and so as not to yield to his temper rather favoured to excess those by whom he was most offended on such occasions as long as the other party didn't seek its salvation in even greater affronts, in which case the clerk would prove his independence most elegantly to everyone who, trusting in their gift, had thought him well and truly bribed.

And now, instead of describing the person of Kenyházy, whom we shall meet frequently in the course of this story, and giving details of his clothes – from the blue spencer (not a button missing in its earlier days), the waistcoat (the present colour of which is due to the effect of the sun), the cravat, wrinkled by time, which now hangs as comfortably on its owner as it must have on any, the mouse-coloured trousers that have slipped up to his knees as he rode and so on down to his spurred boots, which, together with his rotund hat, lend to the person of the clerk a curiously Hungarian appearance, may I draw my readers' attention to a prejudice which, praise be! doesn't in practice exist among us but which is, in theory at least, commonly accepted: I mean that against magistrates susceptible to bribery, which, I am fully convinced, is one of those unjust assertions which, out of pure jealousy, are disseminated against us that are better educated by a thousand mouths of the public.

In actual fact – leaving aside our Hungarian laws, under which our judges are permitted to accept gifts, and which are in this respect not considered outmoded even by the most venturesome innovators – isn't gratitude the basis of all morals? Isn't it one of the virtues without which we can't so much as conceive of a good man? And have we any right to desire of the judge that he alone be ungrateful to him that would do him good? "What thou desirest for thyself, that do unto others also," commands our faith; assuming now that the judge were in the position of him from whom he now accepts a gift, that is, if he were a party in an action concerning the rights and wrongs of which he is not entirely convinced, wouldn't he too wish, in that case, that his judge should accept a gift from him and pronounce in his favour? And has he then no duty, since it's in his power, to treat his fellow man as he would wish himself to be treated in such a situation? According to the general principles of law no judge may deliver his verdict except in accordance with matters declared and entrusted to him in the court proceedings; now if, among considerations finely balanced, one of the parties places a couple of banknotes among its documents and the other simply fails to respond to these disclosures – can the judge do otherwise than ascribe truth to him whose cause is the better defended? And doesn't history hint at the same and set before us a long line of bribes from Jacob's mess of pottage to the Judgement of Paris, indeed perhaps somewhat farther, as examples from which future generations can learn? If the Alcmaeonids hadn't suborned the Delphic Oracle Athens mightn't have been liberated from Pisistrates and his clan; and if the shepherd hadn't been bribed at Thermopylae and led the Persians by that path Leonides wouldn't have died his heroic death. If the Euboeans hadn't bought Themistocles, and he the other generals, the Greek fleet would have retreated and Greek freedom, and with it perhaps civic liberty, would have been lost; space alone prevents my setting out a long price-list of the cost to peoples and periods of remaining free or becoming slaves. And can anyone wish that Hungarian judges shouldn't strive to follow such lofty examples? That in this great market they alone should dispense free of charge the treasure entrusted to them, or that they should give to all in exchange for a little honour – for public esteem depends on the crowd – that through which our noble country might run into no slight danger? True, there have been instances of individual rulers sharing this prejudice and being merciless to certain judges. Thus we know from Herodotus that Cyrus had a judge of the king's bench flayed for judging unjustly in return for payment, and had his skin used to cover the seat on which his son later sat in judgement. Likewise Darius had a judge hanged; but, thank Heaven, those times are long past, and if now and then, here and there, injustice arises – because surely according to scripture it's necessary that there be iniquities – at least we can be certain that what scripture also declares – "Woe unto them that devise iniquity"[19] – will also no doubt come to pass, and that their examples will surely deter those who, like them, would be so impudent as to rise against their judges.

However, it's not for us to argue points of law, but it is my task to tell the tale of a village notary, and so let us return to the company that we left on the Turk's Hill. Kálmán was debating the cruelty of coursing with old Vándory; Tengelyi and Ákos took little part in the discussion – the former because, as he said, the matter belonged among those (like du-

19 Micah 2:1.

17

elling) on which we can theoretically be of only one opinion and yet in practice we all do the precise opposite; the latter, because completely different passions and thoughts filled his heart and mind, and as anyone must have been convinced who saw him when he asked old Tengelyi about his daughter Vilma, there were things that interested Ákos much more than coursing.

Tengelyi replied with dry brevity and manifest ill humour, and changed the subject.

Nyúzó and his clerk spoke about the election and the means of gaining public trust, of which conversation, however, at a distance there could be heard only the names of a number of places and expressions like 'ten barrels', 'a silver thaler' etc., to which the clerk always responded with a 'Well, that's settled', muttered between his teeth, and clinked his spurs together as if he meant to dance, scarcely able to restrain his glee, and he emitted from his pipe such clouds of smoke that I would compare him to a steam engine working at full power – if I didn't consider inappropriate the comparison of such a ceaselessly working item to a Hungarian nobleman.

The company was about to move off when attention was drawn by the servants to two riders who had been approaching the hillock while the conversation was taking place. A man was going on foot in front of the riders, sometimes between them, and Nyúzó, whom this sight interested strangely, had asked more than once if they weren't gendarmes. When the riders came closer it became at once beyond doubt that those approaching were servants of the County, such were the occasional blows with which they struck the man walking in front of them as they began the usual preliminary treatment of the person arrested.

"Ride over to those gendarmes, someone, and tell them to bring the criminal straight here," said Nyúzó to his clerk; "I dare say that's one of Viola's band. It's a case for a *statarium*,[20] and it would be bad to take him into the village. Didn't I say," he added, addressing Ákos, who had also turned his attention to the riders, "that we'd round them up? Even if I'm put out of office, at least I'll satisfy the County's previous trust in me and have another three of the villains hanged on this hillock before the election."

"You mean, if you catch them," said Ákos with a smile, "of which, if you don't mind, I still have my doubts. To turn Tengelyi's views round – he always says that it's hard to find an honest man in this world – that's

20 A court specially convened to deal with outlaws. See below chapter 22.

the only sort that you catch in your nets; and if my eyes don't deceive me, the one that is being brought here – Viola's accomplice," he added with a laugh, "the great villain with whose hanging you mean to favour the County, the new Jaromir and Angyalbandi[21] – is our old Gypsy."

Kislaky, who had now recognised Peti – such was the name of the well-known man – also began to laugh, and none of the company, with the exception of Vándory, whose heart fell at the sufferings of the prisoner, could remain serious.

"Poor Peti," said Ákos with mock regret, "the country has no more useful citizen; if a house is built he makes the bricks; if a lock is broken somewhere he mends it, so that the property may be safer; if a horse loses a shoe or some *táblabíró* his spur, he puts it back on; at weddings he plays the cello, and he digs the grave if anyone needs burying; indeed, wicked tongues say that once in his young days he served as hangman, and now he's treated like this! There's no remedy for it, the world's always ungrateful to its great men and even more so to the useful."

"I don't know how you can be so frivolous," said Nyúzó, frowning. "It may be a case for a *statarium*; I at least don't believe that the man my gendarmes are bringing is your old Gypsy, and if he isn't . . ."

"If he isn't," Ákos interrupted with a laugh, "and if he somehow has the impudence to be innocent, naturally nothing will stand in the way of a hanging."

"Now, that will do," Nyúzó interrupted Ákos's witticisms, adding a couple of words to what he had said which are missing, together with all their original Hungarian quality, from the vocabulary of learned society; "Who has said that this isn't your Gypsy? But who knows, the old villain who you have thought was a harmless cellist . . ."

"He hasn't just been pretending to be a Gypsy, has he?" Ákos laughed aloud, rather amused by the worthy official's anger, "and now the truth will come out. You'll strip the evildoer of his swarthy skin, you'll show that the famous Viola, of whom the whole district is afraid, is none other than Peti the Gypsy and . . ."

"I won't tolerate anyone thinking that I'm foolish," roared the enraged Nyúzó, in whose anger his pipe went out. "If you don't mind my saying so Pál Nyúzó is not a man to be trifled with, and in any case we shall see who laughs last. Who knows what the so very honest old Gypsy finds to do apart from making bricks, and if he's once played the part of hang-

---

21 Jaromir (1003–38) was a duke of Bohemia. Angyal Bandi (real name András Ónody, ? 1760–1806) is the first known highwayman in Hungarian history.

19

man can't he play another part at the gallows? The old villain, I believe, might not look at all bad if he were swinging."

To that the *szolgabíró*, forcing himself to laugh at his witticism, re-lit his pipe and, cursing at the tasteless jokes, the match that wouldn't burn, the gendarmes who weren't hurrying and the old Gypsy, waited for the hapless prisoner.

Poor Peti, who in the meantime was coming ever closer to the Turk's Hill, and at five hundred paces' distance had begun to cringe, didn't even suspect the storm that was gathering over his head as he approached and which Ákos, suspecting the consequences of his levity, now endeavoured by all means to calm – but in vain. Nyúzó's annoyance had risen to full tide, he needed someone on whom to vent his spleen, and Peti saw, at the first words that he addressed to him, that he had come before the distinguished gentleman at a bad time.

"So, you're caught in the net at last, my precious bird," he roared, after completely changing his nature to inquisitor in order to be able to speak with him honestly, "now, never fear, you old rascal, you're going to pay the penalty."

"If you please, Your Honour," sighed the unfortunate one, with the gentlest voice of his cello-pitch husky throat squeezed into a violin, "I . . ."

"Silence!" thundered Nyúzó, "I know everything, and never fear, I'll refresh your memory if you try to deny it."

"Your Honour, Your Lordship,[22] I'm a poor, innocent, old man," sighed Peti. "I . . ."

"Stop snivelling," shouted Nyúzó, "or I'll box your ears so that you'll remember me till the Day of Judgement. Just see, the wretch still dares to deny."

"But I'm not denying anything, Your Worship, not a thing," he added, weeping, "only . . ."

"Better if you don't; we won't ask you anything," old Nyúzó cut him short. "The authorities know everything, and now," turning to one of the gendarmes, "tell me, János, why have you brought this old villain before me?"

"Well, it's like this," replied the man addressed, "because the order was to arrest all suspicious persons."

---

22 Nyúzó is usually called *tekintetes* '. . ', but here Peti calls him by the superior titles *nagyságos* and *méltóságos*.

20

"And therefore," interposed Ákos, who had been visibly riled all through the scene and could no longer control his annoyance, "you've arrested the old cellist and really deserve a gold forint."

"We'll see about that later," said Nyúzó, with a cross glance at the interrupter. "Please continue," he went on, turning to his gendarmes. "So what has this old villain done?"

"Well," the gendarme continued – he seemed as taken aback by Ákos's words as by Nyúzó's unaccustomed civility – "it was like this. It must have been about three o'clock this afternoon, wasn't it, Pista," turning to his companion, who nodded in confirmation, "we were walking from the Gyilkos *csárda*,²³ where we'd had a rest and a bite to eat, towards the St-Vilmos forest. We'd been on horseback from sunrise until noon, and we were beginning to be afraid that we weren't going to be able to comply with Your Worship's order at all events to bring in somebody; then Pista, who's got better eyes than me, saw a rider by the forest and somebody with him that was talking to him. 'What if that's Viola?' said Pista, who was just lighting his pipe. 'Goodness, if only it was!' said I, and I looked that way and saw . . .'"

"Viola?" asked Nyúzó in such a tone that anyone, like his gendarme, that knew him could easily realise what reply was required.

"Yes, Your Worship," answered the one questioned, "I'd bet it was him."

"With your inferior eyesight," Ákos interrupted. "you're really wonderful! Well, what more must Pista be able to see if even you can recognise a man at half a mile."

"We shall see," said Nyúzó crossly. "If thieves and highwaymen can find such support the devil can keep order. Go on, my good man, what happened next, didn't you see the evildoer closer to?"

"No, we didn't, Your Worship," replied János, "we'd scarcely got our horses to move – poor things were so tired we could hardly get 'em to trot – and the villain slipped away, and by the time we got there we only found this old Gypsy making full speed for St-Vilmos."

"Well, what else?" said the magistrate impatiently; his hopes had clearly been dashed.

"Naturally they clapped the collar straight on him and brought him here," Ákos interjected, "because who knows what atrocities he would have perpetrated if they'd let him go all the way to St-Vilmos! If the men sent to hunt down thieves are always as clever as these there'll be

---

23 *Gyilkos* = Deadly, an odd name for an inn!

21

an end to highway robbery tomorrow, because honest men won't dare go out of the house."

Meanwhile the old Gypsy said nothing. He turned his dark, shining eyes this way and that, and realised that he had found someone to speak up for him. He faced his questioner with greater confidence, and only begged for the collar to be taken off him as it was chafing his hands terribly.[24]

"You've learnt to play the cello," shouted the magistrate, "and that little violin[25] looks well on your hands," at which witticism Nyúzó and his clerk laughed loudly. Vándory, however, was visibly disturbed at the whole scene, could restrain his feelings no more and asked the magistrate to release him; Kálmán and Ákos did the same, while Tengelyi spoke of cruelty. Chiefly because he couldn't reply to these requests, which, because there were servants present, had been put to him in Latin, Nyúzó ordered the collar to be removed, muttered between his teeth something about putting a yoke on him and the way that criminals were too well treated, and told his faithful servant to continue.

"And then what happened, after you'd caught up with the Gypsy?" said Nyúzó, turning to the gendarmes, who were busy removing the collar, astonished at their magistrate's unaccustomed civility. "What did you observe after arresting him? Didn't you find anything on this old gallows-bait that would make him particularly suspicious?"

"Well, the way it was," replied the gendarme, stroking his moustache and spitting once with gentlemanly dignity and a sense of noble self-awareness, "when we caught up with the Gypsy – and that was a while later, because the old *more* was running full pelt – Pista said, the Gypsy's scared stiff . . ."

"Scared?" interposed Nyúzó. "Why, I'd like to know?"

At which the clerk, with his customary shake of the head, remarked "very suspicious".

"By your leave," countered the Gypsy, rubbing his aching hands, "when they just pulled out pistols and swore at me like that I could only think they were bandits."

"Silence, you accursed brown dog," shouted the magistrate, "or I'll have you given such a thrashing that you won't lie on your back for six months. Go on, János."

---

24 'Collar' here translates the Hungarian colloquialism *hegedű* (literally 'violin'), placed round a prisoner's neck and also restraining the hands, like a portable pillory.
25 An untranslatable play on words!

"Then," János went on, "Pista asked him where Viola had gone off to? And he said that he hadn't seen him."

"When we'd seen him talking to him," Pista put in, realising that the magistrate approved and anxious to share in the respect that he was showing his companion. "That's not true, Gypsy Peter," said I. "You were talking to him here and we saw you, and if you don't confess we'll make you dance to another tune straight away. He kept on denying it. So who was that man on a horse that you were talking to?"

"Well, what did the Gypsy say to that?" asked the clerk, forcing his face into an expression of profound insight.

"He only said he didn't know him," replied János, "and when I lost my temper at that – because as you know, Your Worship, Peti knows everybody – he started to run."

"Oh, if it please Your Worship," implored the Gypsy, "certainly I would have run when they were going to beat me half to death and meant to put the collar on me."

"The honest man," interposed the clerk, "doesn't fear the collar."

"That's what I thought,", replied János. "So we realised straight away we were dealing with an evildoer and we were after him like the wind, collared him and brought him here to you, sir, and now the truth will out."

"You've done well, the pair of you," said Nyúzó, "now take this old scoundrel to my office ahead of me and stay there; I'll need you, and perhaps we'll send this precious flower to County Hall."

"Oh, please," whined Peti, "when I'm innocent, as innocent as a newborn babe."

"Yes, we know," retorted the magistrate in his sourest tone, "you don't even know Viola; nor did you shoe the villain's horse yesterday, did you?"

"Of course I know him," sighed the Gypsy, "how can I help it when I've lived in the same place as him for twenty years? Before the County got their hands on him, you know, he was such a decent man he could have been elected magistrate. It's true I shoed his horse once, but what can an old man like me do when bandits with axes and pistols come round to make him shoe horses? I'd have died a terrible death if I'd refused."

"So why don't bandits go to proper blacksmiths?" asked the magistrate, with a look at his clerk, who smiled and nodded his approval.

"I think," answered Peti calmly, "they only come to me rather than any other blacksmith because I live outside the village."

23

"And why do you (the author omits the titles used at this juncture on account of the difficulty of spelling them) live outside the village?"

"Because ever since there was a fire in Jancsi Barna's cottage His Worship the *alispán* won't allow us Gypsies to live in the village," answered the Gypsy humbly. "It's quite hard on an old man like me."

Nyúzó, to whom, in the words of Scripture, the 'lost sheep' that he could guide to the right way – that is, to County Hall – was dearer than the ninety and nine that never strayed, saw in every response given by a person under examination an affront to magisterial dignity; my readers can't imagine the effect that poor Peti's simple answers had on that so worthy official. Everyone has their vanity, and will find injuries to it harder to tolerate than more substantial harm; even a better man is in difficulties if he is disappointed in his opinion and will sometimes forgive his fellow men more easily for their failings than for being better than he had thought; no wonder that Pál Nyúzó, who was inclined by self-knowledge (however much we deny it, the basis of our understanding of people) to pessimism, was never willing to regard anyone as innocent that he had once considered an evil-doer. In this case he had been irritated by Ákos's jokes and was doing everything possible to bring the old Gypsy's crimes to light.

"Very well, very well," said he, swallowing his annoyance to the best of his ability, "we shall see if you behave so pertly in my office as well; by tomorrow you'll have a famous companion, and it will all come out when you're confronted with him. Take him away, and don't let him escape, because . . ."

The Gypsy whined and the gendarmes had begun to put the collar on him when Ákos, affected by his tears, offered to stand surety for him and asked the magistrate to let him go. Nyúzó was delighted at the chance of revenge for the jokes and shook his head in refusal.

"You know," he said as gently as could be, "I'm always happy to please you, but on this occasion you'll forgive me – it's impossible! By tomorrow morning Viola will be in our hands and we shall see that this Gypsy is one of his men."

"If you're going to keep Peti until you catch Viola," said Kislaky with a laugh, "you're taking in a permanent guest."

"We shall see," replied the magistrate scornfully. "All I'm saying is that Viola will be in my hands this very day, and if he isn't you can laugh in my face. I know from a reliable source that he'll be coming alone to the Tiszarét inn this evening. As soon as it's dark the inn-keeper's servants and any-

24

one that happens to be there and might give a warning will be tied up and locked in the cellar, and instead my gendarmes and the sergeant will be waiting for him, dressed as peasants. The rest will be a matter of course."

"Yes, if he turns up," Ákos interrupted, "but . . ."

"He'll turn up this time," came the reply with magisterial dignity. "Pál Nyúzó has his spies that he can trust. Now," – to the gendarmes – "off you go."

Anyone that had been watching old Peti during this brief conversation could have noticed the sudden changes that unmistakably crossed his swarthy face. Ten emotions were registered on his oriental face, ranging from the keenest interest at hearing the first mention of Viola's arrest to complete despair as he heard of the preparations, but fortunately for him only Tengelyi noticed his agitation, and when Nyúzó's attention returned to him he was standing penitently between the gendarmes; they prodded him to move as ordered by their chief.

"I humbly beg you, young sir," said he, turning to Ákos, "if I've got to be going now, and put in the cells, innocent old man that I am, tell your father that old Peti's been arrested and it's not my fault I haven't delivered the letters."

"What letters?" asked Ákos.

"The ones that His Worship the *alispán*'s entrusted to me," said the Gypsy. He took a couple of letters, wrapped in rags, from his waistcoat and handed them to Ákos. "I've always been His Worship's messenger, and I wouldn't have been late this time either, because Madam promised me a good tip as well if I took them to St-Vilmos before dark, because she said it was something important; and if these – Peti only thought the required noun – hadn't caught me over there in the forest . . ."

Never before has a document caused such a change in a man's fate as did the handing over of those letters in the case of Peti. And when Ákos had opened one, glanced at it and passed it to Nyúzó, who read it, the perplexity and annoyance that showed on their faces were greater than can be imagined.

"I must confess, you've arranged this cleverly," said Ákos to the magistrate rather more quietly. "If you lose the election at least you'll be able to console yourself with having helped the enemy to win, because if the three hundred St-Vilmos votes go against you, you'll all be out of office, no doubt about it – and that's what might happen."

"No chance," muttered Nyúzó through his teeth – while his clerk on hearing mention of 'out of office' shook his head and sighed deeply – "no chance, because the St-Vilmos people . . ."

"They certainly don't care all that much for you," Ákos interrupted, "and if they elect you it'll only be for the sake of my father, or rather of their notary, who in turn is a supporter of my father for other good reasons, and not because of you. We learned this morning that they'd tried to reach agreement with the notary of Bántornya, but without success. My father has taken advantage of the opportunity and in this sealed letter is promising everything that the village scribe wants. At the same time he's inviting the entire nobility of St-Vilmos to come and shake his hand tomorrow – and now you come with your gendarmes and imprison the messenger so that your enemies can seize the initiative when their wicked ways were being obstructed. This is the stuff of farce – I don't know a better name for it."

"But who would have thought," said Nyúzó, "that your father would send such important messages by a man like this?"

"When I said," Ákos went on, clearly overjoyed at the magistrate's embarrassment, "that old Péter was our loyal man and had carried our letters for years, who would have thought that the *alispán*'s trusty Gypsy would be arrested for no good reason and clapped in irons, and not released even against surety."

"Quite," said Nyúzó, scratching his head in his perplexity, "but when he didn't say, never said a single word, that he was carrying such important letters. Confound you, you old villain," he went on in fury. He was one of those charming people that lose their temper at the drop of a hat and are never more uncouth than when they ought to apologise; so that when they tread on your toes you are almost in greater danger than if you had trodden on theirs – "Why didn't you say that you were going on His Worship the *alispán*'s orders? I've a good mind to have you given twenty-five strokes, so that . . ."

The Gypsy, now sensing for once that his back was being protected, said that the gendarmes had already done that, and that in his pain he had forgotten his errand . "Furthermore," he went on, "Her Ladyship had told me to let no one see those letters, least of all anyone from the County, and I thought that in the end I'd be proved innocent."

"Innocent? Monstrous!" said Nyúzó, wringing his hands. "He's carrying letters from the *alispán* in his bag, and he relies on his innocence. But off you go now, clear off, make yourself scarce, here are your letters, and if you're not in St-Vilmos by nightfall just you look out!"

Although the sun was now low on the horizon the Gypsy bowed and, without a word of protest, set off quickly towards St-Vilmos to obey the magistrate's impossible order. When he had gone Nyúzó turned his rage fully on the gendarmes, and with many a curse expressed his surprise at their impudence in daring to arrest the *alispán*'s own Gypsy. A few minutes previously they had been dreaming of flagons of wine, but now they stared as the clerk entertained them by threatening to put them in irons. Ákos and the rest set off, laughing now at Nyuzó's gesticulations, now at the Gypsy, who, looking back from time to time, unlike Lot's wife ran faster and faster every time that he saw the magistrate like a roaring tempest behind him. Only the notary and the pastor remained unamused, and when the cheery company had taken their leave and trotted towards the village, and Nyúzó's swearing and the accompanying laughter of the others could no longer be heard, Tengelyi took his friend's hand and said: "What do you say, aren't I right? Coursing isn't the cruellest pastime in which those gentlemen indulge, is it?"

"Oh, my God," sighed Vándory. "When I think that those are officials, that the fates of thousands are in the hands of men who can actually laugh when they see their fellow men suffer! . . ."

"But who is there that doesn't laugh at the sufferings of his fellow men?" said Tengelyi sourly. "From the child who trips another up as they play, to the man that plays foul on a grand scale or at least sees it done, there's not one that isn't pleased to see his fellow man tripped up, who doesn't laugh. Why are those any better than the rest? But," he added, after a brief pause, "the sun has set, let us go home as well."

For once Vándory didn't venture to contradict. He stood up and the two set off side by side in silence for the village.

"Look at that," said Tengelyi, who had turned round and stopped for a moment, and was pointing something out. "Isn't that our old Gypsy running over there?"

"It certainly is," Vándory replied. "I've been watching him, but I don't know, it seems to me that he's running this way rather than towards St-Vilmos."

"So it seems, my friend," Tengelyi answered. "This time His Worship the *alispán*'s orders aren't going to be carried out. Either Peti's been bribed by the enemy, or – you never know – perhaps Nyúzó's right after all and he really is in league with Viola and is warning him about the trap, as the magistrate so wisely told him about it. But it's no concern of ours, let's go home, it's getting chilly."

And with that the two moved on towards the village in silence, sunk in thought. The dulcet tones of the evening bell rang out to greet them as they approached.

27

But now we shall leave them to their thoughts, and the description of their lives to be found in the next chapter will bring us closer to a knowledge of their characters than any detailed description by me of their present. Only the past is the key by which the apparent contradictions in men can be understood. As with a river, so for the most part with people too it's not so much their temperament as the course that they have run that determines their nature; anyone that observes it, sometimes at a great distance, will always discover the reason: why are there foaming waves? Why has the manly bosom lost its purity? And God alone is both infinitely merciful and just because He is omniscient.

II

At the point where the Carpathians sink lower and lower, finally shrinking into green hills and the great plain of Hungary, lies the hamlet of Bárd.[26] On either side stretch long hills, the one densely forested with oak, the other covered with vines. It is, to all intents and purposes, a poor Hungarian village; situated as it is far from the highroad, seemingly concealed – even its close neighbours hardly know it – it is one to which, on account of its pleasant situation, anyone that has ever been there is glad to return. Some half-century ago there lived in this village Ézsaiás Tengelyi, pastor of the Reformed community[27] of Bárd and father of Jónás, whom we have now met as notary of Tiszarét. This is the place where his life was spent in his sacred labours, known to few but loved by all that ever met him.

Anyone familiar with the situation of the Calvinist clergyman in this country will readily believe that fifty years ago, and especially in so small a place as Bárd, old Ézsaiás's situation can't have been luxurious, yet there will be few among my readers who spend as many cheerful, truly happy hours in their mansions (if this book, which its sympathies will guide towards cottages, were ever to find its way into mansions) as did the grey-haired pastor of Bárd beneath the thatched roof of his house and the time-darkened beams of the little room. There were days when he wished that the window in his room were a little larger, and indeed once or twice in his life he had contemplated having this deficiency remedied at his own expense, as especially in overcast weather his reading of Holy Scripture was impeded. The stove, which was used for baking as well as for heating, took up a sixth of the room, and especially on summery days, if baking took place indoors, produced rather more warmth than comfort required; and every time that neighbouring clergy came to call great criticism and complaint were levelled at the people of Bárd for not even having boarded the floor of their pastor's room. There were no lack of requests and encouragement that, as others had long since raised sound objections to the circuit about the clay floors of their premises, he

---

26   The ancient village of Bárd was combined in 1851 with the neighbouring Lipótfa, Bánya and Szerászló, and since 1908 has been known as Bárdudvarnok. It is, however, nowhere near the Carpathians, but 10 Km south-west of Kaposvár in western Hungary. Perhaps Eötvös thought that he had invented it!

27   I.e. that of the Calvinist Church.

too should speak out in defence of the dignity of the cloth – his silence was shameful. But when the weather brightened once again and Ézsaiás looked at his defective window and remembered how many holy words he had read beside it, and how many times he had seen – on arriving home of an evening – his wife's dear face behind the little panes; and when he considered what a long stove-bench the big stove provided in winter, and thought that the clay floor on which he paced to and fro was the same on which his father, when he had been pastor, had thought out his sermons, and on which he himself had crawled and taken his first hesitant steps, it became clear to him that when all was said and done window, stove and floor were best left as they were and that no comfort could replace the treasured memories that were linked to them; and the little house remained in its ancient simplicity, concealing beneath a modest exterior, like a pearl-shell, a whole wealth of domestic bliss. And if there are those that believe that contentment depends on worldly goods, they would be convinced, on entering the calm that surrounded that hearth, that true good fortune is not the consequence of outward condition, and that it is a mistake so to strive for things that can do as little to alter the feelings of the heart as a dull or gaudy binding can affect the meaning of the book that it contains.

One natural but unexpected event disturbed the even tenor of this modest household. Erzsébet died; and then the heart which had previously harboured such great happiness knew only great pain. The old priest made no complaint, didn't speak of his grief, did nothing that would increase or dispel his bitterness, but those that had known him previously now sensed that his anguish was not such as time would ease, and that his desires and hopes could now only be fulfilled beyond the grave.

One thing there was that kept the old priest in this world – his small son Jónás. When his mother died the boy was barely five, and what would become of him if he were to lose his father too? The majority of people have scarcely goodness enough truly to love their own: where in the wide world would a stranger and orphan meet with a little affection? And furthermore . . . the boy was so handsome. His sky-blue eyes looked at his sorrowing father with the gentle gaze of his mother, his voice reminded him of her from whom he had learned his first halting words, while in his golden curls there could still be seen the touch of the hand by which they had been so diligently tended: what would become of the child if, instead of parents, he found in the world only a double grave to turn to in time of trouble? And if there is life beyond the grave, if the icy hand of death doesn't break the thread that binds together those that love one another, could Erzsébet be happy in God's heavenly kingdom knowing that her son was alone in this world? Old Tengelyi thought all this over and, like so many men of honour that have forsaken other consolations, derived strength to endure his life from a sense of duty.

Meanwhile young Jónás grew up happily in his father's care. In his happiness he was not even to suspect the misery of being without a mother in this world, where the heart always craves affection, and there is nowhere other than in a mother's arms that it may surely be found. So much pleasure finds a place in the heart of a child that there is no room for pain. As the sapling draws up with its roots the soft rain of summer, thrives and develops in the warm rays of the sun, but doesn't yet know the power of the tempest in the lulls of which it grows – so it is with man: it is only later that he becomes acquainted with the woes of his existence. In the early days after his mother's death little Jónás looked for her ten times a day, and when he could not find her sat weeping in a corner; at night he stretched out his little arms in his sleep and snivelled her name, but as time went by he spoke less and less often of his beloved nurse until finally the happiness that he had previously experienced in his mother's embrace was only like a sweet dream, retained in his heart like the fond memory of slowly fading music, of the entrancing sounds of which only that impression remains that pleases the listener. And how could it be otherwise? Perhaps the capacity for forgetting quite quickly is the child's most enviable privilege. Around him a hundred flowers are bursting into bloom – why would he delve in the dark depths of the past? Around him sing a thousand voices at which his heart leaps: how could he hear the faint sound of words from the past?

Nothing disturbed little Jónás's happiness, and any reader that retains memories of childhood can imagine that better than I might describe it; suffice it to say that as the vessel full of spice spreads its odour all around, so does the child's heart the joy with which it is filled to over-flowing, and that old Ézsaiás himself, whose hair became greyer as the years passed, when he turned his gaze from the heaven where the love of his life awaited him to his earthly surroundings, there too found himself not lacking in pleasure and hopes.

Thus the early years went by; Jónás reached the age of eight, and the old priest began his education.

Let no one expect me to embark on an exposition of educational theory.[28] Old Ézsaiás's sole principle of education was that since he that feels no warmth of love in his heart is incapable of true happiness or of achieving any great thing, only love can educate one for life. This was the principle by which he brought up his son; he therefore made use of that which appeared to be appropriate because it didn't infringe this heart-felt belief, and because in this way he ensured for his son at least the treasure that is worth more than all learning put together: happy memories of a childhood on which one can look back and be reconciled with fate. (Our learning is thus bought at the price of much pleasure; why do we sacrifice for that precious thing – after which we strain, while our hearts are impoverished without our heads feeling enriched – the innocent pleasures of childhood, the only pure enjoyment in our lives?) The boy asked questions and the father answered them in as great detail as possible and in keeping with his pupil's capacity for understanding, and so it was that by the time that he was ten the little boy wasn't behind any of his age in his clear grasp of ideas and concepts, although not actually educated in accordance with the system that is fashionable in our schools – perhaps the only good aspect of which is that the child is taught in a foreign language and is less disturbed by all the follies that he learns than he would be if he learned them in his native Hungarian.[29]

No one should think, nevertheless, that Jónás was one of those child prodigies of whom we find hordes – mostly the children of beautiful mothers, or in houses where good lunches are served. Old Ézsaiás, who, though a poor boy, had obtained himself a good education, was far too sensible to bring up his son on those lines. In his understanding, just as morals didn't consist of individual superior acts but of every action in life being conducted in accordance with certain moral principles, so true learning too was to be sought in the perfect understanding and application of a few concepts – and his every effort was directed solely at confining his mental labours to a narrow circle, so that neither should the weight of subjects be oppressive nor the number of them tend to superfluity. Ancient and Classical languages (within the boy's capacity), a little study of nature and of history, sufficient for him to learn to admire his Creator in the wonderful order of the material world and to love

---

28 Later in his career Eötvös served twice as Minister of Education and Religious Affairs – briefly in 1848 and from 1867 to 1871.

29 Hungarian displaced Latin as the language of instruction in secondary education only in 1844.

32

men through great examples of virtue, and above all the clear, moral understanding of religion – that was all that old Ézsaiás taught his son, together with what he considered necessary for him to respond to his calling.

But there is always something in the heart of a child over which the power of upbringing doesn't hold sway: the child's capacity for imagination, and it is this on which the road that we are to follow mostly depends. As the fruit that the tree bears in autumn comes from the blossom that smelled so sweet in spring, so the actions of the man spring from the frivolous dreams of the child, and who shall determine the limits of those? So it was in the case of young Jónás too. While his father was making plans for his future, planting a couple of fruit-trees in his garden and a fine spreading linden in his yard, and even, indeed, frequently thinking about how he could most cheaply have the floor of his room boarded simply so that the joy of his heart, when he became pastor of Bárd, should be more comfortable, the ten-year-old's thoughts were moving in different spheres, and the youthful spirit, which now felt itself restricted in the homely comforts of that modest dwelling, sought its pleasures in roaming among hopes of a far finer future.

As the sailor yearns for harbour only after experiencing danger, so he whom life has not yet tossed about can't conceive of the delights of calm: and it is the prime need of every young man to find himself an arena in which to test his strength in conflict. Chance soon furnished an occasion to awaken and direct those thoughts. Old Ézsaiás, who had, in his youth, studied at a number of universities in Germany and Holland, had brought back with him a fine, leather-bound copy of Plutarch, a gift from an academic friend, in which each biography was preceded by an engraving of a portrait of the man described. As that was the only illustrated book in the house young Jónás became acquainted with it at an early age, and whenever his father permitted he would spend hours looking at the grave manly faces, until every picture became well known, almost a friend. His father was delighted at his son's thirst for knowledge, and spent many happy hours giving an account of them; before Jónás was eight he could tell the names and stories of almost all the pictures so well that old Ézsaiás's eyes were frequently bathed in tears of joy, and although he regretted that the book wasn't a bible, over which he could have told his son religious stories, every time that the child spoke with enthusiasm of the virtues of Aristides, or when his face blazed as he told the tales of the heroic deaths of Leonidas or Socrates, his fatherly heart swelled with joy and he blessed the pagan writers, the

33

friend that had presented him with the book and all that had had a hand in making it, including the binder. For what could better prepare his son for accepting the teachings of religion than the stories of those men who had been the first to perceive the moral values through which Christianity became widespread?

This book had a decisive effect on Jónás's entire life, and although his father didn't fail to make him aware that the standards of Holy Scripture, which he studied with him later and which deeply interested the sensitive child, were of a much higher order than what he learnt in his beloved Plutarch, first impressions retained their influence, and whenever time permitted he returned to his favourite portraits; he felt more sympathy towards them and their tales warmed his heart more.

Often, when his father had gone to neighbouring villages or was away on official business, Jónás would go into the hills and wander aimlessly in the gloomy forest, as the mood took him. Local people often saw him near the ruined castle of Bárd, looking now at the wooded hills that bordered it on one side, now at the plain that stretched boundlessly into the distance, until the glow of evening spread over the countryside, he woke from his reverie, and went back home. And who can imagine the joy that filled his heart at such times? There is no loftier pleasure in this world than the memory of a truly great deed or person which permeates an untainted heart. As in the first period of the development of every people: the child sees a demigod in every great man, and Jónás was at the age when he could enjoy that splendour in its full purity.

Just as our ideas of physical distance only come to us later, so it is in the sphere of the spiritual world. The child considers everything that he can see to be equidistant, and bravely reaches out for it all. We often catch up with life, and even that which is, so to speak, at our side, by a lengthy approach – the child doesn't yet know of it; he doesn't know that the heights of the world can generally only be scaled from one side, and that what is easy to one to others is impossible, and only because no way leads to the summit from where they stand. To the child, the great man whom he admires is at the same time an example after which he strives and a hope at which his heart leaps, and that makes for his happiness. Like every child brought up in solitude – that is, without the company of other children, for only in the company of our peers are we not alone – Jónás too became given to reverie and serious, and if anyone heard him discoursing on Pericles or the Gracchi they were convinced that they were in the presence of one whom fate had condemned to be either great or unhappy among his fellow men; in fact, the two are not far apart!

Fortunately, these thoughts didn't disturb old Ézsaiás's peace of mind. The enthusiasm with which his son spoke of the ancient virtues, the fiery hatred with which he rose up against the oppressors of mankind and his sympathy for the suffering of others merely convinced his father that his son would make a good clergyman. The fact, however, that this enthusiasm showed itself otherwise than in fiery sermons was beyond the range of his thoughts. Indeed, he himself made every effort to confirm his son even more in those noble sentiments. He often spoke of the misery of the poor, the heartlessness of the rich, of man's indifference to God – and how it was the duty of everyone to devote their lives to the good of their fellow man! So it was that when, at the age of thirteen, Jónás was sent to the Calvinist College in Debrecen all the good and bad qualities that were to mark him in later life were already developing in his heart. Boundless enthusiasm for all that was good and noble, fiery hatred for any form of villainy, sympathy towards all suffering, courage at all times and in all places when there was need to speak or act against injustice – but at the same time that severity of principle which itself sometimes leads to injustice; in brief, all the properties that in Utopia would set Jónás among the most virtuous of citizens, but which in our high civilisation make him insufferable, or at least the sort of man that people avoid. In school, however, where every man's societal life begins, none of these properties were yet forbidden. Among children virtue is always in the ascendancy, and so no one may wonder at the esteem and affection in which Jónás was held by his teachers and his peers alike. The former were pleased with the rapid progress that their pupil, urged on by ambition, made in his studies; the latter respected his love of fairness and his courage, and though their serious class-mate seldom shared in their childish games, as soon as they fell out among themselves or needed advice he was their mediator and counsellor.

So five years went by in happy constancy. They were the best years of Jónás's life, a time of unsullied pleasure, when his heart was not yet at odds with the demands of the world, and pride and ambition, the seedlings of which he bore in his heart, were free to pursue their goals without arousing anyone's hatred. Studying itself too, which is the greatest, indeed, the only pain of other youngsters, filled his knowledge-thirsty spirit with that delight which we can encounter only at the start of an academic career, when – like the sailor who sets off with swelling sails – all that we feel is that we are under way and we yet suspect the immensity of the element upon which we are launching ourselves, nor do we think that there are hard times ahead for us because of which we shall feel no progress, lose sight of our destination and the shore ahead, and lose our bearings on the infinite expanse.

Meanwhile old Ézsaiás lived calmly on. The humble dwelling was quieter now, of course, since his dear son had left its precincts, and the aged priest, whose brow was now fringed by silver locks, now walked alone beneath the fruit trees in the garden where formerly he had watched his child at play; but his heart didn't lose its lightness. Like thin cloud pierced by bright rays of sunlight, the very yearning for his distant dear one which now and then rose in his heart was but another pleasure to that pure breast. But as the river, however placidly it flows, comes at length to the sea; and as the flower sheds its leaves even without the breeze when the time allotted by Nature to its perfume has expired, so the measure of human life passes among calm and dangers alike. Ézsaiás could feel that his days were numbered, and there was nothing in that thought that filled his soul with unease. The idea of death is only frightening when the concept of parting is not matched by that of meeting again, and Ézsaiás was convinced of his immortality. As the tree doesn't cease to put out leaves as long as it lives, so that pious heart did not, to its last breath, lose its expectations; they merely beckoned to him from another, more beautiful country.

He still had one desire: to end his life in his son's arms, and Heaven granted that. Jónás came home to Bárd during the autumn vacation. They had not seen one another for ten months, and when the boy saw his father so broken by years and feeble they embraced in tears – for the former tears of pain, for the latter of joy. Jónás was no pessimist. Just as experience makes us suspicious of people as well as of destiny, and he was still at that blessed age when every pain comes upon us unexpectedly; nevertheless, on seeing his father he was left in no doubt: that dear being's days were numbered. And Jónás was not mistaken.

A week went by, which father and son spent in the delight of those that love one another, and the first rays of the eighth day cast their light on the pious old man's cold cheeks; with eyes brimming with tears the people of Bárd accompanied their friend to his resting-place. A simple stone cross carved by peasant hands marks the spot where lies one of the noblest hearts that ever beat in human breast.

His father's death gave a new direction to Jónás's whole life. He had known his father's wishes and had applied himself diligently to theology. Every career is fine, if by following it we can make one that we love happy, and if his father had been alive and had passed the living of Bárd over to him Jónás would have found in that situation the occasion and place to satisfy his desires. Now, however, that the cause that had held him to a career in the Church no longer existed he was free to follow his own wishes, and those led him to a more lively scene. We shall find few of Jónás's age at the time who would opt for a peaceful career. A young man is sensible of the grandeur of the turbulent sea, not of the calm, and in feeling his strength longs for battles and struggles. Jónás therefore destined himself for politics, and since in Hungary no advancement is possible in that sphere without a knowledge of the law he threw himself into the law with all his might. In a brief course of study he made such great progress that, on the recommendation of his teachers, he was awarded a scholarship and was able to complete his legal studies at a German university.

Just as there are few that experience nostalgia, and even if they have never crossed the frontier of their homeland sometimes feel an indescribable longing for the place of their birth or where they spent their youth, so it is rare for the young especially not to long to be beyond that frontier, and perhaps not one such is to be found among Calvinist students. Naturally, our Jónás too wasn't one to lack this impulse. He therefore turned into money everything that had been left to him by his father, and with some six hundred forints in his pocket set off with a couple of companions for Germany, that Colchis of the sciences, where, guarded by grim-faced professors (perhaps that is why it is so hard to digest), hang dreams of the gold of speculative philosophy, and whence our capped and gowned return with university degrees and certificates instead of the golden fleece. As I say, Jónás too went off in search of learning, and for three years sat on the collegiate benches of the German university. Out of Christian love, however, I shall spare the reader details of those three years, and shall merely mention at this point that he spent most of his time in Heidelberg, and that among others – for what young man doesn't have numerous friends? – became the closest of friends with Réty, the honourable *alispán* in whose village we now find him as notary.

Those three years went by – without doubt the happiest that ever came to his honest heart – and Jónás Tengelyi found himself in Pest, that is, on the threshold of his professional career, with a couple of forints in his pocket.

An old friend of mine (a poor, God-fearing man; while he lived we always thought that he talked a lot, and only now do we know what a great pity it is that he has fallen so completely silent) always used to say, every time that some young man perpetrated some foolishness: "What a shame it is that we're not born old and live our lives backwards, be-ginning with old age and the cold of winter and progressing towards the warm days of manhood and youth. If we entered upon life with aged heads and cold hearts we would gain our experience easily and more cheaply, and when at last, after our labours, we reached a goal at least we'd have the strength to enjoy our good fortune." The old man, who was almost always thinking of such profitable matters, used to rack his brains to defend his thesis, and if only the government of the world had a constitution the equal of Hungary's it would, no doubt, have set his retrograde system in motion – but I can't share his opinion. It is quite possible that you would commit fewer foolish acts under that system and would progress smoothly towards your goal, but if your blunders were erased from your life and the errors among which you proceed removed, and there remained only the goal and the dusty, level high-road by which to attain it – would you be satisfied? True, you would not stumble, would never fall; but if, for example, when you were preparing for a fox-hunt the captured fox were put into your hands when you had just mounted – would you be pleased? And is it not the possibility of stumbles and falls that contributes the greatest delight to your hunting? The world, as Dr. Pangloss said, is best left as the Lord created it. True, in it we lose our bearings a lot, stumble and fall frequently, do foolish things, but finally our pleasure is there among the stumbling and error, and the great question remains: who is the more enviable, he to whom life brings the sweetest fruit – but like the fig, without blossom – or he whose lot is a delightful but fruitless flowering? My vote is for the lat-ter, and every time that I remember where I have erred I bless my God for not creating me more sensible. In the fourteen years that I attended school I could have studied more; as a law student I could have spent my time more profitably; but what would have become of all the fine games of ball, the fights, the walks, the friendships and the later sweet reveries if I had been more assiduous in school and as a law student in hearings? I say again: the world is best as it has been created.

But now that after a brief digression I have reached law students, let us go back to Jónás. (Let no one take it amiss that I speak in the plural. Another Hungarian writer has been criticised for doing so, I know off-hand which – but I always imagine at least ten thousand readers at my back, following the twists and turns of my narrative step by step, and can therefore not speak otherwise.) With us Hungarians political life, like marriage, always begins with a vow, but – because Pythagoras was apparently in high esteem among our ancestors – with a vow of silence, the success of which no one can deny in that law students speak among themselves on legal subjects. Jónás therefore took the oath and for eighteenth months rattled his sword up and down the steps of the majestic courthouse; thus prepared, he became a lawyer.

For quite some time nothing out of the ordinary happened in our hero's life, or nothing that I feel should be noted, with the exception of a negative miracle: in the eighteen months that Tengelyi was a law student he only went into a coffee-house twice, struck no one and gave no cat-calls, the natural consequence of which was that he didn't learn to play billiards and so could count only few friends among his peers. I might also mention, among other interesting events, that despite his endeavours he was awarded only a 'distinction' by the examiner, but it was much more remarkable that a couple of young gentlemen whom he had prepared for the examination passed with 'outstanding'. It would be a shame to dwell on the subject, mainly as this, the first injustice that he experienced in his professional life, hurt Jónás so deeply – but only until he took his seat in a cart, and in that modest conveyance set off for Taksony County on the afternoon of the same day. The first jolts of the cart filled the young lawyer's heart with bright dreams of the future as he approached the theatre where his life was to be played out, and there was no room for the past among so many thoughts. No doubt my readers will be curious: why did Jónás choose Taksony in particular as the scene of his future activity? They will think that he had expectations of property or powerful connections in that county; without such, as we all know, according to law and everyday experience we can't prosper; but I'm forced to confess that on this occasion my readers are mistaken. The principal consideration that sent our hero to those parts was that of the fifty-two counties in Hungary[30] there was none to which he had better reason to go, and furthermore, according to what all his friends from Taksony had told him, no more cultured county was to be found, while his fellow students from neighbouring counties asserted that there was no county in the whole of Hungary so in need of intellectuals, and so in either case a future seemed assured for a well prepared young man like Jónás; in the former case his merits would make themselves evident, and in the latter there would be need of them. Finally Réty, with whom

---

30 The number of counties in Hungary has varied greatly over the years and their history is complex. The maximum was 81 in about 1880, while during the Turkish occupation the counties almost ceased to exist. In modern Hungary there are 19 (plus Budapest) following a number of amalgamations, while in the mid-nineteenth century the number was 64..

he had had the closest friendship as a law student, was the son of the *alispán* of Taksony and had promised mountains of gold if he settled in that county.

At length, with heart pounding and with all those feelings that fill youthful hearts on numerous occasions, and which in their inexperience they consider important, our hero arrived in Porvár,[31] principal town of Taksony County. The traveller that arrives on a market-day might observe that he is in a town. On other days Porvár would seem an undistinguished village, did not the two-storey County Hall, outside the door of which several evil-doers in need of correction lamented daily from the whipping-post the power of Hungarian law, remind everyone that they were in one of the places where the long arm of justice knew no rest.

He delivered the letters in which young Réty commended him to his father and other friends in Porvár, rented a little room from the cantor, published his licence as a lawyer and sought work.

Doctor and lawyer respectively always test their skill on the bodies and estates of the poor, and for that reason our hero too began his life's work in that way; but his heart inclined him towards financially unrewarding work, and never did a defender of the poor exercise his noble craft more enthusiastically or with greater pleasure than he. The love of man and of justice is present to some degree in all young persons; all bring with them a small capital of goodness and nobility which later they sometimes lose among their struggles, but of which no one is completely devoid. In Jónás's case these sentiments filled his whole heart. In him all the oppressed, all the suffering, whom others had deserted could find a friend and defender. He was a martyr – or, as was soon the word in Porvár, a fool – for justice. Now let everyone consider his own county, and imagine what rapid headway our hero would have made in those circles. We can't boast of much success for him in Porvár.

At first he only undertook criminal cases, and his reputation remained quite high. True, one prisoner whom he considered innocent was sentenced to death, and a couple of others whose actions he declared excusable were treated more harshly in court than was customary – because as the magistrates said: "One can only strike back when a lawyer of no consequence tries to lecture the whole bench, for which very reason he has to be shown that no one pays any attention to his

---

31 *Por* 'dust', *vár* 'castle'.

futile speeches," but at least he himself wasn't attacked and was merely regarded with indifferent sympathy. When, however, he also began to appear in civil disputes, and wrote so strong a rebuttal against a very senior *táblabíró* who had been unwilling to pay a poor man to whom he owed money that he (the *táblabíró*) almost lost his case even before the Taksony court, then public scandal knew no bounds and for a fortnight whenever two citizens of Porvár stood talking in the street they talked of nothing but the young lawyer's insolence. The young people with whom he had by then become acquainted dropped him, the cantor gave him notice to quit, and he would surely have been sent to Coventry had not the *alispán*, for his son's sake, spoken out on his behalf and pointed out to the nobility that he was still young and no doubt, once he had lived for a while among them and repented of those mistakes, his cleverness would enable him to render valuable service to the noble public.

These were the first steps in Jónás's legal career, and although they took place under unfavourable circumstances our hero might well have persisted in it had not a worthy colleague, to whom I express thanks on behalf of myself and my publisher, caused him to reconsider. In the heads of all – according to Gall[32] – is to be found an organ of struggle (*l'organ de combativité*), developed to a greater or lesser degree, and this organ, which in our peaceful age leads only to verbal disputes, is often of irresistible power. I call in evidence my honoured readers – have you never experienced this (not in yourselves, of course, there can be no question of that) in your husbands and relatives? And have you never been irritated at being forced into arguments, for all your gentleness? This was Jónás's main fault too. There was no one that debated more readily than he, and it was natural that the legal profession, which offers such extensive opportunities for this inclination, should so attract him, as it also furnished satisfaction for his other passion, which made him eager to take the part of suppressed justice. In addition, there was one further reason that could have kept him in the law. The lawyer retained by the Kályhásy[33] family had recently died, and as that righteous man could, in the words of Scripture, take nothing with him but had left the Kályhásys' lawsuits behind; the head of the family, who had made Tengelyi's acquaintance in Porvár, was quite determined to entrust his legal affairs to him.

---

32 Franz Josef Gall (1758 – 1828), German phrenologist.
33 From *kályha* 'stove'.

As I said, we have one man to thank for this not happening – Pál Hajtó,[34] formerly the best known lawyer in Porvár. (I shall spare my readers a description of him, because our provincial lawyers mostly resemble one another as much as their cases do – some are longer, some shorter, but the outward appearance is identical.) Pál Hajtó, as I say, took an extraordinary interest in our hero. When others found fault with his impetuosity, he it was (when they were *à deux*) that constantly urged him to attack the court more sharply still, he it was that defended his virtue from the dangers which, as many know, attend the legal profession.

"My friend, you're not meant to be a lawyer," said he to his protégé. "Heaven means you for higher things. If I were you I'd go entirely into politics, because, you see, that's the only way you'll really get anywhere. As things stand, despite all your efforts, you're just conducting one case after another, and not only do your exertions bring no reward but they're actually futile. Hungary has to be reformed, and that's what you're born to do; of course, you can be a lawyer as well as a politician."

These words were repeated frequently and in a variety of forms, and in the end Jónás was convinced: anyone who has not believed such things when told them in his youth can safely be called a vain fool or whatever; suffice it that a meeting was imminent, and he prepared for his new calling with full seriousness.

The day came, Tengelyi gave his speech, and the whole public was amazed. Not at the speech itself, which, as everyone may imagine, was given in Latin, imitative of the language of Cicero and so old-fashioned, while its principles were so modern that that alone was cause enough for amazement, but that a young lawyer, scarcely twenty-four years of age, not even a *táblabíró* and even less a landowner, had the temerity to speak was such a surprising, an unheard of thing in itself, that the noble army of *táblabírós* at first could scarcely find words to express their indignation. Finally the long suppressed noble wrath burst forth. The full force of *alispán*, chief notary, public prosecutor and senior *táblabírós* roared into action against the hapless one that had dared to trespass on the preserve of their noble guild. Tengelyi, throwing caution to the winds, returned their blows and scourged *alispán*, chief notary, public prosecutor and senior *táblabírós* collectively and severally, until at the end of the debate the whole audience called for him to be fined. His last twenty-five forints, which he had on him, remained in the merciless

---

34 Another allegorical name. *Hajtó* is the participle of *hajt* 'to drive, urge'.

hands of the public prosecutor, and Jónás, his face ablaze with fury, went back to his lodging, swearing that he would revenge himself for those indignities.

As we can see, our hero's appearance on the political stage wasn't much more fortunate than his legal career, and as the first reward that his endeavours brought, apart from the twenty-five forints, was that Kályhásy, who had received a particularly sharp lesson in the meeting, entrusted his affairs to his friend Hajtó. But Jónás's stout heart wasn't brought low by this. Every *alispán*, prosecutor and notary has at least one enemy: that is, the man who would like to succeed him as *alispán*, prosecutor or notary. So it was in Taksony County too, and since he had come out against the present establishment Jónás had gained not only enemies but also friends. Chief of these was Konkolyi,[35] who was standing against Réty for the office of *alispán*, and could not sufficiently praise his intellect and the courage with which he had spoken out. Konkolyi was a conceited man, or at least was considered such, and therefore had little popularity among the common nobility. In this respect Réty far surpassed every *alispán* in the country; no one could address anyone as 'my dear sir' or 'old chap' in a heartier tone, enquire about their wives and children, or offer them a glass of wine – and this last is what really matters in questions of popularity, because our affection, like the grass in the meadows, has to be watered if it is to grow: no one could hug more noble companions to his bosom at one time and kiss them. It could therefore be feared that although everything had been tried that could convince the nobility of his worth, and the poorer nobility had had enough experience of the stocks and the more distinguished of amicable banquets to point out to them Konkolyi's qualifications for the office of *alispán*, nevertheless Réty's popularity would win in the election. Konkolyi's lawyer Hajtó, who understood these affairs better, and knew that good wine, such as came from its owner's vineyard, a fine mansion and an income of twenty thousand forints and the chamberlain's key[36] as well were the finest possible qualities to make anyone the perfect *alispán*, but in addition to these it was also necessary for the person so endowed to be elected: he lay awake at night over so worrying a state of affairs, and Tengelyi's sudden appearance filled his heart with fresh hope.

---

35 The name is derived from *konkoly* 'corncockle, tare'.
36 The title of *kamarás* 'chamberlain' was conferred by the Habsburg emperors on persons of distinction and noble extraction. The insignia – a golden key, hanging from a golden tassel – was worn on the rear of the coat, level with the right hip. At this date no duties or further privileges were involved, but a formal oath was taken by the recipient.

And so he called on our Jónás on the day when he had made his speech. He said that he had been distressed at the indignity that had been inflicted upon him, that he was certain that they could no longer endure that administration, of whose villainy he had made him too aware that day, that Réty alone was the cause of everything, that vengeance should be exacted for that wickedness, and that Konkolyi too shared these views and would be pleased to make the acquaintance of so outstanding a young man.

Flattery has an effect on us all, and there is perhaps no speaker on earth who doubts the statement if told that someone has been convinced by his speech. That evening Jónás and his friend Hajtó called on Chamberlain Konkolyi, and when he saw the numerous company that were all so well-disposed towards him and approved so much of his liberal ideas he could almost have wept for joy. The chamberlain said almost the same things as Jónás had heard earlier from Hajtó, and in the end he called on him most solemnly to seek office in the coming election. Because, as he said, he didn't belong to any of the great County families and so there was no other way that he might give effect to his words.

At first Jónás was diffident: he was young, poor, and unknown in the County – all these could be seen as obstacles under the circumstances. To which the chamberlain said with a smile "Don't *we* know you? – only by one speech, it is true, *sed ex ungue leonem!*[37] Trust us and we'll make you a *szolgabíró*. You're a nobleman, and in Hungary, however poor and unknown you may be, you can become anything." Jónás was quite convinced, and when that night he could not close his eyes there was scarcely anyone in Porvár through whose head more dreams passed. For Hungary is a country with a constitution, where only the majority decide, and nothing other than merit is needed to win it over, at least *for a nobleman*. Our hero had encouraged himself with that thought a hundred times over, and now, when the king's chamberlain too said the same, since it was his conviction too that a Hungarian noble could become anything, how should he himself doubt the validity of this principle?

Jónás therefore became a Konkolyi man body and soul, and it was Hajtó's task to win for him the greatest possible support among the minor nobility. It was his good fortune that the speech for which he had been penalised turned out especially suitable for the purpose. Jónás

---

37 The lion is known by its claws. A *mot* supposedly coined by Bernoulli on reading Newton.

had spoken of the oppression under which the lower classes live in this country. Hajtó obtained the text and, *mutatis mutandis*, translated it. Where *the poor* had been referred to the term was replaced by *the poor nobility*. Where the length of criminal proceedings and the sufferings of prisoners were spoken of, it now read: so quickly do criminal investigations instituted against the nobility of the County proceed that a number of them haven't actually died before the verdict has been reached. Where Jónás painted a touching picture of the wretchedness into which the tax-payer was forced by public works, especially in that his animals were soon exhausted and died, the translator turned his attention to the way that the nobility's animals became thinner day by day because of the imposition of the weight of such great *abactio* and *invagiatio*,[38] being as they were excluded from all the lands and grazing of the upper classes. Although the translation, when it came into Jónás's hands, perhaps didn't satisfy his requirements, I think (every writer disparages his translators) that nevertheless the speech had much greater effect, and of that there can be no doubt; scarcely had two weeks gone by than the people of Rácz and Pálfalu and the other communities were talking about nothing other than their future *szolgabíró*, in whose honour glasses were raised every day in Konkolyi's camps with the greatest enthusiasm. Once the Réty party discovered this tactic and circulated a different translation as a countering action it was too late. This served to increase Tengelyi's popularity "because the blessed man, defender of the poor, has already been subjected to a fine", which was not so easily undermined. Every time that nobles came to Porvár and called on their new tribune, every time that he went with Konkolyi or another leader of the party to call on some lieutenant of the nobility he was received with acclaim. Everyone brought out their time-stained documents, asked his advice and entrusted their affairs to him. Unsurprisingly, one of the accused that he had defended in court was one of the Rácz nobles, while those of Pálfalu called for the dismissal of the *táblabíró* against whom he had protested so powerfully in the taxation case. Thus these merits as a lawyer were of no little advantage, and on the floods of good red wine on which Konkolyi closed with swelling sails on that of *alispán* our hero too approached the office of *szolgabíró*, for which he had ready in mind the finest plans for making everyone happy.

---

38 *Abactio pecorum*: the driving of herds from lands under dispute; *invagiatio*: their driving to the land of claimants.

That was how things stood when the *főispán*³⁹ came to the County like a veritable angel of peace – as the spokesman of the reception committee said, using a completely novel turn of phrase. There was a significant majority for Konkolyi, and scarcely a word said against Tengelyi's appointment as chief justice. But as many say, "there are two sides to everything, it's the end of the whip that cracks, the chicken that clucks a lot lays few eggs – *audiatur et altera pars*,⁴⁰ in any case it would be good to reach an understanding". But how? From Konkolyi's point of view there was no difficulty, old Réty would gladly pass over the office of *alispán* which he had held for twenty years, but on the one condition that his son János, who had accompanied the *főispán* to the County, became *szolgabíró*, most unfortunately, in the ward where that was intended for Tengelyi. What was to be done? If agreement weren't reached there would be strife in the County and the entire country would suffer harm in its legal system: and if agreement *were* reached? Naturally the Konkolyi party could not contemplate that, and Tengelyi would be disappointed. In this the *főispán* could help. Konkolyi therefore called on the *főispán* and in a private conversation lasting an hour, as he said, requested ceaselessly that Tengelyi stand as *szolgabíró*, but to no avail! The *főispán* would not agree. He must no doubt have been instructed to exclude Jónás from the candidacy; and when that evening the Konkolyi party conferred at their leader's there was no one who, under the circumstances, could offer sensible advice. True, if Tengelyi were willing to withdraw his candidacy, for which, after the *főispán*'s statement, there was no prospect of success, everything might come perfectly into place. The calm of the entire county depended on him, and by that sacrifice he would earn such merit as young man never did; but who could ask that of him? They would have to do their best, even if the County were given a commissioner.

Jónás was at the age when nothing is easier to settle for than sacrifice, and when that had all been said he naturally stated decisively that he would gladly withdraw his every demand if the public good were thus advanced. "You do well," said an elderly *táblabíró*, embracing him, "you're still a young man, begin as a clerk, like everyone else. Réty's your friend body and soul, furthermore he's a young gentleman, he won't pay much attention to his ward, and you'll be able to arrange things as you please. By the next election, however, he'll presumably be promoted to

---

39   The representative of the crown in a Hungarian county, akin to the English Lord Lieutenant or High Sheriff. The *főispán* was usually an aristocrat.
40   Let the other party be heard too.

46

some higher level and you'll be able to take his place without any opposition. The *főispán* too has said that he'll look after you." And so it was decided, and the great day of the election dawned to perfect peace and harmony.

Réty's standing down and the elections of *alispáns*, town clerk, notary and *szolgabírós* took place as planned; until young Réty's election – the last of the *szolgabírós* – no differences of opinion were voiced; anyone that had witnessed the irritation preceding the election and heard all the reproaches affecting those who were now elected unanimously, without any mention of horse-trading, could scarcely have believed their eyes: such was the harmonious enthusiasm with which the patriotic Estates of Taksony were able to drink Konkolyi's red wine and Réty's white that not the least trace remained of the election, never mind the colour of the wine. This was continued with the offices of deputy *szolgabírós* and the first few clerks. The whole affair seemed a masterly performance of a well rehearsed play, and Tengelyi, who was very fond of Réty and anticipated with poetic spirit all the good that a clerk can do for his fellow men, was so confident of his election and heard his name among the candidates with such composure as clerk never enjoyed on appointment. But there are things in heaven and on earth, especially on the occasion of elections, of which our philosophers dream, and so it was that Tengelyi, whom previously public opinion had wanted as a *szolgabíró*, now that he was a candidate for a clerkship suddenly saw himself with the tiniest of support; and although Konkolyi, like Brutus hearing his sons sentenced to death, took the blow in silence, it no doubt hurt him more than anyone else, and Hajtó was so affected that he was forced to leave the council chamber at the scene, while young Réty hung his head sorrowfully and all our hero's friends were struck dumb in their noble anger, it made no difference at all. Tengelyi was rejected and a middling property owner from Rácz was declared clerk; he had been Konkolyi's best canvasser and had secured the affection of the common nobility for himself.

Jónás was embittered. All the hopes of his life – and, what was more painful, his faith in human nature – had been shattered. Instead of a bright future penury beckoned grimly, and there was no one at all on whom he could rely, whom he could trust, amid woes so great. True, there was Réty; but although every time that they spoke they called each other dear Jónás and László and used *te*,[41] the days when there had been

---

41 The use of familiar and honorific forms of address in Hungarian causes problems not only for foreign students! Here in the early 19th century Konkolyi addresses Tenge-

no closer friends in the University of Heidelberg than the two Hungarians were over. I shan't even speak of the others; any of my readers who have failed in an election will know from personal experience that the minority that wanted to elect them is like water on sandy soil after rain, and vanishes under such circumstances. Jónás was completely deserted and would scarcely have been able to endure living had not merciful fate offered him fresh consolation in his misfortune.

Jónás was in love. For the first time in his life and as truly as only he can love who, rejected on all sides, clings with all his might to that one being whom the gracious Godhead brings before him that he too may hope and rejoice. I shan't dwell on this subject, and most of all shall spare my readers a description of Erzsi. Girls are almost all like one another. If you ask their beloveds you will only find angels; if you speak with others (I mean girls that live in the same village or social circle or their mothers, only other men) they are almost certainly good, nice looking, decent girls practically without exception. Such was Erzsi too (we shall soon meet her as Mrs Erzsébet), and the only remarkable thing about her was that Jónás could not abide any other than the personal perfections of his beloved, and that our hero had first and foremost to consider a livelihood if, in this beautiful world, where even lilies are given only very light spring clothing, he didn't intend to go through the process of starvation.

For once fate seemed to be kind to Jónás. Good friends of his father and the good reputation as an excellent student that he had left after him in the college in Debrecen all helped him when he applied for the position of cantor of a quite large community, and although this situation could not be called magnificent it provided for his needs, and the promise that he could count on a teaching post at Debrecen College as soon as a vacancy arose augured well for the future.

Nothing therefore stood in the way of his good fortune, and the happy cantor, chest swollen with pride, led his new wife into their little house, the thatched roof of which could protect them against danger and storm as well as any palace, and in which so much love created them a whole paradise. Only one thing had been omitted from the calculations: Erzsébet was a Catholic. In the fervour of his love and surrounded by so many fine hopes, our Jónás had failed to enquire about her religion, and so it happened that the Reformed community was scandalised that their

lyi (above) with the honorific *ön*, the *táblabíró* a few lines above addresses him with the familiar *te* (as a colleague) and the same would be usual between fellow students.

cantor had chosen himself a Catholic wife, and dismissed our hero a year later – and, as was only to be expected, the hopes of a teaching post also ended up in smoke.

And so Jónás had once more to be anxious, to struggle for his daily bread, and he set about that difficult task calmly, but bitter at heart. "Those whom the gods hate they make a tutor," says the Latin proverb,[42] and so it was natural for our ill-fated hero not to be spared that misfortune, and after a lengthy search he did indeed obtain a post as tutor. The house into which he moved was one of the better ones, that is, one of those in which the tutor, in addition to receiving a good salary and pension, almost ranked with the cook and the bailiff, and although two boys were committed to his charge – which in itself was trouble enough, because two young gentlemen always make more noise and learn less than just one: and although the love of father and mother was shared equally between the two, the tutor's endeavours formed a successful counterweight, and on his difficult path all the trifling troubles and sufferings that embitter the life of a tutor were not lacking. Jónás endured it all. It is the most painful time in the life of every better man when, convinced of the unattainability of his finer plans, he is driven to egoism, and those who previously wished to make happy the whole race of men – or at least Hungary – seek with bloodied breasts a little good fortune for themselves. With regard to Jónás, it had come long before, and he was modest in his desires. Erzsébet was living with him in a house, his future was assured, he was satisfied with his situation. But his fate decided otherwise. The house in which he was working as tutor was Catholic, he Reformed; as when he was a cantor and took a Catholic wife the whole community had been in uproar, so now the father's friends and the mother's relations protested against this religious scandal, and as a sign that in Hungary every religious denomination is equal at least as far as Christian tolerance is concerned Tengelyi was dismissed once again, and set out on the path of his life as an estate manager.

Tengelyi was one of those people who, in the case of every occupation, discover in what it accords with some fine or great idea; from that it follows that just as no one resolved more easily upon a new *modus vivendi*, no one more often felt deceived. So it was on this occasion too. When he set himself to farming Vergil's *Georgics* filled his imagination; later all that remained of his reveries were the high midden outside his window and the much dirtier contacts into which he came through his

---

42 *Quem dii oderunt, paedagogum fecerunt.*

profession. In the *Georgics* there wasn't a word about the *urbarium*,[43] and yet the application of it was the only, or at least the principal, duty of Tengelyi's office, to which was added his master's belief – he was a very free-thinking gentleman, who knew Voltaire and Rousseau almost by heart – that the *urbarium* was an outmoded piece of legislation, unfit for that enlightened age; his attempts to carry out ever greater refinements drove poor Jónás almost to despair.

As his peasants owned far less land than should have been the case according to the socage that they performed, and as he knew that all their time was taken up in the service of God, landowner and County and that they were unable to tend their own plots, the honourable gentleman, innately aware of the dangers of sloth, as a good father took care that his children were provided with work in excess of the duties of socage. Additionally even more, very expedient improvements were introduced on this nobleman's estates. He didn't therefore acknowledge how much the power of devaluation had gone, that is, on his estates only silver money was accepted, and naturally he collected hearth-tax too in this form. Likewise he took thought for the education of his serfs. I mean ordinary education consisting of reading, writing and other such fripperies, but more important practical preparation for life, and because this was naturally most expediently acquired on the owner's premises his whole house was full of the sons and daughters of serfs being trained free of charge for the most useful skills in life as grooms, kitchen-maids or needle-women.

Jónás was a reluctant tool in all these affairs, and ate his daily bread in bitterness of heart; only the all-powerful philosophy of need kept him in his post, which was repugnant to his feelings and his convictions alike. But what was he to do? Erzsébet at least felt happy, and now and then came a tear that he could wipe away, individual sufferings for which he could offer relief even in his situation. Two years had gone by in this way, when suddenly threatening letters were scattered, in which the threat was made to burn down all the buildings on the estate. Investigation produced no results and precisely on Whitsunday Jónás's house, together with barns and stables, suddenly burst into flames. As the other bailiffs' houses were roofed with tiles they suffered no damage. One of

---

43 A comprehensive register of farmland in Hungary, instituted in 1767 by Maria Theresa. Although it brought relief to subjects by curbing and clarifying farmers' obligations to their noblemen, Maria Theresa's main goal was to collect money from the nobility, who hitherto had paid no taxes. Landowners therefore spared no effort to disguise the extent of their holdings.

the malefactors was caught in the act, and he declared publicly both at the summary trial and at the foot of the gallows that he had been driven to crime only by all the cruel injustices perpetrated by the owner and his men, and that if the bailiffs didn't mend their former ways they would encounter others after him who would repeat his action for the sake of their relatives.

The scandal was terrible. The landowner, in whom the County respected one of its most enlightened and free-thinking *táblabíró*, who never went to church, never called even his clerk anything other than 'old chap', and as he walked down the street gently patted every child on the cheek (later, when such children grew into grooms or other servants the pat grew accordingly) – how could such a landowner commit offences with regard to socage? Naturally, the bailiffs were the only possible cause of all the bitterness that existed among the serfs. An example had to be made, everyone could see that, and most of all the honourable gentleman himself: and since there was none of the bailiffs to whom he was less well disposed than Tengelyi, as he was the only one of all to speak out against the owner's clear, though only *viva voce*, orders concerning socage in particular, and who, since the misfortune had occurred, had openly and unsparingly raised his voice against the management, finally it was he, whose house had been burnt and whom in this way the incendiary himself had singled out and against whom irritation had reached its height: nothing was more natural than that once again he was the chosen victim and despite every plea was summarily dismissed.

His few items of furniture and what he had acquired during his period of service had been burnt, and he returned after two years of toil to Porvár, which he had left with such high hopes, poorer than before.

Here begins the most dismal period of our hero's life, though not the most poetic, during which he struggled for his daily bread in the greatest hardship and self-denial, with a detailed description of which I shan't weary my readers. Tengelyi was prepared to do anything, would have undertaken any work, rejected nothing, but in vain! Fate didn't permit him the chance to settle anywhere. When he sought a place as a bailiff, his last misfortune was brought up against him – if he looked for legal work, so was the hostility of the Taksony County magistrates, through which he lost every case – if he offered his services as a tutor, his principles, his religion and the restless nature because of which he had never been able to fit in anywhere were his downfall, and in brief apart from an occasional fee for writing a *rebuttal* or request on behalf of some lawyer or other, and a forint here and there for washing or sewing that his wife earned, despite all his learning and hard work Tengelyi was reduced to penury.

In this way another three years passed, and – wonder of wonders! – without Réty, who had entered into his father's inheritance during that time and become *alispán*, doing the least little thing for his friend. So highly did he esteem him that even in his greatest want he didn't even think to insult him with a subvention or a gift; and as for his influence, by which he might have assisted him to some post or office, Réty was one of those men of rare virtue who never abuse their powers to advance their friends; and being thus hampered by his principles, he found himself in the lamentable situation of being unable to do anything for his most loyal friend. All the same, however, the desire flourished in his bosom, and when our Jónas had struggled for three years with so many woes that he had all but abandoned hope, one day the magnanimous *alispán* appeared in his little room, informed him that the Tiszarét notary had died and asked whether he might not take the post? In an excess of nobility of spirit he went so far as to say that like the previous notary, he too would be free of all liabilities for socage in connection with the land pertaining to the office.

Jónas thanked Réty for his consideration and that same week went out to Tiszarét, where we found him at the beginning of our tale, having served as notary of that place for twenty years, grey of head but sound in body and spirit.

If my readers would care to learn something of interest about this time, I can mention in particular that a couple of years before our story Tengelyi bought himself a little *curia* and piece of land, and took to farming in addition to his notarial duties; that a daughter Vilma and son Pista had been born, whom we shall soon meet as the most beautiful girl and most amiable boy in the whole district; that for some time Mrs Erzsébet had been much more quarrelsome, and that Jónas's friendship with Réty had cooled greatly after the last election. There is no more of interest that I can tell. In that lengthy period Tengelyi had not changed; so much hardship had left him somewhat sour, but the love of justice that we saw in him in his young days, and the courage with which he spoke out against any oppression and lawlessness, remained the same, and Mrs Erzsébet was right when she shook her head and said that her husband was never going to see sense or come to anything.

Tengelyi's exterior gave rise to respect, but the feeling was even more fostered by the seriousness, or if I might say so, solemnity which characterised his conduct even in the closest domestic circles, and by which, even if his company was unpleasant, the village notary was protected from outbreaks of that disdainful friendship known as condescension with which many decent people are so much tormented by their social superiors. No one kept more strictly than he to the rules of courtesy towards them when called on by them for the influence that he exercised on the nobility of the County, but no one rejected their friendship with greater coldness. "Our superiors," he often said, "only respect us their inferiors insofar as they can make use of us, and we them insofar as we fear them; I don't wish to be useful to them and have no cause to fear them, so why should I accept or seek their friendship?" My readers will readily perceive that this quality gained Tengelyi no friends. Since he made the humblest faults of the lower classes his own the upper classes were rather condescending towards him; who would hold it against them that they were reluctant to tolerate in others at least their own faults, such as pride; but I know of no more independent person than a village notary, who feels secure in his office through the influence that he exercises on the nobility and owns the little house in which he lives as a nobleman does his estate; therefore our hero could regard calmly all the ill-feeling that was stirred against him in every breast from the *alispán* to the lowliest clerk. Tengelyi was one of those who are – as he used to say – born Caesars or village notaries; that is, if they didn't happen to become Caesars, they could rise no higher than notary, and he had long had no desire for anything other than what he had – whether out of conviction, as he himself said, or by compulsion, as was proclaimed against him, I can't say; but in any case soberly, because the way by which we can advance to the heights is not such as can be found by one unwilling to seek it with bowed head. But just as these faults of good qualities of Tengelyi's (I know what to call them and shall entrust to my readers the decision on this exceedingly dubious matter, which will certainly depend on whether they rank closer to the *alispán* or to a village notary) rendered him disliked by his superiors, so there was perhaps none of the notaries in Hungary that enjoyed such popularity among those that entrusted their affairs to him. Here too there were those who took amiss the excessive strictness of his principles and were weary of the fierce love of justice with which he sided with every good affair without regard for persons. But when all was said and done, there was perhaps no one in Tiszarét or for ten miles around that would not say of Tengelyi that he was an honourable man; and that was the surest sign that he was in fact such, because just as in wider circles nothing is often more fickle than public opinion, in the tight confines of a village one can safely rely on it. Deceptions grow as the theatre expands, but on a small stage the only faults that are not noticed are those that exist.

Tengelyi was, however, on terms of close friendship with only one man, Boldizsár Vándory, in whose company my readers first saw him on the Törökdomb. It was this friendship that gave him one of the greatest pleasures in his life.

Otherwise, Vándory and Tengelyi were the most different people imaginable, and that was perhaps the reason for their constant friendship. We usually like the qualities that we possess ourselves in one person, that is, in ourselves. These two friends' qualities and inclinations were complementary. They seemed, so to speak, to be set side by side so that we might find juxtaposed in them everything that the human breast can ennoble. After the severity with which Tengelyi spoke of humanity, Vándory's cheerful view of the world – always bringing out the best aspect of everything, always finding something likeable in everything – had the effect of beneficial consolation.

By the age of fifty everyone is either reconciled to the multitude or is irritated by it: and if the latter has occurred in the case of a man like Tengelyi, frequently short of friends, it is not remarkable, nor yet to be held against him, especially if that severity exists only in theory, as it was with Tengelyi. Anyone that heard him speak and compared with his actions the vehemence with which he castigated all wickedness, must have been convinced that there was no more merciful man in this wide world than him, who proclaimed himself the inexorable scourge of all evil. My readers should not, however, accuse him of inconsistency – least of all the younger ones, who only know of life by supposition and are as yet unaware of how many virtues we lose as soon as we have the opportunity to practise them. There is scarcely one in a thousand that would not speak most and most warmly of qualities that they possess, and would not, with regard to the very same matters, have acquired for themselves the purest principles of which they feel the need. Cowards speak most warmly of courage, bad judges of partiality, the selfish of the fatherland: why might my God-fearing notary not sometimes display strict principles? We calmly tolerate villainy and endure, indeed sometimes favour, the vilest immorality if they come to us in pleasant guise: why then should we not be permissive towards little blemishes in virtue? Even if it is not cast in pleasing form no one turns away gold, nor does anyone complain that it is too heavy to shoulder and carry off.

There is little that I can say about Vándory; since the time when he came to Tiszarét as pastor, some two years before our hero settled there, his days had flowed calmly, one much like the next. All that we know of his past is that he had studied in Heidelberg and that there, although ten years his senior and a theology student, he had befriended Tengelyi and no other. He never mentioned his family or childhood. No one that heard him speak doubted that he was a Hungarian, and any that came to Tiszarét and saw the elderly priest among his flock would think that he was a father surrounded by his children, such was the respect that surrounded the godly old man and the love that smiled on the faces of all in his presence. The Réty family themselves shared in this public respect, and there was perhaps no one that enjoyed such esteem in that proud house as the modest pastor of Tiszarét.

That is what I've felt necessary to say about my two heroes' past lives. If I've been rather lengthy and bored some of my readers, they should consider that I haven't exercised my right as an author to entertain them to a long introduction, and should not lay my book aside. My novel means to be nothing if not the image of life, and can't *always* be amusing.

Dusk had fallen and only a few red clouds remained to show where the sun had disappeared by the time that the friends reached the village. Vándory wished Jónás good night and they parted.

Our hero made his way home alone and, possibly because the juridical scene that he had witnessed on the Törökdomb had offended his sentiments, possibly because he had been thinking of his past, more solemnly than usual. But when he saw Vilma at the gate coming merrily to meet him and clasped the dear girl to his bosom the anxiety that furrowed his brow vanished and his heart was filled with a sense of happiness.

He was about to go inside, but his daughter gently held him back: "First I've got a little favour to ask," said she with a smile, "I won't let you go in until you promise me you'll do it."

"And what might that be?" asked Jónás good-humouredly, patting her cheek.

"That you won't be angry," answered Vilma in an imploring tone.

"Angry? Whatever for?"

"I've done something without telling you."

"If that's all," said Tengelyi with a laugh, "I promise."

"And you won't object?"

"That's another matter, but if *you've* done it," he went on with a smile, "that's a promise as well."

And father and daughter went into the house, happily and, it must be admitted, not without a tinge of curiosity on the part of our notary.

III

Meanwhile in Tiszarét itself, to which we have returned with the notary and the pastor, peace and quiet reign. Solitary workers stroll home from the fields, here and there a couple of neighbours chat at their gates or a group of children play in the dusty street, and over everything that we can observe the evening bell tolls out its note, slowly, as if it too were tired and half asleep as it recites the angelus. The inn itself, where at other times the dancing is lively, and Isaac the Jew sells his wine at a fair price – but on credit, for crops as yet unharvested – now stands empty; and if we look in at the door of the tavern we see only the Rétys' Czech gardener and Ákos, their huntsman, reminiscing over cool drinks about the better beer in their native land, like Israel in the wilderness about the flesh-pots of Egypt. We find the same silence in the yard of the big house, which in Hungary, as everyone knows, is always second only to the inn as a noisy place. The young master, as we know, has gone out hunting with his hounds. The *alispán* is closeted in his study with the chief lawyer and the notary, and would no doubt be talking about very serious matters if the twilight of approaching evening and perhaps the wearisome importance of the talk doesn't lull them all to sleep. Her Ladyship the *alispán*'s wife, however, who at other times fills the house with the sound of her voice as the nightingale does the thicket, and who differs from that beloved bird only in that what she says becomes louder and more incessant as she advances in the summer of her life, is walking in the park. Let us follow her.

The park of the lords of Tiszarét, as I have already remarked, was the wonder of the entire region. Hermitage, plum-drier, dovecote in the form of a church, fishpond and accompanying fisherman's hut, grotto, peasant house etc. – for who can list altogether the brilliant fruits of the Rétys' imagination and whims which kept the traveller who had the good fortune to go round their park in a state of constant surprise. All these may be admired but not described. The farthest part of the park was occupied by a wood some twenty *holds*[44] in extent, which His Honour the *alispán* would have felled had not the *főispán* – who praised the wood in particular when staying with the Rétys – saved the towering, venerable poplars from their owners' horticultural taste. The spreading

---

44   A pre-metric unit of area – roughly an acre and a half.

branches of the trees and the green tangle of undergrowth beneath them formed a veritable wilderness, into which the hot midday sun didn't penetrate; and if you could withdraw there for half an hour after the eighteen courses of lunch you could feel at least free and easy. There was only one path in this wood, which wound its way through, or rather led round it, in countless twists and turns; and it is on this that we now find Mrs Réty with her most loyal servant, the lawyer Macskaházy, engaged in very important conversation.

It is October, the evening bell has been heard, as my readers may recall, and at the same time we are walking in the woods, where even in the daytime everything is rather dimly lit, and so my readers will find it natural if I embark on a detailed description of our characters, which, especially in the case of Mrs Réty, I would not care to. If, however, it were daytime, the reader might see that she is between forty and fifty, that is, at the age which those who have turned forty consider the finest time of manhood and which, by that standard, in so manly a woman too may be called the most handsome. Her figure is tall and, like her other properties, nicely rounded. Her hair – but until my readers see her with head uncovered, which will hardly happen, that is no concern of ours – judging by the heavy eyebrows and faint little moustache, is probably black. Her face is pure dignity, and at times, which quite surprisingly recur every thirty months and last for six as an election approaches, is exceedingly pleasant and condescending; at other times it is haughty and arrogant, an effect heightened by two huge warts, one on the right side of her upper lip, which gives her features a scornful cast even when she smiles, the other above her chin. You would think she was a queen if the County footman at her side didn't indicate that you were speaking to the *alispán*'s wife. Mrs Réty is a lady in the strictest sense of the word. Her housekeeping is stylish, her lunches never last less than two hours, her courtyard is full of poultry and guests, the more distinguished of which meet with the most attentive service. To hear her speak you would think you were beside some rich spring, flooding everything with an unceasing flow. Her voice is powerful and resonant, such that all the servants pale on hearing it; even the walls of Jericho would have shaken. What she says stirs all that are impartial to astonishment, not only because it is almost the same, word for word, as what the *alispán* says, and this degree of marital understanding is to be admired in this decadent age, but mainly because of the profound juridical knowledge which in our day is to be found only rarely in Hungarian women, and which imparts to women so unusual a charm and attractiveness. There is not a lawyer in the length and breadth of Hungary that would speak on legal subjects more and more readily than Mrs Réty, and with such great knowledge and profundity; Macskaházy has frequently admitted that his best rebuttals have been drafted entirely in accordance with Her Ladyship's advice.

Macskaházy, whom we now find walking in the woods with her gracious ladyship, must be between about fifty and sixty; he is a short, dry little man, bowed down rather by long habit than by weight of years. A pallid face, pointed nose and chin, an uncertain eye (with which you meet only now and then, as it were by accident, but which withdraws its piercing gaze as soon as it is noticed) and a forehead heightened by baldness and fringed by a few grey curls, form a whole before which all men – with the exception of the Réty family – feel uncomfortable. This family has never had a more loyal retainer. He has spent close on thirty years in the house and has enjoyed so many days good and bad alike as to have become one of the family, and has defended its interests more stoutly, perhaps, than they themselves – whether simply out of self-interest, as his enemies have believed, or out of genuine inclination, as Réty has thought, who can say? Perhaps there is truth in both points of view. The man is such a marvellous blend of good and bad qualities that there is scarcely any that could strive for a villainous purpose without some better sentiment rising in his bosom, just as he is rare among those in whose noble motives there is not also mixed a little self-interest, vanity or other similar ignoble material; and it may be that what was once Macskaházy's pretended devotion has changed into genuine feeling – but it is not for me to pass judgement on the man!

Now, however, it seemed that the agreement between Mrs Réty and her faithful lawyer was under stress. She was walking up and down beneath the trees with rapid steps, while he followed the powerful woman apace behind, stooping even more than usual; he could only insert an occasional word of consent into her flow of discourse, but, it appeared, with little success as she shook her head in annoyance at such interruptions, saying that it was easy to talk and that she knew very well how Macskaházy didn't allow anyone to get a word in edgeways but that genuine loyalty could only be shown by deeds, and more of the sort.

"And I'll tell you straight," she ended, as she stopped, worn out either by constant talking or walking, looking the little lawyer in the eye and striking the ground with her parasol, "What you tell me makes me despair."

"But when I tell you, Madam," replied Macskaházy, who also appeared to be on the verge of despair, though for a different reason, "that there's no need, that beyond doubt . . ."

"Oh, we know," the *alispán's* wife cut him short, "you aren't going to despair; what do you care about our troubles. If we're ruined, or put to shame in the eyes of the whole world, you'll still be a lawyer, and who knows, perhaps . . ."

Macskaházy felt insulted, and after his patience was exhausted he suddenly made the great discovery that we can use so effectively in social life, that we can only act successfully against passion with similar passion. The anger with which he now spoke had much more effect on Mrs Réty's tirade than if he countered it with the niceties of all the philosophies in the world. "So that's the thanks," he said in noble rage, "that's the gratitude that I deserve for thirty years of service? To uphold the honour and reputation of the family I, Ádám Macskaházy, have risked my neck, and by way of thanks I meet with suspicion."

"Don't take it like that," said Mrs Réty in placatory tone, realising that in the heat of the moment she had gone a little too far and that Macskaházy was not her husband, whom she could not divorce without legal action, "but I'm a woman, and my unfortunate circumstances . . . and . . ."

"A woman, a woman! That's all very well," said Macskaházy, seeing that the battle was turning in his favour, "I know you, madam, you're not like other women. What you say can be made into a rebuttal. I can see that it will be better for me to seek other employment."

"But who said that you had lost our confidence?" she interrupted him questioningly. "You're the only one we trust, what are we to do if we lose you? What's more," said the *alispán's* wife, now irresistible, "you know what we've promised. The day that the documents are in my hands we'll go to the chapter and the *inscriptio*[45] that you wish for will be in your hands."

"As for the *inscriptio*," growled Macskaházy in a milder tone, "bless my soul, I'm not doing it for that reason. But if Your Ladyship think anything of me for my services – *ob fidelia servitia* – I'll be grateful all my life . . . but . . ."

"Of course, I know, there's no place in your heart for self-interest, but the *inscriptio* is fine, and although it's not adequate reward for the service that you render to my family, it's a nice share all the same."

---

45   A document testifying to change of ownership of property. It has to be certified by Church authorities.

"Which I'll certainly deserve, although there are still a hundred obstacles in my way," said Macskaházy with feeling.

"Is that really what you think, my dear friend?" said Mrs Réty. "I doubt it."

"Why ever? Because there was failure at the first attempt? That's giving up too soon! Everything that could be done was well and truly ready, but just this once heaven wasn't on our side. The man that broke in at Vándory's is reliable and clever. I told him to take some money and something valuable as well as the documents that you wanted, to make it look like an ordinary robbery, and so that no suspicion should fall on us. That was the reason why it didn't succeed. The stupid burglar could only find a few *garas* in the table drawer and looked for more. While he was doing that the reverend came home and raised the alarm even before Czifra could find the documents. He jumped out of the window and made his escape. Vándory didn't chase him, because as he said next day he was afraid he'd be dealt with summarily – so you can see, sometimes philanthropy does have its benefits. Tengelyi's holding the documents now, as I know from the old servant, in a big iron chest by the door, where he keeps his own documents and those belonging to the community; never fear, Your Ladyship, we'll find them there too. In fact, I actually like it, this way we'll kill two birds with one stone, as I've still got a score to settle with Tengelyi."

"I'm worried," said the *alispán*'s wife. "The notary's house is full of people, what if the thief is caught?"

"We hang him," said Macskaházy, unperturbed. "He'll have been caught red-handed, of course."

"And what if he confesses everything?"

"He won't. We'll promise him that he'll come to no harm if he keeps quiet, but if . . ." added the little lawyer in jocular fashion, "he tries to all the same he won't have time; we'll have him hanged before he has the chance."

"Oh, did you but know," said Mrs Réty with a sigh, in a voice that was almost sentimental, "how much I struggled before bringing myself to take this step, how much I suffer even now when I think that . . . But who can help it. The honour of my name, the good of my children, everything that's dear in life and gives it value forces me . . ."

"What will a mother not do for her children," replied Macskaházy, touched by this and wiping his eyes, there being no need for tears in the gloom. "Only I know what a heart lives in Your Ladyship's breast. If the world knew they would prostrate themselves before you."

"God forbid," Mrs Réty broke into the lawyer's enthusiasm. Otherwise she didn't take amiss the lawyer's vast flattery and was pleased when she heard that, by a slight lawyer's cleverness, what she had done – which a peasant would call theft – could be regarded as noble sacrifice. "God forbid that anyone but us two should know. The world's harsh in its judgment, who knows whether it wouldn't say. . ." Here the *alispán*'s wife broke off, perhaps in consternation at feeling that she was beginning to blush.

"Really, why torment yourself?" interjected Macskaházy, perceiving his mistress's embarrassment. "What's wrong at all in what we're doing? It's just a little suppression of documents; the sort of thing that happens every day – in Hungary it's such a commonplace that anyone that feels offended at it is considered eccentric at most. How often have you heard, madam, that entire cases have been lost – and not cases taking a month or a year, but which have grown fat for thirty years – documents and all, and what has come of it? They've been found and it's been possible to start new ones, and no one's said a word about it. So it is in this case too! Are we stealing promissory notes, financial statements or deeds of gift? God forbid! Everyday personal letters, which, for the most part, the gentleman wrote himself and which he doesn't wish to fall into other hands simply because they touch on family affairs. The whole thing is quite harmless, at the worst objection could be raised against the method."

"Yes, yes, but the method," Mrs Réty sighed. "Housebreaking, theft, I don't know what vile names it all can be called."

"Yes, it's housebreaking, theft," said the learned lawyer calmly, "insofar as the perpetrator of the deed is concerned, but what's that to do with us? If someone says in the course of conversation to someone else, whom no one actually calls a saint but who's not presently a defendant in a criminal trial, and to whom, therefore, *jus connatum bonae existimationis*[46] applies, that in the reverend Vándory's bedroom there's a big walnut cupboard in the top drawer of which, on the right-hand side, there's a bundle of documents, sealed and bound with coloured ribbon, which he – that is, the speaker – so much wants to see, out of curiosity or scientific interest or whatever, that he'd give a hundred forints to anyone that brought it to him, is there, I ask, anything wicked or deserving of punishment in it? Beyond doubt, there is not. And now I'll go further: if that same man, whom, for example, we shall call A, says to the other, B, on the same subject that on Saturday evening the reverend gentleman

---

46   Latin: Natural right to good esteem.

will be dining in the courtyard, and as he's not accustomed to lock the door on the garden side it's to be feared that one evening someone may encounter no obstacle in entering the house over the garden wall, going into the bedroom and to the cupboard, where the documents are in the top drawer on the right hand side, I repeat, if someone says all that in the course of conversation, is there anything about it more wicked than in the previous conversation? And if later this person B, to whom *jus connatum bonae existimationis* applied, breaks in and places the bundle of documents in A's hand, have I broken in and robbed the reverend gentleman? Would he not be foolish that said such a thing? I do what I've promised and pay out the hundred forints, because naturally to keep one's word is the duty of every honest man, but I've no part in anything else."

"True, true," sighed Mrs Réty, who felt her conscience fully eased by this argument, "but the world doesn't reason like that!"

"The world has always judged perversely and will do so until the Last Judgement, which will indubitably be the first to be universally accepted," said Macskaházy gravely – as a good Calvinist he liked to flavour his conversations with theology. "One of the skills of so-called virtuous men is to present the best side of things. Have no fear, madam, the public won't talk about this."

"If Vándory still had the documents, I'd believe you," replied Mrs Réty, "but now that they're in Tengelyi's house in the village, where there are so many people going up and down and there's a night-guard, I have my doubts."

"Leave it to me, madam: the documents are in the iron chest, that's sufficient; the chest has only two keys, and how many locksmiths are there in the world!" Here Mackaházy's train of thought was interrupted by Ákos's *vizsla*, which, preceding its master, ran up to Mrs Réty and pranced fawningly around her.

"The huntsmen are home," said she, "let's go." They were about to move when the *vizsla* suddenly turned to the trees and began to bark. A quiet rustling was heard among the branches, the dog rushed into the bushes with a bark, and it could be made out that someone was forcing a passage. Eventually the *vizsla* gave a squeal and limped back just as Ákos and his sister Etelka came up.

"What's the matter?" asked Ákos, kissing his stepmother's hand – she and her faithful lawyer stood there in silence, trembling.

"Did you hear something?" asked the latter tremulously.

"Yes, my dog was barking, perhaps there was a hare or a fox."

"No, no, sir," replied Macskaházy, his eyes still firmly fixed on the place where the sound had vanished, "I'll bet my life, there was someone there."

"Maybe some poor lad from the village," said Ákos, patting the *vizsla*, "who's found out that we're picking the fruit tomorrow, wanted to have one last chance, and has been in hiding all the time, very likely trembling just like my friend here. Well, you're certainly a brave man, the French have a saying that the brave are only afraid once the danger's past, and I've never seen it as clearly as now."

"This person was listening to us, no question about it, he'd just come to eavesdrop," said Mrs Réty anxiously, while Macskaházy nudged her arm to warn her to be careful.

"I don't think so," said Etelka with a laugh. Macskaházy's a very amusing gentleman, but I hardly think that anyone's going to come out here in the cold in October just to hear him speak."

"Dear Miss Etelka, you don't understand," replied the lawyer, to whom calm and full courtesy had returned, "Madam and I were speaking of important matters, our court case."

"And very likely the opposition's lawyer had hidden under those trees to get advance warning of your professional schemes, you mean?" Ákos interrupted with a laugh. "But if it's so important to you, why didn't you catch the rascal? The worthy and courageous Mr. Macskaházy's the equal of ten, I've heard say, and there was only one . . ."

"Me?" exclaimed Macskaházy, terrified at the thought. "Myself?"

"Why not? Anyway, come with me, now there are two of us; if there really was somebody there, which I still doubt, we'll catch him. If not, we'll have a good laugh."

"But please, *domine spectabilis*,[47]" said Macskaházy nervously, as Ákos took him by the hand and pulled him along, "going like this, unarmed, in the dark, it would be better if we called some servants."

"Certainly not," Ákos laughed, "by the time we find servants our evildoer will escape ten times. Courage, my friend, mother and Etelka will go home meanwhile, and we be off on our little adventure; we shall conquer or . . . run away. Agreed?" he added with a laugh, "if our fright doesn't give us a stroke."

Macskaházy was still so horrified that it never occurred to him to be annoyed at these jokes, and he merely stammered out a few remarks;

---

47 Latin was far from dead in Hungary at the time of writing. *Spectabilis = tekintetes/teins*, and so 'worshipful'.

how much better and more purposeful it would be to take servants with them! But when Mrs Réty too asked him to go with Ákos, and when as a shrewd man he calculated that the evildoer to be pursued was probably beyond reach, the little lawyer bravely buttoned up his cloak, declared ceremoniously that he wasn't afraid, and set off after Ákos.

Mrs Réty and Etelka, the former with many misgivings, laughed at Macskyházy's fears and set off for home. The *vizsla*, which evidently remembered its unpleasant experience in the thicket, followed them for once instead of its master.

Of the various sorts of courage, which no one possesses in equal measure, that which Macskaházy possessed least of all was that required for the capture of evildoers, and although I would not venture to state that he was afraid I can at least say that he felt himself to be in a not very pleasant situation. Imagine yourself in someone's place. Macskaházy was versed in the tortuous ways of the law and was no enemy of obscurity, but the sort of path on which his little feet were now tripping, on which so many roots and branches made his progress one long stumble, exceeded his imagination, as did the darkness too that surrounded them as they advanced beneath the dense foliage in the forest. Let us consider that Ákos, in the impetuosity of his youth, ran rather than walked down the path, so that our lawyer could scarcely follow his lead despite his efforts; he pressed relentlessly on through the branches, leading his follower through an endless flogging. On any other occasion Macskaházy would have been mindful of his letters patent of nobility and would not have tolerated this treatment, but now, when to the modest observations that he made against that headlong progress on the grounds that his face was being lashed, the only response that he won was that he should stay a little farther back, he said no more; and despite all the beating and tripping he remained not a yard farther back but in silent dignity, like the dying Roman, covered his face with his cloak and followed in Ákos's footsteps, encouraging himself with the thought that in such darkness no one could be shot at, but should they unexpectedly encounter the enemy that they sought he would immediately run home to obtain help for Ákos. Of that, however, there appeared no great likelihood. The night was dark, and with his eyes closed and also covered with a blue cloak even a man as clever as Macskaházy the lawyer could not see very clearly. Ákos, however, apparently for his friend's sake, was looking only for the densest places, and on hearing the sound as the branches swung back and struck felt in such a good mood that he would not have wished to cause anyone unpleasantness, be he the greatest villain in the world.

After searching for a quarter of an hour they came to the edge of the forest and Ákos finally stopped, and when he turned to Macskaházy, who had opened his eyes again and was getting his breath back, he said "There's nobody in the forest, we can swear to that, not the slightest sight or sound of human being, so perhaps you'll now believe that you were mistaken, and it was at the most a hare that you were so terrified of."

"It really seemed as if we could hear footsteps, Her Ladyship your mother too would testify to it."

"If that's the case," replied Ákos, scarcely restraining his laughter, "let's go back again – I know two or three dense places where we haven't been yet, perhaps he's there . . ."

"Of course not," Macskaházy sighed, holding back Ákos, who had already turned back. "If there were a mouse there we'd have come across it, we went this way and that so much that my legs can scarcely carry me," and the little lawyer sighed and mopped the sweat from his brow.

"Very well," said Ákos, "if you think that there's no one in the forest let's go this way round the park, perhaps we'll find someone on the other side, it's all quiet here." And with that he jumped the ditch. Macskaházy first climbed down into the middle, then, by a remarkable gymnastic feat, up the other side, and the two searchers set off in silence, shortly to disappear from our sight behind a corner of the forest.

All was silence. The October night was dark and dismal. After the clarity of sunset more and more clouds were rolling up on the horizon, long sobs of autumnal wind swept the region and the twigs and leaves quivered at its cold touch. Only here and there did a star shine out from between the clouds and shepherds' flickering fires shed a little light on the distant meadow. The footsteps of Ákos and his follower had long died away, and in the park all that broke the silence of the night were the distant barking of dogs in the village and snatches of song from the firesides – when out of the ditch, near the place where the two had just crossed, there rose a man. Even if it had not been dark his wide hat and the big sheepskin coat that hung from his shoulders would have concealed his face and figure. He stood there, seemingly listening to the singing, and when he was sure that there was no one anywhere near he stepped quietly out of the ditch and made his way hurriedly towards one of the fires in the meadow.

But we shall leave him to himself – if seems as if that is what he wishes – and return to Tengelyi, whom we left just as he was entering his humble abode, led by his daughter.

IV

Have you ever seen domestic bliss, reader? If so, you are one of those fortunate people that enjoy knowing the blessing that mutual love can pour into a family, and knowing that all the name and fame for which we strive, all the wealth which we so ardently desire, isn't the equal of the least of those pleasures, unsuspected by the world, that pure hearts enjoy in the presence of those dear to them; step, then, respectfully into the Tiszarét notary's dwelling and ask your God to visit his plagues upon exalted palaces but to spare from his blows this quiet house in which the family bless their Creator in home-made happiness.

Tengelyi was led by his daughter into his room, put his coat and stick in their usual places and once again enquired good-humouredly what the request was, then, that he had had to promise to fulfil before being allowed into his own house?

Erzsébet said that she had only agreed for her daughter's sake, and Vilma, at a loss for the best words in which to express her request, still hesitated.

"Well, am I ever going to hear the great secret?" said Tengelyi somewhat impatiently. "You haven't done something naughty, have you?"

"Yes, father," replied Vilma affably, "but you promised that you wouldn't be angry with me."

"Angry? You make me sound like a real villain. Since when have you been afraid of your father?"

"Afraid?" said his daughter, fixing her gaze calmly on him. "Your daughter will never be that. If I do wrong you tell me and forgive me, and so I think that I haven't done wrong. Just a moment, and I'll tell you everything. You know that there's been a sequestration in the village, and so you went out with the reverend, because as you said you couldn't help those poor people and it broke your heart to see them suffer. We stayed at home and saw those terrible things. Our neighbour's last cow was taken away, and just across the street at János Farkas's the quilts were stripped off the beds, and Mrs Péter's pillows were confiscated, and if anyone had a few chickens and a donkey on which they went to town with their eggs and brought things back for people, that was taken as well, and there was bad language and swearing, as if they were speaking to criminals. Farkas's son wouldn't let them take his mother's bed and he was beaten, tied up and taken to the magistrate's, from where, they say, he'll be sent to prison tomorrow. We saw and heard it all," she went on, drying her eyes, "and we wept bitterly. Mother said that that was how it all had to be, because the law lays down the taxes and those people hadn't been able to pay their dues. I just asked God for you to come home, because I thought to myself that in those two fat books that you're for ever going through there'd be one little law to the effect that poor people who can't meet their obligations through no fault of their own can't be deprived of all that they have."

"You'll be disappointed, my dear daughter," replied Tengelyi with a sigh. "It's futile to look for a law like that in those books. Our nation hasn't found time to draft it in eight hundred years."

"Oh, then there won't even be God's blessing on those laws," said Vilma, "but never mind, we can't change them, and if there's nothing about it in those laws at least religion commands us to share the burdens of our fellow men, and so I asked mother's permission and went over to Mrs Farkas to ask if we couldn't help somehow. We aren't rich, but even so God's given us enough for us to be able to share our food with decent people without going hungry, and the Farkases have always been good neighbours."

"You did right, my girl," said Tengelyi, his eyes bathed in tears. "God will bless you for it. I too have eaten the bread of poverty, and now that Heaven has blessed me I'm not going to shut my door in my fellow man's face."

"I thought so too," said Erzsébet, clasping her hands tightly together, "and I let our daughter go across."

"When I reached Mrs Farkas's," Vilma went on, "I found the whole house in despair. The master was sitting there in the yard, supporting his head on his fist and looking at the deserted stable, the mistress was pacing round and round in her room, hands clasped in prayer and wailing for her son, and the smaller children were sitting round the stove, not understanding what was happening and wailing with their mother. In the room there were a couple of broken chairs, some straw that had fallen out of the bed, everything in the greatest disorder as if an enemy had devastated the house, and on top of that the neighbours, some actually making fun, some protesting against the injustice, added to the turmoil. It breaks one's heart even to think about it. After I'd reassured Mrs Farkas by promising that the reverend would speak to the *alispán* and her son wouldn't be sent to County Hall – that was what she was most afraid of, because as she said anybody that so much as goes there comes home a veritable villain – I offered that we'd help. She thanked me very much for our goodwill, but said that as long as her son was freed they would help themselves. "We poor people," she said, addressing the others, who were still standing there, "don't desert one another. Look, this good neighbour will let me have a bed for a few days, and she here will give us a crust of bread, and someone else a couple of *garas*, and in this way perhaps God will see us through. If Mr Kenyházy the clerk, who my husband sold two horses to at Whitsun, had paid up we wouldn't have come to this. But that's the trouble, we're being sequestrated for our taxes, and if you go to law you get no justice anywhere. But there's going to be the election, I'll go and see the *főispán*, he's got their money before now for other people that Nyúzó the magistrate has been in debt to." "Yes, you're still all right," said old Mrs Lipták, who had been standing by her all the time, "you've got your husband and Jancsi, and as the young lady says he'll be freed and will work. You're a respectable married woman, but what's poor Mrs Viola going to do? She's at death's door with her baby and seven-year-old son, with a guard on her, and the magistrate's given orders that everyone that so much as goes near the house is to be arrested as they're all Viola's accomplices. But Zsuzsi was a lovely, nice girl when she was young, how can she help it if her husband's become an outlaw? If you could help her, Miss, God would bless you." I enquired and was told that Viola, who used to be a well-to-do farmer, now can't attend to his land and is completely penniless. His cattle and tools were confiscated long ago, his land's covered in weeds, and whatever else he had was confiscated today as fines, so that the poor woman's completely deserted, she's got nothing, and she's seriously ill and she has the children. I asked them to take me there, because I didn't think I would be taken for Viola's accomplice, and I thought that she simply couldn't be left to die like that with no help."

"You're quite right, dear Vilma," said the notary, patting her cheek.

"The poverty that I'd seen at the Farkases," Vilma went on, "was nothing compared to what now faced me. Even as I was approaching the house I could hear a dreadful din. The magistrate had found out – I don't know who from – that Viola was coming tonight to visit his wife, and he'd stationed three *hajdús* there to hide and arrest him the moment he appeared. They were preparing for their heroic deeds with wine and would let no one out of the house, as they had been ordered, presumably so that no one should inform Viola – a precaution which the noise they were making rendered quite superfluous. The house itself was completely empty, except for a little heap of ashes on the hearth and the bench round the stove, which, as it was of mud-brick, couldn't be removed, and the soldiers were using it as a table for their pots and a seat for themselves. That was all that remained of former comfort, everything else had gone into the hands of the law. When I went into the kitchen the *hajdú* corporal recognised me at once – he'd been to our house a few times with letters – and confronted me: what did I want? I said that I wanted to see the sick woman, to which he remarked that it was a pity that I'd put myself out, Mrs Viola had actually died, and as far as that went it was better so, as if she'd lived till tomorrow the gallows would have taken her husband from her and made her a widow. After a few more jokes in that vein, at which his companions roared with laughter, he took me to the door of the larder, where the sick woman was lying. I asked them to amuse themselves a little more quietly and went in. The larder was so dark that at first I could hardly see. The poor woman was lying in a corner on a little straw with her baby on one side and on the other a seven-year-old boy, who was watching every movement that she made with tears in his eyes. The deathly silence that reigned around the sick woman was broken only by the hooting of the *hajdús*. It seemed that she and the baby were asleep, and as soon as the little boy recognised me he came straight to me and stammered out their misfortune in his childish way. His mother had been ill for three days. At first they'd still had beds, he'd collected dry sticks along the hedgerows, and old Mrs Lipták had been to see them and cooked something. That morning the magistrate had suddenly appeared and ordered his mother to pay a hundred and fifty forints. She'd got no money and so could give him nothing. The magistrate started to swear terribly and ordered his *hajdús* to seize everything. They turned his mother out of her bed, the magistrate himself forced Mrs Lipták out of the house, and he ordered the three *hajdús* that were drinking in the other room to let nobody into or out of the house. Then he went away. "Oh, since then mummy's got much worse still," the little boy continued, wiping away his tears. "I picked up the bit of straw that fell out of the bed, put it together and made a little bed for her, but she could hardly walk to it, and since then she hasn't known who I am. The magistrate and those soldiers were saying such terrible things in the room – my father's coming tonight, they're going to catch him and then they'll hang him. For a long time now mummy's just been saying the same, and the way she's been crying and calling out I've been afraid. Then my little brother started to cry as well, and I realised he'd had nothing to eat, 'cos I was hungry as well, and I went out to the neighbours' to ask for something. Nobody gave me anything. The magistrate's given orders that nobody's to dare give us anything, and we can starve like dogs. All I got was a bit of water and a few flowers that I picked off bushes, so that my little brother can at least have something to play with, so as not to come home quite empty-handed." And with that the boy flung himself into my arms and wept bitterly.

"Poor boy," said Tengelyi, whose eyes had become moist during this account, "he's becoming acquainted with the harshness of life at an early age. I hope," he added, turning to Erzsébet, "you've sent something for the lad, and I'll go myself at once and see. . ."

"Don't bother, dear father," said Vilma sweetly, "they're not there any more, we didn't taken them anything, we brought them here to our house."

"Here, to my house?" said Tengelyi in alarm. "And have you considered the consequences?"

"Yes," replied Vilma calmly. "I thought that if I left her there any longer she'd die, and I asked the corporal and begged him, promised to accept full responsibility, and he let us bring the poor woman away, in fact he himself helped us."

"You did right in not leaving them there," said Tengelyi, pacing anxiously to and fro, "whoever you'd taken them to I'd gladly have paid for them, but here in my house! The family of the greatest villain in Tiszarét in the Tiszarét notary's home! What will my enemies say?"

"And haven't you said, father," replied Vilma gently, "that powerful conviction in our hearts tells us that we've done good and can despise the condemnation of men?"

"Yes, if we're fully aware of ourselves," said Tengelyi. "They say that Viola loves his wife and now that she's sick will come to visit her whatever the risk. What am I to do then? As an official, it's my sworn duty to arrest him, but as a man I shudder at the thought."

"You won't arrest him, will you, father?" said Vilma, snuggling up against him. "You can't do that!"

"And if I don't," said Tengelyi, wrinkling his forehead, "I'll be driven out of office in disgrace, called an accomplice of villains, and we shall be beggars again."

"No, father, that'll never happen," said Vilma confidently, though her eyes were bathed in tears. "God won't punish a good deed."

"God won't," replied Tengelyi solemnly, "but men sometimes do. Don't cry, my girl," he added, "perhaps I'm just tormenting myself with nightmares."

"But you aren't angry with me," sobbed Vilma. "I didn't know all that, I couldn't have imagined being the cause of so much unhappiness."

70

"Angry?" exclaimed the old man, clasping her tightly to his bosom, "angry with you? Aren't you my only good, dear daughter, the joy and pride of my life, the loveliest memory of my past, the hope of my future, a very heaven for which I have this angel to thank," he added, stretching out his hands towards Erzsébet.

"Yes, but if Viola does come," sobbed Vilma, "and if everything happens as you said?"

"He won't come," her father reassured her – now he would have given the earth not to be in doubt – "and in any case, if he does come perhaps no one will know, I always look on the black side, of course. Never mind, there's nothing to be done about it. If I'd been at home and seen this woman's situation I too would have taken her in, even if the whole world were up in arms against me. Dry your tears, my dear," he went on, kissing her on the forehead, "you did the right thing. So go and see the patient and I shall run and fetch Vándory, he is half a doctor. God bless."

And with that the old man hurried out before he too burst into tears; and while the women sat by the sick woman's bed he didn't cease from bewailing his cowardly soft-heartedness, because of which he couldn't refrain from tears even in his old age.

V

The stranger, whom we have just seen emerging from the ditch, now stopped close to the fire but still beyond its light and looked enquiringly around. In the uncertain light of the burning straw a well-sweep loomed out of the gloom like a tall spectre. A man was sitting by the fire, bending to poke among the flames with a little stick, and now he began to sing again to an ancient melody:

> *The world is ruled by other folk,*
> *No place for such as we.*
> *Alas, the Gypsy has no home;*
> *No home – but liberty!*

"So you're singing your Nagyida[48] dirge again, old friend?" said the stranger, as he stepped closer to the singer, and at the final word laid a friendly hand on his shoulder. "What's the matter?"

Peti – for it is indeed he that we meet here again – looked round at once, and on seeing the stranger's face in the firelight leapt to his feet, took his hand and drew him away from the fire. "For God's sake! If somebody sees you," said he quietly as his friend resisted.

"You've gone mad," said the latter, freeing his hand and going back nearer to the fire. "I've been lying over there in the ditch and I'm soaking wet, let me dry out a bit."

"No, no; you must be going," Peti urged him. "The whole village is full of your enemies. Who can tell, there may be somebody near here, and if you're recognised we're finished. You must run as far as your legs will take you."

"Look here, old friend," replied Viola, settling comfortably by the fire, "there's nobody but us in the fields for half a *mérföld*. What are you afraid of?"

"You're recognisable even at half a *mérföld*. You know this afternoon when I was talking to you, we were down by St-Vilmos forest and the gendarmes were here on the edge of the park, and even so one of them recognised you."

---

48 The reference is to the 1556 defence of the castle of Nagyida (now in SE Slovakia) against the Austrians by a force containing numerous conscripted Gypsies. After a three-week siege the defenders ran out of gunpowder and the castle was surrendered.

"Yes, as we recognised them; they thought it was me – and if they feel so disposed to try their strength with me," he added, drawing the pistols from his belt one by one and examining them, "I'm ready. I'm not afraid of anyone at night."

"Viola, Viola! Your recklessness will be the ruin of you," said Peti sorrowfully. "You despise danger and you'll come to grief."

"And isn't it better," said the outlaw, placing his *fokos*[49] at his side, "to die one day than to live as I do? To curse the sun when it rises, because it sheds light on the earth and can lead my pursuers on my track? To be alarmed by every bird that stirs a branch, to see an enemy in every tree-trunk, when I go through the forest in the evening, and to spend my days among the wild animals of the forest, to dream of gallows and jailers after all that torment – that's the life I lead, Peti, believe me, there's nothing in it that I value highly."

"What about your wife and children?"

"Yes, what about my wife and children?" said he, sighing deeply as he looked into the dying flames, which gave just enough light for Peti to see the pained expression on his manly features.

Viola was a handsome man. The high forehead, half covered by raven curls that hung to his shoulders, the intrepid look in the dark eyes, the bold expression that marked the sun-tanned features and the natural dignity that showed in every movement of his tall figure couldn't fail to remind you that here was one of those men, richly gifted by nature, who in their own circle, be it high or lowly, occupied prime of place.

"Don't be gloomy, my friend," said Peti when at length he broke the silence, "everything may yet turn out better. But now, go away, we're not safe here for a moment. The election's approaching. Nyúzó's afraid that he'll be voted out of office and he's doing all that he can to gain credit. The gendarmes arrested me today, after we'd been talking, and hauled me before him; God strike him down, the torturer – the way he swore at me and threatened me, my hair stands on end when I think about it, and if that young Master Ákos hadn't saved me I'd be on the whipping-post now, not sitting here with you. He's got spies among us, he didn't name any names, but he certainly knows every step you take. Even today he knew that you were coming to the village, and it's a miracle that you've escaped. If we hadn't arranged to meet here by the fire you wouldn't have avoided danger. The innkeeper and his servants are lying in the cellar, tied up, and gendarmes dressed as peasants are waiting for you in their

---

49 A traditional light weapon – a walking-stick with a small axe-head in lieu of a handle.

73

place. Likewise, your house is full of gendarmes, and orders have been given in the village that the moment the church bell rings the signal everybody's to turn out with pitchforks. When I was in front of him Nyúzó cursed and told me about his preparations, and as soon as I was free I sat down here and I've been bawling out my song. It is really lucky that we've met."

"Gendarmes in my house," said Viola jumping up. "And my wife – you said she was ill?"

"Don't worry about her," said Peti, "She's not in the house now, and as far as a sick person can, she's doing well. She's been taken to the notary's."

"To Tengelyi's? As a prisoner?"

"No, no. With every care and attention, just out of human kindness. Huh! That's a rare thing, my friend, especially these days, but God bless him for it."

"Human kindness," muttered Viola through his teeth, "what if that's just a trap as well? My wife's in the notary's hands, and do you realise, whoever's hands Zsuzsi's in holds my life in their hands."

"Just for once, you're wrong," replied the Gypsy with a smile. "That's what I thought at first; who can help it, if you're not a count but a Gypsy you don't really trust officialdom, and when I heard that Zsuzsi was in the notary's house I was alarmed. But when I was told that old Tengelyi didn't even know and it was all thanks to Vilma I calmed down. Say what you like about the old man, but his daughter's an angel, I'll swear. But let's not waste time, I've got to be in St-Vilmos by first light to deliver my letters, and every minute that you stay here may cost you your life."

"I'm not moving a step until you let me know how Zsuzsi is. I find it all inconceivable."

Peti knew Viola too well not to yield to a wish expressed in such a tone, and so he gave him an account of his wife's misfortune, of which the reader already knows, as briefly and succinctly as possible. Viola listened, leaning on his *fokos*; you'd have taken him for a statue were it not for the occasional silent prayer in which his chest rose and sank.

"Poor woman, so this is what you've had to come to," said he at length, "you've been forced to accept the bitter bread of charity like a beggar, to seek shelter in another's house like a tramp.[50] My God! What has the blessed creature done to you, that you have to persecute her as well?"

"Come along, my friend, let's be off!" Peti interrupted him. "Your wife will come to no harm, and we've got no time to contemplate the injus-

---

50 Eötvös is remembering Dante (Paradiso 17:58): . . . *sa di sale/Lo pane altrui, e com'è*

74

tices of the world. Perhaps one day the chance will arise to turn the tables, and then we'll exact the price for our present afflictions, and I for one shall see that Nyúzó pays handsomely. People have been in worse trouble than you are at present, and all the same haven't been the losers as long as they weren't hanged."

"Who's talking about me? I've been accustomed to misfortune for a long time – there's blood on my hands, and perhaps it is just that God's curse should be on my head, but that she, she whom I love – who has never done anybody any harm, never in her life upset anybody, who's stood by me like a good angel and stayed my hand when I've raised it in anger, who spends hours on her knees in church, whose only offence is to love me – why is she being punished too? Let me be persecuted, tormented, I don't care; let me be hanged, but don't let her be harmed."

"But who ever would hurt her?" said Peti with growing impatience. "She's never been better cared for. But we must be off, because we're going to be in trouble sure as eggs is eggs, and it'll be your fault."

"Nobody in the village stood by her, you said, nobody would take her in except Tengelyi."

"I told you that – the magistrate had forbidden it and they didn't dare."

"Very well, very well, we can reckon on that – but I've never harmed anybody in the whole village, not a single cow's been lost from their herds, and when my family's destitute there's not a soul in the place that gives them a thought, or who would think that it could all be different, that Viola might set fire to Tiszarét and there wouldn't even be as much grief and lamentation for it as for the famous cities of Sodom and Gomorrah."

"You're right," said Peti, seizing his hand, "sometimes a little revenge does no harm, at least people would remember that there's still justice in the world and they'd take better care for themselves; but now come with me towards St-Vilmos, you can be safe in the forest there for a few days, the swineherd's one of us, and we shall call in the others and take council. There's nothing you could do now here in the village, everybody's on the look-out for us."

"You just go ahead, I've still got something to attend to here."

"Where?" asked Peti, holding Viola back by his coat as he set off for the village.

---

duro calle/Lo scendere e'l salir per l'altrui scale. . . . knows the bitter bread of another, and how hard it is to go up and down his steps.

75

"Go ahead to St-Vilmos, I tell you, and wait for me at the swineherd's. I'll have a little word with the notary and be with you by first light, so have some food ready, I'm hungry."

"Perhaps the crows are hungry as well, and relying on you to hang yourself up as food for them. If you go into the village, and above all to Tengelyi's house, you're as good as dead."

"A likely story! Are you so alarmed at this little plan, then? Viola won't be as easily taken as you think. I'll tell you once more, go and get some nice *gulyás* ready for me, and if it'll help to steady your nerves I'll tie the commander of the *hajdús* up and bring him with me, and I'll hold a court martial on him."

"That was all very well when the Tiszarét people were on your side. Then you went around in safety, every house could have been a hiding-place, and there was nobody in the region that would have betrayed you for anything. But after the reverend was burgled everything has changed. People swear that you did it, and they've all turned against you."

"The truth will emerge about that as well, that's exactly why I have to talk to Tengelyi, so as to clear that up. Never in my life have I owed thanks to the gentry, the notary's the first, so don't let him say that I've been ungrateful. Off you go . . ."

"But what good will it do the notary if you're caught?" pleaded Peti, and seeing that Viola's determination was unshakeable he followed him towards the village.

"There's a shameful plot being hatched against Tengelyi. In fact, they've got a hand in it that burgled the reverend, and I must let him know . . ."
"What, today?"

"Yes, this very day. There's no telling, tomorrow might be too late; those good birds are hungry for their prey. I'll bring everything to order within an hour at the most, so you go to St-Vilmos until then."

"What?" said the Gypsy, shaking his head. "Nothing will come of it, my friend, if you've lost your senses and won't let yourself be restrained, and in any case you can't order me to desert you surrounded by such danger. If Viola's hanged, Peti the Gypsy'll have nothing to live for."

Viola grasped his faithful friend's hand in silence, and the two friends walked rapidly towards Tiszarét, where meanwhile such preparations had been made to apprehend the outlaw as even the oldest inhabitants couldn't remember.

Gendarmes were waiting in Viola's house and in the *csárda* outside the village, as the reader is aware, and furthermore soldiers, gendarmes or at least a town crier or two were keeping watch in the main streets, at the tavern and at every private house where the outlaw had ever called, while Réty's servants, armed with pitchforks and cudgels, lurked in the big barn and every householder, by order, waited in his house for the vital moment when the church bell should ring out and all burst forth against the solitary monster. In addition, a number of *táblabírós*, eager for the public good, who feared especially for their herds, and several enthusiastic ladies had offered a hundred forints as a reward for him that took the thief alive or dead – a difference that would be no more in a mere twenty-four hours – and delivered him into the hands of justice; and if he did indeed come to Tiszarét in the night I too would share Nyúzó's opinion that only a miracle could save him. There were, however, certain doubts as to whether he would come to the village. While Nyúzó and his clerk were enjoying themselves coursing, that is, commissary Kánya, commandant of Tiszarét, in their absence had promulgated all orders with an additional penalty of twenty-five strokes, and although the magistrate had learned of this tactic, cursed greatly, and ordered that no one be allowed to leave the village, it was to be feared that Viola would be informed of the preparations made against him. These doubts eventually became so strong that after ten o'clock, when Viola and Peti were approaching Tiszarét, the weary inhabitants involved, and indeed most of the gendarmes, went to bed.

"Wait for me a while," said Peti to his companion when they reached the threshing-floors, "let me look around. A couple of braided villains were posted here by the road, let's see what they're doing."

Viola stopped, and while the old man slipped like a fox over the ditch and vanished among the ricks he checked his weapons and waited for him.

A few minutes later Peti was back. "They're asleep," he said with a laugh. "Well, if they're all doing their duty like that we're safe." And they crossed the threshing-floors and were soon entering the village.

All was peaceful and silent, and apart from the inn and the village hall only here and there was there a candle shining through the little windows; Peti and Viola advanced with swift and silent steps between the houses, avoiding as far as possible the more frequented streets; round corners, through gardens they went, along hedge and ditch, Peti leading and Viola following in silence.

After the mansion, Tengelyi's house was without doubt the most handsome in all Tiszarét, and indeed any foreigner, whose taste wasn't yet so educated that he favoured the mishmash of Italian and French that characterises mansions in Hungary, would perhaps consider the notary's more beautiful and more comfortable with its green vine branches twining almost to the roof, its four little windows overlooking the main street, and the long passageway that led, between wooden columns covered with beans, towards the neat courtyard. This, however, isn't presently relevant, and I'll only mention that on one side of the house lay a narrow yard, on the other a wider garden, one neighbour was the village hall and the other the house of István the smith; on the other side of the street was the shop of Iczik the Jew – the only one to be found in Tiszarét, but for that very reason twice as excellent not only as a store of fabrics from Europe and the two Indias but also because of its fine yellow colour and the porch supported by those bright blue pillars, beneath which on Saturdays Iczik and all fifteen of his family, dressed in fine velvet pantaloons, were accustomed to sit.

Access to Tengelyi's house was possible by only two ways, past either the village hall or István's smithy, and although the sound of hammering could be heard from the forge Peti considered the latter more advisable, especially when he saw that the candle was no longer burning in Iczik's shop and that the Jewish snake, as he said, had withdrawn to the bags of thalers in his inner cave.

They emerged, therefore, from the dark corner which opened onto the main street from behind István the smith's house and hurried towards Tengelyi's. The smith's fire shed a red light onto the street and the Jew's house, behind the closed door and windows of which it appeared that all were asleep. They crossed that lighted space and Peti, who looked left and right and saw everything and was alert to every sound, suddenly seized Viola's hand. "We've been seen," he muttered, pointing to the Jew's house, where a human form had appeared from behind one of the columns and a moment later vanished behind the door of the house. "Go quickly towards the notary's house, you'll find a gap just between the wall and the fence, dive in there and hide, but for God's sake don't go into the house; once the fuss is over and I can see that we can go safely I'll come back for you."

Peti hurried to the other side of the street and vanished between the houses, while Viola, with some difficulty, eventually found the gap and had scarcely hidden behind the bushes when he became certain that the Gypsy's anxiety was not unfounded. Various voices were heard in the street, a number of lanterns were quickly lit, and finally the ringing of the bell showed that the inhabitants were up and about, and had anyone been in doubt the cursing of Nyúzó the magistrate, rivalled by that of

Kenyházy the clerk, convinced them that distributive justice was sometimes not asleep at half past ten even in Hungary.

My readers will easily see that Viola's situation at that moment was by no means free from danger. Tengelyi's garden wasn't so large that one could hide there safely, added to which the windows of the house that looked onto the garden were lit and shed light onto part of it. It really needed nothing more than for someone to see the gap in the hedge and come looking for him – and no one could have saved him. He was, however, accustomed to such dangers and waited to see how things turned out; trusting in his lucky star and his courage, he calmly readied his weapons.

The fuss, however, subsided again after a little while. The searchers moved off to another part of the village, and the distant voices and the bell, which was still ringing, told Viola that the danger had mostly, if not entirely, passed. On such occasions, in fact, in Hungary only the first quarter of an hour is dangerous for the evil-doer, and once that is over no one seeks anything but a pretext for abandoning all search. We're an Oriental people, and we didn't come to the West in order to tire ourselves again, and indeed, a friend of mine was perhaps right when he said one day that he was convinced that our ancestors had only left their homeland to seek one where the sun rose later and they would be able to sleep longer, and so it would be a real injustice that their forebears should expect of us, having been created by God as the noblest of peoples, that we should regard our lives as a lengthy socage. Having on several previous occasions been in a similar situation, Viola knew this national characteristic, and calmly, as if it weren't he that was being hunted, stood up and crept towards the house.

In that house, behind those windows, was his wife, the only being in the world that loved him, the only one that he could call his own, at whose gentle speech the outlaw felt that, excluded as he was from the society of men, hounded and condemned by authority and the law, there still remained to him something of which the world couldn't deprive him and by which he felt linked to life and to his God; and Viola's heart, which in danger remained calm, throbbed mightily when he stole from window to window and finally stopped outside one of the last.

In the room into which he was looking everything was peaceful. His wife was asleep, or at least lying motionless, in the bed, and beside her Vilma was seated watching over the patient, and farther away old Mrs Lipták was reading her ancient bible, from time to time rocking a cradle with her foot; near to her on a chair, his face turned towards the window,

Viola's young son was sleeping, oblivious of his woes by the fortunate privilege of his age. All was silent in the room, and as Viola looked in he was able to enjoy for a long moment the bitter happiness of seeing them again, which filled his long-dry eyes with pure drops. That woman, who, sick and perhaps at death's door, had been driven from her home and forced to seek the charity of others, that boy, who, his name disgraced and without friends or family, was going to lead a life of beggary and, if he grew up, become an outlaw like his father; that baby, whose very mother must wish for nothing but that it should as soon as possible leave this world in which, if it were taken from its mother's breast, only bitterness awaited it – could there be a more dismal sight than that? And yet, was there anything else in this world that the fugitive could call his own? As he roamed for days on end in the forests or the reed-beds of the plains, what consoled him, what sustained the strength of his spirit other than the hope of seeing again that which now filled his eyes with tears? Oh, none suspects how much pain there can be in the human breast; we can't guess how many noble thoughts, how many fine and exalted feelings often lie hidden even in the heart of the man over whose head the world has long since broken the rod of condemnation!

The baby now suddenly began to wail. Mrs Lipták took it in her arms and began to walk up and down the room. Little Pista rubbed his eyes and looked round as if he didn't know where he was. All of a sudden he glanced at the window and caught sight of Viola, who stood there motionless, forgetful of everything; he jumped off the chair, clapped his hands, and ran towards him with cries of "Daddy, Daddy."

"Merciful God, don't let him be here," said Mrs Lipták as she too approached the window. "You're talking in your sleep, my dear boy, be quiet, you'll wake your mother."

"Oh, aunty," whispered the little boy, "I'm not talking in my sleep, he really was there, standing by the window, I could even see the flowers on his sheepskin coat."

"But you can see, there's nobody there."

"Yes," said the boy, almost in tears, "he's not there now, but he was, you can believe me; when I went to the window he suddenly disappeared in the bushes, he's in the garden for sure, I'll go out right away and call him."

"What are you thinking of, son?" said Mrs Lipták, holding back by the arm. "Your father . . ." and the good woman said no more, because she couldn't find words to tell the boy gently what she meant to say about his father.

"Yes," the boy replied, wiping his eyes, "Daddy has to hide, but it's not true what the gendarmes say, is it, that he's a bandit?"

"No, no, son," whispered Mrs Lipták. "Just you keep quiet and don't say a word to anybody; you understand, anybody, even the young lady, and I'll go out and if your father's in the garden I'll have a word with him."

Vilma had been very alarmed at first when the little boy cried out, but now she too thought that he had been talking in his sleep, and she called him to her and stayed at the bedside while Mrs Lipták went into the garden.

Meanwhile Viola's situation had become very parlous. As he stepped back from the window where he had been recognised by his son he realised that his movements were being spied on by someone else too. Someone was standing by the gap where he had come in. In the poor light from the window he couldn't recognise the watcher, but he saw the figure retreat as soon as it realised that it had been seen, and heard clearly that it was running away. What was he to do? He couldn't stay in the garden; it was much too small and open on every side for him to be able to hide or defend himself there. In the streets there were soldiers and gendarmes as well as village people, and in the house only strangers whom he couldn't trust. Now the bell rang out again, and approaching lanterns and footsteps indicated that his pursuers had discovered his whereabouts and were back on their feet. Such was the state of affairs when Mrs Lipták came and softly called his name; he, seeing no alternative, went straight to her and told her all the dangers of his situation.

"Oh, oh, why have you come today of all days?" said the old woman. "Another couple of days and the fuss will have died down and you could have come in safety."

"That's as may be, but what are we to do now? Can you take me into the house without anyone knowing?"

"Not without anyone knowing, no, but the notary's not at home, and Vilma won't be your Judas, just wait for me here." And she went inside, while Viola leant against the wall and waited calmly for her to come back. Meanwhile the noise was increasing, out in the street swords were rattling and the magistrate's cursing could be heard a long way off when the house door opened and Mrs Lipták beckoned to him; Viola, remaining close to the wall so that the light from the windows shouldn't shine on him, took refuge.

"Where is he, where is he?" roared Nyúzó by the fence. "So the precious bird is snared at last."

81

"Go on, lads, "shouted the clerk from well behind, "go on, there's nothing to fear. Whoever catches him and delivers him bound to the County will receive a hundred forints. Forward, lads, devil take you."

"Is there anyone on the other side of the garden, then?" asked a tremendous voice in which everyone recognised the constable.

No one replied.

"You damned idlers, why are you wasting time here!" shouted Nyúzó again. "Why is nobody on the other side?"

"You told us to come here, Your Worship," said a gendarme nervously, in response to which nothing was heard but a cracking sound, which in the dark might easily have been taken for a slap on a cheek.

"Go round to the other side quickly, but not too many of you, and tie him up tight."

"If he resists," the clerk called out again, "shoot to kill at once."

"Anyone that does," interposed the worthy magistrate, "I shall brain. I'm not depriving myself of the satisfaction of having him hanged."

To the accompaniment of such preparations and orders, given and carried out with the usual Hungarian precision, Mrs Lipták concealed the outlaw behind a couple of barrels in the larder and calmly resumed her place at the cradle.

Vilma was shaking from head to foot.

"Don't be afraid, Miss Vilma", said Mrs Lipták calmly. "We're in a noble house and they can't come in here. If we were in some poor man's house it would be different, there they'd search high and low, but in a nobleman's *kúria*[51] everyone's safe."

On this occasion, however, Mrs Lipták was mistaken, and she was soon persuaded that she lived in a country where the fact that something is enshrined in law is not sufficient reason, and where just as noble privilege is won by gift, so it is only by gifts that it can be enjoyed in full measure. That is to say, after magistrate Nyúzó had surrounded the garden on all sides and received no response to his mighty shouts calling on Viola to surrender and be hanged forthwith, he considered further search necessary and led his men unceremoniously through the gap and from the other side through the unlocked gate, and the disorderly un-

---

51 The *kúria* is, so to speak, a single-storey *kastély* – the residence of a nobleman. It resembles a peasant house in all but size and ornateness. The point being made here is that the nobility, unlike the peasantry, was not only absolved from paying taxes but was also immune against summary justice. The Golden Bull of 1222 enacted that the court of the Hungarian noble – that is, his house and a certain extent of land around it – was a sort of sanctuary which no legal officer might enter without permission.

couth mob pressed forward from both sides with lanterns and cudgels over flower- and melon-beds, trampling Vilma's roses and Erzsébet's fine cabbages, until finally they met in the middle of the garden and instead of the 'gallows-bird' for whom he was shouting the constable saw His Worship Pál Nyúzó in front of him and the whole crowd was staring one another in the face in dumbfounded surprise.

"He must be in the house," said Nyúzó at length, and – it is the case with all mobs that have no decided views on an objective that the most sober or most foolish idea immediately becomes public opinion – in a moment no one had any doubt about Viola's being in the house. Kenyházy, who, first ensuring that he would meet with no opposition, had likewise come up to the rest, advanced the suggestion that they should search the house, which was accepted with general approbation. Nyúzó, who had sent the constable with his *hajdús* into the yard of the house, was approaching the door opening into the garden when suddenly Mrs Erzsébet confronted him and stopped the whole horde with the fortissimo of her weak womanly voice.

Erzsébet was a kindly, gentle soul who loved, nay, idolised her husband and Vilma, and no pleasanter, calmer housewife was to be found in all this land – but there was a point beyond which, with the exception of her husband, no one might put her to the test without discovering that they had a Hungarian woman to deal with, and as this breed of woman, like the rose, blooms more beautifully in its tender younger days, in the days of its autumn it has sharper thorns – and that point had been reached.

Erzsébet knew nothing of what had happened until then. At about nine o'clock Tengelyi had received a letter from the *alispán* on some urgent matter and had gone to see him; Vilma, as we know, was at Mrs Viola's bedside and Erzsébet had gone to bed, where she soon fell asleep, having not the slightest idea that Viola had hidden in the house or that anyone was going to look for him there. When, however, the hubbub rose to such a pitch that her splendid health and even better conscience allowed her to sleep no longer, she sprang out of bed and looked into the garden; on hearing the cursing and seeing the cabbages in which she took pride being trampled she wished to know the reason for it all: my readers, who are at all events Hungarians and perhaps householders too, will be able to imagine the noble wrath that swelled that womanly bosom.

"What's all this, then?" said she in a high pitch, not unpleasant but all the more effective. "Who dares to intrude on decent people's property in the darkness of night? What brigands, murderers, highwaymen are gathered here? Out, immediately, out, the lot of you, this is a nobleman's house, no one has any business here unless I invite them. And you'll pay for the damage."

While she was speaking Nyúzó somehow recalled the law of trespass, and seeing his prestige endangered from another quarter tried, somewhat embarrassedly, to justify his action.

Erzsébet, however, realising his embarrassment and well aware that right was on her side, wasn't prepared to listen to any justifications, and attacked the magistrate all the more vehemently as she loathed him and meant to take full advantage of the opportunity to give him what is commonly, with a little poetry, called a piece of her mind. Alas! everyone has their passions, and the nobler the well-spring from which they come the more irresistible they are. Why should Erzsébet be different from the rest, why might we expect her to consider, when full anger arose in her heart, how much the magistrate's revenge could do to even the most perfect notary.

"Mrs Tengelyi," said the magistrate eventually, in a voice choking with fury, "restrain yourself. I come in the name of the County; consider that your superior stands before you".

"My superior!" exclaimed Erzsébet. "You are the superior of brigands and thieves, not mine! County and magistrate mean nothing to me. I am a noblewoman, and I should like to see anyone enter my property without my permission."[52]

Nyúzó was a well-mannered gentleman, who held himself in check should need arise – if, that is, there was advantage in doing so – but in the end his patience had its limits, especially towards a notary's family, and those had long been exceeded.

"We shall see about that," he roared, almost beside himself. "Forward, men! Into the house! Search every nook and cranny until you find the bandit. If anyone obstructs you tie them up – we shall see who gives the orders here!"

"Give me a stick, a stick!" exclaimed Erzsébet furiously, and raising her husband's walking stick, which a servant handed her, she bawled triumphantly "*Opponálok!*"[53] At that the clerk, who was right in front of her, recoiled in alarm and Nyúzó himself was taken aback. Even with that, however, I don't believe that Mrs Tengelyi's rights would have been

---

52 The Golden Bull also enacts that the noble is subject only to the king.
53 "I oppose," a term used in public debate, claiming the right to be heard.

respected had not Ákos and Macskaházy fortunately come in the nick of time, and on learning all the circumstances, that suspicion was based entirely on the statement of an unknown Jew, possibly an accomplice of Viola who merely wished to lead the searchers astray, they didn't support the infuriated magistrate. In this Macskaházy was much the more industrious, because he was certain that Viola wasn't in the house and could see to what use the whole event might be put in bringing suspicion on Tengelyi.

Inside the house, however, terror reigned. Vilma paced the room trembling, a deathly pallor on her cheeks. "Pray for your father," said Mrs Lipták to little Pista, and while the innocent child, with hands raised Heavenward and tears in his eyes, said the Lord's Prayer she herself watched and listened to events by the window. Only Viola in his hiding-place, where he could hear the approaching danger and had a pistol ready to shoot himself in the heart if he were discovered, and his wife, unconscious in bed, remained calm. When things took a turn for the better on the arrival of Ákos Mrs Lipták became calmer once more and began to reassure Vilma, who now burst into tears. The little boy understood nothing, but on being assured that no harm was going to come to his father he rose and was wiping his wide eyes, when a new event drew the attention of all in another direction.

"Fire!" was the cry outside in the street. "Fire, fire!" was repeated in the courtyard. "Fire!" howled the entire crowd that was standing in the garden, and as the bell sounded the alarm a light spread on one side of the horizon and they began to scatter at the run. Only the jailers and the gendarmes remained in their places on Nyúzó's orders: he was still hoping to be able to find Viola there. But when a driver eventually came from the court and shouted that the *alispán*'s park was on fire and every hayrick was wreathed in flames the authorities too ran towards the threshing-floors to save that which interested the state most – the *alispán*'s hay. In a moment there was no one at Tengelyi's house except those that belonged there.

"For God's sake! Save him," said Vilma to Mrs Lipták, "quickly, before they come back."

"Never fear, Miss Vilma, he won't be caught so quickly. Don't say anything to your parents, your father in particular would never forgive you."

And Mrs Lipták went into the larder. Vilma went with her mother to her room, where the latter, worn out after so much excitement, flung herself into a chair and began to weep.

"Come along, now you can be off," said Mrs Lipták as she pushed aside the barrels behind which Viola was hidden. "There's a fire on the *alispán*'s threshing-floor, so leave the village on the other side and nobody will stop you. In fact, the fire's probably been started for your benefit."

"Listen, dear lady, one more thing," said Viola. "I owe the notary much gratitude – my sick wife's been taken in, may God reward them for that, and my life's been saved, for which I give my own thanks. Tell him this, please: I know that in his iron chest he has documents of great value to both himself and the reverend; he should put them somewhere else and take great care of them. He has powerful enemies, and certain ladies and gentlemen are very eager to have those documents. Do you understand?"

Mrs Lipták nodded.

"Well, tell the notary that, please, and now God bless you."

And the outlaw had stepped out through the garden door and was hurrying towards the fence when suddenly someone caught hold of his coat.

"Who's that?" asked Viola, raising his *fokos*.

"Don't you know me?" replied Peti. "So what do you think of our illuminations?"

"I don't believe I would have come out of my hole if you hadn't started a fire. I realised at once that it was you, God bless you for doing that."

"Now, off to St-Vilmos quickly," said Peti at the gap in the fence, which had become much wider. "Look over there," he added, "I would risk a bet that's that damned Macskaházy standing there."

"Even if it is the Devil's son, let's just be off," said Viola. The two friends walked quickly down the street, while Macskaházy, for indeed it was he, had recognised Viola and made for the threshing-floors, shaking his head.

VI

The day following that eventful night was a Sunday. The slow tolling of the bell of Tiszarét church summoned the people to ancient piety, and the disturbance of the previous evening and life's other woes were forgotten at Vándory's cheering sermon. In the big house, the religiousness of which, like that of other Hungarian great families, was more in evidence at assemblies at which the treaties of Linz and Vienna[54] were discussed than it is in church, everyone was preparing to receive the expected noble visitors. Ákos and his sister Etelka were walking in the park. It was one of those fine autumn days which, I may say without any improper bias, I've encountered only in Hungary, and on which I've sometimes thought that our nation too, like its country, will find its days of lasting sunshine after the uncertainty of spring and the variability of summer. Noon was approaching, and the sun was flooding the landscape with warm rays; the green of newly sown crops was appearing and the observer was reminded only by a remaining ploughed field or a patch of fallow here and there that the days of flowering and harvest were behind him and not ahead. Slender threads hung on the coloured foliage of the trees as if autumn meant to bind the fading leaves to their stems so that they should not fall, not cover with their desiccated skeletons the still-green meadows where tall dahlias and modest meadow saffron still stood in bright colours, though frost had nipped a leaf here and there.

Brother and sister walked side by side in silence on the leaf-strewn paths while Tünde, the only one of Ákos's greyhounds[55] to be granted the privilege, dashed after a bird or a falling leaf and then danced around the walkers and ran off again, enjoying the splendours of the park in her own way.

"What's wrong, dear sister?" said Ákos eventually, as she inspected a wilting dahlia. "You're out of humour today."

"Me?" she replied with a smile, as she turned her great dark eyes from the flower to her brother. "You seem no better than Macskaházy, who

---

54   In the Treaty of Linz (1645) Ferdinand III of Austria recognised György I Rákóczi's rule over the seven counties of the Partium (the region adjoining Transylvania) and reaffirmed the religious liberties of Transylvania. There were Treaties of Vienna signed in 1731, 1738 and 1814; the present allusion is therefore unclear.

55   The dog is an *agár*, the Hungarian greyhound breed, and the name means Fairy.

sees the whole world as a great yellow melon when he looks round with his orange eyes in his perennial jaundice."

"You're right," said Ákos, smiling also, "I'm being dreadfully dull."

"No doubt; but that's one of the rights of the Hungarian nobleman, and an ancient custom among siblings in particular, so don't feel in the least sorry." And she gaily turned her attention back to her flowers and left Ákos to his problems, which is almost always the best way to cheer someone up, but at the same time the sort of thing that we meet with least often. All pain, and especially bad humour, which is so similar that it is not infrequently taken for pain, usually dies away unless fuelled by external causes; and everyone is best able to find consolation in their own mind. Our friends, who can tolerate anything rather than wearying themselves with us, allow time for that, and when they mean to cheer or entertain us not only become insensitive to our feelings but in struggling against our woes they incite our minds to defend them, and the result of consolation is frequently only the conviction that our trouble is greater than we ourselves had previously thought. If my readers recall those whom they once called friends until, in that great bankruptcy of hope through which they themselves were passing, they were devalued to the status of mere acquaintances, do they not remember the bitter hour that was actually prolonged by that excess of solicitude? If you are glum and even yourself know the reason, your loyal friend will enquire until at last you think of it; if, however, some trifling ill humour comes to you, something irritating rather than painful and which you would forget in an hour's time, your Pylades[56] will do his best next day too for you to forget it and will so bind your little wound, which would mend much more quickly left to itself, that you without ingratitude forget either his peerless affection or the ill humour that gave it cause. True, if we meet with great misfortune and are really forced to seek help, our friends desist from their unpleasant error at once and in fact incommode us with their attentions, but do we not at such times think how much better it would have been if that principle of non-intervention had been applied before, or all that good-will, those countless tiny favours, with which they have burdened us had been saved up for this one occasion, and that that which their affection intends for us had been offered all at once rather than in pennyworths, so that even a small amount is unbearable. But what can be done about it? We live in commercial times, and it is

---

56 The bosom friend of Orestes in Greek mythology.

no wonder if even those who are attached to us without evident self-interest at least take advantage of us by that means in order to reap the greatest gratitude at the lowest price, and exchange the smallest possible favours for the most possible thanks. Let him to whom Heaven has granted a friend to whom such remarks apply bless his luck, for certainly he is an exception. Ákos may be reckoned such, and among the many gifts of fortune for which the young master of Tiszarét was considered in the county to be happy were that his father was *alispán* and his mother a baroness by birth, that he was handsome, that a partly uncultivated estate awaited him, and I envy him just one thing, if, that is, one may envy another that which fate has granted to oneself too – his sister.

It grieves me that I can't introduce her to my readers: they won't be satisfied with my description of her. Many a loveable woman goes to the grave having been, as Hegel might say, understood by only one person, and by him misunderstood, because, in his fevered state, the one to whom she opened her heart fully saw her beauty only with the eyes of the imagination; and so poor novelist! how is he to be happy with his descriptions of women, especially if his subject is like Etelka, for whom an actual painter would search his colours in despair? Ink and paper are paltry tools for the description of such blonde hair, such dark eyes and such regular features; and what am I to say of the tints of the delicate cheeks? Perhaps I'll give the best picture if I speak of a snow peak, the summit of which the sun's first rays touch with red while the lower slopes gleam white, and the boundaries where the colours merge into one another are not to be discerned, but will frigid summit and motionless mound of ice bring to your mind the gentle fresh cheeks, the brilliant gaze of the dark eyes, the smile of the ruby lips – in a word, the soul that radiates before you in the lovely features and, like the magical light of a summer evening on the least prepossessing of landscapes, would beautify even the most undistinguished face? Etelka was one of those rarest of individuals whose whole being is so harmonious that one doesn't so much as suspect how outstanding are each of her qualities, and if there were need to counter the presupposition that mind and heart weren't as one – put about for the most part by those who possess neither – a couple of days in Eteleka's company would suffice to convince that it was unfounded.

Etelka was a couple of years the younger, but it was she that tempered Ákos's passionate nature, she, to whom he entrusted the secrets of his heart – and all the more gladly because he knew that they would go by the quickest way to Vilma, whom his sister surrounded with all the friendship of which women are capable only at her age, and even then for a very short time!

At length the two reached the top of the mound, from where could be seen the village, the calm Tisza and the boundless plain.

"Here they come," said Etelka, turning towards St-Vilmos, where a big cloud of dust announced the approach of the expected noble guests. "In an hour the house will be packed."

"I wish to Heaven I could be a hundred *mérföld*s away," said Ákos with a sigh.

"Perhaps you'd really prefer to be there in the village, not so far away, at the notary's, wouldn't you?"

"Don't talk about it, if I so much as think about it I could weep; you know what happened yesterday?"

"You made enough noise for me to hear."

"I've nothing more to hope for."

"Don't say such a thing. Vilma loves you, you aren't going to change, and our father . . . "

"Father? If he were the only thing in the way," said Ákos heatedly. "I respect him, but respect has its limits, and if there isn't room for both Vilma and him in my heart I'd be prepared to cut out the image of a man who'd sacrifice his son's happiness to prejudice, but can I hope that Vilma would do the same? And take my word for it, that old Tengelyi's more obdurate than father."

"Don't you believe it, Tengelyi loves his daughter."

"You don't know him. Yes, he loves his daughter. There's nothing on earth he isn't prepared to sacrifice for her – his property, his life – with one exception, and that's his honour and anything that remotely concerns it, and in that respect the old man's implacable. After the unfortunate conversation in which our stepmother, realising that I was in love, gave him to understand that he and his daughter should come to call on us less often, Tengelyi came to me, told me what had happened, and asked that I should spare his house from my visits, since – as he put it bitterly – it's bad for a young man of my exalted rank to keep company with a poor girl. Since then, if I meet her in the street and walk her home, every time as we reach the gate she curtseys deeply and I can go. I've spoken to his wife, who, bless her, has always taken my side, but although she doesn't quite obey her husband blindly she turned me away saying that he's quite immovable on this one point. I spoke to Vándory, and despite all his optimism the only consolation that I could get from him was that we'd have to wait. And now, just think of the indignities of

90

yesterday, which Tengelyi will blame on our whole family, because we're on opposing sides in the election, or at least he'll think so, because I'm not going to join in party politics; so hope after that if you can."

"And I shall," said Etelka, taking her brother's hand. "When on one side every noble feeling calls out, and on the other nothing but reasons, victory doesn't always go to the cause which can be better defended but to the one which can be most warmly felt."

"You think so?" said Ákos, in his delight kissing his sister's hand passionately. "Oh, if I only knew, if I could only be sure, that my enemies' plotting wasn't going to turn her heart against me."

"Ákos! Really! The things you say!" said Etelka with a smile. "What enemies? What plotting? You young men, as Vándory says, really don't recognise a middle course in anything. You're like recruits in battle for the first time, you either go blindly forward into every danger or you imagine a whole army behind every bush and think that every falling leaf's a cannonball. Who's plotting against you? Tengelyi himself, deep down, probably loves his son no more than he does you, and every time that he sees you has to restrain himself from flinging his arms round your neck; and believe me, even if that weren't so, if her father and mother, the whole village or all Hungary were in league against you and spoke evil of you for a whole year without stopping, that wouldn't change Vilma's mind. We girls are weak, or so they say, and perhaps it's true; but that's what proves our love; if it's proved a hundred times over that we've given our hearts to some undeserving man, even if the arguments convince us, what's the use? We lack the strength to want anyone else."

"Dear Etelka, how happy you make me! Do the two of you talk about me sometimes?"

"When Vilma and I are alone it would be hard to talk about anything else. You know, I'm free of Tengelyi's great ban and I go and see her almost every day, as I did before. The old man used to grumble a bit at first when I went, but after I sat down at the piano and we sang a couple of his favourite songs his frostiness thawed, and whenever he thinks of it again we make music for a quarter of an hour. Vilma worships you, and at first, when she didn't know why you'd stopped going, she was sad, but when she heard from me she was reassured and now that I've cheered her up she's full of hope for the future again."

"If only I could see her again, just for a minute."

"We'll see, who knows, perhaps it'll be quite soon. If old Tengelyi's standing in the election, be patient until then. But now let's go, the canvassers will be arriving soon, that'll be worth seeing."

91

"So you think I'll see Vilma?" said Ákos, holding Etelka back as she set off for the house. "For goodness' sake, don't stop taking my side."

"You can be certain, be patient for just anther couple of days and you'll see her."

Ákos gave the speaker a passionate embrace and the two hurried off towards the house, from where a distant storm of dreadful shouts could be heard.

VII

With us Hungarians every creative action – be it large or small, a luncheon among friends or a vital piece of legislation – begins, alas! not with clarity but with uproar, and so my readers can imagine the din that now filled the Réty house. Coachmen and *hajdús* hurried this way and that carrying all manner of things, and everyone was making a racket; the cook and his staff in the kitchen, the steward and the major domo in the cellar, the housekeeper and her maids in the storerooms – all were giving orders and arguing so that each could scarcely hear themselves speak; Madam was at the central window of the upper storey watching for the arrival of her guests, and had sent her last maid to establish peace and quiet without any result other than the addition of another voice to the hubbub; she was scarcely able to maintain that gentle smile that the county so admired every three years, just before elections.

On the porch *alispán* Réty, Bálint Kislaky, magistrate Nyúzó and sundry other worshipful comrades in principle were smoking, and a couple of poor relatives of the house, who were always summoned for the purpose, now lit a pipe for someone, then used up the gratitude owed for that service with another favour; meanwhile Macskaházy leant on one of the Doric columns and ran his little eyes obsequiously over the whole group.

In no other country would we find its like. In Hungary, however, especially before an election, such are almost everywhere, and though few in number this company is composed of such individuals as constitute the most prominent men in Taksony county.

The first to attract our attention is Bálint Kislaky, the father of him whose acquaintance we made on the Turk's Hill with Ákos Réty. There is much about the old man that one might like, but little that one could describe. A small, stout man with a handsome head of silver hair and ruddy complexion, his lips always smiling and his blue eyes always kindly, he stands before you open-armed. To their great detriment, he always forgets the ends of the lengthy stories which he repeats at every opportunity; they are sometimes boring, but everyone appreciates that there is as little falsehood in this man as in his tales and forgives him, feeling more comfortable in his company than in the most intellectual circles.

There are, however, at least two among the others that are passing the time on the *alispán*'s porch who catch the attention of the stranger. It is

93

necessary for my readers to make the acquaintance of these two persons, who are considered prominent in the county. At all events, these two deserve your attention even though we can't share His Honour the *alispán*'s opinion that their like is not to be found anywhere in the world – because we ourselves believe that the breed of so-called *eccentrics*, which, alas! are to be found everywhere, resemble one another more than ordinary people do. I refer to Ágoston Karvaly, invincible castellan of County Hall, and Tamás Sáskay,[57] its dearest tax collector, and I may say without exaggeration that you would search the whole county in vain for characters like them, to the no little relief of the tax-paying populace.

Ágoston Karvaly was of ancient noble stock – my readers will find it natural for me to begin my description with that remark; in Hungary, where we may pass Scot free through and over roads and bridges with the little phrase *I'm a nobleman*, they will perhaps desire almost nothing from my characters whom I present to them with that forewarning, or will be more gracious towards them than other judges. Karvaly's past, in itself, is one of the most interesting, and it may be regretted that his history, which he related quite in the style of Goethe – blending life and poetry – can't be preserved for posterity. He was the fifth son of a father who, being also a fifth son, had received as his inheritance only that part of the estate at Karval that might be determined by calculation (because the Karvaly family tree resembled the five-times multiplication table), and what came down to our Ágoston was an estate of no great extent – the proverbial seven plum trees[58] had ceased to be applicable even to his father – but at least it was enough to make him a Hungarian nobleman, who, as is well known, keeps himself rather by his rights than by his land and can live on honour. He spent his childhood wrestling with his noble relatives around his father's *kúria* or fighting with village children on the village green; and after a preparation reminiscent of the upbringing of the classical heroes of Homer (at the college in Sárospatak, where he was always last among his fellow pupils, and at hare-coursing, where he was always first) the young man's dormant talents were so perfectly honed that his father, whose eyes were bathed in tears when he heard his son swearing – there was no telling whether it was for pleasure or because

---

57 'Speaking' names continue. *Karvaly* means 'sparrowhawk', while *Sáska* means 'grasshopper'.
58 *Hét szilvafás* 'owning seven plum-trees' is the traditional designation for the nobleman of little or no wealth.

it reminded him of his long-deceased father – could say without any exaggeration that there wasn't a boy like him in the whole county. His siblings sometimes complained that he was a little combative by nature, but we may say in his favour that he never confronted a stronger man, indeed, he would run away rather than expose anyone to the unpleasantness that usually results from *major potentiae actio*.[59]

Fortunately for the Karvaly family – because otherwise after so many trials one of the five brothers would still have been found weak – the brave young man was summoned to the '*insurrectio* of the nobility' of 1809;[60] and we should not be surprised that the nobility elected him lieutenant, who had displayed such signs of martial qualities. That war was soon over; we mustn't forget it, because it was a great tax on the Hungarians, or at least on their nobility, which, with God's help, will one day be paid off with interest, nor must we forget that Karvaly must have displayed extraordinary courage; all that we can say about him is that in the great strategic marvel, which put Xenophon's retreat in the shade, he was surpassed by no one, and that in that time of danger no one in the whole county regiment returned home to the defence of his own hearth sooner than he; about that distinction, however, he rather kept silent, a characteristic mark of virtue.

There is, they say, something about a uniform which women find irresistible; whether it is because, as some believe, they prefer to choose their future husbands from that estate which is more accustomed to subordination than any other, or whether it is because uniform makes men more like one another, and if, as sometimes happens nevertheless – getting no true appreciation from their previous lover – they find themselves obliged to make a change, since their hearts remain with the same regiment and only the face changes in the object of their idolatry they may not be accused of inconstancy, I can't say, but this much is certain: when Mrs Ráczfalvy saw Karvaly in hussar uniform his ramrod figure and wondrously shaped moustache had so perfect an effect that she – who, as the whole region knew, although it would have been her duty, had never loved even her previous husband – could never again have

---

59 An act of violence.

60 Hungary joined Austria in opposing Napoleon, and on 14 June 1809 the army – poorly equipped, untrained and badly led – was severely mauled by the French at Győr. The nobility had voluntarily contributed to military taxation at the time in order to avoid the abolition of their exemption from ordinary taxes. An *insurrectio* was a mobilisation of the nobility for the defence of the realm, and it was a legal obligation to come when called upon.

looked on the blue heaven without Ágoston's blue *dolmány* coming to mind, and his *mente* with its frogging so powerfully beguiled her heart that the spell could only be broken by a priestly blessing.

There were some in the county who accused Karvaly of self-seeking on this occasion, and in particular Mrs Ráczfalvy's relatives, who had been expecting bequests from her, kicked up a fuss; there were some, indeed, who gave out that the bride-to-be was well past fifty. I, however, who believe the lady to have been forty-nine at the most, and who know how her husband endeavoured to spend as quickly as possible the money for which he had allegedly entered into matrimony – indeed, that once everything else had slowly dissipated he also parted with the last thing that remained, that is, his wife – can give credence neither to the one slander nor the other, and I assure my readers that Karvaly, insofar as he had inherited from Ráczfalvy, at least faithfully fulfilled the duties of a beneficiary and not only mourned his death very frequently but – something that many hold to be a sacred obligation – avenged himself on his benefactor in full measure.

After this disaster Karvaly was once more forced onto his own pasture, and if he had been fortunate in not acquiring enemies through his marriage he would probably have disappeared in the great crowd of canvassers. It is, however, a known fact that in a country that has a constitution the best way to advance is by acquiring not the most friends but the sort of enemies that belong to the weaker party; and as Karvaly's persecutors were accounted to the party that remained in the minority and he himself was supported by the majority he was elevated without delay to the offices of Castellan and Captain of *Hajdú*s, and indeed was made an honorary clerk of the court, which was an appurtenance of that position.

His opposite stands before us in Tamás Sáskay. There are societies in which you can't find two friends; perhaps there is none in the world in which there aren't two that detest one another thoroughly; and it was natural for Sáskay and Karvaly to assume those roles. The very exteriors of these men seemed to contradict one another and Sáskay's face, which resembled a yellowed sheet of paper which someone in anger had crumpled into a hundred folds because it contained unpleasant matters, was as little like Karvaly's ruddy cheeks, as his colourless hair, combed forward with great care, didn't resemble the castellan's tousled head, and when they spoke you noticed at once that the cracked, piping voice of the one was never in tune with the other's resonant bass. Karvaly's chief characteristic was candour, and indeed some of the people of Taksony county believed that its captain would not be any the less likeable if he possessed much less of that virtue. Sáskay was an introvert, and even if he were asked what the time was he would reply only after careful thought and with certain reservations, and in his case – oh public! – many again found that it was a pity to be so withdrawn, as in a chemist's shop everyone can read what is in it on the outside of the box that contains poison. Even the many trivialities of intercourse that exist between men in the civilised world and are brought to mind whenever we need a light or have left our snuff-box at home, all the occasions on which we need our fellow men and are driven to them in order to smoke or sneeze away our ill humour didn't exist for these two. Sáskay, to his shame, didn't smoke a pipe; Karvaly wasn't in the habit of clearing his muzzy head with snuff, and there was no hope that these gentlemen would ever be of one mind except at lunch.

Sáskay had suffered many misfortunes in his life; I'll only mention the greatest, about which, by strength of character, he never spoke but which is recorded in the annals of the county. When, that is, he was chief tax-collector a deficiency was found in the funds entrusted to him, and although he said often enough that the money had been stolen and although the whole county believed him, indeed, no one had any doubt that Sáskay had seen the thief leaving the room, what was the good! On this one occasion – in Sáskay's opinion too – the government infringed the laws of Hungary and of nature and suspended the tax-collector from office; and although Taksony county wrote up thirteen times and threatened to protest: a man of such great worth was never again designated for his former office, which he had discharged to the full satisfaction of the nobility, and while clothed with which he hadn't only not enriched himself but had even lost all that he had at cards.

Would one perhaps, think that after such unjust persecution by the government Sáskay had gone over to the opposition? But great characters avenge themselves like that, and indeed there would've been no greater enemy of the freedom of the press or the responsibility of Members of Parliament than he; and as for the representation of the people, anyone that so much as once heard him speak on this topic was convinced that if we didn't wish to throw the business of the state into the greatest confusion it was impossible to grant influence on its handling to those that paid taxes.[61]

---

61   As the nobility paid no taxes the inference is clear.

Immediately after the said misfortune Sáskay's situation in the county was a little unpleasant. Public officials have their enemies, and so he had his. In time, however, every blot that occurs on someone's escutcheon usually fades away – either because the blot itself fades, or because the whole thing becomes dirtier – and so Sáskay too spent his days quite pleasantly, and in fact since he wasn't keeping the kitchen himself he lunched much more cheaply and better than before. As I said: his principles linked him to the conservative party, except on financial questions, in which he took particular interest *ex officio*, and he proposed the most daring innovations with plans for a national bank, paper money and county loans;[62] indeed, it can be said that he became obsessed with the setting up of more and more new public funds with clever financial men in charge of them to whom the entire management would be entrusted.

In the middle of the porch sat *alispán* Réty in a silver-buttoned *atilla*,[63] with a big pipe with a silver bowl; and if I've offended against the rules of politeness in not introducing the master of the house first to my readers, my duty as a writer has commanded me to save the most interesting for last. Every circle has its great man. As nowadays coffee is among the prime requirements of every company, so is at least one great man; and as for lack of coffee we turn to a substitute, which, if we are accustomed to it, gives just as great pleasure and is not as expensive as real coffee, so it is with regard to great men. The army consisting of only one general and nothing but private soldiers would fulfil its purpose badly; and so in life it is necessary, that, with the exception of the highest places to which few can aspire, there should exist a number of degrees to which ascent is more likely; only thus may it be hoped that everyone will attain the object of their ambition and perform their duties zealously. If the hope of eternal fame were all that enthused the soldier not many would remain on the field of battle after the first shot. For the general to control his troops it is necessary for many under him to hope for the rank of corporal or sergeant. And so it is in the world at large, where, whatever may be said, the greatest deeds haven't been accomplished by solitary great individuals but by countless mediocrities.

---

62 At the time of writing, central banking functions in Hungary were carried out by the Austrian National Bank (founded 1816), which was succeeded in 1921 by the Royal Hungarian State Bank. Early forms of paper money in the Habsburg Empire date from the 1760s, while the Austrian National Bank issued banknotes (in the modern sense) from 1816.

63 Not to be confused with Attila the Hun! A short, braided, military-style tunic.

What is true in all parts of the world is doubly so in Hungary, where fifty-two counties stand side by side, each like a little kingdom; and if Réty was idolised by one part of Taksony and proclaimed by the other as the model of all villainy, our readers may rest assured that at least fifty-two men live in similar circumstances, and that he with whom we are now becoming acquainted satisfies neither the one judgement nor the other.

Réty was one of those men whom we can best describe as shrewd, and who – even though the word denoting this quality[64] has only recently come back into use – are, thank Heaven, not lacking among our *alispán*s.

Knowing that, just as there is no better way of rising to the rank of *alispán* than by joining some party, there is no worse means of retaining that office or rising higher, ever since his person was raised by a majority of the county as a banner to which their party rallied, Réty had taken it to be his duty to deal kindly with other banners, or, as his enemies put it, to turn with the wind. He was a man of the *juste milieu*, not in the sense in which that expression is used in Europe, in accordance with which distinct principles are desired from that political colouration and it is easy to fall between two stools, but as men of central principle usually are in Hungary: giving his vote now to one party, now to another – like a clever gambler, backing red and black at the same time, so that in no case may he lose. In politics time, as many believe at least, leads to doubt, and I myself have known several honourable men who, at the age of twenty, if it were desired, would have drawn up for our country the most perfect constitution possible in a single day, yet who later pondered for whole days over individual words in a trifling bill; in the master of the house, however, this contrast was not to be detected. The longer he lived, the more clearly he saw that in his position as *alispán* the most correct of all possible convictions was that which most in the county defended; in keeping to this he had the rare good fortune that he had never been forced to declare a majority contrary to his personal convictions. There were those that took amiss this pliability of his opinions, and it was said that always to lead the way was no great glory and that he that was ejected from an inn, although he was usually first through the door, couldn't, nevertheless, be called a leader; other such

---

64 The word that Eötvös uses is *ildomos* 'proper, well-mannered, decorous' in modern Hungarian. The ancient meaning, however, is *ésszerű* 'in accordance with good sense'. *Ildomos* is the equivalent of 'wise (as serpents)' in Matthew 10:16.

unkind comments too were voiced, but since Réty's enemies were, as I said, always among the minority, and even those that had said such things were reckoned among his most eager supporters as soon as they gained the majority, and in such cases – as is the generous Hungarian custom – cheered on with the greatest enthusiasm him whom they had previously most disparaged; taking everything into consideration, Réty was comfortable with his tactics and – something unheard of in Taksony county – had retained his office for nine years.

For some time, however, the easy relationship that had existed between him and the county had been disturbed. Let none believe that after so long a term in office the *alispán* had become conceited; indeed, never in human memory had his face smiled so gently, never before had his arms embraced so many *táblabírós*; his house was as open and as hospitable as ever, and his new cook, who so cooked that every dish appeared to be an allegory of the Hungarian fear that we shall choke on our own fat, was the greatest *concessio* that he could make to public opinion. The only reason for trouble could be found in the fact that the *alispán* of Taksony had for some time now begun to adhere to certain principles that the majority, who had presented him with their confidence rather because they had not hitherto detected this fault in him, couldn't endure without protest. His speeches had previously followed the models of parliamentary speakers. "I'm not talking about that, Honoured Estates of the Realm!" – so went his discourse usually. "I'm not talking about that, and far be it from me to descend into discussion of this other question which would divert us from the point, or would force us to decide on matters which it is inadvisable to resolve at present. It all depends on whether the Honoured Estates of the Realm want *this* or *that*." And there would follow general views, each finer than the last, about the noble character of the Hungarian people, our liberties that had been bought with blood, and other such novel and magnificent topics; at which the speaker, frequently interrupted by resounding shouts of Hurrah! would end his speech with the incontrovertible axiom that the word of the people is the word of God, and that the said Estates of the Realm would settle the question better themselves for the good of the country. So spoke the Demosthenes of Taksony county at one time. His speech – to coin a totally novel simile – flowed over subjects like a clear river, the smooth surface of which no jutting rocklike principle or conviction disturbed, and in which the whole of the body of *táblabírós* could see its own convictions reflected. But for some time a certain thread had been running through his speeches, slender yet, but perceptible, and some of the county began to speak of a false apostate, though they could swear to it that at the age of fifty Réty appeared to be convinced of something for the first time in his life.

The public always watched him open-mouthed in wonder as they did a conjuror's tricks, even though they had seen them a hundred times, and in the same way they marvelled at the change in the *alispán*; but lest my readers, like the county audience, should search in vain for the reasons I, as a dutiful narrator, will inform them. Great men commonly have ambition, and that is good, because it is usually that which drives them to *great deeds*; great men usually have wives too, and that again is good, because in the opinion of a friend of mine, whose name I shall conceal out of Christian charity, only so can they exercise themselves in that second quality, no less necessary than great deeds for the attainment of true greatness: *great patience without complaint*; but the trouble is that great men's women likewise sometimes have ambition, and that often works in a direction opposite to their men's – and many a glorious name has fallen victim to this. That was the case with Réty too, and I ask: are we to think ill of the temperamentally mild *alispán*, who all his life has paid homage to the majority, for doing in his home what he has been accustomed to doing in the Assembly? After an unquiet conscience, the greatest of worldly woes is a woman who is dissatisfied with her husband's achievements, and who would not strive to be free of her? Look into yourselves, readers, and tell me: have you never done anything against your better judgement merely so that the doors of that Temple of Janus, represented in domestic life by the rosy lips of your wives, remain shut, and that peace be maintained throughout your empires? Now I shall turn to my gentle lady readers, who are always the most severe toward their sex, if not toward themselves, and I beg them to make the same allowances for Mrs Réty too. Women can seldom count on a place in history, and even, indeed, even in our parliamentary records we find few female names, with the exception of those widows who have sent emissaries to the lower house; was it not natural that, knowing this, Mrs Réty wished to see with her eyes in the address of every letter sent to her and to hear with her ears the style of *nagyságos* or *méltóságos*, or even *kegyelmes*,[65] which, it can't be denied, sound so fine especially in the superb Hungarian language? Furthermore, as other angels too have descended into Purgatory not in order to remain there but to raise the

---

65 A series of forms of address (in ascending order) to Hungarian aristocrats and dignitaries. Several more were in use.

damned up with them, who can take it amiss that, being herself an angel, she too, who had been born a baroness – that is, a *méltóságos* young lady – should wish to do that for her husband? all these reasons together explain Mrs Réty's desire, which gave her no rest day or night, that her husband should become a baron?

Réty himself, who had objected for a long time, was now actually proposing a middle course and voting rather for the chancellor's key, by means of which he could assume the style of *nagyságos* even without a barony; he thought it better, if only because he would be supported from behind[66] in his official position; it is certain, however, that since this thought had come to him it was as if a veil had fallen from his eyes and he saw everything in quite a different light, and redoubled his efforts to retain his situation as *alispán*.

The *alispán* was perhaps pondering just this extraordinary situation, which many *alispán*s in Hungary usually go through once in their lives; the others were probably dreaming in silence of similar things a degree lower, for civil servants, and those that aspire to office, gladly undertake the less fine part of public affairs of which the practical fulfilment of their office consists – when the silence was broken by a distant but mighty *Hurrah!* and the distinguished company on the porch was suddenly in motion.

"Hurrah for Réty! Hurrah for Nyúzó! Hurrah for Hungarian liberty! Forward!" and other shouts of the sort, interspersed with a little swearing and the occasional pistol shot, filled the village. Above the noise there rang out the splendid chorus

> *Tulips in flower,*
> *Réty for power,*

indispensable at election-time and unfailingly popular because of the universally applicable rhyme. Imagine to accompany it a whole cartload of Gypsies playing the Rákóczi March and all the village dogs howling, and we have a musical treat at which, to quote Shakespeare, angels might weep.[67]

---

66 The title of Chancellor (*kamarás*) could be conferred on persons of distinction, both civil and military. Later it didn't require service at court and was merely honorific. The insignia consisted of a golden key hanging by a gold thread from a gold-coloured backing, worn on the back of the 'Rock' or coat in the region of the right hip. On appointment a formal oath was administered, which had to be taken in the High Chamberlain's office in Vienna.

67 *Measure for Measure, act 2 scene 2:* Man . . . Plays such fantastic tricks before high heaven As make the angels weep.

"There's enthusiasm! That's popularity for you!" said Karvaly at length, as he twirled his moustache and listened to the voices with obvious delight. "A fine thing, for sure, to command public confidence like you do, sir! I'm a poor man, but devil take me if I wouldn't give fifty forints to be cheered like that just once in this world."

"Just as long as they don't set fire to anything," sighed one of the poor relations, who didn't talk as much rubbish about the previous election as did others, but remembered the bruises that he had suffered three years before. His hair almost stood on end when he thought of the imminent glorification of his uncle – perhaps there would be applause on his back once again.

"Set fire? Damn it all, who're you talking about, you lily-livered so-and-so?" the castellan roared at him, "don't you know you're talking about noblemen, that St-Vilmos has three hundred votes, and that if the whole village is set alight once His Honour is safely elected you should be glad you've come here and not gone to the opposition?"

"Karvaly's right," said Réty, turning to his pasty-faced nephew. "How dare you speak like that about my guests? I know the St-Vilmos people."

"Yes, so do I," Karvaly interrupted, "one jailbird in ten comes from their number, I've never seen more upright fellows: those that do the most stealing, fighting and murdering at home are always to the fore in wars and elections."

"There may be exceptions," Sáskay broke in with his shrill voice. "The way I heard it, in the *insurrectio* of 1809 . . ."

Fortunately for all present and especially for Sáskay, by this time the canvassers had come all the way to the gate, and the huge cheer with which the first carriage was greeted rendered further debate impossible: otherwise Karvaly would have brought up a certain financial matter with which he usually repaid talk of the *insurrectio* of 1809 and would have given a turn to the conversation such that certain actions would be found inevitably necessary and, as experience had shown more than once, Sáskay would have had the worst of it.

The entire noble horde had come in about thirty carts, requisitioned from the peasants of St-Vilmos and neighbouring villages, as I heard, for public works on the perfectly legal pretext that as so many carts broke up the clods on the road it did indeed serve as improvement. On the first and last carts could be seen yellow banners bearing patriotic words. On one side was:

We're not making roads or ditches,
Réty for alispán our wish is.

103

And on the other:

> *Pay no taxes, pay no tolls*
> *Over bridges, through controls,*
> *Never be conscripted and*
> *Make the laws that rule the land,*
> *Setting a high price for salt*
> *Noblemen do as they please.*

On every nobleman's *süveg*[68] or cap could be seen a feather, half green, half yellow, portraying the aspirations of the party and the envy of the opposition, and in addition giving the practical advantage that Réty's adherents should not inadvertently break a head in which the right ideas dominated.

The *alispán* descended to the first step of the porch amid the cheers of the nobility and countless compliments, the visitors formed a big ring and the ceremonial began. To mighty shouts of *Hear! Hear!* the lieutenant of the nobility declaimed that in accordance with custom the notary was to express the feelings of all present and especially his own in fine Hungarian. He that had been called upon began as follows:

Glorious *alispán*!

Great patriot!

Immortal man!

Distinguished sir!

Were I to possess the swelling flood of the divine oratory of Greece or Rome, instilled by the Muses, if, as is said of Orpheus, I were able to build cities with my words, or if I might peal forth above the world as it sleeps a cowardly sleep of ineptitude, a world which so many holy desires haven't yet been able to awaken, which still dozes on, bathed in the bloody dawn light of liberty, and, like a Cato, an O'Connell, a Cicero or a Mirabeau, spur the languishing peoples to action by my mighty words: who would there be that could expound to you, great man, the sentiments of so many pure hearts that beat calmly at your name in St-Vilmos, and discharge with humble loyalty the most sacred of civic duties which consists of paying the highest honour to its great men.

But what am I, that this great task should have come to me, that of revealing in your presence the affection of so many warm St-Vilmos

---

68   A tall fur hat.

hearts! I have scarcely outgrown the time of playful childhood, in which, in the exalted affection of its innocence, the heart opens its calyx, as in springtime do the perfumed flowers on a tall tree, among the spreading branches of humanity, not yet aware that the howling gale of hard autumn is soon to come, and that, falling from their branch, on which they have become sweet fruit, they are to rot on the ground, that new trees may spring from them, a whole forest – scarcely have I embarked on the whirling course of public life, in which, following the compass needle of the heart, guided by the rays of the pure star of patriotism, which shines in the heaven, surrounded by a hundred perils, one rows towards the promised land: being chosen as the spokesman for the noble council of St-Vilmos, where am I to turn amid your so many virtues, great man! distinguished *alispán*!, of which I have the honour to speak etc."

The entire speech was one of those marvellous works of art, the rich imagery of which only he can conceive who is familiar with the poetry of Hâfiz or the financial speeches that are customarily delivered in certain county assemblies, and at which the conviction fills our souls that everything in this wide world, sea and dry land, pyramids and church towers, Caesar and the *alispán* who is about to be voted out of office are like one another.

After the speaker had followed for a while his star and then Moses' pillar of fire, he meandered through Réty's virtues and the zeal of the St-Vilmos nobility; after which he paused for a moment on the mouths of the Danube and the frontiers of Hungary in the time of Lajos the Great,[69] from where he moved to the St-Vilmos district and the boundary dispute that was in progress concerning it, a matter such that the arrangement of it was only to be hoped for through the ardour of Réty and the St-Vilmos nobility, and then declared once more the great devotion of those that had sent him and ended his speech with the Romans: *Si fractus illabatur orbis, impavidum ferient ruinae.*[70] That is, as the lieutenant of the nobility translated faithfully, clasping his hands:

> *Tulips in flower,*
> *Réty for power.*

The speech made a great impression; and although the speaker had been obliged by the council of the nobility to refer to the people, virtues and sentiments of St-Vilmos at all places where people, virtues or

---

69 King of Hungary 1342–82.
70 Horace, Odes III.3. Though the world fall into ruin, the ruins will stand fearlessly.

the like were mentioned, and they had regarded bringing up the said boundary dispute as something that might damage public morale, never had a speaker been cheered as he was.

The *alispán*, taken completely unawares by this honour, as always on such occasions, and scarcely able – another everyday occurrence – to find words in which to respond, spoke very finely for a startled man. He said how weary he was and how he yearned for that domestic peace which he would enjoy in the bosom of his family, from which nothing would tear him were the patriotic confidence of the St-Vilmos people not to call him once more to that path which he had hitherto trodden with so much regret, but on which the defence of the threatened liberty of the nobility perhaps required the full application of his feeble powers.

That speech was received like the former with cheers, and after the lieutenant of the nobility had declared that the nobles wished to proceed to pay their respects to Mrs Réty the entire group pushed their way in-doors to more cheering; and there, for a time, we shall leave them.

VIII

There is no moment in our lives more significant than lunch-time; the greatest part of our view of life and our thoughts, indeed, those feelings that most of all ennoble our human nature, depend on the state of our stomachs, and the man that suffers from liver trouble – as do most writers – can understand the entire philosophies of Pythagoras and the Brahmins, as their moral philosophy begins in the kitchen. It is a matter of wonder that among all the delvers into history who, in our time, excel at devising new systems rather than at describing things as they were, none has yet been found that sought the cause of the great deeds of our kind in the foods of ages and nations – in that way, perhaps, they would have achieved greater results than those who attribute everything to climate and racial difference. Instead of describing in detail the *alispán*'s lunch (which would arouse my readers' appetites), I, who feel in me no ability either to start a new school of historiography or to imitate Homer or Scott, shall merely say that the feast, of which the gentry partook in the *alispán*'s rooms and the nobility in the great barn, was one of the most brilliant and most Hungarian that can be imagined. Up where the gentry were twenty-four courses were served, and the sauces were so lavishly offered that with each of the four fricassees each *táblabíró* spilled some, and the thumbs of the footmen that were serving were as often bathed; Hungarian *pezsgő*, Tokaj wine, ice-cream – indeed, a feast worthy of a Lucullus. Down below among the nobles there were *gulyás* and *pörkölt*, *tarhonya*, cabbage, *túrós csusza*, dumplings, roast meat, wine and *pálinka*,[71] in short a veritable banquet. To the last Gypsy there was none that rose – if indeed he could rise – less than cheerful from the table.

When lunch was over, once coffee had been served, Etelka, after discharging all the time the duties of the young lady of the house with the greatest affability, withdrew on the pretext of a headache; Mrs Réty was conversing with certain distinguished *táblabírós* and clergy, while the remaining gentry smoked their pipes either on the porch or in front of the house; and if we can't see the ambitious notary of St-Vilmos – who

---

71 *Pezsgő* is sparkling wine (one may not call it 'champagne'!); *gulyás* (a kind of soup) and *pörkölt* (a stew) are two of the pillars of traditional Hungarian cuisine; *tarhonya* is a form of grated pasta known in English as 'egg barley'. *Csusza* is a form of pasta served with *túró*, which resembles 'cottage cheese'.

had distinguished himself during lunch by many flowery toasts – the reason is probably that Etelka's maid Rózsi lives on the other side of the house.

Ákos and Kálmán were strolling in the farther part of the park.

They were almost the same in age, and as neighbouring children had been together since their early years; I need therefore hardly mention their friendship, which had become proverbial throughout the County. Such a thing was unknown to human memory, at least among the neighbours. At the age of twenty-two, who doesn't make friends, who doesn't know at least one to whom one's heart doesn't cleave with all its strength, so that you can't even imagine how you might live if parted from him? Like our first love-affair, so our first friendship remains among the finest memories in our lives, and although friendship sometimes brings to mind the keenest disappointment, at the same time there is nothing in our past for which we would curse as bitterly the fruit of the tree of knowledge as for depriving us of it. However, although our young friends had spent part of their lives together and were close in age and feelings alike, the domestic circles in which they were brought up differed considerably, and apart from that similarity that exists between all young men of nobler character – for as in spring foliage hangs in an even green on the branches, so men too change their colours in their autumnal days – there would not have been much more difference between them.

There are those who deny the influence of education; and if by that they mean that a person's character can't be formed to taste, no one is more certain of it than myself, as in the hefty tomes that have been written on education, instead of general systems I see nothing but rules which can lead to success if applied to individuals of a certain character, but which for others are hopelessly inappropriate. But just as the influence that one educator has on his charge is slight, and there is no dearth of examples, in cases of children in whose hearts the desire for freedom is more powerful, of the endeavours of educators leading to outcomes precisely the opposite of that intended: so the circle in which we have grown from children into young men differs from our natural inclinations but always exerts an irresistible influence; and if we look back there is none of us who doesn't feel that he has to thank for the large part of his characteristics the education which he received not from a single person but from society, not in accordance with a definite plan but through circumstances.[72]

---

72 The reader should remember that Eötvös was at one time Minister for Public Education.

This was the reason for that difference too that existed on many points between Ákos and Kálmán. Kislaky senior – he, that is, in whom Kálmán honoured his father and the County its former *alispán* and at the same time one of its most respected men – and his wife belonged to that section of Hungarian nobility which, alas! is nowadays in ever-growing danger of becoming extinct, and for all its errors and weaknesses deserves our respect because it has kept pure the customs and national qualities of our ancestors and the ignorance of our forbears, but at the same time the cordial simplicity of times past and many prejudices which nowadays appear almost ridiculous, but together with them that faith without which our nation would never have sustained itself in its difficult struggles: *that the Magyar shall never disappear from this world.*[73] It is beyond all doubt that the merits of this class of people for the maintenance of our national qualities can't be overestimated, that the future would perpetrate a disgraceful ingratitude were it ever to forget how the branches of that nobler culture, the fruits of which it enjoys, only drew their fecundity from the sap of the mighty trunk onto which they have been grafted; but it is just as certain that like everything, so the Hungarian noble houses seem much more magnificent – and more beautiful – at the distance of history than if we examine them close to.

If, for example, one of my readers were to call on Bálint Kislaky, drive in at the ungated fence and step into the house, the chimney of which smoked out of hospitality as its owner did out of boredom, where apart from the kuvaszes, which all but tore apart any that approached, no one did their duty, and with the exception of tilling the fields no trace of order was to be found, I believe that he would not feel very comfortable despite the master's kindness and Mrs Borbála's ceaseless proffering, and indeed in spite of the roast turkey that was cooked for him. In Taksony County this kind of housekeeping was rather plain, not that the Kislaky mansion was distinguished by its shortcomings, and as most, and the most lasting, acquaintanceships are made by mouth – not because we speak but because we eat with it – no one can be surprised that the hospitable house never lacked visitors, and that old Kislaky's time-worn stories, accompanied by wine that was their equal in age, always found an appreciative audience. This was the circle in which Kálmán grew up, en-

---

73 A refutation of J.G. Herder's prophecy in his *Ideen zur Philosophie der Geschichte der Menschheit* (1791), that 'the Hungarians . . . are now wedged in among Slavs, Germans, Romanians and other peoples, and in a few centuries even their language will perhaps be hard to find'.

vied by all around, loved by his parents, respected by visitors, honoured by the servants, made much of by the pastor and the rector, admired by the bailiff and the steward, and adored by the elderly housekeeper; and if in this house, where every dog leaped for joy at his approach and everybody greeted him affectionately, he felt at home and was at one with its ways, the only person that might be surprised is anyone that regarded him as more or less than a good-hearted but ordinary young man.

Who desired more of the only son of the old Hungarian house than that he should become a young Hungarian gentleman? But Kálmán knew the world too: Pest, where he studied and spent the happiest year of his life – his time as a law student, which a Hungarian recalls with longing until the age of seventy – and his friendship with Ákos, by which he was drawn even against the rich boy's wishes into higher circles, could not have passed without effect on his views, and old Bálint and Borbála sighed for hours on end at times over their dear son's fastidious ways and the new-fangled principles which he brought home from Town, though his new-found bourgeois ways had by no means as corrupting an effect as his worthy parents thought in the sorrow of their hearts. It is true that Kálmán changed in Pest, and the rustic young gentleman, now dressed in Viennese fashion since leaving his father's house, cultivated himself rather than his fellow man's creation and discarded many of the good old ways which at one time were in fashion among the youth under the name of national qualities, and the occasional beating of an inn servant, breaking of windows and bottles, sometimes the lavish rewarding of a Gypsy who had played well, reminded the citizens of that city of the soundness of the old constitution; but "Though defeated, not broken",[74] as our laureate poet wrote, the brigand slumbered in Kálmán's breast, still far from dead; and it only required the opportunity, a little rough company, some music and rather more wine, and the lad of old rose from his long sleep; and his lady friends in Pest, who spoke so highly of his modest ways, would scarcely recognise their dear dancing partner in the rowdy young man who danced Kinizsi's famous dance[75] – not actually with a Turk in his teeth but with a bottle in his hand.

---

74 A line from Vörösmarty's *Szózat*, now the "second Hungarian national anthem". Eötvös misquotes slightly, giving *Legyőzve bár*,"though defeated" for *Megfogyva bár* "though diminished", perhaps reminding the reader that *Szózat* (composed in 1836) had not yet gained its later status.

75 Pál Kinizsi (1432–94), a hero of the Turkish wars.

In this regard Ákos was essentially different, indeed quite Kálmán's opposite. Because of their wealth and connections with aristocratic families, the Rétys were among those mocked by the nobility as *fertálymágnások*;[76] and as for the pride, ambition and indeed faults that are attributed – hopefully merely out of malice – to our magnates, they might much more rightfully be called *five-quarter magnates*, since the Zrínyis, Frangepáns, Thurzós and Czudars never advanced so far in their possessions. In Hungary the *fertálymágnás* is a quite exceptional, I might almost say amphibious being. By virtue of his situation, his noble desires and inclinations, he is linked to the magnate class, but has no place that he can call his element nor yet anywhere that he can feel completely at home. His pride is injured if he goes into the company of those higher on the scale; he is offended by every servant that addresses him as *tekintetes*;[77] the contact with the upper classes that he seeks only increases the bitterness towards them that he has borne in his heart since childhood. "What risible arrogance," he will say, "if one returns to one's own home and among one's own people, what loathsome pride, as if all nobles weren't equal in Hungary, as if the title of baron or count were more than a little word that is attached to many a name simply because it didn't sound as if it would earn respect by itself." But if the *alispán* or the chamberlain made his annoyance known in that way, and in order to maintain equality had rather longer epaulettes made for his footmen than he had seen in the house of his neighbour the count, you that are a nobleman but from whose family no one has even been *alispán* and who could not possibly become a chamberlain, or who have one *forint* thirty-six *krajcárs* less annual income, on any account suppose that these fine principles of equality might apply to you. Everything in the world has its limits, and as far as the extent of equality is concerned everyone usually chooses himself as the boundary-mark for the avoidance of error, beyond which levelling-off can't be without danger. If support is needed in assemblies or a vote at an election your nobility will be acknowledged, and Heading Nine of Part One,[78] the thousand-year-old constitution of the Magyars, the blood of Pusztaszer that was mixed in

---

76 'Quarter-magnates', a nineteenth-century term denoting holders of big estates, who aped the aristocracy and endeavoured to marry into aristocratic families.

77 That is, lower on the social scale than the *nagyságos* or *méltóságos* to which he aspired.

78 A reference to Heading Nine of Part One of István Werbőczi's *Tripartitum*, where the traditional legal rights and privileges of the nobility are specified.

111

the great pledge,[79] haven't yet been forgotten, and when someone needs you, you won't see anyone at your side that would not confess himself your equal. But just go to the house of your free-thinking fellow noble, offer him in the sight of his servants the right hand which he has so often pressed at an election, make so bold as to love his daughter or choose her as your wife; and when you have tried to do that we shall speak again of your constitutional equality, and I shall ask you what you think about it? The Hungarian nobility won its fatherland with blood, fought for its liberty with blood, will defend its common property with blood if it be ever attacked – so says the law – and if instead of blood you say money, which, after all, represents the value of everything, it all remains true to this day, with one small difference: whereas in terms of blood we are all given much the same amount, in terms of money amounts are very different, and the equality that seems to follow automatically from the ancient theory, in modern times is reckoned one of the remotest possibilities.

Every man that would wish to appear more than he feels himself to be is rendered laughable by the efforts by which he tries to achieve his set aims; and the coward, who talks among women of his duels; the pauper, who with second-hand clothes imitates a brilliance by which penury is exposed on every side; the peasant, who brags of his lofty acquaintances in order to be considered noble and has his new armorial bearings engraved on every spoon, carved in stone and blazoned in colours, all become the object of scorn and contempt whatever other qualities they may possess. Society, which only seldom acknowledges such virtues as we *do* possess, is unforgiving towards him that desires more from it, and treats him almost as the usurer is treated, or rather, ought to be, who, unwilling to be content with lawful amounts of interest, plunders people of their capital too. The Rétys were in just such a position. Ancient nobility, fine estate, office of *alispán*, a handsome son who remained unmarried and was in a position to marry – what more was needed for them to obtain a pleasant place in society? But their pride required other nourishment. Just as Frederick the Great sought glory in his verse, Voltaire in his diplomatic cleverness, Richelieu in his dramas and Byron in his riding,[80] so *alispán* Réty too made every effort to seem rather more than he had been born; and in addition to centuries of nobility and a

---

79 A reference to the tradition of an oath taken with mixing their blood by the seven leaders of the Magyar tribes.
80 Boxing or swimming, perhaps!

host of ancestors the parvenu would present you with every ridiculous side that he had, talk about his aunt the baroness, his distant relative the German count, and his very close relationship with this or that prince or general – he had that day received a letter from Baron F. or Count X, etc.

Ákos had been sent to Pest at an early age and had lived with his aunt, Baroness Andorfy, spending his days in the best society. He had far too much sense not to see through his parents' weaknesses and, as often happens in the world, became the exact opposite of what he saw around him every day. He became a villain, or rather did his best to be considered such, and so gained himself boundless popularity mainly among the youth of the County; like a man who, although knowing French and English and having travelled widely, nevertheless imitated their villainies to the utmost of his powers, he served as justification for others. It's a fine thing to be popular, and especially when we are young there's perhaps nothing for which our hearts yearn as much. Later, when we know how little certain hearts care about that affection which seems so great, we lose our pleasure in that possession, which perhaps has been lost even more than gained undeservedly. But we wish to deny that this popularity confirmed Ákos not a little in his forced villainy, since it was this effort on the part of young Réty that sometimes evoked the most striking contrast between him and Kálmán. As, that is, Ákos took pride in villainy, so did Kálmán in culture, the two young men seemed to be examples to one another.

When the nobility of the County gathered on winter days in the big room in County Hall – where, as may be supposed, dance entertainments were held in order that the tax-paying populace, who had built that room by the sweat of their brows, should see the nobility too perspire in that place – or when a biggish company assembled to celebrate the name-day of some distinguished *táblabíró*, beyond doubt the noisiest was Ákos and none appeared more fashionable than Kálmán; but when they were all talking about themselves – or more correctly, about what they wished to seem – as they drank or chatted, all was forgotten: roles were reversed, and instead of Ákos, who in the morning had told all and sundry how often in his life he'd been drunk, in the evening it was Kálmán whose eyes were crossed, although in the morning perhaps no one had opposed Ákos's theory of drinking more staunchly than he. Let no one condemn this changeability of the young men; they are at that time of life when we consider the condemnation of men something worth working for, an affectation shared by us all.

Ákos had controlled himself at the start of the lunch as he acted the fool as usual, but the more he saw merriment around him the more he became silent, and towards the end of the meal gave himself over completely to the doleful thoughts with which his hopeless love filled his heart. Kálmán, on that occasion greatly cheered by sitting next to Etelka and her pleasantness towards him – because wine goes most quickly to your head if it finds the company of merry thoughts there – instead of the politeness with which he distinguished himself over the first courses began to speak more and more in the manner of a young boor, until Etelka's serious looks and curt replies made him realise the error of his ways, and by the end of the meal he too, like his friend, was sitting dolefully in his place, scarcely daring to speak to his beautiful neighbour.

As soon as lunch was over Kálmán dragged his friend into the park to complain to him of all his misfortune.

"My friend," said he, flinging himself onto a bench, "I'm the most unhappy man in the world. Did you see your sister today? She doesn't love me, she loathes me, despises me."

"You're not yourself," said Ákos, seizing his friend's hand warmly. "You're talking nonsense."

"No, no, I know perfectly well; Etelka doesn't love me, she never will, a man like me is beneath her – I give up – I . . ."

"Stop drinking wine, Kálmán – it seems to depress you."

"So you've noticed as well? So it's true, then? How can I show myself to her in my shame? Tomorrow I'm going to ask my father's permission and go travelling, go somewhere that nobody knows me, where I'll never again upset your angelic sister, where . . ."

Again Ákos interrupted and asked the reason for his unhappiness, to which Kálmán explained, with all the detail of which the lover is capable, how nice Etelka had been to him at the start of lunch, that he, word of honour, had hardly drunk a couple of glasses, but that it seemed that the wine had affected him, perhaps he'd said something untoward, and after that Etelka wasn't even looking at him by the time that lunch ended. This was the end of everything, he was so repulsive a creature, he could not yearn for such an angel, he would go mad if Etelka found in the arms of another that happiness which she would not accept from him, but if that good fortune were to go to someone whom he knew he would break his neck, and the like. As in every distillation tiny drops appear in the upper part of the retort, so fractions of the nectar of Érmellék[81]

81   An area to the east of Debrecen, now mostly in Romania.

trickled down Kálmán's cheeks in pure tears, and although Ákos knew very well "whence those tears"[82] he cared enough for his friend to be affected by such sympathy with his pain as if he thought that their cause was important. He said: women really don't like to see a young man intoxicated by anything but their charms, but as the effect of good *pezsgő* soon passes and doesn't leave a headache, so does that of such anger. He assured his friend that Etelka loved him, and furthermore despised the vulgar count, in short, he consoled him so skilfully that Kálmán slowly cheered up and eventually clasped his friend passionately in his arms swearing that he would never touch wine again, and in his joy wept out the last drops that had gathered in his lacrimal glands during lunch. It is the finest privilege of youth, that joy and pain lie so close together; later too perhaps they do as much, and indeed we have more cause for joy, but our hearts lose their flexibility, and if once we are saddened it requires so much to console us that often a new grief comes before we forget the old one.

Kálmán had really been more drunk with love than with wine, and after the fresh air, the walk and his tears was all but completely sober again, and the two friends set off back towards the house to find Etelka and, as Ákos put it, conclude the new peace treaty as quickly as possible; but who is there of us mortals that can count for certain on the next minute? Who is there, especially on the occasion of an election, at which, in addition to destiny and fate, canvassers too decide on the future?

While the young friends were still in the park old Kislaky, who, in the kindness of his heart had drunk a glass, indeed perhaps two, more than was his custom to quench his thirst, had had his mind on other things. The old gentleman had for a long time planned on Etelka for his dear Kálmán. I don't mean that he was brought to this idea by nothing more than her wealth, but as the estates of the two families were adjacent to one another, and very likely had been from the first day of Creation to the present, and as the Réty estate had almost all come through the distaff side part of it must go to Etelka, old Kislaky had every right to say that the children were made for one another. Wine is a great flatterer; it confirms everyone in their desires, and old Kislaky, whose eyes had been fixed on his son all through lunch and who had asked his neighbours to right and left perhaps thirty times: had they ever seen two young people

---

82   Is Eötvös thinking of Terence: Andria I.126 *Hinc illae lacrimae?*

who were better suited to one another? was convinced of the realisation of his hopes, and although to the formal request that he made to Réty senior after lunch the only answer that he received was that he didn't know his daughter's feelings; from Mrs Réty the reply was that it would be better to speak of such an important matter after the election.

The old man, rubbing his hands together in delight, paced up and down in the courtyard. In his imagination all the progeny of Kálmán and Etelka danced around him, and the worthy father's heart was throbbing mightily among those images when the noise bursting from the barn turned his thoughts to another direction. The canvassers, who, like great artists, were making lengthy preparations for the big performance in which they were to play the lead, were now conducting their rehearsal in the barn for the second time, and in so doing just at that moment had reached the *albíró*s, at which the bailiff, who as president was deputising for the *főispán*, had called out the name of the chief *albíró* of St-Vilmos, and three hundred voices cried "Long live Kálmán Kislaky!" The old man – for what father would remain unmoved at overhearing plaudits for his son – all but swooned in ecstasy, and when he saw his overseer going towards the barn his presiding spirit, whether good or evil, whispered in his ear the suggestion that it was such a pity for his son's triumph to resound in a reed-thatched barn and how good it would be if Etelka might witness such acclaim! He therefore called his overseer to him and divulged to him the great family secret, which he must have confided to him all the more indistinctly because his tongue was now moving with some difficulty, and it can't be believed that he abused that confidence and asked: "Wouldn't it be good if the canvassers found Kálmán, who's in the park, and carried him in triumph to Etelka's room?" The overseer fully approved of his master's idea, and as soon as he entered the barn shouted three or four times for silence and delivered such a fine speech that the whole crowd set off at once. It is true that Kislaky's emissary's conception of 'secret' was the same as many another man's, that it meant only something that one would blush or not venture to speak of, and therefore wished to make publicly known through someone else, and therefore the marriage of Etelka and Kálmán was the first thing that he proclaimed and hailed. What is certain, however, is that the three hundred noblemen of St-Vilmos, of whom you could have sworn a quarter of an hour before that, like the three hundred Spartans at Thermopylae, they would be found lying in their places, made their way straight to the park uttering terrifying cheers, and that Kislaky, who almost ran to the

116

park in front of them, mumbled through his teeth, his eyes filled with tears: *Ah, but popularity is a fine thing!*[83]

My readers mustn't despise the good old man for this statement, and although many of them would despise the favours of the common people and grumble about them like those who find them implacable or unfaithful do about their wives; they should consider that Kislaky is one of those that see in this popularity not a tool but the affection of many; and because their only means of winning this treasure has been the kindness of their hearts, they haven't so often experienced wavering. In any case, apart from Helen nothing is so much disparaged as popularity, and yet there are not many who, after the city where the faithless one lived with another had been besieged for ten years, would not have gladly taken her back as Menelaus did.

Kálmán and Ákos were approaching the house when they encountered old Kislaky and, immediately behind him, the whole horde of canvassers, who were making straight for them over lawns and flower-beds. The old man embraced his son and had managed to say "Listen, son, this is what they think of you", but not to explain what was happening, when "Long live Kálmán Kislaky and his angelic bride Etelka Réty" was trumpeted to the heavens, putting an end to all conversation.

Kálmán and Ákos themselves were so startled that for a moment they didn't know what to do. But when the overseer's thunderous bass rang out with "Let's take the young gentleman to Miss Etelka, our beloved *szolgabíró*'s lady," and ten hands all at once reached for the happy lover to sweep him off his feet, Kálmán recovered from his amazement and began to defend himself. He tried to beg, he swore, and old Kislaky himself, who had meant his son to be taken to Etelka and not for betrothal to be announced, did all that he could to have Etelka's name left out of the ovation, but in vain! Only the Last Trump could have competed with the three hundred St-Vilmos voices, and despite his protests matters took their course. Kálmán exerted all his strength against the great enthusiasm, and it can't be said that he didn't make a distinct impression on the many St-Vilmos hearts that were ablaze for him, but what had more effect than his words was that his fine *atilla* was torn to shreds, a bottle of red wine that was being offered to him was broken and soaked him from head to foot as he struggled, and now, dangling between earth and heaven on the shoulders of six hefty lads and beating futilely with his

---

83 Quoted by Kálmán Mikszáth in his 1881 short story *Egy kis tévedés* (A little mistake).

117

fists and heels, he was carried straight towards his beloved's room as the former shouting continued.

At the noise the guests gathered outside the house, and on hearing the names of Kálmán and Etelka some were amazed while the rest began to offer congratulations. The *alispán*, smiling in consternation, alternately nodded and shook his head so as not to be taken as saying yes or no; his wife, fortunately thinking of the election and the Kislakys' influence, said that it was all a mistake; Karvaly, however, joined the shouters and loudly declaimed the praises of the handsome pair, whose admirers had now reached Etelka's door and were dangling her hapless worshipper before the threshold.

Kálmán was beside himself with rage. To appear like that before his beloved when he ought to be asking forgiveness for his earlier faults, with his *atilla* torn, soaked in wine, and surrounded by three hundred people – who would not feel the agony of his situation? He begged, wept, cursed, all at once, and all without the slightest success; fortunately for him the goddess or angel that takes the side of true love so arranged things that instead of Etelka only her maid was in the room, and so the guard of honour could only bellow their good wishes to a blushing Rózsi and the very hopeful St Vilmos notary, whose presence had certainly not been anticipated.

Next to the happiness that we feel at the sight of our beloved – as I have heard from a friend who has become grey in love – comes that of not meeting the idol of our heart under certain circumstances, and no one ever felt that more than Kálmán at that moment. Ákos had been annoyed by the shouting out of his sister's name, and in order to put a stop to it pointed out to the respected gathering that every *szolgabíró* needs a clerk, and that no one in the world was more suitable for this office than Bandi Pennaházy the notary; at that he was embraced, to frightful shouts, by public opinion instead of Rózsi and carried to the courtyard together with his future *szolgabíró*, there to be introduced to the *alispán*, who, smiling all the time at it all, merely expressed his complete approval.

In self-justification – in case any of my readers may regard the law of probability as broken in our finding the notary of St-Vilmos with Rózsi – I can only say that even if – as Hegel believes – not everything that is, is good, at least everything that is true is, it is also highly probable that Rózsi's black eyes and Pennaházy's blonde waxed moustache were the sort of thing that, since they often met in St-Vilmos – where Rózsi came of a good noble family – it was only natural that they should call on each other in Tiszarét, especially as – even if we ignore the black eyes and blonde moustache – two more pleasant people would be hard to find. Rózsi went to the Hungarian theatre when in Pest with her Mrs, had read several almanacs, old and new, and knew a few poems by heart, and so was one of the better educated lady's maids who, because they often went about in the clothes that the gentry wore and said things that they had heard from their Mrses, seemed almost young ladies; and Pennaházy who, during a long national assembly now cheered loudly among the audience, now took an active part in the most important councils through other pronouncements and delighted the readers of *Nemzeti újság*[84] with cryptic words, is too well known for me to need to speak of his qualities. I would also have noted the interesting conversation in which the two amiable persons were surprised by the canvassers if the description of matters of national importance didn't await me, and that conversation, with all its delights, would not have been unusually wordless.

My readers, a large proportion of whom are doubtless aware how unpleasant it is for a lady, and especially for a lady's maid, to be found alone with a man will be able to imagine the embarrassment that filled Rózsi in the presence of so many men; however, after seeing her dear notary being shouldered by the canvassers along with Kálmán, and hearing the public acclaim that greeted his appointment as clerk, she was reassured as to his fate and indeed felt less distress at seeing her idol torn from her arms than if he had left her on his own two feet. She quietly tidied the room, which had been left in some disorder by the canvassers and, sighing at Pennaházy being made clerk and she not Mrs Pennaházy, she was making for the coffee kitchen when the opening of the door to the adjoining room caught her attention.

That room was Macskaházy's, and opened off the same corridor as did Etelka's.

Rózsi stopped on the threshold and could hear clearly what Macskaházy was saying; he shut his door and as he moved away said to someone: "At seven precisely by the notary's garden."

"He'll be there, Your Whorship", replied the second voice, which sounded almost Oriental, rather than Hungarian.

"You know your reward," replied Macskaházy, and the two moved off.

---

84 'National News', a newspaper dating from 1840. It was said of it that "it did not stir up our blood but it did pave the way for our transformation".

"Dear me!" said the horrified maid at length, when the speakers' footsteps could no longer be heard on the flags of the corridor floor. "Macskaházy was in his room and heard everything, as no one in the world had such ears. Perhaps he won't tell Madam!" And with that she shut the door and, cursing the lawyer and the Jew alike between her clenched teeth, she left.

And now, my dear readers, although to some among you the company of Rózsi may seem more enjoyable, more important matters await us. The *alispán* has called a conference for six o'clock and that hour is approaching: let us go into the big room.

IX

There exists in this country – it would be difficult to account for, but the fact is undeniable – there exists in this country a certain connection between lunch and politics. It has been my experience, at least, that just as *táblabírós* that have good cooks and are hospitable are never without political influence, so good places for taking counsel on matters of national importance are always to be found where every chair hints at lunches past or future; and for that reason, if there is a class of nobility worthy of being compared to the Roman patriciate, in my opinion only the Hungarian is that to which Menenius Agrippa's *mot* is completely applicable, when he compares the Senate to the stomach of the Republic.[85] That has happened here too, and the dining-room has been designated the place for consultation; at present, however, it lies before us in quite a different form. Green baize covers the big table instead of a snow-white table-cloth, instead of bottles and glasses there are big inkwells, in front of every chair lies a sheaf of paper instead of a plate, and were it not for the walls and the pleasant scent of cabbage that lingers in the room which is before us, now lit by silver candelabra, we would scarcely recognise the place where, a couple of hours ago, all that noise and proposing of toasts was heard.

Now the whole company was chatting, standing in little groups by the stove, in the windows and around the sofa on which the *alispán*'s wife was sitting. The family portraits themselves, it seemed, as they hung on the wall looked down on the new generation in more dignified a manner than they had done during lunch, and since the fat Jeromos Réty, one of the family's greatest men (who had been a captain in Rákóczi's time, and after the events of 1715, as a sign of how he had been respected by both sides, had received a *donatio*), seemed to look down on his more fortunate descendant with such appetite that we almost felt sorry for him; but the *alispán*'s father, the Chamberlain (I don't know the reason why), had had himself painted from behind, just looking round – and with his clean-shaven face, the tricorne hat under his arm and the little dress sword at his side didn't in the least remind us of that manly strength which our poets are wont to look for in the days of the mighty forebears.

---

85 Roman consul in 503 BC. His *mot* is the fable of the revolt of the other body parts against the stomach.

In addition to those whom my readers have already seen on the porch with the *alispán* there is in the room a numerous company. First of all, two clergymen stand before us, one of whom is perhaps somewhat fatter, the other somewhat drier than their calling demands, but who, as spokesmen for the Church, especially at elections – in which, as we know, religion plays so large a part – are equally outstanding. After them come four or five *táblabírós* and three *szolgabírós*, description of whom would be superfluous because, thank Heaven! my readers are familiar with the distinguishing characteristics of the offices of *táblabíró* and *szolgabíró*. By the door lurked a couple of lawyer's clerks, Pennaházy and an honorary *aljegyző*; a number of estate lawyers walked humbly about the room, and the poor relations – with the exception of one, who had gone somewhere to take a nap as the result of lunch and had not yet reappeared – as befits poor relations were hurrying up and down the room in the capacity of servants.

In one of the windows, apart from the company, and evidently engaged in the discussion of very interesting subjects, stand three men to whom our attention is drawn immediately on entering the room.

One of these, who, with upturned black moustache and upward combed hair, raises his head with such great dignity as if, dissatisfied with his two-metre stature, he wished to seem taller still, is Slacsanek, the estate manager plenipotentiary of Count Kőváry[86] – the biggest landowner in the county – a designation which he retains only out of modesty, since anyone who, like him, has something freely at his disposal and collects the greater part of the revenue might have every right to call himself a landowner.

The tubby little person standing beside this tall man and talking ceaselessly, or at least taking part in the conversation by nodding his head from time to time, making approving gestures and uttering occasional comments such as 'Of course, quite, certainly, goodness, who'd have believed it!' and the like, is none other than His Honour Baron Sóskuty.[87] He is a true gentleman, as the ladies make known, Hungary's most upright magnate in the opinion of men, in whose company no one realises that he is dealing with a magnate – so much so that on one occasion in Debrecen market he was actually taken for a dealer in soap. He is a respectable man, whom few have ever heard speak German and no one French, and whose conservative principles when speaking of the

---

86 From *Kő* 'stone', *vár* 'castle' and the -*y* of class distinction.
87 From *Sós* 'salty', *kút* 'well' and -*y*.

affairs of the country are all the more to his credit when we see that as regards his person he doesn't cling to the good things of old. The baron must be about sixty; his once red hair – we must confess – has begun to whiten, and in the twilight of his life that redness, as is usual at such an age, has moved lower and presently burns so finely on his cheeks that I might compare them to roses, if I would not then have to produce a new simile when speaking of the fair sex.

That in the company of such men – one of whom is a genuine magnate, and another something even more, that is, the estate manager of a very wealthy count, who disposes of almost a thousand votes at elections – so refined a man as chief clerk Krivér can only conduct himself humbly; that we see on his face only that pious smile of modesty and respect with which some saints are portrayed; that his body can do nothing but bow, his lips say nothing other than how honoured he feels his lowly self, and if he were graciously permitted . . . all that my savant readers will see through. If, however, any may esteem such great civility in a chief clerk I can say in explanation firstly, that Krivér wishes to be elected deputy *alispán*, and secondly, generally speaking it has become second nature to him to abase himself. The chief clerk is one of those people who begin their political career as clerk or secretary to the great, and later too display all the more humility towards those from whom they expect something while using all the less of that Christian virtue towards those that are their inferiors. It is written: He that humbleth himself shall be exalted, and since that is precisely Krivér's wish, knowing that he can't advance in any way without being exalted at elections (because that is the one day on which the nobility is willing to see its representatives above itself) he is doing everything in accordance with the words of scripture in order to attain a goal.

"So do you know for sure, sir," said Slacsanek to the chief clerk, "that the unfortunate Veszősy has joined Bántornyi's people?"

"Yes, *domine spectabilis*,[88] I'm sorry to say – for sure."

"Now, didn't I always say?" interposed the baron, "haven't I said a thousand times that I have no confidence in Veszősy? Three years ago now, it must have been about a fortnight before the election, it was in the afternoon, a Friday, if I'm not mistaken, when I met you, sir, outside the coffee-house. There were others present, *in specie*, a number of army officers. I lit my pipe and sat down on the green bench at your side under the awning, *domine spectabilis*, and I'm certain I said, that Veszősy . . ."

---

88 The Latin origin of *tekintetes uram* 'respected sir'.

"Your Honour was quite right . . . but . . ."

"That Veszősy," I said, "is a liberal, and what's worse, one that's always talking about his principles, he's a man of property and . . ."

"Yes, that's true," Slacsanek interrupted the baron as he warmed to his theme, "but Veszősy's a powerful man, we did wrong to make him such, to make him *szolgabíró* in a ward that has most votes, but . . ."

"You mean, sir," the baron went on, having spiced the previous speaker's words three times with 'Quite so', "perhaps we can win him to our side! He must be enticed away, surely? That's the whole secret. Do you know what, gentlemen? I live in the ward, we'll give a hunting party, a legally authorised wolf-hunt. The peasants will have to act as beaters, you'll all be there, and he as *szolgabíró* will have to be present as well, because, of course, if we only shoot hares *praesuppositione juris* [89] we'll be hunting wolves, and then – as I said, the *szolgabíró*'ll have to be there as well – and we'll box him in. I know a way – first . . ."

"Yes," sighed the chief clerk, with a sorrowful expression, "if the young baron, who has even more influence on the county than Your Honour, weren't against us."

"That damned boy," said the baron, shaking his head, "how often haven't I said to him 'Bálint, my boy'. . ."

"Perhaps if Your Honour were to exercise paternal authority . . ."

"That's right, you're quite right, my dear sir, I can exercise parental authority and tell the boy to do anything. We're in complete agreement at all times, and he's obedient in all respects, I wouldn't even advise him to do anything else; but in precisely this one matter . . ."

"If the young gentleman would be so good as to obey you in just this matter," opined Krivér.

"You're right, *amice*! Quite right! I'll disinherit him, really I will."

Slacsanek, knowing that the baron's worldly goods weren't such that the risk of losing them would have much effect on anyone, or perhaps realising that for him to be disinherited would require the baron's prior death and that time before the election was short, proposed other methods. To which the baron replied that he knew many methods: the first straight away – if he would marry; "Your Honour would not believe how great an influence that has on one, especially in our family! Before I married there was no more free-thinking a man in three counties around, and now . . . But the boy won't marry. Never heard of such a thing! But he won't."

---

89   . . . as far as the law is concerned . . .

"So how are we off in this ward?" asked Slacsanek, addressing the chief clerk again when he saw that the source from which the baron's words were now pouring seemed likely to be abundant in the extreme.

"Here too it's risky, we've Tengelyi against us, to begin with"

"Tengelyi!" exclaimed the baron. "Tengelyi! A village notary, that's quite something! Tengelyi? How many Tengelyis does it take for things to go against us in the election?"

"Just one more than we are ourselves," replied the tall estate manager. "Votes, unfortunately, are counted, not weighed, and I know few opponents more powerful than the notary."

The baron shook his head in dissatisfaction. Krivér went on: "Ákos himself isn't with us, even though he doesn't openly oppose us."

"*Ecce*," the baron interrupted him, "my son's model, another naughty boy, who doesn't want his father to be *alispán*; I say *est ad . . .*"

"As long as the Kislakys stay firm, I shan't worry about the ward."

"Yes, but the Kislakys are unreliable as well," repeated the chief clerk. "Kálmán gives his mother orders, she tells his father and he tells the whole ward. And I'm afraid that Kálmán's been dissatisfied ever since Count Havasy came to stay in this house."

"But you know what happened today, Etelka was proclaimed as his fiancée."

"Yes, by the canvassers; and I know," added the chief clerk more quietly, "I'm not saying with absolute certainty, but it seemed to me that the whole thing wasn't to the *alispán*'s wife's liking."

"You're right," said the baron more loudly. "That was my impression too, I was standing just beside the *alispán*'s wife, talking about the weather, when the canvassers came bringing Kálmán. My dear lady, said I, when I heard the shouting . . ."

"We shall have to be careful," said Slacsanek, to whom the baron had already told it all twice, "because we're certainly badly off."

"For my own part, sir," replied Krivér, with a humble smile, "you're aware of my enthusiasm, so at least I'll guarantee that nothing will happen in the enemy camp of which I shan't inform our party."

"And the man that is aware of the enemy's plans," said the baron, cheerfully clasping his hands together, "has half won the battle."

"Oh, if there were only nobles like ours in the county!" sighed Slacsanek."If they don't vote as I wish I'll take their land off them, and then they can go and beg from their new *alispán*, so by now they'll eat out of my hand."

The interesting conversation was interrupted by the *alispán*; the entire company was now present and he summoned them to the table for the conference to begin.

I am writing for Hungarians, and as in Hungary there is hardly anyone that has not seen an assembly – even our ladies too have for some time had the pleasure of attending our sessions, at which domestic affairs can be looked down on slightly less that is otherwise customary – there is no need for me to embark on a longer description of the festive scene. One session is like another. In the middle is a green table. Around it sit a number of *táblabírós* who differ diametrically, sometimes in opinion, but mostly in personal interests, while the majority, taking no interest, doodle on the paper in front of them and only take part in the council because to sit at the green table confers distinction, and what is more:

> *A little session for the fatherland*
> *Will do no harm . . .*

or at least, much less than if we work for it; such is the image of all Hungarian official meetings, and although the one for which the magistracy foregathered in Réty's house differed from others in that it took place without any noise and fuss, the presence of Her Ladyship made that natural.

After the session had been opened by Réty in the usual way, he himself was unanimously designated as candidate for the office of *alispán* as was Krivér for that of deputy, and as is usual at such conferences posts were promised to all present, either personally or to some close relative, while Baron Sóskuty gave long speeches praising all the candidates, which only they that were not mentioned failed to consider excellent – and discussion moved on to the methods by which the necessary majority was to be obtained.

As the worthy Sáskay had won himself so notable a reputation on this subject, and had kindly set out in writing his views on the matter, the chairman was of the opinion that it would be apposite to ask the gentleman to read aloud that excellent document; the proposal was accepted, and after no little throat-clearing and offering of apologies he began to read, during which Karvaly, presumably to demonstrate his scorn, closed his eyes and after a while, indeed, began to snore.

I have the whole document in front of me, and I am proud to say that I know of few more distinguished English parliamentary papers; composed as it is in the same format as those, it is greatly to Sáskay's credit. But lest my readers, in particular those of the fair sex that have read this

126

book so far, should follow Karvaly's example and, most horrid of blows to a writer, close their lovely eyes over my excesses, I shall pick out from the twelve written pages only the points that concern the county more closely.

"It is customary in England" – so Sáskay began to read, as no one exceeded him in admiration for the English nation – "that before any matter is subjected to debate in Parliament, its examination is first always entrusted to a number of men in order that, to facilitate discussion, their views may be presented in the form of what is called a white paper." That is the procedure that he too means to follow, and for twelve reasons, only the last of which we shall mention as the most important, to be found in the similarity between the English and the Hungarian constitutions.

The relationship between the two constitutions is a fact that in Hungary few at most find dubious, and although some maintain that the English and Hungarian *Magnae cartae* resemble one another only in the way that in some great families elder and younger siblings do, in that the eldest inherits everything of value while the rest are left merely an illustrious title; who can deny that both are children of the thirteenth century, that the Hungarian Great Charter – seven years the junior – was granted by a king little better than the English John Lackland, and that with the exception of a number of minor details, such as freedom of the press, trial by jury, ministerial responsibility etc. there are no essentials that we might envy the English.[90] Our wealthy clergy, the discrepancy between written and unwritten law, the length of cases at law, the cost of our lawyers, the power of our judges, indeed, one has only to look for them and so-called "rotten boroughs" themselves won't be lacking. That in this state of affairs so eminent a man as Sáskay could draw a fine parallel and convince all his hearers is self-evident; and although later – when, having established as a principle that the English constitution, like the Hungarian, is founded on free elections he began

---

90 A reference to the Golden Bull of 1222, a *bulla* or edict issued by King András II, who was forced by his nobles to accept it. The adjective 'golden' is derived from the seals attached. It was one of the first examples of constitutional limits being placed on the powers of a European monarch. The *bulla* established the rights of the Hungarian nobility, including the right to disobey the king if he acted contrary to law (*jus resistendi*). The nobles (and the Church) were freed from all taxes, could not be forced to go to war outside Hungary and weren't obligated to finance such a war. It was also a historically important document because it set down the principles of equality for all the nation's nobility. See https://en.wikipedia.org/wiki/Golden_Bull_of_1222

to speak about that and adduced the views on the subject of every great writer – a number began to follow Karvaly's example, in any case a profound silence reigned during the whole reading, which was interrupted by only a single "hear, hear!", when with the words "Now as concerns our present situation," he turned his attention to the current condition of Taksony County.

"There are two things in the world," the reader went on, "for which every Hungarian nobleman, and therefore the nobility of this county, more Hungarian than which I know none (shouts of 'Yes!'), is most ardent of all: his faith and his country." A lengthy 'Bravo!' interrupted the speaker. "That is, to use a more popular form of words: *first*, let the seal of the county be in our hands; *second*, in accordance with the ancient constitution let the Hungarian nobleman pay for nothing. Every enthusiasm that doesn't spring from this noble source and that is not directed to the attainment of one of these goals, thanks to the sensible spirit of the Hungarian nobility! can't be lasting, and although certain deceivers have contrived to lead the Hungarian people – because in the constitutional sense we may only thus refer to the nobility – for a time in a way contrary to its interests, experience has triumphantly shown that this abnormal, monstrous condition can't long persist, and that the Hungarian nobility, which won its liberty with its blood on the field of battle, can retain it with its blood in the sacred halls of peaceful consultation too, of which I could adduce many glorious examples from recent times. Yes, gentlemen!" the speaker read fervently on, "great things have happened." And at this point numerous instances are quoted in which the so-called subversive party, which evidently means to overturn the constitution so as to make embankments for its railways from its ruins, is disparaged on account of the house tax[91] or other matters: these were received with the greatest pleasure when Sáskay stated that after such examples the Estates of Taksony County would not be left behind, that they too were prepared to sacrifice the last drop of their blood, or indeed their last *fillér*, for their constitution. The statement was followed by prolonged cheering.

"We want liberty! Yes, conference, we want freedom of the press, freedom of trade and conscience; above all, we want the autonomy of our

---

91   *Házi adó* or *contributio domestica*. A form of taxation on the servile class to meet the expenses of the county, i.e. the maintenance of members of Parliament and servants, official buildings, bridges etc. It was distinct from taxation for military purposes – *hadi adó* or *contributio bellica*.

county to be preserved from such scandalous meddling as, for example, the recent order of the Regent's Council that nobles living on registered land be subject to taxation;[92] we want progress, we want a bank from which all nobles can receive interest at four per cent, railways, drainage, museums and polytechnics; we want nationalities, but we also want liberty, though greater, to remain *noble* and not to lead to lawlessness; we want the whole nation to advance, but in such a way that the order in which it now is be not disturbed; let Hungarian nationality blossom, but since the nobleman is the sole representative of that nationality, let *the nobility* increase with it. He that is not with us in wanting this, who has extended our rights to inhabitants of every language and origin, seeks to destroy our liberty, which will lose its value like paper money issued in excessive quantities and circulating in the hands of all; he that proclaims such political heresy that our railways and bank would be unable to exist without the abolition of our freedom from taxation and the ancestral provisions, is against us, *et hunc tu romane caveto.*"[93]

"Since the law under which nobles living on registered land have been taxed has, thank Heaven, not yet been implemented in this county the greater part of the nobility is with us wholeheartedly, and because the Bántornyi party is still struggling to assess the house tax and other such matters, the first and principal method of binding the nobility to us consists of our making it known how much Bántornyi's unconstitutional intentions may affect them."

"Of course," the interruption came from the baron, who could no longer bear to remain silent. "That would be easy and good, if the Bántornyi party weren't proclaiming among the nobility that they intend to make the landowners taxable, not the poor nobility, and in that way they're winning a lot of support."

"Madness," says an old *táblabíró*, half asleep. "The nobility needs to be enlightened."

"That's the trouble, they're doing that," replied the baron. "I've seen the figures myself that they're canvassing with. The bishop will be taxed 50,000 forints per annum, Count Kőváry 30,000 and so on; you, sir – he went on, addressing Réty – are down for 5,000, all nobles will pay a *garas*, and the roads will be so good that the price of corn, which is now

---

92 An allusion to Maria Teresa's *úrbér* system, introduced in 1767, not least for the purpose of rendering the nobility liable to taxation.
93 Horace, Satire IV:85 *Hic niger est; hunc tu, Romane, caveto.* This man is a blackguard; beware him, Roman.

5 forints, will go up to 7 forints 30 *krajcár*s. I've seen the figures myself, they're certainly enlightening the nobility!"

"Well, they'll have to be enlightened better," said Sáskay. "We'll issue figures in which the bishop will pay 1,000 forints and every noble 100, and the price of corn will slip to three forints."

"People won't believe it, I tell you, they won't believe it," the baron replied again. "At the last tax assessment of the nobility no one in St-Vilmos was assessed for more than a *garas*, and . . ."

"I didn't mean," said Slacsanek, "that such an assessment would have bad consequences. When the Erzsébet *puszta* was assessed – my count owns half, other nobles the rest – we were charged 137 forints 30 *krajcár*s, the other half 11 forints 36. I must have said a hundred times that there will be bad consequences, because the minor nobility have to be frightened rather than enticed into paying tax, but then . . ."

"I wouldn't be surprised if the count wanted to make a complaint?" said a *táblabíró* on the other side of the table crossly.

"Yes – as if it were unjust for those who can afford more to pay more," said another.

"If, that is, both are noblemen," Nyúzó remarked correctly. "The whole business is, what did you call it just now, Sáskay?"

"Progressive tax."

"That's right, progressive tax, the most liberal thing in the world; invented during the French Revolution."

"What I say," said the previously cross *táblabíró*, now angrily, "is that the Erzsébet assessment was correct."

"And I say that it was not," Slanacsek shouted at him heatedly.

At that the whole company sprang up from the table with a frightful din, amid shouts of "It was right, it wasn't, justice, robbery, lawlessness, hear, hear! order! let's hear the *alispán*!" Whereupon the *alispán*, Sáskay and most of all the baron made protracted efforts at reconciliation and finally reconvened the assembly.

"Let's let bygones be bygones," said the *alispán* at length, once order was restored. "I grant you, His Excellency the count considered the Erzsébet assessment burdensome, but by virtue of the patriotism and magnanimity of His Excellency and especially his widely respected representative, the circumstances will be appreciated which recommended the tax rate of the time, and with regard to the good cause, for which a majority could not otherwise be obtained in this county, it won't be taken amiss that we taxed him more highly on this one occasion, all the

130

more so because the poor nobility can scarcely bear the burdens that have been laid upon them for some time."

After that Slanacsek, pacified by these meek words, declared nobly that he didn't take amiss the inaccurate statements made on this occasion; the *alispán* thanked the baron for his observations, which had displayed such delicate tact, and proposed that rather than the agitation against Bántornyi that was to have been started it should be emphasised that his party meant to impose on the nobility *portió*,[94] maintenance of the army, *forspont*,[95] and road-building.

"That's right," said a lawyer with a laugh. "If the nobility can't be persuaded you only have to speak to them in Latin, like the peasants used to say: nothing scared them as much as being addressed in Latin; the three words that they knew – *conscriptio, portio* and *contributio* – could rouse them to revolt."

"Kindly don't make it a joke," Krivér cautioned him. "A lot depends on the name. We know from examples that many matters that have not been accepted in a county have gone through with a change of name and – vice versa."

"Yes, and especially at elections," interposed the baron. "It's a mathematical truth that anyone with a two-syllable name can be elected with half as many canvassers as anyone with a four-syllable name."

"I think we're straying from the subject," commented Réty. "If the respected conference agrees, Sáskay will record that the nobility is rather to be informed of how Bántornyi's party means to introduce not so much a nobility tax as a veritable *contributio* and *portio* (general approval). Now let's move on."

Sáskay recorded the proposal for the undoing of Bántornyi, and now the reading required his full powers of concentration. He stated that all centralisation is inherently damaging and dangerous, but that at an election it is inescapable if one means to succeed; he proposed a main committee in the *ce versa* as a whole, and a sub-committee in each ward; these were to be in mutual contact and would guarantee the effective organisation of elections.

This proposal, like every proposal in Hungary by which the number of officials is increased, was received with general approval, and after half an hour of slightly noisy discussion the offices were filled, naturally in the main from those present, and – which is even more remarkable

---

94   Provision in kind for soldiers and animals.
95   The responsibility for transporting warlike materials to the neighbouring village.

– without any deadly envy arising, with the exception of five or six cases in which individuals took it badly that they were elected only members of sub-committees and not chairmen. Réty stated that he could not undertake the chairmanship of the central committee, because as a candidate for election he didn't wish to exert influence, and to the unanimous acclaim of those present Slanacsek was chosen for that burdensome but pleasing position.

"I have one more humble proposal to make," said Baron Sóskuty when the choices were finally made. "Everything fine and good in the world takes its origin from the fair sex; woman is the being which etc. etc., for which reasons I propose that in every ward a group of lady canvassers be elected."

General approval greeted this chivalrous proposal, but that didn't prevent the following nine speakers from being variously motivated; only after all the merits of the fair sex had been enumerated was it possible to proceed.

After that Sáskay drew the attention of his hearers to certain arrangements which, however, as they form part of the tactics of elections, will not only be familiar to many of my readers but will have been employed by them on occasion; it will be sufficient to mention them. One of the principal ones was that the two bridges by which the nobility of one of the opposition wards came into town should be completely repaired, but in such a way that, having been taken down, they should be in such condition in the days prior to the election that no one might cross them. In fact this was also proposed with regard to the *hidas*es on the Tisza, because just as it was natural that the toll-owners in question would consider the courage of their dear neighbours they would have the *hidas*es and *komps*[96] repaired just then, so that no one could not take it amiss if the carpenters were able to complete so much work only on the day after the election.

The second major chess-move was that all the innkeepers and butchers from whom the opposition would buy its food should be prevailed upon to serve the worst possible wine and rotten meat; it seemed that with a little bribery this would be quite easy, and harder, in the judgement of all the experts, to bribe these people to do the opposite. Magistrate Nyúzó undertook this exception to the regulations, promising that if the said persons – for the most part good-for-nothings and indeed

---

96 These are different types of ferry-boat. The *hidas* is rather like a very large punt, with sloping ends suitable for loading/unloading animals.

Jews – were terrorised by the threats of the opposition into daring to serve good wine, he would take appropriate steps to bring them to order.

There followed more and lesser devices of election strategy, which in themselves seemed trifling, but taken all together would often have great effect. For example: that the majority of the committees to welcome the *főispán* should be appointed from this party, but that the most excessive and stupid members of the opposition should be added so that His Excellency (who had not been in the county for three years) should immediately gain a clear idea of how things stood. In addition it also seemed appropriate, if His Excellency was to be honoured by torchlight music, for cacophony also to be arranged for old councillor Körmöczy, who was in a friendly relationship with His Grace – indeed, one that many believed to be earning annual interest, if, that is the lawyer brought it in regularly; in view of the irritation with Körmöczy that existed among Bántornyi's people – he always took Réty's side – it would not be difficult. If, furthermore His Excellency's secretary were properly informed, the hall occupied in good time, and a few loyal people with good voices arranged beside the *főispán*, success could not be in doubt. To help with that, however, it was desirable for very influential canvassers specified by Sáskay either to be enticed away from the Bántornyi camp or at least impeded in their potentially harmful intentions; several of those present immediately offered to attend to that and divided among themselves the appeasement of those dangerous opponents.

Only one thing remained, something from the constitutional point of view, perhaps, less interesting, but at elections always discussed with the greatest attention: *money*. Before Sáskay had the chance to read out the election budget a curious stirring was perceptible in the whole company. One judge suddenly looked at his watch and was surprised that it was already nine, and at once wished to harness up, from which he and others that meant to follow his example were dissuaded only with difficulty. The baron held his head in his hands and complained of a headache. One of the lawyers and the fat Tüskey, however, were of the opinion that it was no doubt caused by the excessive heat, and so they went out into the corridor, while another lawyer, who had become quite dizzy from all the work, suggested that the discussion be deferred perhaps to a session a week later, as the majority felt incapable of following the proceedings with sufficient attention.

The company was brought back to their seats by Sáskay's looks, Nyúzó's swearing, and Réty's observation that if the respected assembly didn't deal with this matter that day they might as well abandon all plans

133

for the election, as the start of canvassing could be delayed no longer. Sáskay in particular pleaded in tearful tones that his plan should at least be listened to – people would see that no money was required for its implementation – and at length he continued to read his script.

Pride of place among the unjust accusations levelled at Hungary is that of corrupt practice. Anyone that has actually taken part in our elections knows, of course, that instances of our noble compatriots being passively involved in such wickedness are much more numerous than those in which they take an active role, indeed, in all pre-election conferences no sooner does the subject of financial contributions arise than many otherwise eloquent speakers fall silent; since, however, the above-mentioned prejudice exists I can only correct it: Sáskay began his exposition by showing that the money required for the election was on no account to be applied to the bribing of the nobility.

"Every country," reasoned Sáskay, "in which free elections are held has taken care that this important right should be independent, that is, be entrusted to such as are free of material need. Since our laws have failed to do that, and numerous quite penniless nobles have been clothed with the capacity to vote, certain persons have to make good this deficiency and take care that voters, at least while performing their weighty task, be raised above all need; what can happen more naturally than if, while canvassing and the election itself take place, thought is given to food and drink, and occasionally a few *forints* are given in compensation to those who may suffer loss by neglecting their work in the discharge of their duties as nobles? That this is not done with the intention of bribery, but only in order to guarantee the complete independence of voters, is shown by the experience that every time that this arrangement is neglected by some party, the voters can't follow the inclination of their hearts and they give their votes to the candidates of the opposition. And for example, in the present case not to take thought for certain farmsteads and the maintenance of the well-principled noblemen in them would be tantamount to obliging our fellow noblemen to go to Bántornyi's farmstead; which would unquestionably be one of the gravest dangers that can threaten the county, and indeed the country."

At this point the baron and Tüskey heaved great sighs; Karvaly twirled his moustache and said "Just let anyone try to go to Bántornyi's farmstead," and then began to say something about the Creation, which, however, was spoken in a lower tone and could not be fully understood.

"Our goal is sacred and our method laudable," Sáskay went on, "because far be it from us to adopt the principle, so often invoked by the opposition, that the end justifies the means; our goal and method are likewise pure and indeed praiseworthy. Is there anyone that could take it amiss if we invite our sympathisers to lunch, or assist our penurious fellow noblemen with a *forint* or two? There is nothing that might restrain us from what we propose, therefore courage! Forward!"

This call to action was received with the greatest enthusiasm by all the officials and by those who, like Pennaházy, didn't feel obliged to make great financial sacrifices; the others, and especially the baron, heaved a sorrowful sigh at Sáskay's stirring words, and everything that he later said about the irresistible power of associations, and the enormous power that lay hidden in the *fillérs* of the poor if they were put together by men of understanding and handled for a certain purpose, only persuaded a number to point out that times were hard, the price of rye was rock-bottom, and there was trouble lurking in all those associations, etc.

"Times are hard, life is worthless – true! all true!" said Sáskay; he put down his papers and considered the objections such as could not be allowed to pass unanswered; "but must we not therefore consider all the more how we are to help with the shortcomings of the times, to consider certain customers who are well-to-do if not in absolute terms, at least relatively speaking? And I know of no better way of doing this than if we obtain a good body of officials for the county. Times have been hard for the past three years too, but the Jews, who are working for the ruin of the whole country, have had regard for the lawful magistracy, and as far as I know the lives of the respected *szolgabírós* haven't rotted in their cellars as happened to our tobacco, which we all sold as first class with wool and oak-apples, in fact with everything; and the classic proverb *officium non fallit* remains true if we put it into the passive, and it may be said that officials aren't deceived, not even by Jews."

It seems that Sáskay's words had some effect, and at least the previous objections weren't repeated, but when the speaker announced that, with present circumstances in mind, he had established a basis for his plan for which no cash was needed, there followed a "Hear, hear" that sounded almost like "Bravo", and the undivided attention of all present showed in how much esteem the views of the deeply insightful expert on the national economy were held, even in his own county.

If the author were to give a full account of it, Sáskay's plan would be far too scholarly to find room in this modest tale. I shall therefore present only a brief summary of it.

In the wise man's view three things were required at all elections: *food, money,* and because in Hungary the majority have more magnanimity than capital, *credit*. The principles by which the financial element of the Taksony County election was governed were as follows:

Firstly, everyone might subscribe the assistance that they were willing to contribute only in cash.

Secondly, all foodstuffs would be bought for cash and at prescribed prices, but only from those who had subscribed assistance in cash, and only at prices proportionate to the greater or lesser amount of that assistance.

Thirdly, the Rothschilds of the county would advance the necessary monies, and, thanks to Sáskay's skilful negotiations, at five percent, naturally guaranteed by bills of exchange or verbal agreements. For every hundred that was subscribed the bankers would pay seventy-five, which, as is known, is much more favourable than any loans in Spain. Each bond or bill of exchange would also bear the names of two guarantors. Repayment would only be demanded in a year's time, but the lending establishments would, out of respect for gentlemen, declare themselves prepared further to extend credit at the percentages customary for prorogation.

As can be seen, the plan was suited to the genius of the Hungarian nobility, which, as it relies on the past itself, is accustomed to reassuring with the future those that want something from it. Furthermore, since the money subscribed was to be advanced by others while those that subscribed it were able to sell part of their produce for cash at prices set by themselves – it is obvious that, in addition to the good repute that came to everyone, there were those that found it not unpleasant that they would be able to make money without great fatigue and at five percent into the bargain. The readiness with which all present signed their names was the finest proof of the general approval with which Sáskay's plan met, and never had a man a better right to rub his hands together than had the Law of Taksony County as he now walked round the room with a satisfied look on his face and looked from time to time, his eyes a-gleam with pleasure, at the sheet of paper on which the list of subscribers' names was growing longer.

The business was done, and the company left the table and broke up into little groups as before the session. The baron, as is a vulgar custom, but one considered no less pleasant all the same, rehearsed the entire session substituting for his speeches those that he could have made had he not been cut short. Sáskay and Karvaly, as was their wont, spoke not so much with each other as to each other, and the latter remarked that although he himself had subscribed eight *pengő*s he could not conceive how it could have met with such general approval even though the basis of the whole didn't stand, and for every election, in addition to *food, money* and *credit* something more was needed, and that was *the man for the moment*. To which Sáskay, with a scornful shrug of the shoulders, merely retorted that where there were money and food, men such as certain gentlemen had shown themselves to be in 1809 would not be hard to find. Karvaly spoke about certain persons who, after having been prohibited from handling public funds because they had dealt with them as such good stewards that they had given out less than had been taken in, were always dreaming of new *kasszák*. And the two most estimable men would no doubt have come to blows had the welcome words 'soup is served' not been heard on all sides, and had not the two disputants, knowing the custom by which in Hungary there are sometimes fewer seats to be found than guests, made haste to their places.

Now we shall leave the company in its pleasant situation, and if any of my readers, after the lengthy account of the assembly, are hoping that I shall delve into details of the meal and communicate sundry noteworthy facts concerning the cuisine favoured in Taksony County, let them console themselves with the sure belief that as the nobility of Taksony spend the greater part of their lives at tables, and not only taking council, I shall have opportunities a-plenty to speak on this subject. Let it suffice for me to say this once: the excellent lady of the house occupied her husband's presidential chair between Slacsanek and the baron, and by both repeated chiding of the servants and repeated offering of dishes discharged royally her duty as hostess, and even those who, by the end of the meal, had not seen every dish and bottle before them twice – as many of those present had – considered the repast splendid and the courses beyond number.

X

While these noisy events were taking place in the Tiszarét mansion, the little notary's house was quiet, and only the candle-light that shone from the window showed that the occupants were at home. The house had two rooms, and their windows opened onto the street: in the first, which opened separately onto the yard, Tengelyi himself lived, and it was there that he kept his official documents, while in the other, which connected by one door with the notary's room and by another with the kitchen, lived Mrs Erzsébet and her daughter. As we know, the kitchen had one door leading into the garden, through which Viola had entered, and another into the yard. Immediately next to the kitchen was the larder, where Mrs Lipták had hidden the fugitive. The end of the house consisted of the servant's quarters and the little room where Viola's wife lay sick. Tengelyi had spent the whole day at Bántornyi's in Cserepes, where a similar election council had been held. Mrs Erzsébet and Vándory, who had lunched with them that day, was with the patient, and Etelka was sitting and talking with Vilma in the second room.

There is no greater good fortune – as an old woman with whom I had many a conversation used to say – than to be able to speak; and the pious old soul, who, however, has not spoken for a long time, was right. Particularly in the time when we converse in our dreams and dream in our conversation, there is no greater delight than when we can hear from fond lips that which we know and which fills our hearts; and that afternoon the two friends were enjoying that to the full.

Etelka and Vilma were linked by the closest friendship. Since Réty and the notary had been friends for a long time, the two girls had, so to speak, been brought up together. Vilma spent a good part of her days in the mansion and studied with Etelka from her teachers; while the *alispán*'s daughter went to the notary's dwelling and, together with her young friend, received the instruction that Tengelyi and Vándory gave their beloved pupils in history, natural history, and religion; and although later their parents were always more distant from one another, and Vilma for a time had been unable to call on her friend, their hearts remained unaltered and they were all the more attached to one another. If they had lived in a town, in the wider world, this feeling would perhaps not have been so warm; it is at least a rare event that the two

138

prettiest girls and the two cleverest young men, or generally speaking, that such people as are close together, should have special feelings for one another in the wider world. In a village, where there is no place for rivalry, we experience quite the opposite, and those that live close together stick together; so it was with these two girls.

Vilma was now in her sixteenth year and had never gone beyond the boundaries of Taksony County; all that she knew of the world was what she heard from her friend, who was approaching twenty and had spent a couple of winters in the capital. She took no decisions, in great matters or small, without asking Etelka's advice, and when Vándory sometimes said with a smile that Vilma could only want something if she obtained permission from Etelka, he was right. My young readers – some of whom, being reluctant to depend on anyone, are ready for anything rather than do what they are advised by sober persons – should not therefore think that she was one of those weak creatures who lack strength for good and bad alike, whose circumstances are all that the narrator can describe instead of their personalities. Vilma was one of those who can love deeply and for that reason can trust deeply, and if, being ignorant of the world, she followed her heart rather than her head it is a matter for grave doubt whether we should deplore her lack of caution or envy her happiness. We all stumble, but he stumbles least who advances confidently: and that is not he that finds his own way. Generally speaking, if we sometimes recalled how great a part of our so-called convictions is based on our good intentions – it is only when we build our ruminations on a statement that has become a proverb that we can't say on whose authority we act – we would not look so haughtily on those who follow persons of consequence, and, like Vilma, only want until their hearts have chosen themselves a guide. Etelka returned this sentiment fully, and the two young women – in both station and character apparently so far apart – the gentle Vilma, who always needed support, in whose boundless affection wanting was forgotten, and Etelka, whose will had been hardened by the little warfare that she had waged since childhood with her stepmother – clung together with that friendship which only the tender female heart can feel, but which, simply because it is so much finer and loftier than the feeling that we males call friendship, can't last for long.

"So you didn't see him?" said Etelka, laying aside her work. "That's a pity! I wouldn't mind meeting Viola some time; everything that I hear about him interests me. The reckless courage that even his enemies and Nyúzó himself don't deny him, the fact that he's compelled to live as he does at present, and above all the love that he has for his wife and children, all make that outlaw interesting in my eyes."

"How can you talk like that? Goodness knows I pity the poor man, but I don't yearn for his acquaintance. You're brave, I'd die of fright, because they say terrible things about him, he's even killed people."

"That's just talk – a man that can love like Viola can't be a monster. Tell me one of the distinguished *táblabírós*, whom we see every day, whom everybody – with the exception of your father – considers to be splendid, pious people, who would come to see his wife under such circumstances, expose himself to deadly danger, even risk being hanged to see his beloved when she's sick? Vilma, it's beautiful, it's magnificent, even in an outlaw. I'd like to be loved like that by somebody, then I'd feel happy."

"If that's what you need," said Vilma, also laying aside her work and taking her friend's hand, "there's nothing on earth that Kálmán wouldn't do for you."

"Except just once drink one glass less of wine than usual for my sake, or stop swearing and that unpleasant behaviour that I hate. Kálmán would do anything on earth except what I ask of him, and which he's well able to do."

"You're being unfair, Kálmán would go into fire for you."

"Yes, I'm perfectly certain, especially if there were a couple of people there to tell everybody how brave he was. He's a a brave man, there's no denying it, I don't know anybody that would risk their life for lesser things. It doesn't matter to him, and when honour's at stake his personal well-being won't allow him to ignore the matter or give up. Yes, he's got many good and noble qualities, I'll grant all that, only don't say that he loves me."

"You're annoyed with him, he certainly did a silly thing, but that's all."

"He's incorrigible," said Etelka, standing up. "Just imagine, he got drunk again."

"Perhaps you're mistaken again like the other day, when after you'd been cross for a long time it turned out that Kálmán hadn't had a single glass of wine for a week."

"First of all, I don't think I was mistaken, and I think that Ákos was telling a little fib for his sister's friend's benefit; secondly, there can be no question of a mistake today, I was sitting by him all through lunch. But let's say no more about this unpleasant subject," said Etelka in such a tone that anyone could see that she was far from indifferent about it. "I know Kálmán, I appreciate his good qualities but I'm not blind to his faults, and there's no true manliness in him. Anyone who can't resist a glass of wine after all the times we'v agreed may be brave or momentarily noble of spirit, but he's not manly, and only a strong heart can really love."

"Ákos thinks differently about his friend."

"Yes, Ákos," said Etelka, covering her irritation with a forced smile, "and may one not question what Ákos says? He's the most upright man that I know, but he's a man, and so not capable of judging such a thing. Men esteem in their companions the qualities that they can put to the greatest use; if someone's good at coursing, keeps his word, fights for his friends six times, they can't conceive of more to ask of him. I have a different idea on the subject."

The friends fell silent. Vilma realised that the conversation was unpleasant for Etelka and went on with her work. Etelka stood at the window looking out into the dark garden, which lay next to the house in its usual silence, the damage done to it the previous day concealed by night.

"I can imagine your father being cross," said she eventually, turning to her friend, "when he came home yesterday and heard what had happened."

"I'd never seen him so angry; fortunately Vándory had come with him, and he, bless him, calmed his fury a little, but he swore on his word of honour that he wouldn't rest until he obtained justice for himself. I'm quite frightened when I think about it."

"Frightened of his obtaining justice for himself? Don't worry, my dear, he said that out of bitterness, that's nothing to be afraid of."

"But you know, he blames your parents for the whole affair."

"And I'm afraid, as far as my stepmother's concerned, he has a point."

"Yes, but my father's angry with all your family again, except for you, even with Ákos, though we have him to thank for saving us. If he hadn't come along the house would have been searched, Viola would have been found, and we'd have been in serious trouble."

"Who's fault was it? Everybody's unjust, some because they've no principles, others because their principles are too severe. Vándory is, because he sees an angel in everybody, your father is, because he sees opposition in everything . . ."

"Mother told me the whole story, and Mrs Lipták, I and the whole household spoke up for the way Ákos had behaved, but never mind – father said that it was a shame that the young gentleman had troubled himself to come to his house and prevent the search, which would at least have washed his honour clean; and that Ákos presumably knew

141

all about it in advance and only let things reach such a pitch so that he could gain merit in our eyes. Oh, if father knew that Viola was here! I tremble at the thought."

"He isn't going to find out. We can trust Mrs Lipták, you won't say anything, and . . ."

"But if all gets into court; father's said that he'll make everyone take an oath, from mother to the last servant, and what shall we do then?"

"It won't happen – your father was speaking in anger, and he'll calm down later on. In any case, don't say a word to him about it – if I know him, he wouldn't keep it a secret; and he's got enough enemies, who would use what's happened to do him harm."

"That's what Mrs Lipták says as well. But you can't imagine my situation: I've never kept anything secret from father and I daren't look him in the eye if he speaks to me or feel happy if he gives me a hug. Every time the door opens I tremble for fear my secret has been betrayed and I've lost my father's love. Believe me, Etelka, I can't stand the situation."

"But you must, my dear," said Etelka, embracing her friend as she sobbed. "Your father's peace of mind, his happiness, require it. You owe that sacrifice." "I think so myself," replied Vilma, wiping away her tears, "but you don't know how kind he is. When I sit by his side and he strokes my cheek, called me his good girl, says that I'm the delight of his life, he's been deceived by the whole world and in his old age my love rewards him for all his suffering, and then I remember that I'm no longer worthy of his love, that I'm keeping something from him, when I know that he expects complete trust from me and I can't fulfil that expectation, what am I to do? I'd like to throw myself at his feet and confess everything, but then I think again of his peace of mind and his honour, and I stifle my tears."

"Poor Vilma," said Etelka with a sigh. "And yet I hardly know whether I shouldn't envy your situation? I haven't been able to open my heart to my father for a long time. But believe me, everything will come back to normal – after the election, if, as I hope, my father leaves his office yours will stop being angry. As soon as Viola's wife is better perhaps Vándory will take her to his house; it will all gradually be forgotten and you'll be able to talk to your father as well."

"Yes, but until then! Viola knew that the whole village would be out to catch him and still he came. As Mrs Lipták says, no one can imagine how he loves his wife; what's the betting he'll come again – today, tomorrow or any time! Our house is surrounded by spies and if he's caught? Jesus Christ!" Vilma screamed suddenly, staring at the window on the garden side, "he's here."

142

"Who's here?" asked Etelka, also looking that way. "I can't see anyone."

"He's gone now, but believe me, Etelka, he was standing there, I saw his bearded face clearly by the bars."

"Viola? What gives you that idea? He must be miles away, and while Nyúzó and half the county are lurking here he won't be coming back to Tiszarét. You're becoming over-excited, I'll go out and look round the garden myself if you like."

"Never mind, Etelka, my dear. I may well have been mistaken, I'm being a silly girl."

"You're trembling all over," said Etelka, taking her friend's hand. "If your mother could see you she'd be alarmed at how pale you are. I'll fetch a glass of water, that'll make you feel better."

Etelka was getting up to fetch water from the kitchen, when a quiet knock was heard on the door from the other room.

"Stay with me," said Vilma, seizing Etelka's hand. "Who can it be, at this hour? I'm frightened . . ."

"Perhaps it's the magistrate or someone to see your father; we'll see. Come in!"

The door opened slowly and in came a Jew, with much humble bowing and begging of pardon, who wished the young ladies a good evening.

Vilma's former fear and the Jew's humble bows were in such contrast that Etelka could not repress a gentle smile when she saw the horror with which her friend now looked at the stranger.

The latter, however, stood in the doorway between the two rooms twisting his dirty cap in his hands; he didn't have the appearance of a bandit, and his seemingly feeble physique and lack of weapons gave no cause for alarm, though he was the sort of person that struck even the bravest as unpleasant. Jancsi the glazier – such was the name by which he went, in the county at least – was one of the ugliest of creatures. His spindly limbs, which seemed bowed down by the weight of his enormous head, the pock-marked face half covered by a dirty red beard and the red hair hanging over the forehead, the big black patch on his one eye – as he said himself, it had leaked when he had smallpox as a child – and the unsteady gaze of the other, which rotated constantly and always seemed to be looking for something other than your eye: it all added up to something that had a repellent effect on everyone and that the worn velvet trousers, yellow sleeved jacket and little grey pelisse that completed his clothing could not dispel. Etelka herself felt unpleasantly affected by this man, especially when Vilma whispered in her ear that this was the face that she had just seen at the window.

143

"I said, Master Tengelyi is out," said Etelka, "come later, or perhaps tomorrow morning, you're sure to find him in then."

"Please, miss," said the Jew, still twisting his cap and looking round in the rooms, "I've got terrible trouble, I really need to see the notary urgently."

"Well, come back in half an hour; I think he'll be back for dinner."

"Perhaps I'll wait outside until then," said the Jew, not moving from the spot, "doesn't the gentleman have dogs?"

"Dogs?" asked Vilma in alarm.

"Yes, if he's got no dogs I'll wait in the yard, otherwise I'll be afraid to."

"You needn't worry," replied Etelka impatiently, "there's no dog in the house."

"Yes, but there might be at the neighbours', I'm a stranger, and last year I was almost torn to pieces in a village near here, since then I've been afraid." At this point the stranger embarked on a long account of how he'd had a passing shepherd to thank for rescuing him. "Surely to God, if he hadn't come, my pelisse would have been torn to shreds, but it was quite all right, it's not like new but it's very good, I gave five forints thirty for it in Pest."

The Jew displayed a strange blend of craftiness and comedy that almost made Etelka laugh, while Vilma was more and more uneasy and asked twice more for him to leave and come again in half an hour; to that the glazier replied that he would go into the servants' quarters and wait there. "The servant's room isn't next to this room, is it, miss? I won't disturb you there."

Vilma's alarm was overcome by the impatience aroused by the Jew's intrusion, and replied curtly "There's a sick person in the servants' quarters, and I've already told you three times to come back in half an hour and not loiter here."

The Jew bowed humbly and moved towards the door to the kitchen, which he opened.

"Now where are you going?" said Vilma.

"Beg your humble pardon, please forgive me, I've lost my bearings. Perhaps I can go out into the yard this way?"

"That door's locked, go the way you came." And the Jew, with another bow, went out through Tengelyi's room as he had come; but not before bowing two or three times more in the other room, dropping his cap, and behaving so clumsily at the door that he could scarcely open it – meanwhile seeming to scrutinise every corner of the room with his one eye.

144

"What do you say to that?" said Vilma when he had gone. "I'd wager he was a spy."

"A spy? Perhaps; he looks exactly the sort that would be used, and if the enemy came to Hungary perhaps that's what he would be – but what would he come to your house to spy on?"

"Viola – you know the way Nyúzó is after him."

"That is, the way he was after him yesterday, today, believe me, he's the last thing on his mind. You can calm yourself; the Jew had come to see your father with some complaint or request, and anyone that knows them won't be surprised at his walking in."

"But didn't you realise how many questions he asked, and how he looked around the room?"

"That was because he was afraid of dogs, and perhaps he was looking to see if there was a broken window that he could mend when he comes tomorrow."

Vilma wasn't in the least reassured, and probably would have said much more about her anxiety had Tengelyi not entered the room at that very moment, bowed to Etelka and clasped his daughter to his bosom, thus putting an end to the conversation.

"I never expected," said he turning to Etelka, while Vilma put his hat and stick in their usual places, "to find you here, miss – there are so many guests in the mansion today."

"And do you not realise that that is one more reason for my coming here?"

"Yes, what guests they are," said Tengelyi somewhat sourly. "one can't admire such people sufficiently with an election in prospect."

Etelka was a little offended and could make no quick reply other than to comment that "Master Tengelyi is, it seems, a little out of sorts to-day." To which Vilma, to divert the conversation to another topic, asked "Didn't you meet anyone outside the house, a Jew?" adding "he was here just now, we could scarcely get rid of him."

"Oh yes," said the notary, "not far from the house. He was talking to Macskaházy, and before I forget, he sends word to Miss Etelka that he'll send a servant with a lantern; they'll soon be sitting down to dinner, and the *alispán*'s been asking for the young lady."

"And the Jew, what did he want from you, father? It seemed that he must have serious business, he so much wanted to speak to you today."

"Serious business? A serious matter from the poor fellow's point of view, but otherwise a silly joke. He's been working in the mansion, and the Estates have broken a lot of windows, and because he wasn't prepared to laugh with them in this noble deed, or because he's a Jew, or because he's only got one eye, as he said, in their noble anger they gave him a hiding. It's a trifling matter, as you can see, miss," aid Tengelyi, turning to Etelka, "a lot of people are given hidings at election time, especially Jews, just so that they can complain to the new officials and immediately be convinced that as far as they're concerned everything has remained as before."

"But father, that's monstrous," said Vilma, who was beginning to feel sorry for the Jew.

"What can one do about it, my dear?" replied her father bitterly. "What would Hungarian liberty amount to, if even a Jewish glazier couldn't be thrashed? Anyway, the matter is in order from all aspects: Macskakázy has promised that all the damage will be covered, and the Jew will be satisfied with that, as he'll presumably add the fee for his sufferings to the price of the windows."

Meanwhile Mrs Erzsébet and the Reverend Vándory, leaving the patient to sleep, came into the room, and after a brief friendly conversation Etelka embraced her friend and left the notary's house, where Erzsébet was preparing dinner.

XI

While all these preparations for the election were taking place in Tiszarét on behalf of the conservative party, the cellar-man and cook were, as my readers may imagine, likewise fully employed in Cserepes, the Bántornyi stronghold; as, however, parties that work against one another are only as different from one another as the two sides of a coin, on which image and superscription differ while bronze and dimensions remain the same, there's no need for me to go into detail in describing the conferences held there for the purpose of thwarting the schemes of Tiszarét. Those who, like Krivér, took part in the counsels of both camps could see that the affection of the people, like that of ladies, is always won by the same strategies.

In numbers the Bántornyi party seemed the stronger, and indeed with the exception of Kislaky, Sóskuty and Slacsanek we find almost all the intelligentsia and the bigger landowners of the county there, and if we judge enthusiasm by noise the party's victory seems certain, as all the young people too are attracted by its free-thinking; there are only two reasons why Krivér considers the outcome of the affair to be in doubt. The first is that apart from himself, the County Attorney and a couple of *szolgabírós* and their clerks the entire Establishment sides with the opposition, which is only natural under the prevailing circumstances, since Bántornyi has allied his cause almost exclusively to those who, like himself, have only now wished to devote their talents to the noble community; but it was very risky for *beati possidentes* to extend to official positions.[97] The second reason, the more worrying of the two, was that as soon as the election was called Bántornyi's friends decided that in order to realise their intentions they would rely on *persuasion* and not such scurvy tricks as bribery. The proposal was made by Tengelyi, and met with such widespread approval among all Bántornyi's friends, with the exception of those who seek election, that Krivér, the County Attorney and Bántornyi himself employed all their rhetorical skill against it to no purpose. It's true that Bántornyi and his family didn't fail to do anything that made good his party's shortcomings, and that, to his credit, wine and *pálinka* for his noble supporters were nowhere lacking; however, that ill-considered decision of the opposition con-

---

97 *Beati possidentes* 'happy are those who possess' was a phrase much used by Bismarck. In other words, Bántornyi was counting his chickens before they were hatched.

ference, spread by the Réty faction by means of certain commentaries, had its undermining effect. It was said, for example, that not without reason did the Bántornyi party support the emancipation of the Jews, as in terms of stinginess they themselves were no better; that they despised the nobility, as otherwise they would surely entertain them better, and what use was the would-be *alispán*'s covert generosity against such slanders? As Krivér said, the party lacked the powerful tool of publicity. Réty's men went from village to village, established bases, carried banners round, presented boys with painted eggs and girls with ribbons: the very schoolchildren learnt the names of candidates by heart and were given treats in village market-places, every noble lad knew that three *pengő* would make twenty *krajcár* if he voted for Réty as *alispán*, while we were hanging back like shamefaced beggars! What could be hoped for like that?

It is clear that this difference of opinion – not with regard to the end but (as so many reputable persons will argue) to the means – which existed among the Bántornyi supporters gave rise to some very sharp disagreements, and that a number of those seeking office deserted the party and joined the opposition; indeed, the whole faction would probably have broken up long before had not a delightful piece of news held it together.

The *főispán*, that is, who, every time that he came into Taksony county was met at the county boundary by a delegation, on this occasion had informed Bántornyi in a very pleasant letter that he would be taking the Cserepes road and, acknowledging the old friendship that he had with the landowner, he – his faithful humble servant Count Marosvölgyi, *főispán* – would spend the night of the thirtieth of the month in his house. This letter, written entirely by His Excellency's own hand, was an epoch-making event in the county. That the *főispán*, who hitherto had always stayed at Réty's, should now, for the first time – and just when the latter had abandoned his free principles, and Bántornyi had emerged as the candidate of the liberals – stay in the house of the latter must clearly demonstrate the sympathy which His Excellency had always entertained for the principles of the opposition. So they said in Cserepes; whereas the Réty faction either attributed this unexpected turn of events to the fact that His Excellency, coming into the county by a different route, could not find a suitable inn anywhere and was obliged to stay there, or else called this step the greatest possible political mistake, which sooner or later would lead to the count's downfall. All those who had spoken against the bribery of the nobility – in particular, Tengelyi – naturally attributed this triumph to the fact that the underhand means by which Réty hoped to achieve a majority had become known to the *főispán*, and that by staying with Bántornyi His Excellency meant to show how much he deplored all canvassing. And no one that knows the weakness of our nature can be surprised at that, for few though there are that might bring about some kind of incident themselves, are they not fewer still who attribute entirely to themselves that which has happened that suits them?

Whatever the reason was, however, that led His Excellency to Cserepes the pleasure in the Bántornyi house was none the less, and scarcely a day went by without the opposition faction being increased by a couple of distinguished persons in search of the offices of *szolgabíró* or clerk. On the thirtieth of October in particular the house in Cserepes was full of sympathisers, and although the county deputation was only expected for lunch and the *főispán* was expected for dinner, even early in the morning there was hardly room to move in the place.

A few years previously the Bántornyi house had been one of those which, even if they had not seen it, my readers could have conceived quite correctly, and if I simply said that the Bántornyis lived in a mansion, would, broadly speaking, have needed no further description of the house and its associated courtyards to form the most reliable image of it. There were eight windows in the facade of the house, three in the side, in the middle a double door, painted red, up to which led three steps; on each of the corners a square tower. Who has not seen all that a hundred times, who doesn't know that if he enters through the door – above which hang armorial bearings carved in stone – he will go across a paved courtyard straight to the dining-room, to the right of which lives Her Honour or Her Worship the lady of the house *cum appertinentiis*, and to the left the master, guests etc. Had my tale been enacted a couple of years earlier, as I said, I could have excused myself from describing the house in Cserepes; now, however, since His Honour Jakab Bántornyi – or James, as he prefers to be called – returned from England, Lajos himself scarcely recognises his own house, and the housekeeper, who had previously governed the house totally and even now too since Jakab has married, there is no telling why (perhaps because the captain had been a widower), has retained a good half of her authority, never allowed her daughter out of an evening without a chaperone lest, as had happened twice, she should lose her way again and find her way to the secretary's quarters.

149

There is in England a special thing called 'comfort', which is so much the property of that nation that we may use the word without translating. Some wish to call it *commoditas* in Hungarian, but since 'comfort' was introduced to the Cserepes house everyone in Taksony county has been quite convinced that there is a great deal of difference between the two, and it was soon to the satisfaction of Jakab or James that this term, for which he argued convincingly immediately on his return, was generally accepted.

'Comfort' consists mainly of three things. Firstly, that the house should not be externally symmetrical. Secondly, that in the interior there should everywhere be little passages and in particular little stairs between the rooms. Thirdly, that as far as possible the entire premises should be locked with one small lock of Bramah type.[98] Carpets and good armchairs are very desirable, while one or more coal-burning fireplaces are inevitable, the smell of which greatly enhances 'comfort' in England, and is not for the world to be exchanged for wood.

On James's return from England all this was put into effect in the Bántornyis' ancient seat. Next to the mansion an English two-storey house was built, straight out of Loudon's *Encyclopaedia of Cottage Architecture*;[99] one of the old towers, which abutted on the new building, was raised in height, and, despite all Lajos's comments on fire hazards, provided with a wooden staircase. On the garden side of the house a big glazed verandah was erected, and on the far side of the yard another single-storey building, which contained the billiard table. In brief, anyone who had been to England, or at least had seen paintings of the scenery among which the English lived, would think himself in the Isles of the Blessed at the sight of James Bántornyi's house, and even if the three or four plum trees and the truly noteworthy Masánszki apple[100] failed completely to replace the huge oaks that surround English dwellings, at least the red and white painted walls, viewed from a certain distance, were an excellent imitation of the walls of bare brick that James had seen so often in England.

It goes without saying that the part of the stable in which James's horses lived underwent similar alterations, that the coachmen, as they

---

98 A lock designed by Joseph Bramah in 1784, the earliest known high-security lock.
99 "An encyclopædia of cottage, farm, and villa architecture and furniture; containing numerous designs for dwelling . . . each design accompanied by analytical and critical remarks . . ." by John Claudius Loudon (1783–1843).
100 An old Hungarian species.

cleaned their horses or their tack, might never, for fear of dismissal, stop imitating the buzzing of wasps which the English enjoy on such occasions and which I might perhaps represent in spelling with "pzhoo", and finally that the interior of the house didn't belie its exterior. Stairs, passages and verandah, carpets, fireplaces and armchairs, in other words, nothing was lacking: the Bramah lock, however, with which the bailiff – in his cups – locked up the house so perfectly on one occasion that when he lost the key the servants went in and out through the verandah window for three days until the master, who kept the duplicate key on his watch-chain, returned from Pest – the Bramah lock was too well known throughout the county to require special mention. The old mansion in which Lajos lived remained in almost entirely its old condition, and the sole alteration that the elderly master of the house permitted, after many requests, to please his son was that the dining-room was moved from the middle of the house to that large room that connected with the new building, and that in this last pipe-smoking was altogether forbidden. All the rest remained as it had been, and Lajos could at least feel at home between his ancestral walls, which caused the worthy man no little reassurance.

While Lajos was receiving the stream of arriving guests Jakab and Krivér were walking in the garden and talking; James could not tell marjoram from cabbage, but since his return it had lost the straightness of its old paths and had become as Anglicised as a Hungarian kitchen garden can. Jakab seemed out of sorts. He stood, shaking his head, went on, stopped again, struck his boot with the whip that he was holding, and every time that Krivér said something he replied with a "most true", "yes", or some other such exclamation used in the English Parliament, while Krivér always looked around before he spoke as if to see if there were someone nearby who might hear him. That was an old habit with the administrator of Taksony, and it had reached such a stage that if anyone so much as wished him good morning or asked the time he reacted with the same caution.

"You see," said Krivér, dropping his voice to a whisper, "we're simply wasting our time if we don't open centres and set up banners. All the money that you spend and all your brother's popularity will do no good. People will take your money, they'll like your brother, but they won't go and vote, or if they do go they'll be led astray by Réty's canvassers."

You're right, my friend, but what are we to do?"

"Perhaps you could persuade your brother to do the sort of thing that they do in England, hold a *müting* or whatever it's called . . ."

151

"A *meeting*, from the verb 'to meet, gather'. That's what you mean."

"That's exactly what I meant, you ought to hold some kind of meeting, where people come together for a drink."

"My friend, you're mistaken, that's something else. Where people go drinking, that's a political dinner. A meeting is just a conference, at which people sign big petitions, a hundred or two hundred thousand signatures, that has an effect. I was at a meeting like that myself, in Glasgow actually . . ."

Krivér was alarmed to see that James was about to mount his favourite hobby-horse, and quickly changed the subject. "Yes, I know you signed the petition when you were agitating over the Poor Law; but to return to the subject, in that case we ought to give a political dinner like that. You would make a speech in which you'd set out the party's political principles."

"First they drink to the king and the royal family, because they have to be honoured. Everyone may say what they like about the government, but the king, my friend, the king has to be respected, that's the basis of English liberty, and then . . ."

"To the *főispán* . . ."

"That would be a mistake, you've got the wrong idea. After the royal family we'll need a few general toasts – to the Church, the army, the navy."

"I don't think it's advisable," replied Krivér, with a shake of the head. "That would have an adverse effect, people will given the idea that we're a papist party, and if we drink to the priesthood as well the Calvinists will all desert us."

"That's right, the Presbyterians, that is, the Puritans or Calvinists, as you call them, because, I'll have you know," he added with great satisfaction, "there's no difference between the Hungarian Calvinists and the Scottish Puritans, none at all, even their schoolmasters are paid exactly the same. In Scotland their salaries are linked to the price of oats, and here in some dioceses the teacher receives a pailful of oats per child in kind. No one suspects the similarity that there is between Hungary and England! And you're right: our dissenters too hate the high church just like they do in England. But all the same, it doesn't matter if we drink to the Church in general, everyone will think it refers to their own and we shan't be compromising ourselves, and even if we were accused of papist sympathies that's no bad thing in itself, look at England, there the Whigs and O'Connell . . ."

"Don't speak of such things, my friend! Believe me, I know the county, these people are incapable of grasping your ideas and you can only damage our cause . . ."

"I know, I know," replied Jakab, revelling in the flattery, "and if that's what you think I can leave out all mention of the Church and just raise my glass to the army . . ."

"That too might not be entirely suitable. You know that there's friction between the army officers and the nobility."

"Leave it all to me, I'll single out the Hungarian regiments in the army, and since we have cuirassiers billeted with us my toast can only have good effect. It's true that the officers will take it very much amiss and I might have some duels, but who can help that! A political career can only go like that. O'Connell has fought duels, as has Sir Francis Burdett, and . . ."

"You're right, we'll leave the detailed arrangements entirely in your hands, only let's agree in that regard, because if we don't provide something to drink we shan't succeed."

"Yes, but what are we to do? My brother and I have done everything we could, the election has already cost a year's income . . ."

"It's not money that's lacking, we need to make some sort of public show, and everything will be fine. Until we give our people feathers of a certain colour our party's got its wings clipped. Get your brother to take the plunge and we've won."

"You've forgotten that we've all given our word of honour only to act by honourable means . . ."

"To try to win ourselves a majority," Krivér interrupted, "those are the words of the resolution, that is, granted that entertaining our fellow citizens is not an honourable means, something that I myself deny, and if this endeavour isn't successful we'll think of other, more effective means.

"There's no denying that the resolution can be taken that way too, but there are some who'll think differently."

"There won't be one, and when our conference came to that unfortunate conclusion those that weren't seeking office themselves voted for Tengelyi's proposal so as to escape financial sacrifice. Believe me, you can canvass at your own expense as much as you like."

"What about Tengelyi?"

"Tengelyi, always Tengelyi! And when all's said and done, what does it matter if he breaks away? He's an honourable man, a decent man, I grant you, but taking everything into consideration he's nothing more than a village notary, you make more of his power than the facts justify."

"He's got enormous influence, especially over the clergy, and if he turns against us . . ."

"Against us? Don't you know that that can't happen? He's the most unimportant man in the world. Whether you insult him, do what you like to him or flatter him, you'll waste your time, only an idiot thinks that the beliefs of a village notary are worth more than every other opinion. In the worst case he'd only withdraw, he'll never speak up for the Réty side and, what's more, if he did there's a way for us to destroy his influence."

"And what's that?"

"Tengelyi," said Krivér more quietly, "isn't a noble."

"What are you saying?"

"I know for a fact; as you know, I'm friendly enough with Macskaházy to find out the Réty party's schemes, and he told me on his word of honour. As you know, Tengelyi and the Rétys were friendly years ago before the latter shamefully left the Church, the two of them studied together and knew all each other's secrets. Tengelyi hasn't got a single document to prove his noble status. The County Attorney knows all about it as well, but we must keep quiet about it and if he sides with us at the election we'll let him stay in his nobility, but if he doesn't we'll know what to do."

The County Attorney, who meanwhile had come up to them, likewise confirmed the situation, and Jakab was reassured and promised on his word as a gentleman that whatever his brother might say he would unfurl the banner at once and invite everyone in the district to a political lunch next day. At that the two officials equally declared their approval.

The garden had meanwhile filled with more and more visitors who grouped themselves around James and interrupted the conversation of the three; and whatever amusing things he had to tell his visitors about English horse-racing and the English parliament, good though it was to see the struggle with which he tried to defend himself against the embraces of each new arrival and shook his arriving friends' right hands almost tenaciously with either one or both of his own, we will leave the company to themselves. If some of my innocent readers are surprised at seeing Krivér in Réty's house and now hearing him talking in the garden with Bántornyi, or think the scene improbable, all that I can say in self-justification is that it's a done deed and is presumably ascribable to the fact that Krivér wished, come what may, to serve his country and considered it more expedient for him to be proposed as deputy *alispán* by two parties rather than by only one, but chiefly because if he were to withdraw from them completely the Bántornyi party might, in County Attorney Pénzesy,[101] put up a competitor who would be dangerous through his property and his person alike. And is that anything to surprise one? In Hungary, where, except for rich landowners, famers, serfs, working men, master craftsmen, industrialists, artists, non-noble scientists, lawyers and doctors, businessmen great and small, etc., almost every other man is free, excepting, naturally, those who sell themselves through hunger or, as is commoner in Hungary, thirst; and where this free nation rules itself entirely – except in terms of foreign, domestic, military, commercial, ecclesiastical, educational and a few more affairs – in accordance with the principles of self-government; in Hungary, I say, a hundred greater wonders take place every day? Neither we, and perhaps you neither, dear reader – insofar as I am persuaded of your high intellectual qualities – suspect this. It is in our nature not to be surprised at that to which we are accustomed; and while we look indifferently on the gigantic order of the spheres we declare it a miracle if, as once happened on St István's table, roast meat, and not even roast veal but some roast fowl–, takes flight; therefore it can be appreciated that we, who have been brought up and live among these miracles, notice them, but let us speak to a foreigner without embellishment of the way we handle affairs and we shall see the effect that these matters have on him. If we explain to him our constitution, in accordance with which the executive power never accomplishes anything, and the legislative authority can't bring in laws which can be applied everywhere, and the judge has so much other business that he often has no time left for judging; sometimes proceedings, in civil and criminal cases alike, can last a mere day or take several years, and one that has avoided a summary verdict can wait years for the decision of a moment, sometimes violent occupations and evictions are treated as civil matters and an honest man can lose his all because he didn't raise a hand against someone at a certain opportunity, sometimes in a criminal case much more depends on what the accused's ancestor did than on what he has done himself, as his fate is decided by whether he is noble or commoner, and with regard to the deity of justice, as in ancient times with the Romans, there is one goddess for the patricians and one for the plebeians; sometimes, in accordance with the words of Holy Scripture, from him that has nothing even what he has shall be taken – only he pays who might almost go begging; let us explain our ways to a foreigner, and if after that he hears

---

101 Another allegorical name. *Pénz* means 'money', so *pénzes* = 'moneyed', with the *-y* of nobility.

that Krivér attends two conferences in his county he will certainly not be surprised, particularly if he sees that Krivér doesn't thereby jeopardise his standing, indeed, quite the contrary, is respected by both parties equally. But now let us go into the house.

I know of no situation more unpleasant than that of the country householder on whom many visitors call at the same time. Here in Hungary, where every visitor wishes to be personally amused or bored by the master of the house, and the great majority live in perpetual fear that their personal dignity will suffer through the arrival of someone else, on such an occasion the hapless host doesn't know what to do, especially before an election, when every injury can have serious consequences, and before lunch, when he ponders which of three distinguished judges he should seat on the right of the lady of the house, he suffers such torments as Paris alone can have known when he had to choose between three goddesses with his apple. As, however, in difficult, or rather painful, situations every man always plays a thankless part and is all the more gauche for fearing that he may commit some gaucheness, my readers will permit me to omit an account of the civil greetings and infinite pleasure with which Bántornyi received his numerous guests and in particular the entire committee, and to draw a veil of fraternal affection over the splendid meal.

By now evening was drawing on, and James's wife was putting the final touches to the tea table that had been set out on the verandah of the new house, in which the best rooms had been made ready for the *főispán*. Lajos Bántornyi was walking up and down, bearing in his bosom the unease both of a master of a house awaiting a great guest and of a candidate for the office of *alispán*, and looking at his watch; he went out into the yard and came back in, saying that His Excellency really should be here by this time! To which some of his guests replied "Quite so," or "His departure must have been delayed," while from the card tables there rang out *pagát ultimo* or *contra*;[102] and from the other room a noisy political argument, in which thirty people tried to expound twelve opinions on four subjects all at the same time, rendered the host's words of complaint inaudible. Candles had by now been lit. James had abandoned the political battlefield, on which Baron Sóskuty and his ambitious son had finally achieved monopoly of the spoken word by silencing every competitor and, accompanied by two riders, had ridden out

---

102 These are terms used in Tarot, played with the traditional Hungarian pack of thirty-two cards.

to meet the *főispán*. Sóskuty in his short, blue, gold-braided *díszmagyar* – the whole company was in court dress to greet the *főispán* – hurried to the *alispán*. "*Domine spectabilis*, let's stop arguing, Jánosy's hoarse already and the *főispán*'ll be here any moment. You should all be thinking about the *főispán*! If he's stuck somewhere! After all, we're human! He must have been held up." And so on, while the door opened and in rushed the bailiff, and with the brief words "He'll be here directly" gave every thought a different direction, though the noise increased rather than diminished in consequence.

"That's right, that's right! Where's my sword?" exclaimed Sóskuty, running to the corner of the room where the armoury was and to which some of the *táblabírós* hurried while the rest struggled over the pile of *mentes* in the other room.

"Excuse me, *domine spectabilis*! this is mine, the one with the green fur," exclaimed the County Attorney, holding back a *táblabíró,* who had just put on his *mente* and was hurrying back for his sword – he was not a little annoyed and denied the allegation, which the Attorney too was soon forced to admit was unfounded, but not before his *kalpag* had fallen from his grasp in the crush and been trampled.

"I can't find my sword!" cried Édesy, forgetting in his new misfortune all about the *pagát* and pleading futilely for it to be handed out. While Sóskuty was applying all his strength to getting into the room and declaring to deaf ears – as Cassandra did the fall of Troy – the danger of the president of the reception committee appearing before the *főispán* without a *panyóka*[103] if he couldn't get into the room. "Excuse me! Please, I'm president of the delegation! I've got to be wearing blue with gold fringes! Just think about it." In the end the desired garment had changed colour somewhat, as it had to its detriment fallen on the floor and been trodden underfoot, but it came to its owner with only a couple of buttons missing. He put it on and said "Now let's hurry, gentlemen! You've had long enough to get ready, you know! The *főispán*'s here!" and with other such exclamations he added not a little to the general confusion.

Argument went on, here over *mentes*, there about swords or *kalpags*, and the delegation had not even noticed that the orator, the Venerable Archdeacon Zsolvay, who had been pacing up and down in solitude, rehearsing his address while the rest had been drinking and playing cards, was now standing in the middle of the room bereft of his principal adornments – his tricorne hat and cloak – which he had taken off

---

103 A coat worn slung over one shoulder.

because of the warmth; a second Cicero, who every time that he spoke in public, as he said himself, always turned pale.

"Let's go, let's go!" Sóskuty called out finally, addressing the delegation which was now armed and clustered around him. "We must receive him in the hall."

"*Domine illustrissime*, I'm in trouble!" sighed the hapless orator. "I've neither hat nor cloak."

"What's happened to them? His Excellency will be here any moment, somebody give him a hat, it must be a tricorne!"exclaimed the worshipful president of the delegation as he ran about, and his words gave rise to renewed fuss and searching, all the more vigorous and noisy as messengers arrived thick and fast with the alarming news that the *főispán* was now at the barn, now had entered the village, now was approaching the park: meanwhile the hat was finally found – a couple of glasses had been placed on it either deliberately or by mistake – and at just the last minute a clerical cloak too was hung on Zsolvay's shoulders. After these preliminaries the entire delegation made its way onto the porch with much pushing and shoving.

There are moments in our human lives etc., as Schiller's Wallenstein says, and among them are those during which a *főispán* is awaited for an election, and the welcoming delegation is standing on the porch and can see approaching at speed the torches that light the great governor on his darkened way: it suffers no doubt; and in particular not when the orator who is to express the sentiments of the county on behalf of the delegation is to fulfil this onerous duty for the first time in his life and stands among his braided companions trembling like an aspen-leaf. The County had a famous orator, and what county has not? He is János Kraveczky, and it is a real shame that my readers can't make his acquaintance on this occasion, as I have never known a better orator on formal occasions. People speak more highly of Erasmus's *In Praise of Folly* than of Pliny's panegyric on Trajan because the difficulties of the subject amply supplant the beauty of the words, in which the latter perhaps exceeds the former; and yet what is the worth of Erasmus compared to that of the Very Reverend János Kraveczky, who has made fifty-three speeches on a similar subject, always ending them amid loud cheers. His enemies – for who, and especially what archdeacon? has no enemies in this world, in which from the archdeacon's red sash to the cardinal's red cassock, from the distinction won in an examination by a schoolboy to the Golden Fleece, from the smallest flower given by our beloved to the glorious laurels bestowed by the nation, there is nothing that we can receive without a couple of enemies being added to it – his enemies, as I was saying, maintained that those speeches consisted of nothing but repetitions; since, however, God Himself makes His sun to shine on good and wicked alike I can't see why our archdeacon should not do the same too, especially as he knew, as a great history buff, what great acclaim the famous Cato acquired by the repetition of the same short statement that "Carthage must be destroyed". Only those envious of the archdeacon spoke so, however, and I can assure my readers that the persons addressed never found Kraverszky's speeches dull, and indeed he is heartless that attributes that not to the elegance of the speeches but to that human weakness that makes it always amusing to hear something bad about another and something good about oneself. But the great man was far away. Réty, who was awaiting the *főispán* at County Hall with the cream of his party, had also kept this Demosthenes by him, and Zsolvay, after all that he'd been through, didn't seem to be in a reassuring mood. The delegation, who were well aware that those persons that weren't of the *ultima informatio* were usually of the *prima informatio*, looked anxiously at their orator, whose words – as the first that he would hear in the County – would no doubt have an effect on the *főispán*. An unexpected event, however, gave a new direction to every thought.

The *főispán* was approaching the fence around the park, the paraded schoolchildren and the crowded onlookers had begun to cheer, when suddenly three fireworks exploded in the roadside ditch. The horses which Bántornyi had sent ahead to His Excellency for the final stage of his journey were as startled as he was himself and bolted, raced through the gate, and the carriage was overturned. The mounted torch-bearers, like the Philistines' foxes when Samson tied torches to their tails, aroused consternation in the village. With his chivalrous disposition James jumped down from his horse by the shortest route, that is, over its head. The delegation that was standing on the porch and in front of the house clasped their hands in horror, and once the horses had been halted and the danger of being trampled was over they all rushed together to welcome the beloved governor.

Let no one expect me to describe in detail the scene which my readers might now have witnessed. I'm not, as everyone must have noticed, good at descriptions, and my feeble pen is inadequate to give an account of so great an uproar. Let it suffice for me to mention that everything was said to the *főispán* and his coachman that could be expected in the situation, and that the former, apart from a little blue patch above one eye, was pulled from his carriage unharmed and assured the distinguished company with the greatest civility that he found the whole affair extraordinarily amusing; his secretary, however, who was travelling in the same carriage as His Excellency and had borne at the same time not only the burden of his master's high office but also that of his person too, seemed to be of a completely different view on this point.

"Who dared let those fireworks off?" said Bántornyi at length, once the *főispán* and the entire company were making their way to the house.

"I did, Your Honour," said the under-gardener.

"How dared you play such a trick?"

"'Cause I was ordered."

"By whom, you wretch?

"Well, the young lady, the captain's wife said that we must give His Excellency a proper welcome. They always have fireworks at Tiszarét, and we're certainly no worse."

Was it because of this significant reason, or because of the reference to the young lady? In either case, the previously irate master of the house was wonderfully calmed by the explanation and, muttering something under his breath about the thoughtlessness of women he too went into the house; meanwhile the whole company had gathered in the big room and the County delegation was now addressing the *főispán*.

The delegation was a glittering one – that is, in the sense of the word that is used in very many Hungarian local authorities which consist almost entirely of clothing trimmed with gold and silver. Sóskuty, in his short hussar jacket, the gold braid and piping on which left the colour of the cloth in doubt, with his round red face, on which the white moustache among the much precious metal now looked almost like silver, feeling the dignity of a whole County in his bosom, bowed three times to its *főispán*, and the delegation, ranged in a semicircle, one by one followed the movements of its president with jingling of spurs, while on the face of the honoured arrival, in addition to the blue patch which was now prominent, signs of quite affable condescension could be seen; the solemn silence that followed the bowing, in short everything, filled the hearts of the onlookers with respect, and if, at the sight of it all, Archdeacon Zsolvay seemed paler still and his voice weak and tremulous as he began to recite the *főispán*'s lengthy title no one found it at all surprising. What was more worrying was that the orator's tremor, after taking his script from the pocket of his cloak and unfolding its four pages, became visibly stronger, and towards the end of the *főispán*'s title his voice became even weaker and finally almost inaudible.

After the title, a pause.

Sóskuty stepped quietly to the orator: "Go on, just read it out, whatever it says."

The speaker, who until then had run trembling over the first lines of his manuscript, made an effort to set about reading: Splendid man, you come into the circle of the bright faces of those that honour you! And whereas hitherto so many hearts have sighed and yearned for you, now every heart throbs with pleasure at seeing you."

The *főispán* covered the sole dark spot on his bright face with his handkerchief, Sóskuty felt his anxiety eased and cried "Hear, hear" along with the delegation, and only the pastor of the neighbouring village, who had joined the delegation as he happened to be in Cserepes, fidgeted uneasily between two corpulent *táblabírós*.

"Honour and gratitude follow your footsteps," the orator continued, warming to the task, "and nowhere in your whole county is there a man that would not be proud to be able to name you as his leader."

"He's laying it on rather," said one of the corpulent *táblabírós*, while the speaker continued to read out his finely-turned language in a similar vein and in a voice growing in confidence. "It's a bit strong even for Kraveczky!"

"If you please," said the cleric in growing unease, "I wrote this speech."

"The way these clergy are jealous of one another," said the other corpulent *táblabíró* to the first, turning his attention once more to the speaker, who, however, had turned over a page and begun again to speak in a quieter voice: "The flock which stands here before you – the delegation scratched their heads in surprise – is but a small part of the great host entrusted to your care and which feeds on your pastures, and he that brings it before you – at this point Sóskuty gaped in amazement – is no better than the rest and, though he wears your robes, he can't forego your pastoral supervision."

Some of the listeners sneezed, some began to whisper, and the *főispán* himself could not quite suppress a smile.

"Archdeacon, what are you doing?" whispered Sóskuty. "Turn the page." The speaker did so and, almost beside himself, read on: "Here you will search in vain for knowledge, for meritorious deeds done for the country, anything of which men might be proud – the delegation was becoming more and more disturbed – you see before you peasants – at this point indignation erupted – in festal garb."

"The archdeacon's gone mad."

161

"But all are good Christians," sighed Zsolvay with angelic resignation, "in the entire gathering there is not a single heretic."

"He's out of his mind." Let's give a cheer: Hurrah, hurrah, cried the entire audience.

"I've been given the wrong cloak," sighed Zsolvay and stepped back. The *főispán* briefly, insofar as he could for laughing, expressed his thanks.

"How did you come by my speech, archdeacon?" asked the little parish priest whom we saw being so uneasy as the oration began, as soon as he could reach the archdeacon. The latter had withdrawn into the other room.

"Leave me alone, you've made me look a fool."

"That's nice! You give my speech that I took a lot of trouble over – and now what am I to say at the bishop's visitation the day after tomorrow?"

"For God's sake, why did you take my cloak?"

"Your cloak?"

"Yes, just take a look, my speech must be in your pocket."

And the wearer took from his pocket a similar manuscript and clapped his hands together. "That's right, this is your cloak." The two orators were greatly distressed, and despite every reassurance – and although the *főispán* declared that the incident had been marvellous – didn't share in the good mood in which they left the *főispán* and his Estates, expressing a wish that nothing would disturb that fine agreement before the great election day, on which we shall see them again.

XII

There's nothing in the world more important than a good name, at least there are those that think so, and so my readers will find it natural if now, as I seek for a name for the county town of Taksony, I pace my room in no little anxiety. We shall call it Porvár,[104] which, on summer days at least, fits it perfectly. In the evening, when the herd of pigs has been driven back into town, the dust fulfils all the requirements of a well-built fortress, covering the buildings completely and repelling any that would enter. If my readers can find a better name, let them tell me; and I'll only ignore their advice if this book hasn't by then gone into a second edition, of which, naturally, I don't even want to think at present. If so many in Hungary change their names, and certain writers have even been able to use up three, why shouldn't the principal town of Taksony county do the same?

The ancient Greeks used to build on precipitous crags. The Asiatic nomadic people from which we Hungarians spring chose the most fertile places for its settlements, and where it found rich pasture and fresh springs was where it paused with its flocks. Porvár too was once designated as the site of a town on these grounds. After houses had replaced the erstwhile tents the green grassland disappeared and the fresh streams, the burbling of which had perhaps enticed our ancestors there, grew into a big puddle; anyone, however, that in autumn looked from his window upon the well-manured and vehicle-rutted streets could not have denied that Porvár stood in the land of Canaan, and there were weeks in the year when even the least settled citizen of Porvár could leave his place of residence with difficulty if at all. Apart from two endless streets which bisected the town from opposite directions, meeting at County Hall, the houses of Porvár were separated from one another by mere back-streets and alleys, amid the maze of which it was made harder still to get one's bearings by the householders' way of building to the same plan and, with the exception of County Hall and a couple of tiled residences, it was hard to tell the difference between the other thatched and shingled buildings. I'll remain silent concerning the attractions of the town. I might mention the promenade, which had been made outside the town a few years previously by public subscription,

---

104 Great Homer nods – Porvár has already been mentioned in ch.2. See note 31

163

the trees on which, perhaps because they had been under public supervision, had not grown since being planted; the mulberry orchard, in which three trees remaining from the time of Emperor Joseph waited year after year for new shoots, while instead of new mulberries only cabbage was cultivated around them; I could also speak of the paved road if it weren't, on muddy days such as the present, entirely covered, so that only those coming by carriage noticed its existence because of the jolting. In a word, there's much that I might mention, but as I've more important business I'll go with my readers straight into County Hall and the *főispán*'s office.

The anteroom, like all anterooms in the civilised world – because they hold a curious attraction for certain people – was full of people waiting. Representatives of every party, every shade of opinion were to be found there, who, as befits a soldierly nation, were waiting armed and ready for the moment to tender their most humble and deferential respects to their deeply respected *főispán*. Réty, Bántornyi, Baron Sóskuty, Slanacsek, a long series of officials and the whole corps of *táblabírós* appeared in the presence of their president to commend themselves once more on the eve of the election, or to assist the president with their humble advice. For example: that lawyer's clerk A was determined to overthrow the monarchy, and that for the security of the state it was inevitably necessary to replace him by B; that if D weren't appointed honorary *jegyző* the minutes of the county couldn't be kept; that freedom of religion was at risk if the County pen, which for years had been wielded by a Calvinist chief clerk, were to fall into the hands of another denomination; that because the County seal had been entrusted to a Protestant, to entrust the pen to a person of the same persuasion was tantamount to the destruction of Catholicism. And every time that one of the advisers came out and reported his conversation with the *főispán* to his party faithful – taking twice as long simply to repeat it as it had taken inside – great delight arose among the listeners, because the *főispán* had agreed with them perfectly on everything.

When candles were lit a great number of those paying their respects dispersed, some hurrying to the farmsteads, others to the gentlemen's club, members of which had prepared for the evening candle-lit music for their *főispán* instead of the politically torch-lit music. He himself, weary after so much civility, paced up and down in his room with his secretary.

The *főispán* of Taksony – as I don't live in his county and am not going to be designated by him for any office my readers won't take my judgement for one of the stereotypical eulogies that are delivered on every *főispán* in this wide world, at least on the occasion of their installation – was an excellent man. In the iron age of our nation men in higher positions had need of great character and strong heart which became steeled under blows so as to withstand or shatter, but never to yield. In this century, when everything that's elevated is supported only by paper – whether that on which newspapers or bank-notes are written – it's enough for the heart to be slightly hardened, enough if it learns the Roman '*nil admirari*' not only with regard to the good but also, which is harder, to the villainous; and no one could deny the *főispán* of Taksony these qualities.

If we look first of all at his exterior – which, as is known has the greatest effect on the common people and women, because both frequently change the objects of their affections and can't have regard to such qualities as require time to appreciate – his greatest enemy would admit that a more elegantly waxed black moustache than that sported by His Excellency was scarcely to be found. His hair too, most ornately curled, framed his smooth forehead, while around his mouth played an incessant smile – differing from that which we see around the mouths of philosophers only in that no bitterness was to be detected in it; only so can a real privy councillor smile. What to say of his dress? Because since other novelists consider descriptions of their characters' attire to be a principal item I mustn't fall behind. The world takes on quite a different aspect if in winter we look at it bare-foot rather than wearing a good fur coat; a woman buries herself in our bosom more readily if a fine *atilla* rather than a *szűr*[105] covers it; we novelists may not ignore this difference. In addition to his face, which I have already described and the expression of which is, in highly placed persons, almost an item of clothing on such occasions, Count Marosvölgyi's dress was simple but in good taste. A green *atilla* with agate buttons, velvet waistcoat, black cravat and trousers of the same colour together with highly polished black boots – so shiny that one could see one's self reflected in them – was almost all that can be said of the *főispán*'s dress that day. Unless they themselves have their clothes made in Vienna my readers can scarcely have a clear conception of the perfection with which these items had severally been made. Of the *főispán*'s interior it is hard for me to say more and truthfully other than that he was an inner privy councillor. When nature gave our species two ears and only one mouth it reminded us that we should

---

105 The all-enveloping traditional felt cloak of the Hungarian shepherd.

rather listen to others than give voice to our own feelings, and the count tended to follow this injunction from nature and there's little that might be said about his personal views. It's probable that like his exterior his soul too fully belonged in the place to which destiny had appointed him. The Vienna police enquire into the character of every arrival in that city, that is, the title or office that they bear. This is a very intelligent method of enquiry. In almost everyone, the character sooner or later adapts itself to their situation. We have the power to refuse any title, but once we have borne it for a while we almost always become what it entails, and I'm convinced that if we could look into the interiors of people we would, in this regard, find there the same sort of resemblances relative to position in society as may be observed in the exteriors of doctors, clergy, and certain master craftsmen. At least as far as Count Marosvölgyi is concerned, even at the Last Judgement everyone would immediately recognise in him the great man, and their doubts would mainly be as to whether they were looking at a Hungarian great man, as at the Last Judgement we shall appear without clothing.

"And you believe," said the *főispán* as he sat by the fire – "that everything will go well tomorrow?"

"Except for those who may perhaps be beaten up by public demand," replied the secretary. "Réty has a clear majority. Bántornyi has only stood to please his brother, and won't mind doing badly; his party will be satisfied with a couple of minor offices. The deputy *alispán* is a decent man, he's resigning voluntarily and both parties want Krivér in his place. The whole business isn't worth Your Excellency's worrying about for a moment."

"As long as no disorder occurs."

"There are two companies of infantry in the town, the cavalry will be here in the morning, and . . ."

"Now, you know I don't want to resort to such measures. Everyone will take it amiss, and say that an election in which military force was used is not indicative of liberty."

"Quite the contrary," replied the secretary with a smile. "Your Excellency doesn't believe how much everyone here yearns for the military. Bántornyi and Réty have asked perhaps ten times: have the necessary steps been taken to maintain order? And when they heard about our military preparations they almost fell on our necks. They grew accustomed to the military in Taksony county in Your Excellency's predecessor's time, and some people can scarcely imagine an election without bayonets. If I were to portray liberty to their taste, perhaps I'd paint the goddess standing between an infantryman and a cuirassier."

"Don't make light of it."

"How can I help it if I sometimes can't restrain my good humour among all these troubles. Your Excellency only sees the whole picture in the great movement that is swirling around us – the great distur-bance and disorder, the general ruination, and this is unfortunate; we lesser men, however, who look at the details and the internal affairs of parties – how are we to retain our seriousness? Isn't it laughable when I recall that five or six years ago the parties that are now tearing the county apart were in dispute over the question of whether the *hajdús'* uniforms should be braided with just yellow or yellow and black? And that since then the name of Yellow and Blacks has been mentioned with such loathing by the opposition as if it were associated with treason. If Your Excellency were in the farmsteads I wager you'd laugh yourself. In the one, Réty's patriotism is praised to the heavens because in the last election he brought the price of meat down to nine *krajczárs*; while in the pub next door all the noble butchers in the county place their hopes for the country's well-being in Bántornyi, who stood up so eagerly for ten *krajczárs*! And as I was passing the coffee-house a driver was ar-guing that Veszősy couldn't be elected chief justice because he could never play *tarokk*. Your Excellency has no conception of all the amusing things that are happening around you. Slacsanek's just been to see me, complaining bitterly that his two best canvassers have been kidnapped."

"Kidnapped?"

"Yes," replied the secretary with a laugh, "kidnapped; that is, without any harm or trouble, but all the same to Réty's great disadvantage. The one is the forest ranger on the bishop's estate – perhaps you remember him from the last election? His gigantic strength, with which he carried a whole officer corps on his shoulders, his voice, which can compete with the Haarlem organ,[106] and most of all his unshakeable loyalty if he joined either party, combine to make him the canvasser *par excellence*. Furthermore, his influence by virtue of his position is enormous, be-cause the episcopal lands extend over several noble communities, and as forest ranger he can overlook one infringement after another, and make himself friends on a daily basis. Now he's joined Réty heart and soul, and what do the Yellows do? They promise another ranger – his friend – five hundred forints. He goes to see him, complains about the Yellows,

---

106 The famous organ of St Bavo's church in Haarlem, Netherlands.

saying that while a drop of his blood remains he won't tolerate even one of them being elected *szolgabíró*. Zsoltáry,[107] if I've got the name right, swears and swears in delight; and when he hears that next day there's to be an amicable discussion about the election over a barrel of wine at his friend's house he promises to be there. Next day he goes there and the rest, who are all secretly Yellows, get him drunk, put him onto a cart, and now he's going round the county with them, not so much as noticing Bántornyi's banner flying above his head, and being carried from village to village to give support to the rumour that he's left Réty. This joke's been going on for a week, and Zsoltáry's still drunk, still thinks that he's with the Blacks, and is cheering his head off. The Blacks have tried several times to take him back by force but they've been beaten off and suffered losses, and three noble communities which have always voted with the ranger have either gone over to Bántornyi or are leaderless and don't know what to do. The other kidnap was that of the notary of Pálinkás, who's got into debt for four hundred forints with a Jewish crowd, who gamble with him constantly, and every time that the poor man remembers the election and wants to leave they let him win or lose just as much as they think necessary, so that the poor man has still not escaped their clutches and his whereabouts are unknown."

The *főispán* laughed. "And have you spoken to Tengelyi, the notary of Tiszarét?"

"He'll be here directly, Your Grace. You can't imagine how hard that poor man works. I've never seen more honourable enthusiasm, greater virtue. The good man is approaching sixty, and he hasn't yet realised that the office of village notary isn't the position from which one can reform the world."

"He'll be dull," said the *főispán*, stretching in his chair, "but there's nothing for it, if, as you say, he has great influence."

"Greater, Your Grace, than any village notary ever. Vándory, who, as Your Excellency know, is regarded as an oracle by all the Calvinist clergy in the region, does everything that he wants; he himself is an educated man, was once a lawyer, and now he helps the *félnemesség*[108] free of charge with writing petitions, legal advice and a hundred such things besides. That's the reason why Your Excellency's predecessor appointed him an honorary lawyer's clerk, and Réty was a close friend of his for a long time . . ."

"I know, I know he's a demagogue! I heard about him a long time ago."

---

107 Another meaningful name. *Zsoltár* means 'psalm'.
108 *Félnemes* 'half noble': one who is noble only on the mother's side.

"Perhaps not as much as Your Excellency thinks," said the secretary. "Generally speaking, those who've been forced by poverty to accept a certain position don't sacrifice their principles to their status; they're hapless captive champions in the enemy camp, who are compelled to labour in the fortresses that are raised against their friends, but whose sympathies lie with those against whom they're employed. Tengelyi isn't the sort that is usually called that. The principles that demagogues use as means to their personal ends are to him goals for which he would give his life. Just as he's twenty-five years out of date in his dress, so he's half a century ahead in his thoughts."

"All the worse for him," said the count with a smile. "If he's half a century ahead I don't think he'll be alive when the majority catch up with him. In any case, I'll have a word with him. This kind of people are the most dangerous."

"I don't think so, Your Grace! Men of profound conviction stand apart on the whole, and can't easily gather around them parties which might make them dangerous. The only man to attain power is the one who can find a middle way between the differing values and opinions, and Your Excellency will see that that's not Tengelyi's style. He's inflexible in his convictions, relentless in the consequences that follow. A lot of people are perhaps aware of the truth of what he says, but not many are going to admit it. People that set themselves strict logic as a guiding star are rarely followed by the crowd."

"You sound quite enthusiastic about your notary," said the *főispán*, who made so much use of his secretary's cleverness that he tolerated his liberal principles, especially like this in private, "we shall see. "The notary's a married man with a child, and poor as well. Krivér has told me all about his circumstances, and perhaps there will be a way for us to lead him onto a different path. Sièyes, whom he regards as a great man, actually says somewhere that we can enlighten our contemporaries' ignorance and overcome their prejudices; but there's no cure for the errors of a sixty-year-old mind. But who knows, perhaps Tengelyi's only fifty-nine."

"I'd be very surprised if Your Excellency were right," said the secretary calmly.

"You'll be surprised quite a few more times," said the *főispán*, rising from his chair. "If you come into a room and see women whose faces are redder than the rest – be sure that they use make-up; and once in a hundred times you won't be deceived if you deduce from the unusual redness that *en déshabille* they're even paler than the rest. It's no bad thing to judge along those lines in politics as well. But I think I can hear someone – please take a look, and if it's Tengelyi leave us together."

The secretary went out and a few moments later Tenglyi entered the *főispán*'s office with a deep bow. The latter received him with his customary politeness and returned to the stove, where the notary followed him.

"You will forgive me," said the *főispán*, "for sending for you after you had been reluctant to visit me with the other officials."

Every time that Tengelyi had come into contact with persons in high positions, the less he had bowed to their superiority, the more he had been aware of aloofness – and he replied with cool formality that His Excellency might command him at any time, but that he knew his place as a mere village notary, when so many were troubling the *főispán*, better than to steal a moment from those that were more entitled.

"You are mistaken in me if you think that I can't distinguish between a man and his external position, and that I place you in one line with your colleagues."

"And Your Excellency is mistaken if you think that I would take it amiss. As for our inner honour, there are occasions when it remains independent of the external position, and a great heart and lofty thoughts can sometimes be found beneath the peasant's *guba*[109] too; but in other respects, everyone is worth as much as he can profit by them. It is not intention but power that is respected in us, and if a village notary like myself may sometimes respect himself more than do his fellows he will be very disappointed if he desires the like from another. However – he added, as if regretting what he had said – what can I do for Your Excellency?"

"Some years ago, when you were still on a quite friendly footing with the Rétys, we met on a number of occasions." At the mention of Réty Tengelyi frowned. "Excuse me," said the *főispán*, sensing his irritation, "if I have reminded you of times and relationships which perhaps you find unpleasant."

"Indeed, I feel most honoured that Your Excellency deigns to remember my poor person, though sadly I scarcely have it in my power to feel appropriate gratitude for the kindness."

The *főispán* could not fail to notice the bitterness in Tengelyi's words, and most of all in the tone in which he uttered them. "What I shall de-

---

109 An all-enveloping rough cloak worn by peasants, often quite shaggy in appearance. The poor man's *szűr*, so to speak.

sire of you, or rather what I shall ask you for, is not a matter for which your influence is required. Partly it all depends on you, a little trust and friendship towards me, not much goodwill, and you can make me permanently indebted to you."

Tengelyi was one of those who, having been brought up in the school of experience, are so familiar with the dark sides of life that they no longer believe in the lighter aspects of our existence; and it is not to be wondered at if, being always deceived by those higher than himself in the social scale, he received the *főispán*'s words mistrustfully; he viewed them as perhaps an introduction intended to woo him for some vile or self-serving purpose, and so he only replied drily "If what is desired of me conforms with my principles, Your Excellency can confidently count on me."

"Fear not, I know and respect you, and you couldn't ask anything else of me. The few hours that we've spent together and everything that I hear about you have convinced me: you are one of those people who can't come to terms with circumstances, and if they are not given the occasion to use the talents entrusted to them for noble purposes they will bury them rather than give them on usury to such as will misuse them. My request will prove to you how much I esteem your principles."

Whatever we may say, there are few that remain indifferent to disparagement and none to praise, especially when deserved. Tengelyi bowed, and after a short pause the *főispán* went on:

"As I have been informed, you understand perfectly the state of the county; because of your position, through which you also come into contact with the lower classes of society, you must experience many things that don't come to the knowledge of the *főispán*; speak to me openly, as one who accepts all good advice as a genuine favour."

The *főispán*'s words were gentle and spoken in such a tone that, had they come from elsewhere, would have gained Tengelyi's complete trust. On this occasion he remained silent.

"Don't take it as curiosity!" the count continued after a pause. "Tomorrow we have an election, the status of the county for the next three years will be decided, and if I understand circumstances correctly my influence may perhaps be to the county's benefit."

The *főispán* had never in his life spoken to him in that tone, and Tengelyi opened his mouth to reveal all his innermost thoughts; but he recalled how often he had heard that in private the count would declare the most liberal principles in the most sensitive tone, just in order to attain his ends or to find out something that he wished to know; and he replied merely that since he personally was outside the party movements he could offer no information to assist His Excellency's tactics.

Flattery is a much more powerful weapon when used by the higher on the lower than in the opposite direction, and Marosvölgyi, who wasn't accustomed to so much opposition in Taksony County, continued the conversation with redoubled charm. "You're misunderstanding my purpose, believe me, as far as the state of the parties is concerned I've heard more than necessary, as I have no wish to be involved in party politics. But is there nothing in this county but the parties? Shouldn't I know something of the condition of the common people? Don't I need to know how the previous officials have performed their stewardship? And what may the classes that I see around me expect from them that it is proposed to put in their places?" Tengelyi's eyes began to shine, and the *főispán* could see that he had brought the worthy man to a place in which he could not control his feelings. "Yes, Master Tengelyi, that's what I want to know from you, speak to me freely."

"Your Excellency wishes to know the position of the common people?" said Tengelyi, sighing deeply. "Oh, who has the power to depict it with a worthy brush? Since coming into the county, did Your Excellency not look through the window as your carriage passed through villages? And what did you see? Hovels with dilapidated roofs, half the fields lying fallow, the people going gloomily about the streets or driving out their beasts. Industry and growth, the smiles and happiness that distinguish the lives of the common people in other countries are nowhere to be seen. My lord, the country peopled by happy folk is not like this."

"Forgive me, Master Tengelyi, but I believe that there is a slight exaggeration in these words. The Hungarian people are not as unfortunate as you depict. I know of none more proud or manly. The Hungarian is perhaps the most fortunate that I've ever seen."

"Do not be deceived by outward appearances, my lord! The Hungarian peasant goes about the world with head held high. When I see this people whose necks so many centuries of servitude have failed to bend I too sometimes feel proud. It seems that the people that can still hold its head up after so much repression was created by God only to be free, but anyone who believes that this people is fortunate doesn't know its position. We don't see them in rags, it is true, because they have never been over-dressed, and haven't devised anything other than their linen shirts and *gatya*,[110] but are they any less cold in winter? They don't complain,

---

110 The 'bell-bottomed' trousers of traditional male peasant dress.

because they know that their words have no effect, but nevertheless are they less aware of the burdens that weigh down their shoulders? Does it pain them less to be parted from their sons when they're drafted into the army while their noble neighbour's son tests his courage with his greyhounds on his serf's growing crops?"

"You live among the common people," said the *főispán* calmly, "but believe me, in this respect you are mistaken once again. I know Hungarian peasants who bear comparison with any agricultural class in the world in terms of well-being."

"Yes, but does no one live in this country apart from these individuals, do no others than Hungarian peasants live within the boundaries of our country who are none the less our compatriots, who are none the less deserving of our attention? Look at the Russian population of this county, Your Excellency. We can see them in thirty villages, ragged, their sunken cheeks pale with starvation, and what has been done until now to improve their lot? What has been done to bind these people to our nation, to make Hungarians of them, to make them loyal citizens of this country?"

"You may be right and the nation is soon going to appreciate their value," said the *főispán*. "But what can the county administration do to change this? What can I do?"

"A great deal, a very great deal, my lord!" said the notary spiritedly. "The nobility have used the county system to build defences around themselves, behind which they've been able to shelter for centuries even against the law. But if we're no longer prepared to change this situation, why don't we take the common people behind the defences as well? Would the system which is strong enough to sustain our liberties be so weak that we wouldn't be able, if we wished, to protect the common people from oppression? In Hungary the influence exerted by officials is enormous. Look at Veszősy's ward, Your Excellency, and compare it to the rest. There the humiliating punishment of flogging has been stopped, a healthy prison has been built for minor offenders, children are sent to school, public works are more easily carried out because of the greater order, and all this through the influence of one man, because Veszősy realised that in a country where the common people are not sufficiently protected by the law the elected official can't discharge his function if, in addition to his official duties, he doesn't fulfil his *human* obligations. Oh, my lord, take these poor people under your protection, exert your influence so that officials are elected in this county who will understand their high offices! And your name will be blessed as *főispán*'s never has been in Hungary."

Marosvölgyi was not one to be won over by the voicing of a few lofty principles. Seen from a certain height, mankind seem so puny from both material and spiritual points of view, and he is a rare man that, in such a situation, feels sufficient self-esteem in his heart to look on the whole human race without general scorn. But there was in the notary's words something so warm and convincing that the hearer was affected despite himself. When Tengelyi opened his heart he put into simple words that which had been hurting his spirit for so long; he felt unable to doubt him and it was with an unfeigned sigh that he said "If only you were right, and it were up to me to be what I wish to be to the common people."

Tengelyi realised the effect that his words had had on the *főispán*, and went on more eagerly still. "And is it not up to you, Your Excellency? There are honourable men among the present county officials. There is no need for me to name them, my lord, you know them just as the wickedness of Réty, Krivér, Nyúzó and so many more is no secret to you. Reward the former, come out openly against the latter, call on those who, like Édesy, have retired from service in frustration, or those that out of modesty haven't stood for election. Believe me, Your Excellency, your county is rich in men of good character, and a happy people will live in Taksony under your governance."

"Yes, my friend! If in my position I could do what my heart urges me to, if the man in whose hands are united most of the strings by which he seems able to control public affairs weren't by virtue of that very fact tied to others. Not only the artist but also the man who works in a practical way is often forced to abandon the finest notions because the material with which he works is not the ideal choice."

"But doesn't the artist nevertheless not tire in the realisation of his ideal, doesn't he often stand for years before his marble with perspiration on his brow, working his hard material, until he has been able at least to approach what he has in mind? and isn't it our task in real life, in the sphere of politics, where perhaps no one has achieved their ideals but where even the possibility of progress has lapsed; if no one dares go beyond the existing *status quo* with his wishes, if no one sets themselves such goals as seem impossible of attainment? And the desire that Your Excellency has expressed is not one that is impossible to satisfy. State your wishes clearly and there will be no lack of followers. It is not patriotism but the desire for reward, fear and the habit of obedience that cause whole armies to fight as a single hero. In public life the most noble things are sometimes achieved by people that have personal, often wicked ambitions. The most redeeming feature of power is that even wicked thoughts can be put to noble purposes, and that it can make the finest tools for the common good out of servile spirits who flatter everything that is superior. If Nero had made the happiness of the empire his objective, like Antonin, would there not have been found among those who were the tools of his foul pleasures a number whom we now list among the most virtuous of men? Believe me, my lord, power never lacks followers, least of all when it sets itself noble purposes."

"You're forgetting my position. Réty, Krivér, and the men whose remaining in office you consider the most damaging, I see differently," added the count, who never permitted himself to be so carried away as to forget his status. "They are the supporters of my political views in this county. Can I desert them?"

"My lord, I much rather cling to my own convictions than fail to appreciate the way in which others form their opinions; but may the zeal with which we sacrifice ourselves to our convictions extend so far as to sacrifice the happiness, well-being and security of others, especially if they take no part in our political struggles, are completely indifferent to them? I'm well aware that the shade of opinion that governs my sympathies doesn't work otherwise, but does that which is bad become good if it is the practice of more? What have our political struggles to do with the common people? We have excluded them from all influence, may we also deprive them of that peace to which, if we have declared them under-age, they have a claim? If we have had to deny them all rights, must we also deny them justice when we entrust their helplessness to such as stand beside us in our political struggles but of whose wickedness we ourselves are persuaded. Your Grace! the common people take no part in our political life, why should they suffer because of our victories?"

Marosvölgyi was silent for a while. "Believe me," he said at length, in a more sensitive tone than any had heard him use for years, "I have a deep respect for the sentiments that you have expressed. If you were in my position you would see that there are things – noble, fine things – the realisation of which exceeds the power of a single man. If I have influence in the county, it is only thanks to what little popularity I have gained by the exercise of my office; and if I follow your advice today, tomorrow that popularity will be no more."

175

"That popularity. Yes, my lord, every society has its popularity, from the robber band to Rome; where some purpose unites people he that advances it by his actions, declaims most loudly in favour of the accepted principles and fights, will find recognition among his fellows and can count on applause, wreaths and diadems. But apart from that nobility which fills our assembly halls, does no one live within these frontiers? Is there nothing other than applause for which the noble heart might yearn? And the common people! those millions who live silently around us, that huge multitude which now can only show gratitude in prayer for its benefactors' trouble, but which will, when its day comes, shout out the names of its champions more loudly than all the canvassers in Hungary put together – does it not deserve that we should exert ourselves on its behalf?"

At this point sounds of a distant 'Hurrah!' interrupted him.

"My lord, it's almost time for the serenade and I must go. Your Excellency will be surrounded by ceremonial, applause and cheering, the noisiest and least meaningful outbursts of public esteem. Forgive the frankness with which I've spoken, and don't forget, amid the large body that will surround you, that all that noise, all that fuss, all that enthusiasm, are only to be heard near County Hall. The common people only pay with silent gratitude, but their blessings rise to the heavens and if this country has a future it won't elect its great men from those who applaud most of all today."

Tengelyi bowed. The *főispán* gripped his hand, and when he had left the room he sighed as he looked after him.

"What do you say, my lord?" said the secretary, who now came in. "Wasn't I right? That man's not like the rest, he doesn't belong here."

"Say, he doesn't belong anywhere in Hungary," said Marosvölgyi, and with that moved towards the window, through which by now the light of the approaching torches was flooding the room.

XIII

The candles had been extinguished, the *főispán* had retired after his dinner and all was calm once more in the streets of Porvár, and only in a number of farmsteads – where the canvassers were enclosed to protect them from external influence – could be heard an occasional hoarse voice, calling out sleepily the names of Réty or Bántornyi. Other than that weak sound there was nothing to indicate to any passing stranger the pains amid which Taksony County was about to give birth to its new official body. One of the chief reasons for this silence could be found in the fact that so far only Bántornyi's canvassers had invaded the town, and so apart from individual clashes – which, because of the competitive nature of the Hungarian nobility, occurred even between members of that party – no occasion arose for more serious fighting. Réty's men, as is frequently the way with the stronger party, were only to appear on the morning of the election and until then were approaching the scene of the great conflict in easy stages, thus being secured against enticement and promising greater effect when their appearance took the opposition by surprise.

Let's go to one of the farms, established about an hour and a half from Porvár on a Réty property, where we can find the three hundred champions from St-Vilmos, whom we now know well, having seen them at Réty's house. This is a small inn, the kind of which hundreds are to be seen on the Alföld, where, if we can't find a room for ourselves, at least there's usually the stable to tie up our horses, and where anyone that's brought something with them and the knife and fork to enable them to eat it can also dine well. The stable and the big barn, which have been strewn with fresh straw for the comfort of the guests, are full of nobility. Town clerk Pennaházy, the leader of the contingent, has carefully closed the yard so that no one can escape, and has occupied the Jewish innkeeper's bed, while the innkeeper himself lies with his family on the floor in that solitary room. The inn is silent, as if there were nothing unusual within its walls, and only in the tap-room is there a light to be seen. In that large room, the walls of which are decorated for this great occasion, in addition to a smoke-blackened engraving, by a number of patriotic signs, and in the corner of which the party's banners have been set up, we see two men sitting face to face and whispering in the dim candle-light.

177

One of these, the one sitting facing the door, we recognise as the Jewish glazier whom we last saw in Tengelyi's house. The other, who's just lighting his pipe, is still unknown to us; anyone, however, who's ever been into Taksony County jail in the past twenty years would probably know at a glance that they had encountered Master János from St-Vilmos, more commonly known as Jancsi Czifra; nor had they ever seen the jail when Czifra wasn't in it, nor that on seeing him once they were ever likely to forget his face.

I'm no friend of Lavater's science,[111] indeed, when there are in the world so many things that make a man unjust to his fellows I'm almost afraid of the science that declares a nose, mouth or eye of a particular shape to be a certain sign of various bad qualities, exposing the unfortunate person on whom nature has bestowed such features to the suspicions of others without their committing any crime; but there's something in the expression of the human face, something indescribable, yet which has an effect on us all and draws us to confidence or repels, which arouses liking or horror, even at the very first sight. The warm days of spring and the cold of autumn, like the tempest of summer, pass over our Earth without leaving some trace, and why should not the human face retain the imprint of the feelings and passions that pass over it? Thus his character could be clearly read on Czifra's face. His low forehead, furrowed rather by passion than by time, the bushy eyebrows that met at the root of his nose, the shifty look of his grey eyes, in which blended the fearfulness and the recklessness of the evil-doer, the greying hair and beard that half covered his jutting jaw and pale face formed such an ensemble that if one added his scorbutic lips one could but shudder, especially if one saw the muscular, almost unnaturally powerful limbs and the innate strength which nature had bestowed on this man.

"Well, well," said the Jew, shaking his head, "who would have believed that you would go to County Hall of your own free will?"

"When one is a nobleman and is summoned," said the other with a laugh, "and can go along as a respectable gentleman it's quite a different matter. I've spent long enough in the basement there – upstairs is much nicer."

"All the same, it might be better for you not to go, who knows, there are a lot of people there that will recognise you, the castellan, the *hajdús*, you could still have trouble."

---

111 JK Lavater (1741 – 1801) developed the pseudo-science of physiognomy.

"Trouble? Me? What the devil! Who would dare meddle with me, a nobleman from St-Vilmos?" said the other, banging his fist on the table. "That's exactly why I'm going, so that they'll see who I am. If I walk up and down on the porch and that accursed jailer, who's caused me so much pain, sees that I'm a nobleman while he's just a no-good peasant, I know it'll annoy him. I wouldn't miss this for the world, just so as to see them being angry, and if any of them doesn't raise his hat to me I'll knock the pipe out of his mouth."

"Well, well!" said the Jew, "it must be a fine thing, being a nobleman."

"It certainly is, Jancsi," answered the other, stroking his moustache in satisfaction, "especially for people like me. When trouble comes around and you're under suspicion you can be innocent a hundred times over but you're carted straight off to County Hall, down into the cells, clapped in irons and then you can wait for your case to come up. Meanwhile the nobleman is allowed bail, is given two or three years, and if he just doesn't want it hanging over him and doesn't abscond and is sentenced and goes to jail, at least he doesn't get a beating, and if he's got a lot of relations he becomes a scullion in some *szolgabíró*'s house. Yes, Jancsi, that vote's certainly a good thing, especially when you consider that it doesn't cost anything."

Meanwhile the Jew had been jabbing at the table with his knife, and he gave the speaker a sour look. "You're a hard man, Czifra, but just you be careful. If Viola were to find out that you called on the reverend the other day I wouldn't like to be in your shoes, nobleman or not."

The villain reached for his knife and gave the speaker an angry look. "Don't make fun of me, Jew! Otherwise –" The Jew leapt to his feet, and for a moment there was silence. "Now why lose your temper like that?" he asked, as he sat back down on the bench. "You wouldn't kill me for reminding you that you're in danger? When I heard from Viola with my own ears that he's going to smash the head of whoever broke in at the reverend's, even if it was his own brother."

"Yes, but he isn't going to find out," said the other more calmly, "or perhaps you've noticed that Viola suspects me?"

"No, but . . ."

"Or perhaps you mean to give me away?" Again he reached for his knife. "Jew! Nobody but you know that I was at the reverend's, and if . . ."

"Oh, Czifra," replied the glazier, moving his bench back again. "You're really mad, what do Viola and the reverend matter to me? Aren't you and I friends? Who sold the grey the other day that you stole on the

179

other side of the Tisza? and the piglet, I got ten forints thirty *krajczár*s for it."

"Then you swindled me," retorted the other. "Ten forints thirty for a piglet!"

"If you don't believe me, ask the butcher I sold it to."

"Yes, so that I get caught? All right, all right; never mind, you can't help swindling people, it's your Jewish nature. But not a word about my breaking in at the reverend's, not even to your God;

Viola may find out somehow else, just say nothing now, later you can talk all you like, Viola'll be hanged a month from now."

"Oh? How so?" said the Jew, moving his bench back closer.

"Well, how come he wasn't caught the other day? If one of his cronies hadn't started a fire in the *alispán*'s park he'd be hanging by now."

"Yes, quite right," said the Jew. "I don't suppose you did it?"

"Me?" replied the villain, eyes gleaming. "Is there anybody on earth that hates him more than I do? Viola was still a child running around the streets, and if my friends and I came into the village he'd go and hide behind the stove, and when I was going round the county with a whole gang – he cursed and struck the table with his fist – you should have seen him giving orders! And when I broke him out of jail and put him back in my gang, who was the real top man then? Nobody but me, Jancsi Czifra. I'd led them for years, I know every creek and island all along the Tisza, and I had more control over all the cowboys and herdsmen than their bosses. But of course, they had to have somebody else. By then I'd found that he was the kind, the fake, that trembles like a woman at every drop of blood and is overcome at the crying of a child, but they preferred him and I had to shut up if I didn't want a thrashing. He gives the orders, I obey, but we shall see who has the last laugh."

"You're right," said the Jew, pushing across the *pálinka* bottle that stood between them. "It's almost laughable for Viola to give orders to a man like you."

"Yes," said the other, taking a deep drink, "and what orders he gives! The other day I drove a peasant's ox off the field, and when he found out he cursed and swore and ordered me to take it back, because we mustn't harm poor people. Last year, when I shot a Jew, he said that if I did it again he'd kill me. We'll see whose eyes the crows pick out first: when Czifra vows vengeance on somebody they're in danger."

"Now I see," said the Jew, "so it was you that informed His Worship the *szolgabíró* that Viola was coming to Tiszarét the other day?"

"Shut up, Jew – and if I did, what business is it of yours?"

"Yes," said the Jew in a whisper, moving his seat closer to the table, "but I might know a chance for you to take vengeance on Viola and at the same time to make good money."

"Let's hear it!" roared the villain, suddenly slipping into the role of canvasser, so that the walls of the house almost shook.[112]

"Keep your voice down," said the glazier, seizing his hand, "you'll wake up the whole house." He got up, went to the window, and looked out into the yard; on seeing that all was quiet he sat back down at the table and continued: "Did you get nothing for your trouble at the reverend's the other day?"

"Cursed Jew," said the other angrily, "you're talking about that again."

"Just calm down, and I'll get you twenty-five forints."

"Twenty-five forints?" whispered the other. "And how exactly?"

"If you've got the nerve."

"Nerve?" said Czifra, staring at his companion.

"All right, all right, just you be very careful. The documents that you didn't find the other day are at Tengelyi's . . ."

"I'm well aware of that."

"Hush, hush, he keeps them in the big iron-bound chest and you won't get them out if I don't open it. But see here," – and the Jew took from his waistcoat two keys wrapped in rags – "I've got the two keys to the chest, I'll bring the key to the room as well and . . ."

"Accursed Jew," said the other, his ugly face further disfigured by laughter, "how ever did you get the keys?"

"I looked at the chest and recognised it as one that had been bought from a friend of mine at Porvár market, and I got the keys from him. The notary's at the election, and the whole thing can be done with no trouble."

"Give those here," said the villain. "I want to have a look."

"I'm not giving them to you." Czifra leaped up, snatched the keys from his hand and stuffed them into his pocket.

"There, now we don't need you. I'll see to it myself . . ."

"Don't be stupid," said the Jew, "what would you do with the keys?"

"Well, I'd go in," said the villain with a laugh, "and instead of your twenty-five forints I'd get the whole hundred! Because I know that's how much you're getting."

---

112 In Hungarian he has said *Halljuk,* which is also used for the exclamation "Hear! Hear!"

"Oh, Czifra, you're such a clever man. But are you a locksmith? They don't make money-chests so that any fool that's got a key can open them if he doesn't know the combination, he can stand there a whole year."

"What combination?"

"Czifra, old chap, that's not so easy to learn."

"Tell me, Jew!" said the villain, raising his fist, "or else . . ."

"Stop making such a noise, give me back the keys, just come with me and you'll get twenty-five forints. All you'll have to do is to keep watch outside the house, and if there's any trouble, such as if Viola or somebody comes along, come and help me."

"But twenty-five forints! That's no good, you'll be getting a hundred and you're only promising me twenty-five."

"But who'll be going into the house? Who got hold of the keys? Twenty-five's a lot of money, it'll buy two bullocks."

"Let's go halves – give me fifty and I'll go with you."

"Can't do that," said the Jew, shaking his head, "the keys cost me ten for a start."

"Well, if you can't, so be it. I'll go to the election and you go and pray in the synagogue."

"Give me those keys," said the Jew impatiently, "and I'll get somebody else."

"I'm keeping the keys," replied the villain with a laugh, "and if you need another friend, get yourself more keys as well."

"All right then, make it forty forints, and give me the keys back."

"Fifty or nothing."

The argument went on for some time, and in the end the Jew and Czifra shook hands and the latter demanded ten forints in advance. Both put on their sheepskins and set off.

"Let's go at once," said the Jew, making for the door. "If the officers wake up you won't be allowed out."

"That's true," said Czifra, draining what remained of the *pálinka*. "The way they make people go to elections, it's like cattle going to market."

The two shadowy forms vanished and silence was restored in the room; the candle flared up as it began to burn out. After the departing footsteps had died away, from beneath the pile of sheepskins and *szűrs* in a corner of the tap-room there suddenly emerged the face of Peti the Gypsy. Worn out by the endless music with which he had entertained the canvassers at their lengthy dinner, the swarthy violinist had taken refuge a couple of hours earlier under a bench and, covered by the garments tossed onto it, had slept peacefully until awoken by the conversation between Czifra and the Jew. In his chance hiding-place the Gypsy had heard every word, and once he was sure that the two had gone he crawled out, put his sheepskin over his shoulders, extinguished the candle and stole out of the room. A few moments later we find him out in the fields, where, whistling as usual, he strode towards St-Vilmos.

XIV

Novels, as they say, are the epic poems of our time, and if imitation of the ancients didn't conflict with my principles I might begin this chapter with Vergil's first line.

I sing of arms and a man etc. etc.

Our narrative has reached the eve of the election. Four thousand noble souls are going about in Porvár. The different parties frequently gather in little cabals, *caetera quis nescit,* as Ovid puts it.[113] The augurs of the free Roman people never decided on the future without sticks; who would not understand that when we Hungarians elect a new body of officials and settle the future of various parts of Hungary we too reach for sticks, and that is only the consequence of the classical education that we acquire in school. It is perhaps a shame that instead of the air in which the augurs used to gabble we sometimes cause our *lituuses*[114] to move in more material fashion, but that can only be attributed to the spirit of the age, which looks for the most profitable side of everything and also means to put sticks to the most successful use. That occurred in Porvár too on the day which we have reached with our narrative. We have heard of a reputable and stocky *ispán* who had not previously been involved in politics and now, when he took part in the first election with the Bántornyi faction, bore the state of the county parties noted on his back in blue letters. We have heard of an engineer who wished to vote as an *honoratior,*[115] as was the way in the old days, and was flogged like a horse on the field of battle, and by not one noble hand but by so many that he himself found their honour excessive. There were Papists and Calvinists who went home to their families with their heads bandaged as martyrs to their faith; indeed, I met one Lutheran who complained that he had fled like Servet[116] from obscurantism, only to find among the Helvetians what he had tried to avoid with the Romans. But the newspapers, whose county correspondents give accounts of the state of the parties, also tell of beatings-up, and a finer duty awaits me. The poet finds more in a single loving heart than in all the politics in the world.

---

113 Amores 1.5.25 Who does not know the rest?

114 Latin. *Lituus* meant a curved augural staff, or a curved war-trumpet.

115 Latin. One that is more honoured – a higher-class person, an intellectual.

116 ichael Servetus, who escaped the Inquisition only to be burnt for heresy in Geneva, allegedly on Calvin's orders, in 1553.

Sweet days of our first love! Whose brush is worthy to depict your blissfulness? Who can tell the painful delight that fills a young man's soul when he first feels his heart throb more strongly while inexplicable anticipations and inexpressible desires fill his breast? As the sea becomes turbulent when a storm approaches, his spirit is seized by a strange unrest. Neither the shady forest nor the flowery meadow, neither friends nor learning, nothing on earth can quell the disturbance that fills him, and yet he feels happier than ever before! And when finally the storm has broken, when he has centred all his desires and feelings on a single object, surrounded one dear being with all the power of his youthful spirit; when he has found a woman – no, an angel – and clothed her with all the treasures of his boundless imagination and bowed before his idol, he feels all at once, in a single moment, every delight and woe, everything in life that is monstrous and majestic; he sinks under the burden of his joy, and that which fills his heart is more than he can conceal within himself, greater than he can express. Who can find words to describe his feelings? Happy woeful days! As the setting sun leaves behind a bright strip above the part of the horizon where it has vanished, so you leave behind in our lives the bright trace of your radiance, like the sweet echo of a song that has died away, and the heart which you have filled with happiness retains part of its treasure like a vessel in which we have kept perfume; no one, however, is going to describe your bliss; a sigh, a tear, perhaps, is all that we can give; the dream has gone, and he that awakes has no colours by which to show others his Paradise.

He that has ever been in love – it is said that there are those who have never done so, and I believe that they alone may curse their fate, which has given them the sourness of life and denied them its solitary reward – he that has ever loved will be able to imagine the emotion with which Ákos mounted, on the eve of the election, left the noisy streets of Porvár and sped towards Tiszarét. It was evening when he set off, his departure unobserved. The flat land that lay between Porvár and Tiszarét was covered by a thick fog, and as he rode on over the grass he was scarcely able to find his way. He didn't feel the damp chill that struck through his clothes; a warmth was spreading in his soul that the radiance of the sun can't give, and delights filled his heart such as the gentle breath of spring can't create. Never had the countryside in which he had spent all his life from his earliest days seemed so lovely, never so Eden-like, as it did under that autumnal veil.

As my readers will remember, Etelka had promised her brother that he would be able to visit his beloved during the election. The good sister

185

had kept her word, and Ákos was hurrying, his heart throbbing with happiness, to the house from which he had been banned through no fault of his own, but a couple of hours in which would be able to compensate for the sufferings of absence. Those aware of Tengelyi's boundless authority in his own house may be surprised that Vilma, and especially that young lady's mother, had agreed that Ákos might come, but only if they forget that it was impossible for the notary to come home on the eve of the election and that there is no authority that can maintain itself if the heart opposes it.

The Hungarian housewife that expects a guest can never remain at ease. She regards the maintenance of the fortress entrusted to her as does the castellan that of his castle; her honour and that of the house are inseparably linked; and even if the stranger whom she is to receive at her table is the most unpleasant of guests she will exert herself to the utmost so that the roast piglet to be set before him may be done to a turn. How much care there is on her shoulders, then, when he that is awaited, as in this case, is that young man whom she intends for her only daughter. Only my provincial readers will be able to imagine Mrs Erzsébet's anxiety, only they can know now much has to be put in place on such an occasion even in the best-ordered of households, all the cleaning and tidying, how much can go wrong with the almond *torte*, how careful she must be for the roast turkey, that Hungarian love letter, not to be overcooked, for the soup, which reveals the cook's deepest feelings, not to be over-salted; in a word, that everything may be as the lady of the house wishes, and if, when the lunch or dinner comes to the table and, as is the custom, she disparages every course and apologises for every dish, at least she may be able to smile inwardly as she does so.

And Erzsébet was delighted that Ákos was going to visit. Vilma herself could not have been happier at her love than her mother, who, like good parents in general, for her own part had given up every more brilliant prospect and was quite content with her situation but wished for a more brilliant position for her daughter. Ákos was the handsomest, best educated young man in the county, there was no richer nobleman anywhere around, and he might follow his father as *alispán* – could there be a more fitting mate for her angelic Vilma? God Himself, it seemed, intended these noble creatures for one another. Such were Erzsébet's thoughts when she left the room, where she had been talking to Vilma, to go into the kitchen for the fiftieth time. Why forcibly separate hearts which could only beat happily together? The good woman was now, for the first time in her life, almost cross with her husband; he had banned

Ákos from her house, and whenever his love for Vilma was mentioned by Vándory or herself he called her hopes foolishness. She, who would have declined a throne to share her heart with the poor village notary: how would she suspect that others didn't reckon so, and that it was easier to find pure gold in the mines of this earth than that unalloyed feeling that she bore in her heart? Did I too not face obstacles? she thought on, didn't my parents suggest that I should marry Macskaházy, who could guarantee to look after me; wasn't my father angry? but still, am I not Mrs Tengelyi all the same? and what I, a weak woman, did, would not Ákos do when he can see from our example that it is love alone that makes us happy in this world? And as Erzsébet thought back over her past life her eyes were bathed in tears at the memory of so much happiness, but she also recalled the sufferings of the past, all the deprivation, the poverty in which the prime of her life had been spent, the grim anxiety that she had been unable to drive from Jónás's face with all the wealth of her love, the mundane cares which at one time had even soured the joys of motherhood. Oh no, said she to herself as she dried her eyes, Vilma must never know such trouble, I've been happy as things are, she isn't as strong and wouldn't endure it; I know how hard it is to surrender part of our happiness every day for our daily bread. Vilma will be happier. Ákos is rich, and Vándory, who has educated him, who loves him as if he were his own son, has said so often that he would vouch for him. And the happy mother could already see her daughter in the mansion, see the silken sitting-room, imagine her beautiful Vilma sitting on the sofa, walk with her beneath the big trees in the park, go with her to the farm, and her bosom swelled with pleasure as, beside the crackling kitchen fire, she ran over in her mind all the happiness that awaited her beloved daughter.

And Vilma was sitting in her room, running her eyes over the flowers with which she had prepared her humble abode for the coming of her beloved; the book that he had once given her lay open before her – on its pages she read thoughts and feelings other than those of the author; Ákos's favourite songs were open on her little piano and in her soul was every happiness with which love can fill the pure heart of a seventeen-year-old. She too was day-dreaming, but the big house and Ákos's name and wealth had no place in her reverie. A presentiment of infinite happiness was filling her soul, the description and analysis of which are impossible; and if an occasional tinge of bitterness ran through those happy feelings it was actually caused by Ákos's distinguished position, which made her mother's heart beat faster. Oh, if only he were poor, had no one to whom to cling, could reckon on no pleasures other than those which awaited him in Vilma's arms, with nothing to enjoy or hope for in this world but that love in the possession of which his heart would forget all else. How happy this girl would be if she might work for him and earn her beloved's every pleasure by the sweat of her brow! but was she not happy as things were? After the joy that we feel at the thought that our beloved has us to thank for all that he has, is there any greater than that we have him to thank for all our joys? If the intrinsically most trifling thing reminds us of our beloved's affection, if what we see around us, the satisfaction of our everyday lives, is like an ineffable delight to us, it comes from him from whom we can accept it without blushing because we bear in our bosom the measureless wealth of gratitude and we feel that we can't be indebted to him to whom we have sacrificed everything – is there a greater happiness in the world than this? And Vilma sat there before her open book, and minutes and hours went by without the happy day-dreamer being conscious of their passing.

Not so Erzsébet, who could not ignore the time in her more down-to-earth occupations. The turkey was beginning to brown, the tart to set, and the good woman shook her head when she went into the room and saw that eight o'clock was approaching. When it eventually came Ákos had still not arrived; she looked out through the kitchen door and could not even see the wall of the house next door in the fog and darkness, and was filled with grim foreboding.

She went in to speak to Vilma – her mother's questions had made her watch the clock, and she was pleased to see her cheering up. "Ákos is bound to be here soon," said she. "The only thing is that the whole dinner's going to be spoilt. Don't worry, my dear – she went on as brightly as possible – it's terribly foggy, you can't even see next door, but Ákos will find the way better than other people in broad daylight. There are no wolves about, and for a man like him riding in the night is just amusement." She laughed at Ákos's idea of fun and appeared remarkably cheerful at his being so late.

Those words, however, didn't have their intended effect. Never in all her life had Vilma suffered an accident, and so infinite was her happiness at the moment that it had not even occurred to her that something might have happened to upset it; at her mother's words, however, she immediately realised that it was not impossible that misfortune had come to Ákos, and instead of her previous calm she was seized by inexpressible anxiety. "Oh Lord, if something's happened to him," said she jumping up, "it'll be because of me."

Erzsébet saw on her daughter's pale face the effect that her words had had and did her utmost to reassure her. "Ákos won't be bothered by robbers, his horses are reliable, he knows the roads, and it would be really ridiculous for him to fall into a ditch or lose his way in the marshes at St-Vilmos." So no misfortune could happen to a rider on a foggy October night that wasn't proved completely impossible in the distress of the good woman's heart: but all that made no impression on Vilma.

It is the good fortune and at the same time the curse of our youth that we can't tell the possible from the probable. The happiness that our imagination produces offers to the heart a joy which we later expect in vain from fortune; but when we are convinced of the possibility of trouble we no longer doubt its reality, and, surrounded by our imaginary woes, feel once more infinitely unfortunate. So it was with Vilma.

She opened the window and looked out, and as she saw the fog, the tendrils of which made her wet and looked even darker as she looked out from the lighted room, her heart shuddered at the thought that Ákos was lost out there in such weather. She went out into the yard, and the total silence, broken only by the distant barking of dogs, filled her breast with fear, and her mother's assurances, repeated a hundred times, that the night wasn't so dark to anyone whose eyes weren't accustomed to light, and that it was almost impossible for him to lose the way, only further increased her unease.

Half an hour must have gone by when suddenly the sound of a horse's hooves were heard. Vilma listened attentively, her heart racing. The sound stopped; it seemed that the rider had halted some way away, and the minutes were hours as Erzsébet and her daughter counted the footsteps as someone approached from that direction. We can imagine the disappointment when the waiters saw not the elegant Ákos but Mrs Lipták come into the kitchen. She had her short sheepskin over her shoulders, wished them a good evening and made straight for the kitchen stove to warm her old bones.

"Are you alone, Mrs Lipták?" said Erzsébet after returning the greeting, while Vilma could scarcely restrain her tears and sighed "Oh mother, he's not coming, something must have happened to him."

"Perhaps he couldn't get away early," said Erzsébet to console her, "and when he saw the fog he decided to leave it till tomorrow."

"Leave it till tomorrow," said Mrs Lipták with a smile; her intimate knowledge of the notary's house reminds us of the patriarchal ways of the past, which still persist between high and low in certain country places, and so she knew that Ákos was coming as well as anyone else.

189

"Don't say such a thing, madam. Do you suppose that Ákos wouldn't come if thunderbolts were falling from Heaven instead of fog? Is there a more stalwart young man in the county, I don't mean among the gentry, because that's not saying much, but among us poor folk too, he's so strong you'd think he'd only ever worn *gatya*, and as brave as any young soldier; would the dark stop him coming? Goodness me, young lady, the man with a lover like you would face death for her."

"Don't say silly things like that," said Erzsébet, hardly hiding her pleasure at hearing Ákos being extolled. "My Vilma's nobody's lover, let me tell you."

"Very well," said Mrs Lipták, nodding her head. "I know what you mean, but we poor people say 'lover'. God Himself said 'Love one another and . . .' but what I meant was that whether it's her lover or her mate that Miss Vilma's waiting for, he'll come even if the darkness of Egypt covers the world."

"I think he'll come as well," said Vilma tremulously. "Ákos is so brave, he doesn't know the meaning of danger, but I'm still anxious, the night's so dark, and if something were to happen to him . . ."

"The night is dark," said Mrs Lipták solemnly, but in a voice that filled the listener with confidence, "but doesn't God watch over the darkness? and He except at whose will not a sparrow falls from the housetop nor a hair from our heads,[117] He preserves the good on their way. Don't be afraid, dear young lady – she added in a lighter tone – no harm will come to young master Ákos, he may be a little cold, but when he looks into your black eyes he'll be as warm as that ember in the stove. It would be a fine thing if a young man like him couldn't ride here from Porvár in the dark. If he were some luke-warm suitor that would be different, but Ákos, he's a man, mark my words! He was nourished on my milk, he's not like the rest."

"Oh, Mrs Lipták, if only he were here," said Vilma to the old lady, while her mother went into the room, "I can't tell you how frightened I am."

"I'd like it too," whispered she, "if madam would leave the kitchen for once and go inside. And I know of somebody else as well, who's just come from an even longer journey and who can't come into the house before the young gentleman arrives."

"Oh, goodness," said Vilma quietly, "is Viola here?"

Footsteps interrupted the answer and a moment later Ákos was standing by the stove.

---

117 She is mixing Psalm 102:7 and Matthew 10:29.

I shan't describe what Vilma felt at that moment; human speech lacks words to express such happiness, but anyone that saw her at that moment – saw the boundless joy on her tender face, saw the tremor with which she held out her hands, heard the tone in which she spoke Ákos's name, and when she hurried into the room called her mother – might have said with old Mrs Lipták as, wiping her eyes on her little sheepskin, she looked at the lovely couple "Goodness, that Ákos is a lucky man!"

Ákos's old wet-nurse on this occasion even forgave her handsome nursling for failing to greet her, and nevertheless considered the child whom she had suckled to be the most perfect man in the world–she pulled her kerchief over her head, pulled her sheepskin close around her and went out. "Now I'll call Viola," she muttered to herself, "they love each other as well. Oh dear," said she as she went on, shaking her head, "it certainly brought tears to my eyes to see those two children; I can't help it, I always remember my Jancsi at such times. How I loved him, how happy we were, and now he's lying out there in France, they say. It's in the Scriptures: that which God hath joined let no man put asunder – that's why the honourable county declared itself Catholic all the same."

Mrs Lipták was roused from these thoughts by hearing her name quietly spoken by someone as she approached her house.

"Who's that?" said the old woman, and stopped.

"It's me, it's me," whispered the other, laying a hand on her shoulder, "don't you know me?"

"Oh, it's you, Peti," said she in surprise. "I thought you were in Porvár; where've you sprung from?"

"For goodness' sake, keep your voice down. Is he here?"

"Viola?"

"Who else?"

Since she had heard that even among his own men Viola was surrounded by traitors Mrs Lipták was cautious and said nothing.

"Don't be suspicious of me," said the Gypsy impatiently, "I've been running round since first thing, I must speak to him today. My legs won't carry me, but if you don't know where he is I'll run on straight away."

"And what's your important business with Viola?"

"It's a matter of urgency, I must speak to him."

"Well, come with me," whispered Mrs Lipták, seeing the Gypsy's agitation and overcoming her former suspicion, "people are becoming more careful, there are so many bad men about even among us poor people." With that they came to the little house and went in through the garden gate one after the other; Peti was leaning wearily on a stick, contrary to his custom, as no one in Tiszarét had ever seen him do.

In the notary's house, however, there was a time of joy. Love, it is said, destroys the appetite, but four hours on horseback, especially when one is Ákos's age, restores a lot of things, and Mrs Erzsébet too had every reason to be satisfied with her guest. Ákos had been chilled to the marrow, but now, in the warmth of the room and with her steaming dishes before him, he was enjoying all the pleasures of home; and when he looked at Vilma's blushing face as she sat opposite him and helped her mother by passing things, and addressed her a question or two, he heard her words rather than her answers and felt inexpressibly content.

"Now, a little more of this *torte*," said Erzsébet, when Ákos, with all the will in the world, stopped eating – he couldn't manage another thing! "Of course, it's not as good as Your Honour is accustomed to, but it's the best that our poor house can do. It's a little burnt, perhaps, but Your Honour was so long coming, but it's soft, so please . . ."

At that moment Ákos would have clutched at anything that would save him from the *torte*, and he protested at the form of address. "Am I a stranger then, to be called 'Your Honour'? Isn't there something nicer, friendlier, that you could find?"

Erzsébet was embarrassed, but in the look that she gave Ákos so much affection, such unspeakable delight was expressed that he seized her hand and put it to his lips. "Call me Ákos, my son, there's no title on earth that I would desire more."

"Ákos, son, if that's what you'd prefer," said Erzsébet, and tears shone in her eyes. "Make this girl happy and may God bless you for it. Oh Ákos, you're a good, noble being, there's no one in this world more deserving of Vilma's love, but you don't even suspect what a treasure you'll have in her."

They stood up and Vilma fell into her mother's arms. Ákos kissed her hands passionately, and in his mind's eye conjured up the memory of his mother.

"Aren't I a real baby," said Erzsébet eventually, wiping her eyes, "I'm crying for pleasure at seeing the two of you together like this, I'm thinking of the joy that I might find in your love and forgetting all the obstructions, all the perhaps insuperable obstacles between us and that joy. Go on, my dear – turning to Vilma – take the cloth off and take a look at your brother,[118] see if he's asleep yet." And when Vilma had cleared

---

118 There have been two previous references to a son of Tengelyi, and this is evidently he.

192

the table and left the room her mother watched her go with a gaze that focused all her love; she grasped Ákos's hand and said in a tremulous voice, "Ákos, make her happy."

By way of reply, Ákos returned the warmth of her hand.

"Oh, because you don't know, you can't guess the love you'll have from her; the best, the most sensitive of men has no conception of this. If ever she were to feel deceived, if ever . . ."

"And do you think," Ákos interrupted her, "that I'm the disgraceful sort that might turn out unworthy of Vilma's love?"

"No, Ákos, no," said Erzsébet calmly, "I respect you, we wouldn't talk about such things, I wouldn't have disobeyed my husband's instruction – something I've never done before – wouldn't have received you into my house like this if I hadn't been convinced of your noble intentions. Oh, but you're rich, you've got a great future in the world, that's what fills my heart with anxiety. Look at all the grand houses that you know: how many are there in which you find real love, real happiness? Who is there that has the strength to share their heart among so many possessions when life offers so many pleasures and delights, when wherever they look they find something for them to hope for, to yearn after, when ambition calls them to the attainment of many possible goals, when they're surrounded by honour, distinction and popularity? And Vilma needs a whole heart so as to be able to feel happy; fragments of her husband's love aren't going to satisfy her."

Erzsébet was glad that Ákos was wealthy, felt happy at the thought of seeing her daughter in a brilliant situation; she herself had taken sides, had perhaps encouraged Vilma's love in innocent conversations, and yet at the moment she was full of anxiety over her daughter. Such is the nature of our hearts – none of our desires can be fulfilled without, in the moment of fulfilment, the thought arising within us: would it not have been better to direct our desires to some other goal? But that thought which passed through Erzsébet's mind could not resist Ákos's warm words; he was far too certain of the immutable nature of his love than of failing to convince the other of what she wanted to be convinced of.

"I believe you, my dear Ákos," said she, "I have no doubt, never have had any doubt of your love, so forgive if a mother is sometimes unfairly anxious, especially in such a situation as ours! Have you considered the problems?"

"I shall soon be twenty-four, and then who is to give me orders? The property left to me by my mother and which I already own is enough to support my wife and myself, and if my father's annoyed with me for a while – which I don't believe he will be – there's no affection on earth that I'd exchange for Vilma's love."

"Yes, dear Ákos, I believe that," said Erzsébet, "but my Jónás! You don't know him like I do. He's a tender-hearted, blessed man, a living angel; but if he thinks that something conflicts with his principles there's no power that can get the better of him."

"Except love," Ákos interrupted.

"Not even that, believe you me. Jónás has never loved anyone on earth but me, God bless him for that, but I'd never get anything from him that didn't fit in with his convictions."

"I believe that. But can his daughter's happiness be against his convictions? And can't we hope that however rightly he feels that his pride is injured by my parents' opposition, when he sees our constancy he'll yield to our requests? And why should we despair over my father's consent either? No one knows him better than Vándory, and hasn't he said a hundred times that he'd guarantee that he'll agree."

At last Erzsébet was reassured. Ákos told her that he would take Vilma to the estate that his mother had left him in the next county where she would not come into contact with his step-mother. At that moment Vilma came back into the room and Erzsébet, beaming with delight as she told herself about the furnishing of the whole house, took her in her arms.

"So, children," said she, taking their hands, "love one another faithfully and truly, and the good Lord won't allow anybody to separate your hearts. Look at all the obstacles and difficulties that Jónás and I struggled with, and we came together in the end. Anyone that finds real love in this world is very fortunate and can count on the favour of destiny. So, my dears, – she went on, hugging Vilma and placing a kiss on her forehead – have a good long talk, who can say when you'll be able to meet again."

And she sank into her big chair by the stove and lapsed into a blissful reverie as she watched the handsome couple as they sat side by side at the end of the table whispering together.

"Vilma," said Ákos quietly, and she blushed as he took her hand, "when I arrived I saw tears shining in your eyes – why had you been crying?"

"Laugh at me, I'm a silly girl, but we'd both been worried, mother and I, so you see, when I suddenly saw you there despite all my fears . . ."

194

"Angel, how happy you[119] make me with your love, and when I look into your eyes and see your warm gaze resting on me, when I hear your voice in which there's so much feeling, when I can press your hand to my lips and think that it's going to be mine, that one day, perhaps quite soon, I shall be able to call mine all the happiness that love can give, it's as if I'm dreaming and I'm almost afraid that something's bound to go wrong, because it's not possible to be so fortunate in this world."

"Oh, for goodness' sake, do be careful," said Vilma in alarm. "You despise all danger, face everything, but think of us, my mother and I were so worried today."

"Because I took so long to get here?"

"Yes, and the fog, they say that a lot of people have lost their lives in the St-Vilmos marshes."

"If there's no greater danger than what's on the Porvár road, dear Vilma, you can be at ease," said Ákos with a smile. "The St-Vilmos bog, were I to wander into it, isn't deep enough nowadays for a child to drown in it; the only danger that I encountered today, I'm ashamed to say, was that of not finding the way straight here. The fog was so thick that although I've ridden from Porvár to Tiszarét a hundred times I lost the road and I might have still been wandering about, if when I stopped to get my bearings I hadn't hear the sound of hooves. I made for them, but when I came close to the rider he began to canter and then to gallop. I followed, as far my horse could keep up, and he went in front of me faster and faster until I saw a light in the fog and headed for it and found myself at the Tiszarét *csárda*. That rider must have been someone from the village and took me for a highwayman, but whoever he was God bless him for coming my way just then and leading me here. If it hadn't been for him we wouldn't have seen each other today."

"What about going back?" said Vilma, looking anxiously at her beloved. "Mother was saying that you're going to ride back in the dark."

"What else can I do? If I want my visit to remain a secret I've got to be in Porvár early in the morning. I've tethered my horse to the garden fence and I'll be back at County Hall by first light. I'm not going to get lost twice in one day, depend on it! But – Ákos added more quietly, when he noticed that Erzsébet had dozed off in her happy thoughts – Vilma, this uncertainty can't go on, it's intolerable. I'm going to speak to your father."

---

119 The student of Hungarian will like to know that both are using the honorific *ön*.

195

"Don't do that," said Vilma pleadingly, "we can't reckon on his consent until your father has approved your choice."

"But he will approve. If I open my heart to him; if I say how I love you, that apart from your love there's nothing on earth that will make me happy; if I say that life will be heaven if I can share it with you and a curse if I have to endure it alone, and then ask his blessing, nothing but his blessing: oh, believe me, he won't refuse. He's my father, after all, and how often has he said that he loves no one in the world more. Oh, Vilma, we're going to be happy."

Vilma didn't take back the hand which Ákos had passionately seized and didn't say a word to support his expectations, but she fixed her gaze on him with indescribable contentment.

"Yes, Vilma! We're going to be happy. I've told your mother all about my situation. I've got a house three villages away which came to me from my mother. It's very small and modest in appearance. My father made it over to me for my use. The garden had been neglected for a long time but I've put it in order, and the rooms are small but comfortable. That's where we'll live. Where you are is Paradise on earth. We'll take your parents with us."

"Oh, that would be really nice!" Vilma sighed.

"Yes, my dear, and your little brother, of course? And . . ."

"Old Mrs Lipták, perhaps," Vilma smiled in delight. "She's ever so fond of us!"

"Her, of course, and Vándory will visit now and then."

"Yes, he'll certainly come. We'll have a nice big chair made for him, like that one by the stove, he'll always sit on it if he comes to see us, the moment he steps inside we'll have a glass of cool water brought from the well. Oh my goodness, that'll be really nice. And there's a garden, I suppose?" "A nice big garden," said Ákos, and seeing the pleasure shining on Vilma's face could hardly restrain himself from holding her close, "full of roses."

"Roses?" exclaimed Vilma, clasping her hands together in ecstasy.

"When you come back from hunting, or from Porvár or from here, and I hear your horse's hooves in the distance I'll come and meet you with roses in my hair and in my hands, my whole room will be full of flowers. Oh, we're going to be happy there."

"Vilma," said Ákos, his voice trembling, and he pressed her hands passionately to his lips, "can you suspect, can you even remotely guess, how happy you're going to make me?"

"Who knows?" said she, modestly pulling her hand away. "Will it really happen?"

"Will it really happen?" said Ákos, again pressing it to his lips. "If God shows good luck to two people, can he take it from them?"

Ákos's hands were shaking, and in his pale face and blazing eyes was expressed a passion that Vilma had never seen before and at which she was quite alarmed.

"Ákos," said she softly, "you're ill, calm down."

"Oh, Vilma! Don't take your hand away, call me 'my dear', let's say 'te'.[120]

Vilma said nothing, her hands trembled.

"Aren't I your fiancé? Aren't you mine in the eyes of God, why is there this cold dividing wall between us?"

"My Ákos!"

"Oh, please, call me *te*, I can't speak to you anyhow else, the heart knows no other address. See, it's my first and biggest request, the first I've made of you."

Vilma blushed.

"Oh, say that you love me, say that whatever happens you'll never leave me, you'll always be mine."

"Yours," said Vilma in a voice so quiet as to be scarcely audible. And Ákos took the trembling girl in his arms, and the young man's passionate kiss burned on her virgin lips for the first time.

At that moment a loud crash was heard from the next room, as if some heavy body had fallen to the ground, a stifled cry, a man's footsteps, and silence once more. Vilma tore herself from Ákos's arms and screamed, Erzsébet sprang up from her chair, while Ákos took a candle, hurried to the door and opened it to hear someone slipping away. My readers will remember the conversation between the Jew and Czifra of which Peti had been the chance witness. The partners in crime had been unaware of Ákos's presence, considered the foggy night favourable to their exploit, and as soon as the smith's fire had been extinguished and the whole village was in silence they had stolen to the notary's house from behind the gardens where they had hidden. There too all was silent. The kitchen door had long been locked, the windows were dark and the room where there was a light was shuttered; the Jew had stationed Czifra, his armed companion, on guard at the gate and calmly set about his work.

Quietly, he opened the outer door to Tengelyi's room, took a little lantern from beneath his sheepskin and began to open the iron-bound chest.

---

120 The familiar 2nd person.

He could in fact hear the sound of voices through the door to the next room, but he avoided making any sound and continued his work all the more calmly as he was sure that those talking in there were Erzsébet and Vándory, and he was determined, if the latter caught him red-handed, to use his knife to escape. The chest opened, and with the documents and a little bag of silver coins in his hands the Jew was making for the door as quietly as he had come, when on the threshold powerful hands seized him by the throat and he was stopped in his tracks.

"Give the documents here, thief!" said his assailant in a whisper; the Jew thought that it must be Czifra, but as they struggled in the last flicker of his lantern he recognised Viola.

As soon as the latter had learned from the Gypsy of the intended robbery he had joined him in keeping a look-out. It had been beyond his powers to prevent the robbery before it took place. As a fugitive from the law, if he attacked the Jew before he committed his dastardly act and the alarm were raised he would be exposing himself to the greatest danger, and it would have been possible for the Jew later to attack him. He had therefore waited until the Jew was inside, then sent Peti to the gate to watch for Czifra while he himself crept quietly to the door to the room, where now a terrible struggle between him and the Jew broke out.

"Give the documents here," Viola repeated in an undertone, "be quick or you're a dead man."

The Jew fought in vain to escape the iron grip on his throat. The lantern fell to the floor. Fearing that someone would come out on hearing the noise, Viola tried with all his might to wrench the documents away. The Jew stabbed with his knife at Viola's chest, at which the latter laid him low with a tremendous blow to the face. At the sound of that, as we know, peace was shattered in the other room. Viola picked up the documents and took to his heels, followed by Peti. It was all over in a moment. The Jew, stunned, staggered through the door, and when Ákos came in all that he found in the room were the open chest, a bag of money on the floor, and Viola's sheepskin, which he had lost during the struggle.

Ákos hurried to the outside door, which had been left open, and when he came into the yard with the candle he found the Jew lying on the ground; on seeing Ákos he called weakly for help.

Ákos bent over him. At that moment a shot was heard, at which he fell to the ground.

Erzsébet and Vilma had followed him out and screamed.

At the shot, people rushed out from the house and from next door. As the smith rushed out he saw a man running past, and ran after him, shouting "murderer"!

XV

News of the events in Tiszarét had not yet reached Porvár, and Réty, although annoyed at his son's absence – which he put down to political reasons – looked around cheerfully, his face all smiles, in the huge crowd of his admirers who dragged him from his lodging to the scene of the great national ceremony. It is said that those in high places look down on those to whom they owe their elevation, but that such is not the case in Taksony County anyone must have been convinced that saw the refined expression of angelic humility which the face of the *alispán*-designate bore that day; and it seems to me that the St-Vilmos canvasser that held Réty by the leg often said: what a pity it is that we can't carry our beloved chief on our shoulders like this all through the three years, was giving expression to a desire that not only flattered Réty but at the same time was really practical in the canvasser's situation.

Because of the large number of the nobility the courtyard had been chosen as the scene of the election, and with that, in effect, we have told the reader all that he need know. If the members of the Holy Hungarian Crown[121] hold their court not upstairs in the big hall but, in the strict meaning of the word, downstairs in the courtyard, the arrangements are the same everywhere along the Danube and the Tisza, and a certain difference is to be found most of all concerning that little booth under which the *főispán* and a few distinguished *táblabírós* are seated, in that it is covered with pine- or, as in this case, oak-branches, according to the nature of the nearby forest. In front of the *főispán*'s seat is a wooden table covered, like all council tables in Hungary, by a green baize cloth – by the way, let it be said that it is a general custom, in the opinion of several rummagers in antiquity, that certain speeches are called 'green' in Hungarian. The courtyard is full of nobility, divided into parties, while from all the windows in County Hall, and especially those of the great hall, a host of weak women gazes down on the big arena, where the finest sparks are struck from many a noble eye without flint or steel; where, like the world, the official body is created from chaos; where the faces of so many *táblabírós* not only blaze but truly perspire with their convic-

---

121 A circumlocution for the Estates – the aristocracy, clergy and nobility. For an account of this terminology, see Teszelszky, Kees: *The Unknown Crown. Meaning, Symbols and National Identity*, Historia pro futuro IV, Bencés kiadó, Pannonhalma, ISBN 978 963 9226 876.

tions and the patriot, on seeing this host that offers itself for every office, since he senses the enthusiasm with which so many desire to serve their fatherland, can look around with sweet conviction that Hungary will never fail at least for lack of officials.

Other countries speak scornfully of our constitution. Our nobility's freedom from taxation is mentioned! As if it weren't the custom in every people with a bourgeoisie to maintain retired soldiers at public expense, and as if it weren't natural for the Hungarian nation too likewise to support free of charge its great invalids, who fought for it centuries ago, and is not the exhausted invalid of this nation not the nobility? Our public education is derided! as if in this state of affairs we could educate our people somehow differently without jeopardising its self-satisfaction? Indeed, our county system too comes under attack, as it slowly becomes more civilised! as if that which imparts to all citizens that exceedingly pleasant right to give orders while relieving them of all submissiveness weren't the finest and most blessed of all possible constitutions! But let those detractors come to our elections, and then let them say whether they have ever seen anything even remotely similar. I mean not the act of election, because other peoples too, less favoured by destiny, enjoy that right, but the method of election.

Tremendous disorder is evoked throughout the county, mainly where the election actually takes place; the civil constitution is in abeyance; judges cease judging; the collector of the nobility tax has collected nothing for a year; new rumours come every day, according to which noble persons have been thrashed (in direct opposition to the Hungarian constitution, according to which only non-nobles may be beaten). Can a situation be imagined in which the need of order is more felt, by which all are so convinced that the work of officials is only to the common good? And can there be a conviction more salutary than that? Can there be anything finer than when the official, on entering into office, is hailed as a veritable Messiah? It is one of the chief properties of our electoral system (which, as we can see from what has been said, is based on the rule of strict logic) and, as far as I know, not to be found elsewhere, that before we seek to persuade someone to do something we must first make the need of it felt. The perfection of our constitution, however, doesn't stop at that, and it is the electoral method in particular in which our system is without peer. In Hungary the majority is not defined numerically. The big number is deceptive, and to entrust to it the fate of the nation and, furthermore, a county is impossible. Public trust is not something to be determined by addition or subtraction. In Hungary it is not numbers but that choice that *comes straight from the heart*, not a majority of voters, which in any case is merely material animal force, but the very thing which distinguishes man from the animal world, *the spoken word*. *Pectus est quod movet*,[122] as the Roman could say, but in Hungary the heart not merely moves but makes *alispán*s and *szolgabíró*s, and in reality rules. And why should not a body of officials that comes straight from the inward parts of electors not justify their trust? Even so, it's a wicked world! We have so many unfortunate experiences every day! It is good if the official, even before entering upon office, is confirmed in those qualities which we shall most desire of him in his official capacity: and see! our elections answer that purpose too. We want our officials to be proud and yearn for elevation – but is there a better means to that end than dragging them around for hours above the heads of others and acquainting them with the risks and unpleasantnesses of being lifted up? We want them to stand firm in their places, not to be inconstant – but what can we do that is more expedient than to make them dance around in our arms, in order to arouse in them an aversion to all vacillation and the fervent desire to stand on their own feet.

But let's change the subject, I'm writing a novel, not a political treatise; and although in Hungary, where political literature has occupied the realm of poetry and those that hold forth about the national economy proffer only fresh flowers instead of dry straw, perhaps the poet may not take it amiss if he roams the arid plains of politics. I shan't abuse my rights and shall only inform my readers that on that day, beginning with the green booth and table, everything that they have seen in other counties was to be found in Porvár, and in that case a lengthier description is unnecessary. There was something in it all at which an elderly *táblabíró* or two shook their heads: in the middle of the courtyard a company of soldiers was stationed between the two parties; but since in this world everything is progress the youth, who understood their age, were less surprised at this phenomenon since elections in adjacent counties had been conducted in this way for some time past, so that Taksony might not be in any respect inferior; in fact, the military are indispensable at all spectacular plays!

There is almost nothing worthy of record for me to say about the election. After the *főispán*, rather in order to relieve his bosom of the tension of sentiment than to be heard by anyone, finished his speech

---

122 More correctly *Pectus est quod disertum facit* – It is the heart that makes one eloquent (Quintilian, *Institutio oratoria* X.VII,15).

among ceaseless shouts of *Up with Réty, Up with Bántornyi,* and *Vote!,* Réty, with similar success, took leave on behalf of the body of officials; a court was elected to deal with any events that might occur in the course of the election, and after designation the two committees, one chaired by Baron Sóskuty, the other by another magnate dressed in green, blue and red, withdrew for *secret* scrutiny; the parties picked up Réty and Bántornyi and, not without a clash or two, swarmed out of the door of County Hall; and the courtyard, where in addition to the *főispán,* only a few priests, two Royal Councillors and a lame *táblabíró* remained, became relatively quiet. The weak fair sex was still present; it is never lacking at the birth of bodies of officials – as at other births generally – and is always present at our councils, at least if we expect a lively debate. They had pulled in their beautifully curled and kerchiefed heads and were watching from the other side of County Hall the battle which had now begun around the scrutinising committees.

In addition to the central door of County Hall in Porvár there are another two entrances, one on each side of the rectangular building. With regard to comfort and especially tender regard for those who suffered from gout and could not spend that very wet day in the open, the committees were set up – or rather, sat down – under these two entrances. The nobility were released to the last man through the main door, that was then closed, and everyone, individually and according to the ward to which they belonged, voted at the committee at one of the side doors and went back inside through it.

This parliamentary tactic – permit me the use of this much disliked word! but at Hungarian elections, where this science can't be studied from Bentham's famous work, and where anyone that wishes to inform himself on the subject should rather read Montecucculi's military science; from that they will be able to acquire a knowledge of the disposition of individual armies, and this word is certainly more appropriate that any other – this Parliamentary tactic, then, as I was saying, rendered almost impossible any major disorder – or, because what usually happens can't be called disorder, that I may express myself more precisely, any greater beatings; and if liberty wasn't restricted by these measures to such an extent that members of the different parties met and didn't in the fulfilment of their offices break the heads of their political opponents now and then, all the same such warlike incidents lasted for quite a short time, and there were far too many tough heads among the nobility of Taksony County for there to be any harmful consequences. A greater difficulty arose over the committees themselves.

Taksony County has only five wards and, what is more to be regretted, County Hall has only one right-hand side. Which of the two committees, or rather of the two chairmen, should be the one to which three wards are entrusted, and which the one to occupy the single right-hand side? because as we all know that is the side of honour. Sóskuty is one of the leading *táblabírós* in the county, a Chancellor of twenty-five years' standing, and furthermore one of the leading members of the Réty party; the other was a Chancellor of lesser standing, but a count as opposed to a baron, and from another county. Anyone experienced in Hungarian county life can imagine the difficulties facing the *főispán* in this state of affairs, and the anxiety with which he noticed the dissatisfaction of Sóskuty and all his committee – allotted only two wards – and saw from his presidential seat that both committees and their ballot boxes were making for the right-hand doorway. I have no idea where this complication might have led had not Krivér whispered to Sóskuty that although only two wards had been assigned to him these contained two-thirds of the nobility, and so because of the importance of the matter they could be assigned to none other than baron Sóskuty. As for the right-hand side, however, you would be very disappointed if you looked for it where the count from the adjacent county and his committee hurried to; as County Hall and not the *főispán* was what mattered, the right-hand side is to be reckoned from the middle and it is located at that doorway where His Honour's committee's place was prepared. To this Sóskuty remarked with a smile that he didn't consider such trifles; he sat under his doorway to the complete satisfaction of all parties, and to much talk set about his great task.

The principle of secret voting had been adopted at the previous assembly in Taksony County. The matter was, it is said, only brought up for discussion so that it should be made known whether Réty's party or Bántornyi's had a majority, because the members of the former, as supporters of the current *alispán*, wished for open voting, while the latter called for secret. Secret voting carried the day, and Tengelyi, who thought that under that regulation all corruption was forestalled, carried the county's resolution round with unspeakable delight and read it aloud to anyone that he met. When he now walked in under the doorway to take his place on Sóskuty's committee, and since our tale is played out in the Tiszarét ward, we too shall be present, and perhaps our eyes would have been bathed in tears at the notary's pleasure at seeing the method by which his ideas were being put into practice.

The little table, at which in addition to the baron sat old Kislaky and Slanacsek, and so that the Bántornyi party should also be represented, James, the brother of the would-be *alispán*, and a number of *táblabírós*, stood immediately under the entrance beside the door. A little farther towards the courtyard the ballot-box was positioned between two screens. By the door stood Ágoston Karvaly with two *hajdús*, near the table were Nyúzó and his clerk, who recognised best of all the nobility of their ward, and beside them were the former and, as we believe, future Chief Clerk of the county, while Macskaházy, who circulated now round the *főispán* in the courtyard and now upstairs round Her Honour, appeared from time to time at the voting and enquired how things were going.

The *táblabírós* lit up, the wicket door opened and in came individual voters to vote in secret; every one of them, on seeing the committee, shouted out lustily 'Up with Réty' or 'Up with Bántornyi', at which all those outside responded in similar tone, and after this fulfilment of national duty the individual voter withdrew behind the screens to vote in secret.

"No finer thing in the world than secret voting," said Master James, who had shouted 'Up with Bántornyi' in front of the table. "If it were to be brought into the English constitution there would be none more perfect in the world. *The ballot, the ballot for ever,* we radicals used to shout; *it makes a man feel so independent.*"

"Quite, only don't shout like that," sighed old Kislaky. "My boy!" addressing a canvasser who had just hailed Réty, "Don't shout like that, this is supposed to be a secret ballot."

"Of course, secret," said this latter, "up with *alispán* Réty!" and with that vanished behind the screen.

"Really, I ask you," said Kislaky, jumping up from his chair, "this can't go on, it's an absolute farce."

"Quite," Sóskuty interrupted him, "but who's going to tell our fellow nobles what to feel? At times like this there's no commanding people, feeling shows itself strongly and . . ."

"Yes, let it, God bless! But what are these screens for?" said Kislaky. "They've been knocked over three times already, they're a waste of time."

"Your Worship," Sáskay observed, "it's the clear order of the noble county . . ."

"But when the noble county sees that it's giving an impossible order," said Kislaky, more and more heatedly. "Since people will shout out one

204

at a time they'll shout out all the more. It's as if they each want to show the committee that they know best. We shan't be done by evening, and there's such a draught here, we'll all catch our deaths."

All through this argument – which, however, didn't interrupt the voting – Sóskuty had tried to put a word in; now he took his pipe out of his mouth, looked round in dignified manner and put an end to the noisy and, as he said, scandalous argument by pointing out to the committee, including his friend Kislaky, that as he had been appointed chairman he saw it as his duty to carry out the orders of the noble county to the letter, even if they seemed to be impossible. At which, with the approval of the whole committee, with the exception of Kislaky, voting continued in the former manner.

"But tell me something, Your Honour," said Kislaky, still shaking his head to show his dissatisfaction, "it's absolutely impossible to go on like this."

"But look here," replied James reassuringly, "does it do any harm that these people call out the name of a candidate here, when there behind the screen they can still cast a secret vote? Quite independent."

"Yes, but," exclaimed the worthy Kislaky.

"I mean," James interrupted, "who can tell whom they vote for in there, whatever name they shout here in front of us?"

"But look here," said Kislaky with growing impatience, "in the booth the names of the candidates are all written above each box, but how is anyone that can't read going to vote? I've seen ten go in that I know can't read a single letter. And here comes one out of the cage. Hey, Pista," said Kislaky, holding back one of the canvassers who meant to go into the courtyard after voting, "can you read?"

"Read?" came the answer, "I can't read if you make me."

"But surely you can read," interrupted Sóskay, "you don't care to, but you can?"

"Of course I can't, Your Worship, I'm not a scholar, my old father never learnt either."

"What did I say," said Kislaky, triumph and pleasure on his face "and which hole did you put your ball in?"

"The first, of course," answered the canvasser, pulling his sheepskin tighter, "like the *szolgabíró* said. Up with Bántornyi!" and with that he threw the whole committee into no little consternation.

"That man has come to vote for Bántornyi and has given his vote to Réty," said Kislaky with satisfaction. "Now I ask you, can things go on like this?"

"It's very extraordinary," sighed Master James, while Slacsanek remarked, smoothing down his hair, that extraordinary cases could occur under any electoral system.

"Extraordinary cases? Let's have a look, then," said Kislaky, who had been one of the greatest opponents of secret voting. "Can you read?" he asked the first.

"No."

"What about you?"

"Me neither."

"And what about you?"

"Learnt when I a boy . . ."

"And you?"

"Yes."

To which Sáska remarked that as His Worship could see for himself, those that could not read were a tiny minority; and James went to the door to tell everyone to drop their pebble in the second box.

Kislaky was annoyed. Sóskuty was displaying exceptional ability as chairman that day so that no one might have cause for complaint, and the decision of the county be implemented with full rigour, he stationed two *táblabírós* behind the screen, one from each party, to explain the wording above the boxes to every individual voter; after that the voting of the Réty-ward continued without a hitch.

While all this was happening to the electoral committee under the gateway our Tengelyi, outside among the canvassers, was striving mightily on Bántornyi's behalf; the latter was being hoisted aloft almost continuously now that voting had started and cursed his friends and relations a hundred times for their vanity, which was the cause of his present distasteful situation. He had spent all his life in his quiet country seat and was unaccustomed to the warm embrace of popularity, and could not, like Réty, smile sweetly and urge on the failing strength of those that carried him with encouraging words or inspire them with the occasional distinguished remark, as Napoleon's *mots* are reputed to have been repeated all round his army; and this Hungarian triumph, which resembled those of ancient Rome at least in that around the celebrant there was never a lack of those that disparaged him, was perhaps one of the most unpleasant moments in his entire life. Their parties, however, as everyone who has ever been in a similar position knows perfectly well, assaulted them not as men but merely so that they could be picked up and made into party banners; and when the banner is torn apart, or

206

to put it in simpler terms, when the candidate's *mente* is so reduced to rags as he is carted about that from what remains after so many vicissitudes no one can say that what he sees before him is a *mente*, the victorious party will proudly display its tattered colours with shouts of joy, as the crew which comes into harbour driven by a tempest rather than by a favourable wind greets the shore with noisy delight, though the poor ship is battered and in need of urgent repair. And Bántornyi pleaded, cursed, indeed kicked as he struggled to be put down, but in vain: he was held all the more tightly.

At the last minute, when he learnt of Master James's *public dinner* for eight hundred canvassers, Tengelyi was not a little cross with the Bántornyis who, as he said, had broken their word by resorting to the deplorable methods of the opposition and made themselves undeserving of the sympathy of all high-minded people; he therefore resolved to take no part in the election under such conditions. But what could be done about it! The law which Solon had given to the citizens of Athens, that no one might remain indifferent in conflicts between parties, was planted by nature itself in the heart of every honest man; and since Tengelyi, at the scene of the election, could hear the shouts of the Réty party, when Macskaházy, rubbing his hands together, told him that things were going well, and when Nyúzó was carried right past him by six St-Vilmos men, our honest Jónás could not resist and we find him making a speech among the nobility – or more precisely, Réty's opponents – in front of County Hall with more enthusiasm than any of Bántornyi's adherents. On this occasion the notary, like many another honest man in politics, was merely in the grip of reluctance to rejoin the party which he could no longer call his own. It goes without saying that the notary could not be as dangerous an opponent to Réty as those who had by then laid him on the floor together with his bearers for the third time – Tengelyi could not distinguish himself by those athletic or gymnastic feats which, as everyone knows, play a leading role at elections. But he knew all the faults of the county administration, and when he enumerated those through which the nobility suffered, he made a certain impression on not only the clergy, notaries, estate officers and better educated middle-order nobles – with whom he was always influential – but also on the canvassers, even though no small part of his address was lost in the uproar and, as many an honest man painfully experiences in addressing a crowd, the reasons which he considered most convincing had the least effect, and Réty's adherents were delighted to see the importunate speaker go into the gateway to vote and thus be separated from his audience.

But who could describe the amazement with which, on entering, Tengelyi saw the arrangements that had been put into effect on Sóskuty's advice to enable secret voting. "Really, Your Honour," said he to Sóskuty on seeing the two *táblabírós* instructing individual voters at the ballot boxes, "how can you permit this abuse, which is directly contrary to the county's resolution?"

"Abuse?" exclaimed Sóskuty, gaping in surprise. "What abuse, may I ask?"

Tengelyi had come under the gateway with Kálmán Kislaky, the St-Vilmos notary and a number of other nobles, and he turned to the assembled company and asked "Was secret voting not decided on at the last assembly?"

"And because that was the decision," said Sóskuty, "we are implementing the order. Or does Your Honour think that were it not so we would be sitting here under the gateway, would have erected that screen, and would not have been doing our work all this time? Secret voting! What else is this but secret voting?" said the baron, becoming more and more incensed. "Do I no longer suffer from rheumatism? And yet you dare to say that we're not carrying out the county's orders."

"Things can't go on like this," said Tengelyi with growing indignation, when he could see voting continuing in the old way contrary to instructions. "I'm going to report to the *főispán*, the whole election will have to be restarted."

"Notary, sir," exclaimed Slanacsek crossly, "apologise! And don't think that you're in front of a parish church council; vote, if you wish, but we don't take lessons from anyone, least of all – with a scornful glance – a village notary like you."

"Whether or not you take lessons," said Kálmán, who had always liked Tengelyi and had lost patience at Slanacsek's rudeness, "Mr Tengelyi is right, voting in the presence of two witnesses isn't secret."

"That's what I thought myself," interposed old Bálint. Now that he had found supporters his former doubts re-emerged. "But the wise majority . . ."

"I beg your pardon."

"*Rogo humillime.*"[123]

"Let me speak."

"I'll explain at once," exclamations all came at once from Slanacsek, Sóskuty and even a *táblabíró*, while the chairman succeeded in shouting them all down with his piercing voice.

---

123 Latin – I beg most humbly.

"Please, my dear young sir, as your father has most wisely observed, the wise majority of the committee has decided on the manner of voting, and so there can be no question of error. But even if not, in Hungary is not *testimonium legale* required, two judicial persons, to be able to give evidence of an event? But see here, my friend, those two worshipful gentlemen in there by the chest will testify that the nobility has voted in secrecy, *absque ira et studio*,[124] quite independently."

Kálmán laughed, Tengelyi – inaudibly in the din – commented on the sanctity of resolutions, and voting was abandoned until at length Nyúzó, with whom Macskaházy had exchanged a few words, with an expression of anger on his face and with a dignity that none can attain without spitting seized Tengelyi by the fur on his *mente* saying "Take yourself[125] off home, non-nobles have no say here," and pushed him towards the door.

Never did the words of the world's greatest orator have such an effect as did those simple words of Nyúzó's. When a year previously, after the great robbery carried out at the market in Porvár, it had emerged that it had been committed only by nobles, and indeed two distinguished gentlemen had been among the ringleaders; the entire county had been astonished; amazement had overcome the *táblabíró* body at the last court hearing too, when in wishing to call for a death sentence in the thirty-year-long action of a landowner the Chief Clerk announced with regret that the defendant had died the previous spring; there had not been such surprise in Porvár when Karvaly brought news of the battle of Győr from forty *mérföld*s away on the second day. Sóskuty clasped his hands together, Sáskay looked heavenward with a sigh, Slacsanek cast a scornful look at the whole company, and old Kislaky, who most of all felt sorry for Tengelyi, could only sigh inwardly "Who would have thought it!"

Tengelyi stood among the others, his face ablaze with fury, and his feelings didn't permit him to speak a single word.

Nyúzó looked around during the entire scene and perhaps enjoyed the discomfiture of the proud notary more than Macskaházy, who could scarcely conceal his heartfelt satisfaction.

"Yes," said the magistrate, addressing the committee, "astonished though Your Worships may be this person is not a nobleman, and since

---

124 Tacitus *Annals* 1:1 . . . without bitterness or partiality . . .
125 Students of Hungarian will note the use of the style *kend*, used only to peasants. A grave insult. See Aladár Schöpflin, *Nyugat* 1914, pp. 262–266.

I am duty-bound to report this I demand at the same time that he be prohibited from voting."

All those who had cast their votes were crowding in from the courtyard, and, attracted by the disturbance, milling around the committee. The entrance was packed with people.

Tengelyi slowly recovered his composure. "And who is going to prove to me that I am not noble?" said he with dignity.

"*Onus probandi semper privato incumbit,*"[126] replied the County Attorney; his little grey eyes blinked, and so fat was his belly that he could scarcely reach to the table.

"That's true," exclaimed Sóskuty, "*incumbit privato*, that is to say, it's up to you to prove your nobility." Here he broke off and was replaced by the County Attorney.

"Has the gentleman a royal deed of gift, a certificate of nobility, any authentic *transumtuma*s or just *statutoria*s with *cum nos* clauses, or at least what Werbőczi Part 1 heading 6 requires, evidence of the payment of the daughter quarter?"

"If you please," said Tengelyi testily to so many questions – which, like so many questions in this world, weren't being asked in order that they might be answered, "no one in Hungary can better prove his nobility than I, but . . ."

"Then simply do so," the County Attorney interrupted him, "perhaps we shall prove nearly sixty years of custom, but forget, sir, that for that too documents are necessary. Genealogy is proven by authentic letters of class or baptism, and by attested witness statements, if you please, Mr Tengelyi."

"My documents are in my house."

"Be so kind as to produce them. As soon as Mr Tengelyi produces his documents he may vote, may he not, Baron?"

"Yes, just let him produce the documents," exclaimed Sóskuty reassuringly.

"But I've always enjoyed the privileges of nobility, I've contributed to nobility funds."

"*Fraus et dolor nemini opitulatur,*"[127] interjected Sáskay. "Why has Mr Tengelyi not had his nobility proclaimed in the county?"

"But no one doubted my nobility," rejoined the notary, shaking with rage, "when I was a candidate for *szolgabíró*, when I was nominated for lawyer's clerk."

---

126 The burden of proof is always on the plaintiff.
127 Fraud and trickery assist no one.

"It's always good to make one's nobility publicly known," said the County Attorney didactically, presumably aware of what was useful if an opinion was required from the law department on such an occasion.

"You see, if you do that you'll have no more trouble. However, that you stood for office, indeed for a nobleman's office, proves nothing; how many similar cases have there been in which County Attorneys have been careful that the nobility don't increase contrary to the law, as a burden on the taxpayer."

James was unable to suppress the emotions which this last statement stirred in his heart. "Indeed, you're a noble being, Your Worship! If only the tax-payer were always to meet with such a defender!"

"But we can't waste our time," said Sóskuty impatiently. "Let's carry on with the voting, and let Master Tengelyi go home for his documents."

"I wish to vote," said Tengelyi with calm dignity, "a nobleman can't be deprived of his rights by a mere statement, and in a legal case over nobility everyone remains in his former condition as long as it lasts."

"Mr Tengelyi is right," interposed a young lawyer, one of the few that had taken the notary's side throughout the scene. "The royal proclamation . . ."

". . . of 21 July 1785," said the County Attorney, nodding.

". . . orders that," continued the lawyer, "while a suit for ennoblement is in progress everyone shall remain in their previous condition."

"That is, the condition of peasant, like the notary, until he produces his documents," replied Slanacsek.

"I've always regarded him as noble. You say something," said he, turning to Macskaházy, who had approached the table in the meantime. "We've known each other almost thirty years."

"All that I can say," replied Macskaházy, "is that His Worship the *al-ispán* has always treated the notary as a nobleman; however, His Worship is known to be a very generous man, whose kindness many repay with ingratitude. I've never seen Master Tengelyi's documents, and all that I know is that his nobility has never been publicised in the county, he comes from elsewhere, and there have been instances . . ."

"Throw him out! Out with the peasant!" howled the crowd, and Karvaly, his voice ringing out above the rest, pushed forward and took hold of Tengelyi's clothes. "Come here. you who love your life!"[128] shouted Kálmán, who had been turning from one to another throughout the scene, looking for those that would take Tengelyi's side. "Mr Tengelyi's

---

128 Presumably a reference to Luke 9:2g *He that loves his life shall lose it.*

my friend. Lay a finger on him and you're a dead man, even if God's given you sixteen lives."

Karvaly drew back in alarm, and old Kislaky hurried to his son's side and reminded him of his relationship to the Réty family. Baron Sóskuty, with great dignity, pointed out where he was, and the Chief Clerk cleared his throat and spoke of legal consequences.

Kálmán, however, wasn't one of those who, once their blood is up, can be guided by tactful advice. Cheerful, indeed frivolous in everyday life, there was something in his youthful bosom that raised him above ordinary men; and anyone that saw him in that moment as, his face ablaze, he defended the old notary among so any enemies, who heard his voice quivering with emotion, felt that he was looking at one of those men that, like certain gold-mines, are all the richer the deeper they are dug. Old Kislaky himself could not have said whether it was not pleasure that drew the tears that filled his eyes when he heard his son say "What do I care about relationships! When I see shameful behaviour, such as this is, I know only one relationship, that which exists between all decent men and makes it their duty not to suffer one of their number to be done down by wicked scheming."

"But, *domine spectabilis*, we're in County Hall," said Sáskay, raising his eyes to heaven.

"So help me God, one might forget that's where one was," said Kálmán in growing anger. "This house was built for the maintenance of public order and courage, and a decent man is being threatened with being struck down in it; here every citizen expects justice, and finds nothing but what the proverb says is found in wine; here we look for judges and we find cudgels. Really, one would think one were in a den of robbers on looking round in here."

"What! he objects to cudgels?" exclaimed a lieutenant of nobility. "He's abusing the nobility! Prosecute him!" The whole crowd called for prosecution, while Tengelyi, who had never in his life felt so moved as he was by Kálmán's unexpected behaviour, began to fear that he would be carried away by his noble temper and come to harm; he therefore requested to be escorted out of County Hall to find some means of going home for his documents.

"Prosecute him! Very well, gentlemen," said Kálmán scornfully, turning to the nobility. "Just do it in such a way that at least we can show from the documents in the case that it's enough in Taksony County for a person like this" – he gestured with inexpressible contempt at Nyúzó – "to just say something about an honest man for him to be immediately stripped of all his rights." And taking the signet ring from his finger he threw it onto the table, took Tengely by the hand and led him out.

"Come along, my friend, my horses will get us to Tiszarét in two hours, I'll drive myself, and by evening we'll be here with the documents."

There was a murmur among the nobles present, and Slanacsek, turning to Kálmán's father, said in a loud aside "If young Kálmán doesn't become a *szolgabíró*, Your Worship won't have us to blame." At which the old man gave a great sigh and the secret voting continued, though the screens had long ago been knocked over.

XVI

In the notary's house sorrow and anxiety prevailed after the recent events. The shot had only hit Ákos in the arm and the wound wasn't so very serious, and that young man, as soon as he came to himself, was taken to the mansion that very night; the robbery, however, the loss by which Erzsébet could not assess; the condition of Vilma, who had been trembling and weeping almost ceaselessly ever since Ákos had fallen to the ground; but mainly the fact that she had secretly received Ákos into her house despite her husband's prohibition – the whole tale was no doubt to be noised abroad salaciously to the detriment of her daughter's reputation – filled the good woman's heart with profound anxiety. Vilma was lying in her bed, the servants were running hither and thither, Mrs Lipták could scarcely keep the horde of enquirers at bay – their curiosity greatly increased the disorder – and anyone that had seen the house twenty-four hours previously now must have been truly sorrowed at our human fate, which gives such power to the unexpected not only over the fortune which we seek in the treasures of the external world, but also over that which only our hearts offer.

The family's only consolation was Vándory, and it was only thanks to his gentle encouragement that Vilma at length became calmer and towards midday dozed a little, while Mrs Erzsébet herself looked somewhat more bravely forward to the moment when she would confront her husband. Vándory had come to the house after the misfortune and hadn't left, and on examining the opened chest could see that his documents were all present but that most of Tengelyi's had been stolen. He realised the extent of the damage, but his belief that God would not desert the good on earth spread to the others too, and even Erzsébet herself, who, for the first time in their long marriage, was awaiting her husband's arrival with trepidation, calmed down to some extent.

"She's asleep," said Erzsébet as she came out of the adjacent room and closed the door quietly behind her. She went up to Vándory, who was reading by the window. "The poor thing's asleep. Oh my God! if Jónás sees his daughter looking so pale! She's usually so full of fun, so rosy-cheeked!" and tears flooded the mother's eyes.

"By the time that Tengelyi gets home," said the clergyman reassuringly, and closed his book, "Vilma will be well again. Ákos has forbidden any of the servants to tell anyone anything and the serfs have too much to do with the sowing to be put out, my friend can hardly be home before the election's over, and until then let's trust in God that Vilma will recover."

"Oh, I'm eternally unlucky!"

"Calm yourself, Mrs Erzsébet," said Vándory, laying his hand on her arm, "Praise be to God, Ákos's injury isn't serious and the loss in the robbery won't be irreplaceable. For the most part documents were taken, and those may be returned.

"Yes, but the faith that Jónás has had in me until now – who'll restore that? Who'll give me back the love, the respect, all the happiness that I had and which I've lost? Please don't let Ákos into our house, don't let Vilma speak to him, my daughter's peace of mind and reputation require it, and I'd promised to do as he wished, and now! My daughter's reputation! Oh, I've disobeyed him!" And Erzsébet sobbed in her agony.

"It's a bad situation, very bad," said Vándory consolingly, "but Tengelyi's too good to be unable to forgive. Be assured, I'll speak to him. And as for your daughter's reputation there's no cause for anxiety. Vilma and Ákos are engaged, and you never know, perhaps the light wound that he's received will be for the good, because at least neither the Rétys nor Jónás will be able to go on opposing the marriage."

"Oh, the Rétys!" rejoined Erzsébet tearfully.

"The Rétys? You're making them seem worse than they are. Réty's a weak man, but he's sound at heart, and she . . . is there a woman who'd stand in the way of her son's giving satisfaction like an honest man for his lack of caution, after such an incident? All can still go well."

"And when I think," said Erzsébet bitterly, wiping her eyes, "that Viola has brought all this upon us, when we'd taken in his wife and child in their hour of need."

"Who can say whether it was he?" said the clergyman solemnly. "You mustn't judge hastily."

"There's no doubt. As soon as the Jew had recovered somewhat he told us: he'd been going home in the dark when he saw that our gate was open; he knew that my husband was in Porvár and immediately suspected something wicked and came in. He found the door to my husband's room open as well and went in to see whether he'd come home. At that moment Viola was just coming out with his booty and knocked him to the ground. The blacksmith, who chased the would-be murderer, swears that it was none other than Czifra, one of Viola's men; and Mrs Lipták herself has admitted that he was in the village this evening, in

215

fact in her house. There's no doubt! The Jew's still sick in bed after being struck by Viola, you can question himself if you like."

"The Jew's lying," said a female voice, at which Erzsébet turned in surprise and Vándory calmly. It was Zsuzsi, Viola's wife, who had come in quietly during the conversation and, standing by the door, had heard Erzsébet's last words. "Viola's never robbed the house of an honourable woman, nor will he ever if he lives to be a hundred."

Words of powerful conviction are irresistible, and if among the many thousands who, since the world began, have tried to explain the mysteries of our existence by establishing one new religion after another, there's scarcely one that hasn't found at least a few adherents, we may ascribe it to the power over others that God has given to those who don't doubt; so too was that which poor Zsuzsi's words had even over Erzsébet in that moment.

"Blessed be the name of the Lord that it be so," said Vándory, who regarded everything that might weaken his faith in men as personal loss and was delighted at the effect which Zsuzsi's words had on Erzsébet.

"It is so, believe me, your reverence," said Zsuzsi, and her voice – deep, yet womanly and weak – shook as she spoke, "Viola's a poor, unfortunate man. He's been driven from his house and land, hunted and persecuted from one place to another like a wild beast, but Viola didn't do this. They can tear him to pieces, cut the heart from his body, but they won't find ingratitude in him."

"That's very nice of you, Zsuzsi," said Erzsébet, touched by this, "to defend your husband, because you swore not to desert him in trouble and poverty; I myself would like to believe that you're speaking the truth, but it's no use, everything points to your husband and I don't mean to offend you, you poor woman, it's not your fault, but when all's said and done he's an outlaw."

Erzsébet saw the expression on Zsuzsi's face at these words, and regretted saying them. Vándory consoled the poor woman with a few encouraging words, and meanwhile she stepped forward and leant on the table as which they were sitting.

"Yes, yes, Viola's an outlaw," she said eventually in a bitter tone, and the furrows on her forehead and the flush that came to her cheeks showed her feeling. "Don't bother, your reverence, the notary's wife is right, my husband's an outlaw and I'm the wife of a bandit; the whole village, the whole County knows there's a price on his head, every child talks of nothing else! But when the Day of Judgement comes round and

God appears on his throne with the angels around him as is written in scripture, and when He passes judgement on good and wicked and everybody's rewarded according to their deserts, he won't ask Viola why he became an outlaw, but He'll ask them that made him, that persecuted him when he'd done nothing. God's eternally just, he makes no difference between poor and rich, He can see hearts, and Viola will be able to stand upright in His presence."

As she said that Mrs Lipták, who meanwhile had come into the room and up to the table in her little sheepskin coat and her white head kerchief, nodded a greeting, laid a hand on Zsuzsi's shoulder and said "You're right, my girl, trust in God and He won't desert you." The others were touched and said nothing.

"Yes, yes, I trust in God," said Mrs Viola as she recognised the new arrival; she stared solemnly before her. "You've said that a hundred times, and what would a poor person do if they didn't trust in their God; but believe me, sometimes when I think of all our misfortunes, when I realise that nobody at all trusts us any more, that the most decent of people such as the reverend here and the notary's wife think that about us, that we're Judases in the sight of our greatest benefactors; then my guardian angel deserts me, and sometimes I just think that the poor have no God at all."

"Don't say things like that, Zsuzsi," said Mrs Lipták solemnly. "It's written that a camel goes through the eye of a needle more easily than a rich man into the kingdom of Heaven. We poor people have no cause to doubt the Lord's mercy, because God's Son chose his apostles from among the poor. If this good lady has said something that hurt you, just consider: she's your benefactor, and the best of people are unreasonable when they've suffered harm; my own husband, God rest his soul, suspected Peti the Gypsy once when our cow was driven off. Bear your cross calmly, like our Redeemer."

"Yes, but he was the Son of God," said Zsuzsi with a sigh, "and I'm a weak human being, and does anyone know what I've endured? I was a poor orphan, my father and mother died when I was young, and if you hadn't taken me in I might have perished like other children that have no mothers to look after them. As it was, God bless you for it, I grew up with the rest and there wasn't a happier girl in the village than me. My mother died giving birth to me, but it never entered my head that anybody could have loved me more than you."

Vándory and Erzsébet were moved and said nothing. Tears gleamed in Mrs Lipták's eyes.

"Yes, I was a happy child," said Zsuzsi, warming to her theme. "I thought I couldn't be happier, and I thanked God from morning to night for so much good fortune. And yet, it had all been nothing. It was only after I got to know Viola that I knew what it was to have heaven on earth. At first I never so much as thought that a man like him could love me. He was rich, he'd inherited a whole piece of land from his father, and his house was the finest in the village after the notary's, his cattle had horns – I was a poor orphan girl, how could I believe that he would love me? When I was out in the fields reaping he would stop with his four oxen where I was working and help me to tie my sheaves, or he would fill my bucket with water from the Tisza, or sometimes at a wedding he would wear a sprig of rosemary and dance with me. I used to think, Viola's a good man, but that he'd marry me never crossed my mind, and I prayed that God would keep me from such vain thoughts. But when he came to our house at Christmas and asked me if I loved him, and when I didn't speak but just looked at the ground, and he took me by the waist and held me close and said that he'd marry me by Carnival-time, the world spun around me and I thought the angels would envy my good fortune."

"Poor woman," said Erzsébet, wiping her eyes.

"Oh, then I wasn't!" she went on, her face ablaze. "Then the whole world was a great wedding-feast, my heart almost stopped for delight, at that moment I could have wept like a child. And yet all that was but a drop in the ocean compared to the happiness that I found later in my husband's house. When our first child was born and we could do every-thing for little Pista's benefit God's blessing was on our house and fields, our cattle came on nicely, our wheat yielded well. Oh, so many brides go happily to their husband's house, but for me every day seemed finer than the last, and I couldn't even remember my wedding, I felt so fortunate."

Mrs Viola, as if overcome by the emotion that the memory of those happy days aroused in her breast, was silent for a moment, and then went on in a hoarse voice, interrupting her account from time to time as if her strained bosom couldn't hold sufficient breath for her to relate all her woe. "Yes, and as you see all that came to an end, and what hurts is that we weren't boastful in our happiness, we never caused anyone at all any grief. My husband paid his taxes, served his fifty-two *marhás* days,[129] and if he saw a poor man he'd share his last crust with him. Even so, God deserted us. Viola could stand up for himself, but he was only a

---

129 *Marha* = farm animals. A peasant would have to work once a week on the landown-er's land with his own animals.

peasant, and he made enemies among the gentry. The lawyer, God damn him," – said Zsuzsi, clenching her hands into fists, "hated my husband because every time the other peasants had trouble, for example when they were often called on for too much socage or something, they always chose him as their spokesman; and the magistrate swore vengeance, because the wretch came after me, and as a decent woman I drove him out of my house, as was right; and I was always afraid, though my husband used to say that as long as he did his duty he wasn't afraid of the anger of the lawyer or the magistrate. But the gentry close ranks, and poor men's innocence is no defence against them. It was in autumn two years ago when my daughter was being born and I was feeling ill in the morning, my husband and Mrs Lipták were with me, when the lawyer sent word, presumably because he'd learned of our situation from the midwife, for Viola to go at once with four horses to the big house, to take Her Honour to Porvár. He went out and told the *hajdú* that he couldn't go that day, he'd already harnessed up as often that year as any of the other farmers, and he'd gladly go at any other time but not that day because I was in child-bed. We thought that that was the end of it, but half an hour later the *hajdú* came back and said that however I might be my husband couldn't escape his obligation and he must go, because nobody in the village had better horses. Viola was cross, but when I asked him to send the horses with our stable-lad, so as to avoid any arguments, he did that, but very reluctantly, because he didn't like to trust anyone else to handle the horses. And again we were left in peace. I'd gone into labour when back came the *hajdú* with our driver and said that Viola was to go, because Her Honour was afraid with any other driver. Viola could see that I was in pain and couldn't be left, and he said that whatever they did he'd done all he could by sending his horses and he himself wouldn't leave me even for the king's son. To which the *hajdú* said that he himself wouldn't act differently, but even so he'd do better to go, because the *szolgabíró* was at the big house and had sworn that if he wouldn't go voluntarily he'd be taken to the big house by force, and then he'd see what he got. My husband's a temperamental man, can be obstinate at times, and he cursed and sent to the *szolgabíró* that he'd harnessed up plenty of times and that that day he wasn't going even for the sake of God. The *hajdú* went away; what happened next I don't know, I was so unwell that I couldn't hear or see anything that was going on, but as the neighbours and Mrs Lipták here tell me, as soon as the *hajdú* got back to the mansion the magistrate and his gendarmes came to our house and dragged

Viola cursing out of the room where I was lying unconscious, tied him up and carried him off to the mansion."

"That's right," interposed Mrs Lipták, and she took up the tale – those present understood that we often do that if something affects us deeply – for Zsuzsi, who was in tears and covering her eyes with her hands. "That's exactly what happened. When Viola was taken away I went after him. It was terrible to see. He refused to go, threw himself on the ground in his rage, and the jailers dragged him like an animal, it made my hair stand on end. The whole village followed in sympathy, but nobody dared help him and we could only weep inside ourselves and complain that an innocent man was being beaten with sticks and *fokos*es simply because he wouldn't go somewhere. The *szolgabíró* went in front, cursing and threatening that Viola was going to pay the price for his stubbornness. I nearly forgot about Zsuzsi and went with them all the way to the big house, as if I could sense the trouble there was going to be. Scarcely had we got there than the magistrate asked the *hajdú*, in front of us all, whether he'd been to Viola's house, and how often, had he told him that he was summoned to the service of the gentry, and what had Viola said, and I don't know how many questions. "Now then," he said at length, as he had him taken to the whipping-post, "we'll see if you won't come to the service of your betters another time, I'll give you swearing, I'll give you saying that you won't come to the service of God or the noble County. Flog him!" Viola was standing there among the gendarmes; if I live to be a hundred I'll never forget the sight. His head had been split in two places by *fokos* blows, his face was bloodied and his lips were so compressed with fury as to be almost blue. His hands had been tied and in the courtyard they were released, and now he tore himself away from the *hajdús*' grasp, bounded forward like a lion and shouted "If you value your life keep clear." Everybody fell back. But Nyúzó cursed and swore by his soul that if they didn't flog him at once he'd have them all disembowelled, and they all rushed at him. Then Viola looked around and caught sight of an axe that had just been brought into the yard, they'd been splitting logs, and which the devil had thrown his way, he grabbed it and swung it round, and a gendarme and the bailiff fell to the ground bleeding. The crowd parted in horror, Viola ran through, rushed home, jumped on a horse and made for the St-Vilmos forest like Cain pursued by God. The bailiff died, and Viola hasn't lived among people ever since."

"And since then Viola's been an outlaw." said Zsuzsi, wringing her hands and shaking from head to foot, while Mrs Lipták guided her to a chair and Vándory looked heavenward with a sigh.

The simple story, the truthfulness of which was as well known to Vándory and Mrs Tengelyi as to anyone in Tiszarét, and even more the inexpressible pain that could be seen on the unfortunate woman's face, made a deep impression on those present, and only old Mrs Lipták's voice broke the solemn silence that reigned in the room as she held Zsuzsi's cold hands and tenderly spoke her name over and over. Where a corpse is laid out people surround the bier in silence; who would find the power of speech when faced with the much more saddening image of extinguished human happiness. Finally Mrs Viola stood up; her pale face was calmer, her voice stronger as she came to the table and said "Now may God bless you, Mrs Tengelyi, for all that you've done for me and my poor children. I'm going to go and find Viola, and if he knows anything about the stolen items or can track them down, fear not, Master Tengelyi will have them back."

"What are you thinking of? I'm not letting you go like this," said Erzsébet, and she stood up.

"Don't be alarmed," said Zsuzsi with a bitter smile, "I'm not going to run away, I'll leave the children here, and you'll see, even if I'm only the wife of an outlaw I won't abandon them."

"That's not what I meant, Zsuzsi," said Mrs Tengelyi gently, reaching out to stop her. "But you're still not very well, and if you go out on a cold October day like this it could make you worse."

"Thank you," said Zsuzsi gratefully, "but I'm feeling better again, I'll just go as far as the fields and the fresh air will bring my colour back. I can't stay here. Viola's under grave suspicion. I know all about it. The Jew and the rest are plotting against him; there's no denying that he was in the village, his coat was found in this room, everything's against him, and other people don't know that what they accuse him of is impossible. I must clear this up and I'd die in agony if I stayed here and heard all those dreadful things about him. God bless you, Mrs Tengelyi." And she turned and made for the door, followed by Mrs Lipták.

"Poor woman," sighed Erzsébet sadly, watching her go. "She too has deserved better in the world."

"Deserved better?" said Mrs Viola sharply, turning at the door as she heard those words. "Believe you me, if I were born again today and could foresee all that I'd suffer as Viola's wife I still wouldn't marry anyone else. They can hang him, and I'll sit under the gallows and thank God that I've been his wife. There isn't another heart in the world as noble as his. God bless you for your kindness." And with that she left.

221

"I'd venture to swear," said Vándory, when at length he stood up and went to the window as Zsuzsi and Mrs Lipták went past, "that Viola's innocent. A man whose wife can love him like that after eight years of marriage can't be bad."

"Who can say!" replied Erzsébet with a sigh. "The female heart's a strange thing, and thorns through which it's been will often hold it more firmly than if fate had laid it on a bed of roses; but it's sure that Zsuzsi's an angel, and you begin to doubt divine providence when you see a fate like that come to such a one."

"Doubt divine providence," said Vándory sharply. "But didn't you hear what she said as she took her leave? The hand of fate has lain heavy upon her and fate often lays the weightiest burdens on the most noble shoulders, but isn't she happy all the same? That love, which fills her breast, which resounds in every beat of her heart, which makes the life of her life, doesn't it give her more joy, more inward satisfaction, than if we amass around it all the pleasures that sometimes accrue to certain wicked persons? Possibly Viola's unworthy of such constancy, perhaps this good woman's deceived, but the good can be so often disappointed, withstand their disappointments for so long, and, like the idolater before the soulless statue, be filled in the presence of the worthless one that has captivated their heart with the same lofty feelings that raise one up in the dust of this world; doesn't that very fact make her happiness? Doesn't it cause us to reckon up the good and bad times of life and reach the conclusion that in the end the scales don't turn against the good? Oh, Mrs Erzsébet! Believe me, we've nothing for which to pity anyone that's loved like that!"

The clergyman was interrupted by the arrival of Tengelyi. He'd set off with Kálmán after the scandalous scene at the voting that we have witnessed, and on the way met one of the sons of Iczik the Jew. His father had sent him to Porvár to take news to Macskaházy, and from him Tengelyi heard what had happened. From that moment the travellers flew as far as the causeway extended, that is, all the way to the Réty mansion, and there Kálmán drove off the causeway with a great clatter and found that there is no urgency that can contend with Hungarian roads in autumn, especially with those that pass through villages, and when the weary horses finally became stuck in the mud as they approached Tengelyi's house they both got down. Tengelyi thanked Kálmán for his kindness and hurried home on foot.

"Is it true that we've been robbed?" said he as he came in, looking round the room.

"Just your chest was robbed," replied Erzsébet tremulously, "everything else . . ."

"My chest? The keys? Where are my keys?"

"Presumably in your drawer, but the chest is open."

Tengelyi threw off his sheepskin and hurried to the chest, flung back the lid, knelt beside it and began to pull out the documents. The others stood in anxious silence beside him, assessing the seriousness of the loss by the expression on his face. Eventually he stood up, collapsed onto a chair and covered his pale face with his hands. "I'm finished!" he gasped. "My documents are lost and no one will help me." Erzsébet and Vándory said all that they thought might console him in his distress, but he, speechless in his pain, made no reply, and it could only be seen from the occasional irritated shake of his head that he could hear what they said.

"Very well, very well," said he at length as he stood up. "Only the documents have been lost, haven't they? I know, I know! You found the money here on the doorstep, didn't you? But do you realise that we've lost our nobility? Yes, my dear wife, don't gape at me like that! We and our children are ignoble, we're peasants! The sort that is despised, trampled underfoot, owns no land, must be worthless; the sort that live in these hovels around us here, not foreigners because they were born here, and there's nowhere on earth that they might call their country, and yet not natives because your country is what you may call your own."[130]

Tengelyi strode up and down the room and the others looked at each other in amazement. The painful silence was finally broken by the notary, as he stood facing Vándory and told him what had happened in Porvár. "Now," he ended bitterly, "you know everything. Proof of my noble status is required. I came here from another county. As a clergyman, my father paid no attention to his status, my rights were never questioned, and so I didn't think to have my nobility declared in this county, and now the documents with which I could have done that have been stolen. My poor son!"

And he sank back onto his chair and covered his eyes with his hands.

"Jónás," said Vándory, placing a hand on his friend's shoulder, "you know, I too have suffered loss, and you don't know how great it is, how much it affects things that are perhaps closest to my heart in this world – but let's have faith in God!"

---

130 Eötvös's point is that the peasantry were not part of the *nemzet*, the nation. They had no say in the running of Hungary, which was the prerogative of the Estates.

"Have you a child?" said Tengelyi, looking hard at Vándory. "Is your loss going to ruin your son's life?"

"I fully sympathise with your distress. You can be sure," – he added, taking his hand – "that if indeed this blow of fate comes upon you and you are deprived of your noble status no one would more share the grief with which you bear it on account of your son; but must we abandon all hope immediately? Isn't it possible, indeed probable, that the documents that are of no use to the robbers will find their way back to you somehow or other? And even if that were not to happen, can you not offer proof? Your documents have been stolen, but both you and your father enjoyed the privileges of nobility. You could petition the king, there are a hundred ways by which you can recover your nobility."

"Me, petition the king? A poor village notary!" "And why not?" said Vándory with spirit. "If we don't find your documents I'll go up to Vienna and prostrate myself at the foot of the throne and explain all that's happened to you, say that you have children, your son, who is now deprived of noble status by misfortune. The heart of one to whom God has granted such power will certainly be softened when he hears of your misfortune."

"Why don't we live in your dream world," said Tengelyi sadly, "the world isn't as nice as that! You, a village pastor of the Calvinist Church, will go to Vienna and ask before the throne for noble status for a village notary! Oh, you're a happy man indeed to have lived so long and not to have learnt from the varied tale of life the one sorry lesson that we can find in it."

"You're going to say that I'm an optimist again, aren't you?" said Vándory gently. "Do you think that because I'm a poor clergyman I daren't appear before the king? Have no fear, I've enough courage for that, and the whole County will support my request. Anybody that gives the king the opportunity to use his power in a charitable act has no reason to blush in his presence; making a request is like offering a present. The king is so exalted that in his presence the village clergyman can feel like the distinguished lords by whom he is otherwise scorned."

"My friend," said Tengelyi, springing up impatiently from his chair, "optimism is a fine, good thing, but everything has its limits! The County will support your request? But can't you see that the whole robbery is no chance affair, but part of a whole plot for my downfall that has been devised by those gentlemen from whom you now expect support for me. Or perhaps you think that it's pure coincidence that my noble status has never been called into question until the moment when my documents have been stolen and I can no longer defend myself? Coincidence that only my opponents were appointed to the committee? Or that it was only this morning, when these gentlemen had learnt that I'd been robbed by their associates, that anyone reminded me that my noble status hadn't been declared in this County yet and I must see about it? Was this all blind chance, mere coincidence? Oh, if you'd seen Macskaházy standing there by the committee table, staring at me with his little grey eyes, wicked pleasure on his face, you wouldn't say such things. I'm the victim of a fiendish plot – Viola's merely an unknowing tool, that you can believe – and because I wasn't prepared to join in the underhand acts, be the tool of the oppressors, become one of the persecutors, my pride had to be stamped out. No one will help me."

"For God's sake, Jónás, don't talk like that," said Erzsébet, seizing her husband's hand. "It breaks my heart to see you so despairing. Think back, how many difficulties we've come through, how often we've felt hopeless, and . . ."

An indescribable pain flickered on Tengelyi's face, he squeezed his wife's hand, which had remained in his own, and in a subdued, tremulous voice enquired what had become of his daughter.

Erzsébet paled and said nothing.

"Erzsébet!" he asked again, looking closely at her, "what's become of my daughter?"

She was appalled at the expression on his face and again said nothing, and Vándory struggled for words with which to give his friend an account of what had happened.

"Is that so?" said Tengelyi at length, pushing his wife's hand away. "My daughter's dishonoured."

Erzsébet was in tears, and Vándory did all that he could to ease his friend's pain, and they took turns in insisting on Ákos's sense of honour, the young couple's love, and that there could be no question of dishonour. Tengelyi stood there, leaning on the table, pale of face, and not a word came from his quivering lips that could console Erzsébet.

"Yes, yes," he said eventually with a bitter smile, "everything's in order, things couldn't be better. I'll recover my noble status and my daughter her honour, isn't that so, Vándory? You'll go up to Vienna and His Majesty will restore everything, everything! Oh, if there were a place in the world where a woman could recover her good name!"

Once more Vándory said a few encouraging words: there was no reason why Ákos and Vilma should not meet if her mother was present; and that Ákos had come to the house with honourable intentions.

225

"So he came to my house in the fashion of an honourable man?" Tengelyi cut in, becoming more and more embittered. "If anyone hears that he rode off from Porvár in secret, tethered his horse outside to the garden hedge, crept into my house in the dark of night like a thief when he wasn't permitted in consequence of my explicit wish, and was here with my daughter at midnight, who's going to believe in his honourable intentions?"

"The future will show that best of all," said Vándory calmly. "When your Vilma becomes Mrs Réty, who will dare say anything?" Erzsébet quietly echoed those words.

"When she becomes Mrs Réty, you say, wife?" said Tengelyi in fury, turning to Erzsébet. "Was that your wish, when it had all taken place did you perhaps inwardly bless your God for the event that had certainly bound Ákos? And do you realise that you've gambled with your daughter's happiness, that she'll curse your memory for having sacrificed the happiness of her life to your vanity? My daughter as Mrs Réty! Because she'd been compromised, because Ákos had no other way out; accepted into the house that she goes to with disdain and hatred by the family, which won't admit her into their circle but will tolerate her, she'll be torn from her natural position, an inferior, accepted out of kindness by her husband, who'll only remember being forced to take her to the altar and not the love which he found in her arms. You've made our child wretched."

Erzsébet wept.

"Weep, weep for the rest of your life, you hapless woman," said Tengelyi in a rage, "there aren't enough tears in the world to wash away your sin. Was there a better, more loving child in the world than your daughter, and what have you made her into? She was the pride of my life, it made my heart young to look at her, I forgot my past, almost began to love people again when I went among them and heard nothing but praise for her, and now! If I'm going to have to blush, to cast my eyes down like an evil-doer when Vilma's mentioned . . ."

"For God's sake, have pity," said Erzsébet, reeling against the chair. "if you love me, if you ever have."

"If I've ever loved you? Almighty God knows how I've loved you; have you ever heard a harsh word from my lips since the day we were married, have you ever wished for anything that I didn't do, has there been a thought that I've kept from you? And what have you done after all that love? You knew my opinion, I asked you not to let Ákos into our house and you gave your word, but the moment that you did so the plan

226

to deceive me was there ready. He knew beforehand the day on which he would disobey my order, you taught your daughter how to trick her father, and while I was confidently away from home and savouring the moment when I would be able to rejoin the only people on this earth that I could trust, the two of you were awaiting your guest and wishing for nothing but that I should not for some reason come home unexpectedly. That's how you've returned my love."

"God can see my soul, Jónás, I haven't deserved this from you."

A wild fire blazed in Tengelyi's eyes. "Don't speak to me," he shouted, beside himself with rage, "go away and leave me in peace if you don't want me to curse the moment when I went to the altar with you, to curse . . ."

Before he could continue, the door to the other room opened and Vilma stepped quickly out, sank at her father's feet and exclaimed in an imploring tone: "Father!"

Jónás had suffered so much that day; he had seen himself attacked in his status as a citizen, offended in his paternal feelings, and deceived by the one person in whom he had always trusted. He hadn't been able to overcome his feelings over the ruin of his former happiness, and his anger was as boundless as the pain that he felt. Vilma's gentle voice gave a different direction to his passion. The hand uplifted to curse was lowered softly to the dear child's brow, the harsh words ceased in her tender presence as she embraced his knees and looked pleadingly up at her stricken father.

"Can you forgive your Vilma?" said she weakly.

"Come to my heart," said Tengelyi, raising her up. Father and daughter lay in one another's arms and wept.

XVII

As my readers are aware, Ákos's wound wasn't serious. The ball had passed through his left arm leaving the bone undamaged, and the young man was almost ashamed, as he put it, of losing consciousness even for a moment because of such a trifle. The surgeon, however, who was summoned post-haste from St-Vilmos, and even more so Vándory – because the former, for all his diplomas, would scarcely have met with acquiescence – ordered the patient to bed because of the inevitable traumatic fever. And it is there that we now find him, in a rather poor humour among the pillows, while his friend Kálmán, cigar in hand, sits at his bedside and his old servant János dresses the injured limb from time to time with a cold compress. The room in which we find the friends is spacious and comfortable. There are newspapers and books on the tables, and on the walls pictures of a number of famous Hungarians and of as many famous English horses; the wall between the two windows is covered in green baize, and the weapons and riding and driving whips on it frame a couple of fox's brushes and hare's ears, indicating that this hunting equipment is not mere decoration; in addition the necessary number of pipes, tobacco and cigars are everywhere, and a couple of elegant caps, made by female hands, decorate the cupboard – in short, everything reminds us that we are in a young gentleman's room, and we must also mention the armchairs which, as is well known, in a Hungarian country house have hitherto only been found in the young master's room; it is not for me to say whether this is because the younger generation didn't care for seated occupations and parents considered it appropriate to lure them into sitting by means of good chairs; or because our elders feel that their debt to the fatherland is only to be paid off by sitting, and so that their worth may be the greater they wish to perform these their duties in the most difficult way possible – by sinking onto chairs each of which is a veritable instrument of torture; or finally perhaps because we have become degenerate and the generation that came before us, to judge by its chairs at least, was ten times tougher; it is, however, a fact that in all the Réty mansion there was not a chair to be compared with Ákos's, and that on one occasion Kenyházy the clerk could not rise all afternoon from the very one where Kálmán is now seated – which those present attributed to the excellence of the chair.

228

However, all this comfort, augmented by the fire that blazed in the stove, failed to raise the young men's spirits. So much had happened since Ákos and Kálmán had parted in Porvár! Since such unexpected trouble had come upon him in the midst of his happiness Ákos's spirit had been filled with premonitions; while Kálmán, who had once again offended the Rétys by the warmth of his sympathy for Tengelyi, though he didn't regret it could see in it a further obstacle raised between Etelka and himself; and the young men, after exchanging accounts of what had happened to them, were deep in silent thought. There was silence in the room, and even Tünde, Ákos's favourite *agár*, seemed to share her master's ill humour and lay curled up on the bedside rug, and if she looked up at him now and then she growled quietly and closed her eyes again. Only old János, as he went about the room from time to time, his spurs jingling as he brought a fresh ice-pack or something else, sometimes shook his head as he saw his young master's gloomy face.

"Your Honour!" he said eventually, as he removed the dressing from Ákos's arm with more willingness than skill.

"Do be careful!" exclaimed Ákos.

"Oh, I'm an old fool!" sighed the old man. "I'm always so clumsy."

"Never mind, it's all right now," said Ákos, feeling sorry for his loyal servant and at the same time smiling at his efforts to be as gentle as possible. "What were you going to say?"

"Just that we're certainly getting some bad weather," replied János.

Ákos turned toward the window and said that it was dreadful. Kálmán stood up and looked out for a while into the garden, where the faded leaves that still hung on the trees, the colourless lawn and the fog that enveloped the whole landscape, indeed the whole gloomy November day, could not fail to dismay even the most cheerful with their funereal appearance; he returned to his chair with a sigh and was silent again, while János put more wood on the fire, shook his head and muttered an imprecation against Kálmán: there he sat gaping with a stupid smile and saying nothing, instead of entertaining the patient.

"They're lifting the potatoes now," said János, going back to the bedside and stroking his long moustache, "and they'll all be rotten."

"Possibly," said Ákos, and the silence returned.

"Well," sighed János, "nobody had better go coursing round here, on a wet day like this they'll ruin all the crops."

No one answered, only Tünde stood up, turned round a couple of times, and lay down again.

"This dog's completely fed up with it, Your Honour!" remarked János, doing his utmost to spark off a conversation but failing. Finally he left the room and returned with a fresh cold compress.

"But you've only just done that," said Ákos irritably.

"It's supposed to be changed as often as possible, Your Honour."

"Never mind, let me have it," said Ákos, and the wound was dressed once more. János was going out with the old dressing when suddenly an idea seemed to come to him, and he stopped. "Your Honour?" he said.

"What is it?"

"Well, it's just, by your leave, don't take it to heart, Your Honour, it's nothing to worry about, no lasting harm done."

"What am I not to take to heart? said Ákos in surprise.

"Well, it's just that little business, the gunshot wound. I know it doesn't feel good, because I've had a bit to do with it myself. I fought at Aspern and later at Leipzig,[131] and I stopped one or two from the Frenchies in France as well, but no harm done! You mustn't take it to heart, Your Honour. They say God made all women from a rib, and where the bone's all there a whole soldier'll still come out of it."

"Fathead, you're not imagining that I'm worried about my injury?"

"What then, Your Honour?" said János cheerily, as a conversation had started, "because I know very well everything hurts worse for a gentleman like you. When we were on the march if one of the young gentlemen in the regiment so much as cut his little finger they didn't half take it badly, some even went into hospital! Eventually they got used to it. Everybody's the same in war, swords and bullets go into one same as another, and they mend up just the same; officers feel hungry same as privates, and if they get anything they eat just the same. In peacetime you wouldn't think . . ."

Ákos smiled, but his face assumed the same sorrowful expression when he said with a sigh: "Believe me, János, if I had no other problems than this scratch you wouldn't see me looking so miserable."

"Other problems? Really! Well now, I must be forgetting," said the old hussar, smiling broadly as he bowed his head in an effort to let it be known that he was perfectly aware of Ákos's problem. "The notary's little Vilma, you mean, don't you? Ah, that love business is like tobacco,

---

131 The battle of Aspern-Essling (22 May 1809) was Napoleon's first personal defeat. That at Leipzig took place from 16 – 19 October 1813, and was the end of Napoleon's military ambitions. János must have been in the coalition force that pursued the French home.

when it's fresh it's so strong it brings tears to your eyes if you so much as look at it. But do you know what I'd do if I was you, Your Honour?"

"What?"

"Marry her."

"Fathead, if it was only up to me!"

"Who then, Your Honour? Really!" said the old man, scratching his head, "you won't be disabled because of this little wound, and even if, believe you me, someone had three hands and you'd only the one, Vilma wouldn't marry anyone else. I'll be damned if Vilma ever marries anyone but Your Honour." And with that the old man shook his head repeatedly and left the room, still muttering something between his teeth.

In the eyes of some of my readers the friendly relationship between János and his master may seem surprising. In order to understand it they need to know that old János, who could read a little but could not write, returned from the wars in 1814 as a corporal with a silver medal and a cross, found employment as a doorman with Taksony County, and shortly afterwards entered the service of Ákos's father, then a *szolgabíró*. Since that time, long before Ákos came into the world, János had not left the Rétys. When his master rose from *szolgabíró* to *alispán* János was, as he put it, promoted with him. He had been present at Ákos's mother's funeral and had gone with his master to ask for the hand of his second wife (whom we have met in this tale); and if the worthy soldier wasn't as much in favour as he deserved with the *alispán*'s new wife, and although Her Honour too was not entirely to his liking, and he often spoke not only to Ákos but in the servants' quarters about the better times past when the first lady in the mansion had been *tekintetes* rather than *nagyságos*, the Rétys and János could not part because, as the latter said: bread becomes flesh in a man, and so the worthy man who has eaten someone's bread for so long becomes his, body and soul; and because if the old man sometimes grumbled and at lunch broke more plates and bottles than was proper the Rétys knew very well that they might find a smarter man and that there were many faces in the world whom the yellow-braided blue *dolmány* would match better than it did János's ruddy cheeks – the colour of red paprika mixed with fine white salt, and adorned only with a long scar on the forehead and a huge moustache – but that nowhere would they find a more loyal man who could be relied on in all situations; and Her Honour herself was much kindlier towards him than to the other servants, perhaps because she esteemed these qualities or perhaps because it pleased her to be served at table by one on whose chest she could see many-coloured ribbons. On such

231

terms were János and Ákos. Habit is the most powerful instrument of influence. Ministers who have held office for a long time become necessary even when their powers wane and even if they lose the confidence of their prince, and though everyone knows their faults it is impossible to part with them; no wonder then that János's importance had risen from day to day, especially when we learn that the office of butler, which, because of her excessive precision, Her Honour was constantly changing, was always filled at such times by the hussar, who, when he spoke of the Rétys, never referred to them as anything but *we*; and he took the honour of the entire house to heart as much as did the *alispán* himself.

We always find friendly relationships between the children and servants of grand houses. It can't be otherwise. It is one of our human weaknesses: we are happy to converse with those whom we regard as superior to us and who nevertheless treat us as if we were the superiors, and nowhere is this desire so satisfied as between children and servants. The servant likes to be able to talk on an even footing to someone whom he calls the young master, whose boots he cleans, indeed, in whose employment he will one day be, even though the young master is now only three feet tall; the child is pleased that at last he has found a grown-up with a big moustache who will chat to him in a friendly manner when his father, mother and the rest whom he meets in the grand rooms take no notice of him, or at all events treat him as nothing more than a child. Young master and footman therefore form a close friendship which fosters more and more countless little services and countless secrets by which parents and the gentry are deceived, and which, even if it sometimes results in the servant being dismissed – forming the first of those sorry experiences which we have in the world through our desire for equality – is none the less pleasant.

During his time in the army the old hussar had liked nothing more than children, and he looked forward to the pleasure of being quartered in villages and being able to carry his landladies' children around in his arms, and every time, as he said, he would become fond of the youngsters and then be quartered elsewhere: but since Ákos came into the world better days had dawned. While the child was still with his wetnurse the hussar, when occasion permitted, danced attendance on him. When Mrs Lipták – as we know, she was his wet-nurse – left the room János would take him in his arms and if Ákos sometimes smiled as he dandled him on his knee he would laugh aloud for joy. When the child began to crawl on his rug and finally to walk János would sit beside him on the floor and take care that he should not fall and hurt himself; and when he first uttered *dada* János's eyes shone with pleasure, because it seemed to him at least that he was trying to say "János". It was only after Ákos's little hands had tugged at it that his long moustache, of which he had always been proud, won its full value in his eyes – in other words, old János spent all his time with his young master, and if his master admonished him at times, saying that the hussar had become a nanny, his heart, into which Heaven had poured so much affection, felt satisfied for the first time when little Ákos returned his feelings in full measure.

Children are sometimes born with a feeling for beauty, and we see not infrequently that the most difficult, who shrink in tears from all strangers, will cling affectionately at once to a beautiful woman; but if beauty has no effect on some children and if Ákos was presumably of that number – there was no one that he was gladder to see than János – that natural instinct by which a child always recognises those by whom he is loved, and by which he is as rarely deceived as he often is by later experience – that instinct sprang up strongly in him too, and Ákos never felt happier or more at ease than when he could be with János.

Réty was one of those men who, once they have an heir in the world, think of nothing but that his inheritance shall be as large as possible; after the death of Ákos's mother, therefore, there were no further obstacles to Ákos and János's conversations, and indeed the young tutor who came to the house when Ákos was seven was pleased to see that he could entrust his charge to the old hussar while himself attending to all the numerous occupations that burden the shoulders of a young gentleman. If there were truth in the world, and indeed if it could be tolerated in novels, I would say that Ákos was brought up by the old hussar; but at least I can state for a fact that there was not one of the boy's pleasures for which he didn't have his old friend to thank. On fine days he walked with him in the park and the fields, if there was a breeze he flew the big kite which he had made himself from fine golden paper; if it rained he worked the little mill and the boats which at such times were launched to the boy's great delight into the channels that crossed the courtyard, and on long winter evenings too Ákos's only pleasure were the wonderful fairy-tales and long stories which the old soldier told for hours, twirling his moustache the while.

János had been born in a great time, when the existence of every country seemed to be questioned once again, when ancient situations were altered or decided on the outcome of battles, and every nation, one might say every man, had to make a great effort to maintain its former place; like his whole generation he had lived through a lot. He had joined the colours at the age of sixteen and had seen close-to and taken part in the events about which he now told his young master in the evenings. János's account had certain shortcomings: to that day he could not conceive, for example, what those damn Frenchies had wanted with their revolution, and although his regiment had kept being ordered to withdraw he persisted in the slight historical error that Hungarian armies had won the war from start to finish; nevertheless, listener and speaker satisfied one another completely. Like all children, Ákos wanted as many details as possible. János, as a man of the people, was always only too glad to provide them, and it can't be denied that Ákos learnt his first history from his father's footman. That this differed from what we learn in school or from books gave him no reason for doubt: just as there is little mention of the common people in our history books, so in János's accounts there wasn't much about the leadership and the upper classes, but there remains one big question: did this render his accounts less truthful or more worthless? Thus all Ákos's powers of imagination were influenced by János. He took his first role model from these tales, and this was naturally not Napoleon but Captain Horvát, under whom János had served, and who seemed much the greater man of the two; from these tales he derived all that he knew, and it is well known that one who can influence a child's capacity for imagination imparts direction to his whole world; János, however, loved in him all the memories of his past, of which he never said as much to anyone as to Ákos. I don't know what would have happened had *alispán* Réty not sent János with him as his valet when he sent his son to school in Pest.

There the relationship seemed to become somewhat less amicable. Ákos made younger friends, and his studies and life offered new interests to his heart and mind, over which János had at one time exercised boundless power, and indeed the old servant, who more than once took upon himself the role of tutor and kept an eye on his master as far as possible – as soon as it rained going after him with half-boots and umbrella, when it became chilly with a cloak – was at times irritating to the young master; but Ákos was far too good to let his annoyance last more than a moment, and if he crossly said something that could hurt the old man he begged his pardon half an hour later and the old friendship was resumed. Ákos never had any secrets from János. In his years at university and as a law student, and after they had returned together to Tiszarét the servant, alert to every change of mood in his master's face, every movement of his heart, had shared his every thought, and so

234

now too the open, friendly way in which he spoke of Vilma took neither Ákos not Kálmán by surprise.

"Actually, the old chap's right," said Kálmán after a brief silence, picking up the conversation where János had left it as he went out. "No one's ever going to deprive you of Vilma's love, my friend! You've no reason to be miserable."

"That's not what's worrying me," replied Ákos, half sitting up in bed. "Vilma isn't the sort whose love is easily lost once it's gained. But shall I be able to make her happy? That's what bothers me."

"You're not used to lying in bed, that's why you're out of sorts," said Kálmán.

"No, no," Ákos went on, "you're mistaken; if anyone takes a positive view of life, I do. Vándory himself isn't a greater optimist than me, he can find the good side of everything, I can see the cheerful aspect. But from the moment last night that this incident occurred I seem to have changed. However hard I try I can't cheer myself up. I'm ill at ease as I've never been before, my whole spirit is full of gloomy anticipations, it's as if some great misfortune were waiting for me that I shan't be able to avoid."

"You've lost a lot of blood, that's all that's wrong."

"That's not it," replied Ákos, shaking his head gloomily, "the first time I took Vilma in my arms, when I felt her heart throbbing, even then in the midst of my happiness I was startled out of my dreams of bliss, and the thought suddenly struck me: was that not the last great pleasure in life that I'd just experienced? Until then, when I'd thought of Vilma I'd imagined nothing but a pleasant, happy future, but now, after being awoken so roughly from my finest dreams, I've been considering my situation more attentively, and I can't see much to reassure me. Nobody can make his wife happy if the situation into which he puts her, the people that he brings her into contact with, are hostile to his feelings! And what can I expect? Vilma's father and my parents are deadly enemies."

Kálmán sighed; he had some idea of the truth of those words.

"Can I hope that our parents will ever become reconciled? I don't mean a reconciliation that consists of realising that they can't obstruct our intentions and will have to tolerate our marriage, but reconciliation from the heart, and that's what it would take to make Vilma happy. It's not enough for love to be tolerated, it requires warmth of feeling, and if our respective parents simply shrug their shoulders when we speak of our happiness or smile doubtfully at what we say, for all its love the heart will feel lonely; and if two people love each other and stick together

235

under such circumstances it'll be with a sense of pain rather than joy. It takes two to be happy, two that understand one another, and in those heavenly moments that we enjoy in the arms of our beloved the whole world will rage against us in vain; but for blissful calm, and that's what we look for in marriage, a lot more is needed than two hearts that understand one another!"

"Perhaps in time things will become easier," said Kálmán reassuringly, "but at present I must admit the old folks are at daggers drawn, you'd almost think they were relatives disputing an inheritance. Just imagine, when today Tengelyi heard from the Jew that his documents had been stolen, and his noble status was questioned just when the robbery had occurred, he immediately deduced a plot the leader of which. . ."

"My father?" asked Ákos in alarm.

"Not exactly; he knows the situation between your families and only mentioned Macskaházy, but I could read between the lines and saw that he regarded him as only the tool of others."

"My father's incapable of doing such a thing," said Ákos pensively.

"Perhaps he doesn't suspect him as much as your stepmother. He mentioned the other robbery as well, the attempt at the reverend's, where likewise only documents were the object, since the thief touched nothing in the room and only broke into the drawer where Vándory's papers were. His documents were at Tengelyi's on this occasion, and on the way here he said more than once that the two robberies had been the work of the same hands, or at least thought up by the same head. By the way," he added after a brief pause, as if he wasn't sure that the question might not be taken amiss, "you haven't heard anything about Vándory's documents?"

"Not I," replied Ákos, "I've been wondering what such important documents might be doing at the reverend's that people might want to steal, or that he might be worried about."

"The rumour is," said Kálmán more quietly, "that they're something to do with your family."

"My family?"

"You know, your father had a brother," Kálmán went on, "the child of your grandfather's first wife, ten or fifteen years older than himself. When your father was born your grandfather's second wife – your grandmother – was so unkind to the poor boy . . ."

"That he left home," Ákos interposed. "I've heard all about it. It seems that the Rétys don't have much luck with their second wives; but what's that to do with Vándory's documents?"

"This poor uncle of yours," Kálmán went on, "is said to have fled to Germany, presumably to some university because he was seventeen by that time and he's said to have been a very well-educated young man; and people think that Vándory met him there and perhaps is still in contact, so perhaps the documents are to do with him."

"Curious," said Ákos pensively.

"You know what people are like. The exceptional friendship that your father shows Vándory, and in particular the influence that he exerts over your stepmother as well, make people think that he has information through which he has influence over your father, and especially now, since the theft of documents, they can't stop thinking about it. Personally, I don't believe a word of it."

"In any case it's a remarkable business," said Ákos, sinking deeper and deeper into thought, "two robberies in a couple of weeks, and both clearly aimed only at documents. But . . ."

At this point János interrupted the conversation as he came in carrying a fresh dressing. He was followed by the surgeon.

"Your Worship, I've brought the ice and the sawbones," said he cheerily. "Now everything will be all right."

The little man gave János a cross look at the title of 'sawbones', went up to Ákos's bedside, removed the dressing and examined the wound. He expressed satisfaction with the patient's condition and renewed the dressing with great care. Old János, who could bear nothing on earth less readily than that someone else should do the least thing for his master, growled between his teeth that he'd already done that ten times and favoured the poor doctor with angry looks. On this occasion he was in fact mistaken. Whatever Doctor Serer deserved it wasn't anger; we find in him a thoroughly admirable character, and during the sixteen years that he had spent in St-Vilmos a man who had never been ill, like János, had had no cause for complaint about him.

There are men to whom Fate deals a strange hand, and Doctor Serer was one such. As his name shows,[132] pure Asian blood didn't run in his veins, and if, in his quiet moments, the editor of the *Augsburger Allgemeine* reckons up the legions of the German race he will presumably list the St-Vilmos surgeon among those by virtue of whom our fatherland will one day be a branch of the German cutting grafted onto the Holy Roman Empire. Just as the Danube can be considered a German river

---

132 *Scherer* is a German and Jewish (Ashkenazi) occupational name for a sheep-shearer or someone who used scissors to trim the surface of finished cloth and remove excessive nap.

– its source is in Germany – so Serer could certainly be taken for a German; nevertheless, the doctor didn't know a word of German, nor did the whole expression of his face, indeed his features, contain anything to remind one of his origins. In him German national quality had been entirely transformed, and if we take in evidence the narrow swarthy face and black hair inherited from his mother and the small moustache, cultivated by his personal efforts into needle-sharp points by the application of much wax, everything about Serer was so Hungarian that if one of our travellers, seeking the origins of our people in the East, were to meet him in Asia he would probably embrace him with tears in his eyes as a scion of the ancient Magyars.

Fate, it seemed, had been unwilling to leave Serer in his natural state in any respect, and both in his national quality and in his way of life the doctor didn't follow in his forebears' footsteps. As far as their history can be traced the Serer family had always followed the trade of boot-maker. Tóni – such was our new acquaintance's Christian name – was the first to exhibit no inclination for that fine craft, and although he outwardly favoured his father's trade, and was especially keen on the pitch, with which he sometimes daubed his whole face, had no real calling to it; his father suspected this early, because although he only entrusted to him the sewing together of ready-made pieces the way in which he performed this seemingly simple task was such that every pair that passed through his hands was returned to his father by the peasants after a few days with no few curses, as they had come unstitched. "The boy prattles all the time," said his father, shaking his head and that of his hopeful offspring. "He's very stupid," said the assistant, at such times striking either the table or his apprentice's back once more. "He'll never make a cobbler," said both of them. And after that negative conviction they might scarcely have known to what to put the boy's excellent talents had not the barber in the little town where the Serers lived taken him as an apprentice; he liked Tóni's talkativeness, and perhaps believed that the boy was a barber born, because – as the entire family complained – he only did his work on the surface.

That was a stroke of luck for Tóni. He was tossed from one extremity of human existence to the other, elevated from the foot to the head; he had not been created for his works to be trodden underfoot, and suddenly he felt that he had found a niche, was in his element. It was true that the soap bubbles that foamed splendidly around his fingers didn't completely replace the delight that he had found in pricks; and the young barber more than once cast a yearning glance at his neighbour's son, who had followed him as apprentice to his father and went around the town black of hand and face; but could not he, who had previously received a grievous punishment for every piece of leather to which he had put his hand, arrange at his pleasure the skins of half the town? Could he not exercise his imaginative powers without restraint on all the heads that he cropped every day, and create on citizens' heads now a flight of steps up and down which cupids seemed to pass, now, if a toupé was required, a splendid mass of curls? Not to mention the delight with which he singed the locks of members of the council and civic notables on feast days? And can't the barber talk more than anyone else on earth? Who can set his knife to the neck of his hearer and threaten bloody vengeance if he interrupts? Who is quicker to find out and pass on the local news? What editor of a news-sheet is more confident of his readership? He soaps up instead of writing a leading article, brings warm water in place of a pamphlet, in his home reports always has more to say that has actually happened and in foreign reports less, and his audience is never lacking. Who would not be happy in such a situation, especially if he is assisted by his father with three *váltó forints*[133] monthly pocket-money, and can go anywhere in town, not even excepting the council, with perfectly clean hands?

According to the Greek allegory the sphinx used to stop travellers and set them a riddle and, if they could not solve it, tear them limb from limb. This allegory is still valid in our day. We are all set a riddle at the time of our birth, and any that fail to solve it – and it means nothing less than the understanding of our calling – perish; the man that can answer correctly, who is clear about himself, that he has been born a military leader, a scientist, or as in the case of Serer a barber, has an assured future. Men, for the most part, perish not in the struggle that they wage with external circumstances but in that with themselves, and he that is beyond that will progress in his chosen career, albeit at a slow pace, and like Serer may rise from small-town barber to barber's apprentice in Pest, from there become qualified and later appointed regional surgeon in some county, without needing particular luck.

The progress with which the young man studied surgery at Pest university was not at all as remarkable as expected. Nature, which had given him such exceptional talent for asking questions, seemed to have denied

---

133 The *váltó forint* 'alternative forint' was a form of paper money in circulation in the first half of the nineteenth century, slightly less valuable than the *pengő forint* 'tinkling forint'.

him the ability to answer, or at least his fellow students attributed to this the unusual silence which they observed in him in examinations. Indeed, as far as practical surgery was concerned Serer didn't fulfil the hopes of his Pest employer, who had noticed that while shaving his apprentice did as much under the skin as on top, and believed that he had the makings of a surgeon rather than a barber. But since in this world it is love, not knowledge, that works miracles, when the surgeon died in Taksony county and his widow, who was at the same time Serer's employer's relative, came to Pest and saw the handsome surgeon, he had no further need of knowledge. He passed his examinations with the aid of money lent by her and was pronounced a master of surgery, and after coming with his wife to the county, where she, by means of the funds left to her by her first husband and which she loaned to certain officials, had no little influence, in a short time he was appointed county surgeon in St-Vilmos, where we find him to this day addressed as Doctor by all and sundry.

Apart from the chief medical officer of the county, who had brought from the university nothing more than his teacher's certificate, the title of doctor wasn't shared by many, and I would not recommend anyone to address Master Serer by any other. The tiniest word that reminded him of his previous occupation; being called 'sawbones' by ignorant persons like János; indeed, if anyone were to so much as sharpen razors in his presence, resulted in the punctilious man being roused to frightful rage; and when on one occasion the barber in St-Vilmos who now tended his beard arrived late and found the doctor shaving himself he said in delight "Your Worship understands the craft as if you too had been a barber," it was common knowledge that the barber had been thrown out of the house in broad daylight.

"The wound is very good, very good," said Serer when he had carefully replaced the dressing. "I'll venture to say, I've never seen one better."

"You should have been in the wars, surgeon sir," muttered János. "You'd have seen some wounds there."

"What do you know about it?" was the reply. "The good wound isn't the biggest."

"Yes, it's the one that's so small that it heals by itself," said the old hussar, "and doesn't need the sawbones."

Serer gave János a cross look. "How have you been sleeping?"

"Well."

"And how are you feeling?"

240

"Again, well."

"No *alteratio*?"

"None at all."

"So complete *apyrexia*, that is, no fever?"

"I think so."

"Perhaps you've got an appetite?"

"Definitely."

"Didn't I tell you? Almond milk works wonders on such occasions." Ákos smiled.

"You wouldn't believe the effect it has! So everything's in order?"

"Perfectly."

"I'm only sorry that I wasn't called sooner, I could have bled you."

"What ever for, if His Worship's all right?" said the hussar.

"Be quiet, my good man! I say that on such occasions bleeding can have a wonderful effect."

"Homeopaths never bleed people," said Ákos, so seriously that Kálmán, when he saw the effect that those words had on the little surgeon, could not hold back. Just as Serer burst into flames as soon as barbers or razors were even remotely mentioned, the moment that the word homeopath was spoken he lost all patience.

"Homeopaths?" said he bitterly. "What exactly do they do? Do they administer emetics, hot-water bottles, tonics, jollop and China tea, medicine to make the patient sweat, antispasmodics to prevent sweating, anti-inflammatories, anti-rheumatics, aromatics, blessed thistle, rhubarb, tartare, Glauber's salts?"

"For God's sake," Kálmán interposed, "I feel quite ill."

"Whoever heard of a homeopath applying a *visicator* or any other plaster for anyone, and a hot, cold or ice-pack, foot-baths, sitting baths and total immersion? What use have I for a doctor from whom I can't obtain even useless Viennese *elixirium viscerale*?"

"The doctor is right," Ákos interrupted him with a smile, "the patient is deprived of a lot of pleasure if he yields to homeopathy. The task of medical science . . ."

". . . is that the doctor should cure," Serer finished the sentence, "and should do his duty, try everything that is to be found in the apothecary's, and if he can't succeed call for advice, until the patient recovers."

"Or dies," said Kálmán with a laugh, at which old János too burst out laughing in great satisfaction.

"Or dies?" exclaimed Serer harshly. "In the hands of a good doctor not one in ten dies, and that only because he has some chronic condition and calls for help too late. And even if the patient is going to die, does that absolve the doctor from his responsibility to do everything that he has learnt at university? Answer me that if you can, Your Worship!"

"Yes, but homeopaths too administer a lot of things," said Ákos, still keeping a serious expression, "and their patients recover."

"I believe so, of course," aid the surgeon scornfully, "but if it weren't for Nature! Oh, Nature works wonders!"

"But isn't it all the same if the patient's going to recover?" asked Ákos.

"Certainly not, if Nature isn't helped and left to itself, as our chief medical officer says, it over-exerts itself which always has damaging consequences later."

"And if your patients have recovered, who knows," said Ákos, "that they haven't been cured by Nature?"

"We know, Your Worship, we that have been to university and studied with our professors for five years, that patients don't recover if certain medicines aren't administered to them," replied Serer with dignity. "Those that lack experience in science, who, like homeopaths, haven't studied chemistry, botany, mineralogy, anthropophagy – I mean anthropology – which are all necessary for medical science, as soon as we perform some great cure state that Nature has cured the patient. We know better; why would we have studied for five years at Pest university if we didn't know even that?"

"That's true," said Ákos. "Why would you have studied so much if you knew no more than anyone else in the country!"

"And if a homeopath has a difficult patient," Serer went on spiritedly, "doesn't he immediately call on an allopath? For example, the other day in Porvár in the case of the old lawyer?"

"Who died on the third day after the chief medical officer took over?" interrupted Kálmán. "I spoke to his previous doctor, and he said that as the disease was incurable, and he could see that the patient was suffering terribly, he called in the allopaths because he himself, with his weak medicines, could perhaps not have freed him from his pain for a month. With the allopath it went more quickly."

This attack was more powerful than the surgeon could endure from his patient. Convinced of the value of his knowledge as only he can be that received from it three hundred forints a year, free lodging, and numerous fat additional fees for diagnosis, and convinced of the validity of his knowledge as he is that had never read anything but a school-book about medical science, and who didn't consider doubts about the Bible half as wicked as if anyone contradicted him, Serer looked round with inexpressible irritation and scorn, especially at old János, whose face was radiant in his delight at seeing the surgeon being attacked as he nodded assent with his head and all his limbs, especially at Kálmán's more comprehensible jokes. "But is there a grain of sense in what homeopaths do?" said he under attack at length. "A strong adult falls sick, for example eats a whole dish of brawn and upsets his stomach, along comes the homeopath and what does he give him? I ask you, what does he prescribe on such an occasion? A millionth of a drop of camomile. I ask you, how can a man in his right mind accept that that will be useful? A whole dish of brawn, and . . ."

"Yes," replied Kálmán with a laugh, "but I can't imagine why China tea would help if I've eaten a lot of cheesecake or stuffed cabbage and have an attack of the ague?"

"It's perfectly natural for you not to understand, Your Worship," said the surgeon with the smile of satisfaction with which experts talk to the uninitiated. "You lack experience in medical science, but this in itself is quite plain and straightforward. China tea has a certain power that stops the ague, nothing is more natural than that, and God has created it so that we may cure the ague with it."

"But how is it that, when God has created sausage and stuffed cabbage from which we get the ague, He doesn't permit china tea to grow here?"

"Your Worship is just teasing," said Serer with a shake of his head, "it's difficult to explain such scientific matters. But no one will deny that if so small a dose of something as homeopaths give can have so great an effect, more will have greater effect; and if a millionth part of a drop of camomile can cure one, I would give at least three coffee-cups or even more. Which is true, too, because camomile in quantity works wonders."

"As I see it," said Kálmán amiably, "it all depends on the way in which we use the medicine. You can sit for hours on a bundle of sticks or a big hazelwood bench, doctor, without any discomfort at all, but if a stick is taken off the bundle and János, for example, uses it in a certain way, then although the whole hazel bench has no bad effect, I believe . . . What do you think, János?" said he turning to the old man, who seemed to feel the stick in his hand; he clasped his hands together and laughed.

"Well, what I think is," he replied, "that the homopath and the . . . I don't know what it's called, never mind. If I've got stomach ache I drink some wine, and when the butler had pneumonia Her Honour gave him some pálinka with paprika, and we just got better. Our lives are in God's hands, like the reverend says, and if somebody's time isn't up he'll last out, even if he calls a hundred doctors."

I don't know what the consequences of János's daring words might have been, but as the surgeon, his eyes flashing angrily, was about to utter he was interrupted by the entrance of Her Honour Mrs Réty. On seeing her he hurried to greet her and immediately began to talk about the effect of ice-packs, almond tea, and that Ákos was now quite out of danger.

Mrs Réty seemed to be out of humour, and neither the doctor nor Kálmán, who bowed deeply, were favoured with great civility; Ákos, however, always had a special power over his stepmother. That lady, who never tempered her mood to anyone, always treated him tenderly, or at least politely, and now too as she sat down at his bedside she asked sympathetically "How are you feeling?"

Serer and János went off for a fresh dressing; Kálmán, sensing that his company was not desired, went and stood in the window and looked into the park. "Do you see, Ákos," said Mrs Réty quietly, "what happens when you go after girls instead of doing your duty at an election."

Ákos said nothing, but his cheeks blazed. "You've nothing to be ashamed of," said Mrs Réty soothingly, "Vilma's a pretty girl and . . ."

"Madam!" said Ákos, drawing a deep breath.

"Vilma," she went on, "is an attractive girl, and you young men, which of you wouldn't on such an occasion put out a hand for something that's being freely offered. It's up to the girl to consider her reputation."

Mrs Réty's words were soothing, all but gentle, but there was something in her tone that brought all Ákos's blood to his face, and she herself, though she affected surprise, understood perfectly the reason for his agitation when he said, his voice unsteady: "Madam, not another word, pray, in that tone of voice. Vilma . . ."

". . . is a very attractive little girl," said Mrs Réty, still soothingly, but in such a way that even a stranger could have noticed the sourness that her words concealed. "A little more couth than I thought, but when all's said and done it's for her mother to take care, girls like her, who are genteelly brought up, get all sorts of ideas into their heads. Tengelyi himself must have thought that it wasn't the upbringing for a notary's daughter."

"Vilma is the girl for me!" said Ákos, exercising great self control.

"The girl for you?" Mrs Réty forced herself to laugh. "The how-manieth, if I might enquire?"

"The first," said Ákos calmly, "and, I swear, the last as well." And Mrs Réty closed her eyes under the calm, purposeful gaze which Ákos fixed on her.

"Are you delirious?" she said eventually, with the sweetest smile possible. "Vilma as Mrs Réty! After such an event."

244

"If Vilma's the girl for me," said Ákos, continuing to stare at his stepmother, "I see nothing out of order in what happened."

"If you take a wife, as my father often told my brother," said Mrs Réty, "never take one who loves you more than her reputation before the wedding, in case after the wedding she loves another more than you."

"Madam," said Ákos, frowning, "don't besmirch your sex and yourself by speaking so of an honourable girl."

"Of course she's an honourable girl, because you were there until midnight, and you'd kill anyone that dared to doubt it."

"Do go on," said Ákos sourly. "Why shouldn't you speak as you like about your future daughter-in-law?"

"My daughter-in-law? And are you aware that Tengelyi's noble status has been called into question?"

"Yes! When Vilma's my wife, that's all the nobility she'll need. Another reason for my marrying her."

"Tengelyi, according to him, has documents by which he can prove his nobility."

"Did have," said Ákos, enjoying the confusion and anxiety that he saw on his stepmother's face. "They've been stolen. The Tengelyi family have no one but me to rely on, but they can count on me."

"But I've heard," said Mrs Réty, and the expression on her face had changed visibly, "that the robbery was unsuccessful and that Tengelyi's documents didn't fall into the criminals' hands."

"Quite the contrary, in fact," replied Ákos, observing his stepmother's agitation. "The money and everything else has been recovered, only the documents have been lost."

Mrs Réty's face radiated pleasure, and despite her best efforts she could not conceal it from Ákos when she asked "Who could the thieves have been?"

Ákos had kept his eyes focused on his stepmother all the time, and said that in the opinion of the entire village the robbery had been carried out by Viola. At that Mrs Réty stood up, said that she had something urgent to do, and hurried out.

Kálmán had heard only the last part of the conversation, and even he had noticed the change in Mrs Réty that the news about the robbery had brought about. He watched her go. Ákos sat up in bed and pondered for a while, scratching his head. "Kálmán!" said he, "did you say that Tengelyi thought that my stepmother was behind the robbery?"

"He practically said as much."

"And you think that Viola did it?"

245

"Viola or the Jew, and nothing was found on him."

"Goodness knows, I can hardly believe it," said Ákos, shaking his head. "But if Viola has the documents he'll return them, that much is certain."

"No doubt, if he doesn't use them for lighting a fire."

"And you said the other day that Viola often goes to see your cowherd. Do you know what? Ride out at once and tell him to find Viola, and promise him and Viola anything if he brings the documents back. You know, Kálmán, I can't move myself because of this damn wound," said he angrily, looking at his bandaged arm. "The happiness of my life depends on it. Please be quick!"

As he said that Kálmán was in such a hurry that he could scarcely put his hat and *bekecs* on. He slapped his forehead in annoyance at not having thought of it before. "We'll get hold of the documents through the cowherd," said he, clasped his friend's hand and hurried off.

Ákos sat in his bed, holding his burning forehead in his hands. "If it were true!" said he to himself, and sank into gloomy thoughts from which only János roused him as he brought a fresh dressing, and said that Her Honour had been with Macskaházy all the time since then. Shortly afterwards the sound of Kálmán's horse's hooves was heard, as was the rattling of the carriage which Mrs Réty had had harnessed up for some reason as soon as she had left Ákos, and in which Macskaházy now set off.

XVIII

"The Hungarian takes pleasure in tears" says the proverb; and why would he take pleasure otherwise? If the features of ancestors are preserved from generation to generation, are we to be surprised if the expression too that gave life to the features of our forebears is passed to later descendants? In former times the Hungarian had abundant cause for tears! With other nations the new age has healed the wounds of the past. Almost everywhere folk-songs have kept the sad tunes that have been invented in days when the feelings of an oppressed people could have been nothing but mournful, but happier words have long been set in place of the former, or at least the singer's more cheerful tone causes the true nature of the song to be forgotten. With us, the lower classes have no reason for merriment in the present either, and folk-songs sound as gloomy today too as in the days when the crescent moon lorded it on the walls of Buda. There are indeed people in this country who know only the affairs of their villages and scarcely suspect that since the Turks were expelled Hungary has undergone a change, and the serf, when he takes his forint of hearth-tax to the mansion, can't shudder at the past half as much as those who discharged their debt to their fatherland to the last *krajcár* a century ago, and therefore, since we have been liberated from the Turks, pay no tax. The sombreness that characterises the Hungarian people, however, in my view, in addition to its history and present situation is attributable to the doleful nature of our countryside. Who is there that can retain his cheerfulness at the sight of its plains? The primeval forest which once must have covered these landscapes was felled long ago, and the impenetrable veil of vegetation which once covered the virgin body of this land has vanished under the axe of man, leaving nothing but *pusztas*. When inhabitants of other countries look around them, how much there is to delight their hearts! On all sides houses, trees, fences, growing crops, everywhere something to remind them of the achievements of their forebears, to urge them to more and more strenuous efforts so that through its working they may leave after them traces of their existence on earth. On our *pusztas* only the boundary mounds show that this land is called the property of some, though we can scarcely call it ownership that merely consists of denying its use to others rather than living off it, and the general backwardness, the silence of lack of industry, that lies over it fills our souls with gloom. How many

247

generations have vanished on this land without leaving any trace of their existence! And how is he that sojourns here not to remember that he too shall go into the grave, vanish without a trace under the vast expanse, like him that the boundless sea immerses in its waves.

When we see such a countryside – the above applies word for word to the whole region of Tiszarét – in the grey light of a November day the heart is involuntarily filled by gloomy forebodings.

Noon was long past when Zsuzsi left the village, accompanied by Mrs Lipták. They paused for a rest at the outer *csárda*, and then Zsuzsi went on alone with a little package under her arm – food for her husband. She headed for Kislak, where she hoped for news of Viola from the cowherd. His farmstead was a good two hour walk from Tiszarét, and when she emerged from the deep thoughts that absorbed her Zsuzsi was aware of the weakness that her illness had left. More than once she was tired and sat down, and then when she looked around and saw the huge expanse and herself alone on it, so forlorn, the great silence – she could only hear herself breathing – filled her with dread. She remembered that she had recently heard talk of wolves, and she thought of her children and her husband, who might at that moment be in new danger; and she set off again, feeling in her heart not renewed strength but renewed and growing anxiety that in her present weakened condition she might not reach her goal before sundown. Suddenly the sound of hooves aroused her from her reverie, and the thought flashed into her mind that Viola was racing after her and she turned, but the rider was Kálmán, galloping homewards. And so she came to the stone crucifix that stood on the edge of the Kislak land, and although it was in a ruinous state since the Papist owner had died that had had it erected to mark her land its steps offered the traveller a resting-place. Mrs Viola sat down beside this crucifix. She thought of all the hapless folk that had knelt on that stone, had complained of their bitter woes to that image of Him who had come to our earth only to learn of the sufferings of mankind in their full bitterness; how many had risen relieved from that crucifix, and into her Calvinist heart from that Papist cross flowed that peace which neither one religious order nor another can confer but only a sense of religion created by God in the hearts of good men, one which many who have written books on their personal religious beliefs have perhaps never experienced in their lives.

She was standing up to go on when suddenly she heard someone call her name. The voice was familiar but not enough to be instantly recognisable, and on seeing Czifra leaning on the cross and nodding a greeting Zsuzsi recoiled in surprise. Ever since she had first seen him Czifra had horrified her. She knew what a villain he was, knew that every act of cruelty committed by Viola's men had been done by him, and the love that she had for her husband had often not been enough to overcome the loathing that she felt on seeing him in Czifra's company. Viola too had after a while begun to suspect his associate's loyalty and had often said that he would turn out to be his Judas. All this accounted for the horror with which the poor woman looked at the bandit as he leant on his cudgel and, with a strange smile that made his face look even uglier, asked where she was going.

She replied, to visit the Kislak cowherd.

"Looking for your husband, I presume?" said he straightening his sheepskin on his shoulders. "The cowherd may know where he is. What's news in the village?"

"Don't you know?" said Mrs Viola, staring at the speaker. "They say that you and my husband were there."

"Viola? Has he been in the village?"

"And you wouldn't know anything about the robbery last night at the notary's?"

"Robbery?" said he with a laugh. "Well, what did I say. As soon as I heard that Viola had access to the house I said in advance that he'd end up robbing it. There isn't a man like Viola for three counties around, you can't play games with him."

"Don't say such things. I could swear that Viola didn't do the robbery."

"Perhaps, I don't know. So who would it have been?" said Czifra nonchalantly.

"Everybody in the village says it was you."

"All of them? Peti the Gypsy, perhaps?" asked Czifra, his eyes blazing.

"I haven't seen Peti since he went to Porvár, but the blacksmith, who chased you, and I mean the whole village . . ."

"The whole village is stupid, and the blacksmith's even worse to chase anybody if he thought it was Czifra. If it had been me he wouldn't be bragging about being daring. All cats are black at night, and I'd like to know how he recognised me, perhaps it was by my sheepskin" – with a laugh he pulled it onto his shoulders – "it's no dirtier than anybody else's. Good luck to you! I've got to be going." And he strolled away whistling down the road to Garacs, which turned off by the crucifix. For a while Zsuzsi watched him go. Shortly after he had gone she heard the rattle of a carriage and saw that Macskaházy too was making for Garacs. Viola saw the carriage stop when it caught Czifra up; the passenger talked briefly to Czifra, who then took a seat on the rear box and the carriage drove on.

Zsuzsi was astonished and redoubled her pace, but darkness was falling by the time that she reached the farmstead.

There she found the old cowherd and Peti. "Don't suppose you've seen Czifra?" asked the latter anxiously as they saw her coming and came out to greet her.

"I have," she replied.

"Where was that?"

Mrs Viola gave a full account of the meeting, during which the gravest despair was to be seen on Peti's face, especially when he heard that Macskaházy had taken Czifra into his carriage and driven to Garacs.

"This is the end of everything!" said he finally, clapping his hands to his forehead. "How could you have told Czifra about Viola? If I don't arrive in time he'll be caught."

"But for goodness' sake, what's happening?" asked Zsuzsi, trembling.

"I can't stop, István will tell you everything. I'm making straight for the St-Vilmos forest as fast as I can. If your horses arrive, come full speed. You know the way, perhaps we can be there before the *szolgabíró's* men. Praise be, the Tisza hasn't flooded yet this year. For goodness' sake, István, don't spare the horses."

And the Gypsy hurried off towards Szt-Vilmos at a brisk pace.

Zsuzsi realised from what Peti and the old cowherd said that her husband was in danger, and asked tremulously "What's happened?"

"Nothing yet, Zsuzsi," said István, "calm down. If anything happens I'll hang myself, but not before I've torn that Czifra limb from limb."

"But what's happened? For goodness' sake, tell me out of pity," sighed Zsuzsi, going into the house and sinking onto the bench by the hearth. With no few curses the old cowherd explained the situation, which was not reassuring from Viola's point of view. Immediately after the robbery, a truthful account of which Zsuzsi now heard from him for the first time, her husband had come on horseback to the farmstead and instructed István, on whom the whole band called almost daily, that if Peti, whom he had told to come there, or any others of his men asked for him, he was to send them to the usual hiding-place in the St-Vilmos forest, where he was going to remain hidden until the fuss created by the robbery had died down and he had managed somehow to return the documents to Tengelyi; at the same time, he asked him to send him food for a couple of days. The cowherd had known nothing about Czifra's treachery, and in his haste Viola had forgotten to speak of it.

The cowherd had not met Peti since he had come after overhearing the plan, and nothing was more natural than that Czifra should come to the farmstead in the afternoon and ask for Viola, and István had given him a flask of wine and a couple of pounds of meat and sent him to the hiding-place in the St-Vilmos forest. Peti had arrived only an hour later, having parted from Viola at the robbery so that he could run away more easily, and now he heard that he had divulged his secret to the traitor. After that, as Zsuzsi saw with her own eyes, there could be no more doubt of Czifra's intentions, and the poor woman sat in despair on the bench, contemplating all the circumstances and sunk in such pain as Heaven doesn't give tears to relieve.

Two hours had gone by since she had seen Czifra and Macskaházy, Garacs was half an hour closer to the St-Vilmos forest, there were cavalry and commissars in readiness at the magistrate's house – how would they, on foot, be able to reach Viola's hiding-place before them and warn him. There was nothing to hope for!

"I wish my cart would come!" said the cowherd, going to the front of his house. "I sent it into the village two hours ago and it's still not back. Just you wait, you wretched boy! If I could get hold of my horses we could still be there in time. Those magistrates don't move as fast as you think, my dear Zsuzsi, especially just after a meal. Who can say whether he's home by this time? Yes, Peti said that the *főispán* had sent him home. But I'm a damn fool too. What the hell can have made me open my mouth to that villain! Well, Zsuzsi my dear, don't worry about a thing, we'll get there in good time, you'll see, nobody's got a better horse. But who'd have thought that Czifra could be such a swine, he's been a bandit thirty years and still he'll give somebody away, but wait a moment! Just a moment! Immediately after Czifra young master Kálmán was here, and he said that the notary's documents had been stolen, asked me to get them back and to tell him where Viola was. He asked in the name of God and cursed me, and I didn't say a word to him, only promised that if I happened to meet Viola I'd have a word with him – and that other dog, I told everything. But," he exclaimed on suddenly hearing the rattle of a cart, "here are my horses."

The little cart and two powerful horses harnessed to it stopped in front of the kitchen door. "Come on, Zsuzsi, get in the back and cover yourself up nicely," said he, helping her up, "but you get out of the way," to the driver, as he took the whip from his hand and pushed him off the seat. "I'll give you what for, wasting your time in the inn."

251

And the horses set off across the field at full speed. The rattling of the cart soon died away, and the *kuvasz* dogs that ran after it had long fallen silent; only Bandi, the driver, remained standing where he stood, staring after the vanishing cart despite the darkness. "István, "said he, scratching his head none too gently, "if you're making off with Viola's wife you're not so daft!"

XIX

Traveller! if you have come to the Tisza-side ward of Taksony county in search of truth – and why might you not do that? since pious truth is often so hidden from us that we would search the whole world for it – and you reach the community of Garacs, pull in your horns! That is how I might begin this chapter if – as many wish – I were capable of rising to that pathos that has recently rendered our most notable Hungarian works all but untranslatable because nothing in them is in its natural place. But as I am a modest writer I can scarcely find words for the expression of even my simple thoughts. I can but envy the wealthy, who are sent into the world to serve up three nouns for every object and three adjectives to go with them and who accumulate embellishments of their words in the rich store of their tropes and figures of speech – but I feel in myself the power to follow their example, and therefore shall return to my simple narrative style. Yes, reader, if you come to Garacs, where I am about to go with my tale, pull in your horns; I say that not because the village is where Pál Nyúzó the magistrate has his home, and is a holy place to you and one that you should respect as such especially if you stay in his ward; nor because according to Augustine it is best to follow the custom of the place where you reside with regard to such religious practices as fasting, and the entire village of Garacs goes barefoot; but leaving aside all higher considerations you should put on boots of good Muscovy leather, without which in autumn weather, such as the present, you will be unable to walk down the street.

I read in some historical philosophy – I can't say on the spur of the moment which, because there was a time when I read a lot of such things, as I didn't yet know that in history, as in every science, people only look for those truths that will be advantageous to them – in one of the many, therefore, I read that the Phoenicians only made their great advances in navigation because they were rich in materials needed for navigation. Anyone that has ever been to Garacs will surely be persuaded of the falsehood of this statement. Never can men have lived in a place more favourable to the plastic arts. The soil is the purest clay, the whole street is such that it could be used for modelling, and where you tread the clearest impression is left, so that when the soil dries out copper castings may be made of your footprints; it is the veritable soul of clay, as the saying goes; yet there is not a single potter, let alone a sculptor, to be found in the village. After that believe in experts! I have an elderly acquaintance, at one time a sergeant-major in the militia, who, every time that he was asked what Vienna was like, humbly admits that he has never been there; but mention Paris, Rome, Lisbon or Constantinople and he will talk for hours on end about the various streets and markets and the happy days that he spent there. It sometimes seems that our experts imitate him. If we speak to them about the present time and its enormous movements they admit humbly that they know what they mean, but if we go back a couple of centuries or a millennium everything is absolutely clear, and the most minute causes of the most trivial acts, lines of thought and consequences of feelings have remained with them without omission. If you were to ask why Pharaoh dreamed of seven fat and as many thin kine, there may well be a man of learning that can give an account of the Egyptian king's dinner to which this dream may be attributed. Poor peoples! Politicians test their theories on you while you live, and when you are dead along comes the delver into history and tries out his theories too. Your fate is not to be envied!

But I digress! Don't take it amiss, gentle reader; you know that it's my old custom, and furthermore it is one of a writer's duties to adapt his style to subjects, and in speaking of Garacs why should I not enjoy a diversion or two? The most outstanding feature of the magistrate's village was that there no one could walk a straight road, so higgledy-piggledy were the individual houses, so winding was the space called a street – wide in one place, narrow in another – that it merited that name at least as much as the peasant dwellings between which it lay might be described as houses; because if taxation, as in England, were applied according to the number of windows or chimneys it would have been hard to tax any house at all in the village, which may be why in Garacs only hearth-tax was demanded.

Taksony county is not one of those in which the villages are renowned for easy living and comfort, and the English farmer would not find many farmhouses where he would feel at home within the mud walls and under the haphazardly thatched roof – and yet Garacs easily surpassed its neighbours in wretchedness of appearance. You could not help feeling sad as you drove between the dilapidated hovels with their tattered roofs and saw the people that lived there, their sunken faces pale, who seemed never to feel at home in that place until one by one they were taken out to that enclosure on the far side of the village, there beneath its crosses to find rest for the first time in their lives. The church itself – that palace of those who on this earth have only hovels, on which people elsewhere look on with pride, which they decorate with flowers and greenery as they never do their own houses – there stood half ruinous. The low walls, which must have been long unprotected by the broken slates from the destructive force of rain, were merely propped up against ultimate collapse; the tower, which served as the entrance, was cracked in several places and could scarcely support the iron double cross which slumped rather than stood atop the roof, and the bells had long ago been removed and hung on a separate wooden frame. All was decay, all bore the mark of poverty, and it seemed that the faith that had been given to men for their consolation had withdrawn under that crumbling shelter so as not to arouse in its adherents insatiable desires. The church and the clergy house standing beside it – in even worse condition, if that were possible – were bordered on three sides by a pond, overgrown with reeds and sedge, while at the back stood the modest gravestones of a couple of clergy; if you happened to come here on a Sunday as the bells were ringing, while in the pond the frogs kept up their everlasting dismal song and the impoverished people of the village made their pilgrimage to their ruinous church a grief would come over your heart that you would scarcely find words to express. Garacs was a joyless place all year, but it was only on Sunday, that blessed day which God ordained for men's rest and pleasure, that you felt how great was those people's wretchedness.

However, we have seen only one side of the picture, and I would be neglecting the veracity that a writer owes to the reader if I failed to mention that from a higher point of view, that is, as far as roofs are concerned that rise above the mud hovels, the same village displays a quite different appearance, indeed a really upper-class one. The gentle families of Garacsi, Báméri, Andorfi, Nyúzó and various others who have inherited the place on the distaff side have built *kúrias*[134] of ever greater handsomeness, and although in these too the building material of the street (or at best, mud brick) has been used, from the contrast that these taller buildings offer to the hovels in the village you would almost think that you were surrounded by palaces, and the many columns, which, as is well known, are among the principal features of every noble *kúria* because of our classical tastes, remind us sometimes of Hellas but mainly of Sparta, where, as we know, the number of helots always exceeded that of citizens. In the hefty tomes which as students we used to call the

---

134 The *kúria* is a type of upper-class house. Not unlike a peasant house in shape, it is in effect a single-storey mansion.

body of the law (our men of learning have disputed much concerning the spirit of that body without being able to reach agreement; even its undying nature has not been proclaimed beyond all doubt) there is a law by which, if a landowner can't give land in the village as a dwelling to one of his children, he is entitled to a serf plot of equal value. There is nothing more natural than that our landowners, as fathers of their serfs and their children alike, should divide their land among them as they please; and if that law was more strictly applied in Garacs than the serfs may have wished, at least that ordinance of nature by which a man's principal task is to ennoble the gifts of the material world had been so fulfilled by joint tenancy that there was scarcely any non-noble land to be found in the village. The nobles of Garacs had long ago grasped the principle of freehold even before it was taken up by the newspapers, and the serfs' freedom of movement was so unquestioned by anyone that several peasant families had moved on and not even needed to worry about a cart to be able to take all that they possessed with them.

Beyond doubt the finest of these *kúria*s that have so beneficial an effect on the village is the home of Nyúzó the magistrate, and even if I weren't to act as guide my readers would not call anywhere else in Garacs on seeing the nicely mended fence, the vivid green wall in which six windows open, its colour offset by the blue of the two elegant columns on the porch. Indeed, only a third of the roof is as yet slated, but as the magistrate has been re-elected for a further three years it is likely that the two-thirds that remain thatched will soon be slated also; and the smoke pours so thickly from the chimney that we must inevitably think of a hearty dinner.

Nyúzó had only returned from Porvár an hour or so previously. The election, which we left with Tengelyi, had afterwards proceeded with unaccustomed speed. The nobility had been informed that there were non-nobles to be found among Bántornyi's people and turned against him almost to a man, and by twelve o'clock Réty had been declared *alispán* by a large majority. As soon as his wife heard that – she had heard of the events in Tiszarét rather earlier – she immediately had herself driven home with Macskaházy. There was no difficulty over the election of Krivér as deputy *alispán* because Édesy, the previous holder of the post, stood down voluntarily; since, however, the party that was defeated over the first officers withdrew on this occasion too, as is commonly the case, the election merely resembled confirmation in office and was over by two o'clock. At that the *főispán* too was informed of Viola's alleged crime and commissioned the magistrate of the ward and his clerk to track and pursue the thief at once.

The *főispán* of Taksony, therefore – so is authority deceived in this world – presumably imagines the magistrate with his clerk, gendarmes and deputies to be in Tiszarét; we shall steal into his room and find the worthy man at his big oak desk, and if Kenyházy the clerk weren't sitting at his side we would scarcely think that we saw him on his official mission. In the movements of the two as they fill glasses and clear plates there is nothing to indicate that they are engaged in catching bandits. My readers are perhaps not surprised; but if we consider that we have just come from an election in which Nyúzó was re-elected for three years, and that the German proverb according to which new brooms sweep best is frequently turned round in Hungary, the greatest effectiveness of brooms being experienced when they wish to be elected – they are certainly no more surprised than in many other matters, especially if they consider the numerous reasons that make our meritorious official go straight home to Garacs instead of to Tiszarét, where he had been sent.

Nyúzó had set out on his official journey straight away, even before eating lunch, to demonstrate his respect for the *főispán*; since, however, every movement – including that which the official designate had experienced on the shoulders of his enthusiastic supporters – increased his appetite, he might truly have wished that the forces of the law in Tiszarét ward should drive on an empty stomach all the way there, rather than go to Garacs, a good hour and a half closer to Porvár? It is written in scripture that they that hunger and thirst after righteousness[135] are blessed (perhaps that is why Hungary, where there are so many occasions for such thirst, is considered by some to be the most blessed country in the world); but it is nowhere written that it is a blessed state if righteousness itself, or what amounts to the same thing, those in whom we see righteousness personified are hungry, and why should Nyúzó carry out the first experiment on himself? Furthermore, Pista and János the gendarmes were in Garacs and presumably in St-Vilmos, and so, as Kenyházy the clerk quite correctly remarked, might the honourable county wish that they should capture Viola themselves? Evening was drawing on, and at such an hour a thoughtful man – especially if, as in the case of Nyúzó, a whole band had sworn vengeance on him – avoids villains rather than seeks them; finally – a reason not perhaps without influence

---

135 There is a play on words in the Hungarian here. *Igazság*, here translated righteousness as in Matthew 5:6, can also mean truth and justice.

on their distinguished official – as the recent robbery had occurred at Tengelyi's Nyúzó and his clerk weren't really concerned if the evil-doers only came into the clutches of the law when the stolen articles were no longer in their possession. Therefore Nyúzó had a hundred reasons for not going to Tiszarét that day, and who, seeing him sitting in his ancient leather chair, pipe in mouth, at the big table on which his father before him had written judgements, and on which wine bottles – two empty and one started – now revealed the occupation of the present master of the house, while a half-eaten dish of brawn, a ham stripped to the bone, and the cheese – why mention it? only the wooden tub was left – reminded one of the delights of lunch: who could say that Nyúzó had acted incorrectly since arriving home? Such great Hungarian comfort was to be seen on all sides in the house; merely to look around raised the spirits of a Hungarian.

The first requirement of comfort, as is well known, is that nothing shall stand in one's way. In that respect, Nyúzó's room satisfied perfectly the most extreme desires. The bed, which stood in one corner, could not have been narrower; a chest, similar in brown colour and narrowness, on which were heaped clothes, documents, hat, stick, and anything that had no other place; a little table at one of the windows, four leather chairs and a matching sofa a foot wide didn't obstruct the visitor's movements; and the big table itself was used for so many things – most visitors to Garacs sat awkwardly at it – that it thoroughly deserved the space that it occupied, which can't be said of everyone in Hungary. But if freedom of movement suited Hungarians in Nyúzó's room, especially in our time, when even in country places, in imitation of Pest, furniture is set about so higgledy-piggledy that it is almost impossible to move among it without tripping, what pleasure can compare with being able to see on entering that one could do as one pleased? Adam and Eve first felt the loss of their Eden bliss when they began to feel embarrassed in front of one another and worried about clothing! And what are our poor fellow Hungarians to say who are surrounded year after year by further restrictions, who if they travel by steam-ship may not spit out what they feel in their hearts for fear that someone may complain bitterly about them; who here and there may not so much as light a pipe in the rooms of our degenerate women even if its bowl-cover is of the purest silver? A comfortable place is where one can feel at home, doesn't have to put oneself out, and anyone that is looking for such a thing won't find better than this room. The walls have long been browned by the smoke of stove and pipe, and their only decorations are pictures of the Magyar chieftains in red and blue *atillas* (all fine, mustachioed Hungarian men, their legs bulging with muscles, *kalpags* on their heads, maces or banners in their hands, their names inscribed at their feet, so that you recognise Attila and his brother Buda as quickly as if you had lived with them for years); the flooring, long covered by earth, the very spiders' webs that hang undisturbed from the beams seem to say to the arrival: Don't put yourself out; and in any case there would be no point, in the light that comes by day into this room through the dim panes of the two little windows or which is given in the evening by the solitary tallow candle.

Nyúzó could feel all these comfortable aspects of his situation, and he leant back in his chair and sank into the kind of reverie that only a *szolgabíró* can that has seen himself re-elected for a further three years. "We're still in office!" he said from time to time with a gentle smile, "we're still in office!" he repeated, striking the table, "just you wait!" and he clenched his teeth so that the short-stemmed pipe rose to his forehead. A sense of indescribable happiness filled his breast, and in his delight he would have flogged half the county. Sometimes a sudden sadness came over him; such is the nature of our humanity. If pleasure draws a tear from our eye we never know whether pain is going to fill our hearts before it has run down our cheek, and for Nyúzó this house was so full of memories. That table at which he was sitting – was it not the same on which, forty-five years before, immediately after his birth, he had been washed for the first time (and, as many in the county said, for the last time); had he not spent at it his saddest and happiest hours, learning from a gowned tutor how to read and from a recorder how to play *ferbli*? Had he not seated there his dear wife when he brought her home, and in his delight become so drunk that even now he didn't know how he got to bed that day? And to how many happy dinners and weighty verdicts had this table been witness, and of how much wine it still bore the stains! He recalled the seventy forints forty-three krajcárs that he had spent on the election, recalled his father, *szolgabíró* like himself in that ward, who had thrashed him more than once in that room, recalled the fur on his *mente* which the canvassers had torn off, and that two years previously his wife had broken her two front teeth, but suddenly amidst his sorrow his lips began to smile once more. "We're still in office!" he said, half to himself, and regret vanished from his brow. There are a lot of Jews in the ward, he thought to himself, and if his father had not died he would not have become magistrate; the fur that had been torn off, after all, had cost nothing, and presumably he would find similar to replace it; and if his wife had broken her teeth, at least they were only her top teeth, and even so no one in the county could make a *tokány*[136] like hers; and all in all there wasn't a happier man in his ward – with the possible exception of his clerk, because if, as some believe, it is true that the less we know about ourselves the happier we are, that we are happier asleep than awake, and happiest of all when our dreams finally trouble us no longer; this has a certain probability. For half an hour the clerk had been singing his favourite song, resting his elbows on the table:

> If you don't like Nyúzó, ho! ho! ho!
> Then the devil take you, ho! ho! ho!

But although his words grew more and more forceful and louder it could be seen from his half-empty glass that they weren't unassisted. His face too showed the same, as although his eyes were open the expression on his features was that seen only on a sleep-walker.

"Hey, Bandi!" said the magistrate eventually, as the clerk's ceaseless singing disturbed his comfortable reverie.

The other continued to sing, but more loudly.

"Bandi, I'm talking to you, stop that shouting." Bandi looked up at the speaker but the singing became louder still.

"He's drunk!" thought Nyúzó. He stood up, not without some difficulty, went over to the clerk and shook him by the shoulder, whereupon he raised his head as if emerging from sleep, stared at Nyúzó and asked "Well, what's the matter?"

"So we're still in office," said the magistrate; it seemed that there was no room in his head for any other thought that day. And the forces of the law began to laugh long and loudly, making the walls vibrate; the Magyar chieftains whose portraits adorned the wall can have laughed no louder in their delight when they obtained all of Svatopluk's fine realm in exchange for a white horse.[137]

"Why are you laughing?" said Nyúzó at length; his face suddenly regained its full judicial seriousness.

"I'm laughing," replied the other, still doing so, "because they'd organised against us and still we won."

"Quite right, my friend, we've won," said the magistrate, smiling once again. "The thing is that the world belongs to those with eyes."

"And ears," added Bandi, and drained the half-full glass.

---

136 One of the four pillars of Hungarian cuisine, a stew containing roast meats, peppers, mushrooms, smoked bacon and sour cream.
137 According to Hungarian legend, they purchased the country from Svatopluk of Moravia in a symbolic act of exchange: they sent a white horse with saddler to Svatopluk

"That's right! We're still in office, so just you wait," said he, banging his fist on the table. "You wanted someone else for *szolgabíró*, now let's see who was right?"

"And whom did they want instead of me?" continued Bandi, flying into an almost noble rage. "That Vince Görögi, a nobody, he's only just finished the final class in school." That the clerk considered so much graver a shortcoming because he himself had never been in the final class and had terminated his studies in the fourth, which, as is well known, is considered more than sufficient in some counties for service in the magistracy.

"That Tengelyi can look out for himself," Nyúzó interjected, and the same sourness was seen on his face as characterised it when sober. "I decided long ago . . ."

"A good thing he's not noble any longer," said the worthy clerk. "It will make him easier to attack."

". . . to set about doing him harm," growled the other.

"Yes, late at night, in bad weather, when decent folk stay indoors," added the clerk, "and villains can shoot at people from behind every bush. Really, who ever heard of such a thing?"

"Well, you see, Bandi," replied Nyúzó, expressing profounder insight, "that only happens because those great men have no experience of the county. Between ourselves, Bandi, our *főispán*'s no better than the rest. But never mind! He'll give orders and we'll do as we please. You see, my boy, every office has its limitations."

"Yes, but people still shouldn't be sent out at night . . ." and the clerk was presumably about to continue his wise observations when the sound of a carriage in the yard attracted his attention.

"Who can it be?" said the magistrate pensively. "I didn't think that anyone knew that I'd come home."

"Some petitioner," said Kenyházy, calmly pouring himself wine from the new bottle. "They'll be here one after another, because we're still in office."

Macskaházy, still wearing his fur coat, came into the room, thus ending further speculation.

---

in return for some earth, water and grass, supposed to represent his country itself. Svatopluk allegedly disavowed this "contract" and then drowned in the Danube in flight from the Hungarians. The legend, in fact, seems (merely to) describe a common pagan rite of concluding alliances which might refer to Svatopluk's alliance with the Hungarians in 894.

"Fancy seeing you, my dear chap," said Nyúzó, warmly embracing the lawyer and kissing him on both cheeks in a manner that would, in another country, have satisfied the most beautiful woman. "Good of you to come, now we can play preference."

"*Servus humillimus,*" muttered the clerk, who found rising as difficult as it was necessary.

"We're not playing games today," said Macskaházy, disengaging himself from Nyúzó, who was poised for a further kiss. "We must be off at once."

"Be off? Where to?" asked Nyúzó.

"Yes, where to?" Bandi echoed him. "We're not moving a step today, we're playing preference, aren't we, Paul?"

"Nowhere, nowhere at all!" said the latter, reaching out for Macskaházy again; the latter, seeing the state that the two officials were in, shook his head in annoyance. "If you won't stay here willingly we'll take the wheels off your carriage, won't we, Bandi?"

"That we will, and then the honourable gentleman can go where he pleases."

"Well, you could surely have drunk to your re-election later on,"said Macskaházy with a shrug.

"Do you mean that you think I'm drunk," exclaimed Nyúzó, "that I'm not in possession of my faculties? Damned lawyer! Who's the principal *alispán*? Réty, and the deputy? Krivér, and . . ."

"Yes, yes, but for goodness' sake let's have a sensible talk."

"And who's the clerk?" mumbled Bandi. "András Kenyházy, three cheers!"

"Very well, then, let's have a sensible talk," replied the magistrate, pulling himself together. "So where are we supposed to be going?"

"To St-Vilmos."

"I'm not drunk enough to go out," exclaimed the clerk.

"Why's that?" asked Nyúzó.

"Viola's there, we must catch him today or it'll be too late; by tomorrow he'll have handed over the stolen documents."

"We'll catch him tomorrow," said Nyúzó with dignity.

"But I'm telling you that by tomorrow we shan't find the documents on him."

"So much the better," said Nyúzó calmly. "I'm sure I'm going out in the dark to break my neck just to get Mr Tengelyi's documents; you go after him yourself if you like."

"Yes, you go after him yourself if you like," repeated the clerk with a laugh. And Macskaházy cast a despairing glance at the two so meritorious officials. Finally he took Nyúzó by the arm and led him to one of the windows and there talked to him for a long time in an undertone, while the clerk returned to his former theme, once more laid his head on his hands and began to sing quietly:

> *If you don't like Nyúzó, ho! ho! ho!*
> *Then the devil take you, ho! ho! ho!*

"Well, if that's the case," said Nyúzó after a while, during which Macskaházy seemed to have exercised on him his full powers of rhetoric, "that's completely different. Bandi! Do you hear me? Go out and tell the gendarmes to saddle up at once."

"Well, that's different," said Bandi, lurching towards the door. "We can send the gendarmes."

"Why didn't you say so straight away?" said the magistrate, who now seemed much more sober than Macskaházy himself had hoped.

"Because I can't rely on your clerk for everything. Send the gendarmes ahead to St-Vilmos and tell the constable to wait for us at the inn by the forest with the gendarmes and a few men armed with pitchforks. Leave your clerk here, he'd only be a nuisance to us."

"True, but if Czifra's deceiving us and the whole thing's just a trap devised to get the better of us," Nyúzó was visibly paler, "Viola's sworn vengeance on him and Czifra's one of his men."

"Don't be afraid, we shan't even need to go close, I don't care for shooting myself. In any case, Czifra's a reliable man and he's in our hands."

After a while Kenyházy came in and said that the gendarmes had left for St-Vilmos.

"Let's be going, then," said Macskaházy, pulling his fur back on.

"Are you going as well, then, Paul?" said the clerk in astonishment, seeing Nyúzó too in his fur.

"Yes, you can stay here."

"But what will you be able to do without me?"

"We'll try and manage," said Nyúzó with a laugh. "You look after the house."

"Strange," thought Kenyházy to himself as the two took their seats in the carriage and Czifra, who had been waiting in the yard all that time, climbed up behind. "A *szolgabíró* without a clerk!"

263

And Nyúzó's abandoned right hand went back indoors when the carriage had driven off, shook his head several times, drank a glass of red wine, and sang on:

If you don't like Bandi, ho! ho! ho!
Then the devil take you, ho! ho! ho!

. . . until at last sleep put an end to the spirited song and only the barking of the dogs broke the great silence of night at the Nyúzó kúria.

XX

If we had the eyes of witches and could see – as our pious ancestors believed – for miles night and day, and if, in the area where our story is played out, there were some higher ground, we would now be able to observe a truly rare event. On the plain, where, especially after the evening bell has rung in the towers of the scattered villages, only the barking of dogs carrying from farms and the occasional distant sound of hooves break the solemn autumnal silence, now a carriage and a cart are both driving towards St-Vilmos. Two travellers, at such an hour, in these parts! A thing so extraordinary that my readers would perhaps find it incredible if I didn't say that on this nocturnal occasion the cowherd from Kislak and Viola's wife in the one vehicle and Macskaházy and Nyúzó in the other are making for the St-Vilmos forest, the one pair to take Viola to the gallows and the other to save him; the one pair as implacable foes, the other as guardian angels. What makes this event more extraordinary yet is that on this occasion the friends are hastening faster than the foes, which, as is well known, is the rarest of occurrences, as no one is more accustomed to heeding the counsel of the proverbial *More haste less speed* than our friends, so that nine times out of ten they come to our aid when we can no longer make use of them and they may complain bitterly of their fate: why didn't they come sooner? We find the contrary in the present case chiefly for two reasons. One is that Viola's friends are not cultured persons and could not have acquired the ways of such; the second is that cultured persons – such as Nyúzó and Macskaházy indisputably are – love themselves more than they hate others, and if they are intent on hanging someone they don't care to initiate the procedure by breaking their own necks, which was bound to happen – in Nyúzó's unshakeable opinion – if the Tiszarét coachman drove his team of five all the way as he started in the village of Garacs.

"Confound you!" exclaimed the magistrate, rubbing his head, which a violent jolt had brought into less than gentle contact with the iron part of the roof of the carriage, "you'd think you were taking sacks to market the way you don't avoid the potholes. Slow down! Slow down, I say! Or I'll give you such a wallop . . ."

"Please, don't be alarmed," said Macskaházy, likewise rubbing his head. "There isn't a safer driver than him in the county. Even Her Worship travels with him."

265

"Safe driver? He's drunk, I tell you, Macskaházy, drunk as a newt."

"He's not drunk at all, hasn't had a drop since we left Porvár."

"Oh dear!" exclaimed Nyúzó, taking his pipe out of his mouth; at a second jolt it had been driven so far in that had it been in the daytime one would have thought that the magistrate meant to swallow his inseparable favourite, so fond was he of it. "Oh dear, this is the last straw. Stop, driver! Stop, I tell you! I'm getting out."

"Just wait a bit," said Macskaházy patiently. "You can't get out here in the middle of the mud. We'll be out onto grass in a moment, that's as flat as a board."

"Nothing there but pigs rooting," sighed the magistrate; he put his pipe away, but for the last pleasure that he sucked from its stem he still spat. "That's more dangerous still. Here at least it's softer if you fall. I'm getting out."

"But if you get out it'll be tomorrow before we reach St-Vilmos."

"Oh, oh, oh! We'll be capsizing any moment!" exclaimed Nyúzó. "My God! Stop! Jancsi, you villain, stop the carriage!" These ejaculations, during which Nyúzó both clutched convulsively at the cushions and considered which side would be best for him to jump out, may be attributed to a downward slope on which the carriage swerved and tilted somewhat. However, before the coachman, so politely addressed, could descend from his high box the carriage righted itself.

"Let's go! Let's go!" said Macskaházy, suppressing his laughter. "We're on the grass, here the road is smooth. We'll be frozen to the marrow if we go so slowly."

"If we've any bones left," remarked the magistrate, who seemed more at ease now that the carriage was upright.

"Yes," said his companion, "but my rheumatism . . . you know how I suffer. The air's so damp, the whole region is full of sick people."

'Really,' thought Nyúzó, 'how can one be such a hypochondriac?' As the horses cantered steadily along and Jancsi, in the traditional Hungarian way, veered from one ridge to another like a magpie he clung first to one side of the carriage then the other. "You'll see," he said grimly to his companion, cursing and crying in pain at every sharp movement of the vehicle, "we shan't have a bone unbroken by the time we reach St-Vilmos."

"My dear fellow, don't be so fearful," said Macskaházy. "You can see I'm not worried and I too am fond of living."

"It's easy for you," groaned the magistrate, "you're a bachelor, but I've a wife and four children to think of."

266

The lawyer may have found the thought that he had neither wife nor children to make him cling to life a powerful reason, and only complained of the damp and the cold wind. "And I haven't even brought my elderberry tea with me," he said in irritation, "and if I can't find any in St-Vilmos and can't warm myself up properly, you'll see me fatally ill."

"Don't be such a hypochondriac," said the magistrate, as the coachman eased the horses' pace to a gentle trot at his ceaseless cries. And the two men sat for a while in silence side by side, each contemplating his companion's cowardice.

Who may be called brave? The question is one of those the answer to which is much harder than appears at first sight. I have often heard an old French friend of mine say that if a well educated man encounters danger he first looks around, and if he's alone, runs away; but if he can see any witnesses he faces up to it; and up to a point this is true; but when all's said and done, what does that prove other than that the educated man is more afraid of the judgment of others than of other dangers; caught between two dangers he retreats from the former, which another won't even have noticed – public opinion; and may that be called courage? If a suicide has taken place one part of society (in the main, the younger) admires the courageous act, while others shake their heads and call the hapless one that dared not further endure the burden of living a coward. Who is right in this instance? Neither or both? There is no one that doesn't fear something in this world; there is no one who doesn't keep their nerve at certain things the mere sight of which will put others to flight; I have a friend, a brave man who would stand his ground against hundreds – but show him a harmless little snake and you'll frighten him away; I used to know a landowner who was afraid of everything – afraid on the water and on land, in a carriage, on horseback and on foot, afraid of dogs and thunder, since the last earthquake afraid of another and of floods since hearing of that in Pest, in the daytime he feared oxen and at night robbers and spectres; I thought that I'd at last found the ideal of cowardice, but you see, then I heard that when the cholera was at its height no one in the county had displayed greater courage. That man laughed endlessly at the cowardice of the rest, and with great magnificence and the delight which the brave feel when they do something that no one dare imitate, ate stuffed cabbage and sweet melons before the eyes of his astonished guests whom the medical officer had threatened with the most dreadful death if they were to venture anything of the sort. You see, my landowner too had his heroic moments, I could not call him entirely a coward, and indeed I don't know that those who

– like many – respect in our deeds only courage and not intention are correct in their judgments. Will they raise their hats to him who will jump a four-foot fence on horseback and eat ice-cream after dancing; or to the doctor who turns pale at the mere sight of a horse, but will touch with his bare hands the swellings of a patient with the plague? There is an element of daring in everyone; presumably people's judgment differs according to whether they feel themselves more capable of taking the fence or touching the patient. For each of us evaluates virtue in such a way as not to exclude ourselves from the ranks of the virtuous; everyone fashions a morality for themselves such as they are able to live by.

I have digressed again . . . but never mind. The carriage left the grassland and ran onto the highroad, and anyone that has this misfortune in Hungary in autumn can't advance so quickly as not to be overhauled after however many digressions. The passengers' situation wasn't altered. The coachman swore, Nyúzó cried out and cursed at every jolt, Macskaházy sighed because of the inevitable illness, while the *hajdú* dodged from one side of the carriage to the other to be greeted by reproaches because he was always too late and clung to one side or other just as the vehicle swayed that way and might have overturned even without that assistance. Czifra was fast asleep all the time at the rear of the carriage, and we can leave the company at this point in the certainty that if they proceeded in this way the cowherd with his two bays would reach the St-Vilmos forest well before them.

István the cowherd too cheered himself and his sorrowful companion with that fact. True, a good three hours had passed since Mrs. Viola had encountered Czifra near Garacs, which was on a good road and perhaps an hour nearer to St-Vilmos forest than István's farmstead. The magistrate, however – Peti had known that he was at home – had perhaps not left at once; and then the gentry were traveling by carriage, and their road was a bad one, whereas he, in his light cart, could almost fly over the grassland. And after all, had anyone in the world two such bays as István the cowherd?

It had already been getting dark when they set off. The first quarter of the moon, which was to appear that evening according to the Debrecen Kalendar, could not break through the heavy veil of mist and the local knowledge of a Hungarian peasant was really needed to keep one's bearings on the vast plain. Here a boundary bank, there an abandoned sweep-well loomed out of the fog like a dark spectre; here a hayrick, left over from the previous year, there the spoil from a ditch, or solitary willows, isolated where they grew on the water-meadows, sometimes rustled their leafless branches in the autumn wind; that was all. The cowherd drove boldly on without hesitation, as if he were on the most frequented highway in the world, and the bays strained at the harness as if racing against the dragons of the *Garabonciás Diák*.[138] The horses ran on and on . . . István was in ecstasy. He cracked his whip above his head, and offered friendly encouragement to his beloved horses: "Gee up, Vércse! . . . Giddy up, Sárga![139] . . . They're really well matched, the devils . . . I say, there isn't a pair like you in Hungary."

Willows and spoil-heaps, sweep-wells and hayricks seemed to hurtle past the cart. The horses' manes flew back from their steaming necks; the cowherd threw off his fur and sat at the front of the cart, his shirt sleeves flapping as if he were driving into a whirlwind; the horses raced on as if the ground were ablaze beneath their hooves, as if to split the veil of mist and reach the other side before that behind them could close up again.

"Don't worry about a thing, my dear Zsuzsi," he said again cheerily, "we'll be there before that confounded magistrate is out of the house. Gee up, Vércse!"

"God willing!" sighed Zsuzsi.

"It'd be the devil's doing, if we arrived late even going like this," replied István. "Tell me, Zsuzsi, truly on your soul, have you ever travelled like this?"

"Never," she replied, but her thoughts were elsewhere.

"I'll believe it! Giddy up!. . . Now, Zsuzsi, don't worry, we'll be there in an hour, and we'll go to the St-Vilmos *csikós* for some stewing meat; if there's nothing else we'll find a foal and that will have to do. Good Lord, the way they're pulling! my whole hand's gone numb!" added the happy driver, taking the reins in his right hand while he dangled his left at his side, like someone tired by carrying a bar of gold and reckoning the worth of his treasure from the pains that he was feeling.

Suddenly the horses gave a snort and shied to one side. "What's up?" exclaimed István, quickly taking the reins in his left hand again and reaching for his whip. "Sárga! Vércse!. . . Ah, that's what's the matter," said he, peering into the fog and catching sight of a wolf; it had been crossing their path and was standing not far away. "You've seen a wolf.

---

138 A figure in Hungarian folklore: a travelling student who had studied magic. He was able to raise storms and conjure up dragons by his book of spells.
139 The horses' names mean Falcon and Yellow.

269

Go to Kislak, damn you, Tisza and Bodor[140] will tear you to pieces. I hope Peti didn't meet it – but what if he did, a wolf isn't interested in old Gypsy meat."

The anxiety, however, which Mrs Viola felt over Peti at the sight of the wolf and which István's observation on natural history did nothing to dispel, could not have lasted long, as they had scarcely set off again when there was the Gypsy himself, standing by a boundary marker past which they had to go.

Peti climbed into the cart. "We're here in time," said he, sitting down beside the cowherd. "The Garacs road, which they're taking, is bottomless mud, and we're going cross-country."

"If only we hadn't seen a wolf," said Zsuzsi sorrowfully. "I've always hear that it's a bad sign."

"Have some sense, Zsuzsi," replied the cowherd with a laugh. "I've seen lots of wolves in my time, and I'm still here. What harm can it do us?

"As long as the cart doesn't break down," said Zsuzsi anxiously. "I tell you, today I'm frightened of everything."

"Of course it won't," said István, cracking his whip. "It's not a *fakó*,[141] nor a carriage. The difference between a carriage and a cart is the same as between a gentleman and a peasant. The one is big, high, all cushions, painted from end to end, quite splendid to look at, but if it gets into trouble on a bad road or is taken on board a ferry, bang! it's had it. . . Nothing but grief and pushing and pulling in all directions, as soon as it isn't on a made road or smooth grassland, it sticks in mud; but a cart like this can go anywhere, and especially mine! I made the wheels myself, and Peti fitted the iron tyres. Giddy up, Sárga!"

Peti didn't entirely share István's lack of anxiety. "I just hope we don't meet any water," he said more than once, shaking his head. "There's been a lot of rain, and if the bogs happen to fill up . . .

"Don't worry, Peti, everything's going to be in order; and you, Zsuzsi, don't be so gloomy. My nephew Pista, who lived over the Tisza, died last week. He'd left his master a long time ago and got a letter of emancipation and a discharge. With those useless documents, with which Pista's wife can do nothing now, you and Viola and your children can be off to anywhere. I myself know a place a hundred miles away where you'll be able to live as decent people. This county's not safe," he added, "and the good thing is that it doesn't extend very far. What do you say, Peti?"

---

140 Dogs' names – *Tisza* is the river and *Bodor* means 'curly'.
141 A cart with wooden wheels but no iron tyres.

But Peti didn't speak, nor did he answer Zsuzsi, who, on hearing the good news, seemed to have seen a new star of hope rise on the dark horizon. She asked, her voice trembling, "Would there be greater happiness than to have some hope in their hapless situation?" The Gypsy sat motionless in his place, staring hawk-eyed into the dark mist, and it could only be seen from an occasional anxious shake of his head that he wasn't asleep. The cowherd sometimes noticed this and cracked his whip and merely said "There's no problem, Peti, we'll be there directly." And they went on in silence, but the fog seemed to have come down thicker still; the region through which the horses were speeding seemed even more deserted; hayricks and dogs had long disappeared, and anyone unfamiliar with the wonderful cleverness of our people at finding the way in the evident lack of anything to give them their bearings might scarcely believe that the travellers had not been lost for a long time.

Splashing was suddenly heard from the horses' hooves and progress was at an end. The cowherd had said nothing, but for a long time had shared Peti's apprehension. He has noticed a few lighter-coloured patches here and there in the fog, and it had occurred to him that the Tisza was perhaps flooding after all. Now no doubt remained. The place where their cart stood was covered by water, though it could not be seen for the rushes. The Gypsy jumped down and splashed forward. In front of him lay a wide expanse of water, the extent of which could not be seen in the fog. He turned back and looked for a way to the right, but there too there was water everywhere with just a few dark patches standing out like islands from the flood; the ripples of the rising water made the flat ground seem to move as they spread. There was what seemed a more promising way to the left, where there was still dry land, and Peti now led the horses to that side. "Perhaps we can still reach the forest this way," said he, resuming his former seat, "the flood hasn't filled all the bogs yet. Be careful, István, keep out of the water or we'll lose our way."

"Jesus Christ!" exclaimed Zsuzsi, in whose heart every anxiety had suddenly been reawakened. "We shan't get there in time, and my poor husband . . .!"

"We can still get there," replied the Gypsy reassuringly, though the greatest unease was to be heard in his tone. "If the water hasn't passed the Frog Pass we shall find the Black Pool dry, and all will be well. Off you go, István."

"Damned Tisza!" said the latter, encouraging his steaming horses with the whip.

"It's not the Tisza! How can you say that," said the Gypsy shaking his head. "when the water's coming from this side. I saw the Tisza in Rét only yesterday, and it was hardly moving. All this is coming from the Crayfish stream, and since the landowners have made a new dam it's completely out of control."

"Damn it all, there's water here as well!" exclaimed the cowherd, reining in his horses, one of which stumbled. Peti went on in the previous direction, up to his knees in water. "Nothing the matter here," he called after a moment; once he had crossed the narrow stream he could see dry land again, came back to the cart and led the snorting horses into the water. "Don't be frightened, you silly horses, you'll live longer than Pista the cowherd." The cart came safely back onto dry land on the far side, and so they went on, at the gallop where the grass wasn't under water, and led by Peti through a number of minor rivulets until a wide sheet of water rendered further progress impossible.

"The Black Pool's filled up," exclaimed the Gypsy, clapping his hands together. "There isn't a horse on earth that'll go through."

"You two stay here," said Zsuzsi in a quavering voice, "I'll go through."

"You're the one to stay here, Zsuzsi," said the cowherd, restraining her forcibly in her place as she made to get down from the cart. "The pool's full of deep places, and especially as you've been unwell if you were once to lose your footing you wouldn't be able to get up and you'd be done for."

"Let go my coat! God will help me! I can't desert my husband in his hour of need – you know they mean to hang him." And with that the poor woman meant to get down.

"Have some sense, Zsuzsi," said the cowherd, likewise getting down. "If your husband is hanged and you're drowned, what'll become of your children?"

Zsuzsi sat down beside the cart, covered her face in her hands and wept bitterly.

"Don't worry, my dear," said the cowherd reassuringly. "Peti and I will go. You can see the forest in front of us, we'll get through somehow. . . Come on, Peti! Peti! you're such an old fool! What have you brought me this way for?"

The Gypsy in the meantime had been looking around in all directions, evidently trying hard to get his bearings, and to that complaint merely muttered that the way that they had come was two hours shorter in dry weather, and when he'd been that way four days previously there'd been no sign of water at all. "Don't be afraid, Zsuzsi," he added, "I'll get through, devil take me if I don't, just let me get my bearings a bit. Isn't that big tree over there, where we were the other day?" said he to the cowherd, pointing to the far side of the water, where the forest loomed out of the fog like a solid black wall, with a taller tree protruding from it here and there.

"Yes, it must be," said István, turning his attention to the tree in question. "If only it weren't for this fog. . . but there are other tall trees on the edge of the forest, devil knows which is which."

"To the left of that tree," continued the Gypsy thoughtfully, "about a couple of hundred paces, there's a gap in the forest. That's the way we came through with our cart, don't you remember?"

"How should I not remember, and to the right, unless it's been mowed, even nearer to the tree there must be a reed-bed."

"That's right!" the Gypsy went on, "and you said what good fencing it'd make. Well, you go to the right and I'll go to the left, and if that is the tree and I find the gap I'll go through. From the tree to the other side of the dyke there's higher ground."

"I'm going with you," said Zsuzsi. She had listened to every word of the conversation like a prisoner to his sentence, and stood up. "I can't stay here all alone being anxious."

"Zsuzsi, my dear," said the Gypsy, turning as he was about to run off, "you've been ill, it's all mud and slime underfoot, you'd catch your death of cold, you stay here and wait for us."

"But will you come back? You won't go through without me? For God's sake, Peti, I beg you, don't leave me here," called the hapless woman after him.

"If we can get through," the Gypsy called back, turning again, "I'll carry you to the other side on my back." Anyone standing beside the Gypsy at that moment could have seen a tear run down his brown, weathered cheek.

The men vanished into the murk and Zsuzsi was left standing there on the edge of the water, staring at the forest that loomed on the far side. "He's so close, and I can't get to him," she sighed, and her heart swelled with all the pains of love.

The poor woman was right; we find Viola and his companions on the far side of the water, scarcely a thousand paces from where his wife was holding out her yearning arms towards him. On the plains of Taksony County, beside the Tisza, there are magnificent oak forests. Just as the sandy soil produces fine swaying birches and tremulous aspens, and in some places we might imagine ourselves in the loveliest of gardens,

273

so picturesquely are the groups of trees situated, if the cultivating hand of man didn't ruin the effect of the whole with its fields of potato and maize; so in the hard clay that forms both banks of the Tisza mighty oaks raise their dark crowns untended by human hand, but lifting heavenward their broad tops in the full splendour of nature, brought low by neither axe, time, nor the Tisza. Since the price of wood is so trifling in this part of Hungary that the felling of these oaks would cost more than their wood can fetch, almost the only revenue that they yield the landowner is from pannage, which in good years makes the forest the most profitable property on the Tisza. Trees that lie rotting where they have fallen are no rarity, as in the primeval forests of America; and the time is perhaps still far off when cultivation will extend its power to here too, and the dark oak-forests of the Tisza will become more profitable but surely no more beautiful that now, since simply thousands of rooks have taken up residence beneath their gloomy branches.

One of these magnificent forests of oak was in St-Vilmos. The forested area, which made that part of the village lands liable to floods and so unfit for other forms of farming, sloped right down to the Tisza, on the far side of which stood similar oaks, extending for miles. In good years, that is, when acorns were plentiful, the forest was full of noise and life. The snorting of animals as they foraged and the songs and whistles of a hundred swineherds echoed beneath the trees, the dark bark of which bore many a wound capriciously inflicted by those herdsmen's axes. If you passed by the St-Vilmos forest at such a time you could see here and there among the trees a big fire and fur-clad figures around it. Now and then a solitary bagpipe or flute made itself heard from the thicket, and sometimes merry laughter, so that you must almost have envied these men their lot, cheerful and content with so little as they were, their every care dispelled by a mug of wine. Now a deathly silence hung over the forest. The oaks had not been productive that year, and the herdsmen's huts, built by the swineherds in years gone by merely to afford them shelter in the greatest storms, were now either deserted or ruinous. The swineherd didn't build for posterity; if the hut that he built collapsed next day when he moved on with his herd, so much the better; when he returned a year later it cost him little effort to build another. The less the memorial of his presence, the more the swineherd's heart rejoiced.

One such hut, the one furthest from St-Vilmos, was the retreat of Viola and his companions. It was their favourite refuge and the safest. No road led that way; the hut itself was surrounded by dense, trackless forest, and since a couple of years previously a commissioner and two gendarmes had been shot dead near there not even the bravest of the county's servants had so much as ventured that way. If there was no fear of betrayal Viola could sleep as peacefully under that roof as any king in his palace. And why should such a thought enter his head? Apart from Peti and István the cowherd, the only people that knew his secret were the sort whom the gallows awaited if they revealed it.

This hut, in which we find Viola sitting on a little barrel in a corner, was one of the larger ones, and although we see nothing in its furnishings to remind us of the conveniences of the age, by the wooden door with which the entrance and exit could be closed and the reed-thatched roof which had been repaired here and there with branches it could be seen that this hut had not been entirely abandoned.

A spluttering fire in the middle shed its unsteady light on all that was to be seen in those cramped quarters: by the wall on both sides a little straw covered by furs which served as beds for the bandits, a board nailed to four legs that was used as a table, a sooty iron cooking-pot hanging on the wall, the weapons of those present and a couple of flasks. The reed roof, which hung so low at the walls that one could not stand upright under it, was black as soot from many fires, but although there was no chimney and the smoke could escape only through the doorway and a number of small holes made for the purpose in the walls it seemed comfortable enough in there beside the fire.

Viola was sitting in a dark corner of the room, deep in thought, while the two companions that were with him at the time were sprawled on the furs, poking the embers from time to time, sighing deeply out of either boredom or dejection – as Hungarians do at the fireside – and watching the steadily dying flames.

* *
*

It has for some time been the custom of novelists to paint crime in entrancing colours. As, in the happily remembered days of the chivalric romance, writers formed in the imagination a wholly new Middle Ages that never existed, cobbled together of the virtues of loyalty and heroism, so that the reader – I myself remember such feelings in my childhood – almost yearned for the happy time when might was right and was almost contemptuous of our faint-hearted century, in which no one sallied forth from his castle to descend upon passing merchants, and with the abolition of the rack and the burning of witches all that was romantic had faded away: so now smiling images of all varieties of crime are created for the benefit of the credulous public, images so fine,

275

so entrancing, that it is almost amazing that no more are encountered that seek to imitate them for their own ends. Poets, like other artists, are more prepared to choose types for themselves than to follow nature in its endless variety, and if one of the greater sets off on a certain road the others rush after him without considering anything but how not to fall behind their forebears on the path. This is what we can observe in almost all the literature of the civilised world in this century.

The Middle Ages had no mercy on the evil-doer, and yet how much there often is in the life of the criminal that, although we must punish his actions in accordance with our human justice, he merits our sympathy and compassion. Our more enlightened age is well aware of this. The unrestrained passions that seized our ancestors have long been muted, and yet our fevered age, after satisfying its material interests, turns unsympathetically away from the sufferings which it has caused by its social conditions, or which it might at least mollify if it extended its caring hands to them. Great writers have sensed this, and since they have exposed society's vilest wounds with reckless hands, by reminding us of those parts of our human nature that can never be wholly taken from the bosom of the evil-doer, and by drawing attention to the fact that, in addition to the loathing with which we shun his deeds, there is also something else that we may feel for the sinner – pity for his misfortune – what they have done has been noble and honourable. They have been inspired to their works by reaction against the insensitivity of the multitude, and for that very reason – the inevitable consequence of any reaction – have often gone beyond their intentions merely so as to soften the loathing and hatred with which people have been clothed not so much against the crime as against the criminal: they have elevated to objects of affection or admiration those for whom they had only meant to show sympathy. I repeat, what they have done has been fine and noble. The writer has a more exalted task than the covering of a quantity of paper with black scribbling, and he that is aware of this won't be satisfied with a couple of favourable reviews or the artistic delight that he finds in the creation of his works. Poetry is reduced to a favourite plaything if he doesn't disregard the interests of the age and shows no ambition to correct the faults that there are and to ennoble the emotions. And he that buries his God-given talents in the depths of artistic form instead of struggling for the most sacred interests of his fellow men just so as not to suffer any kind of blemish, who imagines himself a demigod from the heights of Helicon, sees the sufferings of his time only as a subject for artistic studies, and sings of flowers and the soft evening breeze while the world is bathed in blood and the whole race of men is beginning a new life among the pangs of birth: we may admire him on his frigid height, may envy him – but our respect and affection only he deserves, however, to whom God has given a heart that can understand the sufferings of his fellow men. But if we can't deny the poet our respect – he has toiled for a noble human goal and sacrificed that which is most precious to the artist, the beauty of his work, in order to affect us more strongly – and if we admire the self-denial with which he, who could find diamonds in the depth of his bosom, has rather ploughed his soil with a sharp ploughshare because he felt that he could do less for his own glory by his efforts but more for the benefit of his fellow men, and if we gladly forgive the faults of works thus produced because of the feeling from which they spring, and forget about their weaknesses because we sense that one should admire that to which the critic takes exception, and that what lies before us in the book is not a fine work of art but a fine human deed; what are we to say of those who imitate these works without higher purpose or justification, who, with their corrupt imaginings, revel in everything monstrous or loathsome, pick over the midden on which perfumed flowers are found – not for the sake of the flowers, but because it pleases them to rummage around in filth; who seek in crime not the remaining fragments of nobler human nature but even in virtue always look for those base motives which, in their view, always form the sole basis of our actions; who constantly scour the depths of their imaginings for new monstrosities as Diogenes searched for an honest man with his lamp in the daytime, and are happier to find them than to offer some new comforting thought to their fellow men. Oh, if one day this so romantically depicted outlaw-life were seen from closer to, the hunger, the filth and all the misery in which these adventures are played out, the whole baseness of these heroes, to whom courage is often no more than fear of the gallows. The image would be different from the one that is presented!

*   *
*

"Hey, Mészáros!" said one of them, known throughout the region as Andor Rácz, pushing his grey hair back from his forehead, "what d'you say, wouldn't a bit of goulash be nice?"

"Go to hell," snarled the other as he poked the fire, staring into the flames. "What are you talking about a thing like that for?"

"And a bit of tobacco," Rácz went on with a laugh, "a pipe of tobacco wouldn't be bad, eh?"

"You damn torturer!" shouted the other, and anger flared on his youthful, drink-sodden face. "Why d'you annoy people when there isn't any?"

"Only joking!" replied Rácz. "Maybe you don't like it," he added, gazing at his younger companion with the dignity with which an old outlaw like him, who had followed his trade for twenty-five years in six bands one after another, might look at such a novice.

"All you do is joke!" said Mészáros, poking the burning wood with his foot. "We've been here since first thing this morning, and not a bite to eat. If this is going to go on for long, I'd sooner we were hanged than die of starvation."

"Well, why don't you go and fetch something?" said Rácz, with a scornful smile.

"When everybody in the village is looking out for us?" sighed Mészáros, "Pass me the flask, at least let's have a drink."

"It's there by you," replied Rácz with a laugh, pointing to a big flask on the floor near Mészáros.

"Not that one," said the latter, shaking his head and looking as if he'd been offered poison. "That's only water, I mean that one by you."

"You're not having any of this, my boy," said Rácz, pushing the flask farther away from the extended hand. "There's more *pálinka* than sense in your head, and it gives you stomach ache, you know."

"Give it here," said Mészáros, more crossly, "I want a drink, don't fool with me, nobody gives me orders."

"We'll see about that," said the old outlaw, and as he fixed his dark eyes on his companion he seized the hand with which he was reaching for the flask in his powerful grip, and anyone could see that the regard in which he was held in the band must not come only from his lengthy experience. "Sit down, boy, and keep quiet."

"Just a minute, you old dog," exclaimed Mészáros, "don't you tell me what to do." It seemed that he had made several libations from the flask that he now wanted again. He sprang up and seized his *fokos* from the wall.

Rácz had been watching his every move and now sprang up, seized him by the throat and pushed him hard against the wall even before he could raise his *fokos*, which he wrested from his hand. "I'll give you what for, you bastard," said he, his eyes blazing. "The swineherds have slaughtered plenty of pigs by this wall, one move and you'll be the next."

"What's the matter?" said Viola; he had paid no attention to their conversation until it took this physical turn, but now he got up from his barrel.

278

"This boy badly wants some *pálinka*," said the older outlaw – he released his unfortunate companion and looked at him with a smile of satisfaction as he rubbed his painful neck – "and I'll give him something else in a minute."

"Well, give him some *pálinka* if there is some," said Viola, "we don't need it that much."

Mészáros looked hopefully at the flask, got up and moved towards it.

"I'm not giving him any," said Rácz, blocking his way, "he's drunk more than he should have as it is, and a drunken man always brings trouble."

"But I'm hungry," said Mészáros, with an imploring look at Viola.

"Why did you become an outlaw?" said Rácz with a scornful smile, "nobody made you."

"And who made you?" he snarled back.

"That's different," said Rácz seriously. "I was a deserter. I was in the imperial army for ten years, during the big wars, and when we came home and they wouldn't discharge us, devil only knows why, I thought I'd done enough soldiering, somebody else could take a turn. I threw away my rifle and cartridge pouch and I thought I'd be able to make a living even if I didn't go on sentry duty. If I'd been the son of a butcher, like you,[142] I certainly wouldn't be here in the forest, and neither would Viola, believe you me."

"I don't care," said Mészáros, evidently unimpressed by the seriousness with which Rácz spoke. "Outlaw life, life of crime, I want something to drink."

"Give him the flask," said Viola again. "Let him drink to his heart's content."

"Very well, but he's drunk already," replied Rácz. He picked up the flask from the floor and held onto it uncertainly. "Every band I've been with, drunkenness has meant misfortune."

"There's nothing to worry about today," said Viola, "especially if even Peti doesn't come out and bring meat from István. The magistrate's in Porvár, and the *hajdús* wouldn't come this far of their own accord, that's for sure, and even if they knew where we were they'd avoid us."

"Oh, you must never believe that," said Rácz, shaking his head. "Danger strikes when you least expect it. Here you are, if you want it." So saying he reluctantly handed over his flask, from which Rácz, with certain expressions of animal pleasure, took big gulps despite the reproaches with which he was tormented.

---

142 The name Mészáros means 'butcher'.

After all that the hut subsided into peace and quiet. Mészáros talked about his heroic exploits for a while, and when he could see that Rácz was making no response and wasn't even paying attention he fell silent and slept. Rácz sat by the fire, his elbows on his knees, and Viola went out to the front of the hut.

The night was dark. The tall oaks that surrounded the place, their tops vanishing into the fog, made the gloom darker still, and only the feeble fire, which illuminated the desiccated branches of the bushes in front of the door, shed light of sorts on the scene. After the conversation in the hut had ceased an infinite silence had descended on the region. Now and then the autumn breeze rustled the dried foliage that still clung to the branches, and what seemed a long-drawn-out sigh of pain was heard, always farther and farther away until the faint sound died and the trees stood once more silent and motionless. Sometimes the croak of a rook was heard overhead as birds, thousands of which roosted in the forest, awoke and shook the resonant branches with their heavy wings – then again silence fell all around. Viola stood there outside the hut and an indescribable grief filled his soul. The dark night, the silence, the desolation in which he saw himself and which he felt all the more keenly when he glanced through the door and looked at such companions as he had left in the world – everything filled his soul with pain. How happy he had once been! When work in the fields was over and, as then, autumn brought its long evenings, he used to sit in his warm room dandling his two sons on his knee and watching Zsuzsi as she plied her spindle ceaselessly in the flickering taper-light. Outside fog enveloped the land: the mansion, the peasant houses, the church and the banks of the Tisza vanished beneath its veil, but the bliss that the farmer found in his humble dwelling could not be hidden from his eyes by the changing seasons. Nature spreads mist over the landscape, snow covers the ground, and beneath them every trace of cheerful green and flower vanish; God has not given nature power over the happiness that we bear in our hearts – he has given it only to man. Who would think that the flower, left to the mercy of insensate nature, was safer on its tender root than our happiness, which only sensate man can spoil? Viola had looked calmly into the future, his happiness harmed no one, he didn't interfere with anyone's pleasure; what had he to fear, that desired so little? The poor man thought back over all this and his bosom heaved with a great sigh at the memory. "And all the same," he said to himself, and his fists clenched convulsively, "my happy home was destroyed! I fulfilled all my duty, no, I did more than I had to . . . I carried out all their orders, raised my hat to the torturers, was as submissive as a dog, would have kissed the shoes on their feet, just let them leave my Zsuzsi alone, not disturb the peace of my home, and even so!" – Viola once again thought over the indignities that he had suffered. The way that they had tried to force him to leave his wife when she was in labour: how he'd been dragged through the village: how Nyúzó had meant to have him flogged, and finally the moment when he'd caught sight of the axe and driven the blade into the bailiff's skull, and at first been horrified at the sight of human blood. "No, no," said he, raising his hands to heaven. "May God forgive my sin, I can't repent of what I did, if I were there now, surrounded by the laughing tormentors, and all of a sudden the axe were shining in front of me, I'd pick it up and woe betide anyone in my way. But you whom I have never ever harmed and who have reduced me to misery, made me a criminal and driven me out among the wild animals, because of whom I'm cursed in this world and in eternity. . . you lawyer and magistrate, look out for yourselves, because I swear, as God is my judge, I'll have my revenge on you."

At that moment sounds were heard in the forest. Viola cocked his ear and listened. It sounded as if people were approaching. A rustling of the dry leaves on the forest floor could be heard, the occasional snapping of a stick, the rooks were cawing and taking wing and the forest was filled with their dismal sounds. "Who can it be?" Viola wondered. "Perhaps it's Peti and the cowherd. But how would they be coming from the St-Vilmos direction?" Now a similar sound could be heard from the other side, and the sound of footsteps grew closer and closer. "There are a lot of people coming!" said Viola. "Are they searching for me?" No doubt remained; in the stillness of the night the whispers of those approaching could be heard. Viola rushed into the hut, closed the door behind him, kicked Mészáros and explained briefly to him and Rácz what was happening.

"Didn't I tell you?" said the old outlaw, leaping up and seizing his double-barrelled gun, "and this one here – poking Mészáros – is blind drunk."

In this last remark Rácz was doing a grave injustice. On hearing that enemies were approaching his unfortunate fellow outlaw became completely sober. "Can't we escape somehow?" said he quietly, clutching Rácz's arm with a shaking hand.

"We're surrounded," replied Viola. "If there aren't many of them it won't matter. Are the weapons loaded?"

281

"Four muskets and six pistols," said Rácz, on whose face a look of wild recklessness was to be seen. "Just let them come, there's a good dinner waiting for them."

"Light the taper and put it in the corner so that it won't show through the holes. Cover the fire with ashes." Mészáros trembled as he did so. "Rácz, you and I will stand by the two holes next to the door. You, Mészáros, if you see anybody approaching to the side, shoot them, fire one shot to the right and one to the left so that nobody can put their guns in through the holes. Don't be afraid, son, you won't come to any harm."

These preparations were all completed in less time than it takes to tell. The fire, smothered with ash, filled the hut with smoke, through which the taper in a corner gave only a dim light. Rácz and Viola stood by the door, guns in hand, looking through the little holes which they had made in the wall as loopholes against the possibility of such an attack. Behind them Mészáros walked to and fro, stopping more than once to take a gulp from the flask which stood on the table beside the gunpowder, and which Rácz was no longer guarding. The inspiring potion, however, seemed to be losing its influence over the lad as, growing paler and more tremulous as he felt danger approaching, he paced up and down almost beside himself. "Just let me get out of this," said he, biting his nails, "and I'll become an honest man again. God, if I'm caught I'll be hanged!"

"The birds are here," shouted a powerful hoarse voice, which everyone recognised as Nyúzó's; "I can see a light in the hut. Are they surrounded on all sides? Shout up!"

Forty or fifty voices responded in unison to this call, which indicated to the outlaws that there was no hope of escape. Mészáros crossed himself and knelt.

"I'll shoot you, you dog," exclaimed Rácz. "Get to the hole and if anybody comes near shoot him. If we put up a good defence they'll all leave their teeth here." Mészáros took a big gulp of pálinka and went to one of the holes.

"Give yourselves up, you outlaws," shouted Nyúzó, "if you don't obey the order of the noble county you'll be dealt with summarily."

In the hut there was not a sound.

"Forward, men, break the door down, go on!" shouted the magistrate. Two gendarmes and a few peasants rushed at the door, but before their axes even reached the planks shots rang out, two of the attackers fell bleeding to the ground, and the rest retreated. From the hut came Rácz's booming voice: "Anybody that wants to die, come on!"

At the moment when his companions were firing Mészáros, who was standing at a hole hardly knowing what he was doing, also fired; as luck would have it, a man who had been posted at that side of the hut was also felled by the shot, as the result of which there was such alarm among the besiegers that some of them took to their heels.

After these opening shots there was silence for a while both in the hut and among the attackers. Inside the outlaws reloaded their weapons, while outside some of the besiegers gathered round Nyúzó and the sergeant to take council. It is worth mentioning that in this council of war Macskaházy's voice was not heard: such modesty exceeds our most sanguine expectations.

"I really don't know how we're going to bring it off, Your Honour," said the sergeant, brandishing his pistol in one hand and in the other the sword that had been in the family since the *insurrectio nobilium*[143] of 1741 – there were many such about – the inscribed blade of which must never have come into braver hands.

"Well, we'll have to charge again and again and again," replied the magistrate, stamping his foot, "until we arrest the villains, tie them up and drag them to the gallows."

"If possible, that is," said the other, shrugging his shoulders, "it's not up to me."

"If possible! If possible!" shouted Nyúzó in fury. "If I give an order it's possible." In this Nyúzó, who demonstrated his leadership capabilities by commanding the movements of his force as did great generals but kept himself away from the bullets, gave another sign of the similarity between him and Napoleon, the greatest military leader of the age, who, as is well known, never uttered the word "impossible" to France.

"I don't care," said the sergeant angrily, "I'll go against him if he's the devil himself, only the rest must follow me."

"Anyone that doesn't go," shouted Nyúzó, "is a treacherous cur and must be shot on the spot."

"Then you come with us as well, Your Worship, I can't command these men by myself."

---

143 The "rising of the nobility to the occasion" was the legal obligation on the nobility to take arms in defence of the realm. This happened a number of times in the course of history, including in 1741.

"What are you thinking of, sergeant!" replied Nyúzó much more quietly. "That's not my function, and I have to keep watch over everything."

"I don't care," aid the sergeant, with a scornful glance at his superior; even if that could not be seen in the darkness, from the tone in which the words were spoken it could have been inferred. "Forward, men!" he shouted, and the magistrate repeated the order even louder, and from behind a thick oak some distance away a shrill voice was also heard, in which my readers may recognise the fine words of the refined Macskaházy. The sergeant brandished his sword above his head and, followed by the gendarmes and a few peasants, rushed towards the hut. As the besiegers neared the door shots greeted them again, and the flashes from the barrels flickered over the scene like lightning; after that, all was in darkness and only cries of pain from those on the ground showed that those shots too had found their marks.

The whole company began to withdraw. "Forward now, go forward," shouted the sergeant, "before they can reload. There's no danger." And with that he, together with the bravest in the company rushed once more towards the door, from where again fire was directed at them, by which the sergeant's left arm was shot through and one of the gendarmes was hit in the chest.

The sergeant cursed in pain and anger. "They have no more shots! Charge, charge!" he shouted, and snatching the axe from the hand of a peasant near him he once again rushed at the door. The others picked up their weapons and hurried after him, some because they really believed that the outlaws had no more loaded weapons, some because courage – like fear, always infectious – and the battle itself, the sensation of danger, impelled the more cowardly. From the hut shot followed shot, and almost all brought a man down. The cries of the wounded and the curses of besiegers and besieged together, mingled with the shots, made a din rendered all the more horrifying by the darkness of the sky above it all, only dispelled momentarily by the flashes of shots. The sergeant's words of encouragement and the sound of axes as he and a peasant struck the door rang out above the tumult.

"Give me that gun," he shouted, throwing aside his axe, and seized the weapon from the hands of one of the gendarmes. "This is for you, Viola," and he aimed at the door and fired.

At the shot someone in the hut cried out and fell, but before the sergeant could express his pleasure in words another shot came from inside and the peasant at his side fell to the ground, mortally wounded.

284

"Give me another gun," he exclaimed, but there was no longer anyone there to obey him. They had all fled unstoppably towards the magistrate, who, throughout the entire episode, had not ceased from cursing and encouraging the fighters; but in his capacity as unshakeable leader had not taken a single step closer to the scene of the action.

The sergeant finally realised that he could not overcome the outlaws all by himself, and when another shot came through the chink in the door and took him in the right shoulder he cursed and retreated to join the others.

The siege had been broken; the defeated force was clustered around its mighty leader. Nyúzó was beside himself with rage. The outlaw whom he had pursued for so long was there, two hundred paces away. He had encircled the building with his sentries and forces, organised everything as carefully as any general besieging a fortress. . . and the bandit and his companions were opposing the orders of their magistrate although they knew that the moment they fell into his hands they would be hanged! And then the cowardly people whose task it had been to capture the outlaws, and whom he had brought with him specially for the purpose, had now dared to run away, leaving their magistrate standing there ankle-deep in mud on a cold November night, exposing himself to the risk of catching a terrible cold by setting his subordinates an example and showing that there was no danger that the patriot would not face for the common good. Never heard of such a thing! And even his pipe as well. His tobacco was damp and would not burn, it would not draw, and was Pál Nyúzó not to curse and blame the whole world from the Creation to the present day when he struck five matches one after the other and could not light up. If it had not been too dark for anyone to see the expression of rage on his face the men running from the shots would hardly have stood in front of their magistrate as he puffed with all his might at his blocked pipe; he gave off sparks like a firework, or to draw a more fitting comparison, like a fire-breathing dragon as he stood beneath the lofty oaks.

"Now then, you scoundrels! Where's the outlaw?" he shouted, hurling his pipe to the ground as his best efforts were in vain. "Where's Viola? How dare you come back without him!"

The gathering was silent, and one of the *hajdús* picked up the pipe, which had fortunately fallen into soft mud.

"Clean it out, and properly, you wretch," said the magistrate addressing him. "It won't draw. Didn't I say a hundred times – again to the others – that you were to bring me those outlaws bound hand and foot?"

285

"Your Worship," pleaded one of them in a humble tone, "we've done all we can, three or four are lying dead, half of the rest are wounded and the sergeant's been shot in his left arm."

"There must be at least ten of them in the hut, wherever you look there are nothing but gun barrels," said another. "There's no chance of beating them."

"No chance! Who said there was no chance? exclaimed Nyúzó in fury. "I'd like to know who dared say that. If I give an order . . . Where is the wretch?"

"He's right," said the sergeant, who had meanwhile joined the others. "No one's going to take Viola with men like these. Take my kerchief," said he to one of the gendarmes, "and bind up my arm. Just anyhow, only tight, so that it doesn't bleed so much until we reach the surgeon."

"But when I say that he must be taken," exclaimed Nyúzó, sensing injury to his dignity, "who gives the orders here?"

"Try yourself, Your Worship, if you like, I can't do anything; I've been hit twice, I can't use either of my arms, I couldn't catch a child."

"A pity," said Nyúzó, shaking his head, "that you've just been wounded, sergeant, but those that have been hit, stay behind. You others, line up. Right, my lads! Come on, damn you!"

The magistrate's order was followed by a couple more shots from the hut, and the besiegers were stopped in their tracks as if by the Gorgon's head. Nyúzó also retreated.

"Charge, charge, you good-for-nothings!" he shouted from behind a tree, but no one moved. If they had been defenders rather than attackers no force would ever have borne itself so well.

"Aren't you going to obey orders?" choked out Nyúzó, seizing a man beside him by the throat.

"Certainly not," he replied calmly, and backed away.

"Wait a moment, what's your name?"

"Miska Kovács, I'm a nobleman from St-Vilmos. I won't go even for God's sake."

"I didn't recognise you. And who's this?" he exclaimed, turning to someone else.

"My brother András, he's a nobleman as well, and he won't go either."

"Where are the peasants, then?"

"Those that haven't been killed have run off."

"Cowardly, useless peasants," exclaimed Nyúzó. "I'll teach them!"

"Your Worship," said the sergeant, "let's go home. We've done all that the noble county can require of us, nobody can be called on for more.

There are about fifteen of us, and the others are dead or wounded or have run off home; we shan't catch Viola even if we get ourselves killed to the last man. The minute that he realises that we're so few and that he's no longer surrounded he'll make his escape, and in the darkness of the forest who'll be able to follow him?"

By this time Nyúzó was beginning to yield to these arguments, the soundness of which even he could see, when Macskaházy approached them with a new suggestion; after the din of battle had died away and lengthy experience had persuaded him that the outlaws' bullets weren't doing so much damage he emerged from hiding. "We must set the hut alight," said he, "when they're warm, they'll come out. Let's position men with guns behind the trees, and as soon as any of them comes out, shoot them."

The words were scarcely spoken than they put new life into the attackers. The sergeant laughed with glee. One of the gendarmes undertook to start the fire and was issued with flint and steel, sulphur candles and a pitch-coated torch, and stole to the rear of the hut, where there was no loophole to fear. Those with guns hid in the undergrowth and Nyúzó, who remained with Macskaházy, embraced his friend in his delight at this angelic thought.

Meanwhile the outlaws' situation was grimmer still. Rácz lay on the straw gasping – the shot fired through the door by the sergeant had hit him in the chest, and the ground by where he lay was slippery with blood. Mészáros was pacing up and down the hut, swearing and praying by turns, cursing the day that he had been born. He wanted to maintain his daring with *pálinka*, but the strong drink was having no effect on him, and the thought of nothing but dreadful danger drove all else from his mind. Viola was calm and silent. He was convinced that his last day had come and he looked death in the eye fearlessly, grieving only on account of his wife and children. For a moment, when the besiegers had last withdrawn, he considered escape. If he broke through the roof of the hut and went out at the rear in the darkness of night, perhaps, he could slip away – but then his gaze fell upon his elderly companion lying blood-soaked at his feet. He remembered that at other times he had owed him his life, and would not abandon him in his distress. Now he could hear the enemy moving to the attack once more, and he felt that it was too late and awaited his fate without complaint.

"Just shoot," said Rácz on hearing the noise outside the door; he supported his head on one elbow, and his voice rattled like that of a dying man. "Keep shooting while there's a single one of them left."

"There's no more ball," said Viola calmly, "plenty of powder, but the shot's all gone."

"Hell and damnation!" said Rácz, struggling for breath. "We've got no shot?"

"None," replied Viola, "we've got one loaded musket and two pistols, and the rest are empty."

"Give me one of the pistols," said Rácz quietly, holding out a hand to Viola.

Viola understood what was behind the request and sorrowfully handed over the required weapon, which Rácz grasped tightly in his hand; he fell back on the straw with a sigh. "So," he growled between his teeth, "they can come, but they won't drag me to the gallows alive."

"Hey, Viola," said Mészáros quietly, pointing at Rácz as he lay there, eyes closed, as if unconscious, "he's died."

"No, you can see his chest moving."

"But he's going to die, isn't he? What do you think, Viola," he added in a whisper, "if we surrendered perhaps we'll be forgiven?"

"We'll be forgiven?" said Viola with a laugh. "That's what you find in the psalms of David; if we aren't killed we'll be hanging on the gallows by tomorrow evening, you and I both."

"Not actually forgiven," said the young outlaw, and his voice rose and rose in pitch as if someone were squeezing his throat, "not completely, so that I could go free, but so that I'd be jailed for five, ten, twenty years, I wouldn't care, and I'd be flogged regularly and kept on bread and water and put on hard labour, I wouldn't care, anything as long as I wasn't hanged. What do you think, Viola, they might not do it if I beg, on bended knee, and you see, you know very well I haven't killed anybody, even now I've only fired into the air."

"Poor boy," said Viola, as he released his hand from his companion's trembling fingers, "tell that to the judge. But what's this?" he exclaimed suddenly pointing at a corner of the hut, "it's smoke."

"The hut's on fire!" was heard outside. "Drive them all back into the fire," Nyúzó's powerful voice was heard above the din, while the interior filled with dense smoke.

"They've set fire to the hut," said Viola in horror. "This is dreadful."

Rácz opened his eyes, raised himself on one elbow again and looked round; the fire could already been seen in one corner and a terrible heat was spreading. "Don't let yourself be taken alive," he exclaimed with the last of his strength, "shoot the magistrate, if you can, then die." And with that the old outlaw shot himself. Viola's hand was spattered with his blood, and he stood there, uncertain what to do.

"Our Father!" exclaimed Mészáros, falling to his knees, "we'll be burnt; give me the flask, perhaps I can put it out. This is burning as well!" he shouted in dismay, when the *pálinka* flowed on the ground as blue flames, "who art in Heaven . . . Oh Viola, Viola! why did you steal the notary's documents?. . . that's what's caused all this." The wretch pressed the flask to his lips and drank desperately until the effect of the fumes and the strong drink laid him on the ground beside Rácz.

At those last words Viola remembered the documents, which he had forgotten in the crisis. He had resolved to bury himself under the walls of the hut; at least if Zsuzsi wished to bring her children to the place where their father lay buried let her not have to take them to the gallows. But could he do that now? Tengelyi had humanely taken his wife and children into his home, these documents were very important to him, and now he was going to let them burn along with himself and would leave this world with the reputation of having brought misfortune upon his greatest benefactor. That could not be.

The flames were continuing to spread, and burning straw was falling at the rear of the hut. Viola's hair was singeing, in the hot air he could not draw breath and his eyes were blinded by the smoke. A moment more and his intentions would be beyond his power. He looked one final time at his companions and then, with the documents, wrapped in a kerchief, in his hand, he opened the door and rushed out.

As for a while no sound had been heard from the hut, and although the thatched roof was an inferno the door had not opened and no one had made a move, everyone had begun to think that, as the sergeant had said, the outlaws had taken advantage of the darkness to escape. The pistol shot that had ended Rácz's life didn't alter that view as it seemed only natural that one of the weapons left there had discharged itself in the fire. Nyúzó and Macskaházy were annoyed that their hopes had been disappointed, but they had no misgivings about approaching the blazing hut. So it was that when Viola – his hair on fire, his eyes blinded by smoke and clutching the documents in a kerchief – rushed out of the hut he ran straight into them. Macskaházy snatched the documents from Viola's hand and ran back, while the others gave a tremendous shout and ran to surround him.

The outlaw was unarmed, but the fear in which his name had kept the whole region for so long, and which his desperate defence had only served to enhance, deterred those that still remained; and if he had had a weapon, if there had still been strength in his arms, he might have broken through his enemies and made good his escape. But Viola had no thought of further resistance. The mental and physical torments that he had suffered had sapped the strength of his iron body. He opened his eyes but could see nothing, he drew the cool air into his lungs in long breaths so that his chest swelled as if to burst, and he flung wide his trembling arms and with a great groan fell to the ground unconscious. At that the whole company gave a shout of triumph over their fallen foe, and there was none that didn't wish personally to tie up the arms and legs of the man whose name alone had previously inspired terror.

After Nyúzó had silenced this jubilation – which wasn't easy – so as to make arrangements for his prisoner to be transferred to St-Vilmos, soft moans and cries of pain were heard from the hut. Those present were horrified, and a deathly silence fell all around, broken only by the crackling of the fire and the ever more audible cries of the unfortunate occupant.

"Perhaps I can pull him out," said one of the gendarmes, more humane than the rest.

A tremendous explosion cut him short. The outlaws' store of gunpowder had caught fire, the roof of the hut was blown off, and blazing pieces of it fell among trees without anyone being injured as once again they ran for their lives.

Utter silence lay over the whole area. The cries of pain from the hut had ceased and the light which the burning roof had shed on everything had faded once more to gloom; only here and there was there a little red light where the shattered beams still burnt, and over it all the smoke from the gunpowder descended like a warm fog.

"We might have been killed," said the sergeant, who was the first to regain his composure. "Damned villains!"

"Can anything else happen?" asked Nyúzó shakily from a safe distance back, where he had taken cover behind a tree.

"No, Your Worship," replied the sergeant.

"Yes, but what if there's more gunpowder in there?"

"Gunpowder has a way," replied the sergeant with a smile, "of all going off at once. But you just stay where you are, Your Worship. There's nothing more for us to do. Two strong men, get hold of the prisoner – addressing the others as they slowly reassembled – and take him into St-Vilmos."

Viola was picked up – he was still unconscious – and the whole company set off for St-Vilmos.

"Are the documents safe?" whispered Nyúzó to Macskaházy.

"Yes," came the whispered reply, "I threw them into the fire." At last the sound of steps died away in the forest and the place of horror was peaceful once again.

I mustn't keep my readers waiting for a description of the feelings of Viola's wife during this time.

Shortly after we had left her Peti and the cowherd returned. The one had found the gap, the other the reed-bed, and the tall tree was the one of which they had spoken. They took off their boots and prepared to go through. The horses were hobbled. Peti led the way carrying a long stick, and István took Zsuzsi on his shoulders – she had begged them in the name of God to take her with them – and waded after him. They had, however, scarcely reached the middle of the water when the forest was suddenly filled by the noise of the attack.

"We're too late," cried Zsuzsi. "Take me through, let me die with him."

Shots could be heard, some of the fleeing peasants made their way through that part of the forest, and the three waded close enough to the far side of the flood to hear the sound of the fugitives' footsteps.

The cowherd began to hope again. "Don't be afraid, Zsuzsi," said he reassuringly, "you can see, the villains are all running away."

Peti went cautiously on, and so they reached the edge of the water. But the noise began again with more shots and shouting as the siege was renewed.

Zsuzsi tore herself from the cowherd's grasp; she didn't know what she intended, what she would do, but rushed half-unaware towards the noise. The men held her back by force. She flung herself on her knees, but only one thought filled her heart, and that was of danger to Viola. Didn't every sound come from his enemies? Might not every shot find his breast? She could not pray. In despair she tore at her hair and in her heart pronounced a curse on the whole of Creation.

Suddenly a great light spread through the forest. The shouts of the besiegers, who were less than five hundred paces away, left no doubt as to its cause. Zsuzsi sprang up and raised her hands to heaven. "They've set fire to the hut – they're burning my husband!" she screamed, and fell swooning into Peti's arms.

XXI

By the time that Mrs Viola had recovered and, attended by Peti and István, reached the scene of the battle all was once more peaceful and silent. The footsteps of the victors, as they hastened on the way to St-Vilmos with their bound captive and wounded comrades, had long died away. Their shouts of triumph had faded in the distance and only the cawing of the great horde of rooks could be heard as, disturbed from their slumbers, they flew about high in the trees. Here and there in the open space around the hut, surrounded by bushes, which served as a yard to the building lay fragments of charred wood, and the occasional flame still given off by the remains of a rafter as it hung like a black mourning flag above the burnt-out walls shed a feeble, wavering light on the ruin.

Zsuzsi was reassured. The human heart can endure only so much pain and pleasure; once the chalice is full to the brim the waters of the sea can wash over it without adding a single drop to what it holds; if the scales have once become unbalanced and one of the pans has sunk to a certain point, tons may be piled onto it but it can't be further depressed until it breaks under the weight.

The unhappy woman had reached that point long before. As she came to the hut she covered her eyes with her hands and stood for a moment in silence. Peti and the cowherd, who was guiding her, likewise said not a word; finally she took control of herself, went quickly up to the hut, and looked inside.

She turned round and, her voice choked by the smoke, said "Peti, light a fire, there's plenty of wood and embers lying around, let me look for my husband."

Peti sighed and began collecting fuel. The cowherd, for whom the despairing calm that he saw in the hapless woman was a hundred times more terrible that the sight of her tearing her hair would have been, wiped his eyes. "Zsuzsi, my dear," said he after a pause, "you go back there under the trees and we'll look for him . . . or rather, not for your husband, you can see he hasn't even been here, but for the others, in case someone's hurt. Rest assured, Zsuzsi," he added, taking her hand, "he wasn't even here, I'll swear to it." The poor fellow knew that he was lying, realised that as soon as Peti's fire burnt up they were going to find Viola in the ruin – perhaps half-consumed by the fire – or to discover

292

that he'd fallen into the hands of his pursuers; but he would have given his prospect of salvation to infuse hope into the unhappy woman's heart if only for a moment.

"Stop it, István," said Zsuzsi calmly. "I know exactly what's happened. I'm prepared for anything. You'll see, you'll have no trouble with me even if I find him half burnt; just let me be able to see him again. He's better off here among these burnt timbers than among his enemies; at least he won't suffer any more."

"But when I say that Viola wasn't here," replied István, "Heaven help me, by my soul, I mean he wasn't here! So what the devil would I be looking for in the smoke? And, don't you see, it's not woman's work – if you happen to come across something nasty, who can say, it might do you no good. You go back, and we'll take a look."

Viola's wife, however, was not one of those feeble, delicate creatures that we mostly find among the women of the cultured classes. The softness, the mindless clinging to us that, under the guise of femininity, is considered so irresistible in ladies of the upper classes is not to be sought in country girls tough in body and soul. Nature has made their hearts of sterner stuff. If their husband is beset by danger, instead of shaking in their shoes they share it with him; if they see someone suffering, they don't weep but help; they don't blanch or swoon at the sight of blood, but bandage up the wound; don't sigh over their children but work for them. It was on the edge of the forest, when she heard the shouts of the attackers and the shots, saw the red light in which her husband might have been breathing his last while she couldn't be at his side in his suffering – it was there that the spiritual strength that couldn't avail her had deserted her, and she'd fallen unconscious into the arms of those behind her. The moment of weakness, however, has passed; she felt that her husband and children might have need of her, and the energy with which she would be able to serve her loved ones was restored in her heart.

"Thank you, István, for being so concerned about me," said she warmly, "there's no need to be anxious. I'm feeling better now. Whatever I may see here in the shed, one thing I'll know for certain, and you must see that it's better so. If my husband's dead, let's bury him here beneath the trees – at least we'll know the place where he lies, and the children and I will be able to visit his grave and shed our tears here."

"I tell you, Viola's not here," said the cowherd, "but you'll see, if you can bear the sight of half-burnt bodies . . . but it's no work for a woman. Even if she were in the best of health. God bless you, but it's the truth!

Two years ago there was a fire on my farm and only two cows were burnt, but even so when Her Honour came out and saw the poor blackened corpses she was appalled . . ."

"I'm not a 'Her Honour'," retorted Zsuzsi sourly. "People like her can be appalled and swoon; I'm the wife of an outlaw, I've no time for such luxuries. Oh, István, if you did but know the thoughts that have passed through my poor head since Viola's been outlawed, the dreams I've had, the terrible possibilities I've imagined when I've been waiting for him to come, in my house at night or out in the fields in the daytime, and he's not been able to – if you knew, you wouldn't worry about my being appalled at anything else in this world. Whatever's waiting for me, there's only one kind of unhappiness; I've been enduring all the pains of Hell at once in my imagination for years."

The fire which the Gypsy had in the meantime lit near the hut was beginning to shed a flickering light. Mrs Viola looked around. In front of the entrance lay the body of the St-Vilmos peasant who had been killed by a shot through the door as he stood beside the sergeant, and farther away in the bushes a couple more bodies could be seen. She glanced at them, saw that her husband wasn't one of them, and then, by the light of a burning brand, she looked into the hut.

I'll not describe the sight at which even the old cowherd himself blanched. The table had collapsed and was still smouldering, and shot-guns and pistols lay on the blackened beds. There sprawled the wretches who had ended their lives there, one on a bed, the other in a corner.

"He's not here," said Zsuzsi at length after carefully examining the corpses, even though their features were burnt beyond recognition. "Neither of them has a silver ring on his finger, and my husband would never part with his. He's been captured."

"Never!" said the cowherd, who still meant to arouse hope in the poor woman. "he's probably . . ."

"And what's this?" Zsuzsi interrupted him, as she bent to pick up a double-barrelled shot-gun. "He always took this with him. Here, take it – she added – keep it in memory of him."

"Gladly, and when I meet him I'll give it back," said István.

"And God bless you for your good intentions," Zsuzsi went on, "but if you came any farther with me you too might get into trouble. Peti'll go to St-Vilmos with me, that must be where he's been taken."

And with that the friends parted. The cowherd, sunk in gloomy thoughts, returned to his horses, found them where he'd left them and set off for his farmstead. The outlaw's wife hurried off with Peti towards St-Vilmos.

There the uproar caused by the departure of the party pursuing Viola – and even more by its return victorious – was gradually dying down. Nyúzó and Macskaházy had gone to spend the rest of the night in the house of the lieutenant of the nobility. Of the villagers that had taken part in the siege, some had gone home to rest and others were in the inn, forgetting the dangers that they'd been through. Viola was tied up in the open yard of the village house, guarded by two *hajdús* and two peasants, and had fallen into a deep sleep of exhaustion. As he was being carried through the forest towards St-Vilmos the unfortunate man had come to for the first time after being captured, looked around in the dim light of the torch carried by one of the gendarmes, and realised that his situation was hopeless. He recalled clearly what had happened, and immediately Tengelyi's documents came to mind. As he emerged from the blazing hut he'd been so dazed, so blinded, that he'd not known into whose hands he'd put them – or rather, by whom they'd been snatched away – and he repeatedly asked those who took it in turn to carry him (the magistrate wouldn't permit him to go on his own two feet once he'd regained consciousness) whether they knew anything about them. Those whom he asked replied either not at all or negatively, with the exception of one more forthcoming than the rest, who said that at the moment when he'd emerged from the hut only Nyúzó and Macskaházy had been near the door, and one of them had torn something from his hand; what it had been he couldn't say.

On seeing himself in the hands of the enemy Viola abandoned all resistance and bore uncomplainingly all the torments that he was forced to endure by those who'd been enraged by the long struggle. On arrival in St-Vilmos he asked Nyúzó several times – he was standing there in the lean-to, ordering his constables to bind the prisoner tightly, even if it chafed his hands he must not escape – whether he had his documents. The only answer, however, was a curse and that it was no concern of his, or that he didn't even know what documents Viola was talking about, from which it was plain that the documents weren't going to be handed back by Nyúzó, or that they'd fallen into Macskaházy's possession – he'd endeavoured so long to acquire them that he was certainly not going to give them back.

"So this is what I've sacrificed myself for, what I'm going to the gallows for?" he said at length to himself when Nyúzó and the others had gone away and he was left with his guards; and as they tramped ponderously up and down he flung himself wearily on the ground. – "Why didn't I stay in the hut? Why didn't I shoot myself like Rácz? They're now at peace, while I'm awaiting a foul death and a useless one! I wasn't even able to save Tengelyi's documents. God cursed me the day I was born! . . . Haven't I wanted a hundred times to return to a decent life? And when every way to that was closed to me, didn't I want at least to show gratitude for the one good deed that's been done to me? And what's come of it? God himself didn't want me to do any good in my life. Let me die, then, on the gallows if needs be. You can't get the better of your destiny." – These thoughts restored Viola's peace of mind. It was a sorry peace, like that of one who can see that he can't resist his fate, once he abandons hope and yields himself willy-nilly to the necessity against which he can no longer struggle, but peace it is nonetheless; and the prisoner, fast asleep, forgot his dreadful situation for a while.

So he was when Peti found him; the Gypsy had left his companion outside the village and gone forward to the village house alone. He was unable to enter the yard, as the magistrate had strictly forbidden that anyone, even his guards, should speak to the prisoner; the *hajdú* at the gate, however, had only just arrived from Porvár, and from him Peti learnt that Viola was to be taken to Kislak, where the *statárium*[144] would sit, and that a horseman had already been sent to old Kislaky, who presided over that court in the ward. He returned with this news to Zsuzsi, after one more doleful glance at the lean-to under which Viola lay on the ground, covered in his sheepskin coat.

"Did you see him?" asked Zsuzsi, as she hurried to met Peti when she saw him coming.

"Yes, he's at the village house."

"Inside the village house?" she asked sharply, because my readers will perhaps be aware that as soon as an evil-doer is under cover, that is, in a regular cell, the case has ceased to be one for the *statárium*.

"He's inside," replied Peti, correcting himself, "but not actually in the village house, under the lean-to."

---

144 The *statárium* was a court of summary justice, generally used in times of exceptional conditions of public order and security, for the trial of more serious offenders. The term is derived from the Latin *stare* 'to stand', and cases were heard and judgment delivered without formal *sessio* 'sitting', for which reason such a court was termed in Hungarian *lábon álló bíróság*, 'a standing up court'. In statutory proceedings, after a single hearing the court had to bring in a unanimous verdict, either a death sentence or acquittal, no appeal or clemency was permitted, and sentence was carried out at once.

"Tied up?" exclaimed Zsuzsi, wringing her hands. "Oh my God, the nights are so cold," she added, realising for the first time that she was freezing, "and he's tied up in the open."

"Not in the open," said the Gypsy to reassure her, "under the lean-to."

"Has he got his sheepskin coat?" she asked, starting to take off her own. "If not, you might take this to him."

"Of course he has!" said Peti. "I could see him, wrapped up in a nice big sheepskin. He's asleep."

"Asleep!"said Zsuzsi, seizing Peti's hand. "Can you tell at sight that he's asleep? Doesn't anybody think he's only pretending?"

"Why would they think that?"

"And what do people say to that? Can't they see my husband's innocent? Who ever heard of an evil-doer sleeping? Tell me, Peti, what are people saying?"

Peti only replied that he'd spoken to no one, and that in any case Viola might be released. "As soon as dawn breaks," he added, "he's to be taken to Kislak. If you want to speak to him you'll have the chance there. At St-Vilmos, nobody's allowed to go to him."

"I understand, I understand," said Zsuzsi, her voice choking. "There'll be a *statárium* at Kislak and he'll be hanged. What are they thinking of, he's innocent, his conscience is so easy that he's sleeping on the hard ground better than they in their beds. But come along, let's be going," said she, taking Peti's hand and making a move, "let's go to Kislak quickly, I must see him."

"You poor woman, how could you get to Kislak?"

"Don't you worry," said Zsuzsi, "I'll get there. I shan't have the use of my legs much longer, so why should I spare them?"

Fortunately, Peti had a friend in St-Vilmos, a blacksmith, who, being a Gypsy, lived outside the village; he harnessed up his broken-down nag and took Zsuzsi to Kislak in his trap – apart from his tools and his hovel, the horse and trap were his only possessions – while Peti himself set out for Tiszarét to take news to Tengelyi and, at Zsuzsi's request, to fetch Viola's children.

XXII

There are many sorts of distinction. The foods with which men nour-
ish their bodies differ hardly as much as the objects in which their vanity seeks satisfaction; and if we consider those things by which individuals believe themselves to be elevated to the head of the community
we might be amazed if it didn't occur to us that crabs, snails and the
like, which arouse a certain natural distaste, nevertheless are held to be
the most delicate of foods, although no doubt it must only have been
extreme hunger that drove the first men to sample them. But who can
deny that insofar as the satisfaction of our vanity is concerned such
need always prevails in civilised countries, and the horde of seekers
after distinction exceeds beyond measure the number of distinctions
that can be gained. This being so, it's one of nature's greatest blessings
that, as man isn't restricted to one sort of food for the nourishment
of his body, it has so formed our vanity that it can find satisfaction in
the most various things. It's true that there are people whom we could,
with regard to material foods, call simply carnivores, and we can compare with these in appetite for vanity those who make no distinction of
what brings them profit, be it once or year on year; others, on the other
hand, are harmless herbivores and eat hardly anything but vegetation;
they are gentle, meek souls, worthy of being ranked with those whom a
harmless title, mark or applause exalts to the heavens. But come a time
of need, and carnivore and herbivore alike desire profitable or pleas-
ant-sounding distinctions, and won't be fussy but will reach with equal
eagerness for everything that they can attain, and nature has given
vanity such great precedence over our stomach that the latter, whether
we've starved it or over-indulged it, is incapable of digestion – a feature
that we scarcely find in the former.

In this regard we Hungarians deserve the name of civilised nation
perhaps more than our neighbours, and I scarcely know a country
where so many – and, it must be said, so cheap – distinctions exist as
here. Even if I say nothing of the numerous pleasures that mere popularity extends, from simple approval through unceasing shouts of
"Long live!" to torch-lit musical processions (thinking of which, we can
only regret their rarity in our ill-lit towns, and the fact that we can't use
them to replace the normal street-lighting) how many gradations there
are, and yet how much splendour in each of them! Never has the device

of popularity been made such use of to such an extent and so cleverly as in Hungary. That which in another nation is considered the greatest luxury, on which only those most richly endowed by nature can reckon, among us has become our daily bread, and what would the ambassadors of Pyrrhus say – who were astounded at the sight of the Roman senate and thought that they were in an assembly of kings[145] – if they discovered that within the boundaries of Hungary we possess an entire people of popular persons, each of whom exceeds the next in popularity without, for the most part, encountering any danger of being exiled, as Aristides was by his fellow citizens, for being the most virtuous of all.[146] Everyone knows that I'm not one to praise to excess our domestic conditions, indeed, I have in my time said things that have brought me into conflict with the word of God on earth – by which, as is known, is meant public opinion – although the word of this god has to be explained to a wise man; but I consider the superiority of Hungary to be no less undeniable than that of England in cotton textiles, which lies not so much in the quality of the cloth as in its low price.

Show me a country, someone, where popularity comes more cheaply. Elsewhere you have to devote your entire life to your fatherland, indeed, sometimes even to die. Your body and blood are required in exchange for a great reputation. In Hungary you can attain that goal if the price of beef has been twelve *krajcárs* and you propose that it be reduced it to ten. That's the means by which in England knowledge may be acquired by all through penny editions: in Hungary – glory; thanks to that, popularity, which in all parts of the world – as is known – can easily lead to the aristocracy, in Hungary is one of the most democratic of institutions. Public opinion is so supportive that none of us can feel entitled to the disdain of others, and yet each and everyone is confined to those salutary limits which elsewhere popularity sets only for individuals; but it's well known to what extent these limits are salutary and how impassable they are. Just as, with regard to the command of Holy Scripture that a wife shall obey her husband, many men live in heresy merely in order to preserve domestic peace, so those who possess popularity live for the most part under slipper-government for the sake of that desir-

---

145 In 280 BC Pyrrhus, king of Epirus, claimed victory in the battle of Heraclea and offered Rome a peace treaty, which was rejected. His ambassador Cinea gave the stated opinion of the senate.

146 Herodotus (8:79) calls Aristides "the best and most honourable man in Athens", but his ostracism in c. 485 BC rather resulted from a clash with Themistocles.

able pleasant goal, simply in order that the fickle, from whom there's no escape, may not choose themselves another idol.

But if I remain silent about popularity – although this form of honour is so common among us – doesn't Hungary possess in the institution of *táblabíró* a device of which no other European country can boast for the satisfaction of countless vanities? This is an unceasing fount of honour, a living example of the five small loaves and two fishes in the Gospel, on which thousands dined well and instead of the food running out still more was available; this wonderful invention of the human mind – by means of which each of us can ascend the same single step fifty-two times and always be convinced that we are at the summit, and that each of us may at least have some title at our disposal – puts Hungary in an enviable position with regard to honours; and if we add to this the numerous delegacies to which an ever-growing number are appointed in so many counties and in all the gentlemen's clubs and other organisations which likewise require numerous committee members, all of whom feel themselves specially honoured by the appointment, it can't be denied that hardly anywhere on earth can we find a place where individual citizens can reckon on so many distinctions or – which amounts to the same thing – so many different offices as in Hungary.

My readers may perhaps ask, why am I writing all this? Why can't I say something else? But I'm doing it in order to make known to them that old Kislaky, who'd served the county for a long time as *alispán*, had, on his merits, been appointed president of the court of summary justice in the Tiszarét ward, and because my readers would not understand why that gentle old man had accepted his cruel office if I didn't point out to them the general custom that everyone that has served as *alispán* yearns for an official position, and if there is no other available will be pleased to accept even the presidency of the *statarium,* especially if, as had been the case hitherto, the position of *vérbíró*[147] in the Tiszarét ward was one of those charming Hungarian offices which those who bore it could always say that they too had important work to do, without ever having to do anything.

At Kislak we see an extraordinary commotion; the news of Viola's capture reached there by first light next day as Nyúzó requested the bailiff by official letter to make preparations for the summary court to be convened and the prisoner to be guarded and executed. Early in the

---

147 The judge in a court that can impose a death sentence.

morning the corpulent bailiff, who at other times was so far from any over-enthusiasm that the neighbours had said more than once that he was only kept on at Kislak so that the bullocks for fattening might take example from him, put on his best robe of office with its silver buttons and paced up and down in his courtyard conferring with his young foreman and an elderly farm-hand, who, being a carpenter, undertook to construct the required gallows. "Start thinking so that everything shall be as required," said he, addressing the former, "and you in particular," addressing the latter, "see to it that the gallows be nice and high and especially strong. Make places for the gentry," he turned again to the former, "and make sure that the gendarmes and the servants have theirs as well. Drive a post firmly into the ground here under the lean-to, we'll tie him up there; and the hands are not to go to the fields today, a little example will do them no harm; we must keep the hose ready." And so on, until the worthy bailiff stood there exhausted, wiping the perspiration from his brow, and sighed, "Dear me, there's a lot involved in this," to which his two companions sighed likewise, nodding their heads in agreement.

However, the news caused even greater upset in the Kislaky house itself. The worthy bailiff was making himself busy, it can't be denied, indeed, displaying such industry that anyone seeing him that day was almost sorry that there wasn't a *statarium* every day in the village to make him a very industrious member of society; the sense of personal importance, however, compensated him amply for so much toil. As far as he was concerned, that day a new epoch had begun, in which years would be numbered in the same way as hitherto from the Ice Age. Poor Mrs Kislaky, however, couldn't console herself with that at all, and when she first heard from the bailiff that the court was to sit in her house and Viola to be hanged on her property she clasped her hands in despair as if some great misfortune had come upon her. "Why are they coming here, of all places?" said she in the greatest consternation. "Isn't the county big enough, that it's got to hang its outlaws in front of my very eyes?"

"You're forgetting, Your Honour," replied the bailiff, who would not for anything have forsworn so modish an honour to the village, "that His Worship, as a former *alispán* of the county, was appointed president of the court of summary justice in the Tiszarét ward. It's true that the court could have been convened to somewhere else, but propriety requires the other members to come to their president's house, which causes the least inconvenience. Your Honour will see that it's a distinction, and. . ."

"Thank you very much," the lady of the house cut him short. "If he's hanged here I shan't dare go out of the house."

"Your Honour's mistaken," observed the corpulent bailiff, "indeed, public morale will be greatly heightened by such an example. I personally know of a similar incident that occurred a couple of years ago in a neighbouring county. Theft and fire-raising had been going on for a whole two years; two were hanged for it, but one wasn't even an outlaw and was completely innocent, and from that moment on the evildoing ceased. On this occasion let only one be hanged, and we'll live in heavenly peace."

"But we've never ever been troubled by outlaws," said Mrs Kislaky.

"Quite," replied the bailiff, "but if Your Honour were to see the cowherd's accounts, what they've eaten is the equivalent of a thoroughgoing robbery."

"I'd rather they ate a year's produce than that I'd have to see a hanged man in my own grounds for a whole year." And with that the good lady of the house left to prepare to receive her visitors, while the bailiff, surprised beyond words at his mistress's oddness in being more afraid of a hanged outlaw than of one at large in the region, repeated all his previous orders and paced up and down smoking his pipe as he awaited the prisoner or the court, whichever might arrive first; and outside the gate most of the people of the village loitered, waiting for what was to take place.

Kislak was a mere Hungarian mile[148] from St-Vilmos, and Nyúzó, his prisoner and his clerk – who had received the news and called on his official companion – were the first of the *personae* in the sad *drama* to appear at Kislak. A little later came Macskaházy, who had first been to Tiszarét, and in a final two carriages rode the master of the house and the members of the court, coming from Porvár.

In the first of these latter were Kislaky and Baron Sóskuty, and in the second *táblabíró* Zátonyi and Völgyesy, the assistant county clerk;[149] the latter seemed to occupy only an honorary position beside his all-enveloping neighbour, as he did in his office. The county clerk himself had

---

148 The *magyar mérföld*, a pre-metric unit of distance, slightly variable from time to time and place to place but on average 8,350 metres, roughly five English miles. Eötvös elsewhere appears to use the word *mérföld* (translated 'mile') in the sense of either the English mile or the Roman *mille passuum*, which are much the same thing.

149 More allegorical names. *Zátony* means a shallow place in water, *völgy* a valley.

previously intended to come, but partly because he was one of those rare county clerks that reserved to themselves all civil proceedings – such as consolidation of holdings and registration of land, in which the protection of the tax-paying populace was involved – while charging his subordinates with criminal cases, and partly because the court would need a notary and he didn't wish to undertake the task himself he had sent young Völgyesy in his stead; the latter had only recently been appointed and had accepted the assignment with pleasure, and was quite capable of assisting the others with advice on points of law should need arise. Among the numerous reasons in favour of majority rule one is seldom mentioned, but none the less is of no little significance: when several have equal rights in deciding on a matter, the majority almost always follows the lead of one person, whereas when decision is entrusted to only one he frequently resorts to several advisers, and thus where we might expect the greatest unity we frequently find the least; and anyone versed in Hungarian public affairs, especially with regard to the courts, will admit that as our majorities possess this quality to a high degree it doesn't interfere with the most expeditious settlement possible of everything that our majorities should, instead of advisers, sometimes choose favourites, and they, as is always the way with favourites, are often changed.

There was nothing in Völgyesy's outward appearance to impress the onlooker favourably. His short and slender stature, his slightly humped back and wan, sickly, pockmarked face placed him among the young men who, having no quality, can't even make a claim to be regarded as elegant; his refinement, however, and most of all the modesty with which he concealed his knowledge rather than flaunted it before others, made him one of those rare people whom almost everyone praises because they see nothing about him to envy. The almost universal opinion in Porvár was that *despite it all* (meaning his humpback) Völgyesy was a nice man, and old Kislaky, on learning that Viola had been taken and that he would have to preside over his condemnation, was perhaps even more alarmed than his wife, and was no less pleased than the baron and the fat *táblabíró* to hear that they were taking the young lawyer with them as notary. Kislaky was glad because the notary was well versed in the law, the baron because Völgyesy could remain silent for hours, and Zátonyi because he played a good game of *tarokk*.

When this company reached the Kislaky house Nyúzó and Macskaházy were already waiting on the porch. On seeing the members of the court the latter rubbed his hands together with no little warmth,

303

convinced that there was none of them whose excessive philanthropy he need fear.

On hearing the carriages the lady of the house also came out onto the porch, and with the greatest civility invited the visitors to breakfast; this, however, was declined at Macskaházy's truthful observation that the hour was almost eleven, and that as the days were short they had to hurry if they were to bring anything to a conclusion.

"We really shan't be able to reach a decision today," commented Kislaky calmly.

"Really, *domine spectabilis*, why not?" asked the corpulent *táblabíró*. "Please keep it in mind that until the delinquent has been executed the *statarialis sedria* has to remain together, and tomorrow they'll be sowing and lifting potatoes on my land, I absolutely must go home."

"Quite so, quite so," said Sóskuty, "why all the argument? We've been sent to act as a summary court and summarily we must pass judgement, therein lies our main responsibility. The delinquent is here, we five are present. This young man," he went on, turning to Völgyesy, "with his customary skill will record the verdict in half or a quarter of an hour and that will be that. God forbid," he went on with a gracious bow to the lady of the house, "that we should inconvenience you for long, Your Honour."

"It's no inconvenience," said she with her usual courtesy. "but do you mean that you may not be about to hang this poor man?"

"Not at all, dear lady," said the *táblabíró* with a laugh, "he's as good as hanged already. I've been on fifteen *statarium*s in my time and we've hanged somebody every time. No one in the county has more experience than I."

Viola's wife and children had been with Mrs Kislaky for an hour before this, because by order of the magistrate no one might speak to the prisoner before he appeared before the court. The kindly woman had given the unfortunate three their own room and, moved by poor Zsuzsi's sobbing, had promised to do all that she could for Viola's life to be spared. The resolute manner in which Zátonyi spoke shattered her hopes at a blow, and she only commented that Viola might not be as wicked as many believed.

"I beg your pardon, Your Honour," replied Sóskuty with his usual civility, "whether he is or is not so wicked is a matter of complete indifference to us. The question is whether the man brought before us is an outlaw or not. Whether he's killed a hundred men or none at all, whether he's stolen a million *korona*s or ten *krajczár*s, is nothing to do with us.

All we ask is: is he an outlaw, and how was he captured? If he was armed and resisting – he hangs."

"But really, Your Lordship," said Mrs Kislaky more heatedly, "a man can't be hanged for a couple of *garas*?"

"He certainly can," interposed the *táblabíró* with dignity, "for a couple of mites, if the incident is otherwise under the jurisdiction of a *statarium*. I myself have been present on two occasions when the man that we hanged wouldn't have been given three weeks in prison if he'd gone before a regular court, but hanged he was none the less."

"I'm only a weak, ignorant woman, said the lady of the house even more heatedly, "but if I'd been there it wouldn't have happened."

"I believe you, Your Honour" replied Sóskuty, who as a matter of principle and usage never missed the opportunity when a woman said something fine, "you're mercy personified, simply an angel of grace; but you see, we are men, and that makes all the difference; such permissiveness doesn't befit us. The county has sent us out to make an example, and we have to fulfil this fine commission."

"Look here," now Macskaházy spoke; he had been showing signs of irritation for some time. "Let's get to work, time's going by."

"That's true," said Kislaky, who had been warming his hands at the stove in the greatest distress, looking now at his wife, now at the *táblabíró*. "We've still got to hear witnesses and. . ."

"We shan't have much trouble with the witnesses," said Nyúzó, "everything's perfectly clear. If you please, everything's ready in the bailiff's house, and we can get it all over with twice by lunchtime."

"Viola's deserved to be hanged ten times over, you know," said Macskaházy, already making for the door.

"That will emerge from the evidence," said a clear man's voice, at which all turned towards Völgyesy. "No one may be condemned without a hearing."

"I don't like this man," at those words Macskaházy turned to Nyúzó and whispered into his ear. Mrs Kislaky, who until then had scarcely noticed the little young man, gave him a friendly look on hearing what he said; nature had given his words the beauty that it denied his body. "You're right," said she sweetly, "we mustn't pass judgement on anyone until we've heard them. His Worship will surely treat this poor man fairly."

"I'm not a *táblabíró*," replied Völgyesy, "I have no part in the proceedings." And with that Völgyesy bowed and left with the others, and

Mrs Kislaky was left alone with her husband, who remained for a few moments.

"Just think about it, Bálint," said she taking her husband emotionally by the hand. "If not everyone agrees, a death sentence can't be pronounced. If homicide is committed it'll be on everyone's conscience."

"My dear," he replied with a sigh, "if it depends on me, if it's only possible, I certainly don't want anyone to die; but. . ."

"I know, my dear," said she, "you do your duty; but just think, a man's life isn't something that you can restore; be inclined to mercy."

"If I can, my dear, certainly."

"One more thing," said the kind-hearted woman as he left, "without neglecting your duty you can allow the poor man's wife and children to go to him, at least let them have a couple of hours together."

"As soon as the court permits it," said the old man, scarcely able to hold back his tears; and with that, sighing and repeatedly cursing the day when he had accepted the presidency of the court, he set off for the bailiff's house.

There, all had been made ready to receive the court. Outside the door farmhands and peasants with pitchforks were holding back the crowd, which consisted mainly of women, as is usual on such occasions. Under the lean-to, where ploughs and harrows had been pulled to one side, Viola awaited his fate, tied to a stake and guarded by *hajdús* and gendarmes. In the passage stood Czifra and Jancsi the glazier, who were called as witnesses, and on the other side Mrs Lipták and the Tiszarét blacksmith, who had come of their own accord, and when the members of the court had been led inside by the deeply bowing bailiff and the door had closed behind them the solemn silence that suddenly descended on the crowd revealed the importance of the moment.

"God have mercy on him," whispered Mrs Lipták to the blacksmith, "I've no hope."

"I certainly haven't either," said he. "I'm only sorry that those two aren't being hanged instead of him." Anyone who at that moment looked at Czifra and the Jew could scarcely have failed to share his opinion – anyone that perhaps remembered at that moment how close they had often been to meeting a similar fate – and especially the former, as he looked around anxiously, his cap pulled down low over his eyes, and not appearing at all as a fair-minded witness usually does.

"I'd like to know who's going to be the hangman," said one old woman to her neighbour; despite her best efforts she could not break through the ring of men with pitchforks. "I hope he's skilful, so that the poor victim doesn't suffer too long. They say that if the hangman doesn't know his trade the hanged man can live for as much as a day."

"That's right, my dear," said the other; meanwhile she wriggled forward to a better position but lost it again to a push from one of the farmhands. "Well, all I know is that some Gypsy's going to do the hanging. Perhaps it's the *alispán's* Gypsy, see, that's him there. Look, what a sight, it's surely going to be him, he almost frightens me."

"Don't talk such nonsense, Verus," interrupted an elderly man that was standing by them. "Peti's Viola's close friend, it was he that brought his children from Tiszarét, and you should have seen the friendly way he spoke to his wife. If he was the hangman Mrs Viola wouldn't be speaking to him like that, even you wouldn't have done as much when your late husband was alive. You didn't need a hangman, did you, you tortured him to death yourself."

"How can you say such a thing," said the widow loudly, "when I called a doctor to him the last time he was ill."

"Yes," said the other woman, "so who's going to be the hangman?"

"How do I know?" replied the man.

"It's got to be a Gypsy," commented the town crier's wife, who'd been unable to go into the house despite her husband's influence. "János the gendarme, the brother of my mother-in-law's child's godfather, said that every Gypsy has to go hanging if they can find no one else who'll volunteer for it, they're forced to it in lieu of *contributio*."

"Perhaps he won't actually be hanged," said the first woman.

"Myself, I'd rather he wasn't," replied the man, "because if he's hanged inside the village, you know, it'll be windy all year long."

"Perhaps he'll be pardoned," said a portly young woman; she had been listening to the conversation, with much sighing and clasping of hands.

"Pardoned?" said the man. "he should be so lucky; once those in there get together you know what to expect. It's a *statarium*."

"What's a *statarium*, then?" asked the woman.

"What is it? It just means that the gentry hold a session and then somebody's hanged. That's how it has to turn out."

"But what if there's nobody to hang him?" she asked again curiously.

"Oh, you do ask some silly questions," came the answer. "To get himself hanged a man has to be caught; but who ever heard that a man couldn't be found to hang somebody else?"

"Yes, but if it were to happen all the same?" the little woman's questions continued.

307

"How do I know. . . In that case the gentry would hang him them-selves, or perhaps hang themselves on the door-post in their regret at not being able to hang somebody else."

So people talked outside the door, and the crowd of idlers which, in town or country alike, is never satisfied with its situation, rather as if it were standing in front of a wall behind which something is happen-ing, watched every movement with keen attention. Everything that took place in and around the house, when the witnesses were called in and the prisoner taken before the court, aroused a stir and countless ques-tions and observations: did you see Viola? how pale he was? his long hair had been cropped etc. Meanwhile the court had begun its session.

The *táblabírós* were sworn in in the usual way, the rules of the court of summary justice were read out, and Nyúzó, who had also taken a seat among the *táblabírós*, submitted his written statement. When, however, Völgyesy's behaviour was very unusual during the reading of the rules, as he read them out in their entirety, slowly and as intelligibly as possible, which irritated Nyúzó not a little; and when, during the tedious reading, he tried to speak to his neighbour, the young lawyer admonished him that while the rules were being read out they must be listened to; and when Zátonyi regretfully indicated to Sóskuty that after all this young man lacked experience, otherwise he would know that the reading was a mere formality, that a clever notary could achieve it in four minutes, reading only the beginning of each clause; what was the amazement and anger of the whole court when the magistrate read out his statement and tried immediately to summon the prisoner, but Völgyesy stepped in at once with the declaration that from that statement he could not consid-er Viola's case appropriate for a court of summary justice.

"What, not appropriate for the court?" said Nyúzó, astounded. "Is Master Völgyesy instructing me, the oldest magistrate in the county? That's a bit rich!"

"Your Worship is most mistaken," said Völgyesy calmly, "if he finds even the slightest intention on my part to give offence in saying that. . ."

"Intention to give offence!" interrupted Nyúzó, "I find no intention but actual offence, and that's a fact. Please consider, Your Worships," he continued, addressing the others and snatching up the rules from the table where they lay, "what it says here in section six, subsection eight: *A full account of the event is to be laid before the assembled court, in which the prisoner's offence, surname, forename and age (in letters not numerals)* etc. etc. – and does my statement not include a complete ac-

308

count of the event, are there not given the prisoner's offence, surname, forename and age, and not in numerals but look, gentlemen, written out in letters. So would I not know how to give a full account, would I not be capable of spelling out a person's age? Really, this is vexatiousness, pure vexatiousness, and I will rather walk out than be treated in this fashion."

The president and other members of the court interrupted and calmed somewhat the worthy official's rage, but if that outburst had been calculated to frighten Völgyesy out of saying any more – he was known throughout the county as the mildest of young men – that calculation proved incorrect. As soon as the young lawyer could get a word in he pointed out that he had no doubts of Nyúzó's stylistic ability, but from the statement in question, which was obviously reliable, it didn't appear that the prisoner had been arrested in hot pursuit, which was a basic requirement of any court of summary justice.

"Not in hot pursuit," said Nyúzó, scarcely moderating his fury, "there's a price on his head, we've been chasing him from one end of the county to the other for more than a year, and yet you won't accept that as hot pursuit."

"It's true, Your Worship," said Zátonyi with a smile, "it was really a poor argument; but then, youth. . . but now let's have the prisoner brought in."

"And I'll say once more," continued Völgyesy, still calmly, "hot pursuit is not in evidence from this statement. Viola's last criminal act was the burglary at the notary's in Tiszarét, and pursuit from that time wasn't continuous."

"If this is no longer a case for a *statarium*," said Kislaky, grasping with delight at anything by which he could escape his unpleasant office, "let's send the prisoner before the ordinary court. . . and have done with it."

"For goodness' sake, Your Worship, please don't allow yourself to be fobbed off, it would be an unheard of disgrace if we were to send Viola before the ordinary court. If that happens, I'll venture to wager, the county will lose its *statarium* straight away – why should it have one if it can't make use of it even in a case like this?"

"It seems as if His Worship the notary has forgotten," said Macskaházy, in his usual piping voice, "that courts of summary justice are set up precisely to deal with highwaymen and outlaws, and as soon as one such is pursued and resists by use of weapons there can be no question of the appropriateness of this court."

"That's exactly what I've not forgotten," replied Völgyesy, "but how does it emerge from this statement that Viola is in fact a highwayman?"

309

"From what does it emerge?" said Zátonyi, clasping his hands together. "Isn't it clearly stated in the statement that Viola's a well-known outlaw and highwayman?"

"If you please," Sóskuty now cut in; all through the debate he had been making his observations quietly known only to Kislaky. "I'll explain to the gentleman at once, he's still young and no one holds it against him that he lacks experience, one can't learn such things from books. Here in the instructions there's a lot about who may be called an outlaw, but it's all impractical. Anywhere in Hungary an outlaw is anyone that's called an outlaw. *Vox populi vox Dei*. If an attempt is made to arrest one such and he resists, he's brought before a *statarium* and hanged."

"Just for resisting?" said Völgyesy sharply.

"Just for resisting," replied Sóskuty with dignity. "No one may resist the law, except," he added, "a nobleman within reason."

"We haven't come here to hold a debate," said Zátonyi at length impatiently. "Actually, Master Völgesy has no say in the matter. Let's vote."

"Yes, but even so," said Kislaky.

"I say *luce meridiana clarius*, things are clearer in daylight!' exclaimed Zátonyi. "The matter must clearly and by law be within our jurisdiction. Let's vote."

The *táblabírós* voted. With a sigh, the president declared that in the opinion of the majority the matter belonged before the court of summary justice and the witnesses were summoned.

Since my readers are aware of the relationship that existed between Czifra and the Jew, they won't be as astonished at the perfect agreement of their evidence as I – the novelist, whose task it is to surprise the public – might wish.

"*Duo testes omni exceptione majores*, two honest witnesses," said Zátonyi when the witnesses had withdrawn, and passed his snuff-box round.

"True," sighed Kislaky, "but we put them on oath, and when the Jew called down all manner of curses on himself I was horrified, it was impossible for him to lie."

For lack of space Sóskuty's words can only be given in summary form, but he spoke very finely about the sanctity of oaths and especially the unpleasant incident concerning Dathan and Abiram[150] mentioned in the Jewish oath, and remarked that he had never heard such great agreement as between these witnesses since his wife, God rest her soul, had died and in the three *consilium*s that were held on her so many doctors

---

150 See Numbers 16.

expressed their conviction that she had been treated as expediently as possible.

The magistrate spat once in his delight and ventured to state that never in his long judicial experience had better witnesses appeared before him.

"Permit me, Your Worship, to express slight doubt about that statement," said Völgyesy; he could see that with the exception of Kislaky the members of the court had inwardly pronounced a death sentence on the prisoner even before hearing him, and took it upon himself to do his utmost to save him. "I see in the unusual accord of that evidence a reason for us to be more circumspect. Especially having regard to the characters of the witnesses I can't avoid thinking of collusion."

"Ah, *amice*, this is too much!" said Zátonyi, shaking his head. "You're even finding fault with the fact that the witnesses agree, this is terrible."

"When the witnesses agree so completely," sighed Sóskuty, "agree in every word, every letter, to speak of collusion is monstrous. *Denique prokátor*."[151]

"Insofar as the final words were perhaps intended as an insult," replied the young lawyer, looking Sóskuty in the eye, and his tone was such that the latter desisted from whispering something to his neighbour and fell silent, "I can assure Your Lordship that that purpose was not achieved. The title of *prokátor* can be the finest or the vilest, as he that bears it either understands his true calling or doesn't. However, as for the witnesses, to return to the subject, I will point out once more to Your Worships that such exceptional accord as exists between the evidence of those two most suspicious persons arouses in me the certainty that they have colluded."

"Master Völgyesy clearly believes that," said Kislaky uneasily, "so perhaps we should rather . . ."

"Of course he does," said Macskaházy, forcing a smile, "the worse a case is that we lawyers are defending, the more pleasure we take in obfuscating."

"Master Macskaházy is mistaken, "replied Völgyesy. "The matter of which we speak is so important that anyone that feels disposed to show off at this moment is only to be pitied. But His Worship himself says. . . Czifra is an evildoer known throughout the county, an outlaw . . ."

"Excuse me," Nyúzó interrupted, "János Szentvilmosi – because it is inappropriate to call a person by a nickname before the court – is now

---

151 Typical lawyer.

an honest man, and I can state officially that since being released from the county prison he has reformed completely, has detached himself from Viola's men, and has gained no little merit from the arrest of the criminal who is before us."

"Very well," Völgyesy continued, warming more and more to Viola's defence, "let's allow that, but this Czifra or János Szentvilmosi or whatever he's called, who is now an honest man, but has been a villain all his life and spent most of his days in prison, what does he have to say? Firstly, that Viola informed him in advance of his intention to commit robbery. But if we disregard what a wonderful thing it was that that should have happened, if the witness has taken up an honest way of life and ceased to be an associate of Viola, why did he do nothing to stop him?"

"That's true; you're mistaken, Nyúzó, my friend," said Kislaky, "he can't be an honest man."

Nyúzó scratched his head in perplexity. "Secondly, the witness states that as he approached the village of Tiszarét on the night of the robbery he suddenly heard a shot and saw Viola running past him with a gun. But why was the witness coming to Tiszarét when, as he said, he was preparing for the election, along with the other nobles of St-Vilmos? How was it that no one in Tiszarét saw him? How come that, as he said in answer to my question, he didn't go into the village when he was so close to it and where he no doubt must have had business, otherwise he wouldn't have come all the way from Porvár by night."

"Suspicious, very suspicious," said Kislaky, while Zátonyi took another pinch of snuff and remarked that in that state of affairs it might do no harm to clap Czifra in irons.

"But where does that leave the two fair-minded witnesses?" said Völgyesy triumphantly.

"True," replied the *táblabíró*, quite unruffled, "the investigation of Czifra must be postponed, and at present we need his evidence."

"But surely we aren't going to sentence a man to death on such evidence?" said Völgyesy, scarcely able to conceal his inward horror.

"You have no say in the matter, Your Worship," replied Zátonyi drily. "We'll see what we'll do. Now perhaps we might summon the prisoner," he continued, addressing Kislaky.

"But I beg the court," repeated Völgyesy, seeing that he had laboured in vain, but not abandoning the cause all the same, "if we don't take the quality of the witnesses' evidence into consideration, if we regard these two men, one of whom is a dubious character just out of the county prison and the other an unknown Jew, as perfectly reliable, be so good as to remark that these two men give evidence of the same facts, and so can't be regarded as two witnesses."[152]

"Two men are not two witnesses?" said Zátonyi. "Never heard of such a thing!"

Sóskuty began to check on his fingers that two was actually two and no fewer, and Kislaky himself wasn't entirely clear, though Völgyesy made a quite thorough effort to prove that since the Jew and Czifra had spoken about completely different things – the one about the robbery itself, the other about what had preceded and followed it – only one witness had testified about each solitary fact.

Sóskuty counted up on his fingers perhaps ten times that twice two was four while once two was two and not one; this casuistry had an irresistible effect on the mathematical heads of our *táblabírós*; and all present were convinced that the young lawyer had spoken a great sophism, which, if it were declared before a less intelligent company, could lead judges into error.

As soon as Macskaházy realised the direction in which the discussion was leading he could not sufficiently praise his young colleague, who could wash the devil himself white with his legal tricks. As a result of these clever tactics Kislaky, on whom Völgyesy's words had previously been so influential, was slowly losing his confidence, and that was precisely what Macskaházy wanted, as he had no reason to doubt the other judges.

Völgyesy sensed the situation, gave a sigh and fell silent, but as the court was about to have the prisoner brought before it the *hajdú* at the door reported that there were a further two witnesses that wished to be heard. With the president's permission Mrs Lipták was brought in.

Concealing the fact that she had seen Viola in Tiszarét that day, she only gave evidence about how Viola was so grateful to Tengelyi that he could not possibly have committed the robbery, all the more so because Viola, an old acquaintance and whose wife was a relative of hers, had told her, Mrs Lipták, two weeks previously that there was a plan to steal the notary's documents, and she should warn him.

"And did he actually say who proposed to steal the documents?" asked Nyúzó scornfully.

"He didn't name them, only said that they were powerful men."

---

152 Völgyesy is invoking the principle that "One witness is not a witness". See Deuteronomy 9:15, Numbers 35:30 etc.

At that Macskaházy forced himself to smile. "A fiction," said he disparagingly.

"It's as true as I'm standing here, Your Worship," said the old woman, raising her hand. "I swear to it and I wouldn't lie, if I could gain all the treasure in the world by it."

"And did you tell the notary what Viola had said?" asked the magistrate.

Mrs Lipták hesitated.

"Speak up, my good woman," Kislaky encouraged her gently, "you've nothing to fear."

"Your Worship, I admit," said Mrs Lipták, "I couldn't lie if I wanted to; the only reason I didn't tell old Tengelyi was that he'd said it in his house, and I was afraid that if the notary found out that poor Viola had been in his house he'd be angry, and turn poor Zsuzsi out."

Macskaházy and Nyúzó looked at one another and smiled.

"Have you nothing else to say?" asked the latter, at which Mrs Lipták was dismissed.

The blacksmith, who came after her, only stated that on hearing the shot and rushing to the notary's house he'd chased the murderer, who had at that moment sprung through the door with his gun, and he'd recognised him as Czifra, and he would venture to swear on his life that it hadn't been Viola but Czifra.

After he had been dismissed, the two pieces of evidence were summarised in writing and signed by the witnesses, who had been recalled for the purpose. The court than had the prisoner brought in from the lean-to.

"These two items of evidence," said Nyúzó while they were waiting, "as the court can see, aren't worth the paper they're written on. The old hag is a close relative of Viola, and so can't give evidence on his behalf; the Tiszarét smith is drunk every evening, and in that state could easily have taken Viola for Czifra."

"Quite," said Kislaky.

"In any case, these witness statements are worthy of consideration," remarked Völgyesy, "at least as far as the assessment of the evidence of Czifra – or Szentvilmosi, as the magistrate likes to call him – is concerned. There have been hundreds of cases of malefactors giving evidence against others."

"That's true too," said the president.

"Tell you what," said Zátonyi, through whose head a marvellous idea had flashed, "let's hang the pair of them."

"What are you thinking of, *amice*," replied Sóskuty, while Kislaky and Völgyesy stared in amazement at the speaker. "The other one's not before the *statarium*."

"If that's where he's put, that's where he is," retorted Zátonyi, evidently quite taken by his spontaneous thought. "I know of a case. A criminal was beneath the gallows when he recognised an accomplice who happened to be passing and pointed him out to the magistrate. The latter sent after him, he ran off but was caught, he defended himself, was brought back and hanged straight away along with the other, and when the magistrate went back to the *statarialis sedria* he reported that he'd hanged two instead of one."

Zátonyi laughed, and Völgyesy raised his eyes to the heavens.

"Goodness, there must have been a row," said Sóskuty. "I wouldn't have liked to be in that magistrate's shoes."

"A row . . . yes," replied the *táblabíró*, still smiling. "There was a bit of a row, because in Hungary every gallows-bird has someone to take his side; the magistrate was reprimanded, I think, perhaps he might even have been dismissed if he didn't resign; there was no more trouble, and anyway the villain had been hanged."

"Absolute murder," said Völgyesy. "Monstrous!"

"*Amice*," said Zátonyi, giving the young lawyer a pitying look, "*denique* you've no experience; I know even better stories about *statarium*s. Anyway, I don't want to force my opinion on the court, I'm just saying that it's really a pity that we aren't hanging the pair of them. But here comes the prisoner."

Now the door opened and Viola, surrounded by guards, stepped into the room.

The prisoner's entrance had a noticeable effect on the whole court. Kislaky's heart was filled with the compassion that every decent man feels at the sight of great misfortune, even when they are quite sure that it is not entirely undeserved; Völgyesy, who, after what he had by then seen and heard, scarcely dared hope for a favourable verdict, shuddered at the thought that this man, whom he now saw in his presence in perfect health, would in a couple of hours' time be leaving the ranks of the living – not because God so ordained but because his fellow men wished it, because among them there wasn't one to be found willing to allow time for the seeds of virtue which doubtless lay hidden in that breast to develop. Macskaházy looked around with evident calm on hearing the rattling of chains, while on the face of Sóskuty, who had never before seen the famous outlaw, there was expressed as much curiosity as on

315

Nyúzó's there was *Schadenfreude* when he that was to be condemned appeared before them; Zátonyi offered his snuff-box round with the greatest composure, as if there were nothing happening that aroused more than distant interest.

"So you're[153] finally caught, you fine bird!" the silence was broken by Nyúzó, as he turned towards the prisoner. "Well, who's going to hang whom this time?"

At this sudden outburst the president looked in amazement at the magistrate, who continued with a laugh: "Your Worship is unaware of the relationship between the two of us. Viola and I are old acquaintances. Aren't we, Viola?" He added addressing the prisoner scornfully. "We've had our sights on one another for a long time, and Viola's taken an oath that if he gets his hands on me I'll hang. Isn't that so?"

"That's not true, Your Worship," said the prisoner, and his deep manly voice was almost pleasing after the magistrates rasping tone. "When I swore vengeance on Your Worship everybody knows I had reason, because I've had nobody but you to thank for not dying an honest man; but that I'd hang you, that I never promised."

"We know, we know," the magistrate jeered, "now you're just pretending to be meek and mild, but if ever I'd got into your clutches you certainly would have kept your vow. You see, when I heard that that was what you'd got in store for me I also swore that if you came into my hands I'd hang you. A solemn oath. So, who's turned out right?"

"I know perfectly well I'm done for," said Viola, fixing his dark eyes on the magistrate, "nobody's going to help me, I'm a dead man, but it does you no credit, making fun of a man in misfortune."

Völgyesy had been scarcely able to control his feelings throughout this scene, and his voice shook as he pointed out to the court – in Latin, so that the prisoner should not understand – that there was deadly enmity between the accused and one of the judges, and that a different judge should be found; that only gained attention in that Nyúzó was told by the president in rather bad Latin that such jokes were out of place. The interrogation of the prisoner began at once.

Viola answered each question calmly and simply; eventually, as if bored with the length of the proceedings, he turned to the president and said: "What's all this lengthy questioning for? It's a pity to waste the court's time; the magistrate said in the first place that you were go-

---

153 It is noticeable that Nyúzó and Zátonyi address Viola as *te* while Völgyesy uses *kend*, as does Macskaházy later.

316

ing to hang me, why should I chatter for my life? I'll confess anything and everything, I don't care. Believe me, Your Worships, if it weren't for my wife and children I wouldn't have waited, I'd have hanged myself on some tree in the forest."

"How can you make a confession," said Völgyesy, moved, "when you don't know what you're accused of? See, you're in front of just judges, speak as you would to God, clearly and truthfully. The court hasn't passed judgement on you yet."[154]

"Thank you, Your Worship, for your kindness," said the prisoner, "but no one's going to help me. I'm an outlaw, I was captured armed, and nothing but the gallows awaits me and sooner rather than later. Let me be spared the questioning."

"If he's obstinate and won't reply," said Macskaházy, who could see the turn that the affair was taking and was becoming more anxious, "we can't make him, it's stated clearly in the instructions that the use of force is forbidden in such a case. We'll read out the questions and if he doesn't reply we'll take it that he acknowledges all charges."

"Yes, but first of all", said Völgyesy, "this man must understand that his fate is not dependent on Pál Nyúzó's wishes alone; that the court will gladly listen to his defence and in its verdict won't be influenced by anger or hatred but by truth alone, and then he will perhaps not remain obstinately silent. You can see, my man," he went on, turning to Viola, "your life is in these gentlemen's hands, and they will answer for it only to God. Consider that if you don't speak nothing on earth can save you, think of your wife and children, and speak out: is there nothing that you might say in your defence?"

Kislaky's eyes began to be moist; Macskaházy favoured the speaker with an angry look, while Zátonyi yawned.

"I shall say nothing in my defence," replied the prisoner.

"Think carefully," Völgyesy urged him. "Look, the court will pay attention to every word you say; these gentlemen are exercising a very weighty responsibility, they don't wish for the death of anyone, and will certainly pass judgement in accordance with truth. If you have any defence, speak out."

"I draw the attention of our esteemed notary to the fact," Zátonyi interrupted, assuming an expression of the greatest sagacity, "that section

154 Even Völgyesy accepts that the prisoner has not been charged, though evidence has been taken which he didn't hear, and now he is being questioned.

ten of part six of the instructions forbids the making of promises to the prisoner."

Völgyesy paid no attention to those words, and once again begged the prisoner to speak in his defence. Kislaky repeated the plea.

"Your Worship," said the prisoner, obviously touched by the sympathy that he saw in Völgyesy, "God bless you for your kindness in wishing to help me, but you can see it's quite futile. No, it seems that there's nothing that I can say to save myself, and indeed, when I appear before God, where all things are known, then I'll expect a merciful judgement; here on earth nothing can save me. You see, Your Worship," he added after a brief pause, "if I say that I was once an honest man, to which I could call on all Tiszarét to witness, would that do me any good? If I say that I became an outlaw not of my own volition but by necessity? That I've never done harm to the poor, and from the rich I've only stolen enough to be able to eat; that except in defence of my life I've never harmed anyone – shall I be punished any the less? What my fellow outlaws have done has been laid to my account; I'm an outlaw, and that's all there is to it."

"All that can have a great effect on the court's verdict," said Völgyesy. "How did it come about, as you said, that you became an outlaw not of your own volition?"

"Ask the magistrate, Your Worship," said Viola, glancing at Nyúzó, at which the latter averted his gaze. "He'll tell you why I became an outlaw." And with that the prisoner, his voice trembling with passion, recounted the tale of his first crime.

"Every word of that is the truth," sighed Kislaky. "I went to Tiszarét the very next day and the alispán told me himself."

"*Nihil ad rem*,"[155] remarked Zátonyi. I shan't describe Völgyesy's feelings.

"But what good will all that do?" continued the prisoner; during the narration his pale cheeks had begun to blaze, and his hands had clenched involuntarily into fists. "What good is it if I relate all the nastiness that has been practised on me and at which my blood boils when I think about it? Does it make me any the less an outlaw? Shall I go to the gallows any later? Should I have endured the flogging, kissed the torturers' hands, or should I have left my wife there in her agony when Her Honour wanted me to drive her to Porvár? I was a worthless peasant for having the nerve to love my wife, and for daring to resist when the magistrate order me to be stripped, wasn't I, Your Worships? Fool that I was,

---

155 Nothing relevant.

I thought that although I was a peasant and discharged my obligations I would be allowed to stay with my sick wife; I didn't stop to think that a poor man's a dog, and that anyone that likes to can beat and torment him. Here I am, Your Worships, string me up."

"That we will," said Zátonyi angrily; for all his obtuseness he had perfectly caught the sense of the prisoner's last words, such was the tone in which they were uttered. "You deserve to die twice for your insubordination, of which you still don't seem to repent."

"You see, Your Worship," said Viola, now calm once more, addressing Völgyesy, "as I said, there's nothing that I can offer in my defence before men. But I have one request to make of the court."

Macskaházy was wringing his hands with obvious misgivings. The prisoner continued: "When I came out of the burning shed, where Rácz had shot himself and I couldn't possibly stay, I brought with me certain documents which had been stolen the day before from the notary in Tiszarét."

"You mean, you admit the theft?" Zátonyi interrupted.

"I , and as God can see my soul I'm innocent of the robbery." replied the outlaw, raising his hands to heaven. "But that's not what I mean. I'm only saying that the documents were in my possession and that I brought them out of the shed with me."

"A fiction," muttered Nyúzó.

"It's not a fiction, Your Worship, but the plain truth!" replied the prisoner, looking steadily at him. "When I came out of the burning building I was blinded, I came out unarmed and only held those documents to my chest. I distinctly felt someone tear the packet from my hand, I could swear to it. I immediately lost consciousness and fell to the ground, and when I came to I found myself trussed up and in the hands of the gendarmes and peasants, being carried off towards St-Vilmos. I enquired at once about the documents, because they were Mr Tengelyi's, and I'd only surrendered so that they shouldn't be burned with me, because he seriously needed them. But everybody told me that when I came out that there was nobody near me except the magistrate and Mr Macskaházy, and the magistrate has denied that I had any documents on me. I beg the court most humbly to be so good as to order the magistrate to hand over the documents."

"Devil take me," said Nyúzó in a rage, "if I've seen a single document." "Your Worship," said Viola calmly, "look, I'm in your hands, you're free to have your will with me and hang me when you like, but don't deny me the documents. I owe much gratitude to Mr Tengelyi, he took in my wife and children in their great need, and I meant to show my gratitude by getting those documents back for him as they're important to him. I'm letting myself suffer a shameful death. . ."

"You utter villain," exclaimed Nyúzó, jumping up from his chair. "How dare you ask me for such a thing! This is disgraceful, I demand satisfaction from the court."

"I'm in the court's hands," said the prisoner heatedly, "you can beat me, torture me, I don't care, only give back those documents."

"Absolute nonsense," whispered Macskaházy to Zátonyi. "Tengelyi says that his certificate of nobility's been stolen, goodness knows what that's got to do with this man."

"Quite," nodded Zátonyi.

"You're not going to say," shouted Nyúzó, even more furiously, "that I stole the documents, are you?"

"I'm only saying that I brought the documents out with me," replied Viola, "that somebody snatched them out of my hand, and that the court is in a position to question all those that were present about them. Nobody other than the magistrate and Mr Macskaházy were near me, and I'm prepared to swear to that on oath. May God, before whose face I'm to appear this day, be merciful to me as I'm telling the truth."

"Curious, very curious," muttered Kislaky.

"The court isn't going to tolerate," said Nyúzó, pushing his chair aside, "one of its members being called a thief by this outlaw."

"This is going too far," said Zátonyi at length in noble rage, staring angrily at the prisoner. "If you don't immediately retract what you said and beg the court's pardon we'll have you given fifty strokes and then you'll say something different."

Viola replied calmly that he was in their power, but that what he had said he would repeat to his dying breath, and Zátonyi would perhaps have pronounced sentence there and then, certainly not without partiality, had Völgyesy not reminded him – in Latin – that in the very same tenth paragraph of the sixth section which the *táblabíró* himself had quoted earlier, threats and beating were no less prohibited than promises of mercy.

To that, however, Sóskuty remarked that such an interpretation of the instructions led to nonsense, because if it were accepted the prisoner could make fools of the entire court and indeed beat them without having anything other than hanging to worry him; perhaps the prisoner might not have escaped this further punishment had Völgyesy not stated in all seriousness that whatever decision the court might take, if

320

the slightest injury were inflicted on the prisoner in the course of questioning he would register a complaint not only at county level but in higher places too. To that Sóskuty merely muttered something about the impudence of modern youth, Zátonyi said something indistinct about underhand denunciations, and the matter was dropped.

During that brief conversation, which was conducted in a language that he didn't understand, Viola stood there calmly, only his facial expression showing the interest with which he followed the movements of the various speakers. Macskaházy and Nyúzó whispered together.

"The court will permit," said Macskaházy eventually, with that gentle smile that he commonly used, and because of which everyone in the county said that the Tiszarét lawyer was probity its very self – although in other countries, where the word "probity" is not used to express politeness, it might meet with a quite different interpretation – "that since the prisoner is accusing me too, I may address a few questions to him. You say, my man, that when you emerged from the shed I too was standing there. Did you see me, my man?"

"I couldn't," said Viola, "I was so blinded by the smoke and flames in the shed that for a while I couldn't see anything. But the *hajdús* and peasants all tell me that Your Worships were there, and I felt somebody snatch the documents out of my hand."

"So the smoke was very dense in the shed?" Macskaházy went on.

"Something terrible, Your Worship, we could hardly see one another. The flames gave a bit of light, but we were nearly blinded."

"And you brought your documents out?"

"Well, they were just there at my side on my fur. I grabbed them and took them out, wrapped in a blue kerchief."

"This man is telling the truth," Macskaházy smiled at the court, "or at least, he believes so. When he rushed out of the shed he was holding something in his hand; in the first moment I didn't know whether it was a weapon with which to defend himself, and I took it off him; only then did I see that it was only a harmless kerchief with something wrapped up in it. But," he added with a laugh, addressing the prisoner, "if you think that you'd brought documents out with, you poor man, you were sadly mistaken. Your Worship, please bring in what we took from Viola when he was arrested."

Nyúzó left the room.

"All there was in the kerchief was my documents," said the prisoner. At Macskaházy's words his face had first registered the greatest delight, then the greatest disquiet. Surprise and fury beyond description seized his whole being when Nyúzó returned and placed the kerchief on the table; Sóskuty and Zátonyi laughed when all that was taken from it were some underclothes. That was his kerchief, the same one in which Tengelyi's documents had been wrapped for safe keeping; how was he to prove that they'd been removed? If Nyúzó and Macskaházy persisted in denying that they'd taken something out of it, with so many present perhaps someone might still be found that had seen him bring something out of the shed, and could give evidence of it – but like this, what means had he left of proving how underhand these two were being? He, the outlaw, against two men who were about as judges to pronounce a verdict on him.

"The court can see," said Macskaházy, showing the greatest sympathy to the prisoner, "that this poor man had no wish at all to deceive the court by lying. I believe, indeed it's very likely, that Tengelyi's documents were in his possession and that he intended to bring them out with him; but as he said just now, smoke and flames had rendered him blind and instead of documents he brought out his underwear. It's quite understandable. . ."

"Of course," said Sóskuty, "under such circumstances I wouldn't know what I was doing myself; perhaps you recall, when fire broke out in the tax-gatherer's premises in a neighbouring county the poor man was so frightened that he only saved a pair of boots and the cash office was burnt to ashes. When the inspectors came round all that they found in the safe was a pile of ash instead of banknotes."

"Your Worships," said Viola after a pause.

"Please don't take umbrage," Macskaházy interrupted him, still suavely, "what this man is perhaps about to say, I'll venture to swear, he'll say purely out of conviction. He'll not deserve punishment, he's suffering from what we lawyers call *ignorantia invincibilis*."[156]

"Quite, quite," remarked Sóskuty. "One of the *remedia juridica*."[157]

"Your Worships," the prisoner repeated in the greatest agitation, "I'm a hapless, condemned criminal, and His Worship the magistrate and Mr Macskaházy are powerful gentlemen, that I know; but what reason have I, that am to appear this day in the presence of God, for lying? May I be damned to eternity, and may God punish my children to the tenth generation, if my documents weren't wrapped in that kerchief."

---

156 Invincible ignorance. Ignorance for which one can't be held responsible.
157 Legal redress. Relief from legal responsibility.

"As I've told the court," said Macskaházy, still smiling, "this man is obsessed; if he's put to the torture he'll say nothing else. It's quite natural. You're mistaken, my man," he went on, addressing the prisoner, "calm yourself. Just consider, what reason would His Worship the magistrate or I have for not producing them to the court if in fact you had brought them out with you, as we have this kerchief and underwear?"

"Yes," said Sóskuty, "what reason could these honourable gentlemen have? What do you suppose?"

Viola was silent for a moment, gazing into space as if sunk deep in thought; at length he looked up and asked that the *hajdús* be sent out, and on noticing that Sóskuty and Zátonyi were perturbed he said "My hands are tied, and there are six of you honourable gentlemen – you have nothing to fear."

The *hajdús* were dismissed. Then Viola stared at Macskaházy and spoke:

"What I'm about to tell Your Worships will certainly surprise you all, with the exception of Mr Macskaházy; I would never have spoken of these matters, and I've asked for the *hajdús* to be dismissed so that nobody other than the court shall hear my statement, because my wife and children live in Tiszarét and after my death perhaps the gentry would show the orphans mercy. But since you ask what reason Mr Macskaházy may have for concealing Mr Tengelyi's documents, I will only say that the honourable gentleman presumably knows best of all, and, furthermore, that his reason must have been very compelling, otherwise he would certainly not have stolen them, but the whole robbery was carried out on his orders."

Macskaházy paled.

"I must say, this is a fine piece of mischief," said he, still smiling, though his voice trembled. "I'm curious to know how the prisoner can prove this allegation against an honest man."

"Let's not even listen to him," repeated Sóskuty; he had looked at his watch several times, clearly anxious about his lunch.

Völgyesy called on Viola to speak, and he, with several interruptions from Sóskuty and Zátonyi – who could not restrain their feelings, especially when they heard the respected wife of the *alispán* mentioned – told the whole tale of the theft of the documents as my readers know it, starting from when he overheard Macskaházy and the *alispán*'s wife talking in the park until the moment when he laid out the Jew in Tengélyi's house and took the stolen documents off him. His account was entirely truthful, with the solitary exceptions that, as he didn't wish

323

to involve anyone else in his trouble, he mentioned neither that he had spoken with Mrs Lipták when he was being pursued in Tiszarét and had been in the notary's house, nor that he had heard from Peti that the Jew and Czifra were planning the robbery.

Macskaházy heard the long tale out, with a scornful smile on his lips, and then requested the others to allow him to address a few questions to the prisoner. "It's not as if we need any defence for myself or Her Honour, least of all against such an accuser," said he contemptuously, "but so that this man may be persuaded of the senselessness of his lies. My man," he went on sharply, turning to Viola, "that alleged conversation that you heard between myself and Her Honour Mrs Réty, you haven't spoken about it to anyone else?"

"No."

"Think back carefully," the lawyer went mockingly on, "you didn't tell anyone, anyone at all, that someone intended to steal the notary's documents? It would help if we knew about your associates too. For example, you never said anything of the sort to Peti the Gypsy, or to Mrs Lipták?"

Viola knew perfectly well the consequences that he might bring upon his friends if it became known that he had remained in constant contact with them, and denied that stolidly.

"And when you were being pursued in Tiszarét, where did you hide?" asked Macskaházy.

Viola said that during the pursuit he had not been in Tiszarét.

The lawyer had Mrs Lipták recalled and had her earlier statement read out, according to which Viola wanted her to inform Tengelyi of the intended robbery, and asked whether she stood by it. To that the old woman offered to take an oath, and said that he had.

"Viola has confessed," said Macskaházy to Mrs Lipták, "that he spoke to you on this matter when he was being pursued in Tiszarét and was hiding in the notary's house. How could he also have spoken to you at another time?"

Mrs Lipták, in the belief that Viola had actually made that confession, said that it was quite true, but that Tengelyi had known nothing about the fugitive being in his house.

Macskaházy's face lit up when Mrs Lipták had been dismissed and he turned to the court and asked: "Have you ever heard more bare-faced lies? One of them says that he hadn't spoken to anyone about the robbery of which he accuses me, but the other says that she had been informed about it in advance so that she might warn Tengelyi, but failed to do so and gave no reason. The prisoner states that he wasn't in Tiszarét while being pursued; the witness says that that was where and when he spoke to her on the subject. Do you hear that?" he added, turning scornfully to Viola, "if you ever again while you live have the opportunity to tell a lie, be better prepared. But let's go on. From whom did you receive the information that the Jewish glazier and Czifra were planning a robbery at the notary's?"

"That I can't say," replied Viola; he would have suffered six deaths rather then involve his most loyal friend.

"That's really a pity," continued the lawyer, "I'd really like to know the precious flower who brought you such information, as long as it's not some evil spirit."

"I tell Your Worship," replied Viola calmly, "all I can say is that I knew that there was to be a robbery."

"And how?" came the next question.

"Czifra and the Jew were talking in an inn near Porvár."

"And you heard them yourself?"

"No, I was told by somebody else."

"The devil whispered it to you, you amazing man," said Macskaházy with a smile, "but if you were so certain that there was to be a robbery, why didn't you report it at once?"

"Your Worship knows that there's a price on my head."

"Yes, on your head, that's true," replied Macskaházy. "But this other person, the one that told you, could he not have alerted the county? Or if perhaps he doesn't like dealing with officials, why didn't he tell Tengelyi himself? Or Vándory, who, I understand, is also affected by the robbery?"

"I don't know," said Viola. "Perhaps he couldn't find Mr Tengelyi and knew that I'd be able to prevent it, so he only told me."

"It's remarkable," said Macskaházy, still sneering, "that anyone wanting to forestall a robbery should have recourse to an outlaw, of all people. And so in fact you went alone to prevent the robbery? Why didn't your associate, or the person that informed you, go with you?"

"I didn't need him," said Viola.

"All the same, you knew that there were two planning the robbery," said the lawyer. "It's odd that both of you didn't go. You can see how valuable your associate's testimony would be now. Because if you only went to prevent the crime you could safely name the other person and he could reckon on a reward from the county."

"I was by myself," said Viola, gradually losing hope, especially as he could see from Nyúzó's face how he was enjoying his discomfiture, and

325

the inexpressible satisfaction with which Zátonyi and the Baron were nodding approval of the shrewd questions.

"Very well, so you were by yourself," Macskaházy continued. "Whom did you see at the crime scene?"

"Only the Jew, who was standing outside the house," replied Viola. "Nobody else."

"You didn't see Czifra there?"

"No, the Jew was there by himself."

"But the Jew says that you carried out the robbery, and will swear to it," Macskaházy went on.

"I don't care," answered the prisoner. "I stand by what I've said."

"Have you nothing more to say?" asked Macskaházy.

"No."

"Perhaps the prisoner might be taken out?" said the lawyer, turning to the president, who gave the order. The *hajdús* were called in and escorted Viola from the room.

Of the hundred arguments that take place daily in this world, before audiences greater and smaller, with lesser or louder volume, hardly one is conducted for the sake of truth. Most people only endeavour for the majority to grant that they are right. In our day it isn't the fruit of the tree of knowledge that men strive after; the majority are satisfied if they can persuade others that they have eaten of it, though they know themselves that they have never even been near the tree. It's so pleasant to be able to say 'I was right all along!' Never can the discovery of the truth offer greater delight. Nowhere has this natural tendency of ours – by virtue of which the philosopher will accept the most dreadful consequences of his theory rather than acknowledge its error, and in accordance with which Lysippos, the collector of antiquities, declares to be gold that which he has bought as such for a large sum, although it's only imitation – so great and harmful an effect as in our criminal proceedings; and my readers – if they know men who deal with such matters – have certainly experienced the way that those who are the meekest in public life are so irritable if, in some prosecution, the offender can't be found guilty. As my readers are aware, Macskaházy had other reasons for wishing Viola to be found guilty by the court, and so they can imagine the joy with which he realised what an impression that he'd made on the judges by his interrogation of the prisoner.

The contrast between the statements of Viola and Mrs Lipták, together with the improbability of the whole accusation that the prisoner had made against Macskaházy, and especially against the so respected wife of the *alispán,* convinced those present that – as Nyúzó put it – the whole thing was a disgraceful fabrication, and Völgyesy himself, despite the goodwill with which he had tried to help the prisoner, could hardly believe otherwise. If the Jew and Czifra had in fact conspired to rob the notary, and on that occasion had been so careless as to let their conversation be overheard – which wasn't likely, considering how experienced Czifra was – who was going to believe that a third person, wishing to prevent the crime, would turn to Viola, Czifra's sometime associate? Or that the Jew and Czifra, if they knew themselves to be guilty, would come forward as witnesses, although the latter had not even been called? And finally, had not Viola admitted that the robbery had been carried out by the Jew alone, and that he had not encountered Czifra on the scene? While the blacksmith had sworn that he had seen Czifra and given pursuit, from which it was clear that either this witness was lying intentionally or that in the darkness he had mistaken the man running in front of him for Czifra.

"Things are clearer in the daylight," said Zátonyi, once all these circumstances had been rehearsed several times by the members of the court. "The prisoner denies nothing, so we'll quickly sign the witness statements, hold a little confrontation and then we can pass a summary judgement. It's nearly two o'clock, we're obliged to allow the prisoner three hours to prepare for death, and at five o'clock it's dark. If we mean to finish the business today we'll have to hurry up."

"That'll hardly be possible," said Kislaky, who seemed all the more uneasy as the moment of judgement approached.

"Not a bit of it," replied Zátonyi, "only let's be quick, I need to get home today, I want to see to the potato lifting and then the ploughing."

"Let's just get on with it," nodded Sóskuty too, who, it seemed, was more concerned over the delayed lunch than the impending verdict, "we really mustn't keep our angel of a hostess waiting any longer."

"This matter can't be finished today," interposed Völgyesy. "The prisoner's statement was a long one, I'll need at least two hours to write it up from my notes."

"That won't be necessary," said Nyúzó. "As soon as Viola came into my hands I interrogated him in the presence of my clerk. As the court is aware, the prisoner has altered nothing; even if it's not in quite such elegant Hungarian as His Worship would produce it's good enough – once it's signed by the prisoner – to be annexed to the record."

The *táblabírós* unanimously accepted this proposal with the readiness that we can commonly observe in our assemblies if they extend beyond the hour of lunch, when all mouths are preparing for movement more congenial than talking, and only Völgyesy shook his head in objection, pointing out that since the prisoner had in fact neither withdrawn what he had previously said nor altered it, but had admitted numerous things of which there was no sign in his former statement, he considered it his duty to note all those precisely.

"To note what?" asked Sóskuty in astonishment. "That the notary's documents were stolen by Mr Macskaházy and Her Honour the wife of the alispán?"

"Everything that the prisoner stated before the court," replied Völgyesy calmly.

"This is unheard of!" exclaimed Nyúzó.

"Your Worship understands his duty as a judge," said the lawyer, "and I understand mine; he will pronounce his verdict in accordance with his conscience, while I, who have no vote, shall record everything that, as I see it, is relevant to the matter in hand."

"*Sed rogo domine spectabilis,*"[158] said Zátonyi, in one hand holding his open snuff-box and raising the other heavenward, his fingers clenched together, so alarmed was he, "what are you thinking of?"

"My duty," said Völgyesy calmly, "which commands that in the account of the proceedings which is entrusted to me I omit nothing that may be of importance."

"But there are things that are certainly not relevant to the matter in hand," remarked Sóskuty. "If the prisoner preached us a sermon, or recommended some treatment for corns, would Your Worship record that too?"

"As I see it, the things that the prisoner has said here are important." replied the lawyer.

"But my friend," said the baron with all possible courtesy, "have the goodness to consider that Mr Zátonyi must still go home today for potatoes to be lifted; and if you intend to write down word for word the criminal's prattle that's impossible. Furthermore, our hostess has been waiting for us long enough already; politeness demands that we hurry."

"When a man's life is at stake, Mr Zátonyi's potatoes can wait another day; and under such circumstances I at least care little for the rules of courtesy."

"So it seems," muttered Zátonyi.

"Monstrous ill manners," sighed the baron.

---

158 But I ask you, Your Worship (Latin).

"Well, perhaps even so," said Kislaky affably, "we can leave pronouncing the verdict till tomorrow, and until then His Worship will write up the statements and Mr Zátonyi. . ."

"Quite impossible," replied the latter. "No one is more zealous in fulfilling his duty to the county than I; there's no criminal court in which I wouldn't take part; but like this, because of pure vexatiousness, I won't neglect my property."

"God forbid," said old Kislaky gently, "but when the notary states that he feels himself obliged conscientiously to record the prisoner's full statement, and when we can see that he can't do that in half an hour."

"Oh, rubbish!" said Zátonyi angrily. "I've been on fifteen *statariums*, and believe me, Your Worship, some of them involved such cases that if they'd come before an ordinary court they'd have been dragged out for months, yet we got through each of them in a day, and is this the only time that I've got to be held up? Never in all my life have I heard such excuses as the notary is making. In the instructions it simply states that the prisoner shall sign his statement, in which his name, age, crime and manner of arrest are to be included. Nowhere in the instructions is there anything about the recording of all the nonsense that the prisoner cares to prattle before the court; and let Mr Völgyesy give me just one sound reason why he wishes to do that, since after the questioning of the prisoner by Mr Macskaházy he won't, I hope, maintain that the things that he said are true."

"My reason," replied Völgyesy, "is that the faithfulness of the record demands it; and even if that weren't so, please understand that an action has been begun against the Tiszarét notary concerning nobility, and that Viola's statement may be of the greatest importance, at least insofar as it acknowledges the theft of certain documents from Tengelyi's house."

"Since that appears to be the case," said Macskaházy sharply, "it will greatly trouble a number of people that I, and in particular Her Honour Mrs Réty, should be mentioned in the documents pertaining to the case in a manner injurious to our good names; as far as I'm concerned, if a majority of the court so desires it I shan't oppose it, and at least the respected lady will be able to see who her friends are, because the mentioning of these matters is not necessary, as is, I believe, clear to all."

"God forbid," said the baron, "that anything should be brought up in those documents that might be even remotely unpleasant for Her Honour, and . . ."

329

"Everyone has his own opinion," Macskaházy interrupted him, "and the worshipful court will be able to judge in accordance with its wisdom how pleasant it will be to Her Honour the baroness and to myself, if Viola's disgraceful slanders have been rehearsed in the legal proceedings and we go through every court, especially if the outlaw receives the punishment that he deserves, and we're not permitted the means of proving that the accusations are unfounded. Slander away, goes the proverb, something will always stick! Everyone will be able to judge how fitting and reasonable it is that Mr Völgyesy, who was in the opposition to Mr Réty in the election, now takes the opportunity for revenge."

When the Italians curse, although they rebuke God and all his saints, they always make an exception of the patron of their city; however, it would perhaps be better to utter dishonouring words against St Antonio in the main square of Padua than to do the same against a powerful and freshly elected alispán in his own county; and it is only natural that, after Macskaházy had pointed out how offended the Réty family would feel if the part of Viola's statement that referred to Her Honour were included in the document, the whole company was seized by an almost holy dread.

"That is truly infamous!" exclaimed Nyúzó.

"As long as I'm sitting here," roared Zátonyi, thumping the table, "not a word of the outlaw's perfidious statement shall be mentioned in the record."

Sóskuty shook his head and lamented the partisanship that reigned in the county, in accordance with which individuals sought to make use even of judicial proceedings to score off political opponents.

Old Kislaky himself wished to avoid any clash with the alispán for his son's sake; he was alarmed at the idea that anything should occur under his presidency that might cause Réty, and especially his honourable wife, to feel offended and make his dear Kálmán lose what little hope remained to him after his defence of Tengelyi at the election. "I'm sure," said he in a placatory tone, "that Mr Völgyesy has no such intention. To give offence to our respected alispán was certainly far from his thoughts, he had merely not considered that the prisoner's complete statement would necessarily have an unpleasant effect on that noble family. If the record were to remain here with us, in the county archive," he added, turning to Völgyesy, "that would be a different matter, because as things stand our respected notary himself can't wish that one of the most prominent families in the county should be dishonoured, especially as, if the prisoner receives his punishment, as Mr Macskaházy has remarked, those so basely slandered will lose the principal means of clearing themselves."

"Who is to prevent Mr Macskaházy from preserving that essential means of his defence?" said Völgyesy; his otherwise pale cheeks were suffused by an unaccustomed flush.

The others looked at one another in amazement. Völgyesy went on:

"According to our instructions only a single vote in his favour is required for the prisoner to be spared from death. If Mr Macskaházy considers himself or Her Honour Mrs Réty to be slandered by the statement made before us, nothing more is required for the lack of foundation of such slander to be demonstrated than that Viola remain alive, the examination of him be continued, and proof be offered that he was lying, and that he later retract his statement himself: why would not Mr Macskaházy, or any of those who have a vote here, exercise that saving vote?"

"That's right," said Kislaky, who had brightened completely, as he thought that in this way his two main desires could be united – that the prisoner's life be saved and the Réty family be placed under obligation. "I myself would be prepared, if only to show my respect for the *alispán* . . ."

"*Per amorem,*[159] *domine spectabilis,*" said Zátonyi, leaving his snuff-box open once more in his alarm, "are we not to hang this criminal?"

"This is monstrous!" said Sóskuty, raising his eyes to the heavens. "The greatest of outlaws has fallen into our hands, Mr Nyúzó, may his name be praised for ever, arrested him at risk of his life and brings him before us, we are a *statarium*, and we are to set him free! What will this lead to? And if anything else. . ."

"For my part," Nyúzó interrupted, "I shall be no one's fool any longer, the devil's life may be at risk if such a villain is acquitted after all that!"

"Not to hang such a man!" exclaimed Zátonyi. "I've served on fifteen *statarium*s, and such shameless behaviour has never come my way. This is siding with criminals."

"Quite," protested Sóskuty, "it's rewarding robbery; a dreadful example!"

"If this goes on, even the devil won't maintain pubic morale," roared the magistrate, and around the table uproar broke out, in which merely individual words – such as scandal, public, unheard of, *fautores criminum,*[160] shame – could be made out, while Völgyesy, with difficulty,

159 Latin: For the love [of God].
160 Latin: those that favour crimes.

contrived to be heard informing the judges that he proposed not that the prisoner be entirely acquitted but brought before the regular court.

"Of course, of course," answered Zátonyi crossly, "as if we didn't know the way that regular courts pass sentence. I remember three instances – I wasn't present myself, otherwise, I swear, the scandal wouldn't have occurred – of prisoners being referred by *statarium*s to the regular court, and what was the result? One was given three months in prison, another a year, and the third was acquitted, and I'd bet ten forints he was an outlaw. Never fear, we aren't going to be so foolish. The county hasn't been given the *statarium* so as not to use it."

"The power of the court of summary jurisdiction," said Völgyesy, with a withering glance at the speaker, "has not, in my view, been granted to the county on condition that it show that it is worthy of it by hanging a certain number annually."

"It's clearly stated in standing orders," said Sóskuty, having meanwhile turned over the pages, "that *punishment can be none other than the gallows*; therefore no one's going to deny that it's required of us that we hang criminals, that this is our duty by virtue of our office. . ."

"Permit me," Macskaházy interrupted him, "since the question has been raised, at least by our deeply respected president, of the acquittal of the prisoner or his referral to the regular court, for the sake of Her Honour Mrs Réty and in a certain regard of myself, as I have the good fortune of handling Her Honour's affairs and know her lofty character, I will state on her behalf that it would greatly grieve that most sensitive lady to hear that personal opinions with which the court is clothed towards her had obstructed the service of justice."

"A noble declaration," said Sóskuty, and beamed in all directions.

"As for myself," the speaker went on, bowing and with an almost pious expression, "well aware as I am of what sharp weapons may be raised against me by this outlaw's statement, and though for my own part I would desire nothing more than that the prisoner remain alive for me to be able to demonstrate even more clearly than I have already done before the court the falsity of all that he has said: yet I recognise all the more my duty not to sacrifice the public good to my personal interests; and who can't see the consequences if we set an example such that even an outlaw like Viola is able to escape the severity of the process of summary jurisdiction by giving voice to base and incredible slanders?"

Sóskuty stood and embraced the lawyer after that noble announcement. Zátonyi, who all his life had always shown himself to be independent whenever he could find a decent opportunity – that is, one in which his independence offended no one – stated that for his part even if the noble announcement had not been made he wouldn't have pronounced a less stern verdict; the judge's prime duty was complete independence. And at that moment Kislaky wouldn't have known what to do had he not been reminded by Macskaházy that the question still remained to be settled: was the prisoner's statement made before the chief justice to be signed or a completely new one made, which would cause the verdict to be postponed until next day?

"The former statement must be attested," said the others with one voice; only Kislaky said that in his humble opinion it might yet be better, as Völgyesy had opined, to present the prisoner's statement in another form. To that, however, Zátonyi remarked that according to the highest authority unanimity was required only in the case of a death sentence, and that the majority had already decided.

"In that case," said Völgyesy, "the noble court will graciously relieve me of the office of notary; because I for my part declare that, as I have said, I won't edit it."

Kislaky was apparently unpleasantly affected by that statement, and the confusion in which he sat in the chair grew further still; Zátonyi himself was nonplussed, and the baron jumped up from his seat and rushed to Völgyesy, shook his hand, and asked his deeply respected friend not to take it amiss if his opinion had not been accepted by the majority. "When all's said and done, we're all human, even the cleverest of us can make a mistake," said he kindly, "indeed, we all respect your noble intention and outstanding ability, but no one may take exception to the majority; kindly consider that we're all obliged to submit to the majority. You'll see later on," etc. The baron, perhaps because he had caught a cold on the journey, or perhaps because his lunch was being delayed, had until then said remarkably little, but on this occasion displayed his rhetorical powers to the full, but without the slightest success, as Völgyesy listened to all his reasoning and only replied that no one was happier to respect the decisions of the majority than he, but that there were matters in considering which a man of honour could count only on his convictions, and that in the present case he was one such. At that the court was embroiled in even greater confusion and would perhaps have acquiesced to the wish of its steadfast notary had Macskaházy not helped it with the recommendation that since no one might be forced to act against their convictions, and that it wasn't stated in standing orders that there had to be a notary additional to the five justices; if it was so desired he would gladly undertake the office himself; there only

333

remained the matter of signing the statements and the brief note of the verdict.

"Accepted, accepted with the greatest gratitude!" exclaimed Zátonyi. "Mr Völgyesy, who has only recently entered the service of the county, will see what a fruitful thing it is when someone doesn't insist on performing the duty entrusted to them to the letter, but as the majority wish. He'll see how far his so-called convictions will get him."

"My dear Völgyesy," said Macskaházy, with all the amiability in him – which nevertheless his rasping voice made to sound like scorn – "no doubt you have only taken matters to this point in order to spare the criminal from the punishment that he has merited. That purpose, I grant, can be fine and noble, at least in our philanthropic century, and most understandable, especially in so young a gentleman; it would, however be an unforgivable error on the part of us older men if we allowed ourselves to be deterred by it from the service of justice. As I have said, I will undertake the office of notary, but perhaps, now that you can see that your purpose can't be achieved by resignation, you yourself will be prepared to resume your office, and from so excellent a lawyerly pen I . . ."

Völgyesy was one of those people whom we commonly consider cold. Even as a child he had been unable, through frailty, to take part in his contemporaries' rough games and had become accustomed to a solitary life; the longer he lived the more he felt the great misfortune that afflicts one on whom nature has bestowed a faulty body, and he had withdrawn more and more from society. "I'm a hunchback," he often told himself, "What am I to look for in society, when I'm the object of either contempt or pity? Beware of those marked out by nature, says the proverb; rather you should beware those whom nature has cursed with some bodily defect; you won't find sympathy for your trouble or return of your feelings in society. My feelings!" he thought on, and sometimes a bitter smile played on his lips, "indeed, if I went into society and eventually found a being to whom I felt irresistibly attracted – for my heart is not shrivelled like my wretched body – and to whom I would give my life for a word, my salvation for a smile, would there be anything more ridiculous than me? Me, a dwarf, a hunchback, prostrate at the feet of a beautiful woman asking for her love! Anything more preposterous has never been heard of. What great thoughts, what exalted feelings have I? If I speak up for justice it can only harm the case, make the most sacred laughable, when a poor hunchback speaks up; there is no word or deed so exalted that lips would not curl in a pitying smile when people heard that it came from me. I have nothing to expect in society!" These thoughts naturally made Völgesy reclusive. If anyone is wounded it's certain that painful touches will come, and so every time that he went into company the young lawyer must have been reminded of his deformity either by a carelessly spoken word or because such were studiously avoided, and felt ill at ease. A certain constraint or timidity could be detected in his behaviour, and that forced his otherwise excellent qualities, especially his mental powers, into the background, and close acquaintance – to which, because of his character, few were admitted – was needed for one to assess his virtues correctly. "Poor Völgyesy, there's no more modest man in the world," was the sort of thing that everyone in Taksony County said of him, and since there, as everywhere else, people are accepted for their money and by outward appearance rather than inner worth, there was hardly anyone that looked for anything but modesty in the young lawyer.

The more universal was this opinion of Völgyesy's character in Taksony County, the greater was the amazement that seized the whole court when it saw the calm manner with which the young lawyer conducted himself on this occasion – and Sóskuty, Zátonyi and old Kislaky himself looked at one another several times. Völgyesy, whose first official appointment this was, and who for the first time in his life could see before him the opportunity to benefit someone and at the same time fight for his convictions, forgot everything in his sense of duty. He was opposed to the death penalty altogether, but doubly so when the judgement that could not be reversed was linked to proceedings that didn't insure the judge against mistakes. It was beyond him to understand how on the one hand the summary court might not hand down any but a sentence of death, and on the other hand might ignore all the proceedings in which much lesser punishments were available and which were considered indispensable, and he'd only been glad to accept his commission because he was certain that as notary to the court he would find a means of averting the death penalty. For the first time he could consider himself useful and necessary, and all his self esteem rose in his breast. At least those of my readers who have experience in minor affairs will realise that the endeavours of a junior prosecutor could not lead to success against the beliefs of so many *táblabírós*. In a country where, may we say, the right to speak depends on our birth, it is only logical that what is taken into account is not what is said but the speaker's social status, and it merely demonstrates Völgyesy's inexperience that we see him in this difficulty. But since he had not yet learnt that just as in our enlightened century it is not good to be born with a hunched back, neither is it good to be fearlessly honest – because those whose upbringing doesn't provide their spirit with the necessary crookedness have always been condemned to the minority – this experience was painful to the young man; it was almost natural, and we can't be surprised if, on perceiving the scorn that Macskaházy's sweet smile concealed, he couldn't restrain his temper, and on rising from his chair he handed over to Macskaházy the documents, saying that not all the treasure in the world was going to make him take the least part in proceedings which he could not regard as anything but judicial murder.

It's a pity that I'm not an epic poet. Never would I have had a finer field in which to display my calling than when I described the consequences of those words of Völgyesy's. Homer opens his Iliad with the wrath of Achilles, but what's a single Achilles compared to five *táblabírós*? And where can words be found to describe the temper which, as is well known, reveals itself not in the drawing of profitless swords but in an unstoppable flood of words?

"This is villainy!" exclaimed Nyúzó.

"*Infamia!*" said Zátonyi.

"Withdraw that remark!" screeched Macskaházy.

Sóskuty was babbling so fast that even his first words were incoherent, while Kislaky himself, insofar as could be made out from his reddening cheeks, was saying something amid the din.

"Worshipful *táblabírós*," said Völgyesy at length, when he was able with no little effort to make himself heard, "I had no wish to give personal offence. Permit me to explain what I said."

"Explain, explain what?" shouted Zátonyi in rising fury. "That the court consists of murderers? Do you know that you have no say in the matter? Anyone that discredits judges is in contempt; you're in contempt."

"Indeed," interposed the baron, "let's find him in contempt."

"Summarily?" Völgyesy cut in with a bitter smile.

"Summarily or otherwise, it's all the same to me," the baron continued, "anyone that speaks in that way against a court is in contempt, it's in the *corpus juris*, there can be no doubt, and rightly so. To discredit our system of jurisdiction is appalling!"

"*Est ad horripilationem!*"[161] shouted Zátonyi. And the universal horrification which all present expressed, in Latin and Hungarian, at the

---

161 Latin: It makes one's hair stand on end.

daring of their former notary, didn't permit the speaker to be further heard. Our Hungarian system of jurisdiction, according to the experts, was brought here from France in the time of the Anjou kings;[162] it's quite probable that *kocsonya*[163] too became popular in Hungary under them, because at least its French name *cochonade* seems to indicate that; perhaps that foreign royal house has those two national benefactions to thank for the fact that one of them has been honoured with the style 'Great', of which we didn't esteem our own Hunyadi Mátyás[164] worthy. Völgyesy had only himself to blame for the exasperation with which everyone turned on him; he was criticising one of the two foreigners most popular in Hungary. The threats of being found in contempt, however, seemed not to have effect, and he looked calmly on the company until he was at length able to put a word in again.

"Find me summarily in contempt if you like," said he unemotionally, "but permit me, not for the sake of those who, it appears, wish for nothing but the prisoner's execution, but on account of the deep respect in which I hold our president . . . "

"*Captatio benevolentiae!*"[165] Zátonyi's exclamation interrupted. "Our respected president doesn't need flattery from the likes of you!"

". . . to draw the attention of the court . . ." continued Völgyesy.

"The court doesn't need its attention drawn to anything," shouted the baron.

". . . to the weighty burden of responsibility that will devolve upon all members that have been here present if they take these present proceedings to a regrettable conclusion."

"What the devil! Calling judges to account? Never heard of such a thing!" said Sóskuty.

Zátonyi held out his snuffbox and commented that Völgyesy was only trying to frighten them.

"Hear, hear!" said Kislaky most attentively.

With the standing orders in his hand, Völgyesy pointed out to the court that the summary court could only act legally if it strictly obeyed its rules; but these didn't cover the present case.

"That's a fine piece of rubbish," said Zátonyi scornfully. "But these days we're getting used to youngsters; there's never been a more despicable prisoner before a *statarium* than Viola."

---

162 Róbert Károly (1301–42) and Nagy Lajos (Lajos the Great) (1342–82).
163 Cold pork in aspic.
164 Mátyás I (1458–90).
165 Latin: Fishing for goodwill.

"Yes, but what about the other circumstances?" interrupted the young lawyer.

"Terrible ignorance!" said the *táblabíró*, raising his voice more and more. "Perhaps he didn't resist arrest? Or did he steal Tengelyi's documents to eat them? That might serve as an excuse. Or he's not yet twenty? Or out of his mind? Or have the leaders and members of the gang of villains that he belonged to been brought before a regular court?" As he reeled off this list Zátonyi looked around in self-satisfaction with his snuffbox, striking it against his palm with every question as if applauding himself.

Völgyesy merely pointed out that the case was one that the court would be unable to settle in three days.

"Three days?" rejoined Zátonyi with a laugh. "We shall see, in three days we'd have disposed of twenty villains like him; we'd have put an end to their activity if this gentleman hadn't bothered us with his impertinent quibbles."

"And so you've forgotten the prisoner's statement, in which certain accusations. . ."

"That's nothing to do with the matter," Sóskuty interrupted him. "There's nothing in the documents, and I'm going to forget them."

"My dear sir!" exclaimed Völgyesy in amazement.

"His Worship is quite right," said Zátonyi. "All that talk that we heard from the prisoner is not *species facti*; to refer to it all in the record is superfluous. One would have had a lot to do if note had to be taken of all useless material such as what the prisoner said in exonerating himself."

"But the completion of the documents?" Völgyesy interrupted, more and more heatedly.

"A useless formality," replied the *táblabíró*. "In this the instruction of section five of part six clearly orders that this court shall pass judgement without regard to the customary forms of any ordinary process of jurisdiction."

"Yes, we may pass judgement as we please, contrary to all legal forms," repeated the baron with dignity.

"That you gentlemen may hang the prisoner," exclaimed Völgyesy finally, "is not open to doubt; but it's also true that I shall never consider your procedure a judicial procedure and shall never see in it anything but an act of violence."

"What?" exclaimed three voices in unison.

"The court doesn't consist of such persons as are desired to occupy judicial positions."

"That's too much, it really is!" exclaimed Zátonyi, rising from his seat. "Are we not *táblabírós*? Didn't we swear at the beginning of the session that our verdict would be given in accordance with the rules laid down in the highest places?"

"And aren't we versed in the law, men of mature and clear judgement?" the baron went on.

"Out with him! Out with him!" trumpeted Nyúzó.

"Prosecute!" exclaimed Sóskuty.

In the din, it was some time before Völgyesy could make his conviction understood: that impartiality was a quality necessary in a judge.

"Balderdash!" blared Zátonyi. "There's nothing about that in standing orders."

"Yes, and if there were," went on Sóskuty, gesticulating, "who can accuse us of partiality? Is there a single word in the prisoner's defence except what you say, sir, and you, praise be, have no vote?"

"Really, I'd like to know," said Macskaházy in a sharp tone, looking hard at the young lawyer, "how is Your Worship going to prove that we are partial?"

"I can satisfy your curiosity," said Völgesy, as his anger mounted yet he remained outwardly calm. "As for you, since you're unwilling to uphold the one means by which you could completely justify yourself from the accusation made by the prisoner, which is none other than that the prisoner remain alive, it seems likely that your interest is to destroy at once both accusation and accuser. With regard to Mr Nyúzó, there can be no doubt of his partiality; in his judgement seat he has received him on whom he should pass judgement more like an executioner."

"Villainy! Wickedness! Impertinence! Out with him! Prosecute!" came cries from every side.

"Where equality is desired for all votes for the verdict," said Völgyesy over the din, "but it's likely that condemnation of the prisoner is in the personal interests of one of the five, and another makes it plain to the court that he's personally hostile to him, a lawful verdict can't be pronounced."

The hubbub drowned his words.

"I shall do everything to make known to all this crying sin!" the interrupted speaker shouted, almost beside himself with rage, "I shall take my complaint to the highest places in order to bring about the punishment that this despicable conduct deserves."

"Despicable denouncer! He doesn't know the laws of 1805! Disgraceful!" and other such cries, among which the voice of Nyúzó was the most audible, convinced Völgyesy that it would be useless to say more; and he was about to leave when Nyúzó sprang up and reached for his collar, shouting furiously "Out you go, hunchback!"

"You'll pay for that," said Völgyesy as he put on his hat, and he left the room, his face ablaze.

The noise that had arisen during the argument in the room where the hearing was held had attracted the close attention of those standing outside the door. The quiet conversations between the *hajdús* and the gendarmes on the one hand and the witnesses and the servants of the house on the other had fallen silent, and every ear was turned to the door from which came a constantly growing din, and as the listeners, like many, believed that vulgarity and justice went together in the main, the reassurance must have spread that never had juster judges sat together on the bench. Mrs Lipták, it seemed, was of a different opinion. She'd found a place near the door and could hear every word, and more than once said with a sigh to the blacksmith at her side: "Oh, the gentry are very cross with one another; poor Viola, to fall into their hands at a time like this." The remainder listened with unmixed delight to the racket by which the seat of justice was making itself particularly public. As is known, there is no better proof of our civil liberty than openness: just as the deadliest poison – Prussic acid – loses its strength if exposed to the rays of the sun, there is scarcely anything so dangerous that, if fully illuminated, doesn't become harmless; I don't believe, however, that those members of the Magyar *demos* whom we find clustered in the passage by the bailiff's dwelling were thinking of that at the moment, and the delight that spread on every face at hearing that coarse language must probably have originated in the pleasant feeling that fills us all when we hear someone else say what we have privately thought for a long time.

Only Viola, it seemed, didn't share in the general interest. He was standing among his guards, leaning on a support of the passage roof and looking intently at something. By the gate stood his wife, with one of his children in her arms and her small son beside her; in the outlaw's eyes, everything else had vanished.

As soon as the court had begun to sit the poor woman had gone to the gate and asked to be allowed in; and as the guards refused this request she tried to achieve her purpose by force, oblivious of the impossibility of doing so. It was all in vain; acting on Nyúzó's orders, the gendarmes drove her back. When poor Zsuzsi saw that all her effort was wasted, and that although some of the onlookers were sympathetic to her requests and pleas she had been unable to enter the yard, she settled beside one of the peasants armed with pitchforks. Viola saw all that, saw how unkindly his wife and child were repulsed, saw the pain on that dear creature's face and the effort with which she suppressed her tears. He would have given his life to be able to go to his beloved and take her in his arms, feel the beating of the heart the love of which nothing on earth could take from him, while he had to stand there, a few paces from her and yet so far away. There was something inexpressibly bitter in the situation of those two people, and it pained even the guards, none too sensitive as they were; more than one of them felt compassion at the sight of the hapless pair, so far apart and yet so completely immersed in one another

When the door of the courtroom opened and Völgyesy emerged into the passage Viola turned, thinking that he was to be summoned to hear his sentence and longing for the moment after which, as he had heard from the guards, he could be with his wife. "Is it all over?" he asked Völgyesy.

"Not yet," said the latter quietly.

"And Your Worship is leaving?"

"I have no vote," replied the lawyer with a sigh, "I can't do any more for you."

"I realised that," said Viola, and a bitter smile flickered on his face. "God bless you for all that you've done for me, poor man that I am; but if you want to show pity on me, I beg, see to it that my poor wife's allowed to come here. The poor creature's over there by the gate with her children, and she's being pushed around and prevented from coming to me. These people have no hearts. Just let her be here at my side, that's all I ask; here I am, tied up and surrounded by gendarmes, in an hour or two I'll be dead, what harm can it do the county if a poor woman's heart suffers a little less pain?"

"You shall have your wish," replied Völgyesy, deeply touched, and after personally letting Viola's wife and children into the yard he went away, deep in thought.

I'm not going to describe the scene witnessed by those standing in the passage, when the unlucky woman, burdened with her children, came to her husband. The hapless couple didn't speak, but when the outlaw's small son, weeping, kissed one of his father's hands as it protruded from the ropes and his wife, trembling, clasped the other tightly, heavy tears ran down the prisoner's pale face; among the onlookers scarcely an eye remained dry.

Meanwhile, in the courtroom the *táblabírós'* righteous indignation had subsided. Macskaházy had taken charge of the documents and was putting them in order. Nyúzó, growling between his teeth, was criticising Völgyesy's impudence; the rest were whispering among themselves on everyday matters, pleasantly enough, with the exception of Kislaky; his unease had become more and more perceptible since the lawyer's departure.

All that still remained was the signing of the prisoner's statement. Viola was summoned, and as it was read out to him he remarked that nothing was included of what he had told the court that day about Tengelyi's documents; when, however, Macskaházy said that the only question was whether he stated that what was included was true, and that the court would note separately anything else that he had said that wasn't relevant to the subject, he put his name to it without demur.

The case was now ready for verdict to be pronounced, and Zátonyi, with a great yawn, offered his snuffbox round, commenting that never before had there been so much trouble at a *statarium*: while the baron looked at his watch about twenty times, informed the court that it was past three o'clock and that after the long fast his head was aching, and that they must hurry.

Macskaházy briefly summed up once more the facts that had been established by the proceedings, and ended his account by saying that in this case there could be no doubt of a sentence of death. Nyúzó said the same in other words. Zátonyi remarked with a laugh that even a weak woman could say nothing else in this instance. The baron bowed courteously, and shared in full his fellow judges' verdict, supported as it was by so many reasons. That left only Kislaky, and no one seeing the worthy old man as he squirmed on his chair, turning from one judge to another, and heard the individual votes, as he sighed and raised his hands to heaven, until at length it was his turn, his ruddy cheeks became deathly pale perhaps for the first time in years, and the paper began to shake as he took it in his fingers: no one, I say, could have looked on his honest face without feeling pity.

Let's put ourselves in his shoes. Kislaky was a gentle, good-hearted man, one of those happy ones who are endowed by fate with a calm disposition and are comfortably off, have never been forced to contend with fate or other men, and have never had occasion for their will to be hardened by struggles or for their feelings to become embittered. Loved by his wife, who, as if he'd no will of his own, exercised limitless influence on him; loved by his son, his friends, his servants and his peasants, and loving everyone in return, he showed nothing but good and kindness to everyone. Kislaky had grown old without encountering the dark

342

side of life; without ever having to resolve on something that conflicted with the feelings of his heart; and now he, who had the greatest respect for life, who could hardly even disturb a dog, was suddenly required to pronounce a sentence of summary execution on a fellow human being! The others had given their verdicts, but if just one of the voters spoke against, the prisoner's life was saved – not only for the time being but presumably entirely; because it was unlikely that Viola, even if he were later condemned to death, might not count on a royal pardon, since he had endured all the torments of fear of death once already. A man's life was in his hands. One word and he could save him; one word, and it would be he that handed him over to the hangman. And on the other hand it was his judicial duty in the interest of public security, which he, like many honest men in Hungary, believed could only be preserved by the strictest measures. The president sat in silence on his seat and couldn't bring himself to take a decision.

"But really," said Sóskuty, taking out his watch again, "we simply can't keep our respected hostess waiting any longer."

"That's true," said Kislaky, woken from his profound thoughts. "It's already late, we'll leave the verdict till tomorrow; the poor fellow's execution can't happen today in any case."

"Why ever not?" asked Zátonyi in amazement. "I've absolutely got to get home today, otherwise I shan't be able to do the ploughing tomorrow."

"But we have to allow the prisoner at least three hours," remarked the president, "and at five o'clock it will be pitch dark, and we shan't be able to carry out sentence in the dark. "

"Our president is right," Sóskuty chipped in. "Let's have a game of *tarok* this evening, I already owe him for a pagát-ultimo that he won. But I don't see why the verdict can't be pronounced today so that we'll have less to do in the morning."

"Because, because," said Kislaky uneasily, "the sentence of death depends on me and me alone; I'll confess, I'm not clear in my mind."

"*Domine spectabilis,*" said Zátonyi, clasping his hands together, "in the past and since then you've borne so many offices, and you aren't clear in your mind! I've been in fifteen *statarium*s and I've always been clear in my mind from the first moment. It's a good thing you're among friends, otherwise you'd be censured."

The others looked at one another in amazement, and Nyúzó could scarcely restrain himself from giving free expression to the scorn which this feebleness aroused in him; but Kislaky remained firm in his inde-

343

cision, and continued to request that the whole thing be postponed to the next day.

When Völgyesy left, Macskaházy had thought that his purpose was achieved, but he was becoming anxious again. He knew his man, and was aware that if Kislaky went home before the verdict was pronounced he would be unable to resist the requests of his wife and Kálmán and Völgyesy's arguments, and so he tried to do all that he could for Viola's death sentence to be pronounced forthwith – its implementation meant more to him than to anyone else.

"As far as we're concerned," said the lawyer, with the great possible calm, "it's immaterial; if you want us to pronounce tomorrow, so be it. For myself, I'd like to have it all finished to make it easier for the prisoner. If sentence were pronounced he'd be able to spend time with his wife and children, prepare for death more calmly, put his affairs in order if there's still anything to be seen to. But if it's going to cause the president the least difficulty, of course, that's a side issue."

When Zátonyi saw the effect that those words had on Kislaky, he added: "Of course, Viola's a great criminal and would no doubt deserve ten days in the death cell." But a man's a man, and he commended what Mr Macskaházy said to the court's practised humanity, since there could be no doubt among sensible people with regard to the nature of the verdict, and to save Viola's life would be a real civic crime.

Macskaházy said that it had certainly not been the president's intention, such weakness could never have entered his head, and no one knew better than he that in a judge's verdicts there must be no regard for personal tendencies or enthusiasms, and that Kislaky, though with bleeding breast and self-denial, would never abuse the trust placed him by the county. Sóskuty spoke at length on humanity and proved how much philanthropy required that Viola be immediately sentenced to death. He referred to the need to set an example, and to the fact that he who forgives the wicked punishes the good. Nyúzó spoke of ever more heinous evil deeds that Viola and his crew were said to have perpetrated and would perpetrate in the county if fear of the summary court were to lapse; until the worthy old man, beset on all sides, seeing no one with him who shared his secret anxieties, didn't know how to respond to those reasons which all his life he'd regarded as irrefutable and to which even now only his heart objected, with a heavy sigh pronounced the verdict expected of him.

"God can see my soul," said he, raising his eyes heavenward, "I don't know what I'd give if I could save this man's life; but I can't neglect my duty."

Macskaházy immediately set about writing up the verdict, and the others tried their best to cheer up the president, on whose breast, after he had pronounced the verdict, the full sense of his responsibility had descended.

At that moment the door opened and in rushed Mrs Viola, holding her son by the hand and followed by two *hajdús* who were futilely trying to restrain her.

After coming into the passage the poor woman had handed her smaller child to Mrs Lipták and stood for a while calmly at her husband's side, where the sympathy of the guards had permitted her to be. In the room where the judges were in session, silence had arisen since Völgyesy had left and the prisoner had signed his statement, and that, together with the quiet observation of the *hajdú* at her side that the verdict must now be in preparation, filled her soul with the utmost anxiety. "If only I could go in," said she time and again to those near her, "if I plead, they can't possibly condemn him," and her eyes remained fixed on the door behind which his life was being decided on. Finally she could stand the situation no longer, went to Mrs Lipták, who was sitting just by the door, and as no one was watching her she rushed inside with her son before she could be prevented. "Mercy!" cried the hapless woman, flinging herself at Kislaky's feet. "Mercy, Your Worship! Don't kill my husband!"

Kislaky was touched by the scene and tried to raise her from her knees.

"No, no," she sobbed, "let me kneel, my child too. Kiss His Worship's hand, now, your father's life depends on him," said she, drawing Pista to her side, "he's such a good man, we shall be eternally grateful to him."

"Please don't let my father be killed," wept little Pista.

"What impudence is this?" exclaimed Nyúzó. "The court isn't killing anyone."

"No, God forbid," said Mrs Viola softly, "don't listen to this silly boy when he says don't let my father be killed. He doesn't know what he's saying, he's a poor peasant child, has no education; I don't know what I'm saying either."

"You poor woman," said Kislaky, "it's hard for a judge, but he has binding obligations and . . ."

"I'm not asking, Your Worships," said Zsuzsi, still on her knees, "for him to be spared punishment. Punish him as severely as you will, only don't kill him. Oh God, I've said that terrible word again! Don't be angry with me. Punish Viola with a long prison sentence, I don't care, if need be for life. Perhaps he said himself that he doesn't care about dying, oh,

345

he often says things like that. Don't believe him, that was when he hadn't seen his children; now that he's kissed little Pista again he wouldn't talk like that. And my little one as well, the lovely smile she gave him! Oh, if you could see her, hear her little voice when she calls him father, you wouldn't believe that Viola wants to die!"

"What's the good of this useless woman's whining?" shouted Nyúzó. "Who's let her in here, I'd like to know. Clear off, your husband's going to die, and if he doesn't like the idea so much the better."

"So did I say that he doesn't like the idea?" sighed Mrs Viola, and at those words had a fresh thought. "My God, what am I saying! Indeed, Viola actually wants to die; see, it isn't punishment to him at all. If you want to punish him, lock him up. He's said a hundred times, he'd rather die than be in a cell."

Kislaky looked at the poor woman and his heart ached, tears gleamed in his eyes. Sóskuty looked at his watch with the greatest impatience.

"Don't you see, Your Worship, you ought to lock him up?" Zsuzsi went on, sensing Kislaky's disturbance. "What is death to him, a moment and it's all over; but to us! I've got my two children, this one here and another outside with Mrs Lipták. What are we to do if the children's father is hanged?"

Zátonyi remarked that as far as the children were concerned it made no difference whether he was hanged or spent twenty years in prison.

"No, no," said Zsuzsi, "it makes no difference to Your Worships, but it does to us. My husband will behave himself, and I'll go on foot to Vienna, go on my knees before the king until he gives my husband a pardon, and if he won't, at least I'll be able to go to the prison now and then, let him see his children grow, take him food and clothing. . . Oh, if only he were locked up, I'd be in heaven. Death, that's terrible."

"Half past three, that's what's terrible!" sighed Sóskuty.

"Stop bothering us, woman," said Zátonyi, taking a pinch of snuff. "It's too late, the sentence has been pronounced."

"The sentence! the sentence of death!" exclaimed Zsuzsi, springing up in horror.

"There it is," said Nyúzó scornfully, pointing to a sheet of paper that Macskaházy was just sanding.

"But when it's a bad verdict, a mistake," said Zsuzsi tensely, "when I tell you that it's worthless because death would be no punishment to Viola, it'd only make us unhappy."

"The facts are the facts," said Zátonyi. "Don't bother us with your futile pleading."

346

"Heaven help me, it's a quarter to four," interposed the baron. "At this rate we may be here until tomorrow."

"But I beg," said Zsuzsi, in growing distress, "what's that piece of paper, surely you could take another and write something else, and my husband will live."

"Of course, we haven't taken enough trouble," Nyúzó baited her. "Mr Macskaházy will write another straight away for your benefit."

"Not for my benefit, for a man's life."

"You poor woman," Kislaky now spoke, wiping his eyes. "we're not allowed to alter the sentence."

"Not allowed!" exclaimed Zsuzsi, raising her eyes to heaven.

"It can't be done," replied Zátonyi calmly, and the poor woman fell to the floor with a scream.

"Thank God," said Sóskuty quietly to Zátonyi, once the poor woman had been taken out and the sentence read to Viola, who remained perfectly calm as he heard it, and the members of the court were making their way to the mansion, "we've got that over with!"

"It was enough trouble. I've never known such a *statarium* session," came the reply.

"What's to be expected if the president's weak?" commented Sóskuty.

"Quite, when the president of a *statarium* starts to snivel when a woman carries on like that," Nyúzó put in. "There was no telling whether we'd finish today."

"It's turned four o'clock, I'll wager there's no lunch left," sighed Sóskuty, "and there's nowhere you'll eat a better roast."

While the *táblabírós* made light of the situation, Kislaky was hurrying home at a distance from the others, deep in thought. His spirit was filled by a new sensation, one that he had never suspected: unease of conscience. "My God!" he said to himself, "that man's life is on my soul, I'll never again be at peace! Why did I pronounce that sentence of death?"

Oh, why are there laws of the need for which the mind can't be convinced, and at the implementation of which the hearts of good men are filled with horror!

XXIII

On his way back to the mansion Völgyesy met Kálmán and Ákos's hussar, old János, walking up and down in conversation in the courtyard. Kálmán had an opened letter in his hand and was walking a little way in front of his companion. The agitation with which he now stood still, now went hurriedly on, then seemed to turn and ask a question, indicated his excitement; whereas from the old hussar's serious expression and the way he stroked his moustache from time to time it appeared that the news that he had brought must not have been pleasant. On the far side of the yard a groom was walking two horses, and from the way that they were sweating it could be assumed that their riders had had regard for time rather than the well-being of their mounts.

Völgyesy was rather too disturbed at that moment to want anyone's company, and as he realised that Kálmán had not noticed him he was approaching the house when the latter, alerted by János, came running after him and took him by the arm. "Is it all over?" he asked in the greatest agitation. Völgyesy stopped, startled by the emotional tone in which the question was put.

"Insofar as an affair of which we know the outcome can be called over," said Völgyesy, "it is, indeed, verdict had been pronounced even before we sat down; however, they're still sitting."

"What are you doing here, then?" Kálmán went on. "I thought you were a member of the court."

"Yes, a non-voting member," replied Völgyesy bitterly, "and I've come away because . . . this is not the place," he added, interrupting himself, "for us to talk about these things. If you want to know what's happened, let's go to your room, we can talk there. And I've got a favour to ask of you."

"Go and have a word with my groom, János," said Kálmán turning to him, "and have yourself given a glass of wine. He'll see to your horse."

"That's not the way, sir," said the old man with a shake of his head. "Horses first, men afterwards, fodder first, wine afterwards, that's the old hussar rule, and can't you see, sir, I've come on Master Ákos's Fecske?[166] I won't trust a lad like that with the horse."

"As you wish, János," said Kálmán with a smile, "only when the horse has been attended to come straight up, we'll be having a chat."

---

166 The horse's name means Swallow.

And with that Kálmán and Völgyesy went to the former's room while János walked his horse for a while longer, went with it to the stable, and while the groom was unsaddling and grooming it he imparted to the coachman no few rules for the best way to keep horses, and in proof of them he brought up the example of the unforgettable bay that had been shot from under him in the battle of Leipzig.

"For God's sake, what happened?" said Kálmán as soon as they entered his room. "Why did you leave the court?"

"Because I didn't mean to have a hand in murder," said Völgyesy as he paced the room passionately, "I wasn't going to be the means, even the reluctant means, of the doing of a deed in which personal grievances and criminal interests were pursuing their vile ends under the sacred cloak of judicial office."

"You're really stirred up," said Kálmán, surprised at the passionate tone in which the normally calm Völgyesy said that. "It can't be that anything of the sort would happen when my father was there."

"That's what I thought too," replied Völgyesy. "No one could respect your father more than I do. He's a good, blessed man, and if I'd never known him, after what I've witnessed today I'd say the same. But – forgive me if I speak frankly – he's weak, and that's what renders the noble sentiments of his heart useless. Believe me, my friend! The responsibility for the bad and immoral things that have happened in this world lies not only on those who devise them in their wickedness but to a great extent on the decent people who tolerate evil out of weakness. The power of the wicked lies not in themselves but in the weakness of the good. They proclaim their lies at the tops of their voices, and we daren't speak up for the truth; they pursue their goals with heads held high, and we humbly give way before them; there's no weapon that they won't use to attain their wicked desires, and we cowards are afraid of the fight, the most we do is raise our voices, and that too we sometimes do in such a way as for God's sake not to give offence; like Pilate, we wash our hands in satisfaction when the vileness that we could have prevented has happened, and we merely haven't contributed to it by what we've said. If anyone lacks the courage to speak up for his convictions, his goodness is a reed bent in the wind which sighs when danger threatens, but all its dismal words won't hold back the hostile element in its course."

"That's perfectly true," sighed Kálmán, "and I'm sorry, but my father is like that at times. But please, tell me what happened?"

Völgyesy did his best to give a short account of events and of his personal injuries, for which, as he had said, he meant to seek satisfaction

349

from Nyúzó as soon as the court adjourned. Kálmán listened to it all with the greatest possible unease. "That can't be," said he eventually, and jumped up from his chair. "Sentencing a man to death in such circumstances! Don't believe it, my father will never agree."

"Yes, he will," said Völgyesy bitterly but calmly. "It will pain him, and perhaps he'll reproach himself for his weakness for the rest of his life, but he'll agree, or quite probably has done so by this time. You can be sure of it. When it was decided that the part of Viola's statement referring to Tengelyi's documents would not be admitted, the verdict could no longer be in doubt. In every other respect, Viola's case was one for a summary court; the one thing that could have been brought up to resist a sentence of death was the circumstance that there were other matters to be clarified. As soon as clarification of these was not required the prisoner's death was certain, especially when – as everything indicated – some of the judges wanted it in their personal interests."

"This is dreadful!" said Kálmán, pacing up and down the room. "And here's this letter that I've had from Tiszarét. I've got to save him, even if he's been condemned a hundred times over."

"You've had a letter? From the *alispán*?" asked Völgyesy.

"No," replied Kálmán, "you know that Ákos's right arm is injured and Etelka has written for him. Read it yourself," he added and handed over the letter, while his cheeks flushed at the mention of Etelka's name.

The letter said:

The documents that have been stolen from Tengelyi are of the greatest importance. We have reason to believe that the good fortune of Ákos and perhaps our whole family depends on the finding of these documents, which are presently in the hands of a criminal. The theft wasn't committed by Viola. Throughout this affair, Viola has conducted himself more nobly than anyone in the world under similar circumstances; it would be appalling to think that an innocent man had suffered death.

Some will do their utmost to bring about his conviction, because if Viola is not alive no one will be able to offer evidence concerning Tengelyi's documents. Save him! It is the first request that I've ever made to you, and the noble manner in which you behaved towards Tengelyi during the election gives me grounds to hope that I've not made it in vain, and both Ákos and I will be bound to you in eternal gratitude for this noble deed.

Etelka

"You see, I must save him if it costs me my salvation," said Kálmán passionately as he strode up and down.

350

"There's a fine piece of villainy afoot," said Völgyesy pensively. "This letter confirms everything that I suspected during the session."

"But what are we to do?" said Kálmán, in ever growing distress. "I'll go straight down to the court and tell Macskaházy that he's a villain, he's the thief, and . . ."

"Steady, my friend," said Völgyesy, catching Kálmán's arm as he made for the door. "We must avoid every semblance of a fuss. By what I've heard about it all, Macskaházy himself is a mere tool, and I'm afraid that there are interested parties whom you, and even less Etelka and Ákos, could not wish to involve in action in the criminal court."

"But perhaps, even so, if there were," said Kálmán, sensing that these observations were correct, "surely a word in mitigation is needed."

At that moment in came János with the news that the members of the court were coming and that Viola had been sentenced to death.

Kálmán clutched his forehead in desperation. "Curses!" he exclaimed. "I would have to be away from home today of all days! I came home yesterday evening at Ákos's request, because I knew that our cowherd was a good friend of Viola. When he told me that he hadn't seen Viola I rode out into our *puszta* at daybreak to speak to the mounted lads. When I went out, it wasn't yet known that Viola had been caught and was being brought here. The *puszta*'s a good three hours' ride away, and it was only after I'd let my horse have a good rest and was on my way back that this letter came to hand."

"Of course, because I didn't know you were on the *puszta*, sir," said János. "I rode here and there all morning, and then I heard from a shepherd that that was where you'd gone."

"János, it's not your fault," said Kálmán. "We're accursed! If I'd been at home Viola would have come to no harm, I'll swear to that! But now that he's been sentenced to death . . ."

"What then?" asked János, stroking his moustache.

"You know what it says in this letter," said Kálmán. "How am I to save him now that he's been sentenced?"

"If you want to save Viola for Miss Etelka – I mean, for Master Ákos," János corrected himself on seeing the flush that coloured Kálmán's cheeks . . .

"If I want? I'd give my life if I could."

"Well then, this bit of a verdict isn't much of a problem. Look, sir!" János went on, "if everybody that was sentenced to hang in Hungary actually were to be hanged we'd run out of rope."

"You're forgetting," Völgyesy cut in, "that we're talking about a *statarium*, that's slightly different, but. . ."

"Of course, of course," said János aloud, then in an aside to Kálmán, "let's not talk about such things in front of strangers."

"You can safely speak in front of Master Völgyesy," said Kálmán aloud, "he knows all about it. And if he can find a means of saving this poor man's life he'll do all in his power to help our honourable plan forward."

"That's different", said János with a smile. "The gentry certainly don't like it if they've sentenced a man to the gallows and somebody interferes. Sometimes they're annoyed if a pardon is granted, so how could they not be cross with a man like me!"

"But how do you intend to set Viola free?" asked Völgyesy.

"I don't know yet," János replied. "First we'll have to carry out reconnaissance; but we'll find a way. He won't be hanged today, and it would be a strange thing if I couldn't free him in a whole long night. Because the master's at home, his cellar's full of wine, there's all the money it needs, a key, a ladder, a rope, a horse, I say!" he added with a laugh, "have you ever heard the story of Trenk?"[167]

"Dear János, if you could pull this off!" exclaimed Kálmán, flinging his arms round János's neck in delight. "Ask for anything you need, spare no expense, you can call on me for anything."

"That's good, very good," said János, stroking his moustache. "Old János isn't the fool that a lot of people think. When you've served the emperor all those years you pick up a thing or two. But there's the bell, go and have your lunch otherwise it'll be noticed that we're plotting something. I'll look round and we'll have a word after lunch."

"You can count on my lifelong gratitude," said Kálmán as he and Völgyesy left.

"That's good, very good," muttered the old hussar. "When you've served the emperor all those years, won the battle of Aspern and then taken Paris into the bargain, you don't need gratitude, especially when you've got a master like mine and you needn't worry about being looked after in your old age. But wouldn't it do Master Kálmán a bit of good if the young lady was grateful to him," he thought on as he left the room, "and I don't mind that; he's a decent chap, and the way he sits his horse he's almost like my master, and he learnt from me. Kálmán and Etel-

---

167 There were two Trenks, the Hungarian Ferenc and the Prussian Friedrich, both disreputable characters in the eighteenth century, the subject of late works by Jókai.

ka make a fine couple, he'll fit in well with our house." And with that thought he set off for the bailiff's house, where Peti came to meet him.

Lunch, as my readers will realise after what had happened, was not one of the most cheerful. The hospitable lady of the house didn't offer her dishes to anyone, nor did she apologise for the poor cooking even though the roast had been turning for a good three hours more than usual, and to put it mildly, was on the brown side; and old Kislaky, who had noticed the change in his wife and understood the reproachful looks which the worthy lady was bestowing on him for the first time in his life, sat silent over his plate. Nyúzó and Kenyházy resumed their official custom and sat side by side, and did their best for good humour, which would not come from outside, to be replaced from within by that which, according to scripture, maketh glad the heart of man, but without the large glasses that they drained having any effect on those two worthies other than that the former set his features into ever crosser wrinkles while the latter yawned greatly.

All were glad when the long meal finally ended, especially Kálmán, who could scarcely conceal his impatience during the final courses, and as soon as the others rose from the table he and Völgyesy left the room.

"Now then, how do things stand, János?" said Kálmán on seeing the old hussar smoking his pipe in the corridor.

"Well, sir!" said János. "Let's go into your room and I'll tell you everything."

"So you think that we'll be able to set the poor man free?" said Kálmán as they did so.

"No doubt about it," replied János. "If the commandant wants to let somebody into a castle, or how can I put it, if the guard – because you gentlemen are now the guard – wants to let somebody out, there's no difficulty."

"But how? By what means? Tell us!"

"Well, just like that," said the hussar in a quieter tone, almost a whisper. "Our reverend from Tiszarét is here, and the minute he saw that Viola was tied up in the open air on this cold November night, with just a bit of straw for him to lie on, and his poor wife and children with him – the way the poor things were shivering, and goodness, aren't they both fine children, the little one was always smiling and tugging at my moustache, you could hardly bear to look – anyway, as I was saying, as soon as the reverend saw that he said at once that it wasn't right, it was sheer torture, and in the king's orders it states that when the weather's cold prisoners may not be held in the open. I thought to myself, now,

353

that's a sensible order, how shall we be able to free him if he stays there under the lean-to, and the asses have set up four lanterns round him so that every movement can be seen. But of course, I didn't say a word about it, but I said to the bailiff, who was there himself, that it would be better – simply because it's more secure – if the prisoner was under lock and key.

"But what use is that?" said Kálmán impatiently. "If Viola's locked up, how much nearer are we to our purpose?"

"Oh, much, sir, very much," replied János with a grin. "When you're alone and can do what you want, and nobody can see, then you can get a lot done. One man's got many more brains than a hundred, and you can do wonders under your own power, you get the chance to try your strength. But when people can see you and look at you from every side, even the strongest will lose confidence. The moment you make a move, ten come running, and all your courage is just something for them to laugh at. Just let Viola be put in the chaff-store, because the bailiff said that he's got nowhere else to put him – and by tomorrow they'll be looking for him."

"But how?" asked Völgyesy, almost losing patience at the hussar's long-windedness.

"Well, like this, gentlemen," said he, whispering even more quietly than before. "The chaff-store's at the farther end of the bailiff's house. There's a door opening directly from the granary, which is on the other side of the house, into the bailiff's loft, isn't there?"

"That's right, yes!" replied Kálmán eagerly, "go on."

"Well, as I said, there's a door from the granary to the bailiff's loft. If the granary had been mine, I wouldn't have made it like that, but it's for the convenience of the bailiff, and now it suits us as well."

"Go on, go on," said Kálmán with growing impatience.

"The granary key," János went calmly on, "is in your mother's possession, and you'll get hold of it, can't you, sir?"

"Yes."

"That's all we need. At night, when everybody's asleep, we'll go out to the barn, from there through the door to the bailiff's loft, from there onto the store. The store's just abutted against the house and the roof of it is only planks. Peti the Gypsy's familiar with it all. We carefully take up two planks, lower a ladder into the room, Viola comes up it and comes back with us through the granary door. Once he's outside, your cowherd, sir – Peti's gone to see him – will have a horse ready, and that's the end of it."

Kálmán clasped his hands together in delight, and Völgyesy confessed that the plan was no doubt the best that could be devised under the circumstances, but its execution depended on so many things that rejoicing would be premature.

"When Viola's in the chaff-store and the granary key's in my hands," said János, "I'll vouch for the rest. There's no window in the store that anybody could see through, and if Viola's sent everybody away and gone to sleep we'll be able to do as we please."

"Yes, but what about the guards?" commented Völgyesy. "And the bailiff, who can hear every sound in the loft and give the alarm?"

"I'll take care of the guards myself," replied the hussar scornfully. "The sergeant is sick in bed, and if the master will get Nyúzó and Kenyházy drunk so that they don't go and check, and like a good host gives the guards some wine to keep out the cold of night, the bailiff can raise the alarm all he likes. But there's no need to worry about that – once the bailiff's asleep he's not easy to rouse. We just need the key, then for Viola to be locked up, otherwise there'll be a problem."

"If that's all that's needed," said Kálmán cheerfully, "there's no problem," and with that he called Völgyesy and hurried with him back into the big room. "He's a good lad, that Kálmán," said the old hussar to himself, as he strolled towards the bailiff's house. "It'd be a sin to give our young lady to anybody else. Yes, but what if she doesn't love him? Impossible!" he encouraged himself inwardly. "Nobody sits a horse better than he does. We shan't find a young man like him for Miss every day of the week."

Of those previously mentioned the young people found only Vándory in the big room. He had presented his request to the members of the court and was protesting strenuously against the rejection, mainly from Zátonyi and the baron, with which it had met; the former because, as he said, in the popular conception malefactors brought before a summary court were to be held in the open; the latter, because it would not be right to cause more disturbance to this gentleman's house. But the clergyman's wish was so heatedly supported by Kálmán's parents and in particular his mother that the young people's intervention wasn't needed for the purpose to be achieved.

"I really don't think it necessary, "said Macskaházy unctuously, "for the prisoner to be locked up. Orders clearly specify winter conditions, and Viola is, I think, not unused to the cold wind that blows outside."

"If his neck's cold," mocked Nyúzó, "he'll be getting a tie tomorrow."

355

"Don't make light of it, "said Macskaházy with a sigh, realising the bad effect that Nyúzó's words had on everyone except Kenyházy, "it's a very serious matter. As I said, I don't think it's so very necessary for the prisoner to be held elsewhere, especially with regard to the said order. If, however, we can win the slightest favour with our esteemed hostess in that way, I have no objection to Master Vándory's request – providing that security be taken into consideration. The windows must be barred, the door locked, and the necessary guards posted."

"If you gentlemen so order," said the bailiff, "I can put the prisoner in a place where there are no windows."

"Yes," remarked Zátonyi, "the cellar. I thought of that straight away, that will be best."

Vándory gave a sigh.

"No, no," said the bailiff, "There's wine in the cellar, I can't let anyone in there, I've got to look after the master's property that's entrusted to me; but I can put him in the chaff-store. That can be locked, there are no windows on any side, and if only a single sentry is posted outside the door Viola'll be as secure as he'd be in the castle of Munkács."[168]

Vándory and in particular Mrs Kislaky were against that plan too, but after their objection – that the room could not be heated, which Kálmán too thought unimportant – had been settled, it was resolved that the prisoner be locked in the store, and that Nyúzó himself, together with Kenyházy and Macskaházy, who meant to see with his own eyes that the prisoner was securely held, should escort Vándory to the bailiff's house to be present when the transfer took place.

"Watch yourself," said Völgyesy to Kálmán, as they followed the rest at a distance. "When you spoke in favour of the unheated store Macskaházy gave you a suspicious look."

"You're right," said Kálmám, clasping his forehead. "When I need to be a little political, when I need to have a bit of sense, there's stupidity ready and waiting. But I'll put it right; as soon as we see the store, I'll object to it so much that. . ."

"That would be wrong as well," interrupted Völgyesy with a smile. "Let them get on with it, and if the chaff-store is the worst place on your property you can be sure that that's where Viola will be locked up."

Events proved Völgyesy right; and after Macskaházy had asked, with excessive zeal, whether the walls were of sound material, and the bai-

---

168 Now Mukacheve in Ukraine, a huge fortress on a high crag, formerly in Transylvania and in the hands of the Rákóczi family.

liff had replied curtly that Master Kislaky wasn't in the habit of building his farm buildings of mud, a table, a bench and a little straw were brought in, two sentries posted outside the door, and to the complete satisfaction of all present Viola was left alone in the icy store with Vándory, who, since he could do no more for the prisoner's bodily comfort, wished at least to cheer the final moments of his life with his consoling words.

Meanwhile old Kislaky, followed by his wife, withdrew to his room on the pretext of a headache. Zátonyi and the baron paced up and down in another room discussing the ridiculous softness of the master and mistress of the house, Vándory's foolish philanthropy and Völgyesy's insolence, and cast longing glances at the table where the *tarok* cards lay; Nyúzó and Macskaházy were keeping them from starting to play. Kislaky, his head supported on his hands, sat by the stove, so deep in thought that he had forgotten that his pipe had gone out long ago.

"Trézsi, my love," said the old man at length, turning to his wife, who was sitting beside him, untypically not engaged in work, looking now at her husband, now at the flickering flames in the stove, and likewise deep in dismal thoughts. "Trézsi, my love, I'm a wretched man."

Mrs Kislaky sighed but didn't speak. It seemed to that good lady too that a dark cloud had enveloped their happy life since a man had come to their house, and evildoer though he might be Kislaky could have saved his life.

"You aren't going to love me as you used to, are you?" he went on gloomily, "nor Kálmán either. When you see me you'll always be thinking: there now, that old man could have saved a man's life and didn't."

Mrs Kislaky spoke a few words of consolation, but her husband shook his head sorrowfully. "No, no, Trézsi my dear, I'm well aware I could have saved that man, but he's going to die. His blood will on my soul."

The good lady's heart fell in her sorrow, and instead of reproaching him as she had intended she tried to console him: the burden of responsibility for the verdict, if in fact it lay on anyone, lay equally on each judge; he had taken part in a criminal trial more than once in his time, and had surely always judged in accordance with the law and his conscience.

"That's different, quite different!" replied Kislaky dolefully. "In other courts people give their votes in accordance with their simple convictions, and the outcome is what the majority decide. A situation in which the prisoner's life depends on the vote of one man doesn't arise. The verdict goes up to the high court, to His Majesty, and even if in the end the malefactor receives the harshest punishment nobody can reproach themselves that they alone were the cause of his death. But in this case, when I consider that all that it needed was my vote in mitigation – indeed, not even that, but just that the prisoner be referred to regular judges – and that I voted for his death, that I with my own hand gave the poor man to his executioner: that is terrible! Can anyone that has a heart do such a thing? Does the man that has done it deserve that anyone should approach him lovingly?"

"But if that's how you feel about the matter," said Mrs Kislaky, her eyes filling with tears, "why, for God's sake, did you vote for death?"

"Why?" said Kislaky, rising from his chair and walking up and down the room. "Because I'm a cowardly, useless man, and because when everybody around me said that I would make myself ridiculous if I didn't condemn the malefactor; because Macskaházy and the rest were shouting that Viola's confession would be added to the documents, and that the Rétys would be even more annoyed with me, and I thought that in that case our Kálmán wouldn't get Etelka. And Völgyesy went away and left me to it – it was as if everything was conspiring against me."

"I can't imagine the Rétys being so horrid," said his wife thoughtfully.

"Neither can I," replied Kislaky. "The whole thing is Macskaházy's wickedness. . . and I've lost my good name and peace of mind through it!"

"Reassure yourself," said his wife, pressing his hand. "Nobody's going to attack your good name."

"Oh yes they will! Perhaps Völgyesy's right; now, when I think it over calmly, it seems to me too that the record wasn't correctly taken. Who's going to be blamed for that? As president, I am. But never mind; let people say I'm an ass, let them say what they like, I don't care, but when I go out of my house and see that poor hanged man out there on my land, whose life I could have saved, when I think of his wife and children begging at my feet for his life: I'll never know peace."

"Yes, you will," interposed Kálmán, who had come in quietly and had heard his father's last words. "If you don't object, father, Viola will be free this very day, and his blood will be on nobody's conscience."

The parents turned to him in astonishment. "Don't make jokes, my boy," said old Kislaky. "What you say is impossible."

"In legal terms, perhaps so," replied Kálmán cheerfully."Just as, in legal terms, it's considered impossible for two witnesses to lie as one, or for a judge to be partial or deceived; however, thank Heaven there are still other possibilities too."

"There's no appeal to a higher court from a *statarium*," sighed his father.

"Oh yes there is," said Kálmán, "the appeal that there is in all worldly affairs. The appeal to the future."

"I don't understand you," said the old man in surprise.

"I do," his mother cut in. Her eyes had been glued to her son's smiling face. "You mean to let him out, don't you!"

"That's right, mother. We'll challenge the verdict. If Viola's at liberty he'll appear either before another judge or, at the end of his life, before God, and there the verdict of today's court will be examined. By legal means it's impossible; so I keep those unstudied laws in mind and don't give a damn if the whole world says that saving Viola was incorrect procedure in legal terms . . . my guts will tell me that I've done right."

Mrs Kislaky adored her son, and my readers can imagine the feeling that his words – spoken with a smile but with deep emotion – stirred in her. "You're right," said she, her eyes radiant with joy, "it's an inhumane law that orders a poor, unfortunate man to be hanged on our property. God bless you if you can save him."

"Yes, but," interposed old Kislaky; joy had shone briefly on his face when he heard of the possibility of saving Viola, but now the same uncertainty could be seen again that came over that worthy man if ever a decision was called for. "I don't understand how . . ."

"Leave it to him," Mrs Kislaky cut him off, "the moment I heard what Kálmán said I was convinced that his fertile young mind had thought of a way . . ."

"This time you're mistaken, mother," laughed Kálmán. "The fertile young minds that have found a way of setting Viola free are those of old János and Peti the Gypsy." And he gave an account of János's plan, the achievement of which had already begun with Viola being locked up in the store.

"So that's why you were against Viola being put in a better room?" said Mrs Kislaky. "I couldn't make that out."

"Precisely," said Kálmán. "But as you can see, for our plan to succeed we need two important things: the keys to the cellar and the granary. In Hungary, especially in legal affairs, we can't achieve anything without those two. Just this once, mother will have to trust me with them."

"With all my heart," said she; her good humour was now fully restored, and she took two big keys from the many in her drawer and passed them to Kálmán. "Spare no expense, let them drink the cellar dry, give the *hajdús* Tokaj wine if need be, just save that poor man."

Meanwhile old Kislaky was striding about the room, evidently in the greatest agitation. "What's the matter, dear?" asked his wife gently, and she went up and put a hand on his shoulder.

"I've been thinking," said the old man, and he stood still, "what a terrible situation my weakness has brought me into. It was in my power to save that poor man's life, I could have done it legally, it would have been quite in order, and now, for my son to make good my mistake, he'll commit a real criminal act, perhaps ruin his prospects, and I can't so much as tell him not to."

"Don't torment yourself with bad thoughts," said Kálmán. "How might I ruin my prospects by helping this hapless man?"

"If the Rétys find out that it was you that rescued Viola," replied his father, "you know how passionate women can be. And what's more, who knows whether you'll ever be forgiven for what you did for Tengelyi at the election?"

"As far as that's concerned," said Kálmán calmly, "there's no cause for anxiety. I want no favours from Réty or his wife; and as for Etelka, from these lines you can see that she thinks differently about the affair." And with that he handed his father the letter that János had brought.

"What an angel!" said his mother, as she read Etelka's letter along with her husband. "You're right, my boy, You must save Viola."

"This is the first letter I've ever had from Etelka," said Kálmán with spirit, "and if she wanted me to commit a crime I'd do it, never mind this!"

"God forbid I should hold you back," said the old man, handing back the letter, "your purpose is sacred and noble. But even so, in the eyes of the law it's a crime. If anything went wrong! If you were discovered! I shudder."

"If anything went wrong?" replied Kálmán cheerfully. "But what more is needed than to make the *hajdús* drunk and to keep Nyúzó and his man indoors on this cold night? The door from the granary to the bailiff's loft is locked from our side; there's no difficulty, we've got the keys to the cellar and the granary!"

"But what if it's discovered?" said his father, still uneasy." What if you're prosecuted?"

"Prosecuted? Don't you know, father," said Kálmán with a laugh, "that only a general assembly can decide on criminal proceedings? What have we to fear?" With which he triumphantly brandished the keys, pocketed them, and left.

"He's a splendid boy!" said his mother, looking lovingly after him. "How could Etelka not be in love with him!"

360

"Splendid!" sighed Kislaky, taking a seat by the stove. "As long as nobody finds out what he's doing it's a fine action, but it's still a criminal one."

"Stop tormenting yourself with thoughts like that."

"And when I think that all this could have been avoided if I'd voted for acquittal."

"Why worry about that? Viola's going to escape and you can relax."

"It's still a terrible law," sighed the old man, "that leaves a decent person unable to sleep in peace for the rest of his life if he implements it."

And the worthy pair sat side by side in silence, until Mrs Kislaky left the room, mindful of preparations for dinner, and Kislaky lit his pipe and went to join his tarok-playing guests who, amid their many cries of *contra*, had long ago forgotten him and the alleged headache that had caused his absence.

XXIV

It's said that there's nothing harder than to bring people to their senses, and that may be true! For since this earth has been turning on its axis and mankind going about on it, how many have attempted that weighty task! and how many have found that they've wasted their time!

Bringing people to their senses may be difficult, but there are occasions when it's also difficult to do the opposite, and that evening Kálmán cursed his fate a hundred times as it seemed that it wasn't permitting him to make Nyúzó drunk. I won't even speak of Macskaházy. The lawyer was one of those unfortunate beings who is always sober. Kálmán was no longer even trying. The others, including even the baron, seemed to be voluntarily, almost effortlessly, fulfilling the wish of their young host. But Nyúzó, like a rock on which the tempest beats leaving no trace, or an island washed to no purpose by the floods of the sea, resisted the power of the best wines red and white alike. He usually drank ordinary, common-or-garden wine, and Kálmán made use of his cellar key to replace the good but everyday red and white wines which Kislaky's guests were usually served with the strongest from Eger and the Hegyalja. Nyúzó wasn't one of those of whom, as the saying goes, weakness never got the better, and my readers themselves saw him at Garacs in the condition to which Kálmán was now hoping to reduce him; but the presence of the hated Völgyesy, Macskaházy's admonitions, and most of all the noble ambition of not jeopardising his reputation as the best drinker in the county so perfectly counteracted the effect of the wine that even after he'd drunk an amazing quantity there was still no sign of him becoming drunk.

"You'd like to make me drunk, wouldn't you?" said Nyúzó, looking at Kálmán after downing another glass of red wine; his face showed that it might have been some bitter medicine. "Don't be so silly. No one's ever seen me drunk."

"I have, old chap," said Kenyházy with a friendly grin, "and you were well and truly drunk."

"What? Me?" shouted Nyúzó.

Zátonyi looked up at the sound – he had been resting his head in his hands, both elbows on the table, deep in thought while Macskaházy shuffled the cards – and commented that it had been a fine summary case that they had seen that day. "The sixteenth at which I've been present, and every time we've executed somebody."

"That's irrelevant." said Nyúzó crossly, "I'd like to ask this clerk of mine . . ."

"Irrelevant?" Zátonyi interrupted him, as sharply as his impeded tongue permitted. "Don't we still constitute a *statarium*? The court remains together until sentence has been carried out."

"Rubbish! that's irrelevant as well," said Nyúzó, shaking his head angrily, "when I want to ask Kenyházy what . . ."

"Rubbish!" Zátonyi cut him short, and slapped the hand that he had just been dealt down on the table in a dignified manner. "When I say . . . what was I saying . . . yes, it's not rubbish, *domine spectabilis*, kindly take that back and think who you're speaking to and where you are. Have some respect to the sanctity of the situation, we're still a session of a *statarium*."

Nyúzó was becoming more and more irritable. Kálmán hoped that a quarrel might be even more conducive to his purpose than his Hegyalja wine, and gestured to Zátonyi to desist, but he went on working himself up: "Indeed, indeed, it's no joke! not a laughing matter! Until the malefactor's been executed we're still in session as a *statarium*. It's all in standing orders. We eat together as a *statarium*, play tarok as a *statarium*, we . . ."

"Would you mind not shouting like that?" bellowed Nyúzó, covering his ears.

"If I want to shout, shout I shall," Zátonyi went on, more heatedly still, "and I'd like to see anybody stop me. I'm a *táblabíró* of Taksony County like any other; I've just been proposed for *alispán* for the third time."

The baron had been looking at his cards and anticipated playing a mighty hand; he gestured to his companions with the greatest possible patience to continue with the game, but in vain. Of all the subjects over which people quarrel none is the source of such noise and acrimony as when the question is which of them is sober, and many people who have never ever raised a glass of wine to their lips have fallen out with their best friends rather than have their sobriety called into question. Who will expect either Nyúzó or Kenyházy to calm down so easily on this occasion? especially when Kálmán has done all that he can to increase the bitterness of their argument, and Nyúzó has thought that he saw a smile of contempt on Völgyesy's lips, which he could not attribute to anything but that the hated opposition was in doubt as to the feasibility of his reckless offer that he, Pál Nyúzó, would drink three glasses to every one drunk by Kenyházy without becoming drunk.

"Now, my friend, that's going too far," said Kálmán, "I'll never believe that as long as I live."

"You don't believe it?" exclaimed Nyúzó.

"I certainly don't," replied Kálmán, "I'll bet anything."

"Very well; two milch cows against my *agár*."

"Agreed, though the *agár* isn't worth much, but you'll lose it in any case."

"It's a bet, let's have the glasses."

Kálmán could scarcely conceal his inner delight. Macskaházy did all that he could to have the wager cancelled; Kenyházy, however, emptied his first glass with a laugh. Nyúzó, as promised, followed that with three, and the sport continued rather more noisily.

While Kálmán was thus attending to the gentry, János was operating with no less success among the *hajdús* and guards, so that after nine o'clock, with the exception of one Kislak peasant and one elderly *hajdú*, himself a veteran soldier, there was scarcely anyone to be found in the yard whom the greatest flatterer could have called sober.

In the prisoner's cell, at the door of which the two most sober guards were stationed, a deep silence reigned. After Vándory had left, after preparing him for death with the consolations of religion, the prisoner's wife went to him, and from then on, if the guards occasionally put their ears to the door they heard only the muffled whispers in which the hapless pair were taking leave of one another; by Nyúzó's strict order, no one was to speak to the prisoner after nine o'clock.

That external silence filled the hearts of Viola and his wife with indescribable unease. He had often thought in the course of his life about the death that he was now about to suffer. His fate had been sealed from the moment of his capture in the St-Vilmos forest, and he had not pleaded, not tried to exonerate himself before his judges not so much out of pride as because he knew that all his efforts would be futile. What was death, after all, but the loss of life, and what had life to offer this unfortunate man that he might have regretted losing? His wife herself and his children, whose love was the sole thing of value left to him in this world, would they not be happier, or at least less troubled, when the misfortune that constantly threatened and made their whole lives a torment was finally at an end? For what could he do for his wife, who had been deprived through him of the happiness of marriage and reduced to beggary? What could he do for his children, the name of whose father would be a mark of shame on their lives, and for whom he could wish, from whom he could ask nothing but that they should not follow his example? "When I'm no more," he thought to himself, "nobody round here will speak of Viola. Who knows? perhaps my wife too may at length forget the accursed creature who has brought nothing but pain and disgrace on her whole life. My children will change their name and seek their fortunes elsewhere, and all will again be well. Better to die today than tomorrow . . ." and Viola awaited his fate as calmly as one struck by a long foreseen blow, the thought of which he has long ago befriended. This indifference towards life isn't as rare among our people as my readers may perhaps think. Just as we're amazed at the levity with which, in the time of the worse Roman emperors, so many gave up their lives either voluntarily or at the tyrant's command, and as the reasons for this phenomenon are not to be found so much in stoic philosophy as in the practical conviction that there was little to lose in life; so our people part lightly with their lives, in which their daily earnings are all too often not commensurate with the toil with which they are gained. Viola's wife herself, once she had regained her senses after hearing of the sentence of death, was calmer than anyone seeing her previous despair could have thought. The imminent disaster that had hung so long above their heads had struck – there remained nothing in this world for them to fear; and as the final hope vanishes, so does our unease.

Old János's good news disturbed this calm. At first the old soldier had intended not to divulge the whole rescue plan to Viola until the last minute. "God forbid!" said he to Kálmán, when the latter had declared his wish not to leave the poor people any longer in their hopeless condition; "You'd spoil everything, sir. If the lady knew that we'd be getting her husband out she wouldn't be able to control herself, it'd be noticed, and it'd be all up. It's best for them to have no expectations, then at least nobody's going to notice any change in them."

János's reasoning seemed so sound that it was accepted by Kálmán without protest, and the old hussar experienced for himself later how dangerous it was to trust anyone with secrets, because when – in a moment of madness – he had scarcely met Mrs Viola all alone, scarcely seen her wordless despair, than he'd divulged the whole plan himself; on seeing the expression of indescribable joy that immediately suffused the poor woman's face, in his pleasure he didn't think that if at that moment someone came into the room they might have suspected a lot from the joyful smile with which she looked at him. Who can help it! However much we talk about plans and calculations made in advance, life is not a game of chess. The subtlest of players knows that his victory depends not entirely on his skill but to a great extent on fate or the unexpected;

365

the pieces with which we carry out our plans are not insensate wooden figures but sensate beings, suffering and rejoicing as we ourselves do with our manifold emotions and moods . . . under such circumstances, who is there that can stick to his plan? When the old hussar entered the room where Mrs Viola and her children were sitting and saw her pallid face as she cradled the sleeping infant in her arms and, sunk deep in gloomy thoughts, didn't even notice him come in; when little Pista, his eyes red from weeping, came to meet him and with irresistible gentleness led him by the hand to his mother and asked him to cheer her, and when the child in Zsuzsa's arms woke at the sound, smiled and looked up at its mother, whose eyes were bathed in tears at that smile: then all of János's stipulations went up in smoke, and when Mrs Viola pressed the little one to her lips and sighed "The poor thing doesn't know how soon she's going to be an orphan . . ." the old man wiped his eyes with his calloused hand and could not have made any other response than "She certainly isn't, Zsuzsi, my dear, any more than you're going to be a widow . . ." and it was only from the look of astonishment that she gave him that he realised what he had said.

After that the secret could no longer be kept; little Pista was therefore sent out and in a whisper János told her all about the plans. "You see," he added cheerfully, "we've thought of everything. No problem, in a couple of hours' time, when the gentry and the guards are snoring, your husband'll be a free man, onto a good horse, and they'll wonder what's become of him. No need to give up, no need to despair. That is, I mean," he corrected himself, "you certainly must be sorrowful, desperate, moan and groan, otherwise the gentry'll notice. I'm an old fool, shouldn't have said a word, you won't be able to pretend and it'll all be ruined."

Mrs Viola, still in a whisper, asked János all sorts of questions about her husband's escape.

"Give me the little one for a bit," said he, as he answered them, "let me look at her, dandle her on my knee. Oh, what a fine child!" said he, and his face was wreathed in smiles as he carefully took the baby into his arms. "I've never seen one finer . . . and the way the rascal laughs, it's as if I'd carried her round a hundred times; we simply mustn't let harm come to your husband! Oh, Zsuzsi, if I'd got a child like this!"

"Mine are going to love you like a second father," said she, giving János a look in which were mingled all her gratitude and the love of a mother hearing her child praised.

"Yes, like a second father," replied János with a sigh, "but being loved as a first father must be something completely different. Do you see,

Zsuzsi, I've often wondered why God hasn't granted me children. They say it's because I've never married. True enough, but why was that? If I hadn't had to go to war I could have grandchildren by now, and believe me, I'd give my gratuity silver and my medal this very day for a child like yours . . . both for just a single one. But God bless! Perhaps the reason I haven't got children is that I'd want them all to be the same even then. When children are little they're all equally beautiful, there's no difference between them at all, they're active, lively as little fish, and later half of them become frogs."

At that moment János saw Vándory coming, led by little Pista, to take Zsuzsi to Viola, and had only a moment to gesture that on no account must she betray herself. He left the room not a little anxious to think of the risks that might arise from his divulging the secret if Mrs Viola were to betray his hopes.

In that regard, however, János's anxiety was quite superfluous. The good news which he had brought to Mrs Viola, and which she shared with him the moment the two of them were alone, filled their hearts with unspeakable unease. Such is our nature . . . the leafless tree stands calm, and the strongest wind scarcely moves its dry branches; the young green shoots quiver at the touch of the lightest breeze . . . and anyone seeing Viola at this moment, when his liberty seemed so certain, and who didn't know the reason for his excitement could only have thought that fear of death had at last taken hold of this stalwart man. And could be surprised? Didn't the vital force pulse in his every vein, that force which flows among all our misfortunes and binds us instinctively to life? Could he not see his wife at his side? Did it not inevitably come to his mind that his children needed him so? – Viola had long been thinking of changing his way of life. Now a definite prospect opened before him. The Kislak cowherd's nephew, having obtained his certificate of discharge from his previous landowner and his passport from the county, had died as he was preparing to leave with his wife and three children and go three counties away, to where he had been promised work as a cowherd on the commendation of his uncle, who had worked there in the past. Old István had the documents, and he would take Viola there himself in his nephew's stead. There, twenty miles away, no one would know him: wouldn't a new life, new good fortune begin for the victim of persecution? But didn't all the happiness which he could now see so close before him hang by a thread?. . . If it occurred to someone in the house that only one door separated the bailiff's loft from the granary, and sentries were stationed at that door? If the noise made by taking up the boards in

367

the loft were to rouse the guards? – a hundred possibilities, and in each of them instead of the happiness that he could now see before him lay a foul death and the wretchedness of his wife and children!

It was in such a condition that Nyúzó found his prisoner. At almost ten o'clock he entered the store accompanied by Macskaházy and the bailiff; he was none too steady on his feet, but he had caused his clerk to be taken to his room dead drunk. The change that had taken place in Viola was much too conspicuous to escape the attention of Macskaházy and the bailiff. . . and after Nyúzó had gone round the store, tapping the walls with the greatest care and turning over the straw with his stick, the bailiff whispered to him that the outlaw had lost all his courage.

"Has he?" Nyúzó laughed loudly. "Is that so, where's your courage now, Viola?. . . Why are you so humble now, previously you were full of yourself?"

"Your Worship," replied Viola, biting his lip, "the step for which I must prepare is no child's play, and a man has a heart. I'm leaving a wife and children behind, and who knows what's to become of the poor things."

"By your wife I suppose you mean Zsuzsi?. . . well," said he with a smile, "I'll look after her."

Viola's blood boiled, but he kept control and said nothing.

"And your children? Well, when they grow up," he went on cheerfully, "they'll go where you're going. But why all this prattle?" he interrupted himself with full magisterial dignity. "You, Zsuzsi, clear off, the two of you've had enough time whining, and you, Viola, prepare yourself for the morning."

The agonising sense of the uncertainty of his situation arose again in the prisoner as it did in his wife. They embraced tremulously, and the hapless Zsuzsi couldn't bring herself to part from her husband. She clung to him convulsively, hugging him to her with all the passion of her agony.

"I said, you've had enough time!" exclaimed Nyúzó, impatiently striking a chair with his stick. "Out you go, and that's that." As Zsuzsi didn't obey at once he caught her by the kerchief, separated her unresisting from her husband and steered her to the door; Macskaházy and the bailiff followed. Nyúzó remained a moment longer, his eyes fixed on the prisoner and smiling in satisfaction at his pale face and the tremor that he observed around his lips, and which he took for fear. "Well, Viola," said he at length with a laugh, "who'll be hanging whom tomorrow? We promised one another, didn't we? See, I'm keeping my word." With which he left, locking the door after him.

As I've said, the two most sober guards were positioned beside the door; but as the novelist too is confined to the strict bounds of probability I must confess that after all the wine with which János had plied the two their sobriety wasn't sufficient to satisfy Macskaházy, and he was just sighing and complaining to the bailiff that through the excessive hospitality of the master of the house everyone in the house was drunk, when Nyúzó emerged.

"Who's drunk? What do you mean, drunk?" said he crossly to Macskaházy, having heard his last words. "Excuse me, nobody here's drunk, nobody can be drunk, I say so and that's the end of it."

"Don't make a fool of yourself," whispered Macskaházy into his ear. "Who was talking about you? But these men here, just look and see, are as drunk as newts."

"So they are!" Nyúzó now exclaimed. "You're both drunk, you worthless pair, I'll have you hanged. If the outlaw escapes one of you will swing for it, so watch yourselves. It's disgraceful for people to drink themselves mindless as animals."

Of course, the guards swore that they hadn't so much as seen a drop of wine and that their prisoner, be he the devil himself, wouldn't be able to escape. Macskaházy, however, thought it safer under the circumstances for him to lock the door and keep the key; but Nyúzó took that as direct interference with his office, all the more so as he realised that Macskaházy wanted the key because he had no confidence in his sobriety. He therefore pocketed the key himself and went off to bed, cursing freely against, among other things, the vile sin of drunkenness.

All became silent once more in Kislak. After their great exertions the judges had made for their beds. The moment that Nyúzó had gone away the guards posted at the gate and around the house lay down and snored in praise of Kislak wine. The bailiff pulled his nightcap onto his head and vanished beneath the quilt with a sense of his importance and the cleverness that he'd displayed that day . . . and while Mrs Viola sat by the bed in which the children were asleep, heart pounding in her breast with all the torments of uncertainty, and for the first time in her life didn't feel her heart assured when she saw the angelic repose on their faces. . . and while Kálmán paced rapidly up and down his room, hardly able to wait for the moment to set about accomplishing his plan, and old Kislaky himself, for the first time in years, could not find sleep and tossed and turned, sighing, in his bed: all was silent around the yard, and only the dogs, responding now and then to those that raised their voices in the village, broke the solemn silence with their barks.

In the prisoner's cell likewise all was silent, and the guards stationed at the door, as soon as the fear induced by Nyúzó had passed off, yawned vastly as they awaited their reliefs.

The night was dark and cold. The clouds which had covered the sky all day had sunk to spread a clammy veil of mist over the yard, and though both of them had, with János's assistance, warmed their stomachs well enough, the damp that came from outside through their clothes began to gain the upper hand over the noble fluids which their inward parts concealed, and although the *hajdú* with military experience bore his fate quite stolidly his companion sighed and protested against the cold, in which, if not soon relieved, he was surely going to freeze.

János was satisfied with the night – so dark that one could scarcely see three paces – and with the external guards – all fast asleep – and meanwhile met Peti, who was waiting with Viola's horse outside the fence of the park. The old Gypsy had brought a crowbar, pincers, in short, all the equipment needed to tear up the boards, and had brought news that István the cowherd would be at the farmyard before midnight with his horses and cart to take Zsuzsi and the children away. Peti's advice was that they should not be left in Nyúzó's power, and István thought it best for him to take them straight off to their new abode; Viola himself could follow on horseback.

At that news old János stroked his moustache with no little satisfaction, and after giving Viola's good horse a pat he tethered it to the fence and ordered Peti to hide near the granary; he himself went back once more to the sentries outside the store, and found them still awake.

"Isn't it ten o'clock yet?" asked the one on recognising János; he was worn out and had sat down, and so as better to pull his sheepskin coat round him had put his rifle down at his side on the ground.

"Of course it is," said the other, "I'd rather do six days of socage.[169] Even for a soldier this is a lot. My mate here was in the war, and even so he says that he was never on sentry-go this long."

"What can you do about it," said the *hajdú*. "Orders is orders."

"That's right, it's an order," sighed his friend. "It's easy for the gentry to give orders. Come here, go there, stand here, freeze, go hungry! . . They go to bed on a full stomach. They might at least give us something to eat, or a drop of *pálinka* . . . just so's we don't freeze to death."

"Now wait a minute, you fellows," said János. "When I arrived today young Master Kálmán gave me some brandy, it's up there in the room, and the bottle's almost full. I'll go and fetch some."

---

169 Work, usually agricultural, done by a serf for his master over and above the norm.

And with that János set off, told Kálmán how things stood, got from him an almost full bottle of slivowitz and some bread, and went back.

"You see," said the old hussar, after taking a gulp from the bottle and offering it first to the *hajdú* and then to the other sentry, "it all arises from the fact that there's nobody in the house that really knows how to give orders. If Nyúzó, or any of the other gentry, had been in the army you wouldn't have to be standing here, your relief would have been arranged and you'd now be taking it easy, but as it is . . ."

"We'll surely be relieved sooner or later!" said the peasant, alarmed at the prospect of spending the whole night there.

"It's a happy man that can trust the gentry," said János with a laugh. "I'd like to know who's going to relieve you when the rest are all asleep."

"Give me that bottle again, I'm still cold," said the peasant, shaking his head impatiently, while his companion leaned on his weapon, sighing deeply.

Before passing the bottle over as requested, János pretended that he too was drinking and by that action prevailed on the *hajdú* to follow his example. All the time he entertained the two with his certainty that no one was coming to relieve them. Meanwhile the bottle went from hand to hand until at length the peasant guard yawned and swore that as far as he was concerned he could stand it no longer, and lay down at once; the *hajdú* also, although he had spoken about strict orders, admitted that he wouldn't be able to remain awake until morning.

"Tell you what," said János in a friendly tone. "I've been a soldier, I've been on sentry-go often enough in my time and I'm not at all sleepy. You go under the lean-to and lie down on the dry straw, and if I feel that I'm getting sleepy I'll wake you. You can get your sleep until then, and tomorrow, when the magistrate comes, you can be wide awake."

This offer was accepted straight away by the peasant sentry, and by the former soldier after some hesitation – he still retained traces of military discipline – and shortly afterwards János could hear snores coming from the lean-to, indicating that there was probably no further obstacle to the accomplishment of his plan.

The old hussar put down the weapon that he had taken over from the *hajdú* and stole quietly over to the lean-to. Once he was certain that both sentries were asleep he hurried to the granary, where Peti and Kálmán were waiting most impatiently for him.

János took off his boots – the Gypsy didn't need to – and after the lantern on the stairs had been lit they hurried silently up to the loft. Kálmán stopped at the door and watched them go; enveloped in his cloak, his heart pounding, he pricked up his ears: was anything going to happen to obstruct their plan at the last moment?

He hadn't been standing there long when he heard steps approaching from the house where the members of the court were sleeping. Kálmán moved to the other side of the granary and was cursing that he hadn't managed to make Nyúzó sufficiently drunk, when in the form that was pacing slowly towards him, carrying a big stick and a lantern, he recognised Macskaházy. At first, Kálmán was uncertain what to do, and there was a moment when the crafty lawyer was in the greatest danger of being laid low, had the young man not realised that that could not be done without making a noise and that every moment that it took would reduce the probability of rescuing Viola.

Macskaházy continued to advance towards the store with his lantern, and his surprise and fury on finding that the prisoner had been left unguarded can scarcely be imagined. "I thought straight away," he thought, "that there was dirty work being planned. Young Master Kálmán has made Nyúzó and all the guards drunk. They mean to set him free, that's obvious! They didn't succeed in court, and now the plan is to use force. I'll have to go back, rouse a couple of men, even stand guard myself here until morning . . . Viola must die! If his case comes before a regular court he'll involve me with his statements, and who knows, with all the enemies that I've got, what the outcome might be?"

The lawyer had just turned away when a sound from the prisoner's cell caught his attention. He thought that he could hear creaking. He put his ear to the door and it sounded clearly as if someone was taking up a board in the loft and lowering something into the store. "They're breaking in through the loft!" he exclaimed. "Curses! Isn't there anyone here? Just you wait, you villains, I'm coming!" And Macskaházy, for all his deviousness, so far forgot himself that he would have gone into the store had Nyúzó not locked the door and kept the key.

Not only those working in the cell could hear the noise, as they lowered a ladder found in the loft through the hole that they had made, but so could Kálmán, and it woke the sentries sleeping in the lean-to, though not to full consciousness; all the greater was the terror that filled the poor bailiff's heart – he had for some time been suffering every degree of mortal dread, as if it were he that the court had sentenced.

As I've said, never had the bailiff put on his nightcap with a greater sense of pride than that evening. The condescending manner in which all the members of the court – especially the baron (who, after all, was likewise a wealthy landowner) – had addressed him all day, the impor-

372

tance at county, indeed, national level of the task that he had fulfilled that day, the admirable ingenuity that he had displayed in all the appropriate arrangements, talk of which would no doubt be widespread, seemed to redouble his esteem in his own eyes – though the worthy fellow had never been in the habit of looking down on himself. He was completely self-satisfied. "Ah!" he was dreaming, "this is the sort of thing I was born for! Who cares about this stupid farming! Muck-spreading, ploughing, sowing, treading, these aren't for me. I should have been a lawyer, that's what God made me for." He thought over what he might have been if he'd studied law. An *alispán*, who knows, perhaps a judge of the Bench of Seven,[170] a *főispán*, *kamara praeses*, a *zászlósúr*? What can a lawyer not become in Hungary? His imagination, assisted by the strongish wine that he'd drunk at dinner with the rest, stopped at nothing, and the fat man tossed and turned in his bed as if all those offices were about to weigh on his shoulders.

We know, however, that there is no stronger opponent of sleep than such reverie. It seems to demonstrate the principles of homeopathy that our waking dreams, drawn before us by love or ambition, drive off the more valuable ones that come of their own accord, and in which our souls as much find repose as they are weary of the others, and however the bailiff closed his eyes, however often he forced himself to yawn, he simply couldn't go to sleep, which to others is unpleasant but more so to a bailiff, who isn't accustomed to it. The hapless man, who at other times was able to send all present to sleep with his conversation and whose skill was now shown to fail to work on himself, tried everything to escape from that intolerable situation and lull himself to sleep. He began counting. That didn't help, counting brought on thoughts of official accounts, and the deeper he sank into addition and subtraction the more it seemed that the figures didn't work out. He opened his eyes and looked around. In the light of the stub of candle everything in the room took on nightmarish form. The accounts of past years, kept in the fashion of old Hungarian farmers on top of the beams, cast big shadows, all huge sticks that stretched towards him and in the flickering light seemed to be brandished, menacing. He shuddered and put out the candle, but what good did that do? The thought of accounts was replaced by that of robbery. The greatest outlaw in the county was captive in the house,

---

170 Originally consisting of seven judges, the *Hétszemélyes Tábla* had 21 members by this time, with 11 required for it to be quorate. It was one of the two divisions of the King's Bench (*Királyi Tábla*).

under sentence of death, but who could say how many there were in his band? If they broke in, intent on saving their leader, what would happen to the poor bailiff – it was he that had had the bandit most closely guarded, had himself given the carpenter orders for the gallows, and had said many a time in the yard, in front of a hundred people, that Viola must hang, of which the outlaws must surely know by that time. And hadn't he slept with every window open for the last two years, for fear of a stroke? Couldn't the outlaws come into his room with nothing to stop them, since the *hajdú* that slept in the yard at other times was on sentry duty that day? In his anxiety the bailiff began to perspire. At that moment he thought that he could hear footsteps in the loft above his head. He sat up in bed in terror. His ears were ringing, but all the same he could clearly hear footsteps and immediately afterwards the sound of creaking, caused by the prising up of boards. There could be no doubt . . . "Merciful God!" said he quietly, and involuntarily clasped his hands together in prayer. What was he to do? Should he lock his door? – but his ears were ringing as if they were flying round him with the wing-beats of a big bird, his heart was throbbing, his chest was so tight that he could hardly breathe, while the cold sweat on his brow and the tremor in all his limbs were the clear symptoms of an imminent stroke. "If I lock the door and nobody can come to my aid, I'm lost," he thought, and hid beneath the quilt. On the other hand the creaking grew louder and louder and, in the silence of night, sounded as if the floor in the next room were being torn up, and who could say how many outlaws there were and what cruelties he would have to endure if he didn't lock the door, so that at least he would gain time to call for help while it was being broken down. This made his death more certain still. Finally, wasn't it likely that, if he got up sweating like that in his cold room, he would have a stroke there and then the moment he got out of bed? In his torment the poor fellow sighed and prayed; he swore ten times over that he would never sleep alone in a room again, that next day he would marry his housekeeper, never again drink wine at dinner; but those conditions would only be of help in the future, while in the present those two monstrous dangers faced him which filled his soul with dread and between which he could not choose. In the end, when he heard Macskaházy's shouts, in his fear he didn't recognise his voice and the apparently ever more imminent danger overcame every other consideration: he wrapped himself in his quilt, got out of bed and made for the door. But imagine his horror on hearing the porch door open suddenly and someone hurry quickly towards his room. He too hurried, dropped his quilt and was reaching for the key when his door burst open and before him stood a man in a sheepskin.

There is a moment beyond which fear becomes desperation and transforms coward into hero, and this came to our bailiff. Half out of his mind, as frantic as a man fighting for his life as mercilessly as one that expected no mercy, he closed with the arrival and in the moment that followed bellowed for Macskaházy to help.

"Villain!" shouted the bailiff. He seized his opponent by the throat, while the other rained blows on his head and shoulders.

"You've gone mad!" shrieked the latter, grabbing his assailant by the ears and likewise defending himself tooth and claw, until people came with lanterns, drawn to the tremendous din, and the two fighters, clinging tightly together, were pulled apart, bleeding from noses and mouths, and were astonished to recognise one another.

"Was Your Worship meaning to rob me, then?"said the bailiff in amazement.

"The bailiff's gone mad!" exclaimed Macskaházy, "it's obvious, let's lock him here in his room; but come quickly, the prisoner's escaping." And with that they all followed that call, left the panting bailiff to himself, slammed the door and rushed after Macskaházy to the chaff store. The bailiff stood there in his white nightcap, astounded at the lawyer's affront and shaking with the aftermath of fear, rage and exertion. At length the chill in the room reminded him of the possibility of a stroke and he took refuge in his bed, continuing on his pillows to contemplate the wickedness of the world.

It was only natural, when we consider the time that he had spent in the bailiff's arms, or rather talons, that Macskaházy found the prisoner no longer there when his cell was broken open. Macskaházy was still shouting at the door when Viola was already in the loft, from where a moment later he was at Kálmán's side, and after a brief word of thanks saw himself at liberty. Kálmán locked the granary and hurried to Mrs Viola to take her the news and to let her and the children out through the rear door to the park; scarcely were they there than the sound of receding hoof-beats showed that the prisoner was in safety. She kissed Kálmán's hands fervently and likewise hurried away; he himself, happy at having done a good deed, went back towards the bailiff's lodging, from where a constantly growing din could be heard.

I shan't describe the din and disorder that Kálmán found there, as my readers are familiar with the characters and the condition to which they had been reduced with the aid of the Kislak cellar. Suffice it to say that the entire house – gentry, servants, gendarmes, and peasants from the village crowding to the noise with lanterns and candles – was milling around in wild confusion, and after everybody had looked into the chaff store and had explained that the prisoner had clearly escaped through the ceiling – of which no one had been in doubt – everyone gave advice and orders, but no one found it necessary on their own account to pursue the prisoner, so that Macskaházy was left with only a bloodied nose and broken teeth as a reward for his wakefulness.

Dawn was breaking by the time that all had heard with surprise that no one had been sent after the prisoner – there being no great likelihood that he would return of his own volition – and all began to feel that they had spent a sleepless night and made for their beds for a short rest after so much trouble; all except Kenyházy, whom neither the noise, the *hajdús'* repeated shaking, Nyúzó's curses, *nec ardor civium, nec frons instantis tyranni*[171] had been able to wake.

When Kislaky entered his room with his son, the good old man flung his arms around Kálmán's neck. "Whatever the consequence may be," he said with feeling, "God bless you for saving my soul from eternal reproach. Never again will I be a *statarium* judge as long as I live."

Kálmán was moved, squeezed his father's hand and likewise went to his room, and silence was restored around the mansion and the bailiff's lodging.

---

171 A slightly selective (mis)quotation from Horace *Odes* III:3. The original has *non civium ardor ... non vultus instantis tyranni* '... not the ardour of the people ... not the face of the tyrant towering above him ...

XXV

There is no more painful situation in the world than when a working man is forced into retirement by sickness or other circumstances. We feel this pain especially in our younger days, when we consider our personal influence much more important than later, and it seems as if the world, or at least the circle in which we move, can't advance if we don't put our shoulder to the wheel. This was Ákos's situation all the time that the events that I described in the previous chapter were taking place – and I scarcely believe that the serious admonitions of the doctor and Vándory could have kept him in his room had Etelka not come to Tiszarét with her father and told her brother how Vilma – whom she had visited at once – wanted him, as a sign of love, to follow the doctor's advice.

The *alispán*, as I said, arrived in Tiszarét a few hours after his wife. Réty was much too subtle a man not to speak of Ákos with infinite anxiety as soon as he saw that the election was over and his wishes had been carried through to the last lawyer's clerk, though he knew that the wound wasn't dangerous in the least. "A father's always a father," he told those who tried to reassure him; among these baron Sóskuty distinguished himself mainly for his reasons and their number. "Ákos is my only son. It's not as if I wouldn't behave with the same love towards my daughter . . . everyone knows how much I adore Etelka . . . but Ákos is my only son, and who can say whether the news that his wound is trifling is correct . . . injuries to the hand, as I've often heard from our respected senior medical officer" – this latter was present – "can lead to tetanus and death . . . and if I were to lose my poor Ákos!. . ." Every time that the *alispán* reached this point in his speech he sighed deeply and wiped his eyes. It was touching to see him in his distress. A couple of hours after the first, a second messenger had arrived from Tiszarét; through him the butler had – contrary to Ákos's orders – sent written word to the *alispán* because he thought that news might have reached Porvár by other means, saying that in the opinion of Serer and Vándory the whole thing was a trifle. But although on hearing this Réty announced that he would stay in Porvár until the morning and lunch with the *főispán*, his paternal anxiety had by then visibly increased so much that the *főispán*, noticing his unease, told him to leave the lunch and hurry home to see with his own eyes what condition his son was in. Réty obeyed with expressions of eternal gratitude, and with his daughter and the chief medical officer – whose enthusiasm on this occasion can be shown by the fact that he rose from the table before the ice-cream – he hurried home, while the other guests extolled his limitless paternal love. My readers know that he arrived home to find his son completely out of danger – as, between ourselves, he had privately never doubted that he would; however, on learning of the patient's condition the chief medical officer immediately prescribed lemonade to replace Serer's almond milk – it goes without saying that in the presence of those who at some time in their lives have called two doctors to one patient I wouldn't mention that if I didn't reckon on a few healthy readers. After this medical consultation and a good dinner the whole Tiszarét *ménage* went to bed early, of which the master of the house in particular was in great need after his exertions of the morning.

No one in the entire family was as upset by Ákos's misfortune as Etelka, not only because no one in the house loved the patient as much, but because she was at the same time also the most devoted friend of Vilma, and felt the consequences that would come to her from this event, because of which she now reproached herself, as it was she that had prevailed on Vilma and her mother to agree to Ákos's visit. After she had wished her brother good night and dismissed her maid, who slept in the side room, she remained pacing up and down the room alone . . . and the more she thought about the whole affair, the greater the anxiety with which she looked into the future. She knew her stepmother far too well to hope that she would ever consent to Ákos and Vilma's marrying, and under those circumstances her father's consent too could not be expected, and indeed it was certain that he would do everything possible to thwart his son's plan . . . and what was Ákos to do? Either to withdraw his promise or merely to delay the fulfilment of it would be dishonourable . . . and Etelka was too good and noble a girl for the thought not to fill her heart with pain that father and son would perhaps, in a few days' time, part after falling out.

There was one memory of that unfortunate day that warmed her heart – the way in which Kálmán had behaved towards Tengelyi. Etelka knew she loved him. They'd been almost brought up together, and had been in each other's company from very early childhood like brother and sister – Kislak was the neighbouring estate, so there was every opportunity – and she couldn't have been indifferent to her brother's friend. If I say nothing about his good looks, which, however much many people may find fault with the statement, do have their effect on the female heart,

Kálmán's character too was such as caught the interest of the ladies. The frankness that his features expressed, his boundless courage and that masculine sense of honour that showed in his every word made him interesting especially to the sort of girl that neither demeaned herself into a puppet nor expected a man to do the same, but looked for manly qualities . . . and she'd told Ákos more than once that she'd never love anyone but Kálmán. But Etelka was one of those ladies whose feelings are profound rather than passionate, who don't allow themselves to be fooled by a tear . . . and as no one recognised her admirer's good qualities better than she, no one saw his faults more clearly either. Kálmán's passionate nature, the weakness with which he was carried away by the impulse of the moment, last but not least his vanity – a fault to which none of us is entirely immune, and yet to which, perhaps for that reason, we all make such a show of severity – had not escaped her, and every time that Ákos spoke in his friend's defence his sister said that she wasn't going to entrust her future to a man who displayed those faults to the degree that Kálmán did until she saw signs of improvement . . . The girl who could realise that she was really loved and remain indifferent doesn't exist. As the god of love shoots his arrows blindfold, it's when passion blinds our eyes and we don't know what we're doing that we have most effect on the hearts of those dear to us. However, the man that wished to conquer Etelka had to win not only her heart but her conviction, and this so far had eluded Kálmán, but the way in which he had behaved towards Tengelyi in the election had raised him much higher in his beloved's estimation. His action had been noble in itself . . . In his situation, aware of the hostility between Tengelyi and the Rétys, he felt that in coming to the notary's defence he had built another wall between himself and Etelka with every word he said; to do such a thing had required true self-denial, real virtue, which in the last analysis is nothing other than the subordination of self-interest to conviction. She was fully aware that he loved her, and anyone that could have looked into her heart would probably have seen that Kálmán had come much closer to his goal rather than, as he thought, been further distanced by his courage . . . At least, as Etelka thought about him she had never counted up his failings less than on that evening.

When Etelka finally went to bed these thoughts denied her sleep for a long time, and scarcely had she dozed off than the sound of carriage wheels woke her again from her dreams, in which there featured a weird mixture of the election, outlaws, her brother's bleeding figure and Kálmán's face. She sat up in bed. Rapid footsteps were heard as someone came up the stairs, went along the corridor, and opened the door of the adjoining room. It was Macskaházy, returning to Tiszarét with the documents after Viola's capture, and – as my readers will know from their recollection of previous parts of this narrative – his room was next to Etelka's, only separated from it by a thin wall; and as the maid had been worried when, after entertaining the notary from St-Vilmos during the recent election conference, she later realised that Macskaházy had been in his room all the time and could have heard every word of their conversation, so now, in the silence of night, Etelka could make out every movement in the adjacent room. "Where's he been so late?" she thought, but she attached no greater importance to it all and was beginning to go back to sleep when what Macskaházy said aroused her attention.

The lawyer had presumably lit a candle in the meantime, and now, judging by the sound, was looking through some documents. "Here they are," said he in an undertone, enunciating each syllable distinctly. "Here are all Tengelyi's letters patent . . . now you've lost your nobility, you arrogant notary!. . . And here are the documents that Her Ladyship has been after all this time: so, into the desk drawer they go, and nobody's going to get me to part with them cheaply." With that Macskaházy closed a drawer, rubbed his hands together and walked up and down the room. Shortly afterwards footsteps were heard once more in the passage. The door of the adjacent room opened and Macskaházy's usual grating voice said "We've got them, Your Ladyship. We've caught Viola, he defended himself desperately, but we set fire to his shack and smoked him out like bees. And all the documents came into my hands."

"Where are they?" said the other voice more quietly; Etelka immediately recognised it as her stepmother's.

"I threw them into the fire as soon as I got hold of them," said Macskaházy. "That way there'll be no more trouble. They were all there together, Tengelyi's documents and Vándory's letters, which Your Ladyship was so anxious to obtain."

"Keep your voice down, for God's sake!" the *alispán's* wife cut him short. "Etelka and her father came home last evening, and if she's awake she'll hear every word." Macskaházy hadn't known that they'd returned, and at that reduced his voice to a whisper so that Etelka didn't hear another thing; once her stepmother had gone she tossed restlessly on her bed until morning, then went quickly to her brother and told him what she had overheard. As soon as Ákos knew what had happened he asked her to write the letter to Kálmán, and old János galloped with it to Kislak.

380

It has seemed necessary to relate all that so that my readers can fully appreciate the anxiety in which Ákos and Etelka sat together in the morning of the next day when János returned from Kislak. Viola had been saved . . . but what was to be done now? From what they knew there could be no doubt but that the theft of Vándory's documents had taken place on the orders of their parents, or at least their stepmother. Could it be – as he had recently heard Kálmán say – that those documents had to do with his father's unfortunate brother, who had left home at an early age, and that Vándory was a party to this family secret? And if that were so, why the secrecy, why had he not spoken previously, why did he not speak now? Could it be supposed that, if this unfortunate member of the family was still alive and the intention was to deprive him of his rights, Vándory would lend a helping hand in such a despicable act? . . But if it was all nothing of the sort, what documents could the pious clergyman have, that their destruction meant so much to their stepmother that she would sink to evildoing on their account? . . It was all a great riddle, uncertainty was equal on all sides: what were they themselves to do?

The documents, including Tengelyi's certificates of nobility, had not been destroyed. Etelka had heard Macskaházy shut them in his drawer . . . and precisely because he had lied to Mrs Réty about burning them there could be no doubt that he meant to retain them and use them for other purposes. How was Ákos to come by those documents, in some of which he had so close an interest? Was he to confront Macskaházy, demand an account? But wouldn't he deny everything? Wouldn't he actually make such an approach the reason for destroying them? How was he to force him to give up his ill-gotten gains without coming into the open, and how would he be able to do that if the evildoer was merely his parents' tool? And again, if he kept silence, wouldn't Macskaházy, with the documents in his possession, perpetrate a hundred crimes, the burden of responsibility for which would in part devolve upon him because he could have stopped him? There are times when we curse our intellect, with which we envisage every danger of our situation, and look with envy at animals, which follow their instincts and follow the path laid before them by nature; times when we feel that our so-called freewill is nothing more than the unhappy privilege, accorded to mankind alone, of having doubts.

"What are we to do?" said Ákos eventually, after listing all the possibilities one by one; he jumped up from his couch with his bandaged hand and paced up and down the room impatiently. "Are we to let Tengelyi be deprived of his rights by a villain in front of our eyes, while

381

we fold our hands and remain silent witnesses of this wickedness, which we might be able to prevent? Or are we to speak out, we, the Rétys' children, against our parents?... A dreadful situation!

"Let's do nothing until we're quite clear about what must be done, that's always the wisest thing," said Etelka. "Macskaházy isn't going to destroy the documents for a day or two, nor will he use them for any underhand acts without our noticing. Until then, let's keep our eyes open and watch what's happening around us. It's not my habit, in fact it's against my principles, but as I'm a woman I won't suppress my curiosity so much as not to put an ear to my neighbour's wall. If we notice anything, or if we have a good idea, we can take a decision later."

"The direct way is best," said her brother, shaking his head. "Eavesdropping, spying, isn't for us. These people will fool us ten times over, and you can be sure that if you stand by Macskaházy's wall for years you won't hear another word. The most natural thing is for me to speak to father."

"If you want the documents to be destroyed this very day," said Etelka, "that's all you need do. Either, God forbid, he's aware of what our stepmother and Macskaházy are doing, or he isn't: all that's certain is that as soon as anybody suspects that we know part of the secret the documents will vanish immediately and for ever."

"You're right," said her brother, dropping onto a chair. "We must be patient, keep our eyes open, as much as we can at least."

"Be careful what you do," said Etelka, as she stood up from the sofa about to leave the room. "I can hear father coming down the corridor ... I expect he'll talk to you about Vilma ... Control yourself and stay calm."

And with that she held out a hand to her father as she met him in the doorway, kissed his hand and left.

The relationship between father and son had never had the warmth, the full, boundless confidence by which family life is made blissful. However close we may be to one another, if our hearts have no desires in common we're never going to become inseparable; blood-relationship can't take the place of those bonds through which shared convictions unite the whole being of two persons. Let no one think, however, that perpetual disagreement and ill feeling existed between the *alispán* and his son – alas! a frequent occurrence between father and son in our noble houses – indeed, Réty *père* behaved towards his son with obvious affection, and the respect that the latter owed his father was never forgotten, and perhaps neither suspected that the peace in which they lived wasn't agreement but only the result of agreement: since there was no subject on which they agreed it was possible that they might clash. Distance, intellectual and material alike, is a concept that we can approach only through experience, and as a child thinks that everything is equally close until he has learnt to measure the space that separates him from individual objects: so father and son presumably had not yet suspected the distance that stood between them as the former pursued his plans for advancement and the latter the promptings of his youthful spirit, although from the embarrassment with which the *alispán* shook Ákos's hand, as he had now come to speak to him about Vilma, it could be seen that he at least at that moment perhaps had an inkling of the relationship in which he and his son stood.

After the customary enquiries about health, which Ákos's appearance rendered unnecessary, the two of them sat in silence for a while, until at length the *alispán* pulled himself together and began the conversation.

"My boy," said he, forcing his lips into a smile, as he usually did when he couldn't be quite certain of the most appropriate turn of phrase for the occasion, "I really should be ticking you off for your latest escapade. Just think how a father feels at such a time."

"Dear father," said Ákos, and from the tremor in his voice the depth of his emotion could be sensed, "I'm glad we're talking about this, the matter has to be clarified and as soon as possible, better now than in an hour's time."

"Let's not do anything rash," interrupted the *alispán*, not liking the way in which his son took the initiative. "You're excited, let's talk about something else, perhaps you still don't feel very well."

"No, father!" replied Ákos briskly. "Your son's good name is at stake, there can be no question of doing anything rash. You know that I love Vilma" – the *alispán*'s lips shaped a smile, which Ákos noticed and blushed – "but don't worry, I'm not going to describe how I feel, I don't think I'd be able to make you understand. But you'll recognise the indiscretion to which Tengelyi's obstinacy drove me – he didn't want me to go to his house."

"In certain regards, Tengelyi always was a rational man," interposed Réty.

"Quite! I won't dispute how rational it is or not," Ákos went on, more warmly, "to want something of a person which can't be done, what point there is in struggling against feelings which we can only conceal, not suppress. That's all irrelevant. You know what happened, you know that although Vilma's done nothing wrong her good name has suffered, that I shall keep my word, and . . ."

"My dear boy," the *alispán* butted in, shaking his head, "don't let yourself be carried away! Vilma's good name – I don't know how that could have been affected? The whole business, it must be said, does Tengelyi's house no credit, least of all Vilma's mother; but as for the girl, goodness, she *is* seventeen!"

Those words, and especially the way in which they were uttered, hurt Ákos very deeply, and the change in his voice when he spoke alerted his father at once to the mistake that he'd made. "Let's leave out the irony, father," said he gravely, "and speak about the subject calmly. As a result of what has happened, Vilma's good name has been made to suffer. If I'd had a moment's doubt, the way in which mother spoke of her in this room would have been enough to enlighten me. The way things stand, there's only one way for me to make good my error, and as I had long ago been clear in my mind that I would choose Vilma to be my wife, I'm now determined to delay no longer, and I therefore request your consent."

Réty had a peculiar dislike of questions being put in such a way as to be answerable only with either a simple yes or no, and especially with regard to the importance of the subject the perplexity into which Ákos's words plunged the worthy man can scarcely be imagined. He merely mumbled something about acting in excessive haste, and that the matter was too important to be decided in such short order.

"As far as I'm concerned," said Ákos, "and this matter is of the greatest importance from my point of view, I can assure you, father, that it's been more than a year since I made up my mind; furthermore, please consider that after what's happened Vilma can only appear in public without embarrassment as my fiancée, and I don't want to prolong the painful situation into which I've brought the family by a single day."

"My dear boy," said Réty, his emotion betrayed by his change of tone, "I fully appreciate your weakness, and you may rest assured that you can count on my assistance in everything that we can see as expedient for remedying your youthful lack of caution . . ."

"So I have your approval?" Ákos interrupted, passionately seizing his father's hand.

". . . and for everything," continued the *alispán*, "that is necessary to prevent the Tengelyis suffering harm through your frivolity. God has blessed us/you with property, and if you regard it as necessary we'll give them an *inscriptio*, we'll arrange a brilliant marriage for Vilma, and . . ."

Ákos released his father's hand and sprang up from the sofa. "Father!" he said, and his face blazed. "Are you forgetting that I love Vilma more than anyone in the world, that she returns my love, and that I'd rather forgo everything than see her in another man's arms?!" The *alispán* ran a hand over his hair in perplexity. "Yes," Ákos continued, "don't think that I'm asking for help in maintaining a house. My mother's estate, which is already in my possession, is sufficient to provide for my wife and myself. Do as you please with your estate, father, I ask for nothing but your consent . . . Don't deny your son that!"

The *alispán* wasn't an unfeeling man, and those words of his son's touched him deeply; but he'd reached that time of life when our principles, which we generally choose to match our interests, become as strong as they are weak in youth; and the influence that Mrs Réty exercised over her husband was greater than he would have acknowledged; and everything that Ákos could extract from his father by way of an answer was merely couched in those stereotyped terms with which those who have never been able to understand deep feelings customarily argue against their passions, and which generally either consist of the denial of feeling or a hundred variations on the ancient theme that the heart of man is fickle, and in time recovers from all its wounds, which is as true of the heart as of other illnesses, only in this case too the cure is often brought about by death, and in fact there is nothing about which to be pleased if, together with its wound, the heart also loses its sensitivity.

Ákos was unshakeable, and he was also reluctant even to hear any suggestion of delay; however, at length his father solemnly stated that if he went travelling now and his intention hadn't changed in a year's time he wouldn't oppose the marriage.

"But I beg you, my boy," said the *alispán* eventually, as he paced the room in the greatest consternation, "think carefully what you're doing; think that you're sacrificing your whole future to your passions. Nobody knows better than you yourself how much I love you; you haven't heard a word from me of resistance to your wishes. Your political ideas are contrary to those that I hold – but never mind! I respect your convictions and I trust that time will set you, like others, on the right way; it's the warmest desire of my heart to see you with the right woman . . . and although I believe that I know several that answer all that I wish . . . Have I not entrusted the decision on your future entirely to yourself? Have you not enjoyed such freedom as perhaps no son ever has, whose parents are alive? . . . Only now yield to my request! Consider the step that you mean to take as one from which there is no way back."

"I've considered everything, and I'm made up my mind," replied Ákos calmly. "There's nothing in the world that could satisfy me other than having Vilma."

"And do you know the world?... And have you any idea what heart-felt needs will arise once your present youth is past?" continued the *al-ispán* sharply. "At your age we're modest in our desires, a thatched roof and the love of our beloved is all that we demand; whatever is missing our youthful imagination will supply... and if, as they say about savages, who give up their gold in exchange for little mirrors or glass beads, we throw away our entire wealth in our youth for a few transitory pleasures, the only reason is that we see inexhaustible treasures in those passing delights. But believe me, my boy, the heart has requirements that we can't know about at the age of twenty-one, which only arise later, but the satisfaction of which is just as necessary. A man yearns for distinctions as youth craves love; after putting all our happiness in the love of a single heart, we don't find ourselves satisfied and look for a substitute in the respect or at least the worship of many."

Ákos smiled and shook his head.

"Don't shake your head," Réty went on. "The time will come to you as it does to us all. You're a young man of noble character, far from any selfishness or self-interest, as I'm well aware; but when all's said and done you're a man, and no one can deny the nature that we share. There are countless differences with regard to physical and spiritual properties which we detect in people, and because a liking for one seems good while we turn from another in distaste, and there are certain essential points to be found in all, though in differing forms, as the loveliest and the ugliest faces alike have mouths, noses and ears: so we find every-where those principal features which depict by their various combinations the nature of our souls. Believe me, my boy, the time will come when the desire for distinctions will arise in you too; days when the thought of how your great talents lie fallow will embitter your soul, days when you see that your contemporaries, in all respects your inferiors, have risen so far above you – and you'll curse your foolishness in ex-cluding yourself from the competition."

"But even if so," said Ákos; he wasn't convinced by his father's words, but they touched him deeply because he could sense the feeling with which they were spoken, "even if the demon of ambition were to arise in me one day, who can guarantee that I should be able to satisfy it even if I followed your advice to the letter? And whose thirst is quenched by the apples of Tantalus,[172] for which so many reach out? Who has

---

172 For attempting to serve his own son at a feast with the gods, Tantalus, wicked king of Sipylus, was punished by Zeus to forever go thirsty and hungry in Hades, despite

ever yearned for distinctions without, at the end of their life, feeling that what they've achieved was useless, and gone dissatisfied into the grave?"

"That may be true of people who set themselves unattainable goals," replied the *alispán*.

"But if I'm not one such?" Ákos interposed. "Until now ambition hasn't troubled me; but I feel that if ever that passion arises the goal that I'll set myself will be such that its achievement will be granted only to one out of millions. Becoming the great man of a county, being addressed as Your Worship and Your Lordship by the couple of thousand who know me, holding my head high like a reed rising out of a swamp, surrounded by the rotting element to which I owe my growth, bending and swaying so as not to betray my weakness as I resist the wind . . . that isn't the goal to which I could ever aspire . . . and what else could I set myself?"

"Why not?" answered the *alispán* briskly; although he sensed that his son was aiming his bitter words at his own situation he was glad of the turn that the conversation was taking. "A young man like you could become simply anything. I agree, the way by which one tries to reach the upper échelons in Hungary is not a pleasant one. In your position you can't avoid serving in the county; but you're young, aren't you? Isn't the way open to you to begin where others finish? In three years' time I'll be resigning and handing over to you. You know my situation, and you know that I'm promising what I can deliver. There's no need for you to abandon your principles, and in fact the more you oppose me the more certain are you to be elected, and once you're *alispán*, the world's your oyster, you could become *országbíró*[173] if you try."

"But my dear father," said Ákos, not entirely able to suppress the smile that came to his lips on hearing these brilliant prospects, "if the career that you see for me were such as I wish to follow, if in fact I feel any desire for it, after following a certain course for a few years, as soon as I saw that I could make no further progress, that is, gain no further promotion, but on the contrary, if I too wanted to be one of those who, like Mahomet, command the mountain to come to them for a while, and then, when it doesn't move, themselves get up and go to the mountain: how could Vilma actually prevent my attaining my goal?"

---

being placed in a pool of water and almost within reach of a fruit tree. His terrible punishment was set as a warning for humanity not to cross the line between mortals and gods.

173 At the time, the third-ranking official in Hungary, subordinate only to the king and the *nádor*.

"My boy," said the *alispán*, looking at Ákos in surprise, "are you forgetting where you live? Don't you know that in this county you can't get anywhere without family influence? Personal merit . . . is a cipher; it enhances your worth if you can show social standing, but without that it's nothing. Do you suppose that I'd ever have become *alispán* if your late mother or your stepmother had not been noble?"

"Why need my wife be noble if I am myself?"

"Not at all," replied Réty, in the heat of debate exposing his fundamental thinking, "if she that you had chosen weren't Vilma, not the daughter of a village notary. Take to wife, say, an ignoble girl, the daughter of a rich tradesman, a stockbroker, a converted Jew, as you please, I shan't object, shan't cling to any family prejudices, and I'm well aware that we're not of aristocratic descent; but choose a rich girl, and your social standing would not be harmed but improved. Family trees are only respected these days insofar as they can be of use as evidence of claims of inheritance, and the peasant ennobled two generations back looks down scornfully on the nobleman with a century-old pedigree when the latter goes on foot beside the former's gleaming carriage; if you mean to rise in the world, my boy, you need wealth. My estates, much though I would give to be able to change the fact, will go to both sides of the family. If your wife brings nothing to your house, you'll only have half of what I possess, and . . ."

"Dear father," Ákos interrupted him, "let's not go on with the conversation, it can only be unpleasant for both of us and it won't change my intentions. My mind is made up. If it were only a question of my feelings I might feel able to sacrifice my entire happiness so as not to cause you pain; but now my honour and Vilma's future will be in question, so I can't alter my decision. Please don't make me do the most important thing in my life against your will by denying your consent."

"Just consider, my boy," said Réty in a pleading tone, "how much trouble your grandfather and I have gone to, to raise our family to this level; do you mean to sacrifice the efforts of half a century to your passion at a stroke? Consider your poor father's domestic peace, which you'll shatter permanently because my wife and Vilma will never ever be friends, and your mother will leave my house sooner than consent to this unfortunate marriage. Think of your sister, whose entire future you'll also ruin, because who'd want to marry into the family of a village notary?" And the worthy *alispán* would probably have adduced several more points, if at that moment the door hadn't opened and Her Ladyship entered the room, and the whole conversation took a different turn.

388

No doubt Réty's detailed arguments were just as little able to convince his son as the latter would have been able to explain to his father how, in a state of complete sobriety, one could value the daughter of a poor village notary more highly than the office of *alispán* in Taksony County; but Ákos loved his father and the tone in which he spoke was too warm for his admonitions to leave his heart entirely untouched. When his stepmother came into the room and, as usual, took upon herself the role of speaker, Ákos's blood boiled at the imperious tone and in his every word there was nothing to be perceived but the contempt that he felt for that woman, especially since he had regarded her as the accomplice of evildoers.

"Have you spoken to Ákos, then?" said she curtly, addressing her husband. "What has he to say?"

"I have," said Réty in embarrassment, "and Ákos says that . . . at this moment in time . . . that . . ."

"That he won't give up Vilma," interposed Ákos calmly, "neither at this moment in time, nor ever."

"We'll see about that," said Mrs Réty, favouring the speaker with a baleful stare. "If the young gentleman thinks that we're ever going to consent to this marriage . . ."

"As far as Your Ladyship's concerned," said Ákos, in a tone from which both could sense his depth of feeling, "we've never counted on your consent; furthermore . . ."

"Your father won't consent either," she interrupted testily. "Your father never said anything else, I'd bet on that."

"Your Ladyship is right," Ákos went on in growing irritation, "but I've always enjoyed my father's love, and I don't think it's impossible that he'll change his mind."

"Your father won't change his mind," said Mrs Réty more heatedly still, "will you, husband?" And when the *alispán* nodded a couple of times, "Never! Never! will either he or I will give our consent to this madness."

"In that case," replied Ákos, looking at her with icy contempt, "without my father's consent, I shall do what I feel obliged to do as an honourable man and leave the house which, it seems, others have so completely occupied so that no place remains for me."

"And where will the young gentleman go?" said his stepmother scornfully, "if we are no longer to have the pleasure of his company? Perhaps he'll withdraw to his girl's place?" And she forced a laugh.

389

"That won't be necessary," replied he; in his fury a deathly pallor came over his face and he was scarcely able to choke back the feelings that filled his breast. "The property left me by my mother is sufficient for me to live decently. If she were alive I wouldn't be forced to leave my father's house in this fashion."

"You scoundrel! You ungrateful boy! You viper in the bosom!" shrieked Mrs Réty, no longer restraining herself. "I was born the daughter of Baron Andorházy, I wasn't forced to marry a useless common nobleman; it was no kindness to me, I did your family an honour. Don't count on your mother's property, you wicked boy! You aren't twenty-one and your father won't give you anything."

"Be so good as to remember," replied Ákos calmly, "that in two months' time I shall be."

"And I say no! No, a hundred times no! This marriage shall not take place!" shrieked the *alispán*'s wife, beside herself with rage. "I won't stand for this disgrace being inflicted on us. If there's nothing else for it, your father will disinherit you, he'll curse you, you wicked boy. I won't stand for the name that I bear being besmirched."

Ákos's face blazed and tried to speak, but his fury stifled his voice.

"I won't stand for the daughter of a nondescript, penniless, ignoble village notary being my daughter-in-law, whom I despise."

"Your Ladyship!" shouted Ákos.

"Yes, a loose woman, she's been your bit of skirt before you get married!"

At these last words, which the *alispán*'s wife spoke with the greatest malice, Ákos's temper knew no more bounds . . . half out of his mind he rushed at his stepmother, and his father was barely able to hold back his raised fist. "How dare you say such a thing, you swine!" he shouted, "you're in with villains, a thief, who's going to bring shame on this house, and if I chose to speak you'd find yourself in the county jail!"

Anyone seeing the *alispán*'s wife at that moment would have pitied her, as she blanched, trembled, and fixed her eyes on the ground; and I don't know what the *alispán* would have done – he knew nothing of what had happened, and saw in his son's behaviour the most appalling ingratitude that ever son showed to father – when at that very moment in walked Vándory and put an end to the painful scene.

When the clergyman came in Mrs Réty took her husband by the hand and left the room with him. Ákos, weakened by his illness, threw himself onto his sofa and burst into tears.

Not a quarter of an hour had passed, during which he told Vándory briefly what had happened, when a footman brought Ákos a letter from his father informing him that he was to leave his house as soon as his health permitted, and although the elderly cleric promised to smooth it all out Ákos was unwilling to remain there an hour longer. He quickly took leave of Etelka, who had hurried to her brother on hearing what had happened . . . and within the hour had left with Vándory for his house.

XXVI

We have a lot to say about the wounds that love inflicts on our breasts: but isn't it unjust that, as we complain, we don't remember its healing power? that we forget how the feeling that can be the source of so much pain at the same time hardens our hearts to withstand the blows of the world, and when the latter floods us with new pains, previously unknown, it defends us from those which otherwise would try our patience . . . No one experienced the healing power of love more than Ákos – exiled from his father's house, deprived of his brilliant prospects, which we can resign only with regret . . . and yet because of his love he felt that he was the happiest of men.

As soon as he had escorted his guest to his house Vándory went to call on Tengelyi. The notary had only returned home late the previous evening; he had been to see a friend who lived some distance away, to inform him of his situation and ask advice, and was on the point of leaving for Kislak to speak to Viola when the news of his escape reached him. My readers must imagine the distress with which he saw himself deprived of the hope of hearing something about his documents, especially when what he heard had happened at Kislak further confirmed his suspicions about the Rétys. Vándory's gentle words of reassurance, however, did much to calm him, and the outcome of a conversation lasting almost half an hour – during which the clergyman also told his friend that Ákos had been banned from his paternal home – was that Tengelyi promised that for his own part he would raise no further objections to his daughter's choice. At that Vándory, eyes gleaming, embraced his friend, hurried to Ákos and brought him back with him.

To what extent his friend's sermon influenced the notary's change of mind, or whether it was the conviction that, after what had happened, he would only be able to ensure Vilma's future if she became Ákos's wife, or whether, in the end, it had been Vilma herself, whose every look was an irresistible plea to her father . . . I shan't decide; suffice it that when Ákos came to the house with Vándory the notary shook him warmly by the hand . . . and when Ákos, adducing in his defence only his boundless love, asked forgiveness for the past event, he granted that request much more quickly than could have been hoped for in view of his customary severity.

"So," said he, returning to his room after taking Ákos to his daughter (I'll leave to my fair lady readers the description of the emotions with which she received him: either they've been through them in the course of their lives or one day they surely will), "so," said he, "what are we to do? They love one another, and it appears that fate itself wished it to be so."

"I've said all along," replied Vándory with a smile, "only you wouldn't believe me . . . those two are made for each other."

"Let's hope you're right! I used to think differently," said Tengelyi gravely. "When we give up freedom, we must at least have equality in exchange if we're to feel happy . . . and love is easily exhausted if it has constantly to rise or descend towards the object that it used to surround. I wanted a different husband for my daughter, one like her in outward situation too, one in whose arms she would never think how painful it is to accept a great deal even from those dear to us, if we can't return it with similar gifts; but fate has willed otherwise . . . and as it has frustrated my wishes, so I hope in the future it will give the lie to my reasoning. Ákos is an honourable man, who will perhaps be able to take the side of my poor and now ignoble son . . . Vilma's good name can only be restored if she becomes Réty's wife . . . and one can imagine what steps the *alispán's* wife will take to defame her . . . it would be unthinkable to obstruct this marriage any longer, however much it goes against my principles."

"Forgive me, my friend," said Vándory, shaking his head, "but your principles are erroneous. To esteem someone on account of their wealth is foolishness; but is it any less of an error to do someone an injustice merely because of their wealth?"

"No doubt," replied Tengelyi, "but will the oak that you've planted in the confines of a greenhouse raise its crown as much as the one that puts forth its branches in the middle of the forest? . . And isn't the fruit tree barren that you plant in permanent shade, where the warm touch of the sun can't permeate its trunk?. . . And isn't it the same with people? Doesn't the germ that is planted in them by nature either grow or wither away depending on the situation into which they're born? . . Believe me, my friend, I speak from experience. If in judging a man's worth we subtract his financial value from his personal qualities, we're less often deceived than if we add them together. However, there are exceptions, and I hope that Ákos is one of them." The cheerful expression on his face showed that he was not only saying that but believed it, as he had seen his daughter, with Ákos at her side, as she basked in all the delights of requited love.

The affair which shortly before had thrown the notary's peaceful house into disorder now imbued its occupants with every pleasure . . . and Erzsébet, realising from her husband's warm handshake that her wrongdoing had been forgiven, looked with tears in her eyes now at the happy pair, now at her husband – that he was satisfied meant more to her than all the treasure on earth.

All the greater is the agitation that we find in the Tiszarét mansion.

Immediately after the scene which we witnessed the *alispán* was admitted by his wife into the secret of what had happened until then and heard from Macskaházy about the argument that had taken place in the court; he paced up and down in his room, deep in thought. Meanwhile Mrs Réty abandoned herself to a bitter mood on the cushions in her boudoir. "So this is what I've done it all for, this is why I've risked my peace of mind, my good name, my whole being, for this ingrate to treat me so in my own home?" said she to herself. "Why did I bother, why did I let myself get into the hands of this unscrupulous Macskaházy, whom I loathe? Wasn't it so as to increase the esteem of the family for him, to obtain a valuable property for him, the worthless wretch, to open a bigger prospect before him?. . . And now look!. . ." She wept in rage. "Oh, how unlucky I am! What has my life been but a long struggle in which I've always sacrificed my feelings for goals I couldn't reach. I was in love, but the man I loved was poor, and I thought that my heart desired more than the calm good fortune that I might have found in the arms of my beloved, and I went to the altar with Réty, because it seemed that through his estate and wealth I could raise him to a position in which I'd be comfortable . . . and here I am, wife of His Worship the *alispán* and that's all I'll ever be. My husband hasn't got the spirit for me to expect anything better. I gave up my fanciful dreams and began to base my plans on something else. Perhaps Réty's children could rise to the place that their father was too feeble to occupy? What were they to do with me? They weren't of my blood, not my children; but after all, their name was the one that I bore . . . and however much they loathed their stepmother, I too would share the status that they attained. As they rose in the world, so would I. My life took a new direction. All my endeavours were directed to that . . . and now everything's being ruined, all my plans, the years of calculation, everything! And just because Ákos Réty's in love . . . the world's his oyster, and he throws it all away for a notary's daughter . . . And I can't even take revenge on him!" Again and again she thought over her situation, trying to find a way of obstructing Ákos in his intentions – to no purpose! A sense of helplessness depressed her as did the certainty that the hated notary was going to triumph over her.

She was sitting on her sofa, sunk in these painful thoughts, when the door opened and in came Macskaházy. She turned towards him and enquired about her husband.

"The *alispán*'s very upset," said the lawyer, sinking comfortably onto the sofa beside her, at which liberty Mrs Réty was not a little startled, as at other times Macskaházy had only taken a seat in the presence of Her Ladyship after numerous invitations and at a respectful distance. "You can't imagine, Madam, how worried the good man is; he's even taken me to task. And no wonder, it's a capital offence . . . and in his situation, of course . . ."

Evening was now drawing on and twilight was spreading in the room; but there was something in Macskaházy's voice and manner which caught Mrs Réty's attention. "You're in a strange mood today," she interrupted him, "a strangely good humour, and I see no reason for it."

"It seems to me, dear lady," said Macskaházy brightly, "that when one's been trying for a long time and can see oneself at one's goal, one has every right to be in a good humour."

"Yes, but have we reached our goal?" replied the *alispán*'s wife with a sigh. "Viola's at liberty again and we'll be under much suspicion."

"That's ridiculous!" said Macskaházy, in a better humour still. "What harm can Viola's being at liberty do us? Hasn't he been sentenced to death? Aren't you aware that if he turned up today to lay a charge against us, tomorrow he'd be hanged? And do you think, Madam, that an outlaw is going to appear before the court just in order to say things about Her Worship Mrs Réty and my humble self that no one's going to believe? Our being under suspicion is a bad dream and it's not worth tormenting ourselves with it; the more serious the accusation that Viola makes, the less he'll be believed."

"Oh, if you'd heard Ákos today you wouldn't talk like that!" replied the *alispán*'s wife. "He must have reliable information."

"Piffle!" said Macskaházy, "piffle, I say . . . Ákos have reliable information? Where from, pray? No doubt he's heard what happened in court, and was speaking in anger, just as Your Worship might call some old woman a witch if she crossed you, without for a moment thinking that she went up Gellért Hill on a broomstick to join the coven. Good news is like capital, anyone that gets some lives on the interest afterwards, indeed, with a little ingenuity he'll get three times as much credit as it was worth in the first place just because everyone thinks that he's rich."

"You really are in a good humour today, you're seeing everything through rose-tinted spectacles," said she, amazed at the lawyer's frivolity; at other times he tended to overstate problems.

"And why not?" said Macskaházy, in his best, most confident tone, "when one's devoted all one's life to the service of a family, and exposed oneself to such danger as I've done recently, and the moment for a reward finally arrives. He'd be a miserable character that wasn't pleased."

"I don't understand you," said Mrs Réty, fixing her gaze on him.

"Of course you do, dear Madam!" replied the lawyer, in a gentle, flirtatious tone, grasping the *alispán's* wife by the hand, "how can you joke like that with your poor servant! Haven't I been promised an *inscriptio* for my faithful service, if I could lay my hands on Vándory's documents? . . . We spoke about it a few days before the last election conference was held. Surely Your Worship remembers; we were in the park . . ."

"I know, I know," Mrs Réty interrupted.

"And then," he went on, "what did Your Honour say? . . My dear Macskaházy, the day those documents come into your hands we'll go together to the Chapter . . . Oh, Your Honour, I remember it all clearly, those words, by which you bound me to you in eternal gratitude, are written in letters of gold in my breast, and . . ."

"Why are you bringing up that promise?" she interrupted him. "Perhaps you doubt my word?"

"God forbid!" said Macskaházy, taking her hand again. "Quite the contrary; I'm perfectly certain that you mean to keep it . . . I just came to ask, in what form are we to draw up the deed of *inscriptio*? You will realise, Madam, that it will be necessary to refer in the certificate to my merits, and modesty . . ."

". . . doesn't permit the merits on which you've obtained the *inscriptio* to be listed." And Mrs Réty laughed bitterly. "Never fear, I'll see to it, and the required certificate will be in your hands; but it's not so urgent, I hope, that it has to be done today or tomorrow?"

"Who can say!" replied the lawyer with a sigh. "Man is mortal, and . . ."

"I hope I don't look as if I'm dying," said she, beginning to lose patience with Macskaházy's unseemly importuning.

"Heaven forfend," said the lawyer, sighing again, "that such a blow should strike its most faithful servant!. . . But after all, who is certain of the morrow? And how should I risk my all, I that have acquired nothing for myself in Your Honour's house other than this promised favour?"

The *alispán*'s wife choked back the temper that was rising in her at Macskaházy's impudence, and pointed out to him with the greatest possible composure to what great suspicion it would give rise if the *inscriptio*, which could not be kept secret, were issued at this moment. "Let's wait a little longer," she added as graciously as could be, "only a little longer, until the present fuss has died down . . . and I promise once more, on my word of honour, that you can count on your reward."

"I ask you," said Macskaházy, kissing her hand in delight, "is there a woman in all Hungary like my Mrs, so thoughtful, so clever, so subtle?! . . . There aren't many lawyers who conduct their affairs with such forethought. You're right, Your Honour, at this moment an *inscriptio* might involve us in the greatest trouble . . . and I myself have actually come here to point this out to Your Honour and make another suggestion through which your noble heart can reward my services almost as generously, and everything remain secret. It's all quite simple," said he, after a brief pause. "Your Honour will give me five notes of hand, each for only ten thousand *pengős*, duly endorsed by His Worship, and naturally, so as to cause Your Honour the least inconvenience, so dated that I can only encash them one at a time at six-monthly intervals, and then . . ."

"You can't be serious!" said the *alispán*'s wife, looking at him in astonishment. "Fifty thousand *pengős*!"

"Never have I spoken more seriously," replied Macskaházy softly. "I'm sure that you'll appreciate that . . ."

"But that's three times as much as the promised *inscriptio*'s worth!" Mrs Réty interrupted, jumping up from the sofa in indignation.

"Approximately, if we take the land at current value," he replied after a brief consideration, and he too stood up, "that's how it would work out; but as I said, you'll appreciate that obtaining the documents involved much more trouble than we could have anticipated; all the dangers I've exposed myself to . . . and the extent to which my good name too has been compromised by Viola's statement. In addition, I've had to pay the Jew a lot; who's to say how much his silence is going to cost me even after that, and that's just as much in Your Honour's interests too, because he's very well aware, I believe, of how one thing's linked to another . . . therefore it's only right that . . ."

"And do you think that I'm going to comply with your impudent wish?" said Mrs Réty, absolutely furious, "and that we're so foolish, my husband and I, as to burden our estate with debt?"

"I'm quite sure," replied Macskaházy calmly, "that if Your Honour weighs up the circumstances with your usual wisdom and takes into account my desserts, your innate magnanimity will . . ."

"Never! Never!" she cut him sort. "Don't count on it. Really, Macskaházy! Now we're getting to know each other, now I see the enthusiasm with which you have at heart only the good of my family!"

"I believe that there's no need for us to get to know each other any differently," said Macskaházy in his usual harsh voice, "and it's only to be regretted if Your Honour damages her precious health by losing her temper, whereas I know in advance that, as I've said, when you've considered all the circumstances you'll gladly accept my proposal."

"Your proposal?! It's downright impudence!" shrieked Mrs Réty angrily. "I'd like to see anyone make me . . . Doesn't it depend purely on my generosity whether I even fulfil my promise? Where are your witnesses, where's the magistrate that would hold me to it? Everything's down to my free will, my generosity, especially as you haven't actually fulfilled the condition on which I promised the *inscriptio*, and I've not so much as set eyes on the documents which you undertook to put in my hands, and even now they must still be in the possession of Vándory or someone, while you have the unspeakable nerve to try to get money out of me and you've lied about burning them."

"If that's all that worries you, Your Honour," said the lawyer in a scornful tone, "and I think that that's quite natural . . . it seems that each of us will do well to obtain as much assurance as possible; I'll dispel that anxiety, as the documents are in my hands and you may examine them in my presence at any time."

The *alispán*'s wife stood there in front of Macskaházy rigid, as if lightning has struck just in front of her, and in her alarm said, her voice unsteady: "Don't you remember saying that you'd thrown the documents into the fire?"

"Yes," said the lawyer, scornfully once more, "what's more, I didn't only say that I'd burned the documents, but the moment that they came into my hands, and that was what I wanted to do. Praise be, I didn't! At least I can convince Your Honour that I'm as good as my word."

"But why haven't you given them to me, then?" said she, her voice trembling; it was obvious that she was beginning to guess Macskaházy's reasons.

"Why not?" said he with a laugh. "Do you need to ask? Simply because I didn't want to, since I've dedicated my whole life to the service of this family, being ordered about like a common servant; because I didn't

398

think it advisable to trust the reward that my work has deserved to your innate magnanimity; and because in any case it makes better sense if I don't allow anyone to think that I'm a fool."

"Let's speak to one another calmly," said the *alispán*'s wife, forcing herself to smile, "old friends like us ought to be more tolerant, even if I did let my annoyance get the better of me. The documents are in your possession, and everyone sets the price on their own property. But you can't really expect fifty thousand."

"I won't accept one *garas* less!" replied Macskaházy calmly. "Documents such that a woman of Your Honour's character is prepared to sink to the sort of crimes that we've committed in order to obtain them are beyond price, no doubt about it."

"You torturer!" growled Mrs Réty between her teeth, as she paced the room in anxiety. "My friend," said she at length, as she choked back her anger and stopped in front of Macskaházy, "consider my situation, I personally can't dispose of such funds. For the notes of hand to be valid they'd have to be endorsed by my husband; how can you expect me to be able to prevail on him for an amount like that?"

"I know the power that Your Honour exercises over all the family in this house," replied Macskaházy, once again scornfully, "and it's just up to you to persuade him to endorse the notes in your usual charming way. Everyone knows that Your Honour is irresistible."

She made no reply to those scornful words, and the room was too dark for Macskaházy to see the tears which fury forced from her eyes; but any that heard the swift steps with which she paced up and down could imagine her feelings. The lawyer looked out of the window and quietly drummed his fingers to the rhythm of a tune. A lengthy interval elapsed, and she stopped suddenly in front of him and asked in a firm, determined voice: "Is what you've said your last word?"

"It is," he replied, likewise decisively.

"You won't hand over the documents for less than fifty thousand?"

"Certainly not," he replied, startled at the tone in which the questions were addressed.

"Keep them, then," Mrs Réty laughed aloud, "and do what you like with them; what do I care? Ákos will have more or less estate after treating me like that and marrying the Tengelyi girl; that's very little to do with me, and the documents will be of no further use."

"I'm to do what I like with the documents?" said Macskaházy, surprised at the turn that events had taken. "Anything at all?"

"Yes," continued Mrs Réty, laughing again. "I can hardly see how I failed to realise straight away that as soon as I knew Ákos's decision these documents were of no interest to me, and after your behaviour today you can just whistle for that *inscriptio* – I withdraw my promise."

"We shall see!" said Macskaházy quite sharply. "Since Your Honour knows Ákos's decision the documents have lost all their value in your view, but perhaps – a woman's heart is fickle – to me sheets of paper that are regarded as trivial retain their worth. The way in which we acquired them, Madam," he added, seizing her hand, "sets the price of the documents."

"What do you mean by that?" asked Mrs Réty in alarm.

"It's very simple, Madam," he replied, in his former scornful tone. "At the recent court session Viola accused Her Honour the wife of the *al-ispán* of incitement to commit theft. One witness, and an outlaw at that, accuses a person of lofty character, speaks disgraceful slander which no one believes. But if after that one witness another were to come forward, myself, for example, to confirm the outlaw's every word with a sound account of circumstances, and as evidence of what I said display the documents which we had stolen jointly and from the content of which everyone could see that their theft benefited no one outside your family, wouldn't there be quite a scandal in the oucnty?"

"Frighten someone else with that," said the *alispán*'s wife crossly, "while I know that you can't harm me without harming yourself too, I'm not worried."

"Don't be too sure," said Macskaházy sourly. "Perhaps just this once your calculation might be wrong. We aren't quite equal in the affair. To me, the stolen documents are completely without value. It was very much in Your Honour's interests to obtain them. If I now go before the court as a poor lawyer[174] and testify that having spent all my life in this house I allowed myself out of gratitude to be pressed beyond the call of duty and offered a helping hand to Your Honour in the obtaining of these documents; but that having at length seen the unfortunate result of my action I am unable to resist the twinges of my conscience and prefer to surrender myself and place the documents in the court's hands

---

174 Two Hungarian words for 'lawyer' are used in this paragraph. The first is *prókátor* (from the Latin *procurator*), a general term which (as here) can have a pejorative sense. At the end of the paragraph we find *ügyvéd* 'affair-defender', a recognised branch of the Hungarian legal profession. The *ügyvéd* promotes (under the law) the assertion of his client's rights and the fulfilment of his obligations, and assists in the settlement of legal disputes with similarly interested parties.

– won't the whole scene be interesting and touching? May I not reckon on a gracious judgement from the judges, each of whom would like to have a lawyer like me?"

"You devil!" exclaimed Mrs Réty and threw herself onto the sofa, her face blazing.

"Indeed, the whole affair, if not exactly to my credit, doesn't seem as bad for me from the material point of view as it appears at first," continued Macskaházy, as if thinking aloud. "There's nothing that Ákos wouldn't give me if I could recover Tengelyi's papers. If I first made certain conditions I might be able to turn a nice profit. Vándory himself, who delights in nothing more than a repentant sinner, would speak in support of me. On the other hand Your Honour . . ."

"Don't taunt me, you torturer! exclaimed Mrs Réty, wringing her hands convulsively

"An *alispán's* wife in the county jail!" he went on as before. "I grant you, you'd probably only be given three or six months. But jail, all the same! and what's more for theft, committed in partnership with a Jew! And then the cross-examinations, the witness statements . . ."

"Macskaházy!" shrieked Mrs Réty, jumping up from the sofa, "you're not capable of such a thing."

"Capable enough," he returned calmly, "for the whole business to be reported to the court if I don't receive those notes of hand within a week."

Mrs Réty strode up and down the room a couple of times in the greatest agitation. "You shall have them," said she at length in a tremulous voice as she stood facing him.

"Five notes of hand, each for ten thousand, and with the *alispán's* endorsement," he continued.

"I know."

"The expiry of each note . . ."

"I know, I know! Just leave me!" the *alispán's* wife was almost screaming.

"As soon as the notes are in my possession the documents will be handed over," he added, taking his hat. "Your humble servant." And with that Macskaházy left the room. Soon afterwards the footman brought in candles, and couldn't have been more surprised on finding Madam standing by the table, pale and shaking from head to foot.

As Macskaházy's footsteps faded down the corridor the nearest stoke-hole opened and the tousled head of Peti appeared. Suspecting that Tenglyi's documents would still be in Macskaházy's possession the stoker

401

had set himself to eavesdrop on returning to Tiszarét. When, in the evening, he saw the lawyer going to call on the *alispán*'s wife he hurried quietly after him, put his ear to the stove (which was luckily not working) from his usual workplace, and heard the entire conversation.

"Good heavens, Peti," said János as he met him in the corridor, candle in hand, "your face is covered in soot and ashes."

"I'm not surprised," said Peti, wiping it with the sleeve of his shirt, "when I go from one stove to another."

"Keep up the good work," said János, "make it nice and hot here in the house, let 'em get used to Hell. I'm off to join my master, put a few things together, there's nothing more for me to do in the mansion."

"So you're leaving as well?" asked Peti with a sigh.

"I certainly am," replied János. "I'd never have thought that I'd leave this house, where I've been in service all these years, without anybody saying so much as God bless you; but it was the same for my young gentleman too. Good night!"

And with that János put his candle down in the kitchen and set off for Vándory's house, while Peti put on his sheepskin and stole into the garden; there he broke into a brisk trot and vanished in the gloom.

XXVII

On the day following the event described in the previous chapter everything outwardly resumed its usual orderly course in the Réty house. Perhaps the *alispán*'s face had a more careworn expression than at other times, and Etelka's usual cheerfulness had deserted her; but everyone went about their work and the name of Ákos was uttered only in the servants' hall, where no one tired of the praise of the young master and his old hussar now that they had gone. For as we know, the surest means of gaining affection is to go away, or actually by death to assure our dear friends and neighbours that they aren't going to meet us before the Last Judgement. It's almost a shame that it doesn't occur to us in the course of our everyday lives that we're all preparing for a great journey and the day is perhaps not far off when we shall have to part for ever; perhaps we would then be more forgiving of one another. The *alispán*'s wife was paler that usual, but she too seemed at ease in her situation, and if the gentle smile with which she received Macskaházy's hand-kiss was a little more tense than usual no one noticed it except the lawyer, who assumed his customary public cringe. Mrs Réty was one of those people who never lose sight of their situation and their goals, however excited they may be. There were moments when her passion broke out, but those were like the night riven by lightnings, and we tremble as we see what thunderclouds tower in the dark; scarcely might we catch a glimpse into the secrets of her heart than her coldly smiling face was before us once more. Macskaházy knew her far too well to trust in her simulated calm, especially after seeing the outburst of her temper the previous evening, and he had heard from her maid that she had not gone to bed all night but had paced up and down her room and as dawn approached had flung open the windows with such force that two had broken; hardly a sign of inner calm. He therefore watched her every move with the closest attention, but as I've said, nothing was to be perceived, and only the maid saw that instead of having the broken windows taken to the glazier she'd summoned him to come at once that morning and, more surprising still, all the time that he was working not only had she remained in the room but hadn't so much as once raised her voice in complaint – an extraordinary thing that was attributed to an indisposition; she'd complained several times that day of feeling unwell.

403

On the third day Mrs Réty went with her husband and daughter to a neighbour's estate, and Macskaházy was left alone in the house.

He was feeling unusually ill at ease. "That woman," said he to himself as the carriage rolled through the gate and he returned, deep in thought, to his room, "is plotting revenge on me. She's certainly got some plan clear in her mind, otherwise she wouldn't be so relaxed. I wouldn't care if she were to reproach me and make a fuss. But what's she thinking about, I wonder?" He pondered all the possibilities and it seemed to him that the *alispán*'s wife couldn't do him any harm without harming herself. "But in the end, isn't it possible that she'll sacrifice her own security to her desire for vengeance? And in that case that I shall be the victim of it all? Wasn't I the one that had a personal hand in the robbery? And how am I to prove that she was implicated? Then there's Viola – when might he turn up? The Jew will deny everything, and is the word of an accused lawyer going to stand up against the powerful *alispán*'s wife? I must think about some support," said he to himself, as he paced his room, "everyone hates me, and a single man, however clever, can't hold out against so many. But how can I go about it?"

As he pondered his situation two ways were open to Macskaházy. The first was to regain the *alispán*'s wife's favour, for which the most certain means would be to prevent Ákos's marriage. The second was to win Ákos's favour . . . and why shouldn't that be possible, and without doing himself the slightest harm? . . When he had the notes of hand, he thought on, he could retain some of Vándory's documents; she didn't know how many there were and so couldn't realise. Later, he – Macskaházy – would give them to Ákos, together with Tengelyi's and explain how he'd come by them and the part that his stepmother had played. For the sake of his good name, Ákos wouldn't tell anyone; Macskaházy's admission would thus be completely truthful, and Mrs Réty would refrain from taking any steps that would damage her rather than him.

Macskaházy felt quite reassured at this prospect, and because he was one of those whose plans succeed because they don't put off anything without good reason he only waited for a suitable opportunity to make contact with the Tengelyis. In the afternoon, as soon as he was sure that the notary, Vándory and Ákos were taking a walk and that he'd only find the women at home, he made his way to the Tengelyi house . . . On the way he continued to think out his role and encouraged himself with the thought that however cool a reception he received he would, after all, have only the women to deal with. So thinking, he arrived, knocked quietly and stepped inside.

404

Erzsébet and Vilma were sitting side by side, busy on female tasks, and looked up in surprise as he entered . . . and Erzsébet's tone, as she enquired to what they owed the honour was not the most friendly. However, Macskaházy said with such aplomb that he merely wished to pay his respects . . . that in the end the lady of the house had no alternative but to offer the unexpected visitor a seat.

This Macskaházy had foreseen, and had so chosen a moment for his first visit in which he could be with her, because he guessed that if Tengelyi found him in the house he'd scarcely have the opportunity to say the fine words by which he expected to make peace with the family . . . as it was more than likely that the notary would open the conversation by throwing him out.

At first they talked about the weather, the harvest and other such matters, and Erzsébet was beginning to think that the lawyer had come, as he said, for no particular purpose, just to pay a visit, when Vilma left the room and the conversation took a quite different turn.

"I'm glad that the dear girl has gone out," said Macskaházy, drawing his chair a little closer, "I've something to say to you, dear lady, that would concern all your family closely, the angelic Vilma too, but which I can only say to a sensible and experienced lady such as yourself."

These compliments, together with the sugary tone in which they were expressed, didn't have the desired effect on Erzsébet; but in the hope of learning something from the lawyer that could concern her family she restrained herself and asked him to speak openly.

"My dear Mrs Erzsébet," Macskaházy went on, in as delicate a tone as he could, "permit me once again to use that name which once was so dear to my heart and at which memories of my youth rise before me."

"We'd do better to leave such matters, my dear sir," said Mrs Tengelyi irritatedly, "you know that at the time to which you refer . . ."

"Quite, quite!" sighed Macskaházy, "Twenty-odd years ago, when I offered my heart and hand to you, dear lady, my proposal was rejected with contempt, and the poverty into which you married Tengelyi seemed more acceptable that the tranquil bliss that you'd have found in my arms . . . and how much suffering might we not both have avoided had my dear Erzsébet had less regard for Tengelyi's seemingly illustrious qualities, which in the end have been of little worth!"

"If you please, sir," Erzsébet interrupted him with a look of disdain, "let's leave such irrelevant matters. We know each other. We have enough evidence of the respect and affection that exist between us; it would be a great shame to waste a single word on the subject."

405

"I see," said Macskaházy with a sigh, "that you are of the same opinion as Tengelyi himself, as if I were the cause or prime mover in the unpleasantness that came his way recently in Porvár. I won't take it amiss if anyone says that of me . . . the future will show that the accusation is quite unfounded."

"Heaven grant that that should be so!" sighed Erzsébet, "and however much cause for complaint we may have for what's happened, you can at least count on my greatest gratitude if there's anything that you can do to help my poor children."

"Don't mention it, dear Erzsébet," said the lawyer warmly, "don't mention it. Nothing will give me greater pleasure than to show that the affection that I once felt hasn't faded without remaining friendship. I'll feel perfectly satisfied if I can prove that by action, and I believe that I now have an opportunity."

Erzsébet couldn't overcome her surprise at the candour with which Macskaházy was suddenly speaking . . . and although she suspected some wickedness in it all, she said, with all the gentleness in her, that no doubt in the lawyer's position and with his considerable influence he must have many opportunities of helping a poor village notary's household.

"Don't believe, dear lady," said Macskaházy modestly, "that my influence is as great as people say. A lot of people talk as if nothing happened in the Réty household but what I want. They blame everything that the *alispán* or his haughty wife does on me, and you wouldn't believe how many enemies that makes me . . . but God sees my soul, and if what I want were to happen in the mansion things would take a different course. But let's change the subject," he added after a brief pause. "It can't be denied that when all's said and done, I do have a certain influence in the Réty house, and it's by virtue of that that I can perhaps be of use to you all. As I understand it, a case has been brought against Tengelyi over nobility?"

The quiet way in which that question was put by him of all people, whom Erzsébet believed to be the prime mover in the plot against her husband, so startled her that she didn't reply.

"And the documents with which Tengelyi might prove his nobility," he continued, "have all been stolen, if I hear correctly?"

"I think," replied Erzsébet, finally tiring of the lawyers impudence, "that you know that as well as anyone."

"I take your point," said Macskaházy with a quiet smile, "though I confess that I find it extraordinary that suspicion is cast on me, to whom it's a matter of complete indifference in whoever's hands the stolen documents are – apart from the fact that such an action is so contrary to my

406

nature that the suggestion can't be a sober one. Or are you saying that I might possibly have some interest in Tengelyi's dog-skins, when we have no blood relationship at all or disputed inheritance?"

"I don't understand any of it," said she with a shrug. "All I know is what my husband says and what I've heard of Viola's statement, and after that . . ."

"But really, dear lady," Macskaházy butted in, "if that were so, do you think that I'd come here myself, to your own house? I'd have to be the most insolent man in the world, indeed the most foolish," he added, noticing that Erzsébet didn't find the former as incredible as he thought, "yes, the most foolish, my dear Erzsébet, if, after putting myself to so much trouble merely to involve Tengelyi in unpleasantness I were to do it all again in order that the affair should be straightened out and no trouble should result for your house."

"Until now, sir, you haven't given much evidence of that," said Mrs Tengelyi drily.

"Heaven can see," said Macskaházy, looking upwards, "how unjust you're being to me! If you knew the trouble I've taken to restrain . . . but that's irrelevant . . . you wouldn't speak like that. But as I say, I want to show my friendship by actions, and I believe that after that Tengelyi himself will retract his harsh judgement."

"God grant so!" said Erzsébet. "You can count on our greatest gratitude, and," she added rather more proudly, "perhaps in future we'll be able to show it to some effect."

"Nothing to be grateful for," Macskaházy interrupted her, understanding what she meant. "Don't speak of gratitude, you'll surely offend me, I merely seek friendship. So the documents," he added more quietly, after a brief pause during which he looked around and made certain that there was no one else in the room, and pulled his chair closer to Erzsébet, "those, I mean that have been stolen from Tengelyi, as you believe, are such as would completely prove his nobility?"

"Beyond all doubt," she replied, more and more surprised at Macskaházy's odd behaviour.

"Hmm, hmm!" he continued, as if to himself, "important documents! Baptism is no more necessary for salvation than nobility is in Hungary if one is to live a respectable life: and I can quite understand the pain which you feel at this loss, especially if you consider the future of your little son . . ."

"For God's sake, don't torture me!" Erzsébet broke into his ruminations. "If you know something about these documents . . ."

"But, dear lady," Macskaházy asked, ignoring her request, "were really all the documents stolen by which your nobility could be proved? Have you nothing left at all?"

"Nothing," Erzsébet sighed. "My husband, tidy man that he is, kept everything in a single bundle, and that's what was stolen. If you know something about them," she added pleadingly, "don't make my children unhappy. If ever I've offended you, for God's sake, don't avenge yourself on the innocent."

Erzsébet hated and despised Macskaházy, but as soon as the belief arose in her that he could be of use to her children all else faded into the background, and as a mother she clasped her hands together and begged him, though at other times she turned from him in disgust.

Macskaházy could scarcely conceal his delight on seeing the effect that his words had. "Ah," said he at length with a sigh, "if it were only up to me!. . . Believe me, my dear Erzsébet, if I knew where those documents were no one could be happier! If need were I'd walk to the end of Hungary, know no rest till I'd found them."

"So you don't know where they are?" asked Mrs Tengelyi in surprise.

"How should I?" he replied sweetly. "Just consider. Everything that Viola said about the robbery was a tissue of lies. However important Tengelyi's documents may be to his own family, as far as the *alispán*'s wife or myself are concerned they're of no interest at all, and one can't suppose that anyone would, without the most compelling reason, expose themselves to such danger as would come to persons of our rank if we kept the company of thieves. The accusation levelled at us on that score can only be laughable; and in any case, how could I have acquired information on the said documents?"

"Then how, my dear sir, can you be of use to my children," Erzsébet repeated her question, more drily, "if there's nothing that you can do to restore our nobility?"

"But who said that there was nothing that I can do? Or that I'm not going to do very much?" said Macskaházy with a smile. "What need is there of documents?"

Mrs Tengelyi took those words as irony and stared at him. Macskaházy continued to smile. "My dear Erzsébet, you live in Hungary but it seems that you don't really know what goes on around you. Whoever heard of nobility being conferred or maintained only through documents? Certainly, that's one way; sometimes His Majesty does ennoble someone by a gift or by letters patent; but that's only one way, and God forbid that it should be the commonest. If everyone that enjoyed privilege had to produce their documents our numbers would dwindle like they did after the battle of Mohács. Look, dear lady, there's another method of ennoblement, much better and more expedient . . . *usus*. These days, when Hungarian names are invented for everything, it's called *legal custom*; but that doesn't really explain the term, because where there's law there's no need of *usus*, and in fact the chief property of *usus* is that it means a sort of custom that isn't based on law nor actually on custom. Let's take an example: you have a certain property, I have an adjacent piece of land. Every year I go farther with my ploughs and and turn over a little more until my holding is three times as big as it once was. Eventually you bring legal action. I show that I have had *usus*, that I have always customarily ploughed and sown so much. You say that this is a bad custom, because the land is yours . . . That I have *usus* is irrelevant . . . and you can bring a legal action, but it will drag on for a hundred years. Or I state that we're joint owners, half of the land is mine and the rest yours. I've always, within living memory, kept sheep. . . you haven't; eventually you too mean to keep sheep . . . I won't permit it . . . if your flock comes onto our joint property I drive them off, and why? Because I have *usus*."

"But what does all that matter to us?" asked Mrs Tengelyi impatiently

"Simply that," replied Macskaházy with a smile, "that like everything else, here in Hungary the privileged status of nobility is mainly acquired through *usus*, and there is no need of documents."

"I don't understand," said Erzsébet.

"It's quite natural," Macskaházy went on, as if giving instruction. "Say A or B has no document by means of which to prove his nobility. Let's suppose that perhaps he himself knows that he comes from an ignoble family; he has friends in the county, however, and for that reason taxation has never been levied on him, and the whole county speaks of him as *nemzetes*[175] or even *tekintetes*. Now if some ill-wisher calls his nobility into question, wouldn't it be a great difficulty for him if he had to prove, shall we say, that his ancestors had gained their nobility by shedding their blood for the fatherland?. . . Instead of that, he'll show that he's never paid taxes . . . and his nobility is saved! Especially if he can also show that he'd been beaten up at some election, or that he'd beaten someone up . . . No one would dare question his *usus*. I know of a nobility case in which someone only showed that his father had been

---

175 Strictly speaking a form of address of last resort for a noble. In a broader sense, used for persons deserving respect by virtue of status, whether or not noble. *Tekintetes* 'worshipful' was used of lower-order dignitaries.

frequently arrested for stealing horses without ever being sentenced to a flogging . . . and *usus* was established. Believe me, dear lady, anyone that believes that documents are required to prove nobility is mistaken. In many counties hundreds are ennobled at every election, and they're just as good nobles as any; it just requires friends and . . ."

"Yes, but have we any friends?" sighed Mrs Tengelyi.

"Certainly you have," said Macskházy, with a friendly nod, "and what's more, such friends as will do their utmost on your behalf, and should it be required any number of witnesses could be found to swear that Tengelyi is directly descended from a line of counts. The *alispán* himself . . ."

"The *alispán* will do his utmost against us."

"You're mistaken, dear lady," the lawyer cut her short. "When the *alispán* sees the part that I take in Tengelyi's affair, he himself will take steps so that either the case begun by Nyúzó will fade into oblivion or that the outcome will at least be as we wish. His Honour the alispán is a very good man at heart, and if the sole cause that's given rise to disharmony between the two houses were removed, I'm convinced that he'd have the same affection for Tengelyi as when they were at university together in Germany."

"I don't understand you!"

"The reason for the disharmony," Macskaházy went on confidentially, "is the love that Réty's son feels for our angelic little Vilma. Believe me, dear lady, that's all it is. If that's removed somehow, everything will be in order. Who can help it? Marriage, as they say, is heaven on earth! It's not surprising that everyone thinks that they must rise higher when they're preparing for it . . . and the alispán . . . when all's said and done, we're all human . . ."

"But don't you know, sir," asked Mrs Tengelyi, in a sharper tone – she was beginning to suspect the lawyer's little game – "that if that's the reason for the *alispán*'s ill-feeling, it can't be removed? Ákos asked for my daughter's hand on his own account . . . and as she loves him she's had our consent as of yesterday. You do understand? My husband's consent too! If you know of no other means of our gaining the *alispán*'s friendship than by sacrificing my daughter's happiness, let's not waste another word."

"But who's talking about sacrificing Vilma's happiness?" said Macskaházy, likewise in irritation. "Who takes that angelic creature's happiness more to heart than myself? Do you mean that the dear girl can only be happy if she marries the *alispán*'s son?" Erzsébet was about to speak,

410

but the lawyer went on: "No doubt a fine name and land are good things; believe me, dear lady, no one's more aware of that than I. It's nice for you to see your daughter in a mansion, going about in a carriage and four . . . but that in itself doesn't make anyone happy!. . . There was a time when you too might have found a husband, not perhaps quite so rich, but with whom you'd have at least been spared everyday anxieties . . . and yet you gave your hand to Tengelyi . . . and so . . ."

"If you think, sir," Erzsébet cut in, "that we want this marriage because Ákos is rich, you're seriously mistaken; I wish heaven would grant that he were of the same class, as poor as we, at least no one would spoil my daughter's pleasure; God has created the two of them for each other!"

"Don't you believe it, dear lady," replied Macskaházy with a shake of his head. "God's only arranged a marriage once; and when that turned out badly, and Adam and the wife made for him were put out of Paradise together, he hasn't interfered since. For my own part, if I had a daughter I'd never give her to anyone higher in society or rich. True, such can give their wives much pleasure that they can't expect in less wealthy houses . . . all sorts of luxury, ease, and so on . . . but real love, you see, Mrs Erzsébet," said he, changing to a sentimental tone, "real love, as we understand it, isn't to be found at all in a wealthy house."

"Ákos isn't like that," said Erzsébet, "he adores Vilma . . ."

"No doubt," Macskaházy cut her off, "who doesn't he adore? There's no softer heart in the world! But, you see, dear lady, adoration's quite a strange thing; one kneels down, raises one's hands to heaven, is almost in a state of ecstasy, and in the end, when one's said one's prayers one gets up and goes one's way."

Human nature is strange; people never believe anything so strongly that it's never in doubt . . . and again, never regard anything as so impossible that they don't sometimes believe it; particularly when we want something badly, or are very afraid of something, we're all inclined to believe in miracles . . . and although Erzsébet was fully aware of Macskaházy's deviousness the doubt with which he had spoken of Ákos's love had a visible effect on her; nevertheless she merely replied that she knew Vilma's betrothed and if she didn't respect him she certainly wouldn't have given him her daughter.

"You're right to have a high opinion of Ákos, dear lady," said the lawyer, with a nod of approval, "there's no one better or more honourable in the world! Of course, I've known him since he was a child . . . The times he's sat on my knee!. . . I couldn't love a son of my own more. Who could take it amiss that he's soft-hearted, not as constant in his affections as we

411

more mature people wish?. . . You see, dear lady, in a young man of rank like Ákos it's all but impossible."

"But that's what I do want!" said Erzsébet, somewhat heatedly. "If I'm giving him my daughter I don't want him loving anyone else."

"That's asking too much," said Macskaházy with a smile. "If Ákos were our sort of person your wish would be perfectly reasonable, but in higher social circles it's ridiculous . . . what would people say if a man like him didn't pay court to someone that wasn't his wife? There'd be talk!"

"But you don't actually know anything bad about Ákos?" asked Erzsébet, more sharply still.

"Anything bad? God forbid!" said Macskaházy calmly. "Nothing in the slightest unfavourable to him. He has his lovers, but . . ."
"Has his lovers!" exclaimed Erzsébet in alarm.

"Well, what's wrong with that?"

"What's wrong with it? replied Erzsébet, forgetting in her excitement whom she was talking to. "If he's got lovers, when he's told my daughter a hundred times that he loves nobody else in the world. . . It's a pack of lies!"

"But I tell you," said Macskaházy reassuringly, "it can't be taken amiss in young gentlemen."

"But I'll take it amiss," Erzsébet interrupted, "rather than have such a thing happen I'd. . ."

"Dear lady," said Macskaházy, looking round again and pulling his chair a little closer, "I understand your views, and therefore, as an honest man with the greatest interest in your wellbeing, I'm obliged to express my belief that Ákos will never meet your requirements. He's a good, honest, clever young man . . . but as I say, to ask of him faithfulness, lasting love, is foolishness!. . . If that's what you look for in a son-in-law," he added more quietly, taking Erzsébet's hand, with all the sweetness in him, "I know one."

Erzsébet stared at him.

"Yes, my dear Erzsébet," he went on with increasing warmth, "I know one whose faithfulness will pass every test, whose constancy is unshakeable. A man who, perhaps, has less to offer your daughter by way of outward brilliance than Ákos, but in whose arms Vilma will be able to find all the quiet happiness the value of which you must so esteem. I myself, my dear Erzsébet," he added, with a questioning glance at her as she sat beside him, unable to utter a word in her astonishment, "I'm prepared to take Ákos's place."

"You, sir?!"

412

"And why not?" he went on sweetly. "True, I'm not as young as I was when I offered my hand to yourself; but I'm not an old man. . . in the prime of life, I can say . . . furthermore my situation has improved, and instead of the decent provision that I was able to offer then, I now bring to my wife a certain wealth . . . I've got more than a hundred and fifty thousand tucked away. If Vilma is my wife, there'll be no more questioning Tengelyi's nobility . . . indeed, I might also expect some property from the Rétys. I'm much too sensible to take amiss what's happened to Ákos, and . . ."

In enumerating the benefits that his marriage to Vilma would confer Macskaházy failed to notice the effect that his words were having on Mrs Tengelyi, and he fell silent with the greatest surprise when she suddenly leapt from her chair, pointed to the door and shrieked that he must leave her house at once.

The lawyer wanted to speak. As my readers know, the feeling which that smooth man had for Vilma was of the least passionate. The thought of taking to wife one of the most beautiful girls in the county wasn't unpleasant to him, especially if by so doing he could at the same time advance his other plans; but if he didn't succeed Macskaházy would take a different path, and it was unlikely that he would feel much heartache on that account. Love – that I too may use a simile for that state, which is compared to as many things as there are people that speak of it – is not to everyone a Pegasus by which they allow themselves to be borne aloft. There are those who use it as a well-schooled mount or even a carriage-horse by which they themselves and their belongings are taken wherever they wish, and Macskaházy was one such. If Mrs Tengelyi had allowed him to speak he would no doubt have revised his words or at least given a fully satisfactory explanation of them; but she wasn't in a mood to give him time for that. The very thought that she had for a moment believed his slanders, even though she knew his deviousness . . . that she'd doubted Ákos even for a moment, so infuriated the otherwise placid woman that the lawyer, after all his fabrications, couldn't find a word to say and was about to leave and let the rest wait for another occasion, when the door opened and to his no little horror Tengelyi himself came into the room.

"What's this gentleman doing here?" asked the notary, frowning severely.

Macskaházy was about to answer, but Mrs Tengelyi spared him the trouble, and gave her husband an account of what had happened, spicing her account with such expressions as she considered that the lawyer deserved. No exception could be taken to the truth of her words, except that she attributed the whole to the *alispán*'s wife's orders, although, as we know, just this once Macskaházy had acted on his own initiative.

"Clear off this minute . . . and don't let me see your insolent face in this house ever again!" were the only words that the notary said to Macskaházy, and though he did his utmost to restrain himself anyone that heard the tone in which he uttered them could guess at his inner distress. This very moderation, however, misled Macskaházy, and when instead of leaving he began to offer an explanation of his action and spoke of the friendship that he felt towards the whole family, Tenglyi's fury knew no bounds . . . and Erzsébet herself was alarmed to see her husband's outburst of temper.

"Out of my house this instant! Out, you good-for-nothing!" shouted Tengelyi, "if you[176] don't want me to throw you out."

"But I beg you, my dear sir" said Macskaházy soothingly, "be so good as to hear me out; I think that the offer that I've made doesn't warrant the treatment that I've received; if Vilma . . ."

"Don't say that name," the notary cut him short, "don't dare speak of her again, you wretch!. . . You, my daughter's husband? You thief, you villain, you dregs of the human race!"

At the noise Vilma and Mrs Lipták came into the room, while several passers-by stopped at the window and looked curiously in. Macskaházy thought that these witnesses would save him from a thrashing, and at the same time felt that if he tolerated this treatment he would seriously lose face. He raised his voice.

"That's going too far!" said he in his grating voice. "You'll regret saying that, notary."

"Regret! Regret!" shouted Tengelyi, ever more furious.

"Yes, indeed, my dear notary," continued Macskaházy sardonically. "It appears that you're forgetting that you're no longer a noble, ha! ha! ha!"

"Are you reminding me of your wicked ways?" and Tengelyi raised his walking-stick, while his wife and daughter could barely hold his arm back.

"And though I've lowered myself and asked for your daughter's hand in marriage, you should never forget the difference that exists between us."

---

176 In the Hungarian, Tengelyi switches to addressing Macskaházy contemptuously as *te* and continues to do so, while Macskaházy uses the honorific third person in his replies, clinging to dignity.

"Yes, a difference, that between a decent man and a villain. Let go of me!" this last to his wife. who was still holding back his hand. Macskaházy shrewdly calculated that the moment had come beyond which it would be dangerous for him to remain, and with a couple more threats reached the door just as the master of the house broke free and rushed at him with his stick.

"That man will die by my hand!" said Tengelyi, once he had been escorted back into his room by Vándory, who happened to be passing – he had chased the fleeing lawyer into the yard. He flung himself onto a chair, exhausted by his outburst, and could scarcely recover his composure even though the others – and later Ákos, whom Vándory went to fetch – said again and again that that wretch wasn't worth a decent man's upsetting himself for a single moment.

XXVIII

While Tengelyi relaxed in his family circle and began at length to cool down, and while those who had witnessed the uproar in his house, either at the windows or by the yard gate, had scattered and told their neighbours that Macskaházy had been thrashed and thrown out, that Tengelyi had tried to kill the lawyer, and that he had been able to escape only by flight, the subject of these conversations, whose dressing-down was received with *Schadenfreude* throughout the village, was pacing up and down in his room in the greatest agitation.

My readers know the reason for his call on the Tengelyis. "How could I have been so mad?" said he to himself, "as to ask for Vilma's hand in marriage? Only the foolish loyalty that I show to the Rétys could have induced me to do it. Even if I married Vilma, what would I gain?. . . I wouldn't in any case be able to extract from them any more than the fifty thousand forints that I've agreed . . . and even if I can prevent Ákos's marriage now this ungrateful woman will never forgive me for spending so much. I've done a foolish thing, that's obvious!. . . But who'd have thought that that woman would be so incensed, that she wouldn't let me get a word in edgeways?. . . And when Tengelyi came home, what didn't I have to endure in front of servants and peasants? and I can't even take revenge!. . . I mustn't offend Ákos . . . when all's said and done, there's nothing for it but to hand over to him Tengelyi's letters patent and one or two of Vándory's documents once I get the promissory notes in my hand, and to reveal all to him so as at least to save myself from criminal proceedings."

Even by that decision Macskaházy didn't feel entirely reassured, as the possibility remained that Ákos could prefer charges – he'd hated him for a long time – even if he were to reveal the robbery personally and hand over some of the documents. But, he thought, first I'll ask for his word of honour; people like Ákos set great store by such prejudices, and what's more he can't get me into trouble without involving his stepmother, and he'll be reluctant to do that however much he hates the woman because she bears his name and he won't want to besmirch it. Thus cheered, he lit a candle and began looking through Vándory's documents.

Eleven o'clock was approaching by the time that he'd finished; most of them were letters, and he selected a few and put them into a separate drawer. The rest he replaced where they had been previously, and prepared for bed.

Macskaházy was no longer worried about the affair as a whole . . . After looking through the letters he was convinced that the Rétys would avoid all publicity and that he had nothing to fear from legal proceedings. He walked up and down his room a couple of times. "So," said he to himself, "another couple of days and I'll be fifty thousand better off. If I disclose everything to Ákos and give him all the documents that I've selected I'm insured against that woman's revenge as well. At last I shan't have worn myself out all these years for nothing!" With which he made for the door to lock it.

He turned the key and tried the door, but it remained unlocked. He tried again; the key turned, but the door didn't lock. He shook his head in perplexity: he'd never had trouble with that door, so what was suddenly wrong with it now? He tried to move the bolt, but try though he might it wouldn't budge . . . and the door remained unlocked. "Goodness knows what's gone wrong with it," said he in irritation. He hit the door several times and tried again to see if he could lock it. He realised that since Ákos had moved out and Etelka was away with her parents he was the only one living in that part of the house. He'd heard so much talk of bandits of late that the thought of having to spend the night alone with the door unlocked filled him straight away with dread, and in his aroused state it seemed to him that he heard something moving in the stove; but when he went over and listened he found everything silent again and calmed down. "Have I gone mad?" said he, and went back to the door and tried once more to lock it. "What reason is there to be afraid if I can't lock my door?. . . The servant strained the lock when he closed the door after he'd been in to tidy up, that's obviously why the bolt won't move . . ." And with that Macskaházy undressed, got into bed, and abandoned himself to the delightful thoughts that only a man can entertain who has come into possession of a substantial sum and is devising schemes for the application of it.

But the lawyer was soon disturbed in those delightful thoughts by a sound. Quiet but distinct footsteps could be heard on the stairs. Macskaházy was quite sure that he wasn't mistaken. He could hear how, stair by stair, step by step, someone was coming up and approaching along the corridor . . . and he was just on the point of jumping out of bed when the door opened quietly and there before him stood Viola.

"Viola!" said Macskaházy in a tremulous voice. At seeing himself alone with the outlaw he was so horrified that he lacked the strength to cry out.

"I'm glad you recognise me," said the other, closing the door behind him and making straight for the bed. "If you call for help, you're a dead man! In any case it would be futile, there's no one on this side of the house to hear you."

"I shan't call out, shan't make a sound," said Macskaházy, and a deathly pallor came over his face. "Only don't hurt me. If it's money you want, I'm a poorer man than you think, but you can take what I've got. Why would you hurt me, a poor, sickly man? I'll give you everything I possess."

"Why would I hurt you?" said Viola, giving the wretched lawyer a look that froze his blood. "Perhaps I might have good cause. Don't suppose that I've entirely forgotten the past. Nothing that I could do to you, if I were to spill your blood drop by drop, would pay for what you've done to me."

"You're very much mistaken," said the lawyer, with a despairing look around, "I . . ."

"Who was the cause," said Viola grimly, "of my becoming an outlaw? Whom have I to thank for being hunted like an animal, roaming forests and *puszta*s, while my wife and children are forced to seek the bitter bread of charity? . . Say that it wasn't you . . . that you didn't do your utmost to have me sentenced to death . . . that you haven't yearned to take my lif . . . that you aren't my deadly enemy?"

"But I give you everything, every single thing that I posess," Macskaházy replied in pleading tone.

"I'm not after your money," the outlaw interrupted scornfully, "give me the documents that you and a low-down Jew stole from the notary's house."

"Documents?" said the lawyer, staring in surprise at Viola. "What documents?"

"Those documents," said Viola with a frown, "that you tore from my hands when I was being arrested . . . those instead of which you displayed clean laundry in court . . . if you don't hand them over you're not going to rise from that bed."

"I know, I know," said Macskaházy. He could tell from Viola's tone that it would be unwise to try his patience. "I had them . . . it's true that I tore them from your hands . . . but you see, as soon as I had them I threw them into the fire. Why should I keep it from you, you shall know everything: Mrs Réty very much wanted those documents destroyed, and I, as you know, have always . . . always been her loyal man . . . as soon as

418

I had them in my possession I threw them into the burning hut so that there'd be no more trouble about them."

"Tell that to somebody else," said Viola calmly. "I know you've got the documents here . . . and that you're asking the Rétys for fifty thousand forints for them."

"Who told you that?" Macskaházy interrupted in astonishment. At the same time it occurred to him that Viola was in the pay of the *alispán*'s wife.

"Never you mind," replied Viola drily, "but if you yourself value your life at fifty thousand and don't hand over those documents at once, you'll see that you've been wasting your breath and that it's worth even less to me."

"But I beg you," the lawyer implored, "just tell me who told you that I'd got the documents? Who's sent you here?"

"Stop blathering," said Viola, throwing open his sheepskin, "and get up and give me the papers, otherwise . . ."

The outlaw's whole demeanour showed that he would stop at nothing . . . Macskaházy felt that he couldn't resist him, and so he got up without a word and went towards his desk while Viola remained in the middle of the room, watching every move that he made.

The lawyer's hands were trembling as he took the documents out of the drawer and put them on the table. There were two bundles: in the one were Vándory's letters, in the other Tengelyi's more important documents; there were also a few letters of Tengelyi's which the Jew had stolen along with the rest, wrapped in paper, and which had been passed to Macskaházy. "Here they are," said he in a choking voice, "but you don't know how valuable they are to me, you can't profit by them, ask me for anything and . . ."

"Keep your money, I tell you," said Viola scornfully as he approached the desk. At that moment the lawyer recalled that in his drawer he had a loaded pistol, which he had put there so as not to be entirely defenceless. If we consider that the documents with which he was having to part were worth fifty thousand forints to him nobody can be surprised that despite his natural cowardice he almost involuntarily reached for the weapon and aimed it at Viola; but it wasn't cocked . . . and next moment saw the lawyer flat on the floor and the pistol in Viola's hand.

That was Macskaházy's undoing. Viola wasn't a cruel man. The thought that he'd shed a man's blood had often filled his soul with horror . . . and although he might have offered himself the excuse that it had been in self-defence and done in a moment of sheer desperation, the

419

ordinary man sees little difference between homicide intentional and unintentional, and calls both murder; so Viola too had forgotten the justification for his act, and more than once had said that he regarded everything that he'd subsequently suffered as punishment for his sin. When Macskaházy handed over the documents he had no cause for alarm. During the struggle in which he seized the pistol from his opponent's hand Viola's temper rose. The hatred that filled his breast for the man from whom he's suffered so much and who was now threatening his life outweighed all else, and almost beside himself he rushed at the wretched man, who was calling for help and trying to rise. "Mercy!" spluttered Macskaházy as Viola seized his throat.

"Were you merciful when you made Zsuzsi a beggar? When you sentenced me to the gallows?" came the reply.

Macskaházy's face was turning blue; but despair gave strength to his weak hands when he saw poised above him the gleaming knife which Viola had picked up from the table. This contest, however, couldn't last long . . . Viola could hear noises in the house . . . the servants had been woken by Macskaházy's cries and were coming . . . he summoned all his strength and plunged the knife three times into Macskaházy's chest.

Viola leapt up, his hands wet with the spurting blood, snatched up the documents from the table and, not noticing that he was dropping a few letters, rushed from the room just in time to reach the courtyard before anyone came running to detain him. There he was glimpsed by the coachman and another man who was coming from the stable with lanterns . . . and pursued by them ran into the fields and vanished among the bushes on the Tisza bank.

The servants rushed immediately to Macskaházy's room, where they found him covered in blood and dying. There were no signs of robbery, and even his watch and wallet were there beside the bed.

"Robbery!" "Murder!" shouted the fat cook, who, in his nightshirt, was the first on the scene with a candle. "After him!"

"A doctor!" exclaimed another.

"A priest!" exclaimed a third.

Everybody was running this way and that in wild confusion, while two of the steadily growing number present laid the dying man on his bed.

"After him! After him!" choked Macskaházy. "My documents . . ."

"What documents?" asked the cook, raising the injured man slightly.

"Tengelyi," said Macskaházy with the last of his strength; the rest of what he was presumably trying to say was incomprehensible. His lips moved, but no words, only choking sounds were audible, at which those present were horrified.

At that moment the *hajdú* was heard in the corridor, saying that the murderer had been caught . . . and immediately afterwards he dragged the Jewish glazier into the room, gripping him by the throat. "Here he is," said he with no little satisfaction, "I found him in the stove."

"Oh, the villain!" exclaimed the cook, pulling the trembling Jew towards the bed. "It was him, your honour, wasn't it?"

Macskaházy shook his head and his lips moved, but nothing could be understood.

"But your honour, it can't be anybody else!" said the cook. "Just nod your head. . . it was him, wasn't it?"

Macskaházy shook his head again, grasped the cook's hand and tried once again to speak . . . in vain! Once more he opened his mouth as if straining for breath, looked around in wild despair, fell back on his pillow . . . and was dead.

"I wish I knew what he was trying to say," said the cook once the deceased was covered, and the Jewish glazier, despite all the oaths with which he protested his innocence, was trussed up and locked in the cellar. "When I showed him the Jew and asked if that was who'd killed him he definitely shook his head . . . but I'd bet my life nobody did it but that no-good glazier."

"While he could still speak," said the cook's wife, drying her eyes – not that she regretted Macskaházy's death, but because she believed that ladies should do that on such occasions – "he spoke the name Tengelyi."

"Don't talk such rubbish," replied the cook. "Saying a thing like that about Master Tengelyi!"

"That's all I know," said she sharply, happy to find the chance of an argument, "but when we asked who was the murderer, he did say the name Tengelyi, didn't he?" said she, appealing to the rest, all of who confirmed the truth of what she said. "And then when he couldn't speak any longer I was watching his lips carefully, and the way they moved, it was as if he was trying to say Tengelyi, always Tengelyi. When my late husband – God rest him – was on his deathbed with dropsy he couldn't speak for three days, but I just watched his lips and could understand everything. Go there, come here, give me a drink, and I did what he wanted . . ." and she began to dab at her eyes again.

"You don't mean to blame this murder on the notary, do you?" said the cook anxiously.

"God save me from anything so shameful! All I'm saying is that when we asked him who'd killed him he spoke the name of Tengelyi, and so clearly and understandably that we all could hear . . . and I'll swear to that if need be."

"Very well, very well," said the cook crossly, "who knows what he was trying to say?"

"Am I making it up?" she went on emphatically. "All I'm saying is that he kept saying Tengelyi . . . and I'll say that till the Day of Judgement."

"The *szolgabíró*'ll interrogate him, I'm sure," said the cook, "and in the end we'll all see that I was right, the murderer was the Jew and nobody else. But for now let's lock the room and send for the *szolgabíró* . . . I know that where there's been a robbery or a murder, nothing must be touched."

And with that they all left the room, leaving the bloodied corpse alone in the darkness.

XXIX

In order to understand what happened after Macskaházy's murder we shall have to go back to the events of the evening of the day on which we last saw the unfortunate lawyer in Tengelyi's house. The notary's family, to which Ákos now belonged, together with Vándory, who for years had spent almost every evening in that house, were sitting together in Erzsébet's room chatting amiably, while Tengelyi himself was in the other room, writing letters.

As he wrote a soft tapping at the window attracted his attention. He looked up, and as he could see no one he resumed his work . . . but when the sound was repeated another twice he got up and opened his window . . . Once more he couldn't see anyone, and he asked in irritation who was disturbing him. And he was about to close the window when a little note was tossed into the room and footsteps were heard as someone made off along the wall without being seen or speaking, and vanished in the darkness.

"What can this be?" said Tengelyi. He shut the window, picked up the note from the floor and took it to his desk; "I don't suppose it's a threat? Such a thing has never occurred since I've been living here . . . and neither I nor the community have given cause for grievance . . ."

The note, which Tengelyi first examined externally, was written on poor-quality paper such as, judging from its many creases, had seen much previous use . . . instead of a seal a krajcár had been used . . . it was addressed to The Honourable Notary Master Tengelyi . . . and on breaking the seal he read, to his astonishment, the following:

I am eternally grateful to Your Honour. People say that I stole the documents from your house, but to say so is shameful wickedness . . . The thief was the Jewish glazier, put up to it by the *alispán*'s lawyer . . . I only took them from the Jew; but it's a long story. Come tonight, Your Honour, to the big poplar tree right by the ferry, no sooner than eleven o'clock . . . before midnight I shall place the documents in your hands if it costs me my life . . . because Your Honour kept my wife and children in your own home. For God's sake, be certain to come, don't be afraid of me, outlaw that I am, I'd give my life for any of your family . . . and if you don't come I shan't know to whom to give the documents . . . I'll have to cross the Tisza tonight, I daren't come into the village. So I most humbly beg you, don't say a word about it to anyone and come alone.

The county has put a price on my head . . . if it's discovered that I'm here I'm a dead man. I put myself entirely in Your Honour's hands.

VIOLA

Tengelyi had some difficulty in reading these lines because of the clumsy writing and occasional mis-spelling, and they caused him no little unease. What was he to do? If he didn't accept the outlaw's invitation the documents would probably be lost for ever. Once Viola had left the county he'd be reluctant to come back, and would rather throw away what were to him worthless papers, which might even be used as evidence against him; and if he went – he, one of those most expected to uphold the law – for a secret meeting with an outlaw without making it known . . . how would that make him look, especially after he'd taken Viola's wife and children into his house; it could be used for an accusation by his enemies that he was complicit in criminal activity. Another thought perhaps came to mind, that he should go himself to the rendezvous, take a number with him, have the outlaw arrested and at the same time take the documents found on him. This, however, wasn't in his nature, and if all the happiness in the world were promised as a reward . . . he simply couldn't do it. He was faced with just those two possibilities, and hesitating between his sense of duty and his paternal love he paced his room in the greatest agitation, now resolved to act on the outlaw's invitation, now on the contrary; and when Erzsébet came into the room to call him for dinner both she and the rest were astonished at how distraught he seemed, something that wasn't lost on the servants and Mrs Lipták either. No one knew anything about the note, which he had burnt so that it shouldn't come into anyone else's hands. Officials sometimes came to see him ten times in a day and asked him about this and that at his window without going into the house, so if Erzsébet or someone in the other room had heard the knock at the window or him opening it, it was quite a common occurrence and would surprise no one; his mood would be attributed to his annoyance with Macskaházy.

When dinner was over Vándory and Ákos left and Tengelyi said good-night to his wife and children[177] and, on the pretext that he had more writing to do, withdrew to his room. After thinking over his situation once more he decided that he was going to meet with the outlaw. "I can't in any case report that Viola's been here," he thought to himself, "no one would wish me to be so despicable!. . . and in fact in what respect

_____
177 Again the plural!

424

am I neglecting my official duties if I do my utmost to recover my rights for the sake of my children? If in fact he's got my documents, so much the better; if he hasn't, I shall at least escape self-reproach for missing the opportunity to obtain what is mine. It's not very likely that my taking this course will be noticed . . . and after all, what have I to fear if my conscience accuses me of nothing?"

It was close on eleven o'clock when, so thinking, he quietly left the house, went through his garden and came to the Tisza. It was a rainy November night, not a star was to be seen in the sky, darkness covered the ground, and Tengelyi needed all his local knowledge so as not to fall into a ditch as he made his way along the narrow path between the gardens. In the village everyone had long been asleep, and he reached the spot designated by Viola without meeting a soul.

In summertime this was one of the pleasantest spots in all of Tiszarét. There was a little grassy place which, protected from the sun in the spreading shade of the huge poplar, was always green even when the torrid heat of July burnt the whole region bare. This place was bordered on three sides by dense bushes and a few stunted trees and on the fourth by the mirror-like surface of the Tisza, to which some of the branches of the big tree reached down. Tengelyi had spent many an hour under that tree with his friend, who had often commented that there was no pleasanter place to be found on the Tisza, and if the Turk's Hill had not been there that tree itself would earn Tiszarét a place in the list of desirable places to live. Now the space beneath the tree was strewn with dry leaves and looked doleful and deserted. The night wind whistled above in the leafless branches, while the Tisza splashed the bank with foam. The notary, enveloped in his cloak, walked anxiously up and down, stopping from time to time if a sound was heard in the bushes, and resuming his ill-humoured pacing once he had assured himself that no one was coming, or taking a look towards the ferryman's house, which could have been a mere two hundred paces away – the kitchen fire was still burning, and cast a little patch of light through the door.

Thus almost half an hour went by, and Tengelyi was beginning to think that Viola had changed his mind or had been unable to carry out his errand, when the shouts of those who were pursuing the outlaw after he had killed Macskaházy came to his ears.

Tengelyi could hear people approaching with shouts of "murder", "thief", and was convinced that Viola had been recognised and was being chased; so as not to be found in that suspicious place he retreated quickly towards the village.

425

Not many moments after Tengelyi had left the place, Viola burst through the bushes carrying a bundle of documents. He stopped for a moment, looked around, saw that the notary was no longer there, could hear the shouts of his pursuers close to the bushes behind him, leapt into a little boat by the bank, pushed off strongly, and began to row.

"He's here! He must be here!" shouted the coachman, who hadn't lost sight of the outlaw all the way there although his lantern had gone out. His companions, who were similarly convinced, searched for the criminal among the bushes making a tremendous din so that they failed to notice the constantly receding sound of oars; at the noise the ferryman emerged from his cottage with his two sons.

"What's up, Ferkó?" called the ferryman, recognising the Réty coachman by the light of a burning piece of wood that he'd brought as a torch. "Has your horse been stolen?"

"No, no!" said Ferkó, relighting his lantern. "Our lawyer's been killed; we've chased the murderer to here, and he's vanished in the bushes. I could see him a moment ago . . . he must be here. Come and help look for him."

"What the devil!" replied the ferryman in amazement. "The lawyer's been killed? . . Well, he's no great loss; but if you're looking for the murderer and you've actually chased him this far, he's not here now. . . Just before you came I heard somebody hurrying towards the village, you did as well, Andris, didn't you?"

"That'll be him for sure, let's be after him!" shouted the coachman, not waiting for the boy's answer, and followed by the others he hurried towards the village by the same path that Tengelyi had taken shortly before on his way home.

"He obviously came this way," said the ferryman. He could hardly keep up with his younger companions in the mud, and simply to slow them down drew their attention to the path. "Look here, you can see footprints . . . all fresh . . . you can still see the water that's splashed up at every step."

"And what's this?" said the coachman, bending to pick something up. "A walking-stick, and a gentleman's, with a brass pick[178]. . . he must have stolen this and lost it here . . . After him! Follow the footprints. He must be hiding in the gardens." And the whole group, led by the coachman who followed the footprints by the light of his lantern, reached the notary's garden fence.

---

178 Clearly a *fokos* is meant, a walking-stick with a small axe-blade in place of a handle.

"What the devil!" said the coachman. He'd gone a couple of paces past the garden gate, and suddenly stopped with his lantern. "I can't see any more footprints here!"

The rest took the lantern from him and also scrutinised the ground. The fresh trail that they'd been following had vanished. "Obviously, there are no more footprints to be seen," said the ferryman. "Don't suppose the ground has swallowed them up? I could still see them back there by the garden gate."

"Perhaps he's hiding behind the fence," said the coachman pensively. "You stay here, I'll climb over and look . . . what if we find him here . . ."

"Leave it, you'll get hurt," said the ferryman holding Ferkó back as he was half over-and one of the others was trying to follow him. "What business is it of ours if the lawyer's been killed? . . If only the devil had taken him sooner I wouldn't have to pay a hundred and fifty a year now." But the coachman, certainly not driven by love for Macskaházy to hunt the murderer, didn't listen to that wise advice, searched along the fence with the greatest care and came back convinced that the criminal's trail had been lost. He was about to climb back when one of the ferryman's sons, who was standing by the gate, noticed that footprints could also be seen on the path from the garden to the house. The coachman ran there with his lantern and the others, who had meanwhile tried the gate and found it unlocked, also went in; everyone could see clearly that the trail that they'd been following led directly to the house.

"He's in the notary's house . . . perhaps he's in the shed," said the coachman; like everyone that has made a great effort for something – even though, as far as they're concerned, it's a matter of complete indifference – he would by then rather have endured anything but see all his efforts wasted, "let's go in and take a look."

"What are you thinking of!" said the ferryman holding him back as he moved off. "You aren'tgoing to search for the criminal on the notary's premises?"

"And why not?" came the answer. "Don't you know that there's been a number of criminals here before? Our young master was shot here."

"But you're obviously forgetting that Master Tengelyi's house is a nobleman's curia," said the ferryman.

"I don't care!" said the coachman, going further in. "When we were looking for Viola we searched this house, and the *szolgabíró* himself was in charge."

"Yes, but those were gentry," said the ferryman. "We shall be booted out."

"We shall see!... I'm His Worship's liveried coachman, and I'd like to see the notary that'll throw me out of his house!" And with that Ferkó without further hesitation, accompanied by the two that had come with him from the mansion, went straight into the yard, while the ferryman and his son, muttering under his breath that it wouldn't do any harm for those stuck-up servants to get a good thrashing just for once, stayed behind.

But great though Ferkó's courage was, when Tengelyi (who had only just returned and hadn't even taken off his burka) suddenly emerged from his room on hearing the noise, came into the yard and asked loudly what they were doing there, he was taken aback and at the first moment rendered speechless, and only after a pause was able to say that Macskaházy had been killed and they had been following the murderer's footprints, which had led them there.

I won't describe the feeling that filled Tengelyi's breast at that moment . . . He remembered Viola's letter, and could have no doubt that the lawyer had been murdered by the hapless man, probably in order to take the documents off him . . . and he shuddered at the thought that albeit unwittingly he'd been the cause of murder. For all their lack of couth, the coachman and his companions saw the effect that the news had on Tengelyi, and looked at one another in amazement, while he, the candle trembling in his hand, once he had recovered from the surprise enquired how and when the murder had been committed.

"We went after him," said the coachman, then looked at Tengelyi's boots which were muddy to the ankle, then turned to his companions in the greatest consternation, "he ran in front of me to the Tisza, I saw him clearly . . . and from there we've followed his footprints."

"That is, begging your pardon," said the ferryman, "that we've followed a clear trail, it's as true as we're standing here; but whether that was the criminal's trail I certainly don't know . . . and I told the others here not to go in because I know the house is a curia, but . . ."

"You're mad," said Tengelyi in the greatest agitation, "if you think the murderer's in my house, search by all means, don't leave any stone unturned."

Slowly the other occupants of the house were woken by the noise. Erzsébet and Vilma dressed quickly and Tengelyi, lantern in hand, went from room to room, to the attic and the stable with his followers, until all were convinced that there was no stranger in the house . . . Meanwhile a messenger came to summon Tengelyi to the mansion, and he went off with the rest.

428

"Did you see," said the coachman, as he was followed behind with the ferryman, "the way the notary trembled when he heard that the lawyer had been killed?"

"How could I not have!" said he. "I've got eyes."

"And then, his boots were muddy up to the ankles," went on the coachmen.

"Very surprising, the weather we've been having!" said the ferryman, surprised at Ferkó's strange remark.

"I swear by God, if I hadn't known the notary these ten years . . ."

"You don't think it was he that killed the lawyer?" the ferryman interrupted him and stood still.

"As we didn't find anybody else in the house, I might certainly think so, my friend," said the coachman quietly.

"Have you gone mad?" asked the ferryman, and with that the two of them, sunk in thought, walked on side by side in silence.

XXX

If people were as generous with all that they owned as they with their thoughts, life would be a real pleasure! As far as our other possessions are concerned we're delighted to exclude others; everybody is only happy to inform of their thoughts, and if they think of something they don't rest until they have shared their freshest fruit with their fellow men. Let something happen, or indeed be merely spoken of, and at once exchange of thoughts strikes up, the most equitable exchange in the world, in which he is a rare man that gives anything other than worthless things, and rarer still that receives anything else in return. We believe that the bliss that awaits us in heaven consists largely of the singing of the angels and the blessed; on this earth human pleasures are by nature to be sought on a lesser scale, and beyond doubt are to be found in the fact that we can talk . . . As the bee can draw honey from every flower, so can people extract all the sweetness of a long conversation from the most disagreeable of subjects, and not only those rare creatures that are blessed by nature and to whom heaven has given its own thoughts, but all of us; because ideas, like money, seem to increase by circulation, and the purse gives a louder sound when it is not over-full. Just as the gold which Croesus once displayed to the Greek philosopher was probably not lost but was minted into coinage, and perhaps even as I write is perhaps being counted out by some banker, his heart throbbing with pleasure; so it is with our ideas too. The thought that occurred to a single person has since been used by millions; thousands have thought themselves rich, thousands have boasted of their possession, because the thought is his that makes use of it. The man who clinks large sums is considered rich, even though every coin has passed through a thousand hands before his. There's another way too in which money and talk are similar, and as I've strayed onto the subject, why not speak of it? . . . Just as in those countries where gold and silver grow in the soil, we seldom find much noble bronze in circulation, and in our blessed country we pay in paper, while in France and England they weigh our gold coins; so it is with thoughts too . . . he that wishes to profit by them doesn't fatigue himself by seeking them but gathers up what others bring to light by the sweat of their brows; the whole value of money consists in our having something to sell, and of thought in our having something to say; the novelty of ideas, indeed the pleasantness of subjects, is a matter of indifference; it's the conversation itself that gives pleasure.

In keeping with this characteristic of the human species, my readers can't be surprised if they don't find the occupants of the Tiszarét mansion as depressed at Macskaházy's murder as at first they may have supposed. The sense of horror which his death caused has abated, and the event now has remained the subject of inexhaustible conversation, in which the whole household have taken part by the kitchen fire. Although almost all the staff immediately rushed after the criminal and hurried almost as one to Macskaházy's room, there was none of them that didn't have a different account, and until morning, although the company had remained together, the incident was presented in almost as many ways as Hannibal's crossing of the Alps . . . Everybody proposed a different hypothesis, to prove which they exerted themselves to the utmost.

The greatest variation in these accounts concerned the dying man's last words. The under-cook, with the support of the butler and everyone else, stated on oath that when asked who had killed him Macskaházy had simply answered with the name of Tengelyi. The cook, who, like many an honest man in a debate, found it impossible when confronted by such arrant falsehood to restrict himself to the truth, felt it necessary to say something rather more, and likewise called on God and all his saints to bear witness that the lawyer was only saying that he wanted to speak to Tengelyi, with which the the kitchen-hand, the footman and a nurserymaid agreed completely. Tengelyi arrived at the house before dawn – the court officials had sealed the room in which the crime had been committed – and the news that the dying man's last word had been his name had a perceptible effect on him; this enlivened the debate not a little. In the morning the *szolgabíró* arrived; the cook and the under-cook had relied all night on his authority.

"Our lawyer's been killed," said the cook, while assisting Nyúzó from his carriage.

"Poor gentleman!" interrupted the under-cook, "and the last thing he said . . ."

At this point the cook reported with great pleasure that the murderer had been caught.

"It was me that caught him," said the *hajdú*.

"That's right, he was caught in the stoke-hole," added the nursery-maid,

"He hasn't been caught!" said the under-cook, rather loudly.

431

"It's the Jewish glazier, you know him, Your Honour," the cook interrupted; as the highest ranking person present he felt himself specially called to be the one to inform the *szolgabíró*.

"Only he escaped," Ferkó the coachman chipped in, almost pushing to the front. "We chased him as far as the Tisza and there . . ."

"He's down in the cellar," said the footman, "I tied him up hand and foot, so . . ."

"Yes, Your Honour," the coachman went on, "the way he ran we couldn't catch him, and when he got to the bushes . . ."

"The door's well and truly sealed, I've locked him up . . . "said the cook proudly.

"It wasn't the Jew, never in his life," the under-cook butted in.

"It certainly was the Jew," exclaimed cook, nursery-maid and kitchen-hand all together.

"Well, if it was the Jew," exclaimed the under-cook, "why did the lawyer shake his head like this?" And with that she began to shake her head alarmingly, while the others outdid one another in declaring that it was and was not the Jew.

"Have you all lost your senses?" the *szolgabíró's* stentorian voice eventually trumpeted forth above the din. "You can't hear yourself think with this row going on!"

All fell silent, and only the under-cook continued to shake her head, and whispered into the clerk's ear – he was standing next to her and she hoped that he would be a more tolerant listener – that the lawyer had done just that when he saw the Jew after he'd been stabbed.

"My dear cook," said Nyúzó at length in a gentler tone, addressing that worthy, "mightn't we have some breakfast? We're absolutely frozen." To which the response came that Their Honours should go to his nice warm room, and he would shortly bring the *slivovic* and bread necessary for breakfast to sustain them until the coffee, or whatever they might like, was being prepared.

While the under-cook complained that no one would listen to her and went grumpily to her room and the coffee-making was entrusted to the nursery-maid, the cook gave Nyúzó a full account of events as he viewed them. In his opinion there was no question that Macskaházy had been killed by the Jew; as soon as he had committed the deed and heard people, even before he could steal anything, he'd hidden himself in the stoke-hole, from where he'd been dragged by the *hajdú*. "If one has only a slight conception of murder," he continued his account, "one can see clearly that it can't be otherwise. Every murderer, if caught in the act,

432

hides under a barrel or a board, or in some stoke-hole, I've read about it in a hundred tales; but that woman knows nothing and argues the toss."

"Of course, cook, you're right," said Nyúzó after his second glass, and as he sank into his thoughts he abstractedly poured himself another. "The matter's clear, there's nothing to investigate."

"Didn't I say so straight away?" said the clerk, nodding his head in expression of the greatest self-satisfaction.

"What did you say straight away, Bandi?" asked Nyúzó, who could only remember that he'd hardly been able to make his clerk get up.

"Well, I said," replied he, "that probably some worthless villain had committed this murder."

"Quite. Bandi said that at once," said Nyúzó, "but I wouldn't have thought that this Jew would have the nerve to do such a thing. Poor Macskaházy, he was a good, blessed man."

"And only the other day when he was playing tarok," said Kenyházy emotionally, "he took Zátonyi's *ultimó* with five taroks . . . and now that Jew!"

"But the Jew will deny everything," said the cook, placing before his guests the coffee – or what passed for coffee – which had just been brought in, "if Your Honour doesn't succeed."

"Not succeed?" asked Nyúzó, looking crossly at the cook for even daring to think such a thing. "Not succeed with a useless Jew! I've been serving the county these twenty years, and I've always extracted what I've wanted."

"Of course, everybody knows that," the cook excused himself. "Everybody's envious of this ward, having Your Honour; but these Jews can be dreadfully stubborn."

"If he won't talk," said Nyúzó, pushing aside his empty cup, "he'll shout."

"Pali from the front, the *hajdú* from behind," said the clerk, "and I'll be at the table with pen and ink. You'll see something, cook, I'll wager, the like of which you've never seen. When we surround somebody they won't hold out for long, I'll guarantee."

The coffee-drinking came to an end. The two officials had restricted themselves to that rather in order to be considered men of culture. Kenyházy was astonished, as always on such occasions, at the stupidity of people in Hungary who lowered themselves to coffee when the best wines and *pálinka* were available, and he washed away the memory of the unpleasant drink with a glass of *slivovic*. Nyúzó lit his pipe, which

433

he had put aside while there was coffee, cleared his throat, walked up and down a few times, and informed the cook that he might have the prisoner brought in and that the *hajdú* should stand ready. The cook left, scarcely able to contain his curiosity, and Kenyházy cheerfully – because he'd found a couple of sheets of paper in the cupboard on which to record the voluntary confession without having to use paper that would have to be accounted for to the county – sharpened some pens and prepared for his task.

My readers are familiar with the way in which Nyúzó usually treats suspicious persons that are brought before him, and so won't expect me to give a lengthy account of the examination of the Jewish glazier. There are, it's true, those that believe that our method should be suited to the character of those that we have to deal with; but this apparently general principle is, for the most part, applied to persons in whose cases we might later regret our method . . . as far as lower orders are concerned, almost everyone regards their method as a Procrustes-bed, which fits all equally. If the individual who falls into their hands doesn't fit it, so much the worse for him; they'll pull and push or break until he can fit in . . . what do they care how he likes it? and Nyúzó was one of this majority. The magistrate was one of those for whom nature, it seems, has made it an obligation always to form a contrast with the person that he spoke to; if the latter holds his head up and straightens his back, they stoop; if the other stoops, they sense their dignity, raise their heads and lean backwards. Such personalities, which I can't explain better than in this geometrical fashion, aren't uncommon in Hungary, and my readers will perhaps even find some among their acquaintances to whom my characterisation applies; for my part, alas! I've encountered many whose treatment of people can only be approved when, instead of the pride that they've displayed towards their inferiors, they've adopted the craven humility with which they're always clothed towards their superiors. If we add together the necessary amounts of respect, more than which is shown to one and less to the other, and re-divide the whole between the parties, it may well turn out that each has been given their due.

The Jewish glazier couldn't expect from Nyúzó treatment different from that given to Peti on the Turk's Hill; indeed, his fate was more grievous, as there was no one there to take his part; and both Kenyházy and the cook (who hated Jews) did their utmost to stir Nyúzó up against his hapless prisoner. But although every question was so contrived as seemingly to contain its answer, the Jew steadfastly denied the murder.

Nyúzó harboured no prejudice against Jews. His antipathy went by no means as far as that of the cook, who naturally could feel no sympathy for a people who despised *hurka* and *kolbász*, turned from ham in disgust, wouldn't so much as hear of *kocsonya*;[179] some, indeed, reproached him with partiality towards the Lord's chosen people, and it was said that it was almost as hard to win a case against a Jew before him as in (I forget for the moment which county). But everything has its limits, and even if the magistrate viewed the richer part of the Jewish people from the enlightened standpoint of our time, it doesn't follow that he might behave in accordance with those principles towards an individual who, like the glazier, carried all his fragile wealth on his back and owned not a single jewel other than the diamond with which he cut his panes. Emancipation is making great strides in Hungary, it can't be denied. The Jews – as they can't emancipate themselves directly – are slowly beginning to emancipate the Christians by all sorts of promises, and that, as is well known, comes to the same thing in terms of outcome. At this time the Jewish population of Hungary is like a mountain the foot of which is still shrouded in gloom, while the risen sun shines on the gilded summit . . . and if the glazier belonged to this part of his people his situation would be quite different; and so, since he might not buy anyone's wool or acorns – indeed, didn't even deal in tobacco, he couldn't count on any favours, and his judge certainly had not forgotten that his forebears had crucified our Redeemer.

After trying every form of questioning on his prisoner – including the surrounding referred to by Kenyházy, for which the *hajdú* and his stick were summoned – Nyúzó paced up and down the room in the greatest rage. "I'll have you put in the *farkasgúzs*,[180] I'll have you beaten within an inch of your life, if you won't speak!" he shouted, prodding the unfortunate man in the chest once again; the Jew trembled and repeated his plea of innocence in a quavering voice.

"Innocent!" the magistrate laughed aloud. "Is this what innocence looks like?" at which Kenyházy and the cook looked at the Jew and also burst out laughing, while from Jancsi the glazier's one eye big tears poured down his face. It must be confessed that there was nothing in his exterior that entitled him to be considered innocent by anyone. His

179 *Hurka* and *kolbász* are types of pork sausage; *kocsonya* is pork aspic.
180 'Wolf-truss', a form of torture. The victim's knees were placed together, his hands were tied and he was made to squat with his arms round his legs. A bar was then inserted between his arms and the back of his knees, rendering all movement impossible.

red hair, which had become wet in the cellar where he'd spent the night, hung even lower on his forehead than usual; his clothes and beard were even dirtier than usual, and his ugly features were made even wilder by the pain that his roped hands were causing him . . . a malefactor might not be depicted otherwise . . . but nevertheless the Jew constantly declared that he was innocent. "But I beg you, Honourable *főszolgabíró*, sir," he whined, "and honourable clerk, sir, and you too, cook, who've known me for a long time . . ."

"Yes, for the worthless scoundrel that you are," said the cook. "Every time I've got you to do something you've swindled me."

"But I humbly beg, I haven't swindled anybody!" sighed Jancsi. "There are big panes in the mansion, glass is very expensive, and I . . ."

"Prattling about yourself again, you gallows-bait!" exclaimed the magistrate. "I'll ask you for the last time, and if you don't confess you'll see what'll happen to you: why did you kill the lawyer?"

"I certainly didn't kill him," replied the prisoner tearfully, "why ever should I have? Master Macskaházy was a nice kind gentleman to me and if he was alive you wouldn't treat me like this."

"If you hadn't killed him, you mean," Nyúzó retorted.

"I didn't kill him," Jancsi sobbed on, "When cook here took me to Master Macskaházy and asked whether it was I that had killed him, he couldn't speak, but he kept on shaking his head. You tell them, cook, sir."

"That's right," said the cook. "When I took this villain to the bedside and asked the lawyer if this was who'd killed him he shook his head. But who knows what he meant by it? Perhaps he didn't know what he was doing."

"No, he never," said the Jew imploringly. "How could he not have known what he was doing when you asked him twice and the poor, blessed man kept on shaking his head?"

"That'll very likely be," said Kenyházy, "what the under-cook was going on about when we arrived."

"Yes, the under-cook," said the prisoner, "and all the servants were there and saw him shaking his head; he was a blessed man! He did nothing else as soon as I came into the room but shake his head all the time."

"Somebody call in that under-cook," said Nyúzó; he remembered the woman's strange behaviour and the way she'd not stopped shaking her head.

"I'm sure it's a mistake for Your Honour to bother with her," said the cook. "She'll chatter like a market-woman, and when all's said and done it's certain that nobody but this damned Jew killed the lawyer."

"That I know," said Nyúzó with dignity, "but with any confession the forms have to be observed," and with that he sent the *hajdú* for the under-cook.

While her natural enemy the cook was present at the examination, Katalin, or as she was commonly called, Mrs Kata – because as she herself frequently remarked, no one gives a poor widow her due, and even her name is cut short as if she were a mere kitchen-hand – had been talking constantly with her adherents, that is to say the steward and the general maid, about the magistrate's stupidity in not so much as questioning anybody that had some sense. "The cook's bound to mislead them . . . there's no more treacherous man in the world! He's the one that causes all the arguments with Her Ladyship, and now he's going to blame it all on the Jew when he's as innocent as a new-born babe. When he was taken to Macskaházy's bedside . . . etc."

Scarcely had the *hajdú* come in with the magistrate's order for the lady to appear before him as a witness than instead of those complaints he became a fine man . . . and Kata straightened her kerchief, using a little mirror in the kitchen window, and informed those present of her belief that truth would certainly now out – then did as she was bidden and appeared before the examiners with no few curtseys.

She'd never before appeared before a court as a witness, and in the first moment was taken aback as she was asked for her name and occupation, which she thought everyone knew, and for her age . . . The scornful grin that spread on the cook's lips when she admitted, in a scarcely audible voice, to being forty-two . . . and even more so when she was warned by the magistrate after those preliminary questions that she must swear to her religion and that if she departed from the truth she'd be punished: it occurred to her that this was all merely the doing of that wicked cook, who wanted to get her into trouble . . . to avoid which she stated immediately after the warning that as concerned her age she'd not seen her certificate of baptism and couldn't say for certain, but that it was her personal conviction that she was even much younger. The cook and Kenyházy burst out laughing, and a smiling Nyúzó told her that as long as she told the truth about other things she could have said that she was twenty-four . . . there was no doubt that she regretted only learning that after the event.[181]

The questions that followed: Had she known Master Macskaházy? For how long? Had she ever seen the Jew before? What did she know about

181 Kálmán Mikszáth's remark comes to mind: No Hungarian woman will admit to

437

him? and so on, did much to compensate her for the unpleasant impression that she'd felt in the first moment of questioning. She was one of those who don't conceal in the earth their God-given talent for speech. Mrs Katalin talked from morning to night simply of her own accord . . . who would expect short answers from her now, when for perhaps the first time in her life it was made her duty to speak, and the magistrate made a point of warning her to omit nothing from her account. Katalin told everything: where she'd been in service previously, how she'd come to the house, what had happened since then, when she'd first fallen out with the cook, how she'd been swindled out of a forint and twenty-four krajcárs by this same Jew when last market she'd had twelve ells of blue calico brought from Debrecen. The good woman literally omitted nothing; if she were a member of our learned society – if all those who study language are so entitled, she would have a strong claim – after that one confession her funeral oration might be written.

Nyúzó paced the room in a sour frame of mind. The clerk, who didn't feel called to write a whole bookful, laid his quill aside; the cook smiled as he looked at first the one, then the other, as if to say "Wasn't I right when I told you beforehand that questioning this woman would be useless?"

"But look here," said Nyúzó, no longer able to contain his impatience, "what do you mean by all this? Do you take me for a father confessor, or an idiot, that you're telling me your life story from the beginning to the present?"

"I beg your pardon," said she, surprised that such things might not be of interest, "Your Honour said that I shouldn't omit anything."

"I meant that you shouldn't omit anything relevant to the subject," he cut her of.

"Yes," she went on, "but if I'm asked for my name and status and I say that I'm a widow, then I've got to name my husband as well, and how long we lived together and, if you please, that we were happy, and when he died, and what of, and . . ."

"Very well, very well," the magistrate cut in, inwardly cursing her chatter. "But now tell me, briefly if you can and only answering this question: is it true that when the cook brought this accursed Jew to the dying man, Macskaházy shook his head?"

"Quite right," replied Katalin, giving the cook a defiant look. "Of course he did, and if Your Honour had seen the way he shook it; since

---

being less than fourteen or more than forty!

438

I was at my husband's death-bed – poor man, God rest him, he'd been a cook . . ."

"Yes, yes, we know," the magistrate intervened impatiently, "he died of dropsy; but now just tell me, my good woman, whether it's true that when the cook put the question to him a second time, he shook his head again?"

"Yes, and Your Honours wouldn't believe," she went on, "the way he shook his head; and as I say, just like my late husband, God rest him, I was at his side the last fourteen days and nights . . ."

"Who can say, perhaps by then he didn't know what he was doing?" the cook interrupted.

"Who? My husband unconscious?" said she. "My husband was conscious right to to his last moment, he couldn't speak any longer, poor man, and nobody could understand him, only me, but what he wanted . . ."

"Who's talking about your husband? "Nyúzó cut in. "God grant him peace, he must have had enough to endure in this world! The only question is: when Macskaházy was asked and shook his head, did he know what he was doing?"

"Didn't know what he was doing?" she asked. "Excuse me, the only sort of person who'd say that" – she gave the cook a look which he understood – "is the idiot that can't understand somebody that can't speak. I could understand my husband to the last, when the water reached his chest and he coudn't speak any longer. He used to make such pitiful eyes at me, as if to say like he used to 'Thank you, dear'. But to get back to the lawyer," she added, drying her eyes, realising that Nyúzó was impatient, "how could the poor man not have known, because when he was asked he could still speak."

"He spoke? What did he say?" asked Nyúzó sharply.

"Well, not much, that's a fact," she replied, "but distinctly, we could all hear that were there. When the cook asked "Who's killed you?" all he said was 'Tengelyi'; after that the death-rattle came on at once."

"Tengelyi?!" exclaimed Nyúzó and his clerk in surprise and almost in unison. "That's odd!"

"How can Your Honours listen to such useless gossip?" said the cook impatiently. "This woman would have her own father sentenced to death so that her tongue could wag."

"Useless gossip is it, what I say?" exclaimed the under-cook. "Well then, why is His Honour questioning me? Why is the clerk taking it down? If I'm a burden to His Honour I didn't see or hear anything; if I weren't questioned I certainly wouldn't have said a word to anybody."

439

The magistrate could scarcely get a word in to warn the cook not to upset the witness; and he asked her again whether she remembered clearly that Macskaházy had actually named Tengelyi before dying.

"Of course I remember!" she continued her interrupted statement. "The lawyer, poor gentleman, spoke as clearly as we're speaking now. He said 'Tengelyi', all the servants were there, everyody heard."

"Nobody's denying that," the cook interrupted, who couldn't restrain himself despite all warning. "The question is, though, when did he name Master Tengelyi? Why did he name him? And here I say . . ."

"He named him when the Jew was brought to his bedside and he was asked if it was he that had killed him," the under-cook broke in; she re-opened the former disagreement, and was still quite insistent. "First he shook his head, then he named Tengelyi, then . . ."

"That's not correct!" the cook interrupted. "He named Tengelyi first and only shook his head after that."

"And I say the opposite!" shouted Katalin even louder, "and anybody who says different is lying, even if they swear a hundred oaths. I can call the whole staff to give evidence." She turned to Nyúzó, her face ablaze.

"And so can I call them to witness," replied the cook.

"To clear the whole matter up," said Nyúzó at length, "there's really nothing for it but to call for more evidence . . ." and while the *hajdú* was sent to summon those of the servants who'd been present when Macskaházy died, the cook and the under-cook continued their quarrel. Nyúzó pointed out to Kenyházy that he should note especially that, according to the under-cook's testimony, when questioned about his attacker Macskaházy had named Tengelyi.

If the magistrate had called before him the other witnesses – the *hajdú* found them all in the kitchen and brought them back to the room – to clarify the point in question, no one was more disappointed in his hopes than he. True, instead of two witnesses he now had six before him, but he was unable to reach among them that criterion of truth which we look for in a majority; the steward and the footman now sided with the under-cook, and the maid and the nursery-maid with the cook – the votes were equal in number on both sides.

"In the end," said Nyúzó shrugging his shoulders after listening calmly to the racket for a while, "opinion is completely divided. Whether Macskaházy raised his head before or after doesn't concern us; what matters is, that when the question was put to him: Who stabbed you? he clearly named the notary, and as far as that's concerned you're all in agreement. That, I hope, you noted down?" This last to Kenyházy, who was still writing and nodded.

The disputing parties looked at each other in surprise; Katalin, whose intention it had not been to arouse suspicion against Tengelyi, and who had only meant to confirm her statement that the lawyer had really shaken his head first and then named Tengelyi, was now alarmed at what the magistrate said and fell silent; only the cook retained sufficient presence of mind to point out to Nyúzó that he'd never agreed with that statement and now too said that the dying man had in fact named Tengelyi, but not when asked about the murderer. Everyone nodded in agreement, especially Katalin, who could see the consequences of her words, and said, near to tears, that she was a poor widow, the cook certainly understood these things better than she did, and that furthermore she'd seen the lawyer gentleman's bloody chest and been so alarmed that she hadn't really known what was going on around her. The magistrate, however, silenced the hapless witness, who wanted at all costs to withdraw her earlier account: what had been said had been taken down by his clerk, and if she withdrew or altered the things that aroused suspicion of Tengelyi she would see what would happen to her for daring to lie before the court. At that she shuddered and made for the stove, and relieved her feelings only in profound sighs lest she might say something else that she would later regret.

The cook was one of Tengelyi's greatest admirers, and despite all the respect that he bore for the magistracy he was visibly distressed at Nyúzó's last words. "I don't know," said he, "what reason there would be in what Your Honour has heard so far for suspecting the notary at all."

"What reason?" said the magistrate with a scathing look at the speaker. "That is in any case not for you to judge; there is, however, certainly reason; when this woman and another two witnesses clearly state that Macskaházy, as he was dying . . . and evidence given in the moment of death is worth as much as if it were supported by a hundred oaths . . . named Tengelyi as his murderer."

"I never said that," sighed Katalin, coming forward from the stove. "I only said that the gentleman first shook his head, then spoke; it could never have entered my head that Master Tengelyi could come under suspicion because of that."

"Because after all it's true," said the cook quite drily, because as a nobleman he took amiss the way in which Nyúzó had spoken, "anyone that cares to can have a suspicion, and it's also true that I shan't be asked: only

441

I think that when it's a matter of murder, a man like Master Tengelyi can't come under suspicion after nothing but wild talk."

"But didn't you yourself say," asked Nyúzó sharply, "that Macskaházy named the notary?"

"That's quite true," replied the cook, "but it's nothing to wonder at as Master Macskaházy had been at daggers drawn with Tengelyi all his life. A lot of people think that he didn't treat the notary as he should have; even yesterday they had a big argument . . . perhaps in his last moment he was talking to himself?"

"Really! So even yesterday afternoon they had a big argument? Note that as well, Bandi!" "It's true! All their lives the two were deadly enemies. And so you say, cook, that even yesterday they had a big argument?"

The cook couldn't deny that that was so; the others likewise confirmed the statement; under-cook, however, thinking that it would help Tengelyi, related what had happened between the notary and the lawyer with the same exaggerations that it had been recounted in the village.

"Strange, very strange!" said Nyúzó, addressing the clerk. "The notary quarrels with Macskaházy and leaves him uttering the most terrible threats. As the under-cook says, the notary swore that my poor friend would die at his hand . . . and then that very same night we find him murdered in his room. I hope you've underlined that, Bandi?" said he to his clerk, who was forcing his face into an expression of concentration, lest it should register the pleasure that he felt at being able to get Tengelyi into trouble.

The cook wanted to speak, but when he saw that Nyúzó was paying him no attention he merely remarked in an undertone to the clerk that if not the Jew but somebody else had killed the lawyer, he didn't know what he might have been looking for in the stoke-hole; to which the magistrate, instead of replying, addressed the same question to the Jew: who was it that had advised him, helped or encouraged him to commit this crime? "Because no one other than you did it, you worthless dog," he added crossly, "there's no doubt about it. Confess the truth! You see, we're on the trail of your accomplices. If you name them without further delay you may be able to help yourself. And if you go on denying it for another moment . . ." at this point the magistrate said no more, but raised his right hand; the Gypsy was no palmist, but he could read his future on it sufficiently to almost instinctively raise one shoulder and shield one cheek, and what everyone anticipated was about to happen, when at that moment the sound of a carriage drew the magistrate to the window.

442

As we know, the *alispán* had spent the previous day on his near-by estate, and as soon as he received the news that murder had taken place in his house he left for Tiszarét with his wife and daughter, arriving at almost the same moment as Serer, who had been sent for in the night to carry out a medical examination. With the exception of Etelka, everyone went at once to the scene of the interrogation, where for the time being the prisoner was left in peace while the master of the house and his wife were being received.

The *alispán* and especially his wife were visibly most upset.

"It's monstrous!" said Réty, on hearing from the magistrate a full account of the event. "A murder like this, and in my own house with all these servants around; sheer effrontery! My poor wife's completely beside herself! It was as if she had a feeling yesterday that some misfortune was going to occur, I've never seen her so agitated."

"Don't say such a thing," said Mrs Réty testily, and a strange quivering could be seen around her lips. "You'll make me out to be a lunatic that can foresee everything. I wasn't feeling very well, and I don't today either, that's all."

The magistrate and his clerk expressed their regrets. Serer immediately reached out to take her pulse. She, however, was looking at the Jew, on whose face there was a strange expression, almost like scorn, but as no one was paying any attention to him no one noticed.

"No one could have perpetrated the crime," said Réty, "who didn't know this house quite well; the strangest thing is that, as I hear, no robbery was involved."

"We don't know yet," said Nyúzó. "The servants say that the murdered man's watch and wallet were found in his room, but we haven't carried out a more thorough search because, as Macskaházy was Your Worship's legal adviser, we thought that his effects might include documents that affect the family, and the court officials have sealed the door and we've left it locked until Your Worship came back or gave some orders concerning it."

"You've done the right thing," interposed the alispán's wife. "Macskaházy had all sorts of legal documents that only concern me . . . I'll go upstairs myself."

"Your Honour," said Serer, clasping his hands together, "in your unwell condition! What are you thinking of?"

"That's my business," she replied drily.

"It would be better if Your Honour didn't go up," the cook agreed most respectfully, "the body's still there and . . ."

"The body? said Mrs Réty, not concealing her horror, "take it away," she added, pulling herself together, "then I'll go up. I know best where he used to keep his papers, and I shan't feel easy until I've convinced myself that nothing has been lost."

Serer, the clerk and the servants left to do as she wished. She paced up and down in the greatest agitation.

"Thank goodness!" said Nyúzó to Réty, who was standing beside him, deep in thought, "at least we've caught the culprit. This Jew," he added, gesturing to the prisoner, "was pulled out of the stoke-hole immediately after the event."

"Jancsi the glazier?" said Mrs Réty, coming to a sudden halt. "That's impossible!. . . "I know that he was always a great supporter of Macskaházy."

"My dear," said Réty, "that proves nothing. I'm sorry to say that there've been many instances of such wretched creatures committing crimes even against their greatest benefactors."

"All the more so," the magistrate cut in, "as it's beyond all doubt that the Jew was acting as the instrument of someone else's vengeance."

At that moment the alispán's wife grew so pale that her husband and Nyúzó asked in unison whether she felt unwell. To which she only asked whether the Jew had confessed to the crime.

"In the strictest sense of the word 'confess'," replied the magistrate, "he hasn't yet; however, that's the least of my worries. I'll get it out of him, however stubborn he remains; and the indications are such that there can be no question of who's guilty," and at this point he related with great satisfaction everything that in his view discredited Tengelyi.

The effect that the magistrate's statement had on both Réty and his wife can scarcely be imagined. The former shook his head and said that such a thing could not be supposed of Tengelyi; the latter looked suddenly relieved and only remarked that as such deadly hostility had existed between Macskaházy and him there was no telling what a passionate man like Tengelyi might be capable of.

"We'll get to the truth," said Nyúzó smugly, "I'll wring it out of the Jew, however much a scoundrel he may be."

"If this is how I'm to be treated," said Jancsi, looking fixedly at the alispán's wife, "I'll certainly confess everything."

"Treated? You'll see how you're treated," said Nyúzó crossly, "if you don't talk well and truly we'll introduce you the farkasgúzs."

"Her Ladyship's known me a long time," said the Jew in a pleading tone, "I've always been an honest man, but His Honour will torture me

444

so that in the end I'll accept everything. The *hajdú*'ll beat me from behind and His Worship himself will poke me in the chest and tear my beard. I'll involve just anybody so as not to suffer any longer."

The *alispán*'s wife called the magistrate to the window and said quietly to him that actually she thought that the Jew was innocent, and that she would think it better if no violence were used in his interrogation. Nyúzó swore by his life that the Jew was lying and that he'd treated him so far with the utmost gentleness, and could not have been more astonished at the Rétys' strange caprices. "The young ones side with Gypsies" said he to himself as he followed the *alispán* and his wife to the lawyer's room, from where the body had now been removed "and the old ones seem to favour Jews; if this goes on, the service of justice will become impossible."

On entering the room Mrs Réty couldn't conceal her feelings. The big patch of blood to be seen by the desk on one side of the room, in the middle of it the still bloody knife which the servants had replaced where it had been when they first came in and found it, the documents scattered on the floor . . . everything was a reminder of the terrible event that the room had witnessed; and on looking round at these things the *alispán*'s wife stood in the doorway horrified. "Female weakness, nothing more!" said she, when her husband and Nyúzó saw how she was affected and asked her rather to go back: "don't worry, it'll pass. Who can help it? Macskaházy was our loyal man, it hasn't yet sunk in that we've had to lose him in such a dreadful way." And with that she pulled herself together and first looked in the desk drawer, then in Macskaházy's other cupboards for the documents for which she'd done so much without so far coming into possession of them, and of which even now she could only find those few letters which, as my readers will remember, the lawyer had put away separately before he was murdered.

She was well aware that those few letters were only a small part of Vándory's documents, and she rummaged through everything in the greatest impatience; in vain! She was now beginning to think that Macskaházy had burnt the rest and kept just that couple of letters to use in order to extract the notes of hand that he wanted, and she was satisfied, when the conversation between her husband and Nyúzó attracted her attention: they were still examining all the objects found in the room.

"As I say, Your Worship," said Nyúzó, "these bloodied documents which we've found on the floor are all Tengelyi's, the two letters there on the desk are to Master János Tengelyi, one addresses him as His Worship, the other as noble and gallant, and here I find on the floor an ac

445

count, half covered in blood, which is entirely in the notary's writing. Books for Vilma, eight forints," he read on, "a dress for Erzsébet, ten forints; payment to workmen etc. etc. Please see for yourself."

"There's no denying it," said Réty, as he took the note from which Nyúzó had read. "This is Tengelyi's writing; but how does it come to be here?"

"As far as I'm concerned," replied Nyúzó with a sigh, "after what I heard at the questioning, perhaps I might say."

"Impossible! Quite impossible!" said Réty, who, for all his faults, was too honourable a man to suppose such a thing of the notary. "You can't be speaking seriously, magistrate. You know I don't like Tengelyi, nor have I reason to; but of all the people I know, he's certainly the last of whom I can suppose such a thing. I can't make it all out."

Mrs Réty, whose close attention the conversation had attracted, understood very well how it all made sense. Once she knew that the documents stolen from Tengelyi's house were in Macskaházy's possession it was quite natural that individual letters to the notary and other documents were there too; what she couldn't understand was that if, as she had begun to believe, Macskaházy had burnt the documents other than the letters which had been found, how could it happen that Tengelyi's individual letters were found scattered in his room? And letters, at that, which were of no importance to anyone apart from the notary, and the thought flashed through her mind that those documents might have been stolen nevertheless – either by Tengelyi himself or someone else doing his bidding. She was confirmed in that thought when she heard that skeleton keys had been found on the Jew, but no stolen items. "The documents have been stolen either by the notary or by someone else engaged by him for the purpose," she thought on, "indeed the man is not hard to find that will maliciously suppose of someone else that which he feels prepared to do himself." And so she too didn't consider Tengelyi incapable of committing the act – "the safest way in which the documents will become harmless is if suspicion of the notary is increased more and more. Tengelyi himself stated that his documents were in Macskaházy's possession, and now, even if they came to hand, he couldn't proceed with them without strengthening the suspicion that had arisen against him."

Those thoughts had passed through her mind in an instant, and Mrs Réty had made up her mind how to act; when she picked up one of the bloodied documents that had been placed on the desk and looked at it,

446

she declared that she was convinced that the affair must at all events be stringently investigated, if only because someone else was accused of the murder, and she, for her part, thought the Jew completely innocent. "It's possible," she added, "that the villain came to the house to steal, but if no trace of blood has been found on him it's impossible that he had any part in the murder . . . there's blood everywhere in the room."

"Investigate! Yes", said Réty. He was so aroused by the idea that the man who in his youth had been his best friend was being accused of such wickedness that in that moment he forgot the submissiveness that he showed to his wife at other times. "I'll investigate, investigate the business myself, so that the vile slander that's being fabricated against Tengelyi may be shown for the complete nonsense that it is this very day."

"I'm surprised at your unaccustomed enthusiasm," said Mrs Réty in a quiet but sour tone, as she and her husband went back down the stairs to the cook's room, followed by Nyúzó. "You haven't usually taken Tengelyi's side so much before now."

"Take his side!" said the *alispán*, also quietly, but in the greatest agitation. "I think we've persecuted that man more than we'll be able to account for in the presence of God!. . . But everything has its limits . . . That man was once my friend, lived for years in my house, and all in all did us no harm that we haven't amply repaid . . . and for him to be accused of a crime that carries the death penalty . . . it's more than I can endure in silence."

The *alispán*'s wife could see that he wasn't in the mood for further discussion of the subject, and she merely remarked that there could be no question of slander about it all, and that for her part she only wanted the indications, which so far all pointed to Tengelyi, to be accounted for otherwise. To that he replied, as he entered the room, that her wish in that respect was surely about to be satisfied.

Serer had by this time returned from examining the body with the clerk, walked up and down and commented on the size of the wounds; the doctor, knowing that the murder had only been committed by a poor little Jew, considered them to be of such a nature as likely to result in death; whereas *vice versa*, in cases where the accused was of higher social class, he usually testified that the deceased had not died because of his wounds but from a stroke suffered at the same time, or some internal disorder. The prisoner with the *hajdú* at his side stood in their previous places, and the former looked around anxiously, waiting in the greatest apprehension for his interrogation to continue.

447

The *alispán* summoned the servants once again, and after reminding them of the consequences of their statements enquired again about the circumstances of Macskaházy's death. The under-cook burst into tears, but couldn't deny that it had seemed to her as if the lawyer had named Tengelyi when the cook had asked him about the murderer, but that she had surely been mistaken, she was only a silly woman who misunderstood everything. The steward and the footman gave the same evidence, and although the rest stood by their previous conflicting statements no one denied that when the Jew was brought to him the dying man had shaken his head and said nothing but the name Tengelyi the whole time, as likewise it was testified by them all that in the evening before his murder the lawyer had exchanged harsh words with the notary and been driven out of the house by him with a walking-stick.

"But surely the Jew must know everything," said the *alispán*, as he walked up and down for a while, deep in thought. "He was found in the stoke-hole, he can't deny that; if he wasn't a party to the murder, he must have heard everything. You good-for-nothing!" said he, turning to the Jew, "What were you after in your hiding-hole?"

"Come to steal, hadn't you, you villain?" Mrs Réty butted in, clearly in a great rage. "Deny it if you dare, after being found with skeleton keys."

The Jew had long ago realised that suspicion was turning to Tengelyi. He seized the opening that was offered, fell to his knees and admitted that he had in fact come to steal. "Your Ladyship's daughter's got all sorts of valuable things," said he pleadingly, "I caught sight of them the other day when I was mending the windows . . . I'm a poor, unfortunate man, and I thought if I could only get some of them I'd do myself some good. The young lady wasn't at home . . . I beg you, Your Honours, have pity on me, I'll never do it again, I'll be an honest man."

"A likely story!" the magistrate cut him short, smiling scornfully. "Now, of course, he'd like us to take him just for a thief, because if he were convicted of murder he'd be hanged. But all the same, it's certain that he had a hand in the killing as well."

"Really, I beg you," pleaded the Jew, still on his knees, "how could I have had anything to do with it? Because the lawyer shook his head ten times to say it wasn't me; and then, how could a weak man like me kill a strong man like Macskaházy?"

"Look here, Jew," said Nyúzó, "think up another excuse. That's the first time I've ever heard of Macskaházy being strong."

"Yes, if you please," the prisoner went on, "but if you want to kill somebody, you don't go without a weapon, like I was when you found me."

"We found a big kitchen knife in the stove," interposed the cook.

"I never knew it was there," sighed the prisoner, "perhaps it belongs to the house and somebody left it there."

"Of course it belongs to the house!" said the cook. "You stole it in the kitchen the day before yesterday."

"But, if you please," the Jew continued, "the knife that was found, was there any blood on it? And if I'd killed the lawyer gentleman with it, wouldn't there have been blood on me as well?"

At this point the steward remarked that the Jews were very skilful, and only the other day there was one such at the house – so he said – who made everybody write their names down on paper, and scarcely had he turned round than the writing had vanished . . . who could say whether the glazier had learnt that trick? And it was well known that blood was more easily washed out than any ink.

With the exception of the clerk and the under-cook, this subtlety made no great impression in anyone, and the *alispán* himself acknowledged that after the amount of blood that Macskaházy had lost it could scarcely be supposed that the murderer wouldn't have some on his person. "But," he added, turning to the Jew, "if it wasn't you that killed him, you don't deny that you were in the stove? You must have heard everything, you must know who the murderer is."

"Of course I heard," sighed the Jew, "from beginning to end; even now I shudder when I think of it! .. Ten times I wanted to go to the poor gentleman's assistance, but first I was afraid, and then I thought that if I was found there and something terrible had happened I'd get the blame."

"So what did you hear?" Mrs Réty cut in sharply. "You're best able to say whether it was Tengelyi . . . as it seems the magistrate suspects," she added as if correcting herself, when she saw the look that her husband gave her.

"If you somehow believe," said the *alispán*, addressing the Jew once more, "that you'll help yourself by incriminating some other honest person, you're mistaken. Whatever you say, you'll remain the prime suspect."

The Jew was far too clever to accuse Tengelyi explicitly under such conditions, and to say something other than that the murderer spoke in a disguised voice, and that he only heard him ask for some documents or other. "I've heard Master Tengelyi named a couple of times," he added timorously, "but as I say, I didn't recognise the murderer. Perhaps the people who chased him can tell you more."

449

Until then Ferkó the coachman had only taken part in the questioning as a spectator, and now, when the *alispán* called for a detailed account of what had happened from these latter, he scratched his head in no little embarrassment. There are people who put boundless enthusiasm into doing everything that is not their duty . . . and Ferkó was one such. When uproar had broken out in the house he and the stable-lad, with whom he happened to be talking, had been the first to give chase to the criminal, although the stable might burn down a hundred times while he did so as he'd left a candle burning. But when his pursuit led to a result quite different from what he'd thought, and instead of catching the murderer he'd followed the trail to Tengelyi's house and finally seen the notary himself – the alertness that he'd displayed all during the chase suddenly dried up and only a single thought arose in him: wouldn't it be better if he hadn't seen anything? We can't be surprised that he had his suspicions about the notary; but either that fear which, in a country such as ours, where personal courage is not perfectly safeguarded by the law, restrains a poorer man from taking action against a stronger; or the fact that he didn't regard Macskaházy's death as such a great misfortune that it was worth upsetting the notary, to whom he too owed a debt of gratitude: Ferkó at the same time decided that he would say nothing by which suspicion of the notary would be increased; and he only related the entire incident as if he'd chased the murderer to the bank of the Tisza, there lost his trail, and returned from there with his companions to the notary's house to report the whole affair to him.

Now the coachman related the events entirely in those terms, and no doubt everyone would have been reassured by his account had the stable-lad, who was also present – he had arranged in advance with Ferkó and agreed with him perfectly – only in order to say something special and distinguish himself – not let the cat out of the bag by mentioning the walking-stick which had been discovered on the path and was in the possession of the ferryman. Then the ferryman was called and one after another the circumstances discrediting Tengelyi came out, and as those questioned – the ferryman no less than Ferkó – tried to avert suspicion from the notary, the whole business seemed so much more suspicious.

"This walking-stick, now, that you're all talking about," said Nyúzó, on whose features the greatest satisfaction was to be seen at this outcome of the examination, "where is it?"

"Well, if you please," replied the ferryman, "the stick which we found in the middle of the path as we were going from the Tisza to Master Tengelyi's house was lying there in full view."

"But where *is* it?" Nyúzó repeated the question sharply.

"Well, if you please," replied the ferryman, "I left it outside in the kitchen, I can't come into your presence carrying a walking-stick."

"Bring it in at once!" ordered the magistrate, and the ferryman went out and a couple of minutes later returned with a black walking-stick with a brass axe-blade in lieu of a knob. If a fairy had suddenly appeared among the company with its wand it could hardly have caused a greater stir than did the ferryman, who now handed the stick over to the magistrate. He in turn, his face radiant with triumph, passed it to the *alispán*, who stood there, hands clasped together, as if paralysed by surprise; Mrs Réty exchanged a few quiet words with the clerk, and the cook, as if involuntarily, breathed "That's Master Tengelyi's stick!" The ferryman and all present stood there astonished.

"You will both swear," said Nyúzó to the ferryman and the coachman, "that this is the same walking-stick that was found yesterday."

The ferryman, who had cursed himself inwardly a hundred times for not having thrown the stick into the Tisza, with all humility merely remarked that the stick was certainly the one that had been found, but that neither he nor his companions had said a word to the effect that the murderer had lost it; as it had been found near Tenglyi's garden it was very likely that the notary had dropped it that day.

To that Nyúzó merely pointed out to him that he should speak only when questioned; and he dismissed the others present with the warning that none was to dare leave the premises on pain of the severest punishment.

The servants trooped solemnly out, the prisoner was led away, and in the room there remained only Réty, his wife, the magistrate and his clerk.

"What did I say?" said Nyúzó, turning to Réty. "I think that the matter is clear."

"There can be no doubt!" said Mrs Réty, looking again at the *fokos* that had been placed on the desk, "I've seen that walking-stick in Tengelyi's hands a hundred times; and there are his initials, J.T., on the brass."

"I'm not so sure," said Réty, in great agitation. "The indications all point to Tengelyi, but there's something inside me that tells me that it's impossible!"

"But look here, Your Worship," said Nyúzó, counting off on his fingers the reasons for his suspicion: "Yesterday Tengelyi quarrelled with Macskaházy and swore vengeance. Last night Macskaházy was murdered. When he was asked as he died who'd killed him, he named Tengelyi. The

451

Jew, of whom I'm beginning to believe that he had merely come here to steal, heard the murderer demand Tengelyi's stolen documents from Macskaházy. The coachman gave chase to the criminal immediately after the crime and lost his trail for a moment on the bank of the Tisza, but when he and the ferryman continued to search they were led by footprints to the notary's room, and there he was, at midnight, still fully dressed and covered in mud, and in a state of great excitement. We find letters to Tengelyi and other papers with blood on them in Macskaházy's room . . . and now there's this walking-stick. Were there ever so many clues all together?"

"I grant you that," said the *alispán* shaking his head, "but all this is out of character for Tengelyi, I've known him these thirty years, and I'm not convinced."

"That's a bit much!" said his wife sharply. "It seems you've become the notary's bosom companion again."

"I'm not his friend," said the *alispán*, "but I'll never believe such a thing of him."

"I'll furnish further evidence," replied Nyúzó, "I'll go straight to his house and question the servants."

"But have you considered, magistrate," the *alispán* had begun, when he was interrupted by his wife with the remark that Nyúzó was right, otherwise clues could be destroyed, "that Tengelyi is a noble?"

"He calls himself a noble," his wife corrected him, "and it was decided in the assembly that until he proved his noble status you would regard him as ignoble. Go there straight away, Your Worship," this to Nyúzó, "if you had him brought here the entire village would come running, and who knows, he may be innocent after all, and I wouldn't want to embarrass him."

Nyúzó and his clerk kissed hands and left, and the *alispán* and his wife were left alone in the room.

"So do you really believe," said he solemnly, taking her hand, "that Tengelyi would be capable of such an action?"

"And why not?" asked she, fixing her eyes on him.

"But he's lived here all his life. You're as familiar with Tenglyi's character as I am myself."

"I only know one thing about Tengelyi," said she sharply, "that he's no friend of mine . . . and never fear, I'm not going to forget that!" And with that she left her husband to himself.

Réty's heart was filled with horror at seeing her soul fully exposed, and it came to him that all his life until then had been governed by the whim of that heartless creature who, even in such a moment, could not forgive. "And if Tengelyi has actually perpetrated this monstrous act," thought he, "what is it that all but forced him to it, what but the persecutions that in my despicable weakness I have permitted? And why? Oh, if only the past were in our power, or if I had ever been able to consider that all that must lead to such an outcome !. . . But now I must at least do my duty. Nyúzó realised long ago that if he harmed Tengelyi he was doing my wife a favour, and is about to bring the full severity of his office to bear on the hapless man . . . on this occasion I myself shall be on Tengelyi's side." And with that intention the *alispán* hurried at once to the notary's house.

XXXI

Although he had as yet no notion of the suspicion under which he had fallen, Tengelyi had spent the night tormented by his emotions. He'd returned home late and flung himself exhausted on his bed, but the aroused state of his spirit would grant him no rest. The conviction that the unfortunate lawyer had been murdered by Viola – the feeling that as he himself had known of the outlaw's presence and instead of obstructing him had waited on the bank of the Tisza for him to do as he had promised, all the benefit of which would be his alone – filled his soul with horror. It seemed to him that he had become the criminal's accomplice; it was as if he, who had hitherto discharged all his duties with almost exaggerated rigour, had now suddenly rendered himself undeserving of people's respect. As soon as it began to be light he went to call on Vándory, to seek his advice in this latest misfortune.

Vándory, who rose at four winter and summer alike, was already up, and on hearing his door open looked up from his book and was not a little surprised to recognise Tengelyi, whom he'd seldom seen at such an early hour and looking so distraught.

Tengelyi gave a brief account of events.

"Monstrous!" sighed Vándory, horrified. "In the midst of his sins, without being allowed a moment to repent of them."

"Yes!" said Tengelyi in despair. "And isn't the full burden of responsibility going to fall on me, when suspecting that Macskaházy had my papers I must have considered that Viola would only be able to acquire them by force, and instead of deterring him I accepted his invitation and received his bloodied booty from him ?. . . "

"What Viola did was monstrous!" the clergyman interrupted him, "I can sense the horror with which your heart is filled by the thought that the wretched man did it solely for the purpose of recovering your documents – but did you know that? And how would it have been in your power to restrain Viola from his action?"

"I should have done my duty," replied the notary solemnly, "which required me to bring about his arrest as soon as I received information that he was here."

"His arrest?" said Vándory, almost startled by the thought. "Have a man arrested who had entrusted himself to you? And under circumstances such that it would be a matter not of his being brought before a

454

court but of being handed over to his executioner?. . . How can you say such a thing?"

"Indeed, it was a burdensome duty that my position as a citizen required me to perform," said Tengelyi sadly, "but was it any the less my duty? If every citizen could excuse himself from his duty every time that what the public good required conflicted with his individual nobler sentiments, wouldn't our state collapse?. . . If mercy serves as an excuse for anyone that defends the malefactor against the punishing arm of justice, who will you punish as a receiver of stolen goods?"

Vándory brought up the point that if this argument were applied to a different incident, in which there was a question of the death penalty, no one could be compelled, even as a citizen, to offer assistance leading to the death of his fellow man; he personally would be more prepared to expose himself to the severest of punishments rather than ever to discharge such a duty; and that in Tengelyi's situation every honest man would surely do the same . . . that is, he put forward everything that could console his friend. To all that, Tengelyi replied only that he took a completely different view of the matter, and that those who would be passing judgement on him would share his opinion.

Vándory could see how harmful it would be for his friend if the letter that he'd received from Viola became public knowledge, and he did his best to dissuade him from fully reporting the whole incident; no good would come of it, and for him the greatest harm if his numerous enemies made use of the news for further slanders, as they doubtless would – they already suspected him for taking in Viola's wife. But Tengelyi was inflexible on this point. "It's only by openness that we can defend ourselves against lies," said he. "If you try to conceal the truth, sooner or later you'll be forced to change your story, and as you know, even if I wanted to, that's not the way I am! In this case, however, I wouldn't even have the right to do that, because a man's under grave suspicion for the murder of Macskaházy and my statement will serve to avert that from him." All that Vándory could get from his friend was that he would delay his disclosure until Réty returned and would make it to him.

"You're right," said Tengelyi sourly. "Who knows, when I relate the whole incident, whether Nyúzó or your *alispán* – whom you consider for no reason that I can see to be better than him – won't send me off to County Hall in chains. It's true! In my situation that's just what they might do . . . At least everyone knows about Réty that he keeps villains in food so that they shan't raid his flocks; but then, they're nobles, and with peasants like me things are different!"

"How can you think like that?" said Vándory reassuringly.

"And why shouldn't I?" answered Tengelyi with a bitter smile. "I've read more than once that in the seventeenth century in a number of courts a poor boy was kept along with the crown prince who was to be educated, and every time the prince didn't learn his lessons or played some prank, this boy was given a sound thrashing so that the prince could see by his example what he would have deserved; it seems that this custom has been maintained with us. The so-called members of our crown[182] aren't punished . . . but so that they shan't lack an example, others are punished all the more! as far as that's concerned you won't find much difference between Réty and Nyúzó."

"Believe me, my friend," said the clergyman, shaking his head, "you're wrong about Réty. I can understand that as you were close to him at one time you're harder on him than others now that you've ceased to be friends; but I know him better. Deep down he's not as corrupt as you think, his fault is simply weakness, which is why he can't stand up to his wife."

"Yes," said Tengelyi, "call it weakness if you like; but if this weakness serves as an excuse for every wickedness, why are you harder on Nyúzó or others?. . . If the man who deserts his best friend in his hour of need, indeed, uses his misfortune for his own advancement; who denies his principles a hundred times; who uses his beliefs as a sail to send him first one way, then another, to reach the desired harbour by every wind – if that man doesn't deserve your scorn, and you regard him as justified if you can point to his weakness: by what right do you disregard the male-factor whose deed arouses horror in you? For he too, you see, has only erred through weakness! The passion that forced him to the evil deed was too powerful for him to withstand. Don't look down on Nyúzó for putting justice up for sale . . . poor fellow, he can't help it! It's weakness, that's all . . . Alas, he can't resist money!. . . There's no reason for you to loathe the liar it's only his imagination that got the better of him, or he lives under such circumstances that he doesn't feel strong enough to tell the truth. Accept weakness as an excuse, and the difference between good and bad disappears; there's no wickedness for the perpetrator of which you won't feel justified in feeling sympathy, because the cause of

---

182 The Estates or common nobility, in whose hands was the administration of the counties, used this collective style. The Holy Crown had, as it were, a life of its own. See Kees Teszelszky: *The Unknown Crown. Meanings, Symbols and National Identity,* (Historia pro futuro IV.) Bencés kiadó, Pannonhalma, 2016, for a full account.

his crime is nothing other than that his interests or passions have enticed him away to misfortune."

"Far be it from me to do such a thing," said Vándory calmly. "I'm well aware that virtue is nothing more than the power by which we cling to our principles . . . and I don't wish to defend Réty for the things that he's done. Only what I say is: however inexcusable his weakness may be, there's a certain point beyond which it certainly won't go, and neither his wife's influence nor any other interest can induce him to do such things as you allege of him. I'm not convinced of that in respect of Nyúzó."

"That's where you're deceived," said the notary testily. Réty's like Nyúzó and all the rest – if you go all through the county you won't find three people that feel themselves obliged to show the slightest mercy to anyone that can't protect themselves with the privileges of nobility; and when I think that my son will presumably belong to the ranks of the ignoble it fills my heart with bitterness."

Vándory was about to speak but Tengelyi went on passionately: "I know what you're going to say. We're well off for men of liberal principles . . . not only in Hungary but here in the county too you can hear ever finer declarations on all sides . . . Liberty, equality, the rights of the common people and whatever! There isn't an elegant turn of speech in the civilised world that we don't translate, which we don't proclaim at the top of our voices; but look at what the words mean, and if you don't mean to delude yourself, what do you find? Liberty and equality? Yes, the liberty with which the nobleman conducts his affairs, without anyone but God being able to call him to account!. . . the equality with which the lowest canvasser looks on the peasant with the same scorn as the medieval lord looked down on his serfs!. . . The rights of the common people? Yes, that common people of which Werbőczi speaks, meaning the common nobility! The magnanimity of those gentlemen of liberal principles extends no farther. Because the Hungarian peasant doesn't vote in elections, doesn't shout hurray, doesn't make music by torchlight, so why should he look for anyone's favours?"

"You're over-excited," said Vándory, "otherwise you wouldn't make such generalisations. There are some, you can't deny it if you're reasonable, to whom your accusations don't apply."

"Some?" Tengelyi interrupted. "Yes, there are some to whom that doesn't apply, who turn in disgust away from the crowd that surrounds you. But is it any consolation that in this country there are a few hundred or at the most a thousand people who feel as we do, whose souls are pained like ours, when they see the great lie under which we live? Will my son be any less deprived of his rights as a citizen, any less despised, trampled under foot?"

"Your son won't be trampled under foot by anyone," said Vándory calmly. "However grim the condition in which the ignoble inhabitants of our country are at present, it won't keep him back any longer . . . and who knows, perhaps times are coming when your son will bless his fate in being deprived of his noble status and pushed back into the ranks of the common people, only so as to be raised up with his entire class to the position which at one time was considered privileged, and which henceforth it will be able to demand as a right? I grant you, those who most assert the principles of liberty these days aren't serious in their intentions; but doesn't what they say convince thousands all the same? . . . and if the stone moves without their will, or even against it, won't it roll all the same to where its natural weight takes it, brushing aside everything that would oppose it?. . . Yes, my friend," he added, enthusiastically seizing Tengelyi's hand, "finer days are coming, a finer future awaits every class in this nation, and grey though my hair may be I still hope to see the time when our present condition will pass off like a bad dream and will seem almost incredible even to those who've spent their entire lives in it."

Tengelyi was about to reply when the door opened and Mrs Lipták rushed in. "For goodness' sake, Your Honour, come home at once," said she, breathlessly.

"What's happened?" asked Vándory and Tengelyi almost in unison, both alarmed at the way in which she had spoken and thinking that some misfortune had occurred in the notary's house.

"The magistrate and clerk have come," she replied, still in the same tone of voice.

"Dear lady, what's wrong with you?" said Vándory in surprise. "What's strange about the magistrate coming to see my friend? Doesn't he come twenty times a year on official business?"

"But do you know why he's come, reverend?" said she. "The magistrate's saying that it was His Honour that killed that damned lawyer Macskaházy! And he's there with his clerk and his *hajdús* questioning every single body one by one."

Tengelyi was accustomed to the blows of fate; so often had he experienced the injustice of men that, as he often said, nothing bad would happen that would surprise him; the news that Mrs Lipták brought, however, had caught him unprepared. "This is too much!" said he, and his voice shook. "I was ready for anything, but that I should ever be accused of a crime, ever have to defend myself before a judge on a charge of murder – that I've never thought!"

"It's impossible," said Vándory, and, no less distressed than his friend, got his hat and coat to go home with him. "It must all be a mistake."

"That's what I thought at first as well," said Mrs Lipták sadly. "When the magistrate told Madam that Mr Tengelyi was under grave suspicion and would have to be interrogated, I thought he was just joking; but when he summoned the servant and the handyman and the neighbours and questioned them one after another, while the clerk wrote down every word, I could see that the villain was pretending that he thought it was a bad business. When he wanted to question Madam she said that she was a noblewoman and didn't have to answer unless she chose; and the magistrate said that Mr Tengelyi wasn't noble any more, and if she didn't answer she'd find out that he'd make her. When I heard that I ran and came here for Mr Tengelyi, so that there should be somebody in the house that understood such legal matters."

"Well, you see, it all makes sense," said Tengelyi bitterly to his friend. "Why did they go to such trouble to deprive me of my nobility if it wasn't their intention to be able to persecute me even more?"

"But . . ." said Vándory.

"Let's be going, come along," Mrs Lipták interrupted. "As I was leaving the house the *alispán* was just arriving as well."

"Come on!" said Tengelyi to the clergyman with greater bitterness yet. "You hear that, we've nothing to worry about, our friend Réty's there as well, we can count on his support." And with that the men set off, followed by Mrs Lipták, for the notary's house.

In the meantime, things had begun to look worse for Tengelyi. Erzsébet clung firmly to her privilege as a noble and could not be prevailed upon to answer the magistrate's questions; but everything that the others who were questioned stated was entirely against the notary. The neighbours had confirmed the exchange of words the day before, after which Macskaházy had been driven out of the house with a stick. One clearly remembered Tengelyi's words, in which he had said of Macskaházy that he would yet die by his (Tengelyi's) hands. The servant had seen his master leaving the house at about eleven o'clock, a thing that he never did usually. All of them recognised the stick that they were shown as the notary's property; in a word, they were in such agreement that the *alispán* – who had urged Nyúzó to be as temperate as possible and had been present during much of the questioning – despite his inner convic-

459

tion of Tengelyi's innocence, couldn't deny that circumstantial evidence was very much against him.

When Tengelyi, followed by Vándory, came into the room every eye turned towards him, and with the exception of Nyúzó there was no one that could not have been moved at the passionate bitterness with which Erzsébet sank into her husband's embrace.

"Calm yourself," said Tengelyi relaxedly, "this isn't the first time we've experienced people's persecution, and as my conscience is clear, with God's help we shan't be crushed by our enemies this time either."

The dignity with which Tengelyi conducted himself impressed no one more than it did the *alispán*, who went up to his former friend and said with feeling how sorry he was if he regarded the magistrate's presence as persecution. "When strange circumstances are conjoined," he went on, "it can be that the most honourable of men is obliged to justify himself, and that, I'm convinced, will cause Master Tengelyi no difficulty at all in the present case."

"I'm much obliged," said Tengelyi sourly, "for the favourable opinion of me that Your Honour has been good enough to reveal, and I'm quite certain that if it depended on Your Honour the procedure would also have been adopted towards me which any person of good repute may rightly demand in such a case; permit me, however, to ask the magistrate: what are the circumstances and situations on account of which the slightest suspicion falls on me with regard to the murder of Macskaházy – of which I hear I'm accused?"

"We'll provide Master Tengelyi with that at once," said the magistrate; now, as always in official proceedings, he included his clerk and spoke in the plural, and he listed one by one the circumstances already familiar to my readers that cast suspicion on Tengelyi, while his clerk nodded his head at each point as if wishing at least by signs to have a share in the glory of the examination so swiftly conducted. "Now, since Macskaházy's murderer is not known," he began his account, "and since no theft took place, it is not known who might have benefited by this man's death; however, Master Tengelyi's hatred of him is common knowledge, and as the most recent proof of which we refer to the notary's outburst of yesterday, in the course of which, as several witnesses state, he said plainly that the deceased would die by his hand; and since it is known that he unjustly suspected the deceased of having stolen certain documents of his, this murder could have been in his interests: this we find the cause for the gravest suspicion of Master Tengelyi, all the more so because as the murder took place at about half past eleven, by the evidence of one witness the notary left his house at eleven that evening, contrary to his custom, and when the coachman and the ferryman and their sundry companions came to this house at about midnight Master Tengelyi, again contrary to his custom, was still up and dressed, and his clothes were covered in mud, and especially as not only documents found at the scene of the murder but also the walking stick which the ferryman found as he pursued the murderer from the Tisza to Master Tengelyi's house were the notary's property. What does the notary say to that?"

That lengthy account was more admired by no one – with the exception of Nyúzó himself – than by the trusty clerk; my readers will see that it was delivered in the style of written Hungarian judicial pronouncements, that is, with as many diverse subjects as possible under the least number of headings; such a compilation of so many pieces of evidence, however, had no little effect on others too, and Tengelyi in particular couldn't conceal his surprise; he could see what it all added up to, the difficulty of justifying himself, and for a moment said nothing.

"Please don't be put out, Master Tengelyi," said Nyúzó scornfully, "just render a truthful account, if you would. As you can see, we are asking with the greatest courtesy."

"Don't say a word to him," interrupted Mrs Tengelyi passionately. "Thank goodness, no one's demonstrated that we aren't nobles, and you can't be forced to speak."

"I wish to speak," said Tengelyi, regaining his composure, "and speak I shall. There's no one on earth that I wouldn't consider worthy of my acquainting him with the state of affairs if I knew that he held me in such suspicion."

"So you see, Mrs Tengelyi, your husband considers us deserving of an answer," said the magistrate, still scornfully, because as the *alispán* had cautioned him to moderation only so could he exact retribution. "Let him speak, I'll wager that as soon as he does so everything will become clear, and as concerns noble privilege I've already said that where there's no written evidence of nobility we, good Calvinists that we are, pay little attention to such tradition."

"If Master Nyúzó thinks," said Tengelyi, the blood surging to his face, "that that scornful witticism can increase respect for his official position, perhaps His Worship the *alispán* here will be kind enough to persuade him of his error. As for the matter itself," he added, holding himself in check, "I don't deny that at first sight many circumstances seem to speak against me; however, I believe that an account of the state of affairs will convince even the magistrate that he has been mistaken." And Tengelyi gave a full account of what had happened. The suspicion that he revealed that Macskaházy had stolen his documents was only natural in his position after the events at Kislak, and nothing confirmed the basis of that suspicion more than the fact that documents had been found in the lawyer's room which he could only have acquired by being complicit in the robbery. In explanation of why he had left his house so late the day before, contrary to his custom, and how it happened that he had been found by the ferryman and the coachman with mud on his clothes, the notary related how he had received the note from Viola in so furtive a fashion.

Nyúzó listened to it all with a smile of disbelief. "And so how does it come about," he asked, "that you responded at once to Viola's invitation? That you went out late at night, alone and without a weapon, as you say, to a quite deserted place only to rendezvous with the most wanted villain in the country, whom others fear when they outnumber him four to one?"

"Never in my life have I done Viola any harm," replied Tengelyi, "and so I wasn't afraid of him, especially after seeing from the note that he felt grateful to me. Furthermore, what else could I do? I knew of no other means of recovering my stolen documents, and I accepted what I was offered."

"And let's ask then," Nyúzó spoke again, "may we not see the note in question? It would be of interest, if only so that we could recognise the famous villain's writing."

"At the writer's request, I burnt it straight away," replied Tengelyi.

"That's a great shame," said Nyúzó, "especially if you lack two well-disposed and unbiased witnesses, with whom you shared the note you received from Viola, and who would confirm this quite extraordinary and at least amazing tale, or rather account."

"I've only spoken of the affair to my friend Vándory this morning."

"Yes, this morning, I see," Nyúzó continued, "by which time I was in the village and had begun my investigation. Have you nothing else to say?"

Tengelyi signified that he had said everything that was relevant to the matter.

"From what we've heard," said the magistrate, turning to his clerk, "what's certain from Master Tengelyi's statement is that he's admitted the intention of murder."

Tengelyi observed that as far as he recalled he hadn't said that.

462

"I consider that in that regard any denial is superfluous," said the magistrate sharply. "You acknowledge that you thought that your documents were in Macskaházy's possession. If that is so, you received Viola's note . . . if indeed it was written . . . and how could you have thought for a moment anything but that he was going to obtain them by force. Indeed," the magistrate went on after a short pause, during which his gaze was fixed on the notary, "by your own admission it's all but certain that you not only knew beforehand that murder was to be committed but also were an accessory, since Viola himself couldn't have known the value of the documents and wouldn't have exposed himself to the risk of obtaining them by such a crime if he hadn't been encouraged to it by some other person . . . and it's obvious that that can only have been you, as obtaining the documents wasn't in the interests of anyone else."

Tengelyi was about to speak, but Nyúzó went on: "And who's doing this? Who's committing this heinous crime? I ask you: a notary, a man who's duty-bound to hunt down criminals, and who uses the confidence placed in him by the county and its authorities to make his house a haven for them. This is too serious a case," he went on, turning to his clerk, "for us to be able to deal with. We must send the accused to County Hall, and under close escort, so that Viola and his gang, who, it seems, are closely associated with him, may not set him free from the hands of justice.

The *alispán*, who was deeply concerned at the turn of events, advised Nyúzó that there was no need for that as he personally would, if it was desired, gladly undertake Tengelyi's security; Nyúzó, however, who previously had been ready to do the *alispán*'s bidding, restrained himself from the coarseness of which he made use at other times and didn't find it necessary to yield to his superior on this point and declared pompously that as the burden of responsibility lay on himself, and that in such a case he wouldn't accept security even had Tengelyi's noble status not been called into question, as the privilege of nobility didn't come into consideration with regard to the imprisonment of the associates of proven thieves.

"How dare you, sir, call me the associate of thieves!" exclaimed Tengelyi, no longer able to sustain the moderation to which he had forced himself until then. "You, of whom the entire county knows that you have used your office to receive stolen goods?"

Concerning Tengelyi's accusation, we must make it known that the notary could scarcely have said anything – in the presence of the *alispán* and so many others – that touched the wealthy magistrate on a more tender spot, as people in the county had spoken of several instances when stolen cattle had been found by their owners in Nyúzó's stables, at which naturally those people had been so surprised that at first they hadn't known what to say, had said nothing, and when they returned later with witnesses the cattle were no longer to be found there. But the momentary embarrassment into which he was plunged merely served to stir his stifled fury to breaking point, and Nyúzó abandoned all restraint. "How dare I call you that?" shrieked the infuriated official. "How dare I, the chief magistrate of this honourable and noble county, call you that? If I weren't so respectful of His Worship the *alispán*'s wishes I'd have clapped you in irons long ago, as it's public knowledge that when we were looking for Viola here in the village before the election the villain was hiding in this house all the time, and when I wanted to enter with my men your wife had the impudence to threaten me for invasion of privacy."

"Who dares to slander my house in such a fashion?" asked the notary, in growing rage. "Viola in my house?. . . I took in his wife and children because they were destitute, but I never saw the outlaw!. . . Speak up, Erzsébet," said he, turning to his wife, "has Viola ever been in my house?"

Erzsébet, like Tengelyi himself, knew nothing about Viola's hiding in the house with Vilma's connivance and Mrs Lipták's help, and she assured him on oath that the fugitive had never been in the house since taking up a life of crime; to that the magistrate, with a scornful smile, called forward Mrs Lipták, and she was unable to retract what she had told the summary court under oath. "It's true, Your Honour," said she with a sigh, "that when Viola was being hunted in the village the poor man was here in the house all the time. I myself hid him beneath the barrels in the pantry, but neither Master Tengelyi nor his wife knew anything about it, I was so afraid that they'd find out that I never even told them what poor Viola asked me to when he left – to tell Master Tengelyi to look out for his papers; and if I had, who knows what trouble might have been avoided."

"God bless any one that believes that," said the magistrate scornfully. "How could you have taken the outlaw into the pantry without anyone knowing?"

"Who said that nobody knew?" answered Mrs Lipták. "I only said that His Honour and Mrs Tengelyi didn't know, she'd gone to bed. When poor Viola came to the house only Miss Vilma and I were awake. I was sitting right by Zsuzsi's bed when we heard the commotion in the street. I went out into the garden and there I found Viola, the house was completely surrounded, there was no escape, and I knew if he was caught he'd be hanged, and I asked Vilma if I might bring the poor man inside. She's an angel, her heart was broken at his trouble and she let me. That's all; let me be damned if anybody but us knew that the one they were looking for was here. . If we did wrong in hiding Viola I don't regret it, you can do what you like to me, I've lived long enough and there's nobody in the wrong but me!"

"Never fear, you'll pay the price, you old witch!" said the magistrate crossly. "Now we'll have to question the young lady, it looks as if the whole family's in it together. Call the girl in," he added turning to Mrs Tengelyi, "let's question her as well."

"What, my daughter?" said Erzsébet passionately. "You certainly shan't! My daughter's engaged to marry Ákos Réty, let anybody try to harm her if they dare . . . My Vilma in front of such people! Being interrogated like a criminal!" And the good woman would probably have said more yet had Tengelyi himself not asked her to fetch his daughter as requested.

"But have you thought this through, my dear Jónás?" asked Erzsébet in amazement.

"I'm telling you, go to your room and call for your daughter." replied Tengelyi seriously. "I'm quite sure that Mrs Lipták isn't telling the truth. My daughter has never kept anything from me."

Erzsébet left and after a short while came back with her daughter. The power of beauty is irresistible, and Nyúzó himself, for all his native harshness, on seeing the young lady led by her mother was unnerved at the sight of the tenderness of that regular, pale face and said with unexpected gentleness that as the clarification of certain circumstances rendered it necessary for her to answer a few questions – that is, if she had no objection to doing so at that moment, because in that case he would gladly postpone questioning her to another time.

"That won't be necessary," said Tengelyi drily. "Speak freely," he went on to Vilma, "is it true that Viola was hidden in our house when he was being looked for in the village?"

"Daddy," said Vilma, and a blush ran at once over her pale face.

"There's nothing to be afraid of, my dear," he went on in an encouraging tone, "you've always been my dear, good daughter, you've never kept anything from your parents. Say without hesitation: is it true that Viola was in our house and that you gave permission for him to be?"

Vilma said nothing; the poor girl was trembling from head to foot, and even Nyúzó began to feel sorry for her when he saw the effect that these questions were having on her.

"I tell you, there's nothing to be afraid of, Vilma," Tengelyi repeated. "I know it's all just slander. I know that you wouldn't have been capable of doing such a thing without my permission, or at least of telling me afterwards. But this woman here," he added, indicating Mrs Lipták, "from whom I expected and deserved something different, is making the excuse that she hid Viola in our house by your permission."

The thought that frank admission of the truth was necessary to justify Mrs Lipták dispelled in Vilma's heart the youthful fear that had her hold back until then, and she raised tearful eyes to her father and confirmed that the woman was telling the truth. "Forgive me, father dear!" she implored, "I'm the sole cause of the misfortune. I told Mrs Lipták myself to hide Viola in the house if she could. I myself told her not to say a word to you, because I knew that however natural it was for me to do my utmost to save a hapless man from death, even so you'd be cross because Viola was said to be a criminal."

"God bless anyone that believes that!" muttered Nyúzó through his teeth, while Kenyházy gave a deep sigh and Réty observed that he saw nothing that made the account seem improbable.

Tengelyi remained silent throughout, looking up to the heavens, but the expression on his face showed that in his heart was one of the pains for which our language lacks words and our eyes tears. Vilma watched him in silent despair, and the painful silence was only broken when Vándory went to his friend, took his hand and begged him not to let the pain get the better of him.

"Never fear," said Tengelyi gloomily. "If I've had to reach the stage where I only hear the truth from my daughter when I'm questioned in front of a judge there's nothing more in this world to surprise me. But let's stop this!" he added with a sigh, turning to the magistrate and his clerk. "Let's put an end to this painful scene. You gentlemen know what you wanted to find out by your questioning, the evidence is all against me, there's no reason for you to bother any more. Give me two hours to put my affairs in order and say goodbye to my family, you can put a guard on my house for as long as you like, and then take me to Porvár."

"If you've nothing more to say in your defence," said Nyúzó as he stood up, "we can indeed put an end to it all. The matter is clear. Your carriage will be ready in two hours' time, have your things ready by then, and I warn you, you'll do well to prepare for a longish stay."

"We'll go with him!" said Erzsébet, as she burst into tears. "I'm not going to desert my husband in his awful predicament."

"My dear Erzsébet," said the notary, touched by this outburst, "you stay here in my house. As such a grave accusation has been brought against me I'll need to prepare my defence, and it's best if you'll leave me to myself for a while."

Erzsébet wept even more, and Nyúzó left the room with his clerk, not before remarking that he had no idea how much time the rules of the prison permitted the accused to spend with their families; and I for my part think that he could have done nothing either kinder for the notary's family or more expedient for himself, as scarcely had he left the house than Ákos entered the room in a state of the highest dudgeon.

After going home with Vándory the previous evening, he'd spent half the night pacing his room full of happy dreams, then at length had fallen asleep in a sense of his good fortune and slept so soundly that although his room was next to Vándory's he hadn't heard either Tengelyi or Mrs Lipták come, and it was only now, having been awoken by old János, that he had learnt about both the murder that had been committed and the steps taken against Tengelyi by the magistrate. I shan't describe the feelings that filled Ákos's heart at this news; he hurried to the notary's house and found his beloved pale at the side of her tearful mother. "For God's sake, what's happened here?" were his first words.

"My dear Ákos," said Erzsébet, clasping his hands, "we're in a desperate situation. Our good name is besmirched. My husband's accused of murder and they're taking him to the county prison . . ." and her tears choked her voice.

"And I let my father down," said Vilma in despair. "Ákos! if ever you loved me, save him . . ." and with that the hapless girl fell swooning into the young man's arms.

Followed by Erzsébet, Ákos carried his beloved into the side room; the notary watched them go in silence, and tears gleamed in his eyes; he grasped Vándory's hand and said quietly: "When I'm gone, you be a father to these poor things."

Réty stood there, deeply touched, while this all took place; but the cold formality with which Tengelyi had rejected his support every time that the *alispán* had spoken on his behalf held him back from expressing his sympathy. Now he pulled himself together, and as the notary went up to Vándory, in a voice heavy with emotion, asked that whatever had happened between them in the past he should be convinced that he would do all in his power to rescue his former friend from this unhappy situation.

467

"I'm most grateful for the warm sympathy for my situation with which His Worship the *alispán* is clothed," said Tengelyi frigidly, when he was able to speak. "I confess, I hadn't even realised that we still had the pleasure, I thought that after the affair that had aroused his interest had been concluded he'd left with the magistrate. As His Worship can see, everything is settled, the crime, it appears, is completely solved and I'm guilty."

"Tengelyi!" said Réty, deeply moved, "don't be unfair to me! Nothing else has brought me to this house but that I may if possible be of use to you through my presence, and that I may cause Nyúzó to be as merciful as the exercising of his office permits in such a case."

"If that was His Worship's intention," said Tengelyi bitterly, "it would have been easier if, in the election, he had not exercised his influence for the election of such a magistrate as only refrains from the abuse of his office when his superior is present."

"I won't argue with you about that," replied the *alispán* embarrassedly, "I merely want you to be sure that however weighty the evidence against you may appear, I'm convinced of your innocence; you may count on me."

"Your Worship," said Tengelyi gravely, "there was a time when I did so count. My friends were good enough to persuade me that the infinite and boundless feeling that we call friendship is far too sublime for us to count on it on this earth. Shortly, perhaps, I shall appear before my judges, and if Your Worship feels strong enough to forget the friendship towards me with which he was once clothed I shall be happy to see him among them; now excuse me if I leave you. I may only spend two hours in my house, and those I wish to spend with my family." And with that Tengelyi bowed deeply and, taking Vándory with him, went into the side room.

Réty looked after him for a long time, than sighed deeply and left the house.

XXXII

Every parting fills our spirits with a feeling of sadness. Even the most cheerful of men can scarcely conceal his distress on shaking his friend's hand for the last time. But what is that feeling compared to the one that fills the bosom when, at one of the doleful moments of our lives, we're forced to leave the circle of our loved ones! . . At such times the heart, which always sees the past and the future in the light of the present, expects that only menacing dangers await it, and can't be free of the thought that the circle which it may be about to leave only for a few days will never be the same when it returns. It was natural that in his perilous situation Tengelyi should be doubly conscious of all this: and indeed it called for all his manliness to find words of consolation for his grieving family when he could see nothing in prospect to which he might anchor his hopes; above all, his daughter's woe filled his heart with a bitterness beyond any that he had ever known.

"Don't cry, my dear!" said he to Vilma. "Look, your father's innocent, you must know that. A few days, and the true state of affairs will become clear, I'll be back home, and you'll be my lovely, happy daughter again, won't you?"

"Oh, daddy!" said Vilma, and her voice was shaking. "You in prison, there among wicked people, if only for a day, for a single hour, and when I think that I'm the cause of it all!"

"You, my dear?" asked Tengelyi in surprise. "How ever do you make that out? Perhaps you think that your confession must make things worse for me?"

"Daddy," said she sorrowfully, "don't speak so nicely to me, I don't deserve your love. Aren't those wicked men going to say that you knew very well that Viola was hiding and that you only wanted to keep it secret, and even if not, what's brought all the misery down on us except that we took in Zsuzsi and the children? And I did that!"

"And precisely because that's the cause of your misfortune," Vándory interrupted, "God won't desert you in your trouble. The ways of providence are wonderful, but doing good has never led anyone to ruin."

At those words Tengelyi sighed deeply; but Vilma felt more at ease, and Erzsébet herself sobbed more quietly when Vándory reminded her that this unjust accusation itself might be the way to the shaming of her enemies and perhaps the recovery of the stolen documents.

469

Tengelyi himself consoled his wife by saying that in any case his imprisonment could only be brief, and for its duration they wouldn't be left without a supportive friend as Vándory would be there with them.

Erzsébet asked again to be allowed to accompany him to Porvár, but Tengelyi felt that if he were to see his grieving family around him as he stepped over the threshold of the prison his resolve would break under so much suffering, and with Vándory's help he prevailed on his wife at least for the present, for the first few days, not to ask.

"If my imprisonment is prolonged," he added, "which I don't fear, you can come later. For the first few days I'll have to busy myself completely with my situation. Völgyesy's an honest man, to the best of my belief, and has kindly offered to defend me. Ákos will find a means of bringing me news of you all as often as possible. But where is Ákos?"

Erzsébet said that when the *alispán* had left Ákos too had gone, presumably to speak to him. Shortly afterwards, as Tengelyi was packing the few things that he meant to take with him, Ákos returned. His face was blazing, and it seemed from his eyes that he had been weeping.

"Did you speak to your father?" asked Erzsébet quickly.

"Yes!" said Ákos, his voice quivering.

"And what did he say?" asked Erzsébet and Vándory, almost in unison.

"The finest, most constructive things that you could believe," replied Ákos bitterly. "He was in tears, he truly wept, flung his arms round my neck and called me his dear son; he said that he was convinced of Tengelyi's innocence, that he was heart-broken when he thought that so honourable a man, one who had once been his friend, should come to so hapless a situation. What do you expect! He said everything that might persuade anyone at all that Tengelyi's innocent and that it's every decent person's duty to take his side; but the outcome of all those fine words was that he can't do as I requested, and since Nyúzó won't accept his surety he can't make him . . . so there's nothing that he can do. But didn't he say that he was heart-broken . . . what more can we ask of him?"

"I could have told you that beforehand," said Tengelyi calmly.

"No, my friend!" Ákos continued warmly. "That you could not have done. If an angel of God were to descend and tell me that that was how my father would respond to my request, I wouldn't have believed him. You don't know how I begged him. I cried like a child, flung myself at his feet, invoked the memory of my mother; I said that if ever in his life he'd loved anyone, if he didn't want to break with me for ever, didn't want me to curse my fate in being given him as a father, let him fulfil this one request . . . and he refused."

"And who's to say," said Vándory, pained by the bitterness with which Ákos spoke of his father, "that he wasn't just telling the truth when he said that he couldn't do it?"

"Well, if you think," replied Ákos bitterly, "that if my father had actually stood surety for Tengelyi, or had, as I asked him, meant to keep him under guard in some room in his own house until this unfortunate business was cleared up, that Nyúzó'd have dared to say him nay? Quite, but what was His Excellency the *főispán* going to say? Wouldn't the honourable Estates have taken it amiss if he sided with Tengelyi, who's hated by many in this county? That's what held my father back from acting in accordance with his convictions, as has always been the case; that's why he's repudiated his son."

"Don't judge your father so harshly," said Vándory, deeply affected by this outburst. "Who knows what a grievous struggle it cost him to refuse your request."

"Never mind!" Ákos interrupted. "As I left the house Nyúzó was arranging the carriages. Time is short – let's not sour it by arguments that can't lead to anything. With your permission," said he to Tengelyi, "I'll go with you to Porvár."

The notary repeated what he'd told his family, and only asked Ákos, if possible, to let him know how Vilma and Erzsébet were while he was in prison. "No need to commit them to your protection!" he added with a smile.

"Oh, if only I had even more right to protect them," said Ákos, seizing Tengelyi's hand, "if I might call Vilma my wife! Who knows, what my father hasn't done for his son's happiness he might do for his name."

"I understand you" replied Tengelyi calmly. "But praise be! I need no protector for the proof of my innocence. I can give my daughter no dowry but my honourable name, but I'll never permit you to be united before I can put that to rights."

Ákos was on the point of replying, but the sound of carriage wheels outside the house gave a quite different direction to all thoughts.

Tengelyi embraced his wife and daughter quickly, so as not to be unnerved by the sight of their tears, put on his fur and took his place in the carriage that Réty had sent for him – to Nyúzó's no little annoyance, as he'd intended to have him conveyed to Porvár by farm-cart and in irons.

Beside Tengelyi sat the clerk, and *hajdús* sat with the driver and at the back . . . and the hapless notary blessed his God when he had once

471

more pressed Ákos's hand and at last the horses set off and took him away from the sight of his despairing family. Whatever awaits him at his destination, there can be nothing more painful to a good man that to see his loved ones overwhelmed with grief.

* *
*

Let's now leave Vilma, her mother and Ákos in their pain, shortly to be joined by Etelka, and follow the notary to County Hall.

When Lord Byron stood on the so-called Bridge of Sighs in Venice, the thought that he could see a palace and a prison on each side gave the great poet occasion for a fine reflection:

> *I stood in Venice on the bridge of sighs,*
> *A palace and a prison on each side.*[183]

The Doge's palace in Venice is, as is well known, equally famous for its resplendent halls and its loathsome dungeons; its brilliance is framed by the tin roof above and the canal below. That's a true image of many states, in which those above or below the happy mean are excluded from the enjoyment of the blessings of the state; and we see on every side inexpressible sufferings among which a couple of hundred fools or impostors take council for the maintenance of liberty. Venice is beyond doubt lovely, the Doge's palace is lovely, lovely too are Byron's lines, which come unbidden to the mind of the traveller as he passes in his gondola beneath the sorrowful bridge over which the Venetian prisoner goes either to appear before his judge or to his death; but that we can see in the Doge's palace both a palace and a prison can't seem remarkable to the Hungarian; indeed, in Hungary every child knows that the prison can't be anywhere but in County Hall, or rather beneath it, which is unquestionably the most expedient, because County Hall has no need of a wine-cellar as every time that the Estates gather in large numbers they first ensure that during their conferences they shan't be afflicted by thirst – and so a place other than the cellars, of which no other use can be made, can scarcely be found for the prisoners.

There are people – because what does this featherless biped, as Plato described man, not think of since it's made good the deficiency of nature with the feathers of the humble goose and rises with those? – There are people, I say, who declare that situation of our prisons to be bad. They're light-minded dreamers, soft-hearted fellows, political eccentrics . . . it

183 From *Childe Harold's Pilgrimage.*

doesn't enter their feeble heads that of all things our prisons demand our attention the least; and when they rejoice that the shores of Pest and Buda are being connected by a chain-bridge,[184] at the same time they don't consider it a matter of indifference that our prisoners – many of whom are perhaps innocent – are burdened with chains weighing thirty pounds or even more. But the silent majority, praise be to our destiny, don't listen to the words of those lunatics, and the Estates of Taksony County have until now kept their prisons free of all profitless innovations. It can't be denied that here too things have happened recently that threatened danger to our penal system, which has developed from the genius of the nation. Not long ago a young *táblabíró* travelled through the county for the sole purpose of inspecting the prisons; and although the castellan had caused a half-*meszely*[185] of *pálinka* to be given to each prisoner that day and had ordered them all to play cards, just in order to persuade the stranger how well Taksony County treated its prisoners: that man, in his inexplicable blindness, caused much outcry against Mr Karvaly's keeping of the prison. An even greater danger threatened the former status quo, when in the winter following that visit the feet of five or six prisoners in the prison of a neighbouring county were frostbitten. Because although the county proceeded with all possible care and amputated the said feet with a wood-saw, and though the patients, with one exception, on whom this surgical operation was performed all died and so didn't complain, and although similar events have happened more than once and have never before aroused special attention; on this occasion an unheard of fuss was made nation-wide about the cruelty of the Estates in the said county. It was as if they had certainly been the reason why the said winter had been unusually cold, and as if it was just when the feet had been frostbitten in the lower dungeon that upstairs, where eighty were held captive in one room, no one would have complained of the heat, it was clear evidence that such wicked people preferred the most contrary charges against their superiors. But when the visiting *táblabíró* had moved on, after giving a fine lecture in the gentlemen's club about how the prisons were to be improved, and the neighbouring county was able to preserve its autonomy concerning those who had been investigated concerning the frostbitten feet, likewise the fuss that had been made on that occasion subsided, and the relevant orders were filed away – and Mr Karvaly adhered to his old, purely Hungarian sys-

---

184 The first permanent bridge on the Danube in Budapest was built between 1840–49.
185 About two-fifths of a pint.

tem, the effectiveness of which is now supported by the fact that the pupils of those educational establishments (for all prisons are regarded as such in recent times) increase in number year on year.

My readers will be aware that in Hungary County Halls aren't simply places where council meetings are held. These buildings, if not actually built by the nobility, are used exclusively by them – with the exception of the jail, where they also tolerate the presence of the ignoble – and are put to more pleasant uses. The great hall, for example, where of a morning the finest patriotic sentiments ring forth at the green table, or sometimes sentences of death are pronounced with a fitting solemnity that nothing, as is well known, so increases as the smoking of pipes, is unquestionably the most suitable of places for the *alispán* to be able to hold his sumptuous lunches . . . This is the place where the lack of order which is our frequent experience at morning council meetings is rectified at evening balls, when a hundred couples move in fine array to the sound of violin and cello. One of the main ancillary purposes of County Hall is to serve as a meeting-place . . . and although almost everywhere in the principal county towns gentlemen's clubs have been coming into being for some time now, and the *táblabírós* could find other premises, County Hall remains unequalled for comfort, and long custom has made it everyone's favourite; we can scarcely go into the office of a notary or attorney general without finding the individuals that work there surrounded by a whole company walking up and down the room, smoking their pipes and conversing in order to assist in the work. There is much in the Hungarian nobility that reminds us of Rome, such is our inclination to spend as much time as possible in County Hall. The Roman only felt at home in the Forum – the *táblabíró* has no dearer place than County Hall. There he finds entertainment, there he works, nowhere does he eat more tasty food than at the table at which he sits in council, his favourite places for cards are the offices of the attorney general and chief tax-gatherer. This custom was in vogue in Taksony County too, and my readers can evince no surprise if Nyúzó, who – as soon as he had completed his examinations in Tengelyi's house and informed the *alispán*'s wife of the outcome – had left for Porvár, on arrival found a whole company in the attorney general's rooms; after being informed by the magistrate about what had happened, they remained there to await the arrival of the once so proud notary, now a prisoner. Together with the host, the former county tax-gatherer Sáskay and *táblabíró* Zátonyi offered one another their snuffboxes and spoke of the rotten state of the modern world. Beside the stove James Bántornyi was explaining the jury system to a number of legal officers who had gone to sleep where they sat and couldn't leave, illustrating his learned discourse with certain very interesting and therefore frequently repeated English examples; while a retired captain, who lived in Porvár, was attributing this case also to the overly mild penal procedures, and a few *táblabírós* nodded their heads, sighed deeply, and encouraged the speaker in his passionate account, mostly with individual exclamations such as "Quite right! It's been two years since anybody was beheaded! We shall end up being killed as well!" Völgyesy himself, although he was no enthusiast for such company, was present that day, and repeatedly declared his conviction that Tengelyi was completely innocent of the charge, much to the offence of the rest and in particular of Nyúzó. Of the great men of Porvár, only Krivér – now deputy *alispán* – was missing; as he had heard from Nyúzó that the *alispán*'s wife wished the prisoner to be held with the greatest possible severity – while the *alispán* had, in contrast, ordered the greatest possible clemency, he was unable to resolve such conflicting demands and found it much more expedient to quit County Hall and leave the reception of Tengelyi to others.

The entrance of Kenyházy and the news that he and his prisoner had arrived safely put an end to all conversation. All attention was focused on the clerk, and I can safely say that for all Bandi's merits never had his entrance made so great an impression – not even when he first put on the *mente* lined with grey lamb's wool in which he now stood in the centre of the room. There's an old Roman saying, that he who hides from the attention of the world has lived a good life; I personally cast no doubt on the truth of that statement. It's in our nature to become as easily accustomed to the applause that we find on the stage of life as we find it hard to accept the pelting with rotten eggs and apples that also goes with the profession; and I believe that few people that have attained distinction would not, at the end of their lives, have confessed to themselves that they'd have done much better to remain in obscurity. In Hungary, however, it seems that this old saw carries no great weight, and there's hardly anyone that has seen themselves acclaimed and thinks it so very unpleasant . . . and who, when they're considered by everyone to be a *mázsa* – when they feel that they weigh a mere half a pound – wouldn't look round with such satisfaction as did Kenyházy in that moment? "Indeed, it's been a difficult journey!" said he, furrowing his brow and assuming an expression of the utmost solemnity. "I'd never have thought we'd have so much trouble."

"So what was the trouble?" asked Nyúzó sharply. "I thought so straight away! You were much later in arriving than I'd expected. I knew that something must have happened to delay you on the road."

"Delay us?" said Kenyházy. "And how! If I hadn't had two *hajdús* with me I don't know what would have happened."

"What the devil?" said the magistrate in surprise. "So did the notary resist arrest after all? Or was there an attempt to set him free?"

"Not exactly," replied the clerk; seeing the interest that the questions had aroused in those present he regretted having to answer in the negative. "But we were held up. One of the bridges is being mended, the driver had to go down off the embankment and the carriage sank axle-deep in the mud. As I said, if I hadn't had the two *hajdús*, and if the notary and I myself hadn't helped to push, we'd have been there until tomorrow, and then, I think, the outlaws would have tried to free the prisoner. Though if they had," he added, raising his fist in a heroic gesture, "they'd have found out who they were dealing with!"

This explanation made his late arrival much more reasonable, but it didn't fully satisfy the audience; the main interest remained, centred on Tengelyi's person, and three or four voices asked in unison what the notary had done on the journey. What had he talked about? How had he conducted himself?

"Well, nohow!" came the answer. "Since His Worship the *alispán* had made a point of instructing me to treat my prisoner with the greatest possible clemency."

"What!" burst out the magistrate, on whom these words had made an even greater impression than on the rest of those present. "The *alispán* actually gave you that order?"

"He certainly did!" replied Kenyházy. "I've never heard him speak so firmly as when he said that he was convinced of Mr Tengelyi . . . he actually called him Mr, I'm as sure as if he were saying it now . . . of Mr Tengelyi's innocence, and that I was to avoid anything that might make his painful situation even more unpleasant."

"Amazing!" said Sáskay.

"That's what I thought as well," continued the clerk, "but as that was what the *alispán* wanted . . ."

"I find this intervention by His Worship the *alispán* perfectly natural," Nyúzó cut in. He'd seen the effect that his clerk's words had had on the chief lawyer and inwardly cursed his Bandi. "Poor chap, what was he to do? His son's madly in love with the notary's daughter. If he doesn't pretend to be taking Tengelyi's part now that he's in trouble who can say what Ákos might resort to in his excitement. However, I know what he really thinks about this affair . . . Before I left, Her Ladyship asked me particularly to proceed with the utmost rigour in the investigation of the crime that has deprived her of her most loyal servant, and everyone knows that the alispán never holds an opinion that contradicts his wife's."

"I don't know," said the clerk, scratching his head, "perhaps I've done the wrong thing; but when His Worship the alispán had said that to me I didn't even put the handcuffs on him. And I tried to talk to him about all sorts of things, but could scarcely get a word out of him."

"A bad conscience!" sighed Sáskay.

"I think so as well," Kenyházy went on, "when he didn't even want to smoke a pipe, though I offered him three times."

"The clerk needn't have done that," said Zátonyi seriously. "We must at all times maintain our authority over prisoners . . . always behave with a certain gravitas, otherwise they'll even be thinking they're our equals."

"Well, never mind!" said Nyúzó cheerfully, seeing how crestfallen his clerk was at this comment. "It doesn't matter, Bandi, you always were a chivalrous young man. Have our prisoner brought in, let's hand him over; he'll be treated with the necessary gravitas in here, don't worry." The clerk left and a few minutes later in came Tengelyi escorted by the castellan and a hajdú, and followed by Völgyesy, who had left the room on hearing of his arrival and gone to meet him. The notary bore himself in a grave and manly fashion as always, equally distant from boastfulness and humility, and the calm with which he appeared before those on whom his fate largely depended didn't fail to make a lasting impression on all with the exception of Zátonyi and Nyúzó.

"Just look at his damn smugness," said the chief justice quietly to the chief lawyer. "We'll break him!"

"Of course, of course! If only the alispán hadn't taken his side," said the latter with a sigh.

The formalities of handing over and acceptance of the prisoner and the paperwork were soon completed, and Tengelyi was waiting in silence for the moment when he would be led as a prisoner to the prison by a warder, when Karvaly turned to the chief lawyer and asked what irons he was to put on the prisoner.

That question was perfectly natural from one in Karvaly's position, not only because he knew from experience that there are situations in life from which we feel a strong inclination to escape, but because there are in Taksony County, as in many other jurisdictions in Hungary, irons and irons, with no little difference between them; it must be a matter of some importance to the prisoner whether a pair of two-pound chains or fifty-pound fetters were fastened to his legs, and in this county the latter had been shown to be so strong that they interfered with not only the prisoners' attempts at escape but also with the orders of authority, by whom the use of such heavy irons was forbidden. In fact, in this county it had formerly been the practice for the choice of irons to be left to Karvaly's discretion, and he in turn delegated it on to the *hajdú* corporal; the present case, however, was one for which he preferred to pass the burden of responsibility to another, as he'd heard Kenyházy say that the *alispán* wished for the greatest consideration.

Routine though the question was, therefore, the *attorney general* was nonetheless clearly embarrassed by it, and could only comment that he thought it best to let the matter of irons wait for the deputy *alispán* to come back.

"What ever for?" said Nyúzó impatiently. "The prisoner's being handed over to the attorney general, and I see no reason why the matter can't be settled. Put simply anything on him, eight- or ten-pounders, and have done."

Before the attorney general could reply to this demand, Völgyesy advanced the view that he could see only purposeless torment in the attaching of irons if it wasn't necessary for the purpose of detaining the prisoner.

"It seems," said Zátonyi irritably, "that every criminal can find a supporter in Mr Völgyesy."

"Not every criminal," replied Völgyesy gravely, "but I consider it my duty to defend the man who is accused of some crime and of whose innocence I'm convinced, and for that reason I've asked Mr Tengelyi to entrust his defence to me."

"So we shall have the pleasure of honouring Tengelyi's defence lawyer in the junior prosecutor," said Nyúzó with a scornful smile, as he looked at Völgyesy.

"*Desperatarum causarum advocatus!*" said Zátonyi,[186] and laughed. "If only Viola hadn't escaped we'd have seen by this time what use your defending is."

"What use my defence is doesn't depend on me," said Völgyesy, with a scornful glance. "I can only state that I shall do everything in accordance with my duty to defend from any ill treatment the man whose

---

186 Latin: defendant of hopeless causes.

defence I undertake, as neither Hungarian law nor the circumstances require ... and I'm convinced that in this regard I can count on the support of our respected *alispán*."

The last words didn't fail to make an impression on the attorney general ... and after he had sent Tengelyi off with the *hajdús* the result of the brief conference that he conducted with those present – mostly in an undertone – was that he was to be incarcerated without irons until further instructions.

Karvaly and Nyúzó took this decision very much amiss, and the former in particular remarked what a terrible injustice it was (since the whole responsibility devolved upon him) that he might not employ the precautions against Tengelyi's escape without which it was impossible to hold a prisoner securely. However, the wish of the *alispán*, especially a couple of weeks after his election, was more than the arguments of a castellan could counter, and by his objection all that Karvaly obtained was a reminder from Sáskay that it was much easier to keep a prisoner in jail than to keep certain men on the field of battle ... and in the general laughter that ensued he couldn't make his witty reply heard, to the effect that in the county everything had to be doubly guarded, as it was well known that although the contents of a certain cash office had no legs and yet were kept in iron, they had nevertheless succeeded in vanishing while handled by certain persons.

The castellan looked around contemptuously, shrugged his shoulders, and once the laughter had subsided – he and the retired captain had laughed rather more temperately – he merely uttered the caution that since His Worship the *alispán* wished them to deal with Tengelyi with the utmost consideration, at least he wasn't to be blamed if that command was not entirely fulfilled, as it was natural that as the prisoner was to be confined without irons he would only be able to put him in one of the most secure cells in the lower prison.

If I don't acquaint them with the Taksony County prisons my readers won't understand the meaning of those words, and even less the horror that was evident on Völgyesy's face when he heard them. The reader mustn't think that in describing them I'm criticising the jurisdiction in which he lives or holds office. I'm describing the Taksony jails; it's not my fault if the prisons of many of the counties of Hungary have remained like them to this day.

In the old days prisoners were confined below ground level, and there is nothing more effective. By this process the sufferings of the innocently chained could cause no scandal; but the fate of the wicked made a still more alarming example if they were secretly held, condemned behind closed doors with no witnesses, taken to an underground prison, and nobody knew where they had vanished to. Those who, in accordance with the word of Scripture, desired not the death of sinners but that they should reform and live, could console themselves with the thought that wine is improved in cellars, and the same may happen with such people as are often induced to wickedness by wine itself. Those of less tender thoughts could say that since hell was well known to be under the ground they were merely shortening the way there for their prisoners.

Our constitution, as a witty friend of mine recently remarked, belongs in the Middle Ages . . . and he's right! Our decadent, prosaic age doesn't deserve that its sons should possess anything so fine and romantic! The state of our agriculture, and the laws that refer to it; our means of transport, whether by water or on land; our school system; the liberty that we nobles enjoy, which in Hungary the liberty of others doesn't limit; our civil and penal legal codes . . . can there be anything more imaginative? Indeed, all it would require is Scott, and Hungary would force Scotland into the background for romantic quality without the poet needing to go back a couple of centuries in his poetry. Here the power of life and death over others granted to some in the Middle Ages is still in vogue; and instead of the romantic medieval scaffold we have brought in very fine alternatives, in our whipping-posts at least. Hungary has, therefore, as I said, a medieval constitution; the whole thing is, to draw a simile, a building in splendid, full Gothic taste! In fact, parts of it are reminiscent of so-called wig-style, but that's true of almost all Gothic buildings. It's also true that here and there this building is beginning to decay and is only held up by struts which make it hard for us to move about inside – but when all's said and done it's Gothic, and that's the main thing, not only for the novelist, who can't feel more at home anywhere than beneath its pointed arches, but also for the reassurance of those who can't conceive of why our prisoners are kept underground in so many places. Whereas it is a well known fact that in Gothic buildings like ours there is nowhere else to put them.

Although Taksony County was in the forefront of higher intellectual matters, it didn't regard lowly material things as worthy of consideration, especially if they cost money; it had therefore kept its underground cells unchanged in the county hall of a hundred years ago. My readers – many of whom have probably only seen cells on the stage – should not imagine long, high-vaulted chambers, dimly lit, in which the solitary prisoner paces up and down, with only a bed, a water-jug, and a bit of bread. The Porvár prison isn't half as dreadful. There's a door in the courtyard, and when it's opened we can see twelve steps in front of us. If we go down these we come to a corridor, and looking down it we see twenty iron grills, each opening onto a separate cell. That's all. No nightmarish lofty vaults anywhere, the keystones of which can scarcely be seen in the gloom. The Porvár cells are nice and low, rather higher than one can reach not only by eye but also by hand. Nowhere a water-jug, but if the prisoners have money bottles of wine and flasks of *pálinka*. There's no solitary pacing up and down – the number of the occupants would make that impracticable, as in every individual cell, three fathoms wide and one and a half in length, one can find eight or ten prisoners; while there are the most entertaining company, pipe-smoking and reclining in comfort, mighty oaths and singing . . . in short, everything that a Hungarian can wish for. As my readers can see from the foregoing, the lower cells in Porvár were by no means as terrible as some maintain – at least as far as those for whom they were built is concerned; witnesses and accused, however, who weren't accustomed to prison life, didn't enjoy its social delights and were sometimes confined there for months – and they complained. It wasn't as if they needed to fear being forgotten by their jailer and dying of thirst, as on rainy days plenty of water always ran into their cells through the windows on the street side; the chief cause of complaint was the air, which – I speak only of those that weren't used to it – seemed bad, and was perhaps the reason why scurvy never died out in this prison and serious outbreaks of so-called jail-fever[187] occurred annually.

Such unhealthy cells are unquestionably very unpleasant, especially since it has become usual through our prejudices to provide every illness with a cure, and chemist's shops are so very expensive; I don't believe, however, that that alone could have persuaded the Estates of Taksony County to build new prisons. When the prices in chemist's shops rose exceedingly high the Assembly, despite the opposition of the chief medical officer, resolved that certain more costly medicines were not to be used . . . later, however, likewise by resolution, it accepted homeopathy for its prisons, by which means expense was reduced to a very modest amount, so that the establishment of new prisons was certainly not approved by miserly financial considerations. But there's a certain number beyond which even the all-powerful Estates of Taksony can't enclose more in a prison of a given size, and it was on account of that cir-

---

187 Epidemic typhus.

cumstance alone that the county eventually resolved to build a prison, even though it had always kept half of its prisoners at liberty on surety. The new prison, as befits our enlightened age, was constructed not underground but in the form of a two-storey building, and consisted of eight medium-sized rooms and one larger; in the former those detained always numbered from twenty-five to forty, and in the later from fifty to eighty. As far as health was concerned, the prisoners' condition was no more favourable in the so-called superior prison than in the cellars described above; this persuaded one section of the older *táblabírós* that the frequent cases of disease were not the consequence of the badness of the cells.

Such were the cells in which Taksony County held its five hundred prisoners; and my readers can't be surprised if Völgesy was horrified at the thought of Tengelyi being incarcerated in any of them. In addition to these cells, however, there were on the first floor four smallish rooms that were used for the detention of prisoners who, either with regard to their social standing or for some other reason, were kept out of the ordinary cells; and the young lawyer requested that his client be placed in one of these for as long as his case lasted.

"Good heavens!" laughed Zátonyi, "a private cell for a village notary! Whoever heard of such a thing?"

"*I say,*" James Bántornyi interrupted in English, "Mr Völgyesy's right. Every prisoner should be held in solitude, *solitary confinement* (again in English). He's got a bed in there, a jug, a table on which to work, a bible, and if he's a Papist, never mind, a crucifix. There's nothing better, I've seen them myself in England. Have none of you read the second report, called the Second Report on Prison Discipline?"[188]

"Really, Your Honour must give up these English frivolities," Zátonyi cut in irritably. "Thank God we live in Hungary."

"But look here, I say," repeated James, "there's no punishment more severe than solitary confinement; the Auburn system,[189] which I saw in Bridewell,[190] is nothing like it."

"Of course, we should even give our prisoners sugar and coffee," said Zátonyi, laughing again. "and rice pudding, as someone said the other

---

188 Reference is to the [Second] Report of the Committee of the Society for the Improvement of Prison Discipline, and for the Reformation of Juvenile Offenders. Published in 1820.

189 A penal method of the 19th century in which persons worked during the day and were kept in solitary confinement at night, with enforced silence at all times.

190 Bridewell Palace in London was built as a residence of King Henry VIII and

day in America, where it's part of the prison regime. But really, *domine spectabilis*, when there are only thirty-three prisons in the whole of the county how are we to lock up five hundred prisoners so that they have a cell each? There's no room!"

"No room?" now the retired captain spoke up in his usual vehement tone. "And why not? Because instead of being hanged as they should be, people are locked up – that's why! If it were up to me there'd be room, I can tell you! Fifty strokes or the gallows! Anything else is sheer nonsense."

"I wouldn't object in the least to Tengelyi being held in solitude," said Völgyesy, turning now to the attorney general, who was visibly much affected by the news that the *alispán* wished him to treat Tengelyi with all possible consideration, "but in fact we have no room . . . The four smaller cells that we use for solitary confinement are occupied."

"So after all there are four cells in which prisoners are in solitary confinement!" James cut in sharply. "What did I say? At last we too are getting to where England is. Solitary confinement has been introduced for four prisoners, and it will gradually spread to the rest. Like O'Connell,[191] I too accept the least amount as part payment."

"You're right!" said the attorney general, afraid that he was about to hear a hundred descriptions of Millbank prison.[192] "But what can we do about it: one at a time in four cells, there's only room for four people, and these solitary confinement cells are occupied."

"Occupied! And by whom, may I ask?" James went on. As he was always saying, nothing interested him more than prison-keeping, in much the same way that we're all interested in what happens to us after our death without the least desire to satisfy our curiosity by experience.

"Well, Your Honour," replied Karvaly, "we're holding a baron in the first. Poor man, he's been there almost three years now, though he's certainly not guilty of anything."

---

was one of his homes early in his reign. Given to the City of London Corporation by Edward VI for use as an orphanage and place of correction for wayward women, Bridewell later became the first prison/poorhouse to have an appointed doctor. It was built on the banks of the Fleet River in the City of London between Fleet Street and the River Thames in an area today known as "Bridewell Court". It was closed in 1855 and demolished in 1863-4.

191 Daniel O'Connell (1775 – 1847), Irish political leader.

192 A prison in Westminster, London, originally constructed as the National Penitentiary, Jeremy Bentham's proposed Panopticon. Opened in 1816, it was closed in 1890 and demolished by 1903.

"*Indeed?* Not guilty? asked James.

"Quite so!" replied the castellan with a sigh; this was perhaps the only one of his charges for whom he felt any pity. "He was a passionate man, and it certainly happened once or twice that he had a few peasants or servants beaten, or he did it himself. How can it be helped when there's no other way of dealing with peasants! It happens to other honest men too and no one says a word about it. He was unlucky! It must have been about thirty years ago that he hit a servant on the head so hard that he happened to die, and a case was brought against him at once. While the case, which everyone's now beginning to forget, went quietly on the baron unfortunately got into more trouble. He thought a very great deal of his garden, and the peasants constantly used to steal his fruit and flowers, so that eventually he swore that he'd take revenge – anyone caught stealing would be given forty strokes. Next day, alas, a boy was caught in the act of picking cherries from the tree. The baron meant to keep his word . . . and what could anyone do?. . . the boy was only ten . . . he couldn't endure it, and died. At that there was a terrible to-do . . . another law-suit, and the county had no alternative but to sentence the baron to six months jail; the Court of Seven[193] extended the sentence to four years, and now he's seventy; it's really cruel to lock up a man like that for four years!"

"*Yes, yes*, I remember," said James, "I heard about it when I came back from England. But I thought that the baron had been set free long ago, because I saw him the other day on his estate."

"If we don't let him out occasionally," said the attorney general, "his entire property will be ruined."

"In the second cell," Karvaly went on," that lawyer is imprisoned – as Your Honour knows –who was sentenced for issuing false bills. In the third is an engineer, who's in jail for forging banknotes."

"So what's your experience, Mr Karvaly?" asked James with the greatest interest. "Doesn't being locked up alone, *solitary confinement*, have a marvellous effect on prisoners?"

"Indeed it does," replied Karvaly gravely. "Since the baron's been with us, he's put on weight; he has no complaint but that, as he says, he's never lost so much at tarok as he has since he's been playing with Sáskay every evening, and for some time he's not been able to find any wine that he likes . . ."

---

193 A section of the King's Bench (*Királyi Kúria*), the highest court in Hungary.

"Wine and cards don't go with *solitary confinement*," remarked James, "but let's leave the very strict punishment in England. So what do the other two do?"

"The lawyer who's been imprisoned for uttering false bills," Karvaly went on, "gives legal advice to people who are looking for money or who want to lend. And the forger writes and draws all the time. Your Honour may perhaps have seen the picture that he drew the other day. There's a portrait of the *alispán* in the middle and all sorts of drawings round it, two or three fivers and tenners, so perfectly copied that nobody could have known."

"Now that's good!" said James approvingly. "Work is the soul of prison discipline, it's the only thing that can reform the wicked."

"But if you please," said Völgyesy at last; he'd been suppressing his impatience all through this conversation. "One of these one-man cells is empty, so why could Tengelyi not be put in there?"

"Impossible," replied the castellan drily. "The honourable county has decreed that one of the cells must always be vacant in case of unexpected events."

"But isn't this unexpected, then?" asked Völgyesy.

"Whether it is or it isn't," said the castellan, stroking his moustache and looking down from his grenadier's height at the little lawyer, "the honourable county has commanded that one cell be vacant, and I see to it that it is. And furthermore, the notary can't be locked in that cell in any case: for the last three years Her Ladyship Mrs Réty's been using it for a larder, and she holds the key."

This last reason was, as my readers will see, the sort against which Völgyesy couldn't win. Even the attorney general himself didn't believe that the consideration with which Réty wished the prisoner to be treated could be taken so far as to have his wife's larder emptied for the purpose, and so he firmly opposed his youthful colleague; Völgyesy displayed extraordinary tact as he understood the situation but continued to argue his case.

"But when all's said and done," said he, when he could see that he couldn't win that argument, "if the *alispán*'s larder can no longer be applied to the purpose for which it was built, what's to prevent us putting two of the three prisoners who've actually been sentenced into one cell, and giving the one thus freed to Tengelyi?"

"That would be the end!" exclaimed Karvaly. "The baron would really take it amiss if I were to put somebody else in his cell, especially if he heard that it was for the benefit of a notary."

Völgyesy reminded those present several times more how insulting and unjust it was for an honest man like Tengelyi to be locked up along with known criminals; but Nyúzó put an end to the long debate when he remarked, with a glare at Völgyesy in which contempt was matched by anger, that it was ridiculous to argue for days over such childishness, and that Mr Völgyesy might defend his notary in the case as he pleased, but he'd do well not to forget that an honorary *alügyész* didn't give orders in County Hall.

"Give up, my boy," said one of the *táblabírós*, when Völgyesy was about to answer. "If you annoy us your notary may yet be clapped in irons." And the young lawyer felt it better to choke back the feelings that were crowding his bosom.

"In any case," said the attorney general to Karvaly, "you must put him in a cell where there aren't too many."

"He'll go into number twenty," replied Karvaly. "There are only five in there, the old receiver of stolen goods, who's been there twelve years now, a murderer and a horse thief and a couple of children as well."

"Very well," said the attorney general approvingly, "he'll be best off in there. If there's anything that he needs, give him anything that you can. His Worship the *alispán* wants us to treat him with all consideration."

Völgyesy followed Karvaly into the corridor, feeling crushed at heart, and there Tengelyi was sitting on a bench, awaiting the outcome of the discussion concerning him.

"I'm surprised not to have had at least half a *mázsa* of irons put on my legs," he said on hearing the decision as he went down the stairs with Völgyesy and the jailer. "I'm in their power; His Honour may be sure they'll make me feel it."

The lawyer said that the inhuman treatment could only continue until the next day, and that he would go in person to see the *alispán*, and as he'd sent word that Tengelyi was to be treated with all consideration he didn't intend him to be incarcerated with the greatest criminals.

"Don't waste your time," said Tengelyi sourly, "first of all because you won't succeed; secondly because I've reached the stage where I don't care whether I have to suffer a bit more or a bit less. You regard my being locked in prison with criminals as a great misfortune . . . when you're a little older you'll see that in this respect prison and life aren't as different as you think." And with that the notary wouldn't allow his young friend to accompany him further than the door to the cells, shook his hand, looked around one last time beneath God's open sky, and went down the stairs with the jailer and a *hajdú*.

Völgyesy stood outside the prison for a long time, deep in thought, and as at length, on hearing the heavy door slam shut, he was slowly leaving County Hall, he met Kálmán Kislaky. He'd come from Tiszarét, as he said, to enquire how Tengelyi was since Ákos himself had been reluctant to leave his fiancée in the state of mind into which recent events had plunged her. My readers can imagine his feelings on hearing of Tengelyi's fate. He hurried back to the inn, where he'd left his horse, and without letting the poor animal get its breath back mounted and galloped off to Tiszarét, convinced that the *alispán* would put an end to this unworthy treatment at once as soon as he heard of Tengelyi's situation.

XXXIII

The sun hadn't yet set when Tengelyi took leave of Völgyesy and was led to his cell. Before crossing the threshold the hapless man took one more look around at its final rays, which for the first time in days were piercing the autumnal mist and gilding the chimneys of County Hall. His heart sank at the thought that sunlight and the open air, those gifts of God that every beggar enjoys, were henceforth to be taken from him. Below in the cells it was already dark. In addition to the filthy panes of the low windows, which were here and there pasted over with paper excluding the light, though in themselves they would have been sufficient, heavy iron grills and wire netting so barred the rays of the sun from that dismal place that even at noon the most that it received was a twilight. As the daylight faded, anyone entering from the yard felt that they were in total darkness until their eyes became accustomed to the gloom. This darkness, and even more so the stinking damp air that began to make itself evident at the fourth step, had such an effect on Tengelyi that he could scarcely hear the warder's encouragements; this last regarded all better-off prisoners as a source of income and didn't fail to show him his usual courtesy. This worthy officer, who bore the rank of warder, made room as best he could for his prisoner to deposit his luggage in the cell, with a curse admonished those who were thus displaced that they were in no way to inconvenience their new companion, and asked Tengelyi once more whether he would require anything for the night.

The notary said that most of all he would like another palliasse or mattress.

"Certainly," said the warder, "of course, I'll have to borrow that from somebody else, and I don't know how much a day they'll ask for it. But if the gentleman will pay, there'll certainly be one."

The notary said that he was prepared to pay.

"Then no problem!" the warder went on. "Anyone that's got money can get everything in here: wine, *pálinka*, meat, anything, as long as they've got money. It wouldn't be a bad idea," he added in an undertone, "to send for a drop of wine or *pálinka* for these here. Every time a new prisoner arrives it's usual to drink his health, and these are in a bad mood today because we've made them move up. It'd be as well to please them a bit, otherwise you'll have a lot of trouble with them."

Tengelyi said that if he thought it a good idea he should bring something, as long as he was left in peace by his fellow prisoners.

"Naturally, if you'll pay."

Tengelyi asked how much was required and immediately handed over the sum desired.

"Do you hear that?" said the warder. "This gentleman's a decent sort. He's having wine and *pálinka* brought for you at lamp-lighting time, so drink his health, and don't do anything to upset him." In the darkness several voices loudly expressed their pleasure at the promise, and the warder left, closing the iron grill. Tengelyi sat down on his luggage and, holding his head in his hands, sank into gloomy thought.

If ever a man deserved the name of man for the resoluteness of his character, that man was Tengelyi. Deserted by his friends, without wealth or supporters, battered by destiny, he had hitherto struggled manfully with his fate, and even if he'd often been without hope he'd never lost confidence in himself . . . now for the first time he felt that he'd lost heart. Previously, whatever his troubles he'd retained his liberty and his good name . . . now he'd lost those too. Imprisoned along with criminals, every decent person would shun him, and he had no means of proving his innocence.

As he thought over all the circumstances of Macskaházy's murder he became convinced that as long as Viola didn't fall into the hands of the authorities and confess – neither of which seemed very likely – suspicion would remain on him, and he could await either a shameful death or lifelong imprisonment; then what would become of his children? All that he'd be able to leave them would be his disgraced name.

He was roused from these dismal thoughts by words addressed from the far side of the cell.

"You mustn't feel sorry for yourself, my friend," said a weak, hoarse voice. "It's pretty cold in this damned cellar, and anybody that grieves, falls sick."

In the darkness Tengelyi couldn't see the speaker, but the cracked voice and the wheezing and coughing that accompanied it told him that he must be very old.

"Now, what's the good of never saying anything?" said the voice, when it realised that the new arrival did't mean to answer. "If we're living together we've got to get to know each other; by and large we don't have such a grim life as a lot of people think. Do we, lads?"

"Not at all," a man's voice and a boy's replied in unison.

"Not at all!" said the first, with a hoarse laugh, "except that young Imre here gets flogged ever three months, and when Pista's sentence is confirmed by Vienna he'll be beheaded; that's a bit of a worry."

"Why do you talk about such a thing?" said the man's voice, shaking audibly.

"Well, never mind!" said the first. "Maybe you'll get a pardon. You were only twenty when you killed that Slovak child, so it was pretty stupid to pick that useless oil-vendor if you had to kill somebody. You only found fifteen *garas* on him. And I've been sentenced to death twice, and I'm still here, and if I'm beheaded, just think, your father was hanged, and maybe even so you'll die after me. Well, when you're ninety-three . . ."

"Ninety-three?" Tengelyi couldn't help exclaiming – the whole conversation filled him with horror.

"Ninety-three," said the other with a cough. "A good age, isn't it? And I've spent fifty-four years in prison . . . and I'm all right . . . and if God keeps me, I'll be out again by St István's day."

"Fifty-four years?" queried the notary in amazement.

"Yes, if not a bit more," came the reply. "I was jailed for stealing a horse as well, I don't know how often for stealing cattle; then I got mixed up in a murder. Twice I've been jailed for fire-raising, but then I was innocent; this time they've accused me of being the leader in the robbery in Pást, in which three were killed. Well," he added with a laugh, "by St István I'll be out; perhaps their honours were right to blame me after all."

"Tell us about when the Jew was killed, granddad," said the boy's voice.

"Not now," said the old man with a cough, "can't you see I've got a cough? Ask Pista to tell you how he killed the Slovak."

"He can't tell a story like you can," replied the boy. "When you talk it really cheers me up."

"Well, never mind, your turn'll come," said the old men, laughing and coughing at the same time. "If you don't kill somebody before your moustache grows, I bet I'll never be out of this cell."

"I'll kill somebody, for sure!" boasted the boy, "just let me get out some time."

"You'll never dare," said the old man, mocking him.

"Won't I?" said the boy in a harsh tone. "You'll see! When they shut me in here I was a timid idiot, I only had to see a knife and I'd run a mile, but since you've told me all those great stories I've changed completely. I still dream at night about the old Jew that you hanged on the tree in the forest. Just let me get another axe, I shan't be cutting sticks with it."

"All right, all right!" said the old man. "You'll be quite a boy, but what's your friend doing?"

"He's asleep again," replied the boy.

490

"Again?" said the old man crossly. "Pull his hair good and hard and wake him up, then slap his face. He's a horrible boy, he'll never come to anything."

The cry of pain that Tengelyi now heard and the pleading tone in which the other boy asked for mercy showed that the old criminal's order had been carried out, and although he had inwardly proposed not to come into contact with his fellow prisoners the boy's cries made him forget his intention. He stood up and went towards the side of the cell from where speech was heard and asked crossly, "Why not let the poor boy sleep?"

"Leave my children alone," said the old villain with a laugh. "I have to knock 'em about a bit now and then, it's part of education. I've got enough trouble with 'em, young Imre might come to something, he'll be a credit to me; but that lazy bastard will never be any good. I've put up with the two for a year now."

"You'd do better," said Tengelyi seriously, "to think about the hour of your death than to corrupt these children in your old age."

"I'm not corrupting them," said the old man with a cough. "In fact, I'm making men of 'em. They can be grateful to the noble county for locking 'em up with me, at least they'll learn something here."

At that moment the creaking of the big iron door of the prison interrupted the conversation. A lantern was brought and hung up at the end of the corridor where Tengelyi's cell was, shedding light on the objects around him. He was horrified when he saw the place into which his luckless fate and the wickedness of his enemies had brought him. It wasn't the brown patches that came into sight on the walls of the cell, while in other places where the lamplight fell drops of moisture shone brightly; it wasn't the desolation of the place, where nothing was to be seen that answered the requirements of human comfort but some rotting straw and a broken jug; nor was it the loathsome filth that surrounded him on all sides that filled him with horror – all that was merely material hardship! No deprivation could alarm him, nor the most agonising physical torment, nor the danger of death itself, which was perhaps all around him in that unhealthy place; but when he saw the heavy iron bars that cast their shadows on the cell wall, and when he heard the rattle of chains around him, his captivity and the foul crime of which he was accused came to his mind, and when he looked around and saw those together with whom he was incarcerated his manly heart sank. The old prisoner with whom Tengelyi had been talking occupied one corner of the cell. He was sitting there, crouched on the straw and leaning his back against the wall, hanging his head so that his features could scarcely be seen; only when he sometimes looked up as he spoke and turned his gleaming eyes to someone could the face be made out on which almost a century of sin had left its mark. It was one of those faces which, once seen, is never to be forgotten; and the warder himself, for all his lack of feeling, approached this prisoner with a certain apprehension; he was, as he said, more like a ghost than a living human being. The white beard that covered almost the whole lower part of his face – the sparse silvery hairs that dangled from his head – the deep hollows of his eyes and temples – all indicated that he was coming to an age that few attain and which in another is an object of respect or at least pity. The look in his eyes – which seemed to have outlived the rest of his body and gleamed in youthful fire beneath his long eyebrows, giving the whole face an indescribable and frightening expression – showed that even if this prison-patriarch lacked the strength to do evil, at least the desire remained in him; and when he raised his desiccated, trembling hands towards you, rather than pity you felt relief that they were no longer capable of holding a dagger. The enfeebled voice, which he used only for relating his past evil deeds and for cursing, filled your soul with loathing, and however wretched the situation in which you saw him, you could not wish that the sufferings of this hapless man, whose heart had never been touched by remorse, should be ended otherwise than by death.

At the old man's side, also on the floor, knelt a boy; judging from his undeveloped limbs and piping voice you would have thought that he was fourteen at the most. His face looked old before its time. You looked in vain for the gentle smile of youth on those pallid cheeks; the young brow was furrowed, and instead of a cheerful glance his eyes looked around with a dull mindlessness except when the old prisoner beside him occasionally addressed him by name, or he felt the touch of his trembling hand as it stroked his hair. Then an expression of emotion enlivened his face and it looked as if the boy was moved by inward instinct to love, and wished to give the whole treasure of his feelings to that one vile creature. The other boy, whose cries had made Tengelyi intervene, went and stood at the iron grill as soon as the lantern was brought to the corridor, and was staring at the wick. When the flame flared up from time to time his face showed an indescribable delight, he clasped his hands together and laughed aloud in glee; when it burnt less strongly he complained sadly that it had been badly adjusted and was going to go out as it had the other day! "Oh, if only I could get out!" he sighed, "I'd light it! I'd pull the wick out nice and high, fill it with oil, and it would burn beautifully with flames of red, yellow and blue, even prettier than now. Look, look! how the flame's stretching up; go on, grow, grow, little flame, right to the roof, above the whole town, bright and warm. Oh, just look, isn't it lovely!" And the poor boy pressed his burning face against the iron grill. "Oh, if only I could get closer! Could reach out to it!"

"Then, of course," said the young murderer, who was lying in the other corner of the cell, enveloped in his sheepskin, "you'd set fire to the whole prison again. Come away from the grill, you young idiot, or I'll grab your hair and pull you away."

"You'll do well to pull his hair, Pista," said the old man with a cough. "We nearly suffocated in the smoke the other day. You can see, the boy's completely out of his mind, he can't hear or see."

Tengelyi restrained the young prisoner who had stood up and was reaching for the boy, and he asked how it could have happened that even in prison the boy had somehow started a fire.

"Well, I never saw such a boy," said the other. "He begged for hours for me to give him my flint and steel. Once he'd got hold of them I had to use force to get them back. He'd have struck sparks until morning, and every time he saw a spark he laughed and shouted like a mad thing. Once he stole a bit of tinder off me, set fire to it and pushed it into the old man's straw, and it caught fire."

"Box his ears, Pista," said the old man, in whom the memory of the danger revived the hatred that he felt towards the boy, and Tengelyi would scarcely have been able to save him from that when the warder came to the grill with some *kalács* and an *icce*[194] of *pálinka*, which gave new direction to the thoughts of the old man, Pista and Imre.

"Bring that *pálinka* here, young Imre," said the old man. "You take the *kalács*, Pista, and leave that useless boy alone, if that's what that chap wants who sent for the *pálinka*; I don't care if he gawps at the lantern until tomorrow, just keep an eye on your tinder. Won't Your Honour have a drink?" said he to Tengelyi. Now that the lantern had been brought he looked at him very closely, and his answer that he wouldn't drink came as great a surprise as his respectable appearance and the unusual – by prison standards – cleanliness of his clothes.

"I don't care!" said he eventually, after his repeated attempts to draw Tengelyi into conversation had failed. "He's paid for the *pálinka*, let's leave the boy in peace. Tomorrow," he added more quietly, "you can

---

194 *Icce* is a pre-metric measure of volume, 0.9 litres. *Kalács* is a sweetbread.

torment him until he sends for *pálinka*, we can use him for a cellar, as it seems he's got money. Drink up, young Imre, just stick to *pálinka*, you're cross-eyed already, don't worry, you'll get used to it, they'll take you in the army just the same."

Tengelyi had the old man's calculation to thank for being left alone from then on, and while his young fellow prisoners became drunk on the strong spirit and expressed their pleasure in ever louder laughter and their ancient chief at last fell asleep he was able to devote himself freely to his thoughts. There are people who can't become involved in public affairs without their personal interests coming to mind ten times every half-hour . . . but also those whom every thought that their personal situation arouses leads to general subjects concerning the whole, and Tengelyi was one such. The unfortunate condition in which he saw himself and the dangers by which he was surrounded made him realise how many lights like his were hidden in the hundred prison walls of Hungary . . . and he forgot his own troubles when he considered the state in which criminal procedure is in Hungary.

If there are subjects that can fill the human heart with horror this is one. There's no need for us to look at our prisons from the point of view of sentimental philanthropy – for I know that philanthropy's been an object of scorn for some time now! Here and there among the gold there's been false bronze, and some have been led to the excessive imitation of sentiment by weakness or because their hearts are not imbued with genuine love of their fellow men; consequently these days everyone makes free with the name of philanthropy. But let's take just a single cold look at our prisons, and can we, as we take pride in our advancement in mid-nineteenth century, tolerate this state of affairs to continue?

Since under present social conditions there are many who, even after long consideration, can't really see that the upholding of the law is in their interests, I can see that severe punishments are desired in Hungary. But is it therefore necessary that, in addition to punishment in the gloom of his cell, the prisoner be exposed to a thousand sufferings which neither he nor his judges suspect, nor those to whom his suffering might serve as an example? Is it necessary that the prisoner's fate should depend rather on the cell into which he happens to come, or the *hajdú*'s disposition, than on the judge's? Or that while we, in our assemblies, make ever finer speeches against the death penalty, underneath the council chamber our prisoners should fall victim to infectious diseases? Let our punishments be severe, even harsh, I don't mind.

494

Let's bring in Draco's code, under which every crime was punishable by death. Let the hangman be the defender of our public security, let the gallows be the foundation stone of our state – we shudder at such laws, but the cruelty is only superficially greater. Nowadays we don't execute our prisoners with the axe, but any that crosses the threshold of our prisons is, in effect, sentenced to death, and the scaffold on which their lives would be ended in a moment is often only replaced by a lengthy wretchedness which takes them to the grave by a more painful road. And how many innocent persons, like Tengelyi, occupy our prisons merely because they are accused of some crime, and how many are there, whose crime was the result of the mere passion of a moment or an accident?

May my readers not take what I've said as a complete digression. I'm in the fortunate position that my views on this subject do not differ from those of my hero, and in what I've said above the thoughts that engage me are more or less those that were going through Tengelyi's soul in the moment which our tale has reached.

As his drunken cell-mates had fallen asleep there was no one to disturb him from these thoughts. Tengelyi was brought back to earth by the opening of the cell door; in came a prisoner who introduced himself as Gazsi Csavargós[195]; he put down at Tengelyi's side a mattress, a blanket and a pillow, and although he was a denizen of that prison he was presently working in the attorney general's kitchen; he'd also brought a little basket containing a bottle of wine, some bread and some roast meat, and he informed Tengelyi that these things were all from Mr Völgyesy; he should be patient for the time being, and next day he would have a cell to himself. "I'll make you a bed," he added cheerfully, "fit for for a king. I've done that for the lawyer gentleman as well. "

"Won't you have something to eat?" said Tengelyi, who hadn't had a thing all day, and despite his unhappiness set about the food with gusto.

"Thank you kindly," said the other, "I've already eaten. There was a dinner at the attorney general's this evening, and I was on duty . . . I shan't need anything until the day after tomorrow. I hope the wine's in order?" said he, stopping in making the bed as he noticed that Tengelyi was scarcely touching it. "Mr Völgyesy insisted that that I should bring the best. I went to the inn myself, and if I go there the landlord doesn't play me tricks, because he knows that if ever he deceives me I'll be straight off to the 'Lion.'"

---

195 From *csavargó* 'vagabond, loafer'.

Tengelyi could hardly suppress his amusement when he heard that. "You'd better try it yourself," said he and passed the bottle over, "I'm not going to drink any more."

"Thank you kindly," said the prisoner as he raised the bottle to his lips. "Ah," he added after drinking, "now that's what I call wine! God bless Mr Völgyesy and His Worship too. If they gave me wine like this every day I'd never leave."

"It sounds as if you're not dissatisfied with being in prison!" said Tengelyi.

"I'm not as badly off as I thought I would be when they put me inside," said Csavargós good humouredly. "I've been in service all my life, and now I'm a kitchen-hand, so there's not much difference. In fact, when the weather's bad and I'm nice and dry in the kitchen, and I remember the way I used to be forced out to work winter and summer at one time, it seems I've never had it so good. The food's good, the clothing's good, sometimes I get a little tip, and the *hajdús* don't trouble me . . . A poor man can always be satisfied with service like this."

"But don't you ever think of freedom?" asked Tengelyi sharply. "Don't you yearn to be free of those chains?"

"The chains, certainly, do bother me at times," said the prisoner calmly, "especially when I'm putting my boots on, you wouldn't believe the trouble I have with them, but now they've put the lightest irons on me. But who can say, if the chains were taken off me wouldn't I just have to earn my living and there'd be much greater burdens on my shoulders? And freedom? Well, if the weather's very nice, especially on a starry evening, it sometimes crosses my mind how good it would be to gallop round the fields with my mates; and sometimes I'd like to be at home, because the wine in the pub there's a lot better than in these damn Porvár inns! But then, freedom has its bad side as well . . . you have to go into service."

Tengelyi gave a sigh. "Now, you mustn't let it grieve you," said Csavargós, who at that moment would have thought anything but that the notary was sighing over his moral decay. "Tomorrow you're being put in a separate cell and you'll have no trouble. If Mr Völgyesy's taking on your defence you'll get out, that's as sure as I'm sitting here. The devil himself wouldn't keep you in this hole of a cellar; there isn't a man worth anything in this whole prison."

"The company can't be very good in other places," said Tengelyi as he lay down on his bed.

"Not a bit of it!" said Csavargós. "I've been in a prison where it was nothing but pleasure. Only people of experience; I never heard finer stories. One had scarcely finished before the next one began, and there were even women there. But this place would drive you to despair."

"So this isn't your cell?" asked Tenelyi.

"Certainly not," came the reply. "I generally sleep in the lawyer gentleman's kitchen or in the yard. I've only come in here today because Mr Völgyesy told me to keep a look-out so that Your Honour should have no trouble."

"Trouble?"

"That old villain is capable of anything," said the kitchen-hand. "He's tormented the one boy so badly a couple of times that he nearly became seriously ill."

"So why are the boys left with him? asked the notary in horror.

"Well, they say," replied Csavargós, as he too lay down on his sheepskin, "that every time only men have been locked up with him they've all committed serious crimes the minute the've been released. Pista's been locked up here because, according to the lawyer, he's certain to be beheaded. Boys like that, even if they get out, can't get up to much mischief."

"What did they do that got them in here?" asked the notary.

"That's the odd thing!" replied Csavargós with a big yawn. "In the village where they come from there was one fire breaking out after another, and investigation showed that they'd been started by mere children, boys of thirteen or fourteen. Mr Völgyesy says it's a disease, and I think so as well; but whether it is or not, the magistrate had the rest flogged and these two, as their parents are deceased, were brought here. They'll be real villains when they grow up. Good night!" And with that he wrapped himself in his sheepskin and was soon snoring.

Tengelyi stayed awake for a while and looked at his sleeping companions by the fading light of the candle. At length fatigue overcame him, caused by the unaccustomed excitement, the travelling, and the sleepless previous night. Let's leave him to rest; may Heaven send sweet dreams to all that suffer.

XXXIV

There are times in life when anyone that has set riches, power or distinction as the goal of his life's work is profoundly aware of the futility of his best efforts. There's a point on the wide road by which most strive for the trappings of good fortune at which he who advances along it – still far from his goal despite all his exertion – finds himself obstructed by the seething crowd around him and yet alone, and comes to the sorry conclusion that the satisfaction that he's been seeking isn't attainable by that road; he breaks with the majority and strikes upwards by solitary ways, not so that the crowd shall admire his exalted position but so that he may feel himself elevated; not so as to be seen by many, but that a wider vista may open to his eyes; not because he means to dominate from his height, but because he yearns for liberty; although he sometimes feels his strength failing on the path that few tread, he can never look back on his past with such great bitterness as that with which the *alispán*, pacing his room as he contemplated his present situation, realised that the whole direction of his life had been misguided.

Réty wasn't by nature an unfeeling man. In his youth there had been no one who so needed to come close to others, to be liked by many. Fate had endowed him with mental powers above the average, though not outstanding, with a good estate and those outward perfections which are perhaps more necessary than inward excellence if we are to be fortunate, and young Réty had every right to call himself blessed. It seemed that there was nothing lacking from either his personal qualities or his situation that could make him such, and if by following his nature he didn't rise beyond the circle in which destiny had placed him we would now probably see in him one of those fortunate individuals to whom life has conferred almost all his desires.

There was, however, a side to Réty's character that frustrated all those expectations: *weakness*, and that which commonly follows (when it doesn't derive from lack of brains) – *vanity*, and these didn't permit him to enjoy at leisure what destiny brought. Torn from his natural situation by these faults, his life became a long series of disappointments and regrets. Just as the tendency to cling to people, which his school-fellows and the friends of his early youth had experienced in him, wasn't the outcome of affectionateness but rather of his constant need of someone on whom he could rely for support, when he returned from the university and entered everyday life the views and advice of his parents couldn't fail to influence the young man; and although he at first rather tolerated than shared his father's ambitious plans for him, it wasn't long before – inclined as he was to vanity – he favoured the prospect that was set before his eyes every day and yearned himself for those distinctions which he had not rejected out of hand because he had been unable to oppose his father's wishes.

My readers know how Réty fell out with his university friend Tengelyi when he first stood for office. The young man felt the unworthiness of his action, and did his utmost to dissuade his father from his intention. He said a hundred times that he'd despise himself if he were capable of treating his best friend in that fashion. But when he heard his father say that he would frustrate his best prospects in that way; when his mother pleaded, and when men said that there had never been so young a chief justice in the county, and the women one so good looking, and yet they had all agreed that Tengelyi couldn't be appointed to that office, Réty hadn't been able to resist, and every finer thought and nobler feeling that spoke out in his heart had only made him realise his mistake and from then on avoid his friend's company so as not to be ashamed in his eyes.

Held firmly in the circle of public life by that action, and accustomed to the little honours and worthless distinctions that county life has to offer, and which serve rather to stimulate than to satisfy vanity (as I see it, these are the main reason why this fault is so widespread in our nation), Réty's natural inclination was further developed; and it is only natural that in succeeding his father as *alispán* he felt quite comfortable surrounded by sycophants.

Some even then accused him of lack of principle and believed that the reserve which he displayed towards everything sprang from a deeply hatched plan, but they were mistaken. All that the *alispán* had wanted for a long time was that he should be the first in Taksony County, the one who was most loved and praised; his caution only came from un-willingness to offend anyone and so deprive himself of an admirer. His vanity made modest demands. He was one of those who have no need of lavish praise or a great sphere of influence in order to feel content, but who are delighted if they can climb slowly, step by step, just as long as they can always find about them men by whom they'll be admired; and since the office of *alispán* of Taksony met those requirements and it didn't occur to Réty that it was the greatest possible shame for a man to be favoured by all parties equally, he desired nothing more.

499

This apparent satisfaction, however, only lasted as long as there was no one around him who would disturb him, and the vain man was only able to enjoy his current distinction while no one aroused loftier desires in him. The death of Ákos's mother and his second marriage brought this about.

In his first marriage Réty had followed his heart, as fortunately on that occasion his parents' wishes hadn't conflicted with his own; but his choice of a second wife was in pursuit of the satisfaction of his vanity, and he brought to his house a woman who, though poor, came from a great family and was fulsomely praised by everyone on account of her beauty and her intellect alike. The thought that he would be envied by all and admired by almost everyone when he, a widower, was able to catch the most beautiful girl in the region meant more to him than any other happiness, and even later, when he'd realised that his wife had qualities other than beauty and cleverness, that thought at least was a great consolation to him. That woman, whom my readers know, was incapable of feeling satisfied in the situation that she occupied as wife of the *alispán* of Taksony.

Impoverished though her family was, members of it held quite high office, and so she was constantly reminded of how much more modest her situation was; at the same time, they were able to offer helping hands for her husband's elevation, and the very possibility of his rise that she had in view made the proud woman's present position more unbearable; from the moment that she stepped into his house she set herself the goal of transforming his vanity into the ambition that she felt herself.

Faced by such influence, the *alispán*'s satisfaction couldn't survive. If he'd previously been happy to be considered first in the county, he was now reminded daily of how trifling that glory was and that it wasn't a worthy goal in life. The loud outbursts of public affection and confidence – which, like swearing, are nowhere commoner than in Hungary – lost their value in his eyes when it was daily hinted to him that he owed them to his wine rather than to his merits. The condescension necessary in his situation was rendered more burdensome yet by the scorn with which his wife chastised him for such self-abasement, as she called it; in short, all his life he'd found happiness in everyone's satisfaction with him, but now he found in his wife nothing but dissatisfaction and scorn, and contempt for all the goals for which he strove; he seemed to feel belittled in his own eyes.

Anyone that believes that he who appears weak in his youth will later acquire a firmer character in adulthood, is mistaken. In fact, just as when a man standing on a steep hill begins to hurry downwards the farther he goes the more involuntary is the tendency to break into a run, so at the start of his career a man can resist more easily than later, when he has set himself on a certain course; and even if Réty never loved his wife passionately, he was quickly induced by the ceaseless influence of the clever and constantly purposeful woman to wish for something higher than the situation that he had hitherto regarded as happy.

Since then his life had become unhappy. The man whom heaven has created vain is not fit to set himself loftier or more distant goals. Vanity yearns for ceaseless satisfaction, finds applause in every word, praise for its every action, requires adulators at every moment, and the attainment of higher goals is granted only to those who are prepared to do without all these. Réty knew that if he intended to rise he had to choose a certain course of action, but when he did that, instead of the general satisfaction with which he bore his office, he suddenly saw enemies in his path, and their attacks and abuse made him unhappy. If he permitted himself to yield to his natural inclinations, abandon his aims and return to his former ways of seeking the satisfaction of all parties, the public acclaim that he gained for a little while was soured by his wife's dissatisfaction. Uncertainty was to be seen in everything that the *alispán* did, and no one felt more keenly than he the dual situation in which he found himself.

The more unpleasant his position became, however, the more he began rather to sense that the greater the power became that his wife exercised over him there was no longer any prospect of reconciliation between him and the party devoted to his higher goals. He'd invested so much in satisfying her that he had at least to strive perfectly to achieve that; every vain man changes the objects of his vanity lightly, and if he sees himself deprived of his hopes in one sphere he turns his desires to other goals which are sometimes diametrically opposed – and so did Réty. He was convinced that the popularity that he had once enjoyed was irretrievable, and now he shared his wife's wishes entirely and followed her advice almost blindly.

The weakness with which Réty was clothed with regard to his wife had led to his friends abandoning him more and more. Especially while his first wife had been alive and after her death, Tengelyi had been on the old footing with him since coming to Tiszarét as notary, but now he hardly ever went to his house. Vándory himself, who used to be an almost daily caller, seemed cooler. Old Kislaky and Bántornyi came less frequently to Tiszarét, where they had previously spent many happy hours. All that remained around the *alispán* was the company of his flatterers, Macskaházy and people like him, who acknowledged his wife's authority and took pains to remain in favour with the ruling power, so that even if Réty had wanted to oppose his wife he'd have found no one beside him on whom to rely. In the end, in order that the humiliating indecisiveness into which he'd fallen should not be noticed by others, he pretended that everything that he didn't oppose was the expression of his own wishes.

My readers know the part that Mrs Réty had played in the theft of Tengelyi's documents. Since, as all must believe, as a result of Viola's statement it had not remained secret, the whole affair had become the subject of gossip, and there was no one in the county that gave credence to the outlaw's account that didn't consider the *alispán* to have been complicit in the whole plan. That harsh judgement too, however, was unjust. Réty had not known of his wife's intention before it was accomplished, and however much he appreciated the importance of those documents which he had known to be in the possession of Vándory and later of Tengelyi, the *alispán*, for all his faults, was too honourable – and even if not, too much a coward – ever to have connived at the crime which his wife intended. After the event, however, and he had been informed by his wife of Viola's statement, what could he do?

In horror, he asked her whether the outlaw had been telling the truth.

"And if everything that he said was true," she replied, "if I've done everything of which I'm accused, haven't I done it for the good of your family, for the upholding of your reputation, for the advancement of your interests? Are you going to prefer charges against me? Will you summon your wife before a judge like a prisoner? Will you yourself besmirch the name that you bear? You'll ruin yourself and you won't persuade people of your innocence. Even now everyone accuses you rather than me. If you proceed against me people will see in that too a further dishonesty and not freedom from guilt. You've got one way ahead of you, only one, by which to save your honour: use all your influence to cover up this unfortunate event."

Réty had never felt unhappier than at that moment. His spirit was appalled at the thought that he had inadvertently fallen in with criminals. He could foresee all the difficulties that covering up the deed was going to bring. He guessed that the serenity of his life was lost and that like those responsible he would henceforth have to tremble at every moment lest the monstrous secret should be revealed – and yet what could he do? His wife had summed up correctly. He would have to act as an accom-

502

plice whether he punished the crime or helped to keep it secret. It was natural, considering Réty's character, that he chose the second option. The influence that his wife had exerted over him for years, the thought that it was possible to keep the deed secret and, if he succeeded, of keeping his good name and present position, scarcely left him any choice; in the opposite case, if he extended a helping hand in uncovering it all, the most secret family circumstances would become common knowledge and he himself would be condemned, if not by the judge then at least by public opinion; the *alispán* saw himself forced to take a course that he deplored, and which indeed horrified his whole being.

This position had been rendered more difficult still by the murder of Macskaházy. A number of documents belonging to Tengelyi had been found in his room. While he was under suspicion their presence there could be explained by presuming that he had dropped them in committing the crime; but if he were found innocent, wouldn't their discovery make it more likely that the *alispán* would be accused of having stolen them? Wouldn't Tengelyi himself use this circumstance as evidence? "To send to the scaffold a man of whose innocence I'm convinced, who was once my friend, and whose daughter is to be my son's wife, is to expose myself to either eternal shame or severe punishment. That's the choice that I'm facing." So said Réty inwardly, and his heart was filled with indescribable torment.

Like weak people generally, Réty had never loved his wife; he was unable to escape her power, and the coldness which he had felt for her had now changed into hatred. Deserted by his friends, despised and perhaps hated by by his children, deprived of the public esteem that he'd craved all his life, exposed to danger and shame – such was the position in which he saw himself; and he loathed his wife all the more as he was less and less able to forgive himself the weakness with which he'd followed her advice.

His wife knew her husband too well not to notice the change that had taken place in his mood. She was a proud woman, however, and returned the evident coldness with the scorn which people like her bear towards such as allow themselves to be used as tools by them; she was indifferent to his anger, as she was convinced that her husband's good was inseparable from the success of her plans.

The *alispán*'s unease was explicable enough by his situation, but on this occasion it seemed to be further increased by a letter which was lying on his desk; as he walked round his room he would stop now and then, pick it up and re-read parts of it in the greatest agitation.

503

It can be seen from the writing that the letter was from Vándory, and as readers of novels enjoy the privilege that certain governments sometimes assume – that of reading at leisure everyone's most confidential letters – I think it will be most expedient if I reveal in its entirety the letter which so disturbed Réty.

The letter said:

My dear brother!

You know that I'm not in the habit of abusing that name, which was once dear to my heart, but which I ceased to use when I realised that use of it could be harmful to you. You are my brother, but I've never claimed any right other than what the heart grants, and now too I only wish to remind you of our relationship so that my words may, if possible, turn you back from the path down which you're going.

You're on the brink of an abyss, Sámuel! Look around! One step more and the wrong that you've done may be irreparable; your honour, which is now in jeopardy, will perhaps be lost; such deeds will burden your soul as your later repentance won't make good. Oh, come to your senses, brother! Consider whether that external brilliance and earthly wealth for which you've already sacrificed so much are worth your risking for ever the peace of your soul.

There was a time when you called Tengelyi your friend; but let's leave that! You saw fit to break those links, and although the friendship of an honourable man is as great a benefaction from God as the affection of a great man you've rejected that benefaction; so be it. But if Tengelyi had never been your friend, if you consider him your enemy, would your heart not cry out to see him in this situation? You're convinced of his innocence, you know the circumstances of which he's the victim, you know who are the causes of all this unhappiness, you know the villains who are making accusations against him to cover up their own evildoing; can you tolerate that the most honourable man on this earth shall be oppressed by his enemies in this way? That the best, the most loving family shall suffer so much, when you can help, when the saving of so many depends on you alone?

I didn't think that I'd be forced to ask for what your most binding duty requires; I was sure that as you yourself have been a major cause of Tengelyi's sufferings you would do everything that making good your own shortcomings required; it seems that I was mistaken, and indeed that your own son's requests couldn't prevail upon you to so much as ease the fate of a hapless family ruined by you. It hurts my heart, but I must remind you of your oft-repeated promise never to refuse my just desire; to bring to your mind that duty which you have so often declared that you will never forget.

504

Yes, Sámuel, if you look back over the past you will be unable to deny that I have always treated you as a brother, and for your benefit have sacrificed much that is of great value in the eyes of men.

I was still a child when my mother died, but even then mature enough to notice the change which took place in my situation especially after our father married for a second time. Since your mother came to this house my happy days were over. She hated me before she bore a child because I reminded her of what she most desired; but later, after you came into the world, of what she feared, that I would share my father's inheritance with you. Everyone pitied my situation, and there were many who tried to rouse me to envy against you; but nevertheless I loved you dearly. It seemed to me that all the pain that I endured in my father's house since you came into the world was nothing compared to the joy that I experienced when I held you in my arms and you called me your brother. My stepmother persecuted me, I thought, my father didn't protect me, I was chastised and tormented, but when all was said and done I had a brother, and when he grew up we'd be happy together.

So unhappy was my childhood that in my hopes I had always to be far away in the future, and the older I became, the more insupportable my situation seemed. When you were seven a tutor arrived for you, and I was separated from you too. My father concentrated all his love on you, and grew daily colder towards me. As your father he hated me more and more, even the servants drew back from me, and it seemed that I was becoming an object of general disdain and persecution. I could bear it no longer. At the age of sixteen we all expect more from life and have more faith in ourselves than fears about risky enterprises. The bonds that will later chain us irresistibly to the sphere of our life's work are still weak, and the young man doesn't suspect that when he ventures on a new course he is usually only going to exchange his woes for new ones, and that such delights as he has enjoyed are irreplaceable. After a long struggle I left that house and sought peace and freedom abroad.

Long years have gone by since I did that, but when I look around your room, which was then my father's, and I remember the moment when I last pressed his hand to my lips, even now grief fills my soul. Had he said a loving word, had he noticed my distress, seen the tears that I couldn't conceal and which were running down my face, and instead of doing as he did at other times and dismissing the whining child out of hand, simply asked the reason for my misery, I would never have found the strength in me to implement my decision. I loved my father even at that moment, one warm word from his lips, and I'd have been spared so much self-reproach and he perhaps so much grief.

505

As you've often said, my father loved me and I deserted him. Oh, Sámuel, that hurts me! And although I was still half a child it hurt me when I left Hungary. But in our young days, when we can't keep what our heart feels a secret from ourselves, who suspects that the love that others feel towards us can be disguised by a cloak of coldness? And I left, convinced that I'd be missed by no one, not wanted back by anyone except perhaps by you, who would feel in your childish games the loss caused by my absence, and who would perhaps wish for your brother to come back.

A close relative of my mother, who had always been very fond of me and had constantly encouraged me to take this step when he saw how everyone was treating me, helped me to achieve my goal. He obtained the necessary documents for me to be able to go abroad under the name which I now bear; I have him to thank that I wasn't in need during the first years of my exile, although I'd set out almost penniless. After three years this uncle died so quickly and unexpectedly that he was unable to tell anyone of my whereabouts and wasn't able to make arrangements for my assistance, and I suddenly found myself left to my own devices in Göttingen, where I'd just started at the university. No one has felt the agonies of homelessness more keenly than I. I make friends very easily, and what experience taught me later I had begun to guess when still almost a child: there's hardly anyone in whom, on closer acquaintance, we wouldn't find much to like, and so I wasn't without friends abroad; but the thoughts that all those bonds which bound my heart to individual people were going to be broken if I eventually went home, that those whom I'd learnt to love would later not be employing their talents in the same circle as myself, that I couldn't enter into any lasting relationship, all soured my pleasure. I was like a man who lived on this earth and doesn't believe in immortality, and so fears death and thinks that it means the end of everything; he can't enjoy his existence, closely confined as it is within the narrow bounds of life. If my companions talked about their homes I couldn't join in their enthusiasm; if I saw that some of them, who had little in common, shared a common memory and treasury of hope in the past and future of their homes, an infinite yearning for my homeland arose in my spirit. But I couldn't rely on my father's love, didn't believe that he could forgive my thoughtless action, and I stifled my desire. The fact that no one helped me after the death of my uncle couldn't constitute justification for changing my decision. My needs were few, and my work was sufficient to cover them, and indeed, like every young man in a similar situation, the thought that I had myself to thank for everything filled my heart with a kind of self-satisfaction which I wouldn't have changed for anything.

506

Thus I spent more than ten years. My memories of home fell farther from me and caused me less pain. Even our language, which I could use only rarely, fell into disuse; I took my degree and began to feel at home in my new land; and although I hadn't given up hope of one day returning to my native land I was at least patiently awaiting the time when I could do so when I received news that you'd come to the university of Heidelberg. I read your name on the list of students there. There could be other Sámuel Rétys in the world, but my heart told me that I would find my brother. I gave up giving the private tuition on which I was living in Göttingen, broke off all my connections, and came to you, to turn to your advantage the experience of my life and the things that I'd learnt.

I'm not writing all this in order to reproach you – I believe that the diligence with which I helped you in your student years was not entirely worthless, and in that my affection pleased you in that distant foreign land – but I know that anyone would have done the same in my position, and if I had any deserts the happiness that I enjoyed in your company rewarded me amply. I could speak about the happy memories of my youth in my native language once more, my brother answered my questions, and for the first time in years the conviction rose again in my heart that I wasn't entirely deserted in the world. No, Sámuel, I don't wish to reproach you, but to make you think back to the happy days that we spent together – the days when there were no secrets between us, when for me to ask you for something that it would have been unpleasant for you to give seemed just as unlikely as your denial of my request. No one suspected the relationship in which we stood, and indeed there were many who were surprised that we could be friends despite our difference in age. Tengelyi himself, from whom we had no other secret, never guessed that we were brothers. But we decided between ourselves that when your university years were over we would return together to my father's house and would together beg his forgiveness for the thoughtless action by which I had saddened his old age.

Heaven ordained otherwise. You knew the angel whose love made me forget all other bonds and choose Germany as my country. No doubt my action was wicked: however slight the strength that one feels in oneself, to desert one's native land is never within one's liberty, and he is a sinner that rejects the portion allotted to him by God and applies to another place his abilities that can only here be profitable. I also knew through you that my father yearned for me; but I loved once in my life, and when I had to choose between my love and my duty I didn't feel in my heart the strength to sacrifice so much happiness. If I took the lady whom I had chosen as my wife to my father's house, he, whose pride I knew, would feel further pain instead of pleasure. The thought that his son had chosen as his wife the daughter of an artisan would have been a greater misfortune in his eyes than the finding of his son could compensate for, and you yourself saw it as better that I should accept the little office that I had been offered and should remain abroad for a while under a pseudonym.

Do you remember the moment when we parted, Sámuel? When we last shook hands the thought that we weren't to see one another for a long time filled our hearts with pain and our eyes with tears, yet we were happy. You saw yourself on the threshold of a life of work in which you thought that you would realise the promise of your youth; I had more modest prospects, and looked to the future bearing in my bosom the full happiness of a requited love.

As you know, that happier period of my life was brief. A few days after your return to Hungary my wife died, and I was left with only the memory of all the happiness with which I had been surrounded. I might best of all have aired my grief to you, but you were far away; Tengelyi had gone back even before you – after you, he'd been closest to me. There had been a time when the delight that I took in my studies and the pleasure of being with my friends brought me contentment; but the heart soon grows accustomed to good fortune, and once I'd learnt the bliss of love and had it taken from me a sorrow beyond words and an overwhelming yearning came over me. I decided to return home, and without letting you know I set off.

I wanted to see my father and the way things were in the house before introducing myself to him as his son. What I found in this house when I first crossed the threshold, known by no one except yourself, persuaded me that I would do better not to say who I was while my father was still alive. If I came forward with my name and my requests your mother's hatred of me would perhaps be revived and the discovery of the lost son could disturb the tranquillity of my father's last days. We agreed not to say anything, and when through your mediation I was chosen as pastor of this village and moved in there remained no reason for me to wish to alter the situation. I lived in our house like a member of the family, and my father, possibly led by a natural instinct, received me with unlimited kindness, and although I wasn't recognised I devoted my days to making his last years more cheerful.

Finally your mother died, and shortly afterwards my father too, the last of his strength rapidly wasted by the pain of the loss of his wife. As his last hour was approaching I prostrated myself on his bed, revealed my secret and begged his forgiveness. Tears gleamed in his eyes, with the last of his strength he clasped me to him, called me his son and pronounced a bless-

ing over me. You were in the room; he called you also to his bed, took us both by the hand and asked us to be together and never desert one another.

After father's death there was no way that I could discard my pseudonym and appear to the world as your brother. But during the time that I spent with you I experienced much that restrained me from what seemed a natural step. Father hadn't been thrifty, and his estates were burdened with debt. You yourself spent quite a lot while father was alive, so you too had got into debt; if I now appeared as your brother and claimed half the paternal inheritance I'd have placed you in such a financial condition that you'd have been unable to continue in your current life-style. To come forward with my name and not to claim my inheritance wasn't feasible, not only because you wouldn't have felt assured for the future by such a disclaimer, but because I didn't want you to seem so beholden to me in the eyes of the world. Furthermore, during the time that I'd been pastor in the village I'd learnt to like my new calling, and I felt that I wouldn't be able to continue with it under the family name without being called eccentric. The very uproar that the appearance of Boldizsár Réty would cause, and my becoming the subject of gossip, held me back from disclosing my secret, and two days after father's death I asked you not to say a word to anyone about our true relationship. Thus I could remain with you, love you as my brother, and I wanted nothing more.

At the time you spoke of magnanimity; what I did was perhaps not that. I'll admit that there were moments before I made up my mind to take that step when what I was about to do seemed a sacrifice. There's no one that hasn't yearned for wealth at some time in their life, and while there are people whose troubles we can ease with our wealth there's no reason to be ashamed of that yearning. But after considering my situation as a whole, the reasons for my taking that decision were quite numerous, and just as I never regretted what I did at the time I did so without self-denial. I was secure against hardship, and you voluntarily promised that I would never be able to ask you for anything and be refused; and so if I occasionally wanted to help someone I had no need of my own estate.

Yes, Sámuel, that's what you promised; the time has come for me to remind you of that promise.

I've left a fine estate, a position in the world which can be called enviable; though I'm far from ambitious, I've felt more than once in my life that I could have been more use to my fellow men if I hadn't declined my birthright. Oh, brother, don't awaken in me the belief that I did it all for someone that didn't deserve it, that I only did so for it to be misused by you!

509

Tengelyi's fate depends on you, you can save him and restore his threatened reputation. There's no need for me to tell you how; but if you've ever loved me, if our father's last wish is sacred to you, if you don't want me to curse the moment when I permitted myself out of affection to subordinate my own interests to your benefit: I, who have sacrificed all my wealth for you, would have given my life for you – and still would, if your good required it – I beg you by the happiness of our childhood, for the sake of your peace of mind, do what duty and conscience require.

Your brother Boldizsár.

The *alispán* re-read once more the final lines of the letter, flung himself onto a chair, fixed his gaze on the burning candles and sank into profound thought. Suddenly the door opened and there in front of him was his brother.

Kálmán had returned from Porvár, gone straight to see Vándory and had told him of Tengelyi's situation. The clergyman had gone to call on the *alispán* at once, to talk to him about his friend.

Vándory's arrival startled the *alispán*; he hadn't anticipated talking to his brother just then, and he extended his hand in obvious confusion. The clergyman didn't take it, and his face, usually so mild, was formally solemn.

"Boldizsár," said the *alispán* gloomily after a short pause, during which he stared at Vándory, "Won't you shake the hand that I offer you in affection?"

"Sámuel," said Vándory gravely, "if hearts have altered, why should our hands be clasped? They won't hold together those whose ways are parting."

"You too, then," said the *alispán* dismally, sinking back onto his chair, "are you going to reject me too? Oh Boldizsár! If you too condemn me, you who are always so gracious and loving towards everyone!"

"I condemn no one," replied Vándory, deeply affected by the pain that showed on his brother's face, "and you may believe, I wouldn't have come to see you if I weren't sure that the kindly disposition that God created in your heart would triumph over the wicked passions to which you've allowed yourself to sink. But there's no time to delay, if you don't come to your senses the harm that you've done may be irreparable. Tengelyi's in prison . . . "

He's a rare man that doesn't feel in his heart a sort of hatred for the one that he's injured, especially if he can't make good his error. The awareness of our sinful deeds is so painful that we try to evade it, go to any lengths and rather declare the whole world unjust than accept the painful truth ourselves; we can't therefore be surprised if Réty was overcome by similar feelings the moment he heard Tengelyi's name; he remembered only what he had suffered because of the notary and cut Vándory off short. "Don't say that name," said he irritably, "I wish I'd never ever heard it!"

"So you've gone so far," said Vándory with a sigh, "that instead of regretting what you've done you speak with hatred of the man whose forgiveness you should be asking?"

"His forgiveness?" said Réty, and his face flushed. "Who's shattered the calm of my life the way that he has? Whom I have to thank for my only son's leaving my house in anger, and cursing his fate in my hearing for making me his father? Who's depriving me of your affection, the last I could hope for? Show me one of my woes that I'm not suffering because of him, and I'll ask his forgiveness on bended knee."

"And who's the cause of all this?" asked Vándory calmly.

The *alispán* said nothing.

"Who's to blame," went on Vándory in censorious tone, "for the breaking of the bonds of affection with which life had previously joined the two of you? Who has been harsh to whom?"

The *alispán* was about to speak, but Vándory went on.

"Tengelyi's in prison, sharing a cell with the worst of evildoers, and you, *alispán* of the county, can only use your God-given authority to torment him who was once your friend and whom you now hate, because you can't forget the very bad thing that you've done to him. Who has cause for complaint in this?"

"I'm not the cause of Tengelyi's sufferings," said the *alispán* crossly, "I'm certain that he's innocent, but I can't restrain the hand of justice even if I can see that it's making a mistake."

"Sámuel," said the clergyman solemnly, "that excuse will do in the eyes of men, but are you going to present it before God when He calls you to account for Tengelyi's sufferings?"

"I did all that I could," replied Réty in growing unease, "I offered to stand surety for him; I asked Nyúzó, gave his clerk orders, that while he's in prison he's to be treated with the greatest clemency; no one can reasonably expect more of me."

"Not even I, your brother? said Vándory, looking hard at him. "I, who have sacrificed for you everything that this world holds precious?"

Réty looked around in obvious embarrassment.

511

"Never fear," said the clergyman, and for perhaps the first time in years a bitter smile played around his lips, "there's no one in the room to hear what I say, no one before whom you would need to be ashamed when I remind you that you're my brother."

Réty tried to say something, but Vándory interrupted.

"Yes, your brother. The documents with which I might prove my birth have been lost, and a mortal judge might refuse me if I were now suddenly to appear and claim my name and my property. You know that I'm telling the truth, and you won't deny that I've behaved towards you as a brother."

Réty mumbled something about gratitude.

"Is this your gratitude?" asked Vándory bitterly. "Is this the brotherly love in possession of which I gave up everything and yet felt happy? Is this the fulfilment of that promise that was not requested but that you have made countless times, that I could never ask you for anything humanly possible that you would refuse?"

Again Réty tried to speak, but Vándory cut in.

"I trusted your word, and all the more firmly because I was certain that I was never going to ask you for anything that would require great sacrifice from you. We have both been happy on those terms, and when I saw the influence that I could exercise for the good of the peasantry I've blessed my God many times that I hadn't allowed myself to be enticed into abandoning this calling. The very relationship that you once had with Tengelyi was restored. That worthy man forgave everything that he suffered through you, he surrounded you with the complete friendship of his steadfast spirit, and it seemed that the affection between you that was almost a byword at the university was going to live on in your children. And who is to blame for the change in those happy days?"

Once more, Réty tried to say something.

"I don't mean to blame anyone," Boldizsár went on, "I just want to ask you: if you compare that time with your later life, in which ambition has seized your soul and you've sacrificed your heart to your plans, when were you happier? . . . You sigh!" he added after a short pause, during which he looked hard at Sámuel as if waiting for an answer. "Oh, Sámuel, why didn't you believe me then, why didn't you follow your inner feelings, why have you said one thing and done another? . . I don't mean the heartless way in which you've treated Tengelyi because Ákos has fallen in love with Vilma. You knew that it had been the greatest desire of my life that those two young people shouldn't be parted, I've seen them grow up, and I've known that they would make one another happy; but your pride couldn't tolerate your son taking the daughter of a notary to the altar, and you've shamed Tengelyi, whom you've called a friend all your life, by banning him from your house."

"I wasn't aware of what my wife was planing," Réty interrupted, "otherwise I certainly wouldn't have let myself treat Tengelyi like that."

"Stop!" Vándory went on. He was beginning to speak more heatedly, almost emotionally. "I'm not going to argue with you about the extent to which that statement agrees with what you've done recently. However misguided the view is, people generally believe that a father has a right to decide on his children's futures, and I won't complain even if you've abused that. But whether the theft of my papers . . ."

Réty seized the clergyman's hand convulsively, and his face blazed. "Not you too?!" said he in a pained tone. "Even you think me capable of a wicked act like that?"

"God can see my soul," said Vándory, raising his eyes heavenward. "When the first attempt to steal them took place, nothing was farther from my thoughts. I'd relinquished of my own accord all the claims to which my birth entitled me, so how might it have crossed my mind that it could be in anyone's interests to deprive me of the documents with which I could establish my rights, and apart from myself who could value the letters that I'd once received from you or my wife? You could see how little I suspected you both as after the event I entrusted my papers to Tengelyi's care, and spoke of my decision to you and your wife. But after the theft had taken place at Tengelyi's, after Viola had overtly accused Macskaházy and your wife in his statement, after I'd thought that Tengelyi's documents couldn't be so valuable to anyone that they would commit such a crime, and that the letters from you that had been in my possession would in fact have sufficed to prove my birth . . ."

Vándory fell silent before he had finished enumerating these individual points. Réty covered his face with his hands.

"I am by nature a trusting sort of person," said the clergyman, on seeing the pain that his words were causing Réty. "It was the greatest bitterness in my life that I had to think of you in this way even for a moment. Explain to me the concurrence of all these dreadful circumstances and I shall bless my God if I can kneel and ask forgiveness for my unjustness."

Réty rose and walked up and down the room a couple of times in the greatest agitation. He had come to one of those moments in which the heart can bear its burden no longer but divulges its most secret feelings. The hapless man would have told everything, even standing before his judge, even if his confession cost him his life. Everything seemed more bearable than not to speak to anyone about his situation. "Despise me," said he passionately after he'd spoken of everything – the part that his wife had taken in the theft of the documents, which he had learnt of only after the event – "despise me, brother, take your love away from me for ever, I'm unworthy of it, but there was nothing else that I could have done. My unhappy destiny willed that I should choose this monster as my wife. I was blinded by her family connections, her beauty, and by those who extolled her as the most outstanding woman in the whole region. Before I led her to the altar I never mentioned my brother for fear that she might change her mind – I was well aware that my wealth had no little to do with it; after she'd become my wife I intended day after day to admit her to the secret, day after day I waited for the right moment, always put it off, never had the courage to do it; so it was that my wife knew nothing about this relationship until I could, I was certain, no longer delay its revelation. The wretched woman realised that Ákos was in love, and – she's prepared to sacrifice anything to her pride – she required me to ban Tengelyi, or rather his daughter, from my house. I'll confess I would have liked my son to choose another, but partly because I didn't want to offend you, to whom I owed so much, and partly because I expected him to come to his senses and change his mind, I continued to oppose my wife's wish. At that she made up for my weakness, as she put it, and did herself what she couldn't prevail on me to do. The thought filled me with unspeakable horror that you'd be so cross at seeing your best friend insulted by me that you'd regret your magnanimous action, which I've repaid with ingratitude. I reproached my wife, and when I was derided by her for being so afraid of a poor clergyman and a village notary I told her of the relationship between you and me, and said that if you were disposed to make use of the documents in your possession, which mostly consisted of letters in my hand, it would be open to you to put yourself in possession of half our estates. The wretched woman didn't trust magnanimity, was led astray by the villain who had her complete confidence, and resorted to criminal acts. Tell me yourself, could I have foreseen, even so much as imagined, that when I told her of our relationship this would be the consequence?"

"My poor Sámuel!" sighed Vándory.

"Oh, brother," the *alispán* continued, raising his eyes heavenward, "no one has any idea what I have to endure! My children turn away from me and despise me, my honourable name is in jeopardy, and even you think that I'm the accomplice of criminals."

514

Vándory tried to say something.

"Don't say a word, don't console me!" said Réty. "The accomplice of criminals! Well, isn't that what I am, as in my position I'm forced to use all my influence to cover up the wickedness?"

"Quite so, the bonds between you and your wife are sacred," said the clergyman after a brief consideration. "You can't abandon her in her trouble, and indeed, whatever depths she's sunk to, you're obliged to defend her as far as your conscience permits. You may, indeed, you must, sacrifice yourself if her good requires it; but when a man's life is at risk and she can only escape punishment if you sacrifice the innocent for her . . ."

"I understand you," said Réty, "and believe me, if sacrificing my wife would be to Tengelyi's advantage I wouldn't hesitate for a moment. I've learnt to understand that woman and to hate her. But if I put my wife in front of the judge, if I besmirch my own name and that of my children, what good will it do? The more certain it is that Tengelyi's documents were stolen by our lawyer on my wife's instructions, the more likely it will be that in the judge's eyes Tengelyi committed the murder of which he stands accused."

Vándory could see that this view was correct, and when he was convinced that the *alispán* could at present do nothing to set Tengelyi free he merely asked gloomily that while he was in prison at least he should protect him from needless torment.

Réty was surprised to hear how his orders concerning Tengelyi were being carried out, and promised to go personally to Porvár next day and see to it that the unfortunate prisoner was as comfortable as could be.

"So, Sámuel," said Vándory, relieved, "do all that you can to ease poor Jónás's fate, and trust to God for the rest."

Réty sighed.

"Don't give up hope,"Vándory went on in a reassuring tone. "You'll see, it will all turn out well."

"Brother", said Réty sadly, "the man accused by his own heart is the one with no hope!"

The voice in which he said that touched Vándory deeply. He had come to pick a bone with his brother; but when he saw his pain that intention had vanished forthwith, and now the pious clergyman could only feel cheered. He listed every means by which Tengelyi might be freed from his grim situation; he reminded his brother of the salutary influence that he, as *alispán* of the county, could exercise on the fate of the accused; he spoke of the happier days which were surely to come, when the love of Ákos and Vilma would once more unite the former friends with bonds that could not be broken. Like fear, hope too is infectious, and Réty couldn't resist the confidence with which his brother spoke of the future; finally he too became calmer.

"Boldizsár," said he at length, "how happy you are – your heart is full of such certainty that the treasure that you bear in yourself spreads to those that come near you."

"Happy? Yes, Sámuel, that I am," replied he, clasping his brother's hand, "but believe me, so shall you be too. You call me an optimist, and you'll see that my view on life is not only the happiest but also the most correct. Anyone whose faith is not just empty words has no doubt of the goodness of God. For my part, I would sooner believe that the sun won't rise again on our horizon than that God didn't create Man to be happy. You've tried to become happy by a road other than that set before you by destiny, and you can't complain if you're unhappy. The miner who seeks treasure in the bowels of the earth, the goal of whose life's work is a thing that fate has hidden from him, works in perpetual darkness, but the rays of the sun shine as warmly on the hilltop now as when he went down the mine. Turn back from your dimly lit path, and you'll find once more this beautiful world, entrancing with all its hopes, just as you left it. But brother," he added, "goodbye, it's past midnight and I must go. I'll go with you to Porvár tomorrow morning, and until then may sweet dreams cheer your spirit."

Réty clasped him to his bosom, and when they parted after that lengthy embrace tears were gleaming in the eyes of both.

XXXV

I've reached the point at which I can abandon the style of my story this far and break the thread of narrative. It is one of the greatest privileges of novelist or historian to be able to skip uninteresting episodes and only include in his work that which he considers the finest and most excellent; why shouldn't I enjoy that privilege, which in real life too we sometimes find so hard to ignore? When the farmer has tilled and sown his land in spring he would sometimes lie to sleep and skip the season between then and harvest; and when we've finished the novel of our life – because every life has a novel, and the driest of teachers has had days on which the little moisture that still remained in him ran down his cheeks in tears – how we would like to sleep after the brief adventure which sometimes leads to so dull a reality! Fate has denied mankind this gift, and only the novelist and the historian retain this privilege.

The novelist and historian; how dare I lump together serious science and genial artistry? But is it in fact such great daring? Do those who publish accounts which are genuine – or which at least they believe to be such – in order to extract from them false moral teachings, stand higher than those who, in order the better to be able to relate certain moral truths, contrive a story which is often more profitable, and indeed more genuine, than much of what we learn in our history books? Doesn't he that, in depicting present morals, reveals the marks left on the character of our contemporaries by the chains that have been borne for centuries, warn people against the same thing as those who rattle before our eyes the real chains in our museums which our fathers bore? Don't they both admonish us to beware of servitude? Novelists and historians alike charge themselves with seeking the truth; and if he can cite human nature in proof of his statements, why should the former blush before the man of learning who proves every fact with ten written documents? The historian deals with the description of great characters, while the novelist sometimes selects his personae from the more modest sphere of everyday life – but is the difference really so great? Are not those characters whom we call great rendered such by their times and circumstances? History is a marvellous microscope, and when you look through it you see giants, but nevertheless the individual that you admire becomes no bigger, and the glorious character is sometimes a perfect copy of the man that has stood beside you unnoticed for years.

517

It's not the place of his actions that makes a man really interesting, not the clamour that attends his appearance, not his title. The single sign by which you can recognise truly great hearts among the cowardly horde that imitate greatness is the great love for some noble cause with which they are filled, and history doesn't always choose such as the puppets whom it makes portray the ideas of individual periods.

But once more I'm losing the thread and, like many honourable men in the world, talking about my duties instead of performing them, that is, going on with my novel. But for three months (such is the length of time that I've skipped) perhaps so much reflection isn't a lot, and if my readers bear in mind that I've spared them the description of a whole unpleasant winter they'll forgive the digression, especially if they consider how much must have happened in the seat of Taksony County because of Carnival, which enticed me into describing it only in order to refute the accusation made against me – that my narrative only moves in lowly circles and contains the apotheosis of peasant sufferings.

It's common knowledge that the Hungarian nobility, which shares fraternally in everything with the other estates of the nation, has arranged its affairs with the peasants like Castor and Pollux, so that in summer, autumn and spring the latter may labour, and in winter they themselves, and not only by day but for whole nights; they have set themselves as a task that the famous *csárdás*, the maintenance of which, as all can see, is in the greatest interests of the nation, may rise to ever greater perfection. It depends on me alone, and if I give an account of the events of those three months I might tell of balls at the description of which my beautiful lady readers would feel their hearts throb, and their estimable mothers, who escort them to dance-entertainments, would feel their whole bodies perspire. Balls, I say, held for the benefit of the poor, from which, after all deductions, thirty-two *forints* and twelve *krajcárs* pure profit remained for the relief of hunger; one that was given for the kindergarten, which, as far as that establishment was concerned, actually showed no material profit, but all the more moral good was achieved after the daughter of a land-owning lady died of whooping-cough while her mother was dancing for the benefit of the children of others, and the need to care for little ones was recognised throughout the county; balls, I say, that were held in the rooms of the civic casino, at which, in accordance with the spirit of our enlightened century the whole nobility took part, although the casino of the nobility didn't ask for the compliment of a return visit. I might speak of lunches at which, if the proverb *in vino veritas* is true, anyone hearing and understanding the toasts – which re-

518

quired the drinking of at least four glasses of wine – was persuaded that Hungary was rich not only in good wines but in great men too; at these I might take my readers into so much good company that the lowest rank of the intoxicated was never less than that of chief clerk. I could enjoy theatrical performances, in which those Frenchmen who opposed the legal prohibition of public performance in their own country might convince me of how erroneous they were in their ambitions, when the theatre can be forbidden by law, and all the same one can amuse oneself just as well at the Faro[196] table, especially if the bank is held by one of the *alispán*s, because – if my critics will permit me the use of Latin words once again – according to the proverb *praesente medico nihil nocet*,[197] when he that is charged with upholding the law is present, infringement of the law can naturally do no harm. I might speak of many excellent evening entertainments, valiant love-affairs, indeed, notable marriages, and those that would like to see my novel move in more noble circles will be delighted to read my third volume – but what's to be done about it! Not everyone has the fine touch required for the description of such things, and I've spent so long with the poor characters in my novel that in the end I've almost become a peasant myself.

No one has more respect for high society than I. There have been times when I've even liked it, and that feeling – as is often the case – has ended with my avoiding as much as possible the subject of my former proclivity simply out of respect. I also know that no novel will interest a maid unless the hero is at least a count; manservants too applaud only if they see a duke die for their money. But never mind! I'm one of those eccentrics whom low society – that created by God – interests more than the so-called high; those who consider the sunrise more beautiful than the lighting of candles in a great man's halls as seen from the street; and I've been unfortunate enough to have encountered more interesting people dressed in linen than in fashionable stuffs; I must leave to cleverer hands the stock-novel, in which every distinguished character has sixteen ancestors – and the one worthy man, who appears to be a peasant, unfastens his clothing at the end of the book to reveal a star, so that everyone recognises him as the prince. My posterity will find many in the higher echelons of Porvár society whom I haven't introduced to my readers, and from whom they can very well profit.

---

196 A gambling card game of late 17th century French origin, superseded in popularity by Poker (with which it has elements in common) in the 1900s.
197 Latin: when the doctor is present, nothing does harm.

First of all I'll mention *táblabíró* Csatlósy,[198] well known in Taksony and the neighbouring counties too for his celebrated patriotism. If you wonder about his favourite foods, nothing is more to his taste than *kocsonya* and pork *tokány*; the works of Beethoven are no substitute for the tunes of Bandi the Gypsy; he never buys foreign clothes – except when they're cheaper than Hungarian. And how much does he love his fatherland?! If you spend some time in his company, fatherland, liberty, all the words on hearing which at other times you feel your heart throb, are so commonplace that the sound of them makes no more impression than if someone says 'Good day' or 'Your humble servant'. This is no everyday love, rendered unacceptable to the beloved by indiscretion, but an extraordinary feeling such as Schiller describes in Toggenburg, where the knight sits outside her convent and looks up at his beloved, looks all the time, looks until his last hour, never does anything but love endlessly. Schiller sings of another knight too, whose beloved throws her glove among wild beasts and calls on him to bring it back. The knight does so, but deserts his beloved. If his one beloved, the fatherland, had demanded such a thing of him Csatlósy would have behaved quite differently. He'd have left the glove, but his love wouldn't have changed – that love has become second nature to him. Everyone knows that there's nothing more dangerous with regard to the permanence of our feelings than that our beloved causes us great expense. Regular payment is the death of our feelings. The *táblabíró* knew this, and so he was careful not to enter into such a relationship with his dear fatherland; at most an occasional small gift or a big promise – that is what doesn't harm our love, and for which he showed himself to be ready. Csatlósy is a member, indeed, a committee member, of almost every society. He's one of those who don't attend committee meetings and don't pay their annual subscriptions, but are to be found in every register; thus they can serve as examples to the many that are indifferent. And so Csatlósy is one of the most respectable of men, probably a popular figure, though not as rare as we might think from all his qualities.

Palaczkay,[199] a former chief justice, is likewise an interesting individual. As Solon threatened with punishment any Athenian citizen who didn't belong to a party, if that law were in our *Corpus Juris* Palaczkay might count on a reward, as he always belonged not to one party but to them all. No one knew better than he that in order to make progress it

---

198 From *csat* 'a clasp', *csatlós* 'hanger-on, henchman', a pejorative term.
199 From *palack* 'bottle'.

is necessary to step forward now with the right foot, then with the left; no one was more convinced that as nature has given us two ears, one on each side of the head, and only one mouth between the two, it meant to point out that we should pay attention to what others say around us, to right and left, but in speaking should always remain between both opinions. That is to say, Palaczkay was one of the most tactful of men.

In addition to these, no small part is played by János Talléros,[200] the Porvár millionaire, who has at least two hundred thousand forints and represents the new aristocracy in Taksony County, the aristocracy of money. We usually ridicule this variety of aristocracy as much as we honour the older one. Can I not see why? The origin of the old aristocracy is obscure, and more than one family can scarcely say from whom it's descended; isn't it so with the new aristocracy too, in which no one knows where their father or grandfathers acquired the first forint on which their huge wealth is founded? The former, distinguished by great families, have often been famous robbers that held whole regions in fear of their mighty arms. The stockbroker is sometimes descended from a famous usurer, swindler or thief. The memorials of great families are linked to the history of the world, or at least of their country; but isn't the same true of our money-aristocrats too, who've made all their wealth by charging three or four per cent? If a ruler dies, great families go into mourning; but has there ever been such grieving as we shall see among the stockbrokers of Europe at the death of Louis Philippe?[201] Sometimes we can recognise descendants of great families by their features, but are there no features characteristic of the money-aristocracy too? They have their tendencies and caprices: sometimes the former despise the ignoble, while the latter always scorn any that have no money; and so the comparison is perfect, and only comes to attention in Porvár when the representative of the new aristocracy is second in public esteem only to the *főispán*.

Many may still remember others such as Mr Zászlósy,[202] who was very sorry when Latin went out of fashion because, as he said, that rendered his schooling entirely futile. And a certain rustic *táblabíró*, who never wrote a novel, but ploughed, sowed, made *pálinka*, fattened calves, and taught himself politics, after which one can believe that he

---

200 From *tallér* 'thaler, a silver coin'.
201 Louis Philippe I (reigned 1830–48), last king of France. His reign was dominated by wealthy industrialists and bankers.
202 From *zászló* 'banner'.

farmed all his life and learned that the latter too could be profitable, at least as far as he was concerned. The county chief engineer, the best of all at *tarok*, and a man of learning, who went around as if he were something special as he couldn't be considered anything else, and eventually attained a great reputation for scholarly qualities; but as I said, I must leave all those to another and return to Tengelyi's family, which was living in seclusion in Porvár.

A few days after her husband was imprisoned Mrs Tengelyi too came to Porvár and took up residence in a little house. The poor woman could hardly bear her distress. Erzsébet was proud of her husband. It's true that the wife of a village notary has perhaps little cause for pride, but the respect in which her husband was held everywhere in the county, his friendship with Vándory and at one time with the *alispán* himself, and the confidence that almost everyone placed in him had justified her in going about with head held higher than the wives of other notaries. Wherever she went she heard her husband being acclaimed; there was no more honourable man in the county than Tengelyi – such was public opinion, and knowing that meant more to Erzsébet than would being addressed as Your Honour. She was a strong-hearted woman; in all his woes Tengelyi had found in her a support in the firmness of which he could trust; what had happened now, however, was more than the poor woman could bear. And now – with her husband in prison, accused of the vilest crime imaginable, exposed to horrifying danger – she went about, seemingly dizzy with pain; the needs of her little household had lost their interest for her; even her daughter could no longer lift her spirits, and those that had known her previously whispered sympathetically one to another that Erzsébet wasn't going to survive her misfortune.

The effect of these circumstances on Vilma was quite different. In her happier days she'd been like a flower shaken with every breeze, to which nature's only defence against being trampled was beauty. In that gentle temperament, the most lovable property of which was weakness, no one would have looked for spiritual strength and steadfastness. Her father's misfortune and the despair in which she saw her mother gave her strength to become what her parents needed – their comforter. Vilma was certain of her father's innocence and had every expectation that the truth would soon be clear, but the situation in which she saw that respected man grieved her deeply, all the more so as she believed that she herself was one of the reasons for his suffering. At night, when she saw that her mother was asleep, she sometimes spent hours on her knees, begging her God to take pity on her parents' agony. She would bury her

522

face in the pillow and weep, often until morning, but by the time her mother woke Vilma had dried her tears and looked calm. Her simulated cheerfulness sometimes reassured her mother too; those who'd known her earlier, especially those who'd witnessed the passionate bitterness with which she'd received her father's misfortune, could scarcely explain the change that had come over her since arriving in Porvár. Few realise that weakness, the well-spring of which is the heart, becomes strength as soon as one has to struggle against great vicissitudes rather than one's friends' wishes. The selfish person, who resolutely opposes his friends' wishes when his interests or merely his fancy so desire, yields like a coward when his will comes into conflict with a greater force; but the blows of the outside world have precisely the opposite effect on him whose heart is filled with love. Therefore that love which can do everything because it's prepared to endure anything strengthened Vilma's heart, and love of Ákos gave her more happiness than all the woes on earth could take from her. At times the poor girl almost reproached herself for feeling so fortunate when her family was so afflicted.

Ákos deserved that love, if ever a young man did.

There is a time in life when each of us grows tired of vague speculation, and finally seeks a definite purpose for himself. This is one of the most unpleasant periods of life; but just as our bodies develop in the fever of spring, so too do our spirits develop, because of which everything that we see about us seems loathsome. Ákos was past that time of life. If he'd lived under different circumstances, if those that he saw surrounding his father hadn't deterred him from the career which he'd taken, or if he hadn't loved Vilma – perhaps he'd have thrown himself into public life; but who can see in their youth that the ideals for which they are ablaze are too fine to be capable of realisation? and that what they'd be able to attain by their activity in public life isn't worth enthusing over? In a different situation, like many of talent in Hungary Ákos too would probably only have toiled to accommodate that which was loftier in his ideals to the mediocrity of the majority; to change his splendid feelings into resounding words and scatter them broadcast among the people; but after the experiences that he'd had in his father's case Ákos could have no liking for such a life. He'd often come into contact with the crowd, and what he'd seen then hadn't encouraged him to strive for its favours. To love, hate, or respect the crowd, or to harbour any human feelings towards it was, he often thought, quite absurd. That soulless mass of humanity which re-echoed indifferently every sound – as long as it was loud enough and came from the place to which it usually responded

– didn't deserve one to love or hate it. Like the column of sand caught up in the desert by the whirlwind and blotting out the caravan, like the avalanche that thunders from the heights into the valley and sweeps away forest and village – such was the crowd in its movements. It was an element the effect of which could be sublime, magnificent and dreadful, but to respect its mindless power was just as foolish as to pretend to despise it. The most sensible thing was to take care to have nothing to do with it. Ákos believed that he who set the making happy of a loved one as the goal of his life had chosen for himself one more attainable but no less fine than his that strove for laurels – and especially after he saw Vilma suffer, he had dedicated his life exclusively to her.

The *alispán* himself no longer opposed Ákos's wish, and the only obstacle to his happiness was the anxiety which he felt because of the uncertainty of Tengelyi's fate.

Kálmán shared his friend's anxiety, and yet never did a man feel happier than he did all the time.

Recent events had given Etelka insight into the better side of the young man's character. The spirit with which he spoke out every time that he saw someone being ill treated, the manly determination with which he came forward if his help was needed – his faults were forgotten, or rather Etelka was persuaded that as complete perfection isn't to be found on this earth it's better to be attached to someone whose mistakes come from the head rather than the heart. In his livelier moments Kálmán was still noisier than decorum required, and despite his love for Etelka he couldn't stop himself going coursing frequently, or indeed hunting whenever weather permitted – but despite all these slight faults Etelka had made up her mind long ago and was regarded by everyone as Kálmán's fiancée even though her stepmother had said a hundred times that she was never going to consent to that marriage.

What Tengelyi himself suffered during his imprisonment had not failed to have an effect on him; as is always the case, however, with persons of more resolute personality, rather than change his character it served to confirm his former virtues and faults. My readers know him. He was one of those individuals with splendid qualities whom destiny has placed in restricted circles. As with the oak which has been unable to grow surrounded by a dense forest, the marks of the struggles by which it has tried to break free of its narrow confines are to be seen on the gnarled branches, tossed hither and thither, so it is with men: we often realise only through their discomfiture that they are meant for spheres wider than those in which we find them – and there's no one on this earth more deserving of our pity than they. Life's a great treadmill, and if we don't want to be carried downward on it we must struggle upward, and the desire to rise that keeps the whole thing in motion is necessary for the happiness of the individual too, but only insofar as it doesn't extend beyond the next step. As in the sciences, so too in life the hardest, but at the same time most necessary thing is to mark out the boundaries within which we mean to confine our activity; anyone that doesn't do that will always be unhappy. Fate is often unfair to us and doesn't fulfil even our most modest desires; and if we have been unreasonable in our demands, what can we expect but that the excessively fine hopes of our youth will later exact retribution? What else can we expect but to experience in ourselves that our hearts are filled with pain, not so much by what we've lost as by what we haven't achieved? All this Tengelyi had felt, and he'd often proposed to himself abandoning every higher desire and restricting his activity purely to his own circle. "Reforming this country isn't the sort of task that the notary of Tiszarét should set himself," he would say with a sigh, "why make myself enemies, my efforts can't lead to anything. A pearl will only be given its full value when it can be pierced and strung in a row; a man is worth most if he doesn't step out of his natural line." But these were the thoughts of his quieter moments, and they only lasted until he heard of someone being oppressed or unjustly treated, and he felt himself called to further fruitless struggles. He was one of those impractical people who will never understand that in our cultured century the man that means always to follow the commands of recognised morals and forgets that every moral command has countless exceptions in everyday life, is much more likely to find himself on the scaffold than in the Kingdom of Heaven.

Now in particular, as his heart had been embittered by his misfortune, Tengelyi had become even more unbending. Vándory's advice and the requests of Vándory and even Ákos couldn't induce him to so much as speak to Réty. Every device that conflicted with his moral concepts, even if customarily used by accused persons, he rejected angrily, even though Völgyesy pointed out more than once the difficulties that he was putting in the way of his own defence.

"I'm innocent," said he on occasion, "and the truth will out sooner or later. If I've now got to prove that I'm not a criminal, I'm never going to do it by humiliating myself." Now too we find him arguing in such terms with his young lawyer.

As soon as the *alispán* arrived in Porvár he had Tengelyi transferred from the underground cell where he had first been confined to that which, as we know, had previously been used by Mrs Réty as a food-store. The prisoner was given such modest comforts as the place permitted and to which he was accustomed in his home; they also made his situation more bearable, especially as there was no impediment to visits from his family. The window of this cell overlooked the street, and Tengelyi looked out through the iron bars at the bright March sunshine, in the rays of which the last white patches of snow were slowly melting off the roofs. Völgyesy was pacing the cell in the greatest agitation.

"But consider, my dear friend," said the latter, stopping by the window, "what humiliation can there be in exchanging a few civil words with Réty, or with the *főispán* – he's shown himself so well disposed on every occasion, asking in a simple letter for the hearing of your case to be delayed."

"And I tell you, it *is* humiliating," replied the notary crossly. "I won't go cap in hand to anyone, won't beg anyone for favours, I'm innocent, let them judge me, that's their business."

"But look, there's no need to beg for favours," said the lawyer with a sigh. "All I'm asking is for you just to be amiable towards them, not to drive away people who show sympathy, as you did the other day Krivér and the attorney general. You've made enemies of them again."

"And what have I to thank for this sympathy?" replied Tengelyi in the same tone. "The fact that I'm innocent, do you think? God forbid! If the *főispán* didn't speak favourably of me they'd be my greatest enemies. Am I supposed to talk to them? When Adam was alone in Paradise he enjoyed himself talking to animals – a lot of people have wanted to do that in our time too, but experience has showed that such conversation doesn't go unpunished. They all kick and bite, the best thing to do is to stay away from them."

"My dear Mr Tengelyi," said the lawyer yet again, in a pleading voice, "think of the monstrous nature of the accusation, and the consequences!"

"They'll hang me or cut my head off, you mean?" said the notary sourly; especially since he'd lost his freedom he was more inclined to follow his passions than his insight in a discussion. "Let them, let my blood be on their heads, I shan't be their first innocent victim. One way or another I'll have to die one day, and people'll soon forget me. The ancients believed that the river of Lethe divided the land of the living from that of the dead, and that it wiped out the memory of those who were still on this side, as well as those who'd crossed it."

"And what about your family?" said Völgyesy sorrowfully. "Think of them, my friend."

A look of inexpressible pain passed over Tengelyi's face; he covered his eyes with his hands, and for a while said nothing. "What do you want me to do?" said he at length, in a voice that quivered with emotion. "Do you want me to go on my knees and beg Nyúzó for sympathy? Must I resort to bribery? Buy a false witness or do something else of the sort, the kind of thing I abhor? Although I'm well aware that such legal devices are much more effective than the ones we learn at law school. In Hungary the criminal law obeys the principles of homeopathy, and anyone that's accused of crime can only help themselves by resorting to it. Our judges here in Porvár want to prove the Oriental origin of our race, which means that no one is allowed to approach an official without a present. I know all about that; but who can want me, in my old age, to bring shame on my whole life by actions that I despise?"

"You're over-excited, my friend," said Völgyesy, taking the notary amicably by the hand.

"Excited?" replied Tengelyi bitterly. "Put yourself in my position, and just tell me how I can stay calm? I started life with high hopes, that was foolishness, but so what? Everybody that God's ever given a soul to has done the same until their experiences ruined their expectations. I've had to abandon my hopes; I learnt that Sisyphus will finish rolling his rock up the mountain, the Danaides' barrel[203] will be full before injustice is ended in this world and before those that want to raise a constantly backsliding nation from its ignominy succeed in doing so – and I chose a small circle for my life. I wanted to pass through this world with neither fame or name, toiling ceaselessly in my small circle and confining my efforts just to that. How many people's lives are like clocks, with all their wheels going round and round and the pendulum going back and forward on the same place, with no other purpose than for the hand to point to their last hour? That's how I too wanted to live. My only desire's been to do some good for the happiness of my family, especially of those nearest to me . . . and now I'm not even doing that! My misfortune will send Erzsébet to the grave, my daughter can't keep her grief from me, I know very well that she'll always be bitter over what she's suffered be-

---

203 The Danaides were the fifty daughters of King Danaos. He summoned his fifty nephews who expressed their desire to marry his daughters. Danaos accepted. For their weddings, he gave his daughters daggers and made them promise to kill their husbands at night. All did except Hypermnestra, who spared Lynceus. Later, Danaos held games to marry off the remaining forty-nine, but Lynceus killed them all in revenge for his brothers. In hell, the Danaides were given a punishment: to spend eternity filling a perforated barrel with water.

cause of me, and my son may go into the world with his name dishonoured, and last of all I'm required to sacrifice my convictions! My friend, it's more than I can take calmly."

"My friend," Völgyesy was deeply touched. "No one's going to say that an honourable man was ever in a sorrier state than yourself; but all I'm saying is that there isn't the least humiliation in asking Réty and the *főispán* to delay deciding on your case, nor any other reason why they should be reluctant to do it."

"If I ask for my hearing to be delayed, what is that but a clear admission that I don't believe in the rightness of my cause?" said Tengelyi with a shake of his head.

"Say rather," Völgyesy interrupted, "admission that the evidence necessary for your defence isn't yet sufficiently clear. We have to admit ourselves that as things stand, all indications are against us. Public opinion is on your side, and your character is so well known that although in a bare rehearsal of the circumstantial evidence we can't offer any contrary proof, none the less your innocence is not in doubt for most people. If we had juries the case could be tried today, but a judge can only give a verdict on what is stated in court, and so for the present we can't hope for anything better than a postponement. With time, who knows what evidence may emerge. Perhaps the Jew, who's now at death's door with typhus, may recover and be persuaded to tell the truth; perhaps we'll be able to find Viola, and then the whole case will simply collapse; perhaps . . ."

At this point the lawyer was interrupted by old János; neither had noticed him coming in as they were talking, and he'd heard the last few words. He had been providing the little service that Tengelyi needed in prison – with the *alispán*'s permission, of course, and at Ákos's request – and called in ten times a day; if there was nothing else for him to do and he found the notary lonely he would try to lighten his captivity with a few cheery words. There were times when this excessive zeal was a burden to Tengelyi, but even then the good-heartedness manifest in János's every word made him forget the dullness of his conversation, and Tengelyi often said that he'd never known a more noble heart that that which beat beneath that livery.

"Well, look here, Your Honour," said the old hussar as he approached the table where Tengelyi and Völgyesy were sitting, "would it really be true that if we could find Viola the gentleman would be cleared of the accusation?"

"No doubt of it at all," said Völgyesy, "just let's get hold of Viola. If he'd confess to the murder of Macskaházy, as we can expect from his previous behaviour, our case would be won."

528

"Well then," said the hussar pensively, "we ought to find Viola."

"We've been trying ever since Mr Tengelyi's been in here," said Völgyesy with a sigh, "We sent out an order to all *szolgabírós*, wrote to every county, but it's been no use! No one can pick up his trail."

"Well, it's no wonder they haven't been able to track him down," said the old hussar, shaking his head. "You showed your hand.[204] Viola won't be daft enough to show himself to a *szolgabíró*."

"But what are we to do? Have you any other ideas?" asked Völgyesy.

"I certainly have," replied János, "there's no other way of going about it. If you want to get hold of stolen goods or a villain, the only way is to go through another villain. You'll have to find Viola's friends, they're sure to know where he is."

"We've asked Mrs Lipták, and Peti the Gypsy . . ." said Völgyesy.

"Well, as far as he's concerned," János interrupted, "I'd bet that old rascal could take us to him this very day if he wanted to; but you never know, he might have had something to do with the lawyer's death himself. And then, he was always Viola's good friend. He'll think to himself that His Honour's got a lot of people on his side and not much harm will come to him, whereas if the county gets hold of Viola he'll be hanged."

"As far as that's concerned," said Völgyesy, "Peti knows, the *alispán* himself told him, that Viola wouldn't go before a *statarium*. And if he were brought before an ordinary court, as he's committed no greater crime than that of murdering Macskaházy, and especially as he's already suffered the fear of death, I'll warrant he wouldn't be sentenced to death."

"Your Honour might warrant, but Peti wouldn't believe you," said the hussar. "Nobody's going to give his best friend away to the authorities if it's a hanging matter, not even if the whole county guaranteed that he'd come to no harm. But there are others . . ."

"Who?" asked Völgyesy.

"Well, Your Honour," replied János, "one or other of the bandits in prison here. Honest men don't know one another, but villains are like a secret society. For example, there's a prisoner here who works in the chief accountant's kitchen, Gazsi Csavargós. Let him out for just two or three weeks. I'll go with him myself, disguised as a peasant, I guarantee I won't let him run away, and if we don't come back bringing Viola, I won't care, nobody need believe me if I say that we defeated Ferkó at Aspern."[205]

---

204 A Hungarian proverb: *Dobbal nem lehet verebet fogni* – You can't catch a sparrow with a drum.

205 The battle of Aspern-Esslingen (May 21/22 1809) in which Austrian forces inflicted

As a county lawyer Völgyesy was aware of the close connections that prisoners maintained with their associates at liberty, by means of which some crimes were devised in prison, and that no one could actually retrieve their stolen property if they didn't enquire about it among the prisoners, and so János's advice seemed so sound that he promised to obtain the *alispán*'s permission to release the kitchen-hand that day so that he'd be able to leave with János on the morrow.

"It'd be better still tonight," said János after a brief pause for thought. "If any of the prisoners or *hajdús* sees Csavargós leaving with me, by tomorrow evening every villain in the county will know about it. We'll be called spies, and we'll never come across Viola."

Völgyesy approved of his caution.

"And then, if you please," the hussar went on, in some embarrassment, "it's not that I wouldn't gladly help Your Honour, God can see my soul, I'd do anything to get you out of this accursed prison; but, well, poor Viola too is a human being, and his wife is a blessed creature, and her children are so nice and the way they stroked my moustache and called me uncle . . . Your Honour, I wouldn't like to have a hand in their father being hanged. Any other punishment, Your Honour, but death's a nasty business."

Völgyesy repeated what he'd said before, and the hussar himself too appreciated the correctness of that.

"Well, if that's so, Your Honour," said he, stroking his moustache, "and why shouldn't it be, if the *alispán* too is going to promise that – as it's up to Their Honours whom they hang – let I not be an honourable man if I don't bring Viola back. It'd be better for him, poor man, to serve time, and my master'll see to it that his wife and children have no trouble. So, just let me have Gazsi, and you'll be hearing from old János before long. Ah, I've been on some odd missions in my time, and I've always pulled it off. No need to give up just yet." And with that he left. Völgyesy and Tengelyi went on talking for a while about the likely success of this move – the former with much the greater confidence – and then the lawyer shook his friend's hand and left to have a word with the *alispán* about releasing the kitchen-hand.

Tengelyi pondered the amazing complexities of human life. Who is there so elevated that he could say beforehand "This man, whom I despise, shall never influence my destiny!" As the most wonderful facts are sometimes the consequences of the least of circumstances, so a life

the first significant defeat on the French under Napoleon.

spent in the most modest of circles is sometimes linked to the greatest events of world importance; and there can be, indeed, there are certainly countless instances of one person or another not becoming a tailor if Napoleon doesn't come to the island of St Helena. Who knows the relationship in which human lives stand one to another, and which determines the fate of good and bad, of exalted and lowly? It's only certain that there is no voice so distant that it can't blend into the harmony of our lives, or spoil it . . . and why are we proud, then?

XXXVI

I've reached the month of March in my tale, and those familiar with Porvár or perhaps other county towns will know that this time of year is that in which most mortality occurs in Hungarian prisons. I know no reason why the year in which our tale is played out should differ from others in this respect, since in the winter months, when everyone seeks a warmer dwelling, the cells have been as damp and filthy this year as at other times, and so it's only natural if now, when I take my readers back to the prisons as my narrative requires, they find among the inmates the annual reign of typhus. In Porvár no one was more surprised at this state of affairs than if it were announced that the office of some tax-collector was plagued by consumption, because everyone has their natural diseases, prisons and offices alike, and the whole county – including the doctors – viewed coffins from the prison with the calm of true Stoics as they were brought out of the County Hall courtyard two or three times a day, always with new corpses.

It's a serious shortcoming of my novel that I ride my hobbyhorses a very great deal – at times I feel sorry for my readers. No one knows better than I how irritating it is if a writer leaves the thread of narrative and starts lecturing every five minutes. I was once walking in the hills with a friend. He was a good, honourable man, who knew as much of the natural sciences as he could comfortably expound in a couple of hours, and so he belonged to that class of scientist who have acquired their knowledge, like summer clothing, not for their profit but only in order to be able to impress others and to seize every opportunity of arousing the admiration of those more ignorant than themselves. Although we'd only set out for the purpose of watching the sun go down from one of the highest peaks, this worthy man stopped every ten paces to break off a plant and talk about botany, or to pick up a stone and talk of mineralogy. Never in all my life have I been so annoyed – and yet a couple of years later I'm doing the same to my readers. You want me to take you to where Ákos and Vilma are seen at the altar as a happy couple, and at every step I'm delaying and boring you. But there's nothing for it! Everyone has his faults (Vándory says the same about good qualities), or perhaps we might say that at various times of their lives everyone runs through almost the whole gamut of faults, and there's almost nothing that they can say against their fellow men that couldn't have been turned on themselves at some time; my present fault is mounting my hobby-horse – I can't help myself! I know that I often tell you things which everyone knows in Hungary and so are out of place in a novel; I also know that people most esteem truth, like gold, when it's quite soft and can be twisted in all directions, and that I'm often insufficiently attentive to that; I should describe more love scenes, from which my young readers can learn how to conduct themselves in certain circumstances, as if from a new Knigge;[206] a few magnanimous deeds would also have increased the esteem of my work, as would no doubt a chapter in which, as English lords scatter gold coins in stage plays, my characters would have revealed noble sentiments by the sack-full: that would have made more of an impression than my dry lectures. It's a well-known fact that the novel is simply a substitute for the childish fairy tale for mustachioed men and kerchiefed women, and is most favoured if what it narrates isn't to be found anywhere on earth. I know all this, and I've told myself so a hundred times, but I've never succeeded in correcting my faults though I've meant to a hundred times. I believe that it was Archimedes that said that he could build a new world[207] if he could be given a place to stand other than ours; who can require of me a world other than the one I live in, which occupies all my thoughts and feelings – I lack the ability even to imagine another. If Danton had asked me whether we could take our fatherland on the soles of our shoes, my answer would have been yes. Let's take our fatherland with us on the soles of our shoes, and indeed, if our shoes had no soles or if we set out barefoot we'd take it with us everywhere, even to the land of dreams, even to the sphere of free poetry. I at least am not enough of a poet to be able to forget the sad truth when composing my work, and if my readers won't forgive my weakness, all that I can do is admit my failings and promise to improve.

But in the present case I've been speaking of the numerous deaths that occurred daily in Porvár prison. Have I ever had a better occasion to discuss our medical system? The natural train of thought seems to lead us to this, and thoroughly reliable data could be compiled from which my readers might be surprised to see the extraordinary way in

---

206 FreiherrAdolph Franz Friedrich Ludwig Knigge (1752–96), German writer and enlightener, best known for his work *Über den Umgang mit Menschen* – How to Treat People, which was much expanded by later writers. His name stands for a textbook of etiquette in today's German, which has nothing to do with Knigge's sociological work in the sense of the Enlightenment. His advice still appears relevant, if taken with a pinch of humour and applied to today's context. See Wikipedia.
207 Not quite! Archimedes offered to move the world, not rebuild it.

which thought is taken for the healing of the sick. I could set out the entire Hungarian medical policy and convince everyone that our happy land is entirely free from policy of that sort, as it is from all public policy in general. But I'll overcome my inclination and say nothing; is that not great self-denial? Especially when we can recognise in the Chief Medical Officer of Taksony an individual who, in the course of his life, has frequently shown that there's nothing on earth less inappropriate, sometimes, indeed, just as profitable, than for instructions issued in a medical context to be observed to the letter.

A couple of years ago much of Hungary was in the grip of cattle-plague. In accordance with the instructions of authority, Taksony County too was sealed off and the bringing in of cattle from elsewhere was banned on pain of punishment. What happened? At the same time one of the senior magistrates had bought cattle in an adjoining county and wanted to bring them home. An official and guards stationed at the county boundary wouldn't let those beasts in and the magistrate was in an awkward situation: although at other times he'd occasionally pastured his oxen on neighbours' land he was now unable to obtain permission to bring them onto his own fields. But the situation which so injured the sanctity of the estate didn't last long. The Chief Medical Officer, that is, saw that the instruction from authority only referred to bringing in *alien* cattle, and was persuaded that oxen which were the property of one of the chief magistrates of the county couldn't sensibly be called *alien*, and immediately gave permission. On another occasion, partly perhaps in consequence of the foregoing, because his action had been disapproved of by the Governor's Council the Chief Medical Officer proposed in the assembly a fortnight before the Porvár market that since for several years cattle-plague had always struck in that month the county should be sealed off in the week preceding the market. There was in fact no plague in the neighbouring county at that time, but it was certain that the Taksony landowners never sold their beasts for better prices in Porvár market, and the CMO gained himself rare public favour.

I could quote many similar occasions on which he did so; but from now on I mean to stick to only the most essential account, and my characters' motivation comes under the basic rules of criticism, that is, in the present case, the revelation of why my CMO was appointed to that office in Taksony County.

One of the greatest difficulties of any Hungarian subject – and perhaps the reason why Hungarian writers so often choose to locate their plots abroad – lies in the fact that we can find hardly anything that wouldn't have the closest connection to constitutional questions. Politics is the daily bread on which we live – many have nothing else to eat and sometimes their stomachs are upset; there's no subject that can be understood without a knowledge of political science, and I can't, for example, speak of my chief medical officer without mentioning the constitutional status of Taksony County. Everyone knows that the appointment of chief medical officer is one of the controversial problems of the county system in Hungary. One might believe that debate might turn on whether the appointment should be made by the doctors of the county, the medical profession as a whole, or the national CMO. God forbid! Because of the autonomy of the Hungarian counties the only choice can be between appointment by the *főispán* and voting at an election, and the decision between the two is rendered more difficult by the certainty that there must be in the world very many people in their right minds that can see as little sense in the one as in the other.

When the present CMO's predecessor died – he'd been a famous man for miles around, he even shot birds with 12-gauge shot, and he gave all his patients the same pills with the same result in both cases, that is, the smaller birds and the patients got safely through – when, as I say, that gentleman died this question naturally arose again. The *főispán* immediately promised the position to a very excellent young man; he was in all respects familiar with good conservative principles, was a qualified teacher, had served for five years as tutor in a noble house, during which he had greatly distinguished himself in 'fine entertainments', publishing a couple of poems and 'hidden words',[208] and furthermore he was a Roman Catholic. The Estates of Taksony, however, exercised their right to nominate another. True, no one in the county knew him, but it was said that he spoke French and English, and what was more knew all about silkworm culture, was an honorary member of several foreign agricultural associations, and not only knew medicine but had studied law at Sárospatak, and furthermore had been born a Calvinist. Under such circumstance the whole county was split into two parties and more than a year went by before the disagreement between the Estates and their governor was smoothed out; this only happened when the candidates of both the *főispán* and the county stood down and the disputing parties agreed on a third, that is to say the present Chief Medical Officer. As a Lutheran, his religious beliefs didn't clash with either the *főispán*'s

---

208 *Rejtett szó*: a popular literary puzzle, in which the spelling of a word is alluded to bit by bit. See Kisfaludy Károly's well known verse *Rejtett szó* on the word *Remény* 'Hope'.

views or the requirements of the Estates, who definitely didn't want a papist, and furthermore as he had neither conservative nor any other principles the new CMO was equally close to both parties, knew neither French nor English nor anything about keeping silkworms, had written no poetry, wasn't a member of any societies Hungarian or foreign, and so was absolutely born to unite the votes of the opposing parties and be proposed as Taksony County's angel of peace.

As my readers can see, by his first action the CMO cured Taksony County of the commonest and at the same time the greatest woe in jurisdictional life, internal dissension. There may have been some that didn't attribute this fortunate outcome entirely to him, but more educated men will know that the CMO has at least as much merit for ending this county plague as his many colleagues of repute have for their most celebrated cures, and the first action would have been sufficient to establish his name as a doctor if, that is, one fact, however marvellous, were sufficient to make one famous in the world of today. In history one can acquire a name for a single great deed, as did Mucius Scaevola, Horatius Cocles, Curtius and countless others – but in life that is not enough. The great men of history can rest easy on the high pedestals where they have been placed by time, and Brutus, even if he never draws his dagger again, will be famous for ever; but anyone that is still in this life can only remind the ceaselessly moving crowd of his presence by pushing and shouting.

Anyone that knows a few literary celebrities will immediately realise the truth of what I say. Some believe that in order to make a name in literature we need a work that bears the stamp of brilliant intellect, with profound thoughts and exalted sentiments on every page. God forbid! What is it that lights our streets, stars or oil-lamps? The former shine more clearly, darting their rays upon us in eternally changeless beauty up on high; but oil-lamps are closer to hand, we can see their wicks, their light, indeed their smoke, and after all there's no day when they won't be lit again. We can forget the stars, but the lamp will even remind us by its smell that, as I said, it should be lit every day – and the secret of a literary reputation lies in that. Readers, if that's the treasure that you seek, follow my instructions and you'll surely be able to find it.

Let any of you write a few little poems, each in a different pocket-book or periodical, so that his name may come up frequently. A friend will make favourable comments on each little poem in various periodicals – or at least comments in which some fault is severely criticised – and they will be displayed as the enormous errors of genius. Such critics open the door to counter-critics, these in turn have to be answered, scandal arises, and the writer of the verses has a reputation. Not much more is required for a name to be made – sometimes the re-publication of one's work, sometimes a little literary scandal or criticism; only as I said, to get oneself talked about somehow or other, by someone at some time – to get oneself talked about, that's the secret. The mole that throws up the soil in the middle of a path where a lot of people walk alerts the passer-by to its activity more than does Achilles, lying far away beneath his magnificent tumulus.

There are certain similarities between the work of writer and doctor, which makes doctors who fail to find recognition in their own field so happy to plunge into literature: the former endeavours to treat the moral faults of the human race, the latter its physical ones, and for the most part both are successful; as for gaining a reputation, however, the doctor can't do better than follow the advice that I offer to the ambitious writer. *Get yourself talked about* – that's the way in which a doctor gains a reputation, and no one understood that part of his profession than the CMO of Taksony. Every year he had at least ten patients who'd been at the doors of death, all of whom had been cured. Every convalescent is pleased to hear that he's been in danger, and so on such occasions the doctor need hardly do anything other than let the patient speak about his miraculous recovery and himself say nothing to the contrary. Every year public expressions of gratitude to him had appeared several times in Hungarian and popular foreign papers, and such notices naturally have had all the more effect because they came from completely unknown persons, and all could see that they had not been inserted in the paper by some friend of the highly praised doctor. Homeopaths, allopaths, hydropaths, and indeed those who found the most reliable guidance of medical science in the counsels of somnambulists were equally enthusiastic in praising his name. The CMO cured all his patients in accordance with the method that they desired, and so not only was in the pleasant position that if something went wrong his patients had only themselves to blame, but also could always reckon on their defending him. If the patient died after being bled the homeopaths to a man blamed only him for having wanted to cure himself by a completely allopathic method, while if bleeding wasn't carried out the allopaths attributed all the trouble to the harmful effects of homeopathy. If to these excellent ways of the CMO is added that he recommended to every hypochondriac old bachelor that he should marry, never prohibited dancing to young women, sent every sick woman that sought his advice to spend summer at a spa, permitted pipe-smoking to men whom he was treating by a homeopathic method, their favourite foods to allopaths and wine to hydropaths – no one can be surprised at the public confidence that this diplomatic man enjoyed in Taksony and the neighbouring counties.

Infectious disease is the touchstone of every doctor. Though the illness threatens the doctor who struggles against it with a hundred deaths, he does his duty and exposes his life, the importance of which no one knows better than he, to danger at every moment: that's the time when the doctor can set the example of marvellous courage and self-sacrifice to which only philanthropy can inspire. I've known such men. The typhus which was now raging in the prison gave the CMO of Porvár too a similar opportunity, and it must be admitted that he remained true to his character and above all did his duty to the full, which in the case of infectious disease means for a CMO preventing its spread, and so that the epidemic should not be communicated to others by him as he daily made the rounds of the most excellent houses, he rather – with great self-denial, for what doctor wouldn't be delighted to be able to visit numerous patients – left his patients completely to their own devices, by which means it came about that the prisoners in Porvár were consigned entirely to nature; the bill for medicine didn't become very great; with so many patients entrusted to his care, of whom a few died every day, no one could accuse the CMO of erroneous treatment and his tender heart was spared much pain.

In Porvár, as my readers know, the cells are not considered by those for whose benefit they were built to be excessively unpleasant places to live. The company of kindred spirits, wine, *pálinka*, cards, singing and conversation, especially in winter, are such perfect substitutes for the joys of liberty that some of the noble and ignoble inhabitants of Taksony County could be found who did their utmost in autumn to secure themselves a place for the winter in this part of County Hall. But any that saw the place now were horrified.

The prison actually has its own sick-quarters. The Estates of the County were reluctant to oppose higher authority, and so in one cell six beds were allocated to sick prisoners. These sick-quarters were generally full, although there were on average only five hundred prisoners in the building, and one may think that in a time of infectious disease it was impossible to isolate the sick with such sick-quarters, and everyone remained where the sickness caught up with them. Some mornings two or three corpses were removed from the upper cells, where anything from thirty to eighty prisoners were held together. Down below, where the air seemed even more deadly, all the occupants of individual cells died with the exception of a luckless one or two.

Among the prisoners a glum desperation prevailed. The image of death, which all could see, filled the bravest with dismay, and the *hajdús* themselves, whose duties took them into the prison a couple of times every day, did their work in the greatest haste and spoke with horror of the sights that they witnessed. At other times a cheerful din of debauchery was heard from the cells, but now they generally stood silent. In the evening hymns were heard from the windows, which were lit from the street, and the doleful choir, which sounded as if were deep under the ground, made passers-by shudder. Sometimes, at dead of night, when all else was silent, the warders would hear the prisoners praying, and when that died away a silence as of the grave returned. Prisoners seldom spoke among themselves, and even then in a whisper. When the *hajdús* came into the cells in the morning to let those still healthy out into the courtyard for half an hour they would find them clinging to the iron grills. Everyone pleaded for the cells to be opened as soon as possible, lest a single moment of those permitted under God's free heaven be lost. There were times when those whom the disease had already taken and could no longer stay on their feet unaided clung to their fellows and staggered up the steps with the last of their strength to draw in once more the life-giving air of spring. Those who remained downstairs, who had passed through the disease and couldn't share that delight because of weakness, watched sadly as their more fortunate fellows left, while sometimes a couple of these would turn back to help their hapless friends up.

In the first cell, next to the stairs, among others two brothers were confined. Both were shepherds, sons of honest parents, and had been sentenced to a year in prison for their part in an act of banditry; they had asked one thing as an act of mercy, that they be locked in one cell. One of them, the younger, still almost a child, had been one of the very first to be taken sick, and never did mother nurse her child as carefully as this poor boy's elder brother cared for him. It had been he that had caused his brother to commit the crime, his fault that he was in prison, and was he now to see him die that had unwillingly become a murderer? When he fell sick, every time that a *hajdú* came round the elder brother asked him in the name of God to call a doctor to his brother, or to take him out of the cell and ask the *alispán* for him, as the elder and guiltier to suffer punishment for the two of them. "Keep me here for two years, if need be to the hour of my death, only let this poor boy go, he's innocent, it was I that led him astray." So he pleaded, his hands clasped in prayer and, insensitive man that he was, the corporal's eyes sometimes filled with tears when he heard his pleas and had to answer that he couldn't do it, because the noble county had given orders that while the disease lasted no one was to be released from the prison. Later, when no hope remained of his brother's recovery, he spoke to no one. He sat there in silence, watching the patient's every movement, holding his head in his hands. When the grill was opened in the morning and the prisoners were let out he put his brother over his shoulder and took him with him. In the yard he sat beside him again, cradling his head like a child's, and waited in silence to be called back in when the half-hour was over. "What are you lugging him round for?" said one of the *hajdús* one day. "Can't you see he's dead?" The prisoner looked at his brother, appalled, as he lay motionless beside him. He put his face to his lips – could feel no breath; put his hand to his heart – it wasn't beating; looked into his eyes – there was no life left in them; the limbs were all rigid, the body cold as ice, there could be no doubt. "He's dead!" he shouted in a terrible voice, and fell unconscious at his dead brother's side. His fellow prisoners carried him back into the cell, but the poor boy never regained consciousness – the fever claimed him too, and a few days later death ended his sufferings.

In the neighbouring cell another prisoner aroused sympathy even in his fellow inmates. He'd been sentenced to ten years and had spent that long in his cell; his hair had turned grey and his limbs had lost their former strength after such long suffering, but he had survived his punishment. The day when he would go back into the world, his body broken but no more in chains, was only a few more weeks away. No one would be waiting for him outside, no one would receive him lovingly on his return, but he would be free; that one thought made him forget all the suffering of his long captivity. When the plague began to show itself in the prison his spirit was filled with an unspeakable disquiet. He walked up and down in his cell, asking his companions at every moment how they were feeling. Every day he enquired of the *hajdús* whether anyone had died. In brief, his entire behaviour revealed that fear of death which he was feeling for the first time in his life, perhaps because he could see before him for the first time a great hope. When he'd only a few days of his sentence left the fever seized him too. His despair was terrible to see. He'd been telling his fellow prisoners that he'd be free in a few more days; he'd spoken of the place where he'd been born, of the future that he meant to spend as an honest man – and now he was going to have to die. Sometimes he prayed and wept, sometimes he cursed being born and swore at God for preserving him through those ten years merely in order – after all the torments that he'd endured – at the moment of his liberation to take away his life. That life was precious to him for the first time, the world, from the enjoyment of which he'd been barred those ten years, stood before him like Paradise, the green fields over which others walked without a thought, the tranquil mirror of the river, the broad horizon, whose beauty he hadn't suspected in the days of his freedom: an unspeakable yearning filled the prisoner's soul, he'd thought of them, dreamed of them for long years, and now, when the hopes to which his heart had clung for ten years were to be fulfilled – must he now die? Now, before he could call himself free once more, before the chains had at last been taken off his limbs. The fever rendered him unconscious, but those tormenting thoughts lingered on among the sick, wild dreams, and the poor man, in his delirium, complained on and on against the pitiless fate which had deprived him of his liberty until death finally fulfilled that desire for him as for so many more – for how many were there in that prison that could only exchange that grim dwelling for the grave?

And if that fate came only to the wicked! Might there not be, among those that death chose for himself day after day, some that had come into that situation having committed no crime? That wasn't so, it couldn't be so. In Hungary, as everyone knows, that most sacred civil right by which no one may be punished before being sentenced by a judge is one of the privileges of the nobility, so that we shan't find a prison in which the majority of the prisoners are not the sort who are incarcerated on empty and often unfounded charges and endure for years similar torments, imprisoned with the greatest criminals. Yes, for years, and will anyone be so rash as to accuse me of exaggeration because I speak of the most recent times? Will anyone declare that the cases that I speak of are rarities? Go through them, you who accuse of exaggeration everyone that alludes to the woes of the present, and call it cowardly philanthropy if someone brings to your attention the cruelties that even now are perpetrated every day. Go through the prisons of this country, you men of outstanding experience, and say how many cases you find in which the penal procedure is not so arranged that some of those accused don't wait for years for their cases to be judged; how many in which, as far as treatment is concerned, any difference is made between sentenced prisoners and those accused and awaiting trial. Chains and fasting two days a week, that's the usual form of punishment in prison; but don't those accused wear chains too? Don't they fast along with those sentenced? And what difference is there apart from the fact that the sentenced criminal knows the length of his sentence, whereas the frequently innocent person accused has nothing to look forward to or hope for? And why are we surprised at this? I could tell my readers of instances – not one or two, nor such as I've dug up in the chronicles of past centuries, but from times when the rights of man have been mentioned as a commonplace in our council chambers, and yet some people, without being sentenced for a crime, indeed, without being so much as charged with one, have suffered lengthy periods of imprisonment. Yes, lengthy periods of imprisonment, and in chains and in the company of criminals, merely as the result of some error or thoughtlessness on the part of the prison governor, who has by mistake had chains put on one or another individual, who, for example, had come to County Hall as a witness, and has then held him with the rest until the mistake was revealed by some fortunate accident – after all, one prisoner more or less doesn't add to his problems, and *alispáns* have far too much to do, to be able to bother about inspecting the prisons. I could, I say adduce such instances, and my readers – those, that is, who know our situation from other sources such as their experiences at the weekly sessions of the Academy – can add to them; but in the first place I can see that since such persons as have been sentenced by a judge to imprisonment are released from our prisons for money and fine words, perhaps the desire is to keep up the numbers by locking up those who shouldn't be in prison; secondly, I wouldn't like anyone to think me too much of a philanthropist, and so I'll restrict my account of these instances to that occasion if anyone thinks it unlikely that, in addition to the very many accused in Porvár prison, a single one such completely innocent person was found, who after five months reflection could not to this day conceive how he came to be in prison.

The poor man, whom his fellow prisoners treated with the greatest disdain precisely because of his innocence, was now sitting apart from the rest in a corner of the cell. His young wife, who had done her all to secure his release and had squandered her little wealth on futile attempts, came three times a day to the prison window and looked inside. Those were the only moments when the wretch was relieved for a little while of his gnawing pain. He would go to the iron grill, through which he could see his wife at the window that opened onto the corridor – he would tell her that he was well and ask about his parents and the children, and when he sensed tears coming to her eyes would himself send the dear creature away as he didn't wish to let his own pain be known to her. At length the poor woman at least succeeded, through Völgyesy's

542

intervention, in establishing her husband's innocence. Next morning, when the *hajdús* were opening the cells, she went with them to inform him, but he was lying unconscious on his straw, and a few short days later death ensured for ever the liberty that he had regained.

There were some among the criminals of deepest dye whom constantly imminent danger made pious, and they would say half-forgotten childhood prayers in little tremulous voices, seeking consolation in their religion. Others tried to subdue the feeling of their fear by strong drink, and the gifts which, when plague prevailed, flowed freely into the prison collecting-box – people are always more kindly towards those in danger, though it's a shame that this kindness is only shown when there's least need of it – those gifts were mostly turned into pálinka and only used to enable the unfortunate inmates to drown their sorrows for a couple of hours. Yet others sat in glum agony on their straw, saying not a word, as if waiting indifferently for the moment when the plague would seize them too, while some cursed their fate in desperation, filling the prison with hideous oaths, sometimes shaking in a fury exceeding their strength on the iron grill that held them in their grave.

The sufferings of these unfortunates were eased by the modest efforts of only two men. One of these was Vándory and the other the Catholic chaplain of the Porvár prison. A debate on religious topics was in progress at that time in the county council chamber, and supporters of the two religions were arguing with unrestrained enthusiasm over the question of the form of the marriage contract. Vándory and his fellow cleric – although accused by many of religious indifference – thought it better if, when so many *spoke* of religion in the House, they *were to act* as their religion commanded. In Taksony the Church Militant was, it seemed, adequately represented; it did no harm, therefore, if at least two men remembered that the Church had business other than militancy; when the upbringing of children yet unborn was debated with boundless enthusiasm, Jerusalem was thought to be ravaged, and men became enraged if they thought that a couple of children had been christened by reversalists[209] in accordance with rites other than theirs, they felt that at least two should use their time so that those of the numberless who, in the legal meaning of the term, were named as Catholics or Protestants should be taught at least something of the tenets of their religions and enjoy the

---

209 A *reverzális* is a statement made to the civil authority by a person engaged to be married to someone of different religion, to the effect that any children born to them shall follow the other party's religion.

consolation of the faith before their deaths. If Vándory and the Catholic chaplain discussed their faiths I don't believe that they would have agreed on many points; while they were doing good deeds there was no difference between them – and although the one saw in Rome the New Babylon, and the other the well-spring of all divine grace; and although the one thought that his religion was in danger as long as reversalists existed, and the other thought the same if they were banned; while the one considered it impiousness if all Rome's decrees weren't accepted, and the other found it idolatrous if anyone found the basis of his faith in anything but Holy Writ, every time that Vándory was able to come in from Tiszarét he spent much of his time in the prison, as did the chaplain every day, and their words of consolation poured fresh hope into the hearts of many hapless wretches, who would have allowed themselves to yield to despair had it not been for those heartening words. There were some who at first rejected these gentle men, and many received their instruction with scathing disdain; but who, especially in the hours of his unhappiness, can go for long without the consolation of his religion? Faith is sometimes not enough for our intellect, we want to understand, and religion offers incomprehensible mysteries – but can the heart find satisfaction without it? Take the doubter out into God's nature, where the horizon is bounded by high hills, and the eye, which needs a distant view, rises to the heaven almost involuntarily; there, where all around you are to be heard the thunder of streams falling from the hills, the song of birds and the sigh of the breeze in the branches, at which the heart is stirred and the mind seeks in vain to understand, show him the lofty heaven, and when the sun is setting in its pool of blood above the horizon or the moon is silently spreading its silvery light among the millions of stars ask your companion whether he still doubts. And all those wonders of nature don't affect the heart as much as does the approach of a truly good man who, inspired by his faith, endeavours to bring happiness to his fellow men by his quiet works.

People have recently turned their attention to the prisons and have established a new form of poetry, a form of the innocent pastorals that are performed in prisons. Everything that we see as great and fine in the world also has its caricature which rises at almost the same time, and this growth of philanthropy, according to which every criminal is merely misunderstood by his fellow men and is portrayed as an honest man that has accidentally strayed from the right way, is beyond doubt just as ridiculous as other similar errors of the human mind; no less in error, however, are those who set out from the opposite point of view, and indeed consider the great majority of criminals to be incorrigible. The great man, whose deeds are praised by hundreds, is only a human being when seen close to, and the great criminal, whom we shun in disgust, is also a human being when all is said and done. The deeds that we admire in the former and by which we're appalled in the latter constitute only individual moments in entire lives, and just as there are numerous defects of human nature in the great man, so there are also various good qualities in the great criminal, and it's for this reason that in many cases such redemption is possible – but always only through such as are inspired to it by religious feeling.

The effect that Vándory in particular had on the prisoners was little short of miraculous. When he went into the prison and the prisoners merely heard his voice or the sound of his footsteps delight shone in every face. The occupants of the prison into which he went surrounded their consoler with respect, and the unusual sympathy, the loving manner in which they had not been addressed for a long time if ever, opened the heart of the most confirmed criminal to his gentle teachings. Anyone that saw Vándory among the prisoners couldn't have been surprised at the optimism with which he declared all his disciples redeemable, indeed, in many cases already redeemed. So it actually seemed when he was there. Most people's character is shaped by external influences; the heart is like an echo and responds to the tone in which it is addressed, and where he sees true sympathy the greatest criminal, made savage by the pitiless blows of his fate and the injustice of men, can seldom resist it.

Most striking was the effect that Vándory had on the Jewish glazier; he had come under suspicion, as we know, for Macskaházy's murder and been taken to Porvár. As the Jew had been found in the stoke-hole after Macskaházy's murder a statement by him was of the greatest importance for Tengelyi's case, and Völgyesy, as the notary's defence, had requested that he be held in isolation. This the *alispán* did as readily as if he were doing it on behalf of his wife. One of the wood-stores was emptied for the purpose, and the basic essentials installed, consisting of a stove stoked from inside, an inferior bed, a strong new lock on the door and little else. That was the Jew's cell, where he could contemplate his unfortunate situation with no one to trouble him. The *alispán*'s wife was convinced of his innocence, as she'd said, and at first showed some sympathy for this unfortunate man, and indeed at the start of his captivity went straight away to visit him on one occasion – which the jailer, contrary to Mrs Réty's clear orders, spoke of to others lest this noble deed should remain a secret. Apart from this high-ranking lady no one had showed the least compassion for his fate, and apart from his interrogators hardly anyone so much as spoke to him. Even the *hajdú* displayed contempt as he gave him his meagre food, then left the cell either in silence or with a coarse joke, and the prisoner felt the full range of the torments of solitude, relieved by neither scant hope for the future nor pleasant memories of the past.

Pleasant memories! for he was a Jew; that was the story of his life. Born to share the wretchedness of his family, prevented in his mother's caring arms from knowing the injustice of the world even in early youth, he'd left the family home to feel abandoned rather than free, toiling for his daily bread not in some decent employment – a Jew is forbidden that – but by cunning and deception, crawling on the ground like a grub to be trampled by the unthinking passer-by, hated and persecuted – that's what the Jew finds in his past, that's what this prisoner's memories were of. The happy days of childhood! The man, when he's achieved all of life's goals, looks back in the finest moment of his triumph on his innocent childhood games and would gladly exchange his laurels for the pure joys in which he then delighted; but what can the Jew find when he recalls that time of life? Scorn, which embittered even his first childish pleasures. The first time that he went through his village streets on his own two feet the village children ran after him calling him names. The battle which he, all alone, has fought with the crowd begins then on the threshold of his life, and derision and ridicule poisons its chalice from the first drop. He too will fall in love, but he'll see her for whom he'd give his life despised by all and sundry – she that he'd raise to the throne in his youthful enthusiasm, he has nothing to share with her but his shame, a shame that he hasn't deserved and from which, for that very reason, he can't be free, the shame that he's inherited from his ancestors and which he'll bequeath to his children, the shame that has been pronounced like a curse on his entire race and from which no virtue, no great deed can relieve him.

And are we surprised if the Jew is degenerate, and if the higher feelings which ennoble human nature are rarely to be found in that race?! Have we given him room in which to exhibit these higher feelings? Has this country acknowledged him as its son, that it might expect his affection? Have we treated him as a brother, and now we accuse him of selfishness? If we withhold every earthly reward for virtue, so organise our society that we take no account of good works either for the honour of our compatriots nor the glory of our name – how many will still follow the path of virtue? That's the situation into which the Jew has been placed in the middle of this enlightened century, at least in Hungary. Such noble sentiments as remain in his soul after so much repression can only find expression in the burning hatred that he feels for us.

Apart from the sufferings shared by his people, the Jewish glazier deserved the sympathy of all for other reasons too. His repulsive appearance, which made him suspicious before he'd done any wrong, and his sickly physique made him doubly unfortunate; and especially now while he was in prison, where the mark of fear was plain on his face, it was hardly possible to imagine anyone more likely to arouse pity. But as I've said, no one felt any compassion for the Jew and it seemed as if he himself didn't count on any sympathy – and Vándory, who didn't restrict his visits to those of his own denomination, had been to see him several times, always found him locked into himself, and soon came to the conclusion that the poor man merely took him for a spy. The clergyman did his best to arouse confidence in this prisoner as he did in all cases, and indeed was all the more hopeful that he would be able to pick up things from the Jew that could be useful to Tengelyi – but in vain! The Jew received Vándory with the utmost humility, answered all his questions, and sometimes even began to talk about being baptised, but it was obvious from all his answers that he regarded his visits as just another form of interrogation; and Vándory became convinced that his visits were a burden to the prisoner and eventually stopped going.

Now, however, this situation had changed completely. After being in prison for some months, during which he had not been allowed out of his underground cell into the fresh air, the prevailing jail-fever also seized the poor Jew, and there was no hope of his recovery except, perhaps, in that he wasn't being treated by the county doctors. He lay forsaken in his cell, even more unfortunate than the other prisoners in that if he ever awoke for a moment from his fevered dreams he couldn't even obtain a drink of water to slake his burning thirst. It was as if he had already died, everyone seemed to have forgotten about him, and even the *alispán*'s wife, for all the sympathy that she'd shown, was completely unconcerned when she heard that there was no hope of his recovering, and that in his delirium he was simply uttering disjointed words in an incomprehensible language.

Vándory was the only one who didn't falsify his reputation for good-heartedness, and just as when he realised that his visits were unpleasant to the Jew he stopped of his own accord, so now he did all that he could at least to ease the poor man's situation. At his own expense he employed a poor woman to spend a large part of the day with the patient, in other words, did everything in his powerthat he felt to be his duty as a pious Christian – everything that is fine and good, from the tiny services by which we show our goodwill towards our fellow men to the loftiest virtues. The human being for whom he did this was a Jew, and furthermore one who, it seemed, had been unwilling to be persuaded by the Christian clergyman's teachings and shown little inclination to be converted; but even as a heathen it seemed to Vándory that the command in the parable of the Samaritan to love one's fellow men didn't only apply to one's co-religionists, and that in the holy book by which he ruled his life it was laid down as a duty that we love our fellow men, and he held to that.

When the Jew awoke from his disturbed sleep he would often see before him Vándory's calm features. When he woke in the night and wanted a little water to slake his burning thirst his nurse would be there, moving quietly to his bed to fulfil his request, and if he asked who had sent her to him, once more he would hear the name of Vándory. He was like a supreme providence that could foretell his needs, like a guardian angel whom God had sent him as consolation in his pain; so this unexpected benefactor appeared in the poor man's imagination, and in the wild dreams that disturbed his fevered bed it seemed that he called on Vándory for help, and the old woman who was at his side said that every time that he spoke that name he immediately seemed more at ease.

Almost three weeks went by without any change in the patient's condition, and finally the fever left him and he became lucid. Even now there was no prospect that he would recover. His body lacked the strength to stand the inevitable crisis, and his mind alone was restored for a short while, as sometimes happens in the final stages of this illness. It's a painful condition: death allows its victim a couple of hours respite only so that he may take one more look around this world, see before him once more everything that he is to lose and cling to life with renewed strength.

The Jew could see his situation plainly, and it appeared that he was at peace with it. He had only one desire, that of seeing Vándory again. He asked his nurse as he came to, and learnt that he hadn't been dreaming when he'd thought that the clergyman was often at his bedside, and that he had him alone to thank for all the kindness that had been shown him during his illness. That day Vándory wasn't expected in Porvár before noon, and the patient became hourly more and more distressed when he saw that his benefactor still didn't come. "I can't die in peace," he repeated to the old woman, "without speaking to the reverend. I'm grateful for all the kindness that he's shown me," he added more quietly, "and I've got a secret on my soul, something that Mr Vándory really ought to know, and I can only tell him. Please go and ask whether he's here yet."

The woman went to see Tengelyi, whom he usually went to see before anything else if he came to town, and returned with the news that Vándory hadn't come yet; the patient fell back on his pillow almost in despair. At last, late in the afternoon the door of the cell opened and the clergyman was at his bedside – he'd sent his nurse to Tengelyi again, and had all but given up hope. I shan't describe the feelings that filled the Jew's heart in that moment. All his life he'd met with only scorn and contempt, had feared and hated people as they'd meant nothing to him but persecution, he'd trusted no one because he'd never met with sympathy – he hadn't hoped for anything good even from God, who'd evidently put him on this earth just to suffer – he'd loved no one, as one who hadn't known his parents and whom no one had ever approached affectionately. Now, for the first time in his life, all the finer feelings in his soul spoke out at once. Vándory was the first person ever to approach him with kindness, and the heart which life had taught to hate opened to that gentle touch. All the gratitude that he would otherwise have felt to benefactors in the course of his life, all the trust the need of which he too bore within him but which he hadn't been able to give to anyone, all the affection of which his soul was capable – these emotions all filled his bosom in an instant, and he could find only tears with which to give expression to them.

"Easy now, my dear fellow," said Vándory, deeply affected by the scene, "God's infinitely merciful and He'll take pity on you too."

The prisoner seized his hand convulsively and his tears continued to flow, but he made no reply.

"Well, you're feeling better," said Vándory, sitting down by the bed, "you're going to get better, you'll be able to live and even become a useful member of society."

"Oh, dear Reverend Vándory," said the Jew weakly, his voice almost choked by tears, "I'm done for, I feel I've got to die, but that's not why I'm weeping. I've not had a lot of pleasure in this world: I didn't even know my parents, and a poor Jew like me hasn't got much to lose but his life. When I'm under the soil maybe I'll find some peace there. But when I think of all the kindness Your Reverence has shown me, all that a Christian has done for me, and you of all people, whom I . . ." and once more his tears burst forth, he covered his face with his hands and sobbed.

549

Vándory thought that the moment had arrived for him to be able to convert the hapless man – he had always been much more convinced of his religion to be indifferent to spreading it; proselytising wasn't an offshoot from a strong faith but its necessary consequence – and began to speak of the infinite grace of God, who would not reject the sinner even though he converted at the last minute.

The Jew grasped the meaning of those words, wiped away his tears and shook his head sorrowfully. "Your Reverence," said he with a sigh, "don't ask that of me. I can't abandon the faith of my ancestors. What a scoundrel I'd need to be, when all my life I've hardly done anything good but refuse to be tempted away from my religion, if I even failed in that and not kept the faith. There's nothing I wouldn't do for Your Reverence, but don't ask that of me."

"You mustn't think," said Vándory, "that I want you to be converted for my sake, you'd be quite mistaken if you took that most important step in your life except by your own conviction. I'm speaking for your sake, for the salvation of your soul, Christianity is the religion of love . . . "

"The religion of love?" said the patient, and a look of bitterness returned to his face for a moment, "ask us Jews what we've experienced! If I'd known any more Christians like Your Reverence," he added hastily, seeing the effect that his words had, "who knows, perhaps I might have converted. And personally, I've not known many good Jews. But," he went on after a brief pause, during which he looked round the room, evidently trying to make certain that no one but the clergyman was there, "I've got a secret on my soul which I must tell Your Reverence before I die . . . and I can feel my strength failing."

Vándory pulled his chair closer to the patient's bed, and the Jew, interrupted several times by weakness, told him what my readers know about the theft of Tengelyi's and his documents, and how the involvement of Macskaházy and the *alispán*'s wife, which many believed after Viola's statement, was established beyond any doubt.

"But who killed Macskaházy?" asked Vándory, after listening closely to every word. "From where you were found, you must have heard everything that happened in the room."

"So I did," replied the Jew. "The murder was committed by Viola, I'll venture to swear to it. He talked to Macskaházy for perhaps a quarter of an hour, and I recognised his voice at once."

"Then why ever didn't you say so in your statement?" said Vándory with a sigh. "Didn't you know that another innocent man was accused of the crime, and that your truthful statement could save his honour and perhaps his life?"

"Why didn't I?" said the Jew, looking hard at Vándory, "Because Her Ladyship threatened me that if I said a single word to put Tengelyi in the clear all the suspicion would fall on me."

"But what were you after in the mansion that night, when the unfortunate lawyer was murdered?" Vándory went on.

The Jew said nothing for a moment. "Why shouldn't I tell you," said he at length. "I promised to keep quiet, but that woman's abandoned me in my hour of need, I owe her no favours. One day, before he was murdered, she and Macskaházy had an argument. He wouldn't hand over the documents, which he'd found in Viola's hands; so she sent for me and promised me two thousand forints if . . ."

Vándory clasped his hands in shock.

"Viola beat me to it," the Jew went on quietly. "Otherwise Macskaházy would have died at my hands."

He fell back on his pillow. Vándory sat at the bedside, deep in thought. What he'd heard filled his soul with horror, and at the same time with hope because he could see that it would be of the greatest importance for clearing Tengelyi. After a short reflection, however, he realised that the entire statement couldn't help Tengelyi if the Jew lapsed back into unconsciousness before repeating it to at least one other reliable witness, because the court wouldn't accept his unsupported evidence as he was Tengelyi's best friend.

"My dear fellow," said the clergyman as he stood up, "pray to your God, who has given you time and strength to repent your sins, and you'll be able to make up for some of them at least. What you've told me, in my view, is enough to clear Tengelyi of the suspicion that he's under at present; but in order to give credibility to your statement it needs to be repeated in the presence of at least two witnesses, and I'll go and fetch someone."

"I've got to say it again, when it makes me shudder?" asked the Jew sorrowfully.

"It's your human duty, the salvation of your soul demands it," said Vándory solemnly. "How can you hope that God will be merciful to you if you weren't willing to extend a helping hand to someone in dire peril?"

The Jew was silent for a moment. "Tengelyi's your friend, Your Reverence," said he then, looking Vándory in the eye. "How better can I show my gratitude?"

551

"If you don't feel up to it," said Vándory, moved by those words and especially by the tone in which they were uttered, "take a rest, and we'll come in a couple of hours' time."

"No, no," replied the Jew, "it's now or never. I feel that I'll only be able to speak for a little while. Come straight back, Your Reverence, bring whoever you like, and I'll tell them everything, and whatever the consequences I'm beyond the vengeance of the *alispán* or anyone else."

"There's no need for you to say anything that'll mean your risking the *alispán*'s wife's vengeance," said Vándory, not wishing to accuse anyone of anything if he could save his friend without doing so. "As you said, you only plotted to steal the documents with Macskaházy, there's no need to say any more. If it's made clear that it was Viola that killed the unfortunate lawyer, the fact that you'd gone to the house with similar intentions and who'd put you up to it won't have any bearing on Tengelyi's position."

"But I won't leave anything out," said the Jew, and his face again assumed its angry expression. "Let me have my revenge on that vile woman, she's got me into all sorts of trouble and turned her back on me in my hour of need when I'm suffering because of her."

"Have you really got time to think of revenge?" said Vándory seriously.

The Jew was silent for a moment. "As you wish, then, Your Reverence," said he, looking hard at Vándory. "I'll do anything you say. You've been kind to me, and I'd have liked to do more to show my gratitude. But," he added, wiping away the tears that had come to his eyes once more as he spoke, "please go and be quick, there's no telling whether I'll be able to keep my promise in an hour's time."

Vándory called in the nurse, who was standing outside the cell, and hurried off. The Jew turned to the wall and, worn out by the conversation, quickly fell asleep.

XXXVII

On leaving the sick man Vándory's first concern was, naturally, to find fully reliable witnesses who would testify to the statement that the Jew would repeat in their presence. He was in County Hall, and the spring meetings were just taking place, so he could be certain that if he merely went up the main staircase he was bound to come upon a committee in session in either the larger or smaller hall from which he could take a couple of members. He hurried that way.

In all countries we can find something that attracts our attention as soon as we cross the border, something that gives its peculiar character to the life of the people. England has world trade; in France the whole nation is enthused by a desire for military glory; in Holland there are the canals, the result and at the same time the symbol of that quiet industry with which that people first won its land from the sea and later charmed it into a garden; God has endowed Germany with its philosophers, who, within those frontiers, impenetrable to the human intellect, have found the country for themselves and their students. In Hungary, beyond all doubt, what immediately strikes every foreigner is the *infinite number of our committee meetings*. Trade and industry, science and art, honour, indeed, even diligence are matters in which we have to yield pride of place to others; but there is one thing in which no one surpasses the Hungarian people – naturally, only in the constitutional sense of the word, that is to say, the privileged as defined by Werbőczi[210] – *our committee meetings*. No people on the face of this earth holds as many committee meetings as we do.

There are those that proclaim that our eight-century-old constitution is still flourishing in the fulness of its strength. In my view, that is a huge deception. The right of the Hungarian nobility to rebel, which the Golden Bull gave it, has been transformed into the right to hold meetings and assemblies, and we can state that almost without exception everything that was once in force in Hungary has now sunk without trace. This land – to coin a completely new simile – has changed into a gigantic armchair in which sit thousands of *táblabírós*; who can question that the method by which so many individuals strike seams of gold will eventually bring to light this country's hidden treasures too? In Hungary, it seems, every-

---

210 That is, the nobility. The peasantry had no privileges under the constitution.

one expects that, and at least it isn't their experience that the public good can be promoted otherwise than by committee meetings.

Foreigners don't esteem sufficiently this form that our patriotism takes. They don't know what it means to take part in a conscription assembly and to sit in parliament in the morning – because it's necessary, in the afternoon at elections of associations – because it's useful, at the card-table in the evening – because it's splendid. If just once in their lives they tried, I wager they'd be quite amazed at the way in which so many people meet in this country, who can endure it? In explanation I can only offer that those who are most eager to attend our committee meetings are at the same time those who rise to speak most often, and so at least sometimes find rest from their onerous sitting. Yes, no one will deny that the number of committees rather than diminishing increases daily: and I really can't understand why the association of Hungarian doctors hasn't offered a prize *for an account of the causes that have brought about and maintained our chronic disease of sitting on committees.* That this question belongs in their sphere is clear from the numerous symptoms that anyone that has so much as seen a committee in session must have observed, and which present themselves in so many different forms. Some are sensitive to draughts and are afraid of catching cold; one perspires, another is thirsty, a third has corns; many yawn – which is, as is well known, the sign of an upset stomach; while some ramble as if delirious. What might an astute doctor not observe in this sickness! What fine books he might write on the causes of the plague of committee meetings!

But where am I? I meant to follow Vándory into the big room, where the cream of the county is holding another meeting, and here I am talking about the great number of committee meetings in Hungary and the reasons for them. These deviations that hold up the thread of my narrative at every trick and turn are, as my readers can see, only to be attributed to the excessive conscientiousness with which I address every single fact. The Estates of Taksony have been in session all morning, and this afternoon we find them there again – how am I to state the reason for this without reminding my readers of the general passion for meetings that prevails in Hungary? It's a simple matter for others. One is a famous scholar, another a glorious patriot, or a great man, perhaps a great landowner. If you ask "How did they become such, and in what does their worth consist?" no one's obliged to answer; that's just how things stand – the reason why is none of your business. Only we poor novelists are lamentably constrained to give adequate reasons for our

554

characters' actions. It's as if we've painted a picture of life and it wouldn't be really natural if at least half of them never really knew why they were doing this or that.

No one, however, especially at this moment, can say that of James Bántornyi, whom we find in the chair as we enter the room. Who can't see sufficient grounds for the formation of the society *for the prevention of cruelty to animals* that he has established, when such a society exists in England too?[211] And where in Hungary might there be a person more suitable for the office of president of such a society than Mr James, who's always keenly active in horse-racing and fox-hunting and so demonstrates in practice his interest in animals? Immediately on his return from England Bántornyi became occupied with quite different thoughts. We know what glory Wilberforce and others won for themselves through the liberating of the black slaves that was enacted in the British Empire after arduous struggles,[212] and James yearned for similar glory. The fact is that really black people – which no doubt would be much nicer – are not to be found in Hungary; however, our many Gypsies are at least brown, and in material terms are not much better off than the slaves in the English colonies ever were; and the society that Bántornyi proposed, which was called *The Society for the Advancement of the Well-being of the Coloured Populace of Hungary* at least had a title that sounded very fine when translated into English. There would be no lack of support. After Bántornyi had explained the English system for the emancipation of slaves in the country, and when the *táblabírós* – who had previously only commented on it in short articles in the papers – realised that gradual emancipation would begin by servants being obliged to work for at least four days a week for ten years as so-called apprentices, they were clothed with a special enthusiasm for that kind of philanthropy and considered it much better than our Hungarian socage, in which there wasn't so much concern for the education of homeless cottagers. However, who would think it: the Gypsies themselves appeared uninterested in such an improvement of their lot, and when this educational system was tried on a number of Gypsies by some of the county's philanthropists and they had fled from the weekly four days of work, Bántornyi saw that Hungary wasn't yet mature enough for such

---

211 The forerunner of the RSPCA was founded in 1824. The founders included William Wilberforce.
212 Slavery was abolished in England in 1807.

555

a society to function and that he must direct his efforts to some other sphere.

The stopping of cruelty to animals was the objective that he chose for himself, and at first sight it appeared that he couldn't have made a better choice. First of all, no one can deny that his ambition in this direction was purely English. Next, it was probable that in this instance those whose benefit was intended weren't going to oppose it. Natural order too seems to demand this, as it is well known that God created animals a day earlier than Man, and if we don't intend to disrupt this sequence we must put the welfare of animals before that of people. But no one will believe how many difficulties Mr James had to contend with in this too. There were first of all the unsympathetic, those who were unsympathetic from the first moment and those, even more numerous, who became such only later, when they discovered that they would have to pay a forint annually into the society's funds. Even Vándory, whose support James had doubted least of all on account of his well known philanthropy, had showed himself to be unusually cool, and as soon as cruelty to animals was mentioned began to talk about hospitals, orphanages, and other such institutions, which had nothing to do with cruelty to animals.[213] It seemed clear that not everything had its right time,[214] and that schools, the abolition of capital punishment and the cessation of flogging might not be spoken of later, as the example of England showed most excellently, where associations active against cruelty to animals were, as we know, in full agreement with the use of the cat-o'-nine-tails. In addition to the unsympathetic, the society was also opposed by those who, Cassandra-like, can see everything more deeply, and now warn their fellow citizens of the possible dangers that can come from stopping cruelty to animals just as the Jacobin club[215] was believed to have been formed at the first gentlemen's club, and it is clear that they who were now speaking only of animals could easily expand to other subjects which may threaten our constitution. Still others saw the ninth title of the first part[216] contravened if the Hungarian land owner, true member of the Holy Crown, was reduced to such servility that he couldn't beat his own beast of burden to his heart's content; and when Mr James, taking as an example the county that brought in mutual fire protection, but

---

213 *Magnus dormitat Homerus!* See ch.1 for Vándory's views on hare-coursing.
214 Is Eötvös ironically echoing Ecclesiastes 5:1?
215 The most famous club of the French Revolution.
216 Reference to Werbőczi's *Tripartitum* – see above in ch.XXXVII.

in such a way that the nobility weren't to be forced to submit themselves to that rule, proposed among its rules that the society should only prevent cruelty to animals among the non-noble inhabitants of the county, further difficulties arose on the question of the extent to which it could be called cruelty if a serf were driving a team and was obliged to beat his horses because of the bad state of the roads, and it was only thanks to Mr James's extraordinary tact that the meeting didn't break up over this ticklish point. When, that is, it was laid down in the rules that beating a draught animal or other beast on the order of a nobleman might not be called cruelty, and also that didn't constitute beating which a serf performed on his team of horses in the course of his master's work, or which took place between the end of September and the beginning of April on the main highroad in the county, on which progress was impossible in snowy conditions without a whip, the principal objections of the meeting were silenced.

Mr James had gone to a lot of trouble; he'd gone round the county so much winning the support of all the more distinguished nobility that two of his four beautiful bays had died; but in the end the society existed, and its founder had been unanimously elected its president. Even now there were those that opposed the society; Vándory, for example – who at other times was so eager to relieve suffering, and one of whose favourite ideas had been to end cruelty to animals – couldn't understand how, while down below in the county jail prisoners were dying because of the poor conditions, upstairs in the council chamber discussions could be going on about relieving the sufferings of horses and cattle; and those who'd paid their annual forint as members of the society – fortunately, these weren't numerous, because the members of Porvár societies were happier to buy the glory that accompanied patriotism on credit than for cash – those, I say, couldn't grasp that no one but the president of the society had yet received anything from the money which had been contributed for the benefit of the cattle; but for all the animosity and suspicion the society existed, and that was no doubt the main thing.

I can't say on the spur of the moment which famous writer it was that said *To live is the main purpose of our life*, nor can I recall in which of his famous works. If my readers don't believe that these words were spoken by a German they will blame me for them – this notion isn't the worst of the foreign ones that we've picked up and the French, English or German nature of which we've Magyarised by an appropriate twirl of the moustache. What is said there about human life is good for a great number of things in this world. They exist that they may exist, that's

557

their main purpose; children need games and men need some form of occupation in order not to be bored, and the greater part of these things, which we carry out with the most serious of expressions and sometimes in the sweat of our brows, are of hardly any other use – with the exception, naturally, of all official business that confers payment, as in that case the use lies in the actual payment. The Porvár Society for the Prevention of Cruelty to Animals held meetings, had a president and voting members, and indeed a paid secretary and treasurer; what more was required? Under such circumstances James had no need of excessive optimism in order to hope for the continued existence, and indeed the expansion, of the society that he'd founded. The Hungarian has a rare inclination to imitate – what he sees done in foreign parts, especially any foreign customs that he regards as excellent, he immediately tries to do in Hungary too. That may be why our most famous men of learning have seen Hungarians in all the peoples of this wide world – there's hardly anything to be found on earth that someone doesn't try to introduce in Hungary. If horse-racing and fox-hunting have been brought from England, why not societies for the prevention of cruelty to animals too? My principal objection to Mr James's thinking is that he has made a mistake in the logical sequence, which now, as I understand it, calls for the introduction of cock-fighting; that, however, is only my personal opinion, and when Mr James sees the rapid expansion of his first society he'll make good that deficiency because of which we've not yet been able to struggle up to England's flourishing condition. The minute-book confirmed that the Society for the Prevention of Cruelty to Animals was in fine fettle and had already achieved good results by that time. The secretary's address to the present session gave very many examples by which any fair-minded person could be convinced of how the spirit of the Society was spreading in Taksony County. Permit me to adduce just a few.

Almost two months ago the attorney general's coachman had encountered a carter and noticed as he passed him that this man was flogging his horses. The coachman called out to his harsh colleague, but the mud was deep and instead of listening to the friendly suggestion the latter lashed his poor horses all the more. The coachman admonished the obdurate horse-beater more loudly, but instead of replying he merely cursed and beat the horses all the harder. At that the philanthropic coachman jumped down from the box and, not mincing his words, ran back and caught up the carter – which was all the easier as the cart was completely stuck – took him by the leg, pulled him from his seat, and thrashed him so that he could scarcely resume his place.

Resolution: The Society regarded the coachman's philanthropic action as especially meritorious. It was pleased to see that, as concerned cruelty to animals, more enlightened views were now spreading among the lower orders of people too. The coachman's name, Péter Katona, was to be recorded with distinction in the minutes.

N.N., a county *táblabíró*, was travelling from his village to Porvár last February and when he was half-way there realised that his horses were becoming exhausted in the deep mud. So that no harm should come to the poor animals the said gentleman immediately unharnessed them and made his coachman obtain eight peasant post horses from a nearby village, and with them continued his journey.

Resolution: N.N. had given further proof of the refined feelings for which the Society knew him, and in recognition of his merit he was elected an honorary member of the Society. The president would arrange for the publication of a certificate to that effect.

I shan't burden my readers with more quotations from the minute-book; suffice it for me to say that the public spirit displayed by two or three in Taksony County, as in a number of others, by now was wholly supportive of the Society, and whatever some might say to the contrary, that it was just so much empty wind, we know that all the same the majority of people turn their cloaks to it and often put their hands to their hats before it, lest they be blown off their heads.

When Vándory entered the room – he made his way straight to where he could most easily find persons suitable as witnesses – a very interesting debate was just taking place about a donkey that had been beaten by its owner. Since its foundation the Society had been divided into three parts. One, that farthest to the left, wanted to extend its good works to all living animals; the second, which consisted of determinedly conservative members, wished to restrict the Society's actions only to horses, while the third, which, like Ancillon,[217] did its best to mediate between these extreme opponents: it was the section that progressed by discussion and took donkeys under its protection, wishing to give them the privileged position of horses. This section had won a significant victory at the previous session, when it had carried a motion to the effect that mules – unfortunately, no such animal existed in Taksony County – be regarded as horses in future. From there it was only another short step

---

217 Johann Peter Friedrich Ancillon (1767 – 1837), Prussian historian and statesman. His main work was *Ueber das Verhältniss des Idealen und der Wirklichkeit* (On the relationship between Ideal and Reality).

to the emancipation of donkeys, and my readers may imagine the zeal with which this section was arguing in the present case, in which it had a close interest.

Fine though the speeches were on this occasion, veritable models of Hungarian rhetoric – under the rules of which the driest political subject calls for almost as many poetic syllables as do the appellations *édes nagysám* and *kedves teins uram*[218] in love scenes – with however many garlands individual speakers adorned the ears of the donkeys that they favoured, while their opponents extolled the extraordinary merits of the services rendered in ancient times to the fatherland by horses, in particular recalling the injustice which would result if special privileges weren't awarded to those animals on which our ancestors had come to the land of Hunnia and been victorious in every battle, so that almost half of the glory of the past belonged to them, and we could scarcely say what might have become of the Hungarian nobility had they not found something to ride: Vándory, it seemed, didn't dignify the debate with his attention, and after he'd called aside first Völgyesy, who was taking no part in the proceedings, and Lajos Bántornyi, who'd been unable to absent himself from the session for his brother's sake, to a whispered conference by one of the windows, the three of them left the room in apparently the greatest haste.

But great though the disinterest had been that Vándory had displayed in the deliberations of the Society, the interest that his coming had aroused was greater, especially as he left hurriedly taking with him Bántornyi and Völgyesy, who'd seemed so surprised and interested in what he'd no doubt told them that the former hadn't even stayed to hear the rest of his brother's finest speech and the latter had even left his gloves behind on the table. Some racked their brains: what had Vándory come for? Others rather pondered why he'd left, and especially why he'd taken a couple of people with him, while many found it most incomprehensible of all that he'd taken Völgyesy and Bántornyi in particular, when he could have chosen so many others. A whole mass of hypotheses sprang up, among which was that Völgyesy and Bántornyi had been summoned to a certain lawyer, then a very sick man, whom no one had yet been able to induce to make a will, and whom Vándory had persuaded; more probable was that witnesses were required for some marriage. The interest with which everyone had previously been following the Society's deliberations fell slack from that moment, and Mr James, after for a

---

218 Respectively *my sweet madam* and *my dear sir*.

while doing his utmost to bring back those present from their frivolous thoughts to the matter in hand, could no longer tolerate the walking to and fro and the whispering. He saw himself compelled to adjourn the session, with the result that the just demands of donkeys were left to a day later.

No one can take it amiss that Mr James was cross at this turn of events both with Vándory for coming and with his brother and Völgyesy for leaving the meeting. I don't know many that would be happy to share the attention of an audience with others, or who, when delivering their finest speech from the presidential chair, heard their listeners whispering and saw them move this way and that, and everyone will be able to excuse him for a little ill humour after such a session. There was, however, someone in County Hall on whom Vándory's conduct made an even less comfortable impression – Mrs Réty.

The *alispán's* wife happened to be sitting and working by the window of her bedroom that opened onto the courtyard when she saw Vándory emerge from seeing the Jew and hurry towards the steps into County Hall. Her attention was attracted by this but she wasn't alarmed. Since she'd known that the Jew was out of his mind and that no hope remained of his recovery she'd not been enquiring after him and was quite as much at ease as if he were already dead. Now, on seeing Vándory coming from the pantry that was being used as his cell, she remembered the unfortunate man. "What do I care whether he's alive or not," said she to herself, "he's lost his mind; that soft-headed priest has probably prattled something to him again of which he won't have understood a word, and now he's satisfied that he's said his piece and he's off to see Tengelyi to do the same again." And the *alispán's* wife went on with her work, thinking of the clergyman's futile efforts with that contempt which so-called practical people feel towards those who don't reckon the usefulness of their endeavours in *forints* and *garases*. A short while later, however, she heard the sound of steps in the yard once again, looked down and saw Vándory return to the Jew's cell accompanied by Völgyesy and Lajos Bántornyi; the nurse attending the sick man came out at once, and the *alispán's* wife's heart was filled with misgiving.

"What ever's going on?" she thought. "The Jew's delirious; there's no hope that he'll recover; what can they be after in his cell? Strange, very strange. Völgyesy, Tengelyi's lawyer, and Vándory . . . what if the Jew's feeling better after all, and . . . I must find out!" said she to herself. "The woman who's been looking after the Jew is standing there outside the door, she must know all about it."

561

Mrs Réty sent down her maid, and shortly afterwards the old woman stepped into the room with a deep curtsey. The poor woman was quite bewildered, so amazed was she at being summoned to Her Honour the *alispán*'s wife.

Mrs Réty concealed her agitation to the best of her ability, and after telling the still bemused woman how long she'd known the Jew, that she believed him to be innocent, and that it was for precisely that reason that she was very interested in what happened to him, and after praising her for her diligent nursing she enquired how he was feeling now, and did she know why Vándory and two gentlemen had just that moment gone to his cell?

The woman's replies, although they were offered in a humble tone, weren't such as might reassure Mrs Réty, and indeed filled her with even greater alarm. Why had the Jew been so desirous of seeing Vándory, now that he had fully regained consciousness? What could the secret be before revealing which, according to the nurse, he couldn't die in peace, why had she been sent out that day when the clergyman had talked with her patient for more than an hour? And now why had Völgyesy and Lajos Bántornyi been summoned to the sick man, if not to witness the revelation that he had made or was about to make?

"Don't you know," asked Mrs Réty in a tremulous voice, after listening to the woman's lengthy account with the closest attention, "what the Jew was talking about to the Reverend Vándory?"

"His Reverence sent me out," said the woman calmly, "though there was no need, I've never been one to talk, and at my time of life, I think, I can be trusted. But His Reverence sent me out, so I don't know anything, I only suppose that he was confessing to some evil deed."

"What makes you think that?" asked the *alispán*'s wife, whose unusual agitation the old woman now noticed.

"Well, I certainly didn't eavesdrop," she said, "and even if I'd wanted to, I'm hard of hearing, and I couldn't have heard anything through the door, I just think that's what they were talking about. I've never seen His Reverence look so surprised as when he came out of the cell. Goodness knows what dreadful things he must have told him! When I went back in the Jew seemed calmer for a while, but I'd hardly sat down than he was restless again. "If they want me to make a statement," said he over and over, "why don't they come?" I told him that His Reverence had only just that minute gone, and he should take it easy. But he kept tossing and turning and sighing – it was terrible to see, Madam, how his conscience was troubling him, and he didn't rest until His Reverence

562

came back with the other gentlemen. Then he just asked if he could make his statement, and when they said yes he seemed quite at ease. But I was sent out. But Your Honour," she added in surprise, seeing how pale Mrs Réty had become, "perhaps you're not feeling very well?"

Mrs Réty gathered all her strength. "No, my good woman," said she with the greatest composure. "Go down to your patient, the gentlemen will very likely be coming out directly."

"Yes, Your Honour," said she. "In any case the poor man won't live till morning, but he may still need me tonight. But as long as the truth emerges. That's the main thing, isn't it, Your Honour?"

"Quite right," said Mrs Réty, her voice subdued. "The truth will out." And with that the old woman took her leave and left, while Mrs Réty locked the door so that no one should see her in her agitated state, flung herself onto her bed and sank for some time into silent despair.

The Jew was making a full statement; after what she'd heard from the woman Mrs Réty could be in no doubt of that, and could she expect that Tengelyi's most loyal friends would not at any price listen to anything that could be to the notary's advantage?

"What am I to do?" said she to herself and shuddered at the situation in which she saw herself. "Is there no escape?" She sprang up from the bed and paced her room. "There is none!" she said at length, and stopped. "Tengelyi's case has roused too great a stir to be smoothed over without a verdict; to whom can I turn in my dreadful situation? Whom can I ask for advice? My husband?!" An expression of indescribable bitterness came to her face. "Can I ask him to take my part? And why would he? Has he ever loved me? Doesn't he now hate me as much as his cowardly spirit can know such a feeling? Can't I be certain that the moment he sees me in danger he'll desert me, and indeed join my persecutors, lest the accusations against me be extended to include him too?... No! Anything but humiliate myself to that man! But what am I to do?" She began to pace the room once more, and it was evident from the anxiety with which she shook her head from time to time that she was unable to come to any decision. At last it seemed that a thought had suddenly come to her; she stopped, and stared at the escritoire in one corner of the room. "No," she said with a shudder, "there's no need of that, that can't be!" and walked on more quickly still, as if trying to run away from her thoughts. The escritoire seemed to draw her gaze by a magic power; she couldn't escape her terrible thought, and wherever she went her eyes remained involuntarily fixed on it. "I shall go mad!" she said at length, as she covered her eyes and stood still in the middle of the room. "Now that this awful idea has come into my mind I can never be free of it. My God! My God! Help me!"

Mrs Réty stood motionless for a while; her heart pounded and there was a sensation of tautness in her chest as if it were about to burst, and no tears wet her yes. "But why would the idea be so terrible?" she thought on, more calmly now that the first surge of despair had subsided. "To die . . . why does my heart shudder at the thought? Death can only take from us what we have in this world, and have I anything that I might regret losing? I've no children, nor have I ever wanted any; but if I had, perhaps I'd feel bound to this earth. My husband I loathe. I haven't attained the status that I desired . . . and now all that awaits me is disgrace and punishment. To hesitate further would be sheer stupidity."

The *alispán's* wife went to her escritoire, opened one of the drawers and took out quite a big glass bottle which was half full of a white powder resembling sugar. "With this arsenic," said she in an undertone as she put the bottle down in front of her, "I could send half the county to the next world. While this is in my possession no one's going to pronounce judgement on me!" She remained for a while deep in thought; so presumably will my readers and, at all events, my critics, who will declare it as unjust as could be that Mrs Réty can find poison at once when she has need of it. It isn't unlikely that there were rats in the Réty house, as in so many noble Hungarian houses, nor that Mrs Réty wished to be rid of them and used the commonest of means to that end. That she should keep arsenic for the purpose, as is practised in a hundred houses in Hungary, in her own possession under lock and key is a rare precaution, but one to be expected of a careful woman like her. Anyone, however, that thinks that the quantity of poison is improbable is speaking of the matter simply in theory, and knows from experience that it's only hard to obtain arsenic from chemists, whereas anyone that likes can buy it by the pound from tradesmen. I myself once encountered a painter's servant, carrying a pound of arsenic which he'd bought for his master down the street in a blue paper bag. Anyone that doubts that should enquire; it would do no harm if those concerned in supervising medical practice did so.[219]

"But they say that death by poison is agony," said she after a longish contemplation, staring fixedly at the bottle in front of her. "I've heard

---

219 Eötvös anticipates by some eighty years the murderous activity of the poisoners of Nagyrét in the Tiszazug, central Hungary, who killed perhaps as many as 300 between 1914–29. These women obtained their arsenic by stewing fly-papers.

of people suffering dreadful pains for hours, and only being able to die cursing themselves after terrible suffering. What if that happened to me too? What if my strong constitution resisted the poison and I'd have to lie there for hours between life and death, feeling the horrible poison tearing at my inside as every part of my body struggled against dying? And no one would sympathise as I suffered in those long-drawn-out throes and infinite agonies, no loving hand would wipe the cold sweat of death from my brow? Would I have to endure all that alone, or surrounded by people whose every word and glance indicated that they desired not the end of my suffering but of my life?" She shuddered, and as if involuntarily pushed the bottle away.

Her resolve had broken. She didn't know what to do, could see no other way out, yet the whole of her being rebelled against the one that there was. There she stood in silent despair, the poison in front of her, now and then reaching out a hand for it and turning away again with a shudder. "I shall take a lot, all of it," said she again to herself, and her fingers closed convulsively on the bottle which she'd taken in her hand once more, "that way I shan't suffer, a moment and it'll all be over . . . But to die now, when I might live another twenty years!" Mrs Réty put the bottle down again, threw herself onto a chair and covered her eyes with her hands.

"But what if the old woman misled me?" she said suddenly, apparently surprised at this encouraging thought that now flashed in her mind. "What if everything that she said about the Jew making a statement was untrue? Or if the Jew had in fact summoned Vándory and made a statement, couldn't it have been about something completely different? What reason would he have for accusing me, when I've always been a benefactor to him?"

These thoughts reassured Mrs Réty for a moment. She replaced the poison in the drawer and locked it, and was almost amazed at the way in which she'd let herself so be seized by fear that she'd immediately fallen into those desperate ideas. But the assurance couldn't last long, She was far too intelligent a woman to consider her situation more calmly and not to see that what she was building her hopes on was mostly possibility, and indeed scarcely probable . . . and she lapsed once more into her former anxiety.

"I must make certain," said she at length. "The Jew's presumably still alive, it'll be best to find out from him what he's said. And if he's been tricked into it by Vándory, perhaps I'll be able to make him withdraw his statement." And with that Mrs Réty, enveloped in a cloak, left her room and made quickly straight for the Jew's cell.

By that time it was evening; no one noticed the *alispán*'s wife as she crossed the dark courtyard; and since the cell where the Jew lay was almost always left open – because of his illness no one was afraid that he might escape – she reached the pantry without anyone seeing her. The old woman who was caring for him was not a little surprised when she suddenly saw Her Honour in the light of the taper and was asked how the patient was.

"Calmer, much calmer," she said as she rose from the chair, where at first she remained seated. "After the gentlemen had gone he said that now that he'd told them everything that had been on his conscience he felt much better. Since then he's been dozing all the time. Poor man, if he even knew that Your Honour was asking about him as well, indeed, that you'd even been here . . ."

"Go outside," said Mrs Réty, her voice unsteady, "and wait for me in the yard. Don't tell anyone, anyone, you understand, that I'm here. I must speak to the poor man before he dies. You know," she added, seeing the woman's surprise, "that Macskaházy, whom this Jew killed, was our most loyal servant; I must speak to him about that. If he actually regains consciousness perhaps he'll answer my questions."

"He's already come to," said the nurse, still delaying her departure, "that's certain. His Reverence had quite brought him round. Only it would perhaps be better if I stayed, all the same. He's more accustomed to my voice, he'd reply to me sooner, and then it's also possible that he'll slip back into his dreadful dreams and then he's quite furious, and Your Honour . . ."

"Go outside, I tell you," Mr Réty cut her off, "and wait for me in the yard; and as I say, don't dare tell anyone that I'm here."

Those words were spoken in such a tone that, for all her curiosity, the woman daren't stay in the cell; she put on her sheepskin and left, grumbling about the arrogance of the gentry who called for a poor woman if somebody needed nursing but the minute he was better they dismissed the nurse so as to hear something interesting from him and were left to talk to him alone.

Mrs Réty went to the door and looked out to make certain that the woman wasn't eavesdropping, then she went to the Jew's bed and spoke to him.

The patient didn't reply. He was breathing unevenly, and the heavy sighs in which his chest rose now and then, while around his lips and all

566

over his body could be seen that strange quiver that is noticeable in the dying showed that his hours were numbered. Mrs Réty stood by the bed, her heart pounding, and looked at the shrunken face, already bearing the mark of death, but the patient's eyes remained closed and he made no reply. He was restless and clawed at the bed-clothes, apparently looking for something, but it seemed that he was still half asleep.

Mrs Réty was convinced that if she meant to speak to the Jew there was no time to waste, and when he didn't respond to her repeated words she shook him gently.

The Jew opened his eyes and looked round, but when he only saw a woman he presumably took her for his nurse and tried to turn back towards the wall.

"Don't you know me, then?"[220] said the *alispán*'s wife unsteadily. "Don't turn away, look at me, it's me."

"Leave me alone," said the Jew weakly, almost inaudibly. "I've told you all that I could, what more do you want?"

"So you don't recognise me?" Mrs Réty repeated, no longer in a questioning tone. "Look at me, I'm Mrs Réty."

"Mrs Réty?" said the Jew in surprise, turning over and raising his lustreless eyes to her.

"Who else would come to see you?" said she gently, "Who cares about you? Who takes your well-being to heart?"

"Go away, you horrible woman," he interrupted her, "at least let me die in peace. What are you doing here? You can see I haven't got the strength to rob or murder anybody."

"You're out of your mind," said Mrs Réty quietly. "How can you say such things? What if someone heard you?"

"As if I cared," replied the Jew quite calmly. "I'm not afraid of anybody now."

"Don't let yourself be fooled," said Mrs Réty quietly. "They say, don't they, that there's no hope of your getting better? But see, they're only doing that to trick you into making a statement. I've heard from the doctor himself that you're completely out of danger, only being ill has left you weak, and that'll soon pass off. But just look out for yourself. This very day, as I hear, Vándory and a couple of gentlemen have been here to see you . . ."

---

220 The Hungarian reader will see that the conversation is in the familiar second person singular. Mrs Réty is being condescending, the Jew is being rude.

At this point the *alispán*'s wife was interrupted by the Jew's laughter, or rather the throaty rattle that hearing those words produced from the dying man. "So that's why you're here, isn't it," he said in a muted tone, and he clutched convulsively at Mrs Réty's hand with his withered fingers, "you want to know which of the crimes I've confessed to that I did with you. Rest assured, I told them everything, understand? Everything. From the moment that Macskaházy first spoke to me about stealing the documents until the evening when you and Macskaházy had fallen out over them and you called me in to put a couple of new panes in your window, and while I was doing it you said that if somebody were to kill Macskaházy . . ."

"Silence, you monster!" Mrs Réty cut him short, as she tried to free her hand from his fingers.

"Monster! Aren't I just, a monster?" said the Jew, and the blunt word that he'd forced himself to pronounce filled her with dread. "But what are they going to call the person that put me up to the actions for which everybody loathes me?"

"You despicable Jew!" said Mrs Réty. "Who'll believe you if you make accusations against me?"

"They'll believe me," replied the Jew. "What I've said, Viola said as well; nobody's going to doubt it."

"You must withdraw your statement," said Mrs Réty, her voice shaking. "I'll bring other witnesses and you can say in front of them that you were prevailed on by promises to make a false statement against me, and that everything that you said was simply a pack of lies, understand?"

"I won't take back any of my statement," replied the sick man, "not a single word."

"Jew," said the *alispán*'s wife in a rage, "if you don't . . ."

"Go and threaten somebody else," he interrupted, "your promises and threats don't matter to me any more; by tomorrow I'll be where the powers of this world can't have any more say even about my being a Jew. But you, you," he added, with the last of his strength, "who enticed me into all sorts of wickedness, and when I got into trouble because of you, you abandoned me, you're going to be brought before a judge . . . you're going to prison, like me . . . to the scaffold. I've had a dream while I've been ill . . . You and me in the middle, the executioner between us with a big shining sword. Czifra was there as well, and Macskaházy, and lots of people all around, they sat us in chairs . . ." Here the sick man's incoherent words became incomprehensible, he went on speaking, but he was

568

delirious, and Mrs Réty could feel from the quivering of his cold hand as he still gripped her arm that his final death throes were near.

She freed herself from the dying man with no little difficulty and rushed blindly from the cell, where the nurse, when she returned, found her patient in his final agony.

I shan't describe the emotions that filled Mrs Réty's breast at that moment. There are monsters in the material and emotional worlds alike the description of which is beyond our powers, and these she was now suffering, trapped among them. Her maid was horrified to see her in such a state when they met on the stairs and she told her to bring candles and a glass of water. A deathly pallor covered her face, her whole body was shaking and she was looking around wildly.

"Are you ill, madam?" said Julis, as she placed the candles on the table. "Perhaps I should go for the chief medical officer? He's here in the house."

"What's it to do with you?" said Mrs Réty, her eyes gleaming. "Put that water here by me and get out."

The girl left, and Mrs Réty locked the door and was alone.

We can deter the sympathy of others, but not their curiosity; and if anyone pretends, especially about a maid, that she'll do as she's told if she's warned off something that is nothing to do with her, I'm perfectly certain that they're very much mistaken. At least in the present case this was so; as soon as Julis was dismissed as described above and was alone in her room she knew no more important task than to eavesdrop at the door that communicated with her Mrs's room.

What she could hear aroused her curiosity further still. Mrs Réty walked up and down. She sat down at her table and wrote. She got up again and appeared to be tearing paper. Again she walked around the room. She opened her cupboard. Again she sat down at her table, and Julis could distinctly hear her sighing deeply. A while later the maid thought that she could hear the *alispán*'s wife stirring something into her glass.

"Sounds as if she's unwell," she thought, "she must be taking some drops. I'd better call somebody, whatever she said."

The maid put her ear to the door again and heard a ringing sound, as if someone had put a glass down hard on the table; judging that her Mrs was in a bad mood, she changed her mind and thought better of calling anyone, but then it seemed that the *alispán*'s wife had flung herself onto the sofa and that she could hear groans of pain from the room.

To continue to hear these without knowing the cause was more than could be expected of a maid's discretion, and after knocking a few times, calling to her mistress, and obtaining no reply she forgot all about her strict prohibition and sharp temper and ran straight for her master.

Not many minutes before that Vándory had been to see the *alispán*. He had been very agitated and had asked whether he had seen his wife.

On hearing from Réty that he hadn't spoken to his wife all day and on being asked the reason for his anxiety, Vándory explained that while he had just been seeing Tengelyi the old woman who had been nursing the Jew during his illness had reported that the *alispán's* wife had been with him just before he died and had had a long talk with him. He gave a full account of what he'd heard from the old woman. "My dear brother," he added, "your wife's a quick-tempered woman and she knew that the poor fellow, who's now no more, had made a statement to me and the others, but she doesn't know what's in it and may think that she's accused of something. Who knows what she's capable of in her despair? Please go and reassure her. The Jew's statement contains nothing that might be dangerous for her. I can give my word of honour that the poor man only accused Macskaházy."

The clergyman was interrupted by Julis, who came rushing in to tell all that she heard at her mistress's door.

"Let's go, quickly," exclaimed Vándory, "we may still be in time." A moment later the men were at Mrs Réty's door.

It was locked. Groaning could be heard from inside.

"We must break it open!" exclaimed Vándory, and when he and Réty applied their combined strength the weak lock yielded.

The purpose for which they'd come could no longer be achieved. The glass, which stood on the table still containing a little liquid, and the bottle of arsenic beside it left no doubt of what Mrs Réty had done. She was beyond help.

When her husband stepped into the room the hapless woman was still alive; she looked at him as if wishing to say something, but when he knelt beside the sofa and took her hand her tightly clenched fingers were cold, her bosom heaved in a last deep sigh, and the light faded from the eyes that looked on her husband.

She was no more.

XXXVIII

Everyone, though they may have spent their life in the most modest of circumstances, attracts the attention of their fellow men on one occasion – when they're buried. At such times the bell in the tall tower tolls for the poorest; people gather together round the coffins of them that have been ignored all their lives; crowds turn out for the funerals of them who, for eternal reasons, might not advance; and the wretched, having all their lives had nothing to call their own, obtain in perpetuity little patches of land which they may freely enjoy until the Last Judgement without being punished for trespassing. The dead are surrounded by sympathy and respect – and why? Perhaps because they that act sensibly deserve respect, and the majority of people can hardly do anything wiser in life than take their leave of it? Or is it perhaps because, as we are persuaded, the dead finally discover that which interests us all alike, but which the wisest only believe? It is true that there is in the world no better teacher than death. If anyone doubts the value of their life and doesn't know whether what they can achieve on earth is worth bothering about, they may see clearly the first time that someone of their acquaintance dies. A bigger or smaller funeral, coats of arms on the coffin or just the name, a mausoleum or a wooden cross over the grave, the costs of erecting which are different but which stand equally deserted; a brief conversation among the neighbours or a printed letter or a notice in the papers, or perhaps even obituaries in the foreign press – an hour, a fortnight, or a month later silence and indifference: *such is glory*. A bit of black veil on the hat, or full mourning clothes, argument among the poor over who's going to pay for the funeral, among the rich, who's going to inherit?: *this is what reminds us of the love that we'd felt*. And as for friendship, however many times we've grasped our friends' hands it rarely happens that anything remains afterwards that would remind our friends of us and our handshakes as much as our corns remind us that our shoes were once too tight. Anyone that isn't satisfied with this reward for their life may console himself that they're one of the exceptions.

Mrs Réty was one of the latter. Her death caused more of a stir in Porvár and the whole county than anything worthy of record that had happened on the Tisza for years. The very fact of her dying would have attracted public attention. If a wealthy land-owning woman suddenly died, and furthermore, one that hadn't reached the age of fifty, kept a good kitchen and went about in the finest dresses it was a dreadful thing even if all the proper forms were observed in her death and the patient passed away only after two doctors had conferred over her. But what could be said about Mrs Réty's case? By the time that the Chief Medical Officer was summoned she was already unconscious, and for all his science he could only say that had he been called five minutes earlier the honourable lady would have been saved. Serer happened to be in Porvár and also came to the house on hearing the news, but could only express his conviction that what the honourable lady had drunk wasn't sugared water; but there could be no question of medical conference or treatment, and indeed there hadn't even been time for Serer to recommend almond tea, which, as he said, sometimes worked wonders. The *alispán*'s wife had been poisoned, and what was more by her own hand, of that there could be no doubt . . . and as the medical profession of Taksony County must have raised a proper objection to such disregard for due legal process, Porvár society applied its full attention to discovering the secret causes of this terrible event.

The Réty family, and those that were closer to it, like Vándory or Kálmán Kislaky, described the whole incident as an unfortunate accident. The poor *alispán*'s wife, according to their account, had often taken magnesium and kept it in the same cupboard where, a day or two previously, she'd put away the arsenic which she'd bought to deal with rats – an unfortunate error explained it all: in the evening, in the poorly lit room, that could easily have happened. The public, unaccustomed to accepting explanations offered voluntarily, and never more doubting than when something was made known officially, gave little credence to that – and as we're all happiest to deceive ourselves when we can't get to the truth, the public preferred to seek enlightenment in its suspicions, in which on this occasion it was more than a little assisted by Julis, who'd been present at her mistress's death. The worthy maid talked so much about the unhappiness that Mrs Réty had shown for some time, and especially the abnormal behaviour which she'd observed on the last day, that no one could be in any doubt that the *alispán*'s wife had deliberately taken poison; and since the fact that the door of her room had been found locked also pointed to that, opinion could only differ over the reasons that had driven her to do it.

Réty himself said nothing about his wife's death to anyone; the cause of her terrible action might have been either mental illness, as many proclaimed, saying that her extraordinarily excitable nature was always considered a sign of such a thing; or she had been driven to that despairing decision by realising her inability to prevent the marriage of Ákos and Vilma, and she'd rather die than witness what she considered a smear on the family's name; or finally, as the women of Porvár explained the matter to their husbands, the *alispán* had no doubt offended his wife, and by the stubbornness with which he'd opposed some desire of hers had murdered her, of which there had been many examples in the world; Réty said nothing to anyone, but those that knew him could see the effect that his wife's death was having on him.

No one should think, all the same, that that pain was evidence of the revival of affection. It isn't actually rare that when one of a married couple dies after a lifetime of mutual ill feeling the survivor miraculously discovers in their heart a sudden boundless love for the deceased. Just as in the vicissitudes of everyday life single failings very easily make us forget all that is good, so when we're parted for ever from our partner in life we retain for the most part the memory of their good qualities, and the weakness of our human nature almost always makes us recall them as a treasure when they're irretrievably taken from us. This, however, wasn't the cause of Réty's grief. He'd never felt real love for his wife, and even if he had at one time had feeling for her he'd recently learnt that there could be no more question of that; the gloom that everyone could see on him after her death stemmed from the reproaches that he gave himself on this occasion. Had he not himself been the main cause of all the misfortunes that he could see around him? After her death he'd found on her desk an unfinished letter which the unhappy woman had been writing to him, in which she reproached him for all her misfortune, and wasn't that at least partly true? When he reflected, didn't Réty have to admit that all the things to which his wife had fallen victim wouldn't have occurred if he hadn't given them the opportunity? If he'd spoken openly with her about the situation concerning Vándory, as duty had required of him, the poor woman would either not have married him, or she'd have accepted the idea that the clergyman was her husband's brother and wouldn't have resorted to the means by which she'd sought to safeguard herself against his demands. It had been his own complacency that had made her what she'd become, and the unconcealed loathing that he'd shown for her recently had pushed her into the desperate decision to which she'd never have come if she'd found support in her husband. These thoughts filled Réty's soul with profound distress, and even Vándory's gentle consolations failed to dispel his gloom.

The Jew's statement, which had caused Mrs Réty's death and had such an effect on everyone in Porvár, didn't have the consequences at which it was aimed, and Tengelyi's position wasn't made much more favourable. Even beforehand, few still doubted that Macskaházy had had a hand in the theft of Tengelyi's papers, but this rather increased the suspicion of his guilt. If the stolen documents were in Macskaházy's possession, as the Jew's statement confirmed, an important reason had arisen that must have driven Tengelyi to commit murder. As the statement of a witness – and a dubious witness at that – the Jew's assertion that Viola had committed the crime wasn't enough to dispose of the circumstantial evidence and for a verdict of not guilty to be based on it. All that could help Tengelyi was for Viola to fall into the hands of the law and confess to the murder of Macskaházy. That was the belief of the notary's friends and enemies, and no one, with the exception of Vándory, had much hope of it. It was more than a fortnight since old János had left Porvár with Csavargós, and when all the municipal authorities in Hungary had reported failure in finding Viola, and when Ákos, Kálmán and Völgyesy – in other words, everyone that took an interest in Tengelyi's fate – had done their utmost to that end without result, it seemed unlikely that an old hussar could succeed.

It did seem likely that Peti the Gypsy knew Viola's whereabouts; but to all Ákos's pleas and promises the swarthy stove-stoker only replied that he hadn't even seen Viola since the statarium, and apart from the oaths with which he confirmed that nothing more could be got from him. The cowherd at Kislak, who we know drove Viola's wife and children away after the escape, was little more forthcoming. He said that he'd taken Zsuzsi to a certain farmstead a mere three miles away, where the poor woman meant to wait for her husband. He didn't know what became of them after that; and curse, promise and threaten though Kálmán might, the old cowherd would have said no more on the rack. Mrs Lipták herself too, for all her love for the Tengelyi family and especially Vilma, excused herself again and again that she knew nothing, and finally confessed to Ákos that even if she had known they'd never have made her say. "You know how much I love you, young sir," she once said to Ákos, when he was besieging her yet again with enquiries. "Whom could I love more? All the other children that I've suckled are dead, and you're the only one left, but don't ask that of me. If I could give my life to save Mr Tengelyi, I'd do it, but don't let anybody ask me to be a Judas. Mr Tengelyi's got friends, he'll get out all the same, and if not, at least he'll be held honourably, and his people are being looked after. Viola can expect to hang

574

and then his family will starve; even if Zsuzsi weren't a close relative of mine I'd sooner bite my tongue off than give them away." Everyone that might know anything about Viola's whereabouts had evidently decided to remain silent; and though Vándory encouraged his friends to trust in God, that trust wasn't going to be justified at all soon, and János himself, when he'd come across not the slightest trace after searching for a fortnight, was beginning to doubt his ability to fulfil his promise.

Neither János nor Csavargós doubted that Viola wasn't in the neighbouring counties. It also seemed likely, as Csavargós said frequently, that he hadn't left the country. But in which of this spreading country's fifty-two counties were they to seek him? That was a question to which old János, for all his strategical knowledge, couldn't find an answer. "This Viola's certainly an awkward cuss," he said many times to his companion. "The way he's retired, the devil himself wouldn't be able to come across him. Goodness, what a general he'd have made!"

"What does *retire* mean?" asked Csavargós on one such occasion. Ever since he'd left with János he'd been listening with endless delight to his accounts, and since he'd been hearing about the war and the former hussar's great deeds he'd looked with little short of contempt on his way of life, the most interesting moments in which didn't measure up to the life of a soldier.

"Whoever heard of such a thing?!" said the hussar in astonishment. "Don't you know what *retire* means? I'm not surprised," he added after a moment's thought, "you didn't serve in wartime, when you'd have learnt. Well, my lad, *to retire* only means being ordered to fall back."

"I see, I see," said Csavargós, after listening to the explanation very attentively, "when you're surrounded by the enemy."

"Fathead!" said János heatedly. "That's when a real man would never retire. Never in my life was I in a fight we didn't win, and yet how often did we not retire!" My readers are aware that János had always been most unwilling to disengage from the enemy when ordered, and was quite convinced that during the whole of his service our forces had never been defeated. "*Retire,*" he went on with his lecture, "is when you've well and truly beaten the enemy, and then you fall back. Now do you see?"

"Yes," replied Gazsi, "only I don't understand why you fall back if you've beaten the enemy?"

"Well, you fathead," said János with a pitying smile, "you fall back because you're ordered to, and if you don't obey orders in the army you get shot."

"But why are you ordered to fall back?" Gazsi asked again; he still couldn't feel that his doubts had been resolved by what he heard.

"That's none of our business," replied János crossly, because that was just the question that he'd asked himself a hundred times and never been able to answer. "A soldier does as he's ordered, and the rest is up to somebody else. Why are you ordered to fall back?" he grumbled on, "that's a stupid question! Well, perhaps so as to advance; because the one that retreats most is ordered to advance most; or maybe it's to let the enemy regroup for us to beat them again. You see, Gazsi, if you were a soldier and came up with questions like that you'd get shot."

Gazsi Csavargós was able to learn a lot from such conversations while old János took no little delight in them, so much that he'd never felt as satisfied as he was with his present companion since Ákos had grown up and no longer listened to his tales of soldiering. However, all that didn't bring the goal of his journey any closer. The Kislak cowherd told him too that he knew nothing. Questions and friendship alike couldn't elicit any other response, and if he asked anyone else he was dismissed with the same answer.

"It's as if they've conspired," said János frequently, and was not amused. "All that they all say is that they know nothing. They're treating me like our stable-lad. If I say anything to him about grooming or feeding horses he comes out with 'I've known that for a long time'; these all say that they don't know anything. Everybody already knows if you want to talk about something, but if you're asking about something they can't help you." But these complaints failed to make the cowherd or anyone else talk: either they didn't mean to or they really didn't know anything. János and Csavargós went on from farmstead to farmstead, and everywhere they were given the same answer.

In this way they roamed through three counties, and although Csavargós was accustomed to this way of life and János could sometimes imagine himself a soldier again – as they rode for days through forest, meadows and marshland, he would stand in the stirrups and look in wordless delight around the plain, where he could see nothing taller than a man on horseback – this fruitless enquiry irritated them both. Almost all of us weary ourselves for goals which others, often everyone, know that we shan't attain. But never mind! Only we ourselves can hold the contrary opinion; but if eventually we lose our conviction and go on simply because our duty, our sense of honour or our vanity (which is precisely the opposite) require it – let's take a deep breath – old János would curse – and go on. According to the old hussar's philosophy, if

576

you go on down a road, even at a walk, you'll always go a long way, and in fact eventually you'll reach the goal that you thought was unattainable – as was the seekers' experience in the present case.

April is commonly accused of being changeable. I don't know how harmful it may be to the good name of the month, at least in Hungary, where we have no need to wait for April if we want to see infinite calm after horrifying tempests – sudden clear skies, clouds and sunshine after showers, winds from north, south, east and west, all in a single hour; what is certain, however, is that in the year when János and Csavargós were looking for Viola no one could have called this month changeable. Although the old hussar had from his youth been inured to hardship he cursed the maddening constancy of April when he was soaked to the skin day after day. On one particular occasion he completely lost his patience.

They were in the third county, almost twenty miles from home. They'd been in the saddle since early morning, and it was late afternoon when Csavargós finally admitted to his old companion that he couldn't find the farmstead to which he was leading him. Since, according to Gazsi, the cowherd whom they were going to visit there knew every shepherd for ten miles around, János had been very patient in the hope that they would at last be put onto Viola's track, but now he spoke severely to his guide: what had he been doing? They were in the middle of a forest, lost, and although János swore that in all his born days he'd never met a man like Gazsi, he wouldn't go any farther, now there was nothing that he could do but hold his sheepskin as close as the wind permitted, and he was consoling himself with the thought that he'd go back to Porvár next day, and meanwhile he walked after Csavargós, who was examining every tree for broken branches or branches placed crosswise on the road, by which highwaymen marked the way in the forests. Evening was drawing on when the light of a shepherd's fire in the trees beckoned the wanderers. At last, in the middle of the forest they came to the farmstead of which Gazsi had spoken, and the pleasure with which János settled down by the fire could scarcely have been greater than that with which the cowherd there greeted Csavargós. It seemed that the old farmer and Gazsi had done much more together than had come to the knowledge of the county.

János asked the cowherd about Viola once he and Csavargós had talked themselves to a standstill, but he knew nothing. At least, that was his first response; later, however, when the question was raised again by Csavargós, he considered briefly and replied that if they would stay

577

with him that day, next morning he would take them to someone who could perhaps tell them more. "Not far from here," said he, "a cowherd's been living since autumn, and he comes from your parts. Otherwise he's nothing special, not very friendly with anybody, doesn't buy and sell cattle, in other words, a useless individual, but as he's from over there perhaps he'll know something about Viola."

"Who can that be?" said Csavargós pensively. "I don't know of a shepherd from down our way that came here last autumn."

"Well, he's the younger brother of the cowherd at Kislak," was the reply. "His brother was a good sort, but this is a useless waster, doesn't even speak to anybody."

"The Kislak cowherd's younger brother?" said Gazsi in surprise. "That's impossible, he died last autumn."

"Died?" said his friend, even more surprised. "I've seen him with my own eyes. He's a good looking man, swarthy complexion, got a wife and children, and you tell me he's dead."

"I only said that the Kislak cowherd's brother was dead," said Gazsi calmly. "The one you think is him must be alive, of course, but he won't be István's brother."

"But when I say that's who he is," said the other crossly, "do you think I don't know István the cowherd? I haven't been over your way much for a long time, but in our younger days István and I were good friends. And now, when he brought his brother's wife and two children here they stayed with me. One of the children was sickly, but the other's a fine child . . . he'll grow up well, takes after his father, he's not called Pista for nothing like his uncle and me. So, do you believe that I'm going to take you to see the brother of the Kislak cowherd tomorrow?" he added, while Gazsi and old János looked at each other and nodded.

"I'll bet my life," said Csavargós, when, after a long conversation, their host had gone to bed and was sleeping, "the man he's talking about is none other that Viola himself."

"I think so as well," replied János quietly, but say nothing until he's taken us there; don't tell him who he's dealing with!"

"He'll have a shock," said Csavargós, "when he hears that his neighbour, whom he calls a waster, was Viola. So, we'll see in the morning." And with that Csavargós lay down beside the fire, ready for sleep, while old János, tired as he was, tossed and turned on his bed. He was convinced that he was going to find Viola, and was beginning to have doubts as to whether it would be better to leave him in peace. "Poor chap, he's evidently become a respectable man", thought he to himself, "why should I disturb him? Mr Tengelyi's never going to be hanged in any case, and who knows, if they get their hands on Viola, will they keep their word? and then, if his wife is left destitute and the poor children are orphaned, whose fault will it be but mine, because I came after him like a despicable spy?" In his internal struggle János was consoled only by the thought that even if he did find Viola it still didn't follow that he was going to hand him over to the county, and if he could speak to him perhaps he'd be able to find a way of Tengelyi being set free without Viola being imprisoned. "The poor man's suffered enough, and now he's surely happy, and he's got such lovely children . . . God forbid that I should spoil his luck." And with those reassuring thoughts beneficial sleep overcame him too.

Now let's go back to Viola, of whom we've lost sight for quite some time as our tale has run on; as my readers no doubt suspect, it is he that is living at the farmstead to which Csavargós's friend has promised to take the seekers, under the name of the Kislak cowherd's brother. I can safely omit a fuller description of this farmstead, as I don't suppose that any of my readers have never seen a cowherd's farmstead, and in Hungary such premises are very like one another. Viola's was one of the better sort, and at all events one in which a poor man could feel at home. His house wasn't as big and comfortable as the one that he'd once occupied in Tiszarét, but the reed-thatched roof, recently repaired, protected its inhabitants from the rain and the freshly whitened walls gleamed afar over the plain, where no other human habitation could be seen for a mile, and the very isolation in which it seemed to the eye of the traveller to be gave the little house a particular flavour of liveability and comfort. Behind it rose a long line of hills, at the foot of which, where the forest had long since been felled, stood sparse but spreading trees, and higher up a dense forest which extended for miles; while below the hills as far as the eye could see, the great plain spread boundlessly, and apart from solitary towers appearing here and there on the horizon, and flocks grazing on the vast plain there was nothing to remind the observer that he was in inhabited country. Close to the house was a stable and beside it stood a few sheds and haystacks; by the door a couple of ill-kempt *kuvasz* sprawled in the warm rays of the spring sun.

Viola could be happy in his new home. He'd found the refuge which he'd been looking for; it was far from the company of men, which, to one like him, that had suffered much from them and could only expect further persecutions, was in itself a kind of good fortune – he could be happy, I say, if our happiness only depends on our present situation. As, however, this was not so, old János was seriously mistaken when he thought him happy. Now his joys were soured only by the fact that he'd been forced to leave the former scenes of his life if similar things awaited him in his new circumstances too. Just as a more cultured man, endowed by nature with a heart, who is banished from his home can never feel satisfied, and even if fortune heaps upon him all its gifts always feels lonely and abandoned among strangers, so too the lowlier orders of the people cling not only to their homes but to their birthplaces. Their lives run their course in narrower confines, and the notion of the fatherland as a whole is generally too remote for them to be able clearly to conceive of it. The peasant loves his fatherland, loves it as something such as he can't completely grasp and define, but before the greatness of which he bows and to which he feels himself tied by gratitude – with a love like that which man feels towards God; but the poor man's real fatherland, which nothing can replace in his heart, is the *village* where he was born, the little place where he spent the days of his youth. Put him ten miles from the place of his birth, and the thought that he's still within the realm of the Hungarian crown won't soften the pain with which he's left his village. The place where his early years were spent, where stands his parents' modest dwelling – or perhaps their grave – the little meadow where he worked for years, the trees beneath which he so often rested, the well, at which he must have met his beloved for the first time – all are irreplaceable . . . his recollections don't consist of the history of the nation, but of his family and neighbours, and even if the people in his new dwelling-place speak the same language, is he going to be able to talk to them about the same subjects, apart from which nothing is of value in his eyes? Isn't he going to be a stranger among strangers, almost as if he'd left his native land? It's as if there's nowhere in the world out of sight of the village church tower where he can feel completely at home. And isn't it a *whole*, our life, from which we can't tear individual moments, the joys of which repose in large part in our hopes, the happiness of which our memories assume? And what was there in either Viola's past or future that he could contemplate with satisfaction? Like the summer tempest that sweeps over a hill, tearing away not only greenery and flowers but sometimes also stripping off the soil and leaving bare rock, so the blows of fate sometimes spoil more than our joys. The bosom over which they pass is left desolate after them, that part in which joys are created is lost, and though gentle days may come again the heart is already barren –

580

such was the nature of Viola's suffering. Could he forget how unjustly he had been treated, the way that he had spent his days being hunted like a wild beast? Could he forget what he'd done himself, at which his entire being shuddered when he thought of it? Hadn't he committed murder? Hadn't he twice soiled his hands with human blood? And how was he to hope for good fortune, he, to whom his conscience gave no peace and who could see himself being at any moment stripped of what he still called his own? The future lay before him as a constant menace. No one in the whole district even knew who he really was, and his master and the people with whom he came into contact thought that he was the brother of the Kislak cowherd; but didn't his entire safety hang on a thread? If any of his former friends came that way or it somehow was divulged that he had come on someone else's name and passport, wouldn't everything be revealed? Viola had reason to be afraid of every person that he saw approach his farmstead; to fear lest his own small son betray his parents by his innocent chatter; is there a greater agony than that? Nevertheless, despite all this Viola would perhaps have grown accustomed to his position, and might have felt at least at ease if not fortunate. Fate had given him so little control over his situation, but had made him instead a heart that could in time grow accustomed to anything. If he'd been able to see that his wife was happy, as he hoped, in the love that he felt for her and the children he might perhaps have been able to forget everything, perhaps even the danger that ceaselessly surrounded him: for the sword of Damocles itself, if it hung above one's head for years, would eventually lose its frightening power. But that didn't happen.

It didn't take much to make Zsuzsi happy. She was one of those beings to whom God, in sending them to Earth, made it their calling to love, and while she was able to fulfil that calling she felt happy. As long as she could see her husband and children at her side, devote every moment of her life to them, care for them, do things for them, she desired nothing more. When the poor woman saw her husband at liberty and was travelling with her children in the cowherd's cart to her new home, she felt completely happy. The greatest hope of her life had been realised, everything that she'd suffered vanished before the joy that filled her soul. For years her only desire had been a new life, far from people, far from the former places, where no one knew her husband – and that had been attained. Once she'd crossed the threshold of her new farmstead she fell to her knees and raised to God a passionate prayer of deep gratitude alone, as if there would be nothing more that she could ask after so much happiness.

That happiness, however, didn't last long. There are people in the world who can be either boundlessly happy or completely unfortunate, and Zsuzsi was one of them. If she could keep those that she loved there was no joy in the heavenly kingdom that she yearned for except the one, that the love with which she embraced her own should be eternal; if they were to be taken from her, was there anything that could console her in her grief? And that is what happened.

Her small child had always been delicate and sickly. "How could it be otherwise," said Zsuzsi often when she saw that doleful expression on the little one's face, the surest sign of illness in little children, "she drank in bitterness from my breasts, and I washed the smile from her face with my bitter tears. From the time they opened, her gentle blue eyes have seen nothing but grief all around; how could the poor thing fail to be gloomy?" The disturbed way of life to which her mother had been forced in recent times and which the poor child had shared with her; the cold air of autumn, to which she'd been exposed for hours, and finally the hasty journey on which the whole family hurried to their new home had all taken their toll on her uncertain health. Agitated as she was in her concern for her husband's life, Zsuzsi didn't even notice the change in the little one; but scarcely had she reached her new house, where Viola too appeared a couple of days later, than she began to fear danger, and at the same time she abandoned all hope. A few days more and the child died, and all that Zsuzsi had left of her little darling was a tiny grave next to the house.

This child's death hurt her mother deeply, more so, perhaps, than it would have done at another time, because the blow struck her heart in the middle of her happiness; but when she realised how saddened her husband was – he took his child's death as a sign of the wrath of God – Zsuzsi felt that he needed something to cheer him up, and that overcame even her maternal grief. "Who knows," she often said, "perhaps it was better for her to leave this world, her life had only been suffering. Perhaps God has only sent us this latest misfortune so that we shan't become over-confident in such great happiness – and then we've still got little Pista, who's growing every day, the sturdiest child I've seen in my life?" And she was right. While a woman has one child left on which to lavish her affection she must feel sorrow, but she won't let herself be completely crushed by fate. The delicate hand by which she leads her child is at the same time the surest support in her life; and little Pista was certainly a lovable child, as full of fun and healthy as a mother could wish, and at the same time as gentle and affectionate as if he could guess that after his little sister's death all his mother's happiness depended on him.

About midwinter Pista caught smallpox. I shan't describe the care with which his mother nursed him; anyone that's seen a mother in such a situation can imagine all the love that there is in a woman's heart, but only she knows what a mother must feel at the bedside of her sick child, cheerful and smiling so that her darling may have some bright moments even when unspeakable pain is filling that heart; she alone knows the strength that enables her to bear everything and that never fades. After three weeks, which she spent between hope and anxiety, her second child too died, and when he was laid to rest next to his sister the poor woman felt that after that there was nothing on earth that could restore her happiness.

Zsuzsi didn't complain, didn't speak of her misfortune, indeed she did her best to hide her pain from her husband; but the pale face that she forced into a smile, the involuntary prayer that sometimes swelled her bosom, her voice, which suddenly trembled if something brought her children to mind while she turned away lest her husband should see the tears that forced themselves to her eyes, all spoke more volubly than any complaint in which the hapless mother might have poured forth her pain; and Viola loved his wife too much to be deceived. He saw the traces of the hidden tears on her cheeks; he understood the pain that was never expressed, and a grief more bitter than any in his life before filled his stalwart spirit. Is there in the world any agony greater than to see someone that we love unreservedly suffer, and to feel at the same time that there's no way for us to ease their pain? And it seemed to Viola that he'd only been saved from death for his lips to taste the bitterest drop in the cup of his life. "Just my luck," said he to himself on one occasion, when he was alone on the meadow watching over the cattle as they grazed, and his eyes wandered over the great plain, "wasn't that enough, then, that I suffered in the past, that I've had to live to see this as well? If I'd been hanged, perhaps God would have had pity on my children, but now he's punishing me in those I love. I've got blood on my hands, but what fault is that of Zsuzsi or my poor children? Merciful God, how have they sinned against you?"

Viola was sitting on the hill behind the house, once more sunk in such thoughts, when his attention was caught by an unusual barking of dogs from the farmstead, and on looking in that direction he saw a stranger making straight for it. As his situation recommended, Viola was living in a remote place, and even the Kislak cowherd had only visited him once; the shepherds and outlaws of the region had realised that Viola had no intention of making friends with them and came that way seldom, and so the approach of a stranger was in itself a thing to arouse curiosity; even at a distance the man looked familiar, and Viola's surprise was all the greater when at length he recognised, as he grew nearer, the *alispán's* hussar, and he was addressed by the name which he hadn't heard for a long time.

As soon as he saw the farmstead in the distance János thanked the cowherd for his trouble and sent him and Csavargós back. So as to speak more confidentially with Viola he went on alone, and Viola could still scarcely believe his eyes at seeing before him the old soldier, usually immaculately dressed but now in peasant clothes and unshaven.

"Is that you, János?" said he, staring in surprise at the arrival. "Why are you dressed like that?"

"Odd, isn't it?" replied János cheerfully. "Never mind, naked we're born and naked we're laid in the grave – except perhaps for our *gatya*; the soldier was a peasant and becomes a peasant again, that's how the world turns; and when all's said and done, these clothes aren't too bad, it's just that for people like me, who've gone round for ages buttoned up, if clothes aren't tight-fitting there's always something missing. The first few days it felt as if I wasn't wearing anything."

"But where've you come from, and what brings you all out here?" asked Viola.

Old János had never been entirely convinced as to the rightness of his journey, and was embarrassed at that question. "Well, I just wanted to come and see you," said he after a brief silence, during which he scratched his head, "that's to say, I wanted to look for you," he added in even greater embarrassment, "I've got something important to tell you. No need to get alarmed, my boy," said he, seeing the surprise with which Viola looked at him when he said that, "I promised to look for you, but it doesn't follow that I'm going to tell anybody else where you've got to. I'll have a word with you and that's all, you can do what you think best. I've never ever given a deserter away, and even if the gentry flay me alive they won't get anything out of me."

At these words Viola's curiosity grew still more, and old János yielded to his enquiry and immediately began explaining why he'd come. There's no need for me to follow the old hussar's rather long-winded account; nor can my readers have any idea of the impression that his words made on Viola. "What an accursed creature I am," said he, looking desperately up to heaven, on hearing of Tengelyi's plight, "I bring misfortune on anybody that I go near, whether they hate me or love me." He covered his eyes with his hands, sank deep into thought, and was silent.

"Look here," said the old hussar reassuringly, "you mustn't think that Mr Tengelyi's all that badly off. He's not even in the prison, but he's held in a separate room; he gets plenty to eat and drink; I see to that myself, and you can imagine I take care of Master Ákos's future father-in-law; there's just that criminal case, or whatever I should call it! There's no telling what he might be sentenced to if his innocence isn't established, and then . . ."

"Didn't I mean to do well by him?" said Viola, interrupting him passionately. "There's nobody on earth that I'm so grateful to. He took my wife and children in; I'd have given my life for him; I shed a man's blood because I thought I'd be helping him . . . and where's my gratitude got me? He's the most honourable man in the world, and I've put him in prison; and if you hadn't come and told me about his situation I might have sent him to the gallows. Oh, János, why did you bother to save my life? It'll be a happy day when I die! Rabid dogs run away from the house where they're fed when they feel the illness coming on, so as not to harm their benefactors; but I'm worse than a mad dog . . . I ruin my best friends,"

Old János was deeply affected by Viola's pain, and consoled the unhappy man by saying that there was perhaps some means by which he could help him.

"As far as that's concerned," said Viola more calmly, "don't worry. We can be in Porvár in three days' time; I've got the documents that I took off Macskaházy, there's still blood on them, and if I state what happened there'll be no more suspicion of Mr Tengelyi."

Old János shook his head pensively. "I don't think that's going to work, my boy," said he, "a thing like this has to be well thought out. Going there is easy. Here I am, I, Viola, killed Macskaházy – certainly you can state that; but if you're once locked up, getting out will be harder, and that's what we've got to think about. Yes, the gentry say that your life won't be at risk, the *alispán* himself has promised; but when all's said and done, can you be sure? The promises that the gentry make to a poor man like you aren't always worth much, so I think it'd be wiser if we tried something else. I suggest you give me the documents, I'll take them along and say that I've spoken to you, and that when you handed them over you told me yourself that it was you that murdered Macskaházy."

"They wouldn't believe you," Viola interrupted.

585

"Very well," János went on, "if they wouldn't believe me, I'll take a witness. Gazsi Csavargós, who's come here with me, is a very good lad, and he's at your neighbour cowherd's place. Two honest witnesses are enough for all evidence; or if Gazsi isn't perhaps entirely honest and does a bit of robbing now and then, we'll call the cowherd himself as a third. While we make our statements in Porvár you move on with your wife and children, and by the time anybody comes here for you they'll find the place deserted. What do you say, won't that be better?"

"I've got no children any longer," said Viola, and an expression of unspeakable pain was on his face, "we buried the second, little Pista, two months ago."

"Pista?" exclaimed old János, "my little Pista? Oh, my boy, that's dreadful!"

"And his little sister," Viola went on, his voice unsteady. "I've got no children, and poor Zsuzsi isn't going to be long after them. She's fading away day by day; she won't live to see the leaves fall that are just sprouting."

The two men sat side by side for a while in silence; Viola was sunk deep in pain, while old János's eyes were full of tears. "Really, my boy," said he at length, and his voice showed his feeling, "God knows why a poor man is treated so harshly. They say we all come to one place in the end, it's as if we're only passing through this world on the way to the next; but I have to say that the men in the rearguard must sometimes lose patience. Those in the front rank get all the glory, all the rear get is the cutting and thrusting. I've experienced this more than once in my time. When the army retreats the bravest are ordered to the rear, and I've been in the very rearmost more than once; but see, my boy, that was when I learnt that you mustn't ever give up. Because in the first place, when service like that is over a wise general will always praise the very last and reward them before the rest, and surely the Lord God'll do just the same in the next world; and then, nobody knows when his luck will change. Thank God, you've still got your wife. You could have another ten children. Of course, there won't be another like Pista – there isn't such a dear child in all the world, nor will there be for a long time – but it 'd be a child all the same, and what I always say is that anybody that can still have a child doesn't know what luck is in store for them. My boy, I tell you, you'll still have plenty of time for that; you'd be a fool to let yourself get into the hands of the gentry."

Viola was not unmoved to hear the old soldier's advice, but when János looked at his younger companion and expected an answer he

586

shook his head sadly. "You don't know how much I've suffered already or you wouldn't give me that advice," he replied. "Are you suggesting that I shouldn't give myself up to my judges to avoid punishment? I'd be sentenced to death, yes, I've deserved it: but what's one death compared to the most agonising, ceaseless trembling in which I've been living ever since I've been here? I've gone twenty miles from home, but what's twenty miles? Like you've done now, anybody might have called on me or happened to recognise me. How often have I gone and hidden in the forest like the greatest coward if I've seen somebody coming? How often have I felt the blood rush to my face if my master or somebody's asked about my previous life, as I've trembled like a criminal before the judge when I've answered questions that were asked casually, without any special intention. Living like this isn't a life, János: if I'm hanged I'll be spared hellish torment."

"You won't be hanged," said János reassuringly. "The *alispán*, thank God, has fallen out with his wife and since then has been a changed man. He's promised that in no case will your life be in danger, and he's certain to keep his word; that is, if he can," he added, "but who knows whether he'll be able to make the others agree? And I always say it's much better if . . ."

"Don't say any more about it," Viola interrupted. "I know you mean well, but my mind's made up. Believe me, since my children have died I've often wondered whether it mightn't be better to surrender to justice? Perhaps if you hadn't come and I hadn't heard of Mr Tengelyi's predicament I'd have done so voluntarily only to be rid of the agonies that I'm living with. Before little Pista died . . . the poor child was so disfigured by the smallpox, you wouldn't have recognised him, but he still had his sweet voice, it's as if I can hear it ringing in my ears now . . . what was I talking about?" said he, wiping his eyes with his hands, "if I think of my son I forget about everything . . . Yes, before little Pista died, all the time that he was ill he kept begging me not to be an outlaw any more. You won't, will you, Daddy? Those were the last words I heard him say; and can I fulfil his request by staying here? If the foulest criminal that I'd met in my outlaw days were to come along and recognise me, wouldn't they be able to force me into all sorts of wickedness, the vilest of crimes, because they knew my secret? As soon as they said my name I'd be in their power, so my good name simply depends on chance."

János realised that what he said was true, and sighed.

"You see, anyone that dips his hands in human blood has to die," Viola went on. "I've often thought about this and I can see that it's natural.

587

You can't know peace after doing such a thing. When my judges have condemned me I'll be content; otherwise my conscience won't let me rest. To tell the truth, it was never my intention to kill anybody; I didn't mean to become a murderer, but destiny willed it; but then it also willed that I should pay the penalty, and what's the use of struggling against it?"

"That's all very well, but what's Zsuzsi going to do!?" János implored.

Viola said nothing for a while; his face showed inexpressible pain, his fingers clutched convulsively at the staff in his hands, and his bosom heaved as if about to burst. "What's Zsuzsi going to do after I'm dead?" said he at length in a shaky voice. "Oh, if I think of that, courage will desert me! But what can I do? If I could see how to ease the poor woman's bitterness, if she weren't so unhappy that I didn't fully believe that she won't be even more unhappy after my death – there's no torture on earth that I wouldn't endure. Even if my conscience pricked me, if I had to live the rest of my life in fear and trembling, if I knew that I was damned for eternity: believe me, János, I'd bear it all without a murmur if I could but see that my life brought her consolation. But the poor woman's heart is full to the brim with bitterness, and there's no room for more bitterness, nor consolation either, and indeed my continued existence deprives her of the relief that she might find in unrestrained weeping. Instead of consoling her I only increase her pain, and she tries to hide it from me, which makes it all the heavier on her soul. No, no!" he continued passionately, "I can bear it no longer; what has to happen, let it happen and be done with. Perhaps, when I've died as well, God will show pity on her and take her from this world where there's no resting-place for them that love Viola; or if not, when I've been hanged she'll have nothing more to fear and good people will look after her. Bind my hands, János, and take me straight to Porvár, that'll be the best thing to do with me."

János could see from Viola's words that his decision was not to be altered and that the less he said against the proposal the more he was aware of the correctness of the reasoning which he advanced for it. "Perhaps you're right after all," said he after considering briefly. "You won't be hanged, that I'll venture to bet, and the best thing will be for you to serve your sentence, after that you'll be a free man. But as for binding your hands, that'd be stupid. If you go of your own free will that'll be to your credit and your sentence will be the less. God forbid that I should take you there a prisoner; to my dying day I'd be ashamed if anybody said 'It was old János that captured Viola.'"

"Very well," said Viola after a moment's thought. "If you prefer, you go ahead and tell Mr Tengelyi not to worry, I'll be in Porvár in four days' time at the most. My lad'll be home soon, I can entrust the cattle to him, and I'll tell Zsuzsi something so as not to alarm her when I leave; even so, it'll be hard enough to part."

"In any case, it'll be best, my boy," said old János, "to say nothing to Zsuzsi for the time being if you've made your mind up. Later on, when you're in Porvár, I'll come and fetch her myself; and when she hears from the *alispán* that your life isn't in danger she herself will be more at ease. Never fear, my boy," he added, slapping Viola on the shoulder, "it'll turn out all right, you'll be locked up for a couple of years, and after that you'll go back to Tiszarét an honest man. But I'd best be off," said he, looking round. "Zsuzsi might come home and if she sees me here, especially dressed like this, she's sure to be alarmed. God be with you, my boy." And with that the old hussar set off back towards the house, where he'd left his horse. Before he'd gone more than a few yards he suddenly turned and came back. "Do you know, my boy," said he to Viola, who was still standing there, "I forgot to say, if you regret your decision, don't come. If you don't, nobody'll find out from me where your farmstead is, you can be sure. The most they'll say is that old János is a bigger ass than he thought, because he couldn't find Viola. That won't matter, goodbye." And with that he set off again, without waiting for an answer; Viola soon heard the sound of his horse's hooves as he cantered away.

"Well, at least my life can have some point," said Viola to himself. "Tengelyi was good to me, I wanted to show my gratitude, and I only got him into more misfortune; I'll rescue him from that. Oh, but what's going to become of my Zsuzsi?" There he was sitting, sunk in painful thought, his head in his hands, when his wife came home, called out to him and disturbed his profound reverie. She could see that her husband had been weeping, but the poor woman had been at her children's graves, and saw nothing remarkable in that.

XXXIX

Viola still had difficult times ahead before he could carry out his intention. His decision was irrevocable, but how was he to find a pretext for going away that would satisfy his wife? Since they'd been living at the farmstead Zsuzsi had been extremely uneasy if ever he was away for a mere couple of hours, and even more so since the children had died. She had nobody in the world apart from her husband, and wasn't he in ceaseless danger if he went to public places where he might be recognised? A hundred times he was on the point of telling her that he was leaving that very evening on a few days' journey, and a hundred times he put off doing so. On one occasion it seemed to him that Zsuzsi was more cheerful than usual, and he was unwilling to upset her at such a time; yet another time her face looked even gloomier, and then he felt that it wasn't the right time to tell her of his intention; and I don't know how he would have accomplished his plan if his wife hadn't noticed him busying himself making preparations for a journey, and hadn't asked why he was doing that. When she heard that orders had come from the *alispán* while she'd been out and he had to leave that very night to drive in cattle from the neighbouring county Zsuzsi's face paled. But what could he do? He couldn't tell anyone the reason why he was reluctantly leaving the farmstead, and poor Zsuzsi even blessed his fate when she heard that the place where he was going was even farther from Taksony County. "I can be even less afraid of being recognised there," Viola repeated, and so as not to make her husband's position more difficult Zsuzsi at least pretended to feel reassured.

Every time that he looked at his wife Viola thought of the pain that she was going to experience when she discovered the true state of affairs, and for all the firmness of his character he could at times scarcely restrain his tears; but he kept control of himself, and when that evening he hugged his wife to his bosom for the last time and mounted no one would have noticed how agitated he was. Zsuzsi herself didn't suspect that when she heard the last goodbye from his lips the poor man's heart was full of the thought that he'd spoken to his beloved for the last time. Viola had long been inured to suffering; like the dark waves of the sea, the constantly grave expression on his face concealed the storm that was rising in his breast; but when he'd galloped far enough towards the forest for his movements no longer to be seen by her that was watching him go, the suppressed bitterness at length burst forth and tears of grief poured down his cheeks.

It was already evening when Viola left his house. The last rays of the setting sun were still giving a faint light on the horizon; the half-moon floated in the sky among light clouds, shedding its silver light beneath which all was calm and solemn silence. The beauties of nature can't make us forget our great woes, but they can dispel their bitterness. Instead of the passionate grief which we feel whether we're with others or apart in our rooms, a soothing sadness fills our hearts: it seems that all of nature is sharing our pain, every star is looking down upon us; we look round the vast horizon and sense how tiny we are, and our personal misfortune seems less when we recall how trifling and fleeting our lives are. Viola too was eventually rendered calmer by the peace that he saw around him. He slowed the horse to a walk, wiped away his tears and looked up at the stars, from where comes so much noble hope to all that suffer.

When he came to the hill from which, a few months before, he had first caught sight of his new home, he stopped and looked back for a few moments. Because of the distance and the uncertain light of the moon all that he could see was a white patch and not far away a faint shepherd's fire. He thought of all the hopes with which he'd come to this place but the disappointments that he'd suffered since – his children, who lay buried on the hillside, the hapless woman on whom the heaviest blow in her life was yet to fall – and at these thoughts tears again forced their way to his eyes; but once the passionate outburst of his pain was over Viola regained his composure. "What can anybody do about it?" said he with a great sigh, as he set off again. "Nobody can escape their fate; I was born unlucky."

He proposed going to Tiszarét and surrendering to Ákos Réty, or if he failed to find him there at least to send Mrs Lipták to his wife; and as that place was a good twenty miles from the farmstead where he'd left his wife, and as, especially after entering Taksony County, he avoided the more frequented roads and travelled mostly by night so as not to fall into anyone's hands, Viola had time during his journey to consider his position. His wife was the main subject of his thoughts. "Poor Zsuzsi!" he often said to himself, "if only I didn't have to worry about her, but when she finds out that I've surrendered to the county she'll be frantic. But what can I do? They'd have found out where I was eventually. Others could come looking for me, like old János did, and then things would be even worse for me. This way, if I surrender, at least Mr Tengelyi's documents can't be taken off me, I'll be able to help him, and who knows,

591

in the end I might be pardoned, as János said." This last thought was no small consolation to him. If ever a man looked calmly on death, it was Viola; but the thought of losing one's life at the hands of the hangman horrifies even the bravest; and Viola, thinking of his wife, was quite prepared to endure anything but that – the dear creature wouldn't survive it. "Let them lock me up for ten years," thought he, "torture me, do what they like with me, the fact that I'm alive and she can be of use to me will keep Zsuzsi's strength up, and I'll endure anything if I can see her now and then. Because everything passes in time, and as old János said, I'll even be able to end my days an honourable man. Such is human nature; if we get into a situation from which there's no favourable outlook we pin our hopes on the least bad one, but we can't go a single day without hope."

The more Viola considered his position, the more at ease he felt. Other than the two homicides, for both of which he could offer so much justification, he'd never committed any serious crime. The very fact that he had endured the fear of death[221] and was surrendering to the court could avert the harshest sentence, and furthermore could he not count on the support of Ákos Réty, and through him that of other respectable persons, if he rescued Tengelyi from his present predicament? On the third night, when he was just a few miles from Tiszarét, his greatest anxiety was that he might fall into the hands of Nyúzó's gendarmes before he could surrender himself and his documents to Ákos Réty or Vándory. He didn't understand why the documents that he had with him were so important, but as they'd been taken from him when he was last arrested and Nyúzó had denied it, he had to fear that the magistrate would steal them again if he had the chance – he knew his character from experience – and he promised himself that he'd rather fight to the last drop of blood than put Tengelyi's documents in untrustworthy hands.

Dawn was just breaking as he came to the St-Vilmos forest. His horse was weary – he hadn't dismounted all night – and from where he was it would take him a further good two hours to reach Tiszarét. Viola felt sorry for the horse, which had been so useful to him, but he was aware of the danger into which he could come if he made for the village in broad daylight and was recognised and dragged off to the magistrate before accomplishing his purpose. The densest part of the forest had been felled that winter, and he could not find concealment in the trees,

---

221 That is, the earlier sentence of death passed by the *statarium*.

especially as they weren't yet in leaf, but on seeing that he felt it advisable to continue on his way even so. "In the open," he thought to himself, "I'll be able to see everybody and avoid them; and you, good old Holló,"[222] he said, patting his beloved horse's neck, "won't have to do any more for me after today, and I'll see to it that you go to a good home. Perhaps you'll find a place in young Master Ákos's stable as a coursing-horse, because you've learnt all about running, you and your former master did plenty of chasing, and I'll never be on your back again." Viola went on his way, once more sunk in dismal thoughts, and his horse, as if sharing its master's grief, walked slowly on with lowered head among the trees through which it had so often raced.

The sound of hooves roused Viola from his reverie. He looked in that direction, and saw, on the far side of the meadow that he was crossing, three mounted gendarmes; they saw him and made for him. Evasion and concealment were impossible, and so he spurred his horse and sought refuge in flight. "Stop!" shouted his pursuers, "or you're a dead man!" and rushed after him, but for all his tiredness Holló was not so easily to be overhauled, and a couple of shots that came his way only made him go faster. Viola galloped straight for Tiszarét, and the gendarmes rode after him at a distance, keeping him in sight.

Ákos happened to be in Tiszarét. Since his wife had died the *alispán* hadn't cared to go out to his estate and had entrusted it to his son, who had just then spent a few days there to attend to the spring ploughing – and because the events of the recent past had been painful for him too he'd been living not in the mansion but with old Vándory. As was his custom, Vándory had risen early that morning too, and when he saw that the sky was clear he'd been unable to resist the desire to see the sunrise from the Törökdomb once again, had invited Ákos to go with him, and together they'd gone to the same spot where we first met them when our story began.

There aren't many young men in the world that readily forsake their morning sleep, and Ákos had been less than eager to follow his elderly friend, who all the way talked ceaselessly about the beauties of the sunrise, anticipating the splendid sight that awaited them on the Törökdomb, and indeed I must say, to the discredit of one of my heroes, that although never had sunrise covered the horizon with colours more glowing, on that day the sight left him cold.

---

222 The horse's name means Raven.

Since the previous autumn, when he'd met Tengelyi and Vándory on the Törökdomb after coursing, Ákos hadn't been on the hill,[223] and it was quite natural that as they came now to the same place the incident came to mind that had occurred then and that he brought it up, almost forgetting the sunrise. "It's as if it were today, I can see it all so clearly," said he to the clergyman. "You and poor Tengelyi were standing where we are now. Our horses were below the hillock, Kálmán was in front of you and I was to the right, over there was the accursed Nyúzó – I can almost hear him swearing now! – and he was looking towards St-Vilmos forest and caught sight of his gendarmes bringing someone with them, and I refused to believe that he'd caught Viola."

As he spoke, Ákos almost involuntarily turned towards the St-Vilmos forest, and with his sharp eyes spotted the riders who were just emerging from the trees into the open. "What's that?" said he to Vándory, pointing that way and drawing his attention to the riders. "They're going flat out, one in front and three behind, it looks as if they're chasing him."

"God forbid," said Vándory with a sigh. "It was enough to have to witness such a monstrous sight once."

"But that's what's happening," said Ákos, who hadn't taken his eyes off the riders, "the one in front is being chased, he's galloping straight over grassland and ploughland."

"God have pity on the poor fellow," said Vándory, raising his eyes to heaven.

"If he's an outlaw, he can't get away now," said Ákos, "he's being driven straight to the village and his horse is tiring as well, the pursuers are gaining quite a bit."

"Perhaps he's not an outlaw," said Vándory, who was watching the movements of the riders with the greatest attention.

"He must be, or they think he is," said he after a short pause. "I can make out the gendarmes' weapons. Poor man! His horse is quite tired, one of the pursuers has caught him up. Now the nearest of the pursuers has fallen off his horse; he's escaped again for a couple of moments; I wish I could give him a fresh horse!"

At that very moment Viola's situation – because as my readers must be thinking, it is he that Ákos can see from the Törökdomb – was more favourable because the nearest pursuer had fallen. On coming to his fallen colleague, who was lying in a ditch along with his horse, the second gendarme pulled up and dismounted to help him; the third had

---

223 Homer nods. See Chapter X.

fallen so far behind that Viola, who now wanted nothing more than to reach the village before them, thought that he had almost achieved his goal of placing his documents in safe hands. "Good old Holló, come on, don't let me down now," said he, spurring the horse again!" But everything has its limits, even the best of horses is exhausted eventually, and Viola could feel that Holló could scarcely bear his weight. The poor horse, which had been travelling for two whole nights and was now being chased over freshly ploughed land and ditches, broke into a canter; Viola could see that in one direction he was near the Törökdomb and so almost at his destination, and looking back saw his enemy coming ever closer; he encouraged the horse with words and spurs, but to no avail. Holló's entire body was lathered and quivering, sweat was dripping off his black mane. Viola could feel his legs beginning to fail and in desperation dug his spurs one more into his flanks. The horse started at the pain and with the last of its strength began to gallop again. But the enemy had caught up. "Stop!" bellowed a furious voice at Viola's back, and he saw in horror that the gendarme was a bare couple of yards away. He could see no other remedy but drew his pistol from the saddle-bow and aimed it at his enemy to warn him off. The gendarme, however, also had pistol in hand, and the moment he saw Viola's gesture he uttered a vile curse and fired at him.

The two were at that moment so close together that the shot could scarcely have missed, and Viola fell onto his horse's neck with a cry of pain. Startled by the sound of the shot, Holló took another couple of strides before collapsing to the ground with his mortally wounded rider.

All this took place so close to the Törökdomb that Ákos ran over on hearing the shot and seeing the result, and arrived just in time to be able to restrain the gendarme from further brutality as he sprang from his mount with his *fokos*.

"Don't you dare harm this poor man, you swine," shouted Ákos in the greatest indignation, as he tried to extricate Viola from under his horse, "can't you see he's no more threat to you?"

"Poor man?" mumbled the gendarme, recognising the *alispán*'s son and not venturing to disobey – in him my readers would have recognised, even in the gendarme's uniform which he had worn for some time, the former outlaw Czifra. "Can't you see, Your Honour? It's Viola. The five hundred forint reward for bringing him in dead or alive to the noble county is mine. I only hope he dies before my colleagues arrive, or they'll want a share."

Ákos didn't hear this inhuman desire, and with the use of all his strength and the help of Czifra and Vándory pulled Viola from under his horse.

"He's dead," said Ákos, as he laid the bleeding body on the grass and recognised Viola by his pale face.

"He's not dead yet," replied Vándory, who had fallen to his knees beside the wounded man and was looking at the wound. "It's a deep wound in the left of his chest, there's no hope that he'll survive, but he may live for an hour or two, perhaps even be able to speak. You mount up," he said to the gendarme, "and gallop into the village at once, and call some men to help me take him to my house."

"I'm not going," said the gendarme. "I'd be a fool. The noble county's promised five hundred forints to anyone that brings in Viola alive or dead, and if I leave here the others'll come along and demand the money for themselves, and Your Honours saw me shoot him."

"If you don't go I'll shoot you myself with this pistol, you dog!" exclaimed Ákos, picking up Viola's horse-pistol, which lay beside the horse. "I'll give you your blood-money if no one else will."

This assurance and the sight of the raised pistol persuaded Czifra to hurry away, and Ákos and Vándory were left for a while at Viola's side as he lay on the grass, still unconscious. One of the gendarmes – after Czifra had been sent to the village, the others also had come up – fetched water, but neither that nor Ákos and Vándory's words of encouragement could bring him round.

Half an hour had gone by and men had arrived from the village when Viola opened his eyes, looked around, and showed signs of life.

"Don't you know me?" said Ákos, bending over him and taking his hand. "Look at me, Viola."

"Yes," said the outlaw weakly, as he regained consciousness. "I'm glad you're here, it was you I was coming to see." He raised a hand to his chest, seeming to feel for something. "Unbutton my waistcoat," said he, as he found that he couldn't do that himself, "and take out the documents . . . They're Mr Tengelyi's documents, that the Jew and Macskaházy stole, that's what I came for, to give them back. There's blood on them," he added, seeing the papers in Ákos's hand, "and more now, but that doesn't matter, because it's only mine. Mr Tengelyi was good to me, I've returned his kindness; give him my best respects, and he's not to think that Viola was such a villain that he could have harmed someone that had done him good."

As Viola was saying this, more and more came from the village and surrounded the dying man.

"My dear chap!" said Vándory, deeply moved. "Perhaps you didn't know that Tengelyi's been under grievous suspicion because of these very documents?"

"I know," Viola interrupted, "I heard from János, that's why I wanted to surrender to the noble county, to clear him from suspicion. Do you hear me, you people?" he said, addressing the bystanders in a stronger but steadily failing voice, "whoever said that Mr Tengelyi murdered Macskaházy was lying; I was the murderer. I only wanted to get from him the documents that he and the Jew had stolen from Mr Tengelyi, but he threatened me with a pistol and I killed him in a fit of rage. May God have pity on my soul, Mr Tengelyi is completely innocent."

Viola tired and fell silent; the people stood there, deeply moved, and tears shone in many eyes. "Hey, my boy," said an old peasant standing by Vándory, "what's made you come to this end? We used to be neighbours, and I thought you'd be the one to close my eyes, like I did for your father."

"Old friend," said Viola feebly, looking firmly at the speaker, "when you go by my house, whether it's standing empty or whether people are living there, spare an occasional thought for Viola; as God is my judge, it wasn't my fault that I became what I have in the end; may God forgive those that were."

At this moment Mrs Lipták arrived. She'd hurried over on hearing what had happened, and now she pushed her way through the crowd and when she saw her kinsman lying on the ground and the people standing round him she asked why they were just standing about, why weren't they taking Viola into the village, where he could be properly attended to?

"Don't bother, auntie," said he, finding it harder and harder to breathe, when he recognised Mrs Lipták. "Nobody'll do anything for me, I'm finished – and I've no complaints. I've spilled blood, and I'm paying for it with my own; it's the will of God. Let me die here, in the fields that I used to plough, under God's free heaven, in the warmth of the sunshine . . ."

Viola's speech was growing fainter; he beckoned to Mrs Lipták, and she knelt beside him to be able to hear what he was saying. "Go to Zsuzsi, auntie" said he, scarcely audibly, "and ask her to forgive me for deceiving her when I left her; I couldn't have done otherwise, couldn't have abandoned my benefactor in his trouble, and if I'd told her where I was going . . ." and his words became incomprehensible; he'd closed his eyes

597

in weakness but opened them once more, looked around, and with his last breath sighed his wife's name.

"God have mercy on all sinners," said an elderly peasant in the crowd. "His soul must be burdened with many sins."

"He suffered greatly," said Vándory, much affected. "May he rest in peace after that hard life."

*   *
*

I might leave the description of the events that followed Viola's death to my gentle readers, who, if they haven't yet tossed my book away, no doubt know as well as I the immediate future of all my characters. The immediate future, I say, because although it's certain that Ákos and Vilma and Kálmán and Etelka became the happiest of couples possible, who would dare stand surety for the future? although in both cases I shall hope, if I return to Tiszarét in twenty years' time, to find the newly-weds settled and looking as satisfied as when the happy youngsters first led their wives to their ancestral homes.

The *alispán* seldom comes to Tiszarét. The memory of what happened there still sours his mood, and he feels so much more at home in Porvár. He's resigned from office on the pretext of ill health, has given up his desire for the titles of chamberlain and counsellor, and since then a more contented man is hard to find. Many thought that he would move to Pest, but they were mistaken. He's the first citizen of Porvár on account of his wealth and merit as *alispán*, and his opinion, as formerly, is that of the majority, for which reason he's still admired by the majority – and in a properly constituted country, what more does one need in order to feel happy?

Old Kislaky had no desire for such an honour, and in fact I can say for sure that after the first occasion on which he presided over the summary court he resigned at once from that distinguished position. Kálmán was happy, and that was enough for the honourable old man and his wife. If Etelka was less pleased with her husband now and then because even now he was excessively fond of coursing, the old man consoled her that even the wine of 1811 had been new once, and that his son too would mature.

At first old Tengelyi was sad. Misfortune such as he'd endured can sour the most cheerful of temperaments, and the notary had been of a serious disposition all his life. His wife couldn't persuade him to move

598

into the mansion. "I was born in a humble house," he always said, "and that's where I mean to die." But the joy that he saw all around him and the great good that he was able, with the assistance of his son-in-law, to do for the inhabitants of Tiszarét finally cheered him too. He set up a seed-store and a kindergarten, had fruit trees planted beside streets and houses, and the ceaseless industry in which his days were spent lightened his old age and testified clearly to all that as the machine that lies idle rusts away in time, while the one that works non-stop is all the brighter; so the man who toils all his life doesn't lose his sparkle in old age.

Völgyesy and Vándory remained the best friends of the Kislak and Tiszarét houses. Völgyesy gradually lost his unsociable ways and began to see that if many are foolish enough to judge one by external appearances, it is no less foolish to withdraw from all society in order to avoid such people; because even if the stupid and wicked are in so great a majority in human society the few sensible and honest people to be found in it are worth searching for, as the pearl-fisher plunges into the murky waves. And how should Vándory not have been happy, living as he did among happy people, in a circle which could serve as proof of his optimism! It goes without saying that on coming into possession of the documents that could prove his birth he didn't change either his name or his situation. Nowhere in this world would he have found greater joy or true felicity than in his little clergyman's dwelling, where any that needed help were made so welcome. The love that filled his pure heart never lost any of its warmth, never did the confidence waver that he had in God's providence and man's good nature. This man's spirituality was like the burning bush of which we read in scripture: the flame that burned in his heart spread light and warmth but didn't consume the altar, for it was no earthly flame.

Ákos made old János his major domo, but for all that he didn't change from his hussar dress and wasn't completely satisfied for the first year; but when Ákos's son was born the old soldier's greatest wish was fulfilled and he could scarcely wait for the time when he'd be able to recount his many victorious battles to this next generation of Rétys.

Some of my readers may, perhaps, wish to know what became of Nyúzó. In order that legal testimony, which has, of course, been present from the outset at all significant points in this conspicuously Hungarian book, may not be lacking at the end, I shall give an account, although the magistrate's end is not as romantic as I would wish. We judge of men as we do of time. The arable farmer blesses a rainy Sunday as the dandy about to take a stroll curses it; there are among dealers in wheat those who extol even hail and persistent drought, and so there's no one who has treated someone quite wickedly that isn't sometimes considered a decent man. No wonder, therefore, if Nyúzó too had friends, only, to his misfortune, after the death of the *alispán*'s wife fewer than he needed in his situation. The magistrate had shaped his whole life according to principles. In his understanding, daily bread was what the wise mean by *the necessary* – which includes a fine house, land, etc. etc., that which is called *useful*; according to this understanding a good name and public esteem count as voluptuousness and luxury, for which the sensible man strives only when he has plenty of the first two. It was the strict application of this principle that got Nyúzó into trouble. Certain public monies which were assigned for the beautification of Garacs and similar matters, of which I shall say no more, to the no small detriment of the Garacs area brought such disrepute on the worthy official that he and his clerk were removed from their positions, after which, to the best of my knowledge, the unroofed third of the magistrate's house is still waiting for its tiles and the fence hasn't been completed.

I've spoken of the gentry so as to confound my critic who complained[224] that in this work of mine I cede pride of place to the lower classes of the common people, and have given a sign of my improvement: wouldn't my readers now like to know what happened to Zsuzsi?

Her story is short and simple. When she heard from Mrs Lipták of her husband's death she swooned into the old lady's arms and remained for a while senseless. When she came to, she went to her children's graves, prostrated herself on the mounds (now becoming green for the first time), took tearful leave of her darlings, and went with Mrs Lipták to Tiszarét. She asked if she might live where she and her husband had lived, and when Ákos, with Mrs Lipták's help, had had the house restored to order she moved in. She spent her days in isolation, shutting herself away from everyone; even Mrs Lipták could see her only rarely and no one else in the village encountered her in the daytime. Only in the evening did neighbours see her door open; then she would go to the Törökdomb and remain there until dawn.

One summer evening Ákos and his young wife were strolling near the Törökdomb when they heard a woman's voice singing this old folksong:

---

224 Eötvös takes advantage of publication in serial form to answer a critic of an earlier instalment!

In the sky this summer night
See the stars, they shine so bright;
Where that star looks down on me
That is where I'm soon to be.

Vilma thought that she knew who the singer was.

Early next morning, as a number of farm hands were setting to work with their scythes, they found a woman lying in the grass near the Törökdomb, at the spot where Viola had died a few months before. They tried to rouse her, but she awoke no more.

*   *

*

I've come to the end of my tale. God be with you, my readers! If there are some among you that are scandalised by the banality of my account and say without restraint that if only they wished they could write a much finer book – let them be assured, it's been my intention to write of real things, rather than exceptional. If a number of you are offended by the frankness with which I've spoken of the darker side of conditions in Hungary, believe me, if I weren't convinced that changing these conditions was in our power I'd rather have sought out the brighter side in order to entertain you and myself with gentle deceptions. If you find the picture that I've set before you to be unreal, convince me that all these things of which I've spoken not only don't occur within the confines of a single county but can't and don't occur in Hungary, and I'll bless you for doing so; likewise it's my warmest desire that this romance should be improbable. It's been my wish to be of use, not to amuse; if my endeavour has not lacked success I wish for no other acknowledgement of my efforts.

And now, God be with you too, great plain of my homeland; in my youth I spent many days, both happy and sorrowful, on the banks of the Tisza, to which my imagination has so often returned as I've been writing this work! Lovely are the hills, lovely is the sweeping mirror of the Danube over which my eyes look out from my lofty dwelling – but don't let anyone speak against you, *green plain*,[225] glory of my homeland! Boundless as the floods of the sea you spread before our eyes, which see no limit to your greatness but the heaven that covers you with its blue vault. No dark ranges of mountains rise around you, the rising sun

---

225 Eötvös may be quoting himself. See the opening paragraph of his novella *A molnárleány* – The Miller's Daughter.

can't inflame golden crowns of snow-covered peaks; your tall grass dries where it stands untouched by scythe, your rivers flow mutely on between their reed-covered banks, and nature has denied you the variety of unexpected hilltops and surprises in bends of valleys; and the traveller, when once he has traversed your level surface, will find no lingering memory of individual beauties – and yet, has he not often stopped in admiration of your impressive magnificence? When the sun rises silently above your grey horizon and suddenly pours its gleaming rays unobstructed over the whole of you, or when in the burning heat of noon the mirage depicts a lake above your shadeless expanse, it's as if the parched land were dreaming of the waters of the sea that once covered it; or when the dark hush of night has shrouded the far horizon, while the only light is that of the stars above, below here and there that of a will-o'-the-wisp, and an infinite silence enfolds the land so that the traveller can hear the evening breeze whispering in the tall grass, doesn't a feeling that defies description fill his soul at such times? a feeling which he didn't find among the majestic wonders of the lofty Alps and which is perhaps more melancholy but more magnificent, as you are more magnificent than all the mountains of this earth, boundless plain of my homeland, you, the equal of the infinite sea, green and limitless as the ocean, where the heart beats more freely and the eye meets with no obstacle!

You are the image of the Hungarian, great plain! Green in hope, you stand uncultivated, created to pour around you blessing through your fertility, but still barren. The powers with which God has endowed you still slumber, and the millennia that have passed over you haven't seen you in your glory; but though hidden, the power still lives in your breast, the very weeds that grow on you in such abundance proclaim your fertility, and my heart tells me that the time is at hand when you shall flower – you our beautiful plain, as shall the people that have inhabited you for a thousand years. Happy the man that may live to see the day! Happy the man who can console himself with the awareness that he has striven with all his might in preparation for that better time.

CEEOLPress 2022

CPSIA information can be obtained
at www.ICGtesting.com
Printed in the USA
BVHW031151071022
648920BV00012BA/1951